The Protector

"*The Protector* will not disappoint readers. Dee Henderson does her homework, and we reap the rewards of a heated, more-than-satisfying tale."—ROMANTIC TIMES MAGAZINE

"A riveting addition to the series! Henderson's magical pen combines the allure of Thrillers, Romances, and Christian books to make one of the best series I have ever read!"—HUNTRESS BOOK REVIEWS

"*The Protector* is very exciting with lots of edge-of-your-seat firefighting scenes. The more I read about the O'Malley family, the more I realize what an extraordinary author Dee Henderson has become.... Her books are some of my most beloved treasured reads."—THE BELLES AND BEAUX OF ROMANCE

The Healer

"*The Healer* is a poignant love story, a five-handkerchief reading experience that readers will never be able to forget because it is so beautiful.... Dee Henderson is a brilliant storyteller."—MIDWEST BOOK REVIEW

"Warning: Be prepared to get nothing else done until you turn the last page of *[The Healer]* and find yourself wondering, 'Well, okay, but what's going to happen next? When's the next book?'"—THE WORD ON ROMANCE

"*The Healer* mesmerized me! A masterful balance of life and death, good and evil is created within these pages, and I could not walk away unchanged."—THE ROMANCE READERS CONNECTION

The Rescuer

"No one blends family and faith with heart-pounding action like Dee Henderson. This author just ROCKS! An awesome ending to a thrilling series."— HUNTRESS BOOK REVIEWS

"Dee Henderson has written another enthralling inspirational romance that showcases a character trying to cope with a terrible trauma."—BOOK CROSSING

"What a page-turner.... We're taken on a wild journey through faith, discovery, puzzles, suspense, and courage. After the O'Malleys, I can't wait to see what Dee has in store for us next. It's sure to be spectacular."— SCRIBES WORLD REVIEWS (www.scribesworld.com)

Novels by Dee Henderson

DEE HENDERSON

THE O'MALLEY CHRONICLES

VOLUME 2

The Protector

The Healer

The Rescuer

Multnomah® Publishers *Sisters, Oregon*

O'MALLEY CHRONICLES, VOLUME 2
published by Multnomah Publishers, Inc.

© 2004 by Dee Henderson
International Standard Book Number: 1-59052-430-6

Cover design by Kirk DouPonce/Dog Eared Design LLC

Compilation of:
The Protector
© 2001 by Dee Henderson
ISBN: 1-57673-846-9
The Healer
© 2002 by Dee Henderson
ISBN: 1-57673-925-2
The Rescuer
© 2003 by Dee Henderson
ISBN: 1-59052-430-6

Unless otherwise indicated, Scripture quotations are from:
Revised Standard Version Bible (RSV)
© 1946, 1952 by the Division of Christian Education
of the National Council of the Churches of Christ
in the United States of America

Multnomah is a trademark of Multnomah Publishers, Inc.,
and is registered in the U.S. Patent and Trademark Office.
The colophon is a trademark of Multnomah Publishers, Inc.

Printed in the United States of America

For information:
MULTNOMAH PUBLISHERS, INC.
POST OFFICE BOX 1720
SISTERS, OREGON 97759

04 05 06 07 08 09 10—10 9 8 7 6 5 4 3 2 1

The O'Malley Family Album

The O'Malleys are a close-knit group of seven men and women, who as children living in an orphanage formed an alliance, adopted each other, and took the surname O'Malley. For over two decades they've held together against all obstacles, surviving and thriving by depending on each other.

Jennifer, the youngest O'Malley, is a pediatrician in Dallas. When she brings the family together to inform them that she has cancer, she's concerned about how her brothers and sisters will react...and whether she will live long enough to share with them her newfound passion and faith in Jesus Christ.

Each of the O'Malleys has successfully taken on the challenge of a high-risk profession, heroically dealing with life-and-death situations every day. But can the family survive when crisis strikes one of their own?

Kate O'Malley decided at age nine, when she was taken from her abusive family, that someone had to kick death in the teeth for the sake of justice. At thirty-six, Kate is now a hostage negotiator for the Chicago Police Department, a legend in the force, willing to walk into any situation. Kate would rather say there is no God than accept that He would allow the ugliness she has seen man do to man. When her sister's life is in jeopardy, can she trust Jennifer's God to be merciful?

Marcus O'Malley grew up watching his mother pray faithfully, but she died when he was eight years old. Now Marcus is a thirty-eight-year-old U.S. Marshal who thinks prayers are answered as much by chance as by a caring God. When he finds out Jennifer is a Christian, as the guardian of the O'Malley clan, he doesn't want her to get hurt by believing in a God who will only let her down. Can Marcus wrestle with the demons of his past to trust a sovereign God again?

Lisa O'Malley was abandoned at birth and lived in seven foster homes before arriving at Trevor House, with a lizard peeking out of her backpack. At thirty-five, Lisa is now a forensic pathologist who is closer to her pets than to people outside her family. She knows more about death than anyone should, yet she doesn't understand how Jennifer can be so confident that God will heal her. Can Lisa overcome her scientific logic to believe in miracles?

Jack O'Malley was eleven when he lost his parents. He learned early on not to waste time worrying about things he couldn't change. Now Jack is a thirty-four-year-old firefighter who likes to make people laugh and takes unreasonable risks to protect those in trouble. Christmas is one of Jack's favorite childhood memories, yet he believes Jesus is a myth, just like Santa Claus. While Jennifer's life hangs in the balance, can Jack discover the real Jesus—that the baby in a manger is also Jennifer's ultimate Protector?

Rachel O'Malley was a child of divorce. Neither parent wanted her, so nine-year-old Rachel arrived at Trevor House broken and alone. Thirty-five-year-old Rachel is a trauma psychologist, whose gift is helping children survive crises. She sees so many lives ravaged by tragedy that she longs for the heaven Jennifer believes in—where illness, evil, and suffering don't exist. Will Rachel come to trust the true Healer before the worry of losing her sister buries her?

Stephen O'Malley was nine when his sister, Peg, drowned and eleven when his parents died in a car crash. Now thirty-five-year-old Stephen is a paramedic who deals with tragedies every day. But Stephen's on the run—from the burden of his profession, from the grief over his sister's illness, and from a God he doesn't want to trust. Will Stephen be able to relax his grip on life and let God be God, knowing that Jesus is the one person he'll never have to rescue?

book four

THE
PROTECTOR

"For God so loved the world that he gave his only Son,
that whoever believes in him should not perish but have eternal life.
For God sent the Son into the world,
not to condemn the world,
but that the world might be saved through him."

JOHN 3:16–17

PROLOGUE

The electricity was out. The candle nightlight on the dresser was barely bright enough to scare away the ghosts. Jack watched the dancing shadows flicker on the wall and wished his mom had brought him the torch flashlight his dad used when they went camping. Dim was worse than dark, and the shadows were laughing at him.

If only there were a full moon, not a storm. He could hear the wind picking up. He tugged on the blanket, ready to yank it over his head when the lightning struck. Sometimes lightning could herald action heroes coming to save him and sometimes it was just angry bolts. Tonight the storm was angry.

"Mom?" He didn't shout it. He wasn't supposed to still be awake; he wasn't supposed to be afraid of the dark. But if she would maybe just come check on him…

Thunder cracked.

His dog raced into the room from the hall.

Overjoyed, Jack hurriedly tugged the sheets back up and buried his face against the pillow so he could pretend to be asleep. Mom had let Shep inside the house. The dresser rocked as his dog crashed into it, squeezing around to get into the fort Jack had built earlier that day with blankets over chairs. The candle toppled and disappeared.

Jack squeezed his eyes shut at the sudden blackness. This was not good. This was very bad. He heard his mom talking with his dad, the sounds echoing as they came up the stairs.

The room started to brighten. He opened one eye a little to see if Mom had come to the doorway with her light to check on him. The door stood open, empty. Jack opened both eyes. Fire peeked over the edge of his bed, licking at the G. I. Joe sheets.

Jack watched, wide eyed, fascinated. The flames grew like marching soldiers in a spreading line.

He reached to move the Matchbox car from the foot of the bed and drew back from the heat. "Mom."

The fire alarm in the hall went off.

The noise deafened the sound of thunder outside.

"Jack!" His mom rushed into the room followed by his dad.

She pulled him from the bed and swallowed him in a hug. She smelled like lilacs. His dad yanked back the rug and the covers, attacked the flames, and stomped them out. *Wow.* They had turned to flames fast; it had been just a flicker moments before. "I'd like Superman sheets to replace mister G. I. Joe," he told his mom, watching his dad save him.

She squeezed him. "Superman sheets," she murmured, her voice choked. "I can do that."

ONE

The house was a total loss. Firefighter Lieutenant Jack O'Malley shone his bright light on the dripping walls, looking for anything that would provide a source for the smoke he was still chasing. Second floor beams above him groaned as the building settled. Fire had shattered what had once been a beautiful, well-kept home. It was like walking around inside a sarcophagus. The place felt like it was dying.

The kitchen smelled of something nasty, the sharp smell of burnt cleaning supplies making Jack's eyes water. Limp bananas were now hanging over a bowl whose apples looked like cooked mush. Coupons fluttered from the counter to the floor, turning to a sodden mass in the standing water. Pictures on the refrigerator had bled away color in the heat, leaving behind the ghosts of people barely discernible.

The big calendar on the wall beside the phone had been reduced to darkened, curling pages. A family's life, documented in dates and times and appointments, gone. Jack let the light linger on the calendar, the month of November half marked off with *X*s, today's date of the fifteenth highlighted by something now illegible in bold red ink. Their vacation dates, he guessed. Thanksgiving was next week and they had chosen to travel early. He was grateful they had not been caught in the inferno.

This was so incredibly senseless. The fire looked like it had been set.

Jack could feel the weariness wash over him again, and behind it, building, the tick in his left eye that showed his growing anger. He'd like to find the man responsible for this and deck him.

A wisp of gray caught his attention as the house breathed. Some smoke was coming through the central air ductwork. Jack touched his radio. "Nate, check the utility room again."

"On it."

Jack walked through what had once been the patio door, stepping out into the night. The massive spotlights from the fire engines in front of the house cast strange shadows onto the backyard through holes in the house where windows had never been intended.

Popcorn.

Jack stopped in his tracks when he spotted the white kernels lying at the edge of the deck protected from booted feet by the waist-high wooden railing. The building anger surged and fury swept through him. Someone had stood and watched the house burn, had come prepared to enjoy the sight. It was a signature he'd seen before.

The white kernels were scattered, dropped as though stragglers from an over-flowing fistful. Jack searched the area. A few of the unpopped grains that had been flicked into the flames lay burnt with hulls split in two. Jack had hoped with a passion this particular arsonist was going to stick to his nuisance fires of grass and trash. Instead, he'd just escalated to his first house.

Fire was supposed to be an accident, not a weapon, not something enjoyed. Jack kicked a smoldering chunk of wood ripped from a window frame away from the evidence. His job was turning into that of a cop.

He hated arsonists. Painful experience from his past had taught him how ruthless a fire starter could become. Destruction of property. Innocent victims. Injured firefighters. They had to find this guy before someone got hurt.

He could fight a fire, but fighting a man... Jack felt like his hands were tied and he hated the feeling of being helpless. He was an O'Malley. He wasn't a man to duck trouble. He preferred to go after it. This was clearly trouble. How was he supposed to go after a man who chose to be a coward and hide behind a match?

Thanksgiving was coming, then Christmas, and he had enough on his plate already with his sister Jennifer fighting cancer to want to add this kind of tangle. The holidays were like waving an invitation to make trouble. He couldn't be two places at once. They had to stop this guy soon. But it was tomorrow's problem.

Around him the firefighters from Company 81 were pulling hose and shout-ing to be heard over the sound of a power saw. They were aggressively searching for hot spots within the burned-out house and trying to find the source of that smoke still rising like a wavering cobra into the air.

Somewhere in the ruins this fire was still alive. Jack pulled back on his gloves and looked over the ruins of the house with an experienced eye. A decade of fight-ing fires had taught him well, for it was not a forgiving profession.

Fire was an arrogant beast. If in control, it challenged with ferocious disdain anyone who approached. If forced to retreat, it liked to lie low, patiently waiting, then exact a painful revenge.

They'd find it. Kill it. And another dragon would be slain.

"Cole." Jack got the attention of the fire investigator.

There were few men who could dominate a fire scene just by being present; his friend Cole was one. Six-two, one hundred and eighty pounds, prematurely gray at forty-two, Cole Parker had made captain at thirty-six, a decade before most. He now led the arson group. Jack trusted the man in a way he trusted few outside his family.

"What do you have, Jack?"

With his flashlight, Jack illuminated the popcorn.

Cole, a big man with a big shadow, stilled for a moment, then walked over to the deck.

"He's escalating," Jack said.

Cole bent to pick up a kernel. "We knew he eventually would. Five fires in seven weeks, he's not a patient man."

"He's ringing fires around the new boundaries of the fire district," Jack suggested, knowing it was at least a clue to figuring out who the man was they had to stop. The smaller, older fire stations had been closing over the past months, their engines and crews dispersed to expanded hub stations. The reapportioned equipment better reflected the new housing construction and demographics of the area, but nothing could change the reality that more territory in each district meant longer response times. This firebug knew how to take advantage of the change.

Cole just nodded. "A dangerous man playing a dangerous game." He ate one of the popped kernels. "Salt. He's bringing his own refreshments."

"I really didn't need to know that."

His friend rose gracefully to his feet. "I thought this had the sound of one of his. Late at night, edge of the district." He looked over at Jack. "Gold Shift."

The implication that his shift was being targeted hadn't escaped Jack's attention. They worked twenty-four hours on, forty-eight hours off, yet all the fires had been fought by his shift, none by Black or Red Shifts. Jack would not easily admit he'd started to sweat when the tones sounded. It was hard to hold his trademark good humor when someone out there appeared determined to make sure he was going to face flames.

Cole brushed his hands on worn jeans. He'd been paged to the scene from his home. "Tell me about this fire."

"It was in the walls."

First on the scene, Engine 81 had pulled up as smoke began to pour from the attic vents and around the eaves. Jack had pushed his way into the front hallway, shining his light, and had watched the paint bubble from the heat inside the walls. No flames had been visible, but as soon as he had poked his ax into the wall, the dragon had leaped out, roaring. "We had a hard time getting water onto the face of it."

Nate on the nozzle, Bruce pulling hose, they'd lost precious time cutting into the walls. With no moon and the neighbors' homes a distance away, the fire had not been reported until it already had a good hold. Jack had been thinking it ignited because of an electrical short until he saw the intensity of the fire. He illuminated the smoke line and burn pattern with his light as they walked.

"Center of the house?" Cole speculated.

They slogged across the yard now turned into mud by the hours of streaming water. Jack stopped by a dogwood tree. "I think so. There was too much ambient heat to assume it started on the second floor and worked down within the walls, not enough fire scarring on the siding to show an origin point in an outside wall."

Arson for profit didn't fit this guy's pattern—probably a guy—Jack decided. It didn't feel like the work of a young offender either. These fire locations were carefully planned. And it was odd for a fire starter who did it for enjoyment to acquire the taste late in life. "Think he's after the press attention?"

"Bold enough to stand around after the fire starts and flick popcorn into the flames, arrogant enough to set fires frequently. Now escalating in the type of fires he sets. Yes, he wants the attention—ours, the media's, and ultimately the public's."

"We'll have a panic on our hands if we don't stop him before the press connects the fires."

"Not to mention copycats."

Smoke twisted in their direction, the heavy ash particles making Jack cough. "What time is it?"

Cole sent him a sympathetic smile. "Something after 2 A.M."

Two and a half hours. Jack felt like he had run a marathon. The fire turnout coat sat heavy on his shoulders and it stuck and rubbed at his neck as he moved. The last hours had turned his blue uniform shirt and cotton T-shirt under the coat into a sweaty mass. Jack knew he could forget any idea of sleep tonight. It would be dawn before they got the fire mop-up complete.

His left knee was still complaining about the force of the impact earlier when he dropped from the engine to the asphalt street with more speed than care. The initial sight of the house with smoke beginning to pour from the roof vents had made him push faster than safety would dictate.

It might have appeared haphazard to the spectators watching their arrival, but the company had executed a well-coordinated attack on the fire. The crew from Ladder Truck 81 had gone after the roof and ventilated the fire; the men from Engine 81 had surged to lay hose and get water on the face of the fire; and the crew of Rescue Squad 81 had hit the ground reaching for air tanks, ready to go in if people were trapped.

The drills and teamwork had paid off; no time had been lost during the attack. There were benefits to working with the best. And a few drawbacks. First engine on the scene, last engine to leave.

He'd kill for a shower. The smell of smoke and sweat was a stench he didn't mind as long as he was moving and was downwind of himself.

"You did a good job of knocking it down."

He was pleased at the praise for Cole didn't give it lightly. "Thanks."

Jack would prefer to be on the roof or pulling down scorched plaster, even coiling hose, than to be the guy tapped to manage the scene. But the captain of Company 81 had been called to the site of a chemical spill, so the job passed to Jack.

He retrieved two bottles of ice water from the rescue squad and handed one to Cole. As he drank, Jack scanned the few remaining spectators—neighbors hurriedly dressed, a couple kids entranced at the sight of the red engine and ladder truck, local media, a cop blocking the street from thru traffic.

Some firebugs were watchers. They acted just so the firefighters would get called out. They'd stand and watch the battle, their own personal entertainment. No one stood out among those gathered.

Jack turned back to the house and watched guys turn a nozzle back on to deal with a pocket of fire found smoldering in the wall between the garage and the breezeway. "This isn't going to be his last fire."

"Safe wager."

"Any ideas?"

Cole drank deeply, then shook his head. "No ideas, no assumptions, no conclusions. You know how this job is done."

Jack did. It took patience he didn't have. "My men are at risk." His words were quiet because he knew the memory Cole carried, knew how the words would resonate.

Cole reached over and squeezed his shoulder.

Jack didn't know if he ever wanted to make captain, knowing how much the privilege and burden of command had cost his friend. Cole had led Company 65 before moving to head the arson group. He'd moved because an arsonist had made it personal. Jack wanted to ask about Cassie, about Ash, but found himself in this situation hesitant to voice the names.

"Lieutenant?" A firefighter from Truck 81 stepped to the open front door. "You're going to want to see this."

The heat from the floor came through his boots. Jack could hear the fire, a rushing sound, huge, consuming. Every step took him closer to it. The hallway turned and he felt the stairwell post. He started up the stairs. There was someone still in the house. They had to get her out.

The smoke was coming down in rolling waves. Fire brightened the darkness ahead of him, surging through the smoke in licks of vicious flames.

The heat was too intense.

The smoke was too low.

No one in this house could still be alive.

It was a grim realization that firmed with each step and by the sixth step Jack stopped. He wanted to rush through the flames, he desperately wanted to change reality. His sister Rachel would be crushed at the news her friend was dead, and Tabitha's husband— Jack couldn't change what had already happened. He was responsible for his men's lives. Jack put out his arm, stopping Ben, the lieutenant of Black Shift who had taken the place of the rookie on Jack's crew for this attempted evacuation. "There's nothing we can do."

Bruce and Nate in the rear of the group turned at his words to lead the way out. Ben Rohr hesitated. Jack squeezed his shoulder. The lieutenant was the veteran of the group, in his early forties but still had more fires under his belt than Jack had ever seen. He understood how torn the man was to turn back from a victim—there was no choice. Ben headed down the stairs.

The fire roared behind Jack, reaching out to touch the back of his heavy fire coat. It had already claimed a victim. They couldn't afford to give it another. Jack felt the post at the bottom of the steps and turned the corner into the hall as the fire roared down the stairway landing and part of the ceiling buckled.

The sound of sirens screaming outside provided direction. Jack followed the noise toward the door they had entered. Water slapped against the side of the house, hissing as it turned to steam. Men rushed to meet them and clipped shakes of heads passed the painful word. Hard hands slapped their shoulders, counting them. "Last man," Jack shouted. "Drown it." The firefighter on the nozzle nodded and pulled hose into the doorway, then opened it.

Jack pushed off his gear. The night air felt cold after the oppressive heat. They would join the fight to stop the fire, but it would be a grim fight with no good outcome. People, property—they had already lost both. How was he supposed to tell his sister that Tabitha was dead? The thought of doing so was enough to drive the sickness deep.

Neighbors, cops, and spectators had gathered to watch the scene and Jack saw the reaction as word a neighbor had died swept through the crowd.

"We could have made it," Ben said, staring at the flames, absorbed in watching them.

"Going up, but we couldn't have made it back out," Jack murmured, watching the veteran firefighter weighing the odds of which could move faster: firefighter or flames. It would have been a suicide mission.

"Get out of my way!"

Jack turned to see a man surging past police. Gage Collier, the reporter a familiar face to local firefighters and police. This was Gage's home. Gage's wife. Jack stepped forward to meet the man before he reached his crew. There were no words for what he felt. "Gage, I'm sorry. I'm so sorry."

Jack saw the punch coming but did nothing to block it.

"She was pregnant!"

Jack jerked awake, breathing hard. He shoved himself upright to get away from the heavy, haunted sleep. The nightmare always came after a fire now. Two years old, and it was still a living memory. It merged with other memories: the victims he hadn't been able to reach, the screams of people caught in flames, the nursing home—always the inevitable memory of the nursing home fire. Jack loved being a fireman but the costs were building. Did the arsonist know what he was doing? Not only destroying property but the firefighters who battled the fires.

Jack would have called his family, just to hear another voice tonight besides the fading ones in his head, but the one person who could help him the most to talk through the trauma was his sister Rachel. And she already had to live with the fact it was her friend who died.

He got up to pace and forced the memories down again. They'd linger and he would live with them. Tabitha died because they had been late to the fire.

Ben still called that the department's blackest day, for a brush fire on the other side of the district had cost them precious minutes in response time. A new lieutenant and a veteran both haunted by the same memory. It wasn't a bond Jack would have chosen, but it was one that went deep. He didn't know how Ben coped. Jack had better learn because otherwise he would have to think about walking away from the profession he loved. This was slowly killing him.

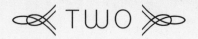
The fertilizer bags were in his way, and after the fourth trip into the garage, he kicked one of them and succeeded in hurting his foot. The Thanksgiving meal today would be chicken from the local fast-food place, the pie a frozen thing that was put in the oven. It was a far cry from the home-cooked feasts of years past, but since the divorce he'd been making do. It had only been a week since the last fire, but he wanted to go burn something. They were destroying him and his family. He had to get their attention, had to get things changed.

The newspaper had relegated the fire investigation to the seventh page in the city section. A short statement by the investigating officer—the fire is under investigation. A quote from the homeowner about how thankful his family was for the support of friends and family at this holiday time. Soft stuff, routine stuff, no hard news in the article. The community had five fires in seven weeks, an arsonist stalking their fire department, and what did they do? Yawn.

Well someone was going to notice; someone was going to hear, if only Jack. He slammed the trunk of the gray sedan. It wouldn't change what he lived with, what his family lived with, but it was a place to start. By the time he was done he would have all of them paying attention.

He'd have to leave a message this time.

The phone rang right next to his ear. Jack was startled awake. His face was inches from the clock on the nightstand, the digits blinking 5:40 A.M. A week since the arson fire and he was finally enjoying sleep again. He hated getting awakened from the dream of his mom hugging him and smelling like lilacs. He loved that memory, it was one of the clearest from his childhood.

A photo of his parents was in a silver frame behind the clock, crowded by car keys, his beeper, and a tattered wallet. His parents had died in a car crash, way before Jack was ready to let them go. He'd been eleven. Another frame beside the photo sat empty, one of his sister's not so subtle ways of suggesting he get a girlfriend. He'd never gotten the courage to move the empty frame to a drawer.

Jack reluctantly reached over to answer the phone. Thanksgiving Day inevitably meant people choking on turkey sandwiches, grease fires in the kitchen, kids playing together banging heads and chipping teeth. It was going to be a long day and he was in no hurry to start it. "Hello?"

"Jack, I need you," Kate whispered.

He wedged the phone tighter to his ear. What was his sister doing up at this time of day, and why was she whispering? Neither fit her. "What's wrong?"

"You really don't want to die, do you? Come on, put it down. Don't eat it," she crooned.

Jack shoved himself up. His sister was a police hostage negotiator, a good one. She was having two conversations. "Where are you?" Where was the rest of her team? She normally tugged in their oldest brother Marcus when she needed help.

"My apartment roof. No, don't go out on the ledge. Don't." Her voice sounded frustrated and that was rare for Kate. She was known for her apparent boredom during a crisis. "I need an extra pair of hands. Marvel got into the turkey bones and he's going to kill himself eating them. I can't catch him. You've got the magic touch."

He had his shirt half on. That stopped him. "Your cat? You woke me up for a cat?"

"Jack—" The phone clattered against stone and he heard the unmistakable sound of Kate lunging. Her apartment roof was flat, gravel topped, with a large concrete ledge around it, and that noise was gravel scattering. "That does it. He's now in the elm tree clutching the turkey leg and hissing at me."

"Let him be."

"Dave gave me that cat."

Jack closed his eyes. Her fiancé, Dave Richman, had given her the cat. And Kate hadn't had a cat since someone shot her last one through her living room window. Jack looked with regret at his pillow and instead reached for his keys. "I'm coming."

"Thank you."

An O'Malley called, an O'Malley came. They needed a cat rescued, gutters cleaned, his sisters called him. If they had a real crisis, they called one of the others. Jack smiled and reached for his billfold, not entirely minding his role in the family.

They'd celebrated Thanksgiving together two weeks ago, as several of them were working this long weekend. He had a lot to be thankful for today, and family headed the list.

The seven of them were close, a group bound together not by blood, but by choice. They were all orphans. At Trevor House over two decades ago they had chosen to become their own family, and had later legally changed their last names. It was unique but it worked. He'd lost so much when his parents died, had been so lonely. By the time the legal logistics had been sorted out, he'd been twelve, at the foster home, and adoption was unlikely. Trevor House had become his home. The O'Malleys had filled the huge void. They were family, even when the calls came at the most inconvenient times for something only family could understand.

Jack found the street Kate lived on in downtown Chicago blocked off, the street and the sidewalks marked with fluorescent red spray paint and big, new drainage tiles sitting on the small strips of grass. No city crew was present to actually work on the project, but they still left the street blocked off. Jack parked a block away and hiked back to Kate's building, taking the outside fire escape up to the roof. Kate often sat on a lawn chair up here at night to watch the city she risked her life to protect.

She was at the east corner of the roof, half leaning over the ledge. Jack summed up the problem in a glance. "You can negotiate with a man holding a gun but can't negotiate with your own cat."

She looked over her shoulder, relief and frustration both showing on her normally impassive face. "Just help me get to him before he gets a bone splinter stuck in his gut and bleeds to death."

Jack winced at the image. He pulled on gloves and opened the canvas backpack he kept for rescuing critters. Fires often trapped pets and he'd learned early on to be prepared. "What were you doing up before 6 A.M.?"

"Do you have any idea how long a turkey takes to bake?"

"Yes. I gather you didn't."

"I try to avoid the actual meal preparation on holidays so that it's actually a holiday. Dave is coming to dinner. I've got to work today, and I do not have four hours to sit and watch a turkey cook. I put it in about one this morning when I got home from a page, and then got up at a horrible hour to get it out."

Kate would have been smarter just to take turkey out of the freezer from all the leftovers or buy her turkey already baked from the store deli. "You had to take the meat off the bones?"

"I don't exactly have room to put that massive carcass in my refrigerator."

Jack stepped up on the ledge. "Let me guess. Marvel got into the trash."

"He grabbed the turkey bones and bolted."

Marvel sank his teeth into the turkey leg and flattened his ears back, offering a threatening rumble. The old yellow tabby was not a house cat, had never been a house cat, and only Kate would try to domesticate him. Dave had been feeling sorry for Kate when he handed her the stray that liked to wander his property. It was doubtful he'd considered what Kate and an opinionated scrapper would be like together.

The old elm tree was one of the few that hadn't been slaughtered in the attempt to rid Chicago of an Asian beetle infestation. Jack hoped the limb hadn't been hollowed out so it would break under his weight. He took the big step from the ledge onto the tree.

"You're not content to set off Dave's alarm system, get in fights and come home bloody, and eat my sister out of house and home. Now you have to pretend you're a squirrel and trees are your home," he said softly, edging out on the limb toward the cat. The next limb was too far away for the cat to jump to and still hold the turkey bone. The cat was cornered.

"Come here, you big lumbering furball." Jack reached for the tomcat. He got a swipe with a greasy paw for his troubles. The claws caught the back of his wrist just behind the glove protection. The turkey bone fell to the ground.

"Nice, Marvel. Very nice," Jack remarked grimly, gripping him. The deep scratches stung. And it was obvious why the cat had acquired the name. It really was a marvel he was still alive.

Jack tucked the cat inside the backpack, then flipped over and latched the canvas flap to keep him inside. He would have tossed the pack to the roof, but Kate wouldn't appreciate it. He worked his way out of the tree back to the roof.

He offered her the squirming bag. "One mad cat."

Kate took the canvas satchel and wisely kept it closed. She patted Jack's chest. "Come down to the apartment and I'll fix you breakfast," she offered over the cat howls.

"Make it coffee to go. I'm due at work."

"Any leads on your arsonist?"

"Sure. He likes to burn things." He was getting philosophical about it. His job was to put out the fires; Cole's was to find the man setting them. And Jack knew better than to bet against Cole.

Her pager went off. Kate glanced down at it on her belt. "Jack—" He took the cat before she asked. Kate was already dialing. The conversation was short. "Someone just shot up a liquor store over on Princeton."

"Sounds like we're both going to have a long day."

She was already jogging across the roof to the fire escape. "Lock him in the bathroom?"

"Go. It's handled. Be careful."

"Always am. I owe you one."

"Remember that next time we play basketball."

She laughed and disappeared.

Jack whistled over the noise as he carried the cat back to Kate's apartment. Her home showed the evidence of her late night return—her gym bag dropped inside the door, tennis shoes in the hallway, her jacket tossed toward the chair, and mail sliding off the hallway table.

Jack warily let Marvel out in the bathroom and watched the cat settle with a huff on the toilet seat cover that matched the rugs. At least the frills were good for something. Jack tugged the door firmly closed.

Out of habit, he checked to make sure the bedroom windows were closed and locked, checked that the fire alarm was flashing to show good batteries. He walked back to the kitchen to fix himself coffee. He could get some at the fire station, but that was a twenty-minute drive and he'd never last that long. Jack wondered how many car wrecks he would work before his shift ended. Too many. And probably at least two kitchen fires. Holidays were predictable that way.

Pulling a piece of paper from the pad, he wrote Kate a note and put it under a magnet on her refrigerator. She'd need a laugh by the time her day was done. Somehow he didn't think her dinner with Dave was going to happen on time and uninterrupted. He understood the hope though; he had major plans for his own evening if he could keep the workday under control. A plaintive howl came from the bathroom. Jack locked Kate's apartment and headed to work, taking the coffee with him, relieved to leave the cat behind.

The Smokehouse Eatery parking lot was crowded tonight. Jack slapped mud off his slacks, splattered from an attempt to stop a dog from darting across a ditch into tollway traffic. He'd rearranged his schedule in order to be here early, even if it meant coming with mud-splattered slacks. He didn't see Cassie's car, but there was always a chance she'd caught a ride with someone.

It was a typical firemen's holiday. They were crowding into Charles and Sandra's restaurant, taking over the Smokehouse Eatery to celebrate Thanksgiving together. The firehouse down the street might have been closed in the department consolidations, but the restaurant had been a tradition for decades and the holiday was just a good excuse to come back.

He worked his way through the crowd, and within moments confirmed Cassie was nowhere in sight. Jack paused to greet their host and was waved with a laugh toward the buffet table. He was grateful; lunch had been a long time ago.

Twenty minutes later he found Cole. "Think Cassie will come?" Jack asked his friend while he watched the door to the restaurant.

Cole picked up a toothpick and stabbed another Swedish meatball from the buffet hot pot to add to his plate. "She won't come."

Jack looked at his friend, hearing the certainty.

"She's tired, Jack."

"She shouldn't be alone on Thanksgiving."

"Her choice. Let her make it. She hasn't been able to make many of them in the last year and a half."

"She won't cook Thanksgiving dinner for one."

"I took her a pumpkin pie," Cole said.

"She was home?"

"I left it at the bookstore. Knowing Cassie, she'll end up there."

Jack fought the disappointment. He had really been hoping to see her here tonight.

Jack kept one eye on the local news, still worrying about Kate in a quiet corner of his attention. The liquor store crisis had ended about noon, but he knew the likelihood that it had just been followed by another page. He kept expecting to see the breaking news banner and a reporter pushing a microphone in Kate's face.

As a substitute for a day with his family, this party was a pretty good replacement. But while the celebration wasn't muted, neither was it complete. They were missing Cassie and Ash.

Tony was here, in his wheelchair from a fall six years before. Chad had come. Ben's nephew was now on temporary disability from smoke damage to his lungs, for fires made no allowance for rookie mistakes. Cassie Ellis and Ash Hamilton needed to be here—to know they still had a place, to know they were still part of the family. And Jack needed to see Cassie, make sure she was doing okay. The guilt from a busy summer and unfulfilled plans didn't sit well.

He turned to reach for a chip he didn't want to cover the emotions that surged back.

He'd been in some tough fires over the years, but nothing that could compare to the event they simply called The Fire. The nursing home had burned, trapping patients and staff alike. Over a dozen firefighters had been hurt by the time it was over but only two still haunted everyone involved. Cassie and Ash.

The ceiling had come down. Burning plaster and beams, chairs, tables, and filing cabinets from the floor above had trapped them. Cassie had been pinned and burned. Ash hadn't been able to shift the debris to get her free.

For an agonizing eighteen minutes, a battle that had been focused on rescuing patients and staff had been overlaid with the grim reality of a missing team. The frantic calls from Ash had been chilling, and then they had gone silent.

Jack had joined up with Rescue 12 for the search, penetrating into the heart of the fire through pitch-black corridors, thick toxic smoke, trying to find a way around the collapsed section of the hallway. The heat had been so oppressive it broiled what it touched.

They had found them just past the commons area. Cassie, facedown with her right arm twisted, pinned down in agonizing pain. And Ash—buddy breathing with Cassie to get her oxygen as her tanks had chimed and went empty, tears pouring from the man as she tried to die on him.

"Has anybody heard from Ash?"

Cole shook his head. "He disappeared after Cassie's final surgery and doesn't want to be found. He left no forwarding address."

"It's been three months."

"He'll be back," Cole replied. "Knowing Ash, he's out on his bike traveling the country, blowing the cobwebs out of his brain. He won't do anything crazy."

Jack had been there. He still occasionally disappeared on his two days off to ride as far as his bike would take him. But three months was a little steep.

"I thought Rachel was coming with you tonight?" Cole asked casually.

Jack narrowed his eyes as he watched his friend reach over to stab a turkey rollup. He'd never been able to figure out if there was something there or not. "She decided to track down Gage," Jack replied, not bothering to hide his opinion of that. Rachel was going to get herself hurt in that relationship, but there was no reasoning with her.

He watched for a reaction, but Cole merely glanced over at him. "Does Gage still hate your guts?"

"What do you think?"

"I think you're a lot like Ash. Feeling guilt you figure you deserve to carry."

Jack acknowledged the hit with a slight raise of his punch glass but countered with the truth. "He really does hate my guts."

"His wife is dead. He's sued the furnace repair company out of business. Money's not going to solve the hurt. Hating you is one way to cope."

"We pulled back from the fire. We were late."

"Tabitha was dead long before you got your air tanks on," Cole countered softly. "Long before the fire alarm came in. Someday he'll accept the autopsy report."

"Kind of hard to read past the word *pregnant.*"

"And you scold me for feeling guilty that Cassie got hurt on my watch." Cole pointed to an empty table. "Sit. We'll talk about our popcorn man and leave the past where it belongs for both of us. In the past."

The bookstore was closed for the holiday allowing Cassie a chance to work uninterrupted on shelving books and updating her inventory. She had begun to play Christmas music a month early. While the rest of the world enjoyed Thanksgiving Day, Cassie set her heart on Christmas and hummed along with "Silent Night."

Christmas was going to be her turning point. There was a new beginning waiting for her—to what she hadn't figured out, but it would at least be a new beginning. She was out of the hospital and was never going back. She was thankful just to have the chance to move on. Last year, no one had been willing to give her odds she'd be through the surgeries within a year.

She missed Rescue Squad 65. Oh, how she missed it. The rescues. The close-quarter recoveries. Cutting people out of car wrecks. Being first to go into the smoke while firefighters from the engine crews worked to get water on the flames. The job was gone for good. She had no illusions that she would ever recover sufficiently to go back on active duty.

Cole wanted her to come work for him. It was a sincere offer but she couldn't generate any enthusiasm for it. Being on the sidelines when rescue squads rolled out would cut into her heart. It was better to move on. But life was boring without Rescue Squad 65.

She hated being bored.

Like a coward, she hid from her friends in order to spend Thanksgiving as she chose to: alone, working. She needed the quiet peace of music, books to shelve, and paperwork to do. She needed the time to think.

Lord, You kept me alive for something, and all I'm doing at the moment is spinning my wheels, waiting…for what, I don't know. What do You have in mind for the future? I know You love me too much to ask me to endure that last year of agony without already having a plan to turn into Your glory.

The questions she'd been putting off until the end of the year were before her now and decisions had to be made. The vinyl records were thirty years old without a scratch on them, the music excellent. The books from the Sandoval estate auction were genuine gems. The paperwork…she planned to ignore it a while longer. Cassie shifted books to fit a copy of *Tom Swift in the Caves of Ice,* copyright 1911, onto the second shelf of the glass-enclosed bookcase. The store was hers, purchased two months ago.

I don't mind selling books, but is this it? For all its challenge, it's a pale comparison to what I had.

She'd been selling rare books on-line as her part-time hobby for years. But she never intended it to become more than a hobby that earned her pocket change. She loved books, but not enough to make them her life. For now, this was a compromise, a place to store her growing collection of books and keep herself busy while she figured out what she wanted to do with the rest of her life.

Thirty, single, burned. The dream of winning a beauty pageant someday could be scrapped.

Her sense of humor was vicious when she was in a bad mood.

Her right hand cramped as she reached down to pick up another book. Cassie closed her hand into a fist, watching the scars on her forearm flex. Fire did strange things to skin.

She was thankful to be alive. She wanted no pity for the rest. Part of it was her independent streak that meant accepting the risks that went with the job. She'd had the misfortune of becoming one of the statistics. Complaining that it had been her and not Ash was anathema. She had pulled nine people from that nursing home and been on her way back for the tenth when the ceiling had come down. She didn't regret the decision she had made.

When she wore long sleeves, the evidence of the surgeries of the last year and a half disappeared. If her glasses were strong prescriptions, they at least allowed her to read. It was a vast improvement over the days of wondering if she would have use of her arm or if her sight would survive.

She was recovering. Friends wanted her to be recovered. It was a fine line that took some maneuvering to manage. She could not yet stop the crushing fatigue that hit when she was around a crowd of caring people. Spending Thanksgiving alone had been the right decision, a necessary one. But not everyone had been fooled.

Cassie was fairly certain Cole had left the pumpkin pie. Only a handful of people had a key to the store. The gift had been left on her desk in a white box with a blue bow on top. It was something her former captain would do.

She should call him. Cole wouldn't mind getting a call at home and it would do her good to make it, to talk with a friend who understood the fine tension that underscored the holidays.

She didn't call.

She wasn't the only one who needed to move on with life. Cole did too.

And Ash. Cassie forced herself to pick up the next book. Her partner had stayed through the surgeries, kept her sane through the pain, only to disappear once she was released. To walk away and give her no clue where he was going…She knew Ash. He'd taken what happened personally. And she didn't need either one of them carrying that guilt.

She needed to see Ash for Christmas. After she hugged him, she was going to slug him for worrying her this way. *Please, Jesus.* She let the two words carry the prayer. The emotions were too deep for more words. She really needed to see Ash.

She'd been a fair-weather Christian before the last eighteen months. But in the recent black days, she'd touched bottom, and God was still there. Still bigger than the problems. She hit Him with her anger, her pain, and He'd taken it in and not reflected it back. Cassie was clinging to that peace she had found. Life was tough, but God was tougher.

Another record dropped on the turntable and "Do You Hear What I Hear?" began to play. She'd never taken the time to really celebrate Christmas before. She let the busyness of the season push aside the deeper meaning. Before this year she wasn't even sure she understood what Christmas was really about.

It wasn't just about a baby in a manger, although that was what the world tried to limit it to. It was a day that had begun the final confrontation between good and evil.

Jesus had won. And in the last year Cassie had met Him. Not the soft Jesus that a commercialized Christmas conveyed, but a Jesus so comfortable and secure in His authority He'd come to confront Satan on his own turf.

Jesus had chosen to lay aside the trappings of power that were His right and come humble and approachable, a servant. Man saw it as weakness; Jesus did it from strength. He had arrived with nothing to prove but His Father's love.

It would be nice to spend this Christmas with a deeper appreciation for the celebration.

What she was going to do that day was still an open question. She didn't want to spend Christmas alone, but she didn't want to get involved in the fire department activities either. She had no family in the area—her parents had died years before, and she'd talked her brother into accepting a job offer in Florida last year. She could get absorbed in events at church, but they would demand energy she really didn't have.

There was no good solution, just a lot of options with different drawbacks. She reached for another book.

What she really wanted to do was spend Christmas with a couple good friends. Ash led that list. And if she had to spend Christmas without him, she was going to give his gift to Goodwill.

"Gage, where have you disappeared to now?" Rachel O'Malley muttered the question to herself when leaning on the doorbell to his town house failed to get a response. Shifting the sack she carried, she pulled out her keys, flipped through the ring to the one marked with a gold crescent, and used it to let herself into Gage's home.

She was invading his space, but she'd done worse in the past. He'd finally given her a key after he found her sitting on the front stoop at 1 A.M., having waited patiently there since 8 P.M. for him to get home. He was shocked sober enough to bawl her out for being careless with her safety. The scowl and the anger had set her back on her heels, but still…it had been nice to see that he cared.

After that, when he'd gone out drinking and knew she was in town, he wore his beeper and carried a phone. He wasn't a man who wanted others to worry; he just wanted to passively kill himself.

Rachel did not like to worry about friends and Gage had her worried. If he couldn't handle Thanksgiving, there was no way he would be able to handle Christmas. She knew what it was like to grieve; Tabitha had been her best friend. And since losing his wife in the way he had, there was a big hole to grieve, but still, Gage was alive. Someday he had to start remembering that.

He was a good man. An award-winning reporter with the *Chicago Tribune*, he fought his battles with the power of his words. And while burying himself in work was a decent short-term answer, it was a lousy long-term one.

He'd fired the housekeeper again. Rachel knew it as soon as she walked into the kitchen and saw the dullness of the linoleum and the stacked, washed dishes in the draining rack. Gage was too neat a man to leave unwashed dishes around. But he wouldn't see the rest of the small details that made a house a comfortable home; he'd only feel them as they accumulated.

She opened the refrigerator to store the Cool Whip to go with the cherry pie she'd brought over. Gage had a sweet tooth.

The milk was sour. She didn't have to smell it to tell; she only had to pick up the plastic gallon to see it. It was the little things that made the grief intense: buying milk by the pint instead of the gallon, cooking for one. Her heart hurt to see the signs of continuing grief.

She was half in love with Gage herself, had resigned herself to living with that fact. Friendships under the stress of the last two years either fractured or melded people together, and Rachel felt like her heart had been soldered together with his. She was going to get him through this if it killed her. She owed it to Tabitha. She'd wrestle with her own emotions later when it was time to move on.

She took off the cap and poured the milk down the sink.

Getting Gage through this second year of holidays was going to be more difficult than she thought. She picked up his phone, saw there were six messages blinking on his answering machine, and since she knew five of them were hers, got further annoyed. The least he could do was listen to her worry about him.

She was surprised when she caught her sister at home. She had expected to leave a message on the answering machine. "Kate, could you rescue my gray-and-white suitcase and shove it in a closet?" She had been planning to head back to Washington, D.C., and already had tickets for an early morning flight out of O'Hare. As Kate had offered to give her a ride to the airport, Rachel planned to spend the night at her sister's place and had already moved her luggage to Kate's trunk.

It was best to put those plans on hold.

On call with the Red Cross and the Emergency Services Disaster Agency to handle trauma situations involving children, Rachel traveled so much she kept apartments in both Chicago and Washington. Staying longer in Chicago would create headaches as she was serving on the presidential commission on school violence next year. The preparation work was just ramping up, but she would figure out a way to work around it.

"That bad," Kate commented.

"If he didn't love so deeply, he couldn't grieve so deeply. But he's drowning in it."

"Drinking?"

Rachel checked Gage's trash and didn't see any liquor bottles. "Doesn't look like it." He'd promised her and he was a man of his word. "But he could use a friend. I'll stick around for the holidays."

"It will be good to have you around. If I'm out when you swing by, help yourself to dinner. I'm buried in turkey; Dave and I barely made a dent in it. There's no need to try and get to the grocery store tonight to replace perishables."

"I appreciate it."

"Give Gage a hug for me? I like him."

At least someone in her family did. Gage's lingering animosity toward Jack had polarized her family. "I'll do that."

Rachel hung up the phone, then looked around the kitchen trying to decide what to do. She had prepped herself to have Gage answer the door, to smile and keep her emotions to herself. She even searched out the *TV Guide* in case he didn't want to talk. For him, she'd tolerate a football game.

Gage called her sticky, sometimes as a compliment, sometimes with a touch of irritation in his voice. She stuck no matter how hard he tried to shake her off.

He thought it was because her overactive sense of doing good wouldn't let her leave him alone. She didn't tell him he was essentially a nonpaying patient. He'd be ticked and she really didn't want to explain the notes she kept out of habit. How did she explain she was just worried enough to want to stay close without sounding paranoid?

She needed Gage. She was thirty-five, and the last few years had drained her more than she would admit even to family. The old stuff she had buried from her childhood was back disrupting her dreams. Her sister Jennifer's cancer had pushed the subject of mortality back to center stage, and she just wanted a chance to stop moving for a while and catch her breath. With Gage, there was a reason to stop. As much as she helped him, he helped her. He listened.

She picked up his jacket from the chair at the kitchen table, caught the faint smell of his aftershave, and rubbed her hand on the fabric as she walked to the closet to hang it up.

Where was he?

A check of the garage showed his car was missing. Knowing Gage, the odds were good he had stayed local. Rachel found her keys and locked his house. Shoving her hands in her pockets, she set out searching.

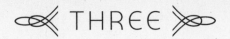

THREE

"Cassie? Open up. I know you're in there. I can see the lights are on." Jack tried to keep the frustration out of his voice. She was going to ignore his thumping on the door. The blinds on the front window had been lowered and the door had stained-glass panels preventing a look inside, but the lights were on and her car was still here. So much for wondering what she'd think about unexpected company.

The street was deserted. The chill in the November evening made Jack wish he'd thought to wear more than a windbreaker. Her bookstore was in the old section of Lincoln Hills' downtown, nestled between a candy store and a bike shop. The businesses were part of one old brick building sharing a common roof and parking lot. He'd leave, but he was beginning to worry and he hated that feeling.

Jack heard a sudden scramble inside to throw locks. The front door opened so fast he saw Cassie wince as the corner of the door caught her left foot. She wasn't wearing shoes. "Sorry, I didn't hear you." He heard the loudness of the Christmas music playing and felt stupid. Deaf, why hadn't he remembered the obvious? She was now partially deaf.

And she was still gorgeous. Her hair had grown back. She'd always looked a bit like a pixie, but now her face was framed by curling brown hair. The suppressed pain had disappeared from those dark chocolate eyes.

She had gone with the oval frames for glasses that had a thin band of gold at the top, and they drew more attention to her spectacular eyes. Thankfully the fire had just brushed her face and those burns had long ago disappeared under the skill of a surgeon's knife. Overall, it was a great face. He leaned against the doorpost, enjoying it.

"Jack. You were looking for me?" Cassie asked, her words breaking into his thoughts.

"I missed you." He saw her blink and realized what he'd said. "At the party. We missed you at the party." She grinned as he dug himself out of the quicksand of words he hadn't meant to say. "Sandra insisted you needed a care package."

"That's for me?" She looked at the sack he held. "All of that?"

He felt like laughing at her stunned expression. "I caught a look at some of what she was packing. I sure hope you haven't had dinner yet. It started with ribs and went on from there."

"Smokehouse Eatery ribs. I've dreamed of them. Come in, please." She reached out and caught his jacket sleeve, tugging him inside.

She stepped out of the way, then closed the door behind him.

The bookstore had been transformed since the last time he visited. Not that he often entered bookstores, but hers was worth a visit. It showed her touches. Whimsical. Rare books. Rare toys. The bold red fire engine sitting on the corner of her worktable had to be from the 1950s.

Cassie stopped at the counter and leaned over to nudge down the music volume. No radio or CDs for Cassie; she had a stack of vinyl records on a turntable. "White Christmas" ended and "Jingle Bells" began. It set a festive mood.

Jack made a place for the sack on the table that dominated the center of the room. It was custom built to be her come-and-linger table where she put out coffee and cookies for her customers. He slid his jacket over the back of a chair.

It was obvious she'd been sorting and shelving books. Several books with colorful jackets were spread out in a semicircle on the floor beside the glass-enclosed shelves. Curious, he studied the two turned his direction: *Wings for Victory,* with its World War II vintage B-52 and parachuting soldier, and *Gene Autry and the Redwood Pirates,* the horse and its rider racing up a trail. Popular children's books from another decade.

"I think you'd like *Uncle Wiggily in the Country.*" Cassie pointed to the book nearest him on the floor. "It's got pictures in it."

He shot her a smile. "That book looks older than I am."

"1940. The jacket is in good condition, and the color-plate pictures are excellent."

"What's it worth?"

"Ninety."

"That's highway robbery."

Her laughter was a delight to hear. "If I wanted to hold it a while and sell it as part of a set, I could get in the low three figures."

Cassie rolled down her long sleeves and looked down to catch the buttons at the cuffs. "Was Cole at the party?"

Jack wanted to tell her not to roll them down for his sake. But he didn't know how she felt about the scars, if they made her self-conscious or embarrassed. If he said nothing, did he make it worse than if he acknowledged them? They looked a great deal better than the day the doctors first removed the gauze to air the burns.

"Cole was there, most of the firefighters, a good percentage of the dispatchers. The place was packed."

She glanced back up and smiled. "I'm glad. Charles and Sandra have been getting squeezed lately with the station closing right after the movie theater. They not only lost the business of firefighters stopping by the restaurant before and after their shifts, but Charles lost the extra income he earned working paid on call with the station."

"He seems to be weathering the transition. And Sandra is happy to have him off the fire runs."

A new record dropped and "Santa Claus Is Coming to Town" began to play.

Their conversation had already veered through its normal course of subjects and she looked to be searching for a new topic. They were casual friends, the kind you could be comfortable around, the kind with whom you could share a laugh and a smile when paths crossed. There was respect, trust, humor…and not much that was personal beyond work.

His plans to change that hadn't worked out as he hoped. Cassie had been in and out of the hospital with the surgeries, and he'd walked into a summer of crises in his family that had absorbed his time and attention.

He hadn't wanted Cassie catching grief because of him. So he flirted a bit when he saw her at a fire scene or a fireman's gathering, made a beeline to sit beside her when they ended up at the same certification training, but otherwise let the relationship drift as casual friends. He should have never let the distance between where they lived, the schedule clashes, what other guys in the small community of firefighters would say keep him from asking her out.

He was paying for it now. He wanted her feeling comfortable to talk about her plans, to stretch beyond that and talk about the holidays, family, what it was like to have dreams about a fire…but he didn't know how to begin. Stalling, Jack reached over and picked up one of the cars on the table destined for her rare toys shelf. "They don't make cars like this anymore."

The Model-T was heavy, made of metal, its black paint still shiny. The tires were thick rubber, the steering wheel an aged white plastic. He turned it over and found stamped on the bottom the signature Hubbley Toys of Lancaster, Pennsylvania.

"Raise the hood and check out the engine."

He did and smiled with pleasure. It was accurate down to the grillwork. "Now *these* are collectibles."

"I think so."

She liked old cars. It was a small thing, but he hadn't known it.

"Have you eaten yet?" Cassie asked.

Jack looked up from the car he held. Cassie pushed away from the counter and disappeared through the side door to the storage room. She came back with plates and napkins. "Say you haven't even if you have. I hate to eat alone."

"Cassie, I never turn down barbecue spareribs."

She moved books from the table to a blue plastic tote, clearing a space for them. "Just stack the pink pages and drop them back into the in-basket on the desk. They're on-line customer wish lists. I'll get back to them later."

"Business is good?"

"It's in the black. At the prices these books command, I only need to sell a few a month to cover the overhead."

When he'd visited her at the hospital he often found her on-line doing deals or researching the value of books she had found, using the hobby as a distraction against the ever present pain. She hadn't been much for TV beyond CNN and old Westerns.

Dealing with the burns, the surgeries, the painful recovery—day after day she had kept moving forward. He'd sat on the weight bench opposite her in the hospital rehab and told her jokes as she struggled to lift a three-pound barbell through twenty-rep exercises. He learned a lot about her ability never to quit. This business was yet another way to move forward. He was proud of her.

The papers moved to safety, Jack started unloading the sack.

She looked tired. As Cassie quietly fixed her plate with a sample of the items Sandra had sent, he could see now what Cole had referred to. There were lines around her eyes and the good mood and lightness in her voice couldn't hide the fact she was relieved to sit down.

He waited while she silently prayed. He knew she was a Christian. It hadn't taken more than a couple visits to the hospital to see her faith was more than words with her. Her Bible on the bedside table, a few of the books she read were on prayer, and the radio had been tuned to a Christian station. Cole believed too, and Jack had at times interrupted some very serious conversations between the two of them.

He found the subject of religion a difficult one. In the last few months four in his family had chosen to believe, and it was no longer a subject he could avoid. Jack didn't understand it. Jesus seemed to be the serious myth that people believed in at Christmas, Santa Claus the childish one. It was the season for children to think someone really did come down the chimney with gifts and for the adults to set aside reason and believe there was a God who had become a man.

Cassie lifted her head, ending her silent prayer, and reached for a napkin.

"You're looking forward to Christmas."

Cassie flashed him a grin as she nudged the box of Christmas decorations on the floor with her foot. "How could you tell?"

He had always loved the color and excitement of the Christmas season, the stocking stuffers, and the excuse to give gifts. It was harder this year with Jennifer sick, harder to retain the smile when there was a chance this would be her last Christmas.

Cassie's gaze sharpened as she must've caught something in his expression. He didn't want to talk about his sister's cancer, didn't have words to keep the emotions he felt in perspective. He spoke before she could. "You need a Christmas tree."

She looked at him a moment, then nodded, accepting the redirect. "I'm going to put a big one in the window and decorate it to the point it wants to topple under all the lights and ornaments. I've got a set of handmade glitter ones that are messy but look beautiful."

Jack seized on that comment. There weren't many obvious ways to put himself back into her world and he would take any opening he could find. She would need help with the Christmas tree.

"Has anyone heard from Ash?"

He wished he could give her a positive answer. He wanted to shake the guy for worrying her this way. Jack knew how close partners got. He had watched Ash and Cassie tease each other mercilessly during speed drills and hose hauls, but let someone else suggest their team wasn't the best and the two of them would turn as one to reply. He envied them both. "No one has heard from him."

Cassie pushed aside her disquiet and picked up the first sparerib on her plate. "Knowing Ash, he'll be back when he's ready and when I least expect it."

Jack didn't think Cassie and Ash had been more than good friends, but he knew they were very close. When your life depended on the person at your side, the trust went deep. And it went both ways between Ash and Cassie. Jack didn't understand why Ash had left without a word.

Cassie closed her eyes as she tasted the first sparerib. "Oh, these are good."

Jack turned his attention to his. "It's the sauce."

"And the smoke and the time and Charles's magic touch." She finished the first one and licked sauce off her fingers.

Jack reached over and wiped a spot from her chin. "Messy."

She laughed. "You can try and clean me up later. Somehow I don't think I'll have to worry about leftovers."

"You didn't have dinner."

She glanced at the box on her desk. "Pumpkin pie."

"Good priorities."

"Absolutely."

"I'll stop asking questions so you can eat dinner now."

The laughter reached her eyes as she picked up another sparerib. "Appr'ciate it."

Jack relaxed. Cassie hadn't changed, not all that much. Her eyes still reflected her thoughts; her emotions still came easily to the surface. "I miss having you at the fire scenes."

She studied him over her dinner. "I miss being there."

The first time he met her he'd been working with Company 81, Cassie for Company 65.

He was facing a grease fire in a restaurant, all his guys committed, with fire leaping to the business next door. Company 65 arrived and he yelled at her as he did any other guy, tagging her number from the back of her helmet, no idea who she was, sending her and Ash into the smoke next door to confirm the building was clear.

When she dumped water over his head to cool him down before cleanup started, he'd taken a mouthful of it as he realized C. Ellis was a woman. She'd laughed so hard at his expression she started to hiccup, then went back to hauling out smoldering bench padding to the street. Jack shook his head like a wet dog and followed her back to work.

"I can image the mop-ups are a bit more boring now," she teased.

"No one to talk literature with," he agreed, smiling.

Cassie put everything she had physically and then some into whatever job she was doing. His biggest caution had always been that she save some of that energy for the end of the fire.

He'd heard that when she returned to her fire station she'd crawl away, crash with a book, and ignore the world to get her energy back. He enjoyed teasing her about that at a scene while they were doing cleanup.

She'd always been one to laugh at his jokes and his gag gifts. She was quieter now, more reflective, and the experience she lived through was there just below the surface. But she was coming back with the same steel that had driven her to excel at her job. He was grateful. She'd had her life upended, but she found the strength to deal with it.

He wasn't sure how he'd handle it if he were put in a similar situation. He wanted to be a firefighter ever since he'd seen the fire in his bedroom as a young boy. His parents had encouraged the dream with trips to the local fire department and to the firefighter museum. The car crash that had killed his parents— It had been the fire department first on the scene to try and save them and Jack had never forgotten that. He'd gotten into the fire academy as soon as he could qualify. Being a fireman wasn't a job as much as it was an identity.

"Do you have plans yet for Christmas?" Cassie asked.

"Working. We'll probably have the O'Malley gathering the weekend before."

"I've heard about those O'Malley bashes."

They were legendary for the fun, family, and food. "If it's one thing the O'Malleys know how to do well, it's have fun."

"I envy you the big family."

He'd love to talk her into coming with him. He looked at her, started to ask, then bit his tongue. If Cassie said no to the invitation, he wanted enough time to convince her to change her mind, and the clock above the door was taking away his options for having such a discussion. It was 8:10. Jack didn't want to leave but knew he'd have to if he was going to get to the fire station on time.

Cassie saw the direction of his glance and wiped her fingers on a napkin. "You're working tonight?"

"I told Greg I'd cover part of his shift so he could get away early in the morning. His family is having a weekend reunion."

"Nice of you."

"I wish now I hadn't said yes."

She chuckled and pushed the frosted pastry his way. "Take dessert with you."

"Can I come back sometime?"

She leaned back in her chair and left his question hanging a beat too long for his comfort. When she answered, her smile reached her eyes. "Come over and I'll put you to work. Next time I'll bring the food."

Of all the reasons he liked Cassie, that undertone of laughter in her voice was near the top of the list. He pulled on his jacket and dug out his keys, then picked up the pastry and took a bite. There was raspberry inside. "Deal."

She was a vision walking in the door of the Smokehouse Eatery. Cole nearly choked on his soda. Where had Rachel gotten a cashmere sweater to match her eyes? Her black jacket hung open, her hands pushed into the pockets. She was wearing jeans and a sweater the color of emeralds.

Rachel was the classic beauty in the O'Malley family with an innate sense of how to dress well to make an impression. She was making one. Tall, slender, she walked like a model with her graceful stride. Cole was aware of men shifting their gaze as she crossed their line of sight. Rachel skirted around people coming his direction where he sat on a stool at the counter. He straightened, hoping…

"Cole, have you seen Gage?"

The vision spoke and he scowled. "Gage wouldn't risk coming here. He might cross paths with your brother."

She winced. "They have got to call a truce."

"Not up to you."

She shot him an annoyed look and turned to scan the room, her shoulder length brown hair swinging across her jacket collar. "Where is Jack? I thought he was coming to this gathering."

"He left an hour ago. I could make an educated guess where he went."

Rachel smiled. "So could I."

She picked up a matchbook from the basket beside the cash register out of habit and slid it into her pocket. He knew it had nothing to do with the fact she smoked—because she didn't—and everything to do with the fact she often worked disaster situations where the electricity was out. She gave new meaning to the adage: Be prepared.

"Sit. Stay a minute. You just walked in." She looked like she was getting ready to head out again.

"I'm looking for Gage."

"He won't be any more lost in five minutes than he is now."

She hesitated, then slid onto the stool next to him. She had a politeness that wouldn't let her refuse the request. She slipped off her jacket. He told himself not to stare. She was beautiful and it was a pleasure to look at her. Her sweater had three-quarter length sleeves, and it set off the fact she still had a tan acquired from her recent work in Texas and Florida. A silver bracelet holding an emerald stone bracketed her left wrist.

Cole turned on his stool and caught the attention of the lady on the other side of the counter. "Sandra, do you have any more of that hot apple cider? Rachel could use some."

"I'm not that cold," Rachel muttered, pushing the hands she had been rubbing into the pockets of her snug jeans.

"Honey, your nose is red, not to mention your ears."

Now her face was red. He watched that blush and was surprised when she didn't say anything as a comeback. He'd always been able to count on her for one. As a silent apology he slid over the basket of deep-fried mushrooms he'd been working on. "Eat. And tell me about Jennifer."

Her straight posture wilted on the stool. She picked up one of the mushrooms and bit into it, her gaze turning inward as she became absorbed in her own thoughts. "Cole, it's going to be a miserable Christmas."

He rested his forearms against the counter and crowded her space and she didn't even notice. "Why?"

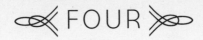

FOUR

"I wondered how far you would walk before you came back here. You should have paged." Caught off guard, Rachel looked up. Gage was sitting on the front stoop of his town house, his gray sedan parked behind her car at the curb rather than in his drive. It was after nine o'clock and Rachel had given up any hope of locating him, having checked all his normal haunts.

"I tried. Your pager batteries must be dead."

He pulled the pager from his belt clip to check. "Sorry. I didn't realize."

Rachel sat beside him on the steps, relief releasing the tension that had built up as she walked back from the restaurant.

Gage picked up her right hand and retrieved the watch she was holding. He fixed the loose link, put the watch back around her wrist, and refastened the clasp. "I was driving. Not drinking and driving. Just driving."

She nodded, appreciating the news.

"I'm sorry you were worried."

She shrugged her shoulder. "I like to worry."

He chuckled and, rather than get up, rested his elbows back on the step behind him and stretched out his legs. "You look good, Rachel."

His mood had lightened since the last time she had seen him. She searched his face and met his gaze, found the first glimmer of acceptance there.

"Thanks. You don't," she pointed out kindly. Thirty-eight, six two; dressing well and staying fit had always been priorities. It was a sign of the grief that what he valued most he'd let go of first.

He stroked his chin. "You don't like the pirate version of me?"

"It's still scruffy."

"Holidays are for beards."

"Is that what you call it?" It suited his chiseled features.

He smiled at her. "Why do I hear an echo of Tabitha in this conversation?"

"She would have started with the hair."

"True."

He let her tease him about it, and that alone told her something had fundamentally changed recently. Hope kindled. Tabitha had softened the man's personality, but the last two years had brought back the edge of cynicism that made his smile rare. Seeing the smile come back was a very good sign.

"I went back to work," he commented.

"I heard."

"No—really back to work. I accepted the Weekend Focus news slot."

A hard-hitting news story for the weekend paper, a chance to go in-depth on stories around the city. He'd won his Pulitzer there four years ago, and the prestige and pressure of that job were some things she remembered. "I'm pleased for you."

"I'm terrified."

He said it so bluntly and with a smile dancing around his mouth that she had to smile. "Welcome back to the living."

"Jeffrey wore me down. My junior partner wants to earn a Pulitzer too."

"He's young, ambitious. Sound familiar?"

"I was never young."

She laughed.

"The piece is ours to research, investigate, and write. I find it somewhat annoying to wear a tie when I go into the office now, but I'll be working from home most of the time."

"Are you ready for that?"

"I'm going to find out. So what were you looking so grim about as you paced back to your car?"

"Cole."

"Not a what, but a who." He got to his feet and offered her a hand up. "You like him; you just don't want to admit it."

"He watches out for my brother; I'm grateful for that." She would be fair and give Cole that. "He's worried about these fires."

"What fires?" Gage's good mood disappeared. Rachel knew how volatile the subject was for him, but she needed his help.

"The house that burned last week…apparently it matches other fires they've had recently. Would you consider taking a look?"

His expression told her no, but he reached out and rubbed her chin with his thumb and sighed. "For you, yes, I'll take a look. As long as you don't rag on me about the housekeeper."

"I'm that predictable?"

He wrapped his arm around her shoulders and turned her toward his front door. "Only to people who like you. So what did you bring me to eat? I'm starved."

"Cherry pie." She glanced at her watch. "I can't stay long. Kate's expecting me at ten."

"Stay long enough to share a piece. I hate to eat alone."

The medallion from Jack's key chain had fallen off. Cassie rubbed the smooth metal between her thumb and forefinger as she walked through the store turning off lights. The man carried a Bugs Bunny medallion on his key chain. It had brought a laugh when she found it. The man was a charmer. And tonight anyone who fed her was in her good graces.

Cassie stopped in the storeroom to retrieve her jacket. She'd have to dig out a pair of needle nose pliers at home and fix the link that had opened. Maybe she would get Jack a matching Road Runner to go with it. They sold them at the corner store, on a spin rack by the cash register right next to the baseball cards and the lock de-icer.

She hadn't intended to stay this late. It was going to be after eleven before she got home. She would get gas in the car, stop by the twenty-four-hour pharmacy, and then it would be home and bed. It sounded like a lovely plan.

Cassie slipped the medallion into her pocket. It was a bit painful to be looking across the table at a young Robert Redford. Rugged good looks, broad shoulders, blue eyes—he was a guy who attracted attention just by walking into the room, who didn't have scars to mar his looks. It wasn't fair to hold Jack's looks against him. Everything she knew about the man she liked. She hoped Jack O'Malley did stop by again.

The fire department community was a small one, and she had worked with his paramedic brother Stephen on a few occasions before the restaurant fire had put her in a place to meet Jack and get to know him.

Dumping water over Jack that day had been a practical way to say hello. It had been a hot day, an intense fire, and cooling down was critical for everyone at the scene. It had also been a laughter-filled way to make sure he would remember her.

She enjoyed his friendship. He was one of the few who hadn't been stiff when he dropped by the hospital to say hi. He was the one more likely to bring her a tape of the Saturday morning cartoons than a magazine. He had always been good for a joke designed to make her laugh.

She saw behind the humor a serious man making a deliberate choice. He made a point to offer her what others were not—a reminder that life outside the hospital walls was still going on, was still there waiting to be enjoyed when she got out. She deeply appreciated that.

Cassie locked the back door of the store. She planned to build shelves in the storage room. She'd see if Jack wanted to help hold boards and swing a hammer some day when he was off work.

Something was wrong.

Cassie stopped, scanning the area and the shadows, searching for why the impression had formed. It was a sensation not unlike being in a fire when she couldn't see but could feel a check from her subconscious not to move, that danger was near.

Her hand coiled around her keys, slipping them between her fingers, turning them into sharp weapons. It was a safe area and she was accustomed to working at night, but if trouble was around the best defense was a good offense.

And then it registered.

Smoke.

She was smelling smoke.

Her head came up like a hawk. She looked toward the sky and saw a faint haze shimmering. Stars began to disappear.

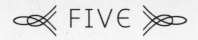

FIVE

Sam was snoring.

Jack turned his head and considered throwing a pillow across to the next bunk to shut him up. That's what Sam's wife said worked. The dorm room at the station house slept twelve, the bunks basic and the mattresses thick enough to be better than camping out but not comfortable enough to make it reach the level of even a cheap motel bed.

Stretched out on top of his sleeping bag, Jack wasn't sure why he couldn't sleep. It was 11 P.M. and shutting off to go to sleep had never been a problem before. He shifted his head over to the right side of the pillow. He was on the fourth bunk and if he moved his head to the left, the triangle of light coming in the window from the streetlight would be in his eyes.

The sleeping bag smelled like smoke and this late at night it was irritating him. He'd have to remember to drop it off at the cleaners to run through their heavy duty washers. Since the bunks were used by three different shifts, most guys stuck to bringing sleeping bags rather than mess with sheets.

It was different down the hall in the women's dorm. There were two women paramedics and one woman firefighter on this shift. They took time to add nice touches to their lives like sheets, even though it meant changing bedding every time they came on duty.

Middle of the night and he was thinking about how women liked sheets and guys went for sleeping bags. He tucked his hands behind his head and wondered what his sister Rachel would say about that. Probably that he needed some sleep.

Cassie would need to get the Christmas tree up at the store in the next week if it was to make any impact on her Christmas sales. Maybe they could look for the tree this coming Sunday afternoon. He knew she closed her bookstore on Sundays for religious reasons so she would likely be free.

He could borrow his brother Stephen's pickup truck and take Cassie to either a nursery or one of the Christmas tree farms. It would be a good excuse to get a couple hours of her time. The more Jack thought about it, the more he liked the idea.

He was going to have to come up with the right Christmas gifts to put under that tree. She'd probably suggest prettily wrapped empty boxes and there was no fun in that. Besides, he was a great believer in quantity in addition to quality.

Jack smiled. There had to be somewhere he could find some old, rare comic books.

Dispatch tones broke the silence.

Cassie slammed her car into park, killed the engine, and came close to stripping the key as she pulled it out. The streetlights were too far away to give more than an impression of a house set back on its corner lot surrounded by century old trees.

The house was big, old, sprawling, with a wraparound porch. She already hated the two turrets because she knew they would have limited narrow access ways going up. It was the kind of place her grandmother had owned, which Cassie had loved to explore.

Smoke billowed in the breeze. Embers were beginning to illuminate the smoke like fireflies set free from the bowels of the earth.

The spectators consisted of one man in his eighties hurrying down his porch steps across the street and his wife tying the belt of her thick blue robe and scolding him for not putting on shoes.

"Did you call it in?"

"Yes." He was staring across the street in disbelief. "I just got up to get a drink and *wham,* I smelled smoke. For the longest time I couldn't figure out where it was coming from."

It didn't surprise Cassie; she knew how fast fires could erupt, developing from nothing to this. "Who lives here? Is anyone home?"

"Carla and Peter Wallis, their daughter Tina."

Cassie flinched at the child's name. "How old is Tina?"

"Six. They travel frequently, but as far as I know they were staying home for the holidays."

Flames weren't visible in the windows but they were now showing at the crown line of the roof. The house was on the edge of the fire district. The firefighters were on the way; traffic was light. Did she have three to five minutes to wait for them?

She leaned on her car horn. The smoke might not yet be on the first floor, but if it had already descended throughout the second floor, anyone inside wouldn't be waking up.

She felt sweat soak the back of her shirt under her jacket. She didn't want to go in. She was afraid. It might be rational but she was ashamed of it. "Pets?"

The neighbor shook his head. At least there wouldn't be a crazed dog waiting for her inside. If someone was in there, she would never be able to live with herself if she didn't go in. Just do it. Think about it later.

She found her flashlight under the driver's seat and grabbed the roll of duct tape she used to seal boxes of books bought at the estate auction. Cassie was relieved to have the leather jacket but wished she had something better than tennis shoes and ankle-high socks.

She had done rescues before. With Ash. With an air tank on her back, a turnout suit that could reflect three hundred degrees of heat, and a face mask to at least keep smoke out of her eyes even if visibility was nonexistent. She had none of those tonight. And it was Ash in the equation she missed the most.

"When the firefighters get here, tell them I'm doing a bedroom sweep clockwise. Remember that. Clockwise."

She ran toward the house. With every step she got closer to her private nightmare.

Lord, give me courage.

She didn't fear the danger; she feared her memories and the fact she might freeze. As long as she kept her focus and kept moving, she could deal with the risks. But if she had to face the flames…the nausea had started and she was only smelling the smoke.

Another spectator. She saw the man as she turned up the drive toward the front door. "Stay back, please. I'm with the fire department."

She didn't need well-meaning civilians entering the house to try and help. The man stood just inside the property line watching the fire. In the dark, he was simply an impression—a tall man, wearing a light brown jacket and jeans. He slipped his hands into his pockets and idly turned to glance toward her. She couldn't see who it was, but the way he moved…

Ash.

She stumbled.

How many times had she seen that still, relaxed consideration of a situation before he acted? "Ash?" she whispered the word in disbelief. He lived near here. He was back. "Ash." Her voice increased in confidence and was filled with relief.

The man stepped back and disappeared into the shadows.

What was going on?

A hot ember brushed her cheek.

Cassie's attention jerked back to the house. It couldn't have been Ash. Not to watch a fire. Not to ignore her.

Smoke spewed out where the roof met the siding like a chimney pointed downward. Since she had arrived the fire had already grown in intensity.

She needed Ash to be here, not some spectator who thought he'd stand and watch.

How would she get in?

In the past she and Ash would have hit the front door with a battering ram and dropped it in two blows. She didn't have the strength to try a brute force entry.

She saw the child-sized rocking chair on the porch beside two adult chairs. There was no need to be pretty. She picked up the first large chair, its metal cold and hard to grip as all her strength was now awkwardly in her left arm. She sent the chair crashing through the living room window. Only a small amount of smoke swirled out. If the fire was high and held in the roof, there was still a chance.

She knocked out the glass at the bottom of the frame with the flashlight.

For a decade she had loved doing this. She'd been crazy.

She went over the windowsill.

Edge of the district. Late at night. Jack braced his hand on the dashboard as Nate made the difficult right turn onto Holly Street, needing every inch of the road to handle Engine 81's length. The neighborhood was old, the streets narrow, the sirens and lights were waking people up. Jack willed the engine to close the distance faster. 1437 Cypress. They were heading to the blocks behind where Cassie's store was located.

This had the hallmarks of one of the arsonist's fires. But it was not Gold Shift on duty this time, it was Red Shift. It was chance that Nate and Bruce had been available when this call came in. Rescue 65 had been dispatched to a car accident, and Nate and Bruce had arrived at the station in answer to the callback to replace personnel just as the dispatch tones for this fire sounded.

Jack had to assume it was the arsonist and plan for the worst case. The address made it another house—but was it unoccupied or occupied?

"Bruce."

"I'll be at your heels with the fire pole."

Jack nodded. He didn't want a team entering a house with a ceiling ready to come down on them.

Cassie whimpered at the heat. It invaded her jacket and penetrated her long-sleeved shirt. The healing skin from the last surgery screamed. She found the hallway and the stairs going up. The smoke was deceptive. It remained wisps of white in her beam of light on the first floor, but her light shining up couldn't penetrate the blackness at the top of the landing.

She wanted to retreat. She knew what was waiting at the top of the stairs.

Go or get out?

Cassie grasped the railing and took the stairs two at a time.

The smoke drove her to a crouch. Coughing, struggling to get her bearings, she moved right, feeling her way. Air was still breathable low but it was hot. Her eyes burned with the smoke and visibility was abysmal. She didn't waste her breath trying to call out. She would be grabbing and dragging.

The roar of the fire in the roof was deafening. The owners had probably filled the attic and never thought about what a decade of dry rot would do to boxes put into storage and forgotten. Plaster was beginning to drop. Outlets were smoking. Flames were shooting from nail holes marking where pictures had fallen from the wall.

Her options were limited. Breathable air wasn't going to be available for long. Thirty seconds. Clockwise search.

She hit the first bedroom with the end of the duct tape already tugged free so that two quick twists wrapped it around the hot doorknob. She let the tape stream out behind her as she dove into the smoke to find the bed.

Find a bed that wasn't made and hope her grasping hands touched an arm or leg, pray she didn't find an empty child's bed. Children in a fire had the deadly habit of crawling into closets or under furniture. There was no way she could do a full-room search without gear.

Her right shin hit wood and the painful gasp cost her precious air as she fell against the bed. The down comforter was stretched taut. She cringed at that realization—this was probably a guest bedroom.

Cassie turned and dove back into the hallway. She dropped to her knees, coughing, getting a breath in the clearer air inches from the carpet. The air was so hot it hurt to breathe.

She scrambled into the thick smoke to reach the next door, ruthlessly denying her fear. The next door turned out to be a bathroom. The third door jammed when she tried to force it open. Had someone tried to get to the door and fallen inside?

Cassie set the flashlight by her left foot. She accepted the blisters she was going to get, wrapped her left hand around the hot metal, and put her weight against the door. Her lungs burned as she strained. She managed to wedge her right hand into the crevice and get desperately needed leverage.

There was fire behind the door. As the door inched open she found herself facing the dragon. The door suddenly opened all the way and the flames slapped at her. Plaster. She'd just shoved aside a chunk of plaster and a beam. Cassie jerked away from the flames back into the hallway. Flames shot across to touch the opposite wall. All breathable air became swallowed in the swirling smoke. There was no time left.

Get out.

There was no way to get past those flames.

Cassie turned...and stumbled on a teddy bear lying in the hall.

SIX

Jack tightened the wrist straps on his gloves as Engine 81 pulled in front of the house and slightly past it so Engine 65 could take the hydrant. They would buddy tank the water, Engine 65 feeding it forward so they could place four attack lines and keep the water pressure even.

Ladder Truck 81 moved past, sirens still screaming, pulling to the east side of the house. Rescue 81 took the street side of the engines. The fire was already crowning through the roof. Jack swung from the seat to the ground relieved they had rolled all engines. They would need the men. They were going to need to lay a lot of hose to get water on the fire.

Was the house occupied or empty? Jack scanned the spectators, dozens of them, searching to spot the one or two neighbors who might have that answer. Two cops were present and a reporter had already made it to the scene.

"She went in to search the bedrooms." Jack locked in on the words of the distraught elderly man now with the captain. "She said to tell you she was searching clockwise. She was real insistent about that word."

"Who?"

Jack spotted the car. There weren't two people who drove blue sedans with white trim who had chili cook-off bumper stickers saying: Firefighters Like It Hot stuck on the front bumper.

"Cassie," Jack hollered, adrenaline surging. "Has she come out of the house since she entered?" He tried to keep the desperation out of his voice as he grabbed his air tank. He ducked and dropped it into place on his back. Bruce and Nate shifted from hose to grabbing fire blankets and spare air tanks, priorities immediately changing.

The two from Rescue Squad 81 were already racing for the door.

"No. She's been in there three minutes," the elderly man said.

Faced with the possibility of people inside, Jack knew she would have had no choice but to go in. He needed a word with more punch than *fear* to handle the emotion that absorbed him. Shingles slid from the roof and crashed with an explosion of embers onto the walkway.

"Jack, backup rescue." Frank keyed his radio and grabbed the attention of the lieutenant for Truck 81. "Five are going in. Tear open the roof but don't drown it until we know we won't be bringing it down on them as they search."

"No one's home!" The cop struggling to get into the garage had just gained entry. No vehicle. Whoever lived here was away for the holidays. Jack wanted to swear. Cassie wouldn't have known that. And that meant she would take the time to try and reach each bedroom.

She knew how fire moved and breathed. She would know the dangers. But that was a two-edged sword. She would stay inside until the last possible moment. And the smoke would take her down. After eighteen months sidelined she wouldn't know her own limits. Stress, heat, smoke…she should have been out of the house long ago.

Bruce and Nate were at his side as he sprinted toward the house. He wished Ben had been called back to duty. He wasn't coming out without her, and he could use the man's intensity right now.

The paint was blistering. Jack's breath hissed inside the mask as his light picked up the sight he feared. Penetrate these walls and flames would surround them. Let oxygen get to the base of this fire and it would roar. The building was primed to go.

Jack followed the guys from Rescue 81 up the stairs while Bruce and Nate veered off to search the first floor.

Where was she?

Flames had the ceiling, a deep red glowing monster that rolled like waves through the thick smoke feeding on the paint. The two men from Rescue 81 moved forward together into the smoke to literally sweep the width of the hallway with their bodies. Jack knew the reality. They were hoping to trip over Cassie.

She was down on all fours crawling. The firefighter in him applauded her smarts; the guy who had visited her in the hospital wanted to weep. His bright light caught the odd color of blue. She was grasping a teddy bear in her left hand. No wonder she had kept searching. The guys from Rescue 81 swallowed her in a fire blanket to protect her from falling embers and lifted her toward him.

Jack did his best to avoid the healing skin grafts on her arms as he took her weight. Cassie was convulsing with coughs. There was no way she would be able to walk the stairs without stumbling. He put her over his shoulder and turned to retrace his steps down the stairs, moving with only one thought in mind—getting her out of the house fast.

The instant he cleared the front door he ripped off his mask. He shifted Cassie, shoving back the fire blanket, alarmed at the first clear look at her face. Tears streaming, she was gasping for air, gagging. Seared lungs could kill. "Where's the ambulance?"

"Here."

The boots felt like lead on his feet when he wanted to run.

Cole was there as well as two paramedics from the area hospital. Jack was grateful to see it was Neal and Amy who had been on duty. They were pros at fire scenes. He still wished it were his brother Stephen who had received the call as he carefully set Cassie down.

Jack heard the order to drown the fire and knew it meant his men and the rescue squad were clear. An incredible rush of noise followed as water flowed.

Cassie refused to lie back on the gurney. "Hot," she protested.

As Cole peeled away her jacket, Jack spotted the burn spots in the leather. She was going to need another jacket for Christmas.

Amy slipped on an oxygen mask over the coughs.

Jack stripped off his gloves. He unbuttoned the cuffs of Cassie's shirt and carefully rolled up her sleeves. The healing scars on both arms were an angry red, inflamed by the heat, her right arm much worse than her left. Neal handed over cold packs and Jack rested them against her forearms. She flinched.

"Better," she whispered.

Jack tipped up her chin looking for new burns. Her eyes were streaming and she couldn't open them to more than a squint. He carefully slipped off her glasses, relieved to see they hadn't been cracked. The exhaustion he had seen earlier in the evening was swamping her now. "The house was empty, Cassie. The family is on vacation."

Her relief was palpable.

Neal slipped an ice pack behind her neck to help cool her down. "Cassie, hold on, the eye drops will help." He brushed back her hair and carefully opened her eyes to add the drops. He blotted her streaming eyes with sterile gauze. "Let them water and clear."

A fit of coughing doubled her up.

It hurt to hear.

Jack had to get back to his men but he didn't want to leave her side. He could only imagine how hard it had been to face a fire again.

A firm hand settled on his shoulder. Jack looked up to find his captain beside him, watching Cassie. "Company 26 is half a minute away," Frank said. "We're covered. Stay with her. Anything she needs, let me know. Anything."

Jack nodded, grateful.

Neal nudged his arm and Jack looked over. Neal had uncurled Cassie's fingers to slip off her watch. There were blisters on the fingers of her left hand and palm, some already open and raw. Jack recognized the pattern: She'd grasped a doorknob. His own hand spasmed in sympathy.

"Cassie, we're going to get you to a hospital." He stroked the inside of her right wrist, feeling her erratic pulse. "We'll get someone to look at the blisters."

Her eyes opened, and in an uncoordinated way she lifted her right hand to push aside the oxygen mask. "No. No hospital."

There was fear in her eyes, but the hospital wasn't a choice. She had to see a doctor, not just for her hands but her lungs. He didn't need a fight with her, not over this. "Cole." He appealed to the one person she would listen to.

Amy tried to get her to put the mask back on and Cassie pushed it away. She tried to look around to see Cole. "No. I won't go."

The man was her former captain. The history between the two of them extended back a long way before the nursing home fire, and Jack could almost see the silent conversation going on. Cole finally nodded. "Neal, do what you can here. She's not going."

Incredulous, Jack turned, furious at him for that. A look from Cole silenced his words before he could speak.

Cassie closed her eyes and let Amy slip back on the oxygen.

Jack moved aside to give Neal room to work. "Cole—" He was ready to argue the point.

"I want my glasses," Cassie mumbled.

Jack glanced at them in his hand. They were grimy with smoke residue. If he gave them to her, she'd just accidentally knock them off, possibly break them. "Later, Cassie. You can't see right now anyway."

She patted her shirt pocket. "Here. Only pair."

"I won't lose them."

She opened her eyes enough to squint at him. "Swear?"

If she wasn't protesting a pair of glasses, he would have laughed at the irritation in her question. "I promise not to lose them."

She was reluctant to believe him. Jack reached down and gently squeezed her ankle. He understood why she would cling to something so simple. She'd spent three weeks with her eyes bandaged after the nursing home fire. Without the glasses her vision was very poor. "Promise, kiddo."

"Cassie." Neal got her attention. "I need to clean this hand. It's going to sting."

She just nodded at that. Jack supposed everything was relative. A sting wasn't high on the pain meter compared to the pain she'd been through.

Jack turned his attention to his friend and pitched his voice low. "Cole, she needs to see a doctor."

"Tell me something I don't know."

"Then why—?"

"She'd have to be dying before she would voluntarily step foot back into a hospital."

Jack supposed if he had dealt with over a year of being in and out of hospitals, he might feel the same. "It doesn't change the fact she needs to see a doctor."

"So I'll find one who makes house calls." Cole pointed to the fire. "One of his?"

Jack forced himself to focus on the problem they had to deal with. "Fire in the walls," he confirmed. "Better than even odds we'll find his signature."

"Peter Wallis owns this house." The quiet statement was underscored by the significance of the information.

"Chairman of the fire district board?"

Cole nodded.

Jack could feel the open question of motive for the arsonist finding definition.

"That hurt."

Jack turned at Cassie's words, saw the taut edge of pain around her mouth.

"Almost done," Neal sympathized. He had her hand clean, was dealing with a blister forming between her two small fingers. Jack stepped back to her side and let his hand touch her shoulder.

Cassie pushed away the oxygen mask. "This fire was set?"

"It looks that way." Jack nudged the mask back on, wishing she was a better patient. She ignored him.

"He set it," she murmured.

"What?"

She frowned and shook her head.

"Cassie, did you see something?" Cole pushed. "Anything?"

"By the drive. Watching the fire. Weird the way he was watching the fire," she whispered. "A tall man, brown jacket, jeans." She looked down at her hand. "I didn't really get a good look. He was in the shadows."

Jack shot Cole a look. They had been hoping for someone to see the man, but Cassie— Jack was afraid of what that meant. She had seen him; that meant he had seen her too.

Cole dug his keys out of his pocket. "As soon as they say she can move, take her to the station and get her statement," he said quietly. "I'll bring her car."

SEVEN

Jack knew Cole used his vehicle as his mobile command center. He hadn't realized that meant there was barely room for people. In the back were empty paint cans to use for evidence collection, metal screens for sifting debris, shovel, rake, crowbar, garbage bags, a large red toolbox, and rolls of plastic sheeting to protect evidence.

Jack nudged down the volume on the radio dispatch calls, keeping his attention on the traffic even as his peripheral vision stayed locked on Cassie beside him. "Leave that oxygen on."

"I'm fine."

"You're still coughing between every other word."

"It's not the first time I ate smoke. It's almost cleared."

He frowned at her. "I can tell."

She raised the mask again.

Cole's jacket swallowed her slim frame. Cassie's system had swung from overheated to chilled as it coped with the crashing adrenaline. Jack was feeling very responsible for her as she'd been entrusted to his care and he wasn't all that happy about it. He wasn't a paramedic.

She should have stayed under Neal's and Amy's watchful eyes for at least another hour. But she'd insisted she was ready to move and trying to stop her was like stepping in front of a steamroller.

"You didn't tell me I shouldn't have gone in."

Jack turned his head long enough to look at her, surprised by the touch of irritation in her voice. He'd cleaned her glasses and her eyes seemed huge behind the lenses. They were still red and watering from the smoke irritation and she was blinking to try to clear them. A fact that just made her look cute. "Because I think you did the right thing." He wondered why she had assumed he would have disagreed with her decision. It might have added about ten years to his life, and until she stopped coughing he was going to be wheezing in sympathy, but it had been the right decision. "You needed to go in."

"I didn't want to."

Jack reached over, avoiding her left hand wrapped in a cold towel and settled for touching the grimy knee of her jeans. "You went in anyway." There was admiration and lingering fear in that. She had been touched by fire once, and she still went in. She'd been touched by it again because they hadn't been in time to help her. "It makes you even more of a hero."

"Heroine."

"You're still lady blue," he corrected.

"Thanks." She sounded pleased...even touched.

"You're one of us. Even if you aren't around nearly as often as we would like."

"The guys crowd me," she said softly. "And it's hard on their families."

Jack hurt to hear that even though he understood it. She was the walking reminder of what families feared would happen. "They don't mean it to be."

"It's just reality. I'm not complaining."

"And it's hard to be around what you once had."

"Yes." She shifted Cole's coat. "I smell like smoke. I don't miss that at all."

As a way to lighten the conversation, she had chosen a great point to make. "We both do." The vehicle now smelled like a campfire gone bad. It was not exactly the way to make a good impression on a lady.

"Did you see where my leather jacket went?"

Jack was grateful she hadn't asked how it had fared. The leather had done its job, deflecting burning embers, but it had been destroyed in the process. "Cole had it. I think he tossed it in your car."

She eased open the cold towel to look at her blisters.

"Don't start playing with the bandage and messing up Neal's work." The cold towel kept the gauze wet and the burns moist, a major factor for how it healed.

"Would you relax? They're just blisters. A day or two and they will be calluses."

"What did they give you for the pain?"

"I've no idea, but whatever was in the shot, it's working."

"Your words are slurring."

"I don't make much sense at this time of night anyway, so it's probably not much of a loss." She lost her voice on another coughing fit.

"I wish you had seen a doctor."

"At this time of night they wouldn't have let me go home."

"That's a big deal?"

"Yes."

It wasn't much of an explanation, but the emotions under the word were deep. Home was critical to her now. He tucked that fact away. Did she dream about the fire, need the comfort of her own bed to help her sleep?

"How are your forearms?"

"They hurt."

She raised her hand, then stopped. "I wish I could rub my eyes."

"There's a clean handkerchief in my shirt pocket if you want it." Jack would have reached for it and given it to her, but his hands were far from clean.

Cassie leaned over and tugged it out with her right hand. "Thanks." She slipped off her glasses and wiped at her eyes.

"Need more eyedrops?"

"When we get to the station." She slipped her glasses back on.

Jack rolled his shoulders and did his best to cover a yawn. It was embarrassing to admit how adrenaline sapped his energy.

"I can't say I miss the middle of the night rollouts."

He heard the amusement under her words. He glanced at the dashboard clock. 12:05 A.M. He could forget sleep again tonight, and it was getting to be a bad pattern. When he was in his twenties it hadn't been so hard to deal with. As he neared thirty-four he now felt every minute of the lost sleep. "At least you got me out of cleanup at the scene."

"Oh, great."

"What?"

She lifted her right knee and braced her foot against the dash. "These were my comfortable tennis shoes." There was a hole in the canvas fabric at the top of her right shoe just above her little toes.

"They look like they were fit for the trash bin before this."

"I like old shoes. New clothes, but old shoes." She tugged at the laces with one finger. "Do you know who has my watch?"

"My pocket," he reassured.

"I feel like I've left bits and pieces of me all over the place. I'm not sure what happened with the leftovers I was taking home. I probably tossed the sack in the backseat of my car when I smelled the smoke and managed to spill the food."

"Cole will deal with it."

"I hope he notices that the car needs gas."

"I'm sure he will notice."

"Is Cole coming back to the office? Or is he going to be at the scene for a while?"

"I'd guess he'll be there until he can get the first look inside and get the security in place to close the scene. Regardless, I'm giving you a lift home. You don't need to be driving with that hand."

"I would appreciate it. I need my hair washed and a change of clothes."

"You look like you walked out of a fire."

"I feel like it. Just don't bump us into someone I know or I'm going to be spending forever explaining."

Jack turned into the Station 81 complex and pulled around to the parking lot behind the building. He parked the SUV beside Cole's personal car. "Stay put. I'll get the door for you."

The cold air swirled in as he opened the driver's door and stepped out. He circled the vehicle and opened the passenger door. Cassie braced her uninjured hand on his shoulder to keep her balance as she stepped down. He leaned in to make it easier. She was hurting, and he wished he had the right to lean in and kiss it better. Her hand tightened on his shoulder. "Don't look like that."

"Like what?"

"Interested," she muttered.

"I am."

"Your timing is awful."

He hadn't placed her as easily embarrassed, but she was now. "I think my timing is just fine," he smiled tenderly, rubbing her chin with his thumb. "But I'll let you think about it a bit." Before she could pull back he turned to lead instead. "Come on, this way."

The light at the back door to the station was on. Jack used his key, then held the heavy steel door open for her. He was here more often than home, and it was a comfortable if spartan place. They walked into a wide spacious corridor, the floor tiled and the walls painted cinder block. The corridor was lined with hooks for coats and jackets. To the right was a spacious kitchen with an extra large refrigerator, stove, two sinks, two microwaves, and a large work area. Whichever firefighter had KP duty for the day was cooking for fifteen to twenty for any particular meal.

To the left was the lounge where guys could hang out while off duty, past it the dorm rooms. The architects had changed the historical layout for this station, and instead put the dorms on the first floor, eliminating the much-loved fire pole. Too many men ended up with shin-splint injuries from repeatedly hitting the concrete floor to make it worth having.

The equipment bays were ahead, a huge part of the building, fifty-two feet long, forty feet deep, with twenty feet high ceilings and fast-rising doors. As large as the bays were, they still felt cramped when two engines, a ladder truck, and two rescue squads were pulled inside at the same time.

He eased the coat from around her shoulders. "Okay?" She just nodded. Nothing could hide the fresh tears. Her arms were really hurting. "I'm so sorry, Cassie."

She sniffed and smiled. "Just get me some Kleenex."

"And I'll go grab more eyedrops and another ice pack."

"Cole's office?"

Jack was surprised to realize she hadn't been here before. "Next door in the district offices. Hang a left when you enter the equipment bay and go through the connecting corridor. His office is on the left past the conference room."

Jack watched her turn that way, her steps slow and measured. The only thing he could do was ease the hurt as best he could and hope she didn't end up with nightmares because of tonight.

The station was quiet, a radio was on somewhere as well as the muted sounds of the TV left on in the lounge. Before he headed to the medical cabinet, Jack paused to nudge the magnet by his name on the status board over to show he was in the offices. He got eyedrops, burn cream, and broke out another ice pack for her hand.

Cassie had turned on lights on her way through the dark office building.

There wasn't room to shove another desk into the packed open office area. There had been an attempt last month to squeeze in a desk for the police liaison by angling it in by the emergency exit, sparking a heated debate over whether the fire department should comply with the letter of the law regarding fire safety or the spirit of the law which was to make sure the exits weren't blocked.

The pragmatic people working on the arson squad suggested if fire crews twenty feet away couldn't deal with the fire, having an exit with clearance of more than eighteen inches was irrelevant. The desk had been put in.

Jack found Cassie in Cole's office. She had settled into his desk chair, slouched to be comfortable. It was cool in this building. Jack wished he had thought to grab a sweatshirt from his locker for her.

"I see he's been decorating," Cassie noted.

Children's hand-drawn pictures of a fireman and engine were taped in a rather haphazard montage on the wall.

"He's been doing a series of presentations at the local schools." Jack pulled out a chair at the small table, swiveling it around and setting down the supplies he carried. The pictures clashed with the pile of books on the table. Two of them—*Investigating the Fireground* and *Fire Investigation*—Jack recognized as course books that Cole was using in his current academy training class.

"What are the latest numbers? Eleven percent of fires are juvenile arsons?"

"Closer to 15 percent."

"Ouch."

Jack reached over for the Kleenex box and set it in her lap. "Eye-drops."

She reluctantly slid off her glasses. "Don't drown me."

Jack chuckled at the warning. "Can't swim?"

"Not funny."

"Bad pun. Tilt your head back."

She leaned her head back but did so by slouching in the chair and looking up. He smiled at her but had his doubts about her ability to see his expression without her glasses. "Don't trust me?"

"What do you think?" She reluctantly leaned farther back.

He missed with the first drop, then got the next four drops sort of in as her blinking messed up his aim. He didn't have the heart to hold her eyes open anymore. "Done."

She didn't comment, just pulled a tissue from the box…and another one and another.

He wisely didn't say anything either as she dried her eyes and slipped on her glasses. He was relieved to see the redness was beginning to clear. "What can you tolerate to drink? More ice water? Juice?"

"Something with sugar. See if Cole has any of his favorite pineapple-orange left."

Jack opened the small refrigerator Cole kept tucked under the side table. He found two bottles of the juice and opened one of them for her.

Cassie accepted it with a quiet thanks, then used the toe of one tennis shoe against the heel of the other to pry off her shoes. "Does Cole like the arson job?" she asked as she looked around the office, sipping the cold juice.

Jack had the odd feeling that Cassie did not want to talk about the fire yet. He set his juice bottle on the table and laced his fingers across his chest. "He's good at it."

"He would be. He's thorough. How are the latest station consolidations working out?"

She was definitely stalling. "There are challenges with learning the new streets and buildings within the expanded district. The station is busier. We're rolling out on probably 20 percent more calls, and it's putting some strain on the paid oncall guys. We'll probably need to move a couple up to salaried positions and put them into the full-time rotation. On the other hand, it is nice having another engine in the rotation for call outs."

"The Company 65 guys are fitting in?"

"Friendly competition," Jack replied, smiling slightly. The drills over the last months were killing them as one engine crew tried to outdo the other, but it was making them all better firefighters. "They seem to be making the transition just fine."

He wished he could read her body language, her expression, better to understand what was going on. He could sort of figure out what his sisters were thinking, but Cassie was a mystery. "What's wrong?"

"What?"

"You're chattering. This place is making you nervous."

She looked away. He waited.

She checked the turned up cuff on her shirtsleeve. It was an interesting tell. He tipped his head to one side and considered why it might be happening. She hadn't been to Cole's office before. She was stalling, and he couldn't figure out why. Curiosity overtook the concern. "Did you ever read the nursing home report?"

"It was offered. I passed."

"I wondered." She had never wanted to talk about the fire when he stopped by the hospital to visit. With Ash it had been the opposite; the fire was the only thing her partner had wanted to talk about.

The nursing home fire had been an unfortunate fire in how it spread. Two of the automatic fire alarms were not working so the fire took hold and spread before other alarms triggered. Two patients died, six had been critically injured from the smoke, and Cassie paid a permanent price. It had been arson. The man suspected of setting it and three other fires had been killed in a car accident in New Jersey two months ago with an outstanding warrant pending for his arrest.

Cassie shifted in her chair. "What do you need to know for your report?"

There was grimness under her words, a reluctance to look at him, a tenseness that extended to her body language. She didn't want to think about the fire tonight. He couldn't blame her, not when he just had to think about that hallway and he saw her trying to crawl out clutching a teddy bear.

"What did you see?"

"Not much."

"Do you want to do this tomorrow?"

"With a crowd around here...no thanks." Jack saw her measure the open floor space with her eyes and shift forward in her chair as she thought about getting up to pace. Then she changed her mind and settled back. "I'm tired, Jack. Really tired. But I know how this guy has been hassling you. This is what, his third fire?"

"Sixth," Jack replied softly. He caught her startled gaze.

"You're serious."

"This makes his second house." Jack found a blank pad of paper. "I need to know everything you saw, from the beginning."

She was distinctly subdued as she answered. "I smelled the smoke when I left the bookstore."

"Who were the spectators at the fire when you arrived?"

Jack didn't hurry as he took her through the evening up to the point when they found her in the house. Part of that pace was not to hit her with a question before she was ready for it. The more serious reason was the fact her answers made it hard for him to breathe.

The fire had a powerful hold before she entered the house. Her description of the bedroom with the door blocked was frightening. A beam could have so easily come down behind her, trapping her in the hallway.

"Tell me again about the man you saw."

"He was standing by the oak tree near the turn in the drive."

Cole had found popcorn near that oak tree. Jack didn't mention that fact. That signature was going to remain a very closely held fact even from someone like Cassie.

"Did you notice anything about him beyond the impression—" Jack checked his notes to get her exact words—"tall, brown jacket with pockets, jeans, black tennis shoes, not teens or early twenties, maybe in his late thirties or early forties?"

"How he stood, watching the fire. It wasn't like he had gone still from surprise or shock. I got the impression he was reflecting on it, like he was watching and thinking."

"Would you recognize him if you saw him?"

She scowled at him. "Maybe. I was hoping you weren't going to ask."

"Would you prefer to try to give a description to a sketch artist?"

"I didn't see him well enough to put it into words. I got an impression."

"You could look at the photos tomorrow." They'd have to work around the delay, but if she wasn't up to it Cole would understand.

"No." She rocked the chair back and forth. "Get the arson photo books and raid a candy bar stash somewhere."

Jack closed the pad of paper, understanding the reluctance, his smile one of sympathy. At this time of night he wouldn't be looking forward to studying the photo books either. "I'll see what I can find."

He left and went to find the keys to unlock the cabinet where the books were kept. He had to raid the receptionist's desk to come up with the bite-sized candy bars. She kept a candy dish on the counter; it was a popular place to stop during the course of the day.

He carried the two thick albums and the bag of candy with him back to Cole's office. "Snickers or Milky Way?"

Cassie opened the first photo album and propped her elbows on the table. "Leave the bag."

Jack did so and tugged a lock of her hair. "Thanks."

"Go away."

With a soft laugh, he left her to it.

Jack placed a phone call as he paced through the quiet firehouse back to the dorm, past ready to change into a clean shirt. "Cole?"

"Hold on a minute, Jack." He heard a muffled conversation between Cole and Bruce. "Okay. What was Cassie able to give you?"

"I've got the notes faxing to the captain's car now. You'd best read them. I flagged page four. This fire sounds different—hotter, faster, probably a different accelerant."

"Hold on, let me get them."

Jack stripped off the smoky shirt and tossed it toward his duffel bag.

"She noticed his shoes," Cole said.

"I wish she noticed his face. She's looking at the books but it sounds iffy."

"Jack—we've got a problem. She saw him."

Jack heard Cole's words, knew the man had just made a leap forward connecting information, and felt totally lost. How did he ask Cole what he was talking about without sounding like a fool? Jack sighed. There were days he felt like he was not playing on the same field. "You lost me."

"She noticed his shoes."

"Okay…" Saying she seemed to have a thing about shoes tonight probably would seal the impression that he was a fool.

"She doesn't notice shoes and not notice a face."

"You know what you're saying—" Jack sat down on the side of the bunk, overwhelmed by the idea.

"Even money she could tell you if the guy had a ring on that hand he pushed in his pocket," Cole replied. "She noticed him. Learn something fast: Cassie does what she thinks is right, not necessarily what is right."

Jack was resigning the title lieutenant and going back to caring about how much water pressure was dialed in so he didn't get knocked flat when they put water on the fire. The people stuff of leadership was never going to make sense. "Cole—"

"I'm here for at least another hour. Where is she?"

"Your office, looking through the arson books."

"She'll give you what she can without crossing her own line."

Jack thrust his hands through his hair. "I think you'd better handle this one."

"I'd just get mad at her. Sit down and tug the information out of her. She's got an acute conscience, so nag and you'll get her to spill it."

"Cole."

"You don't have to like it; you just have to do it. It's one of the joys of being a leader. And Jack—if you make her cry I'm going to be annoyed. So choose your words with care."

Jack rubbed the back of his neck and kicked the metal footlocker. "Let me go talk to her. I'll call you back."

EIGHT

The moon was full and it was shining in her eyes. Rachel shifted her arm under the pillow and turned her head away from the window. She was thirty-five and she was awake in the middle of the night, morose over the fact she was alone. It was a reflection on the choices she had made in her life.

With a groan she buried her head in the pillow. Every time she saw Gage she told herself she was not going to wish for what she didn't have. And every time she did exactly that.

Next year she was going to scale back the amount of energy she put into others and start putting some attention into her own long-term dreams. She had been denying it for a long time. She wanted kids. She wanted to be married. The psychologist in her was amused at the order of those dreams.

Her childhood home had been loud and rough. She tried so hard to be the peacemaker, to fix the problems and the anger and the bitterness between her parents. She was eleven when it had all unraveled. When her parents divorced, she went with Dad. And then her dad didn't have a place for her so she'd ended up at Trevor House.

She wanted a different future. She wanted a happy home and children. Once and for all she wanted to destroy the painful memories of childhood she still lived with.

And her heart was hung up on Gage.

She deserved the mess she was in.

Come the new year, she would be moving on. Her dissatisfaction had been building for a long time but was now ready to be put into words and acted on. She was going to go after those dreams.

All the choices in her life hadn't been bad. Professionally, she could look in the eyes of a hurting child and empathize, reach through and connect with the fear surrounding a trauma. In doing so she could help a child heal. But in putting her focus on her career, she had put her personal life on hold.

No more. The new year was going to be her turning point.

She lifted her head as she heard the distant sound of a siren and relaxed only when it faded. Being around her brother Jack and her sister Kate had made her very sensitive to the sound of a siren.

The apartment returned to silence.

The phone rang.

Rachel tensed even as she reached for it. At this time of night, a phone call for her meant a crisis somewhere and a child in trouble. She did not want to take the call. She couldn't cope with another one. "This is Rachel."

"What exactly did Cole tell you about the fires?"

She blinked at the question. "Gage?"

"Gage. What exactly did Cole say?"

She scowled. "Do you know what time it is?"

"Late."

"I'm sorry you can't sleep. Call me back when it's not late." He was working. She appreciated his help in learning why Cole was worried about the fires but did not appreciate hearing his voice or the question this time of night. "Good night, Gage."

"There was another fire."

She pulled the phone back to her ear and pushed herself up on one elbow. "What?"

"Jeffrey's at the scene; I've got him on hold on the other line. He says the house is a total loss and that Cole is there. Now I need to know what he told you."

She was getting grilled as a source for a story. "Gage, I don't like you."

"Quit thinking and just talk."

Rachel turned on the light. "Deep background, off the record, and all that other reporter legalistic stuff I have to say to get you not to print what I say in the paper."

"I'm not going to quote you, Rachel LeeAnn."

"You've quoted what your wife said in her sleep claiming she hadn't qualified it."

"You are never going to let me live that one down, are you?"

"Never." She had found his Valentine's Day story adorable, if intrusive.

"I won't show Jeffrey my notes. Talk."

It wasn't easy to remember the exact words of the conversation. "As best I can remember—the fires started about two months ago. Cole didn't say what fires, only that there had been a lot of them. That the house fire last week was an escalation and Jack was being kept busy."

"He used the word *escalation?*"

"Yes. He was worried about Jack getting hurt."

"Jack, by name?"

"I don't remember. I could have inferred the concern since we were talking about Jack." She turned the tables on him to get a couple questions of her own answered. "What has Jeffrey said? Is Jack at the scene?" A tone signaled another call coming in. "Hold on, Gage." She answered the other call. "Hello."

"It's Cole."

Cole. He'd never called her before. His tone was worse than grim. She swallowed hard to get back her voice. "I'm dropping the other call. Hold on, Cole."

"Gage, good-bye." She hung up on him. And fought the panic as she waited for the phone to click and give her back Cole. "Jack—he's hurt? Please tell me he isn't hurt. I just heard there's been another fire."

Jack stopped at the door to Cole's office, hating what he had to do.

Cassie was paging through the second arson book. She had her injured hand elevated, idly rocking it back and forth with the melted ice pack lying limp across her open palm. She had neatly arranged six of the bite-sized candy bars end to end, alternating Snickers and Milky Way.

He didn't remember her loving chocolate. He was almost sure she had been a sugar cookie person. Clearly stress changed priorities. The look on her face…

She spoke without looking up. "Do you realize there are kids in this book young enough to still like *Sesame Street?*"

"There's one boy over at Gibson Elementary who has Cole worried. He's already set two fires. The last one did some serious damage to his bedroom."

"Troubled home?"

"His parents were divorced last year. He's an angry young man."

"Sad."

"Yes."

How did he ask? Straight out? Let her talk and see what she said?

Jack sat on the edge of the table, reached over, and closed the album. He'd always preferred directness. "Cassie, what are you not telling me?" he asked gently.

She just looked at him.

"Cole thinks you're hiding something. Is he right?"

Her expression closed up.

Jack was accustomed to people trusting him. Cassie was doing the opposite. On an emotional level it hurt that she chose to respond that way. What was she hiding? He always found it better to face bad news and deal with it than shift into denial mode and lose valuable time.

Who was she trying to protect? And then he tried to get a breath as he struggled to accept the impossible. Another firefighter? "You won't say or can't say?"

The sadness and conflict in her expression… The silence grew.

She'd been biting her nails. Jack reached for her hand and rubbed his finger across the rough edges, feeling that rough himself.

He didn't want to tug it out of her, didn't want to push until she gave him the truth. "I'll take you home."

His quiet words rocked her. "Home?"

She hadn't been expecting him to back off. But if it were a firefighter starting the fires, it was likely someone Cassie knew. Cole could talk to her tomorrow.

And as cruel as it was to consider, it made sense that it would be a firefighter. The fires had been carefully set to make a point. They had started recently. And tonight it had been the chairman of the fire district targeted.

Those facts suggested a motive. Someone laid off in the consolidations, angry enough to be their firebug, might be using fires at the edge of the district line to prove the closed stations needed reopening. And given the location of the fires…it was probably someone from Cassie's old company. If that was what she suspected, Jack couldn't blame her for wanting to keep quiet.

Cassie wouldn't be able to ignore her suspicion. But what would she do if she didn't tell either him or Cole? If she tried to confront the person herself…the thought was horrifying.

Jack found himself backtracking on the decision he had just made. He needed her to tell one of them. He had to at least keep her from trying to act on her own.

Stalling for time, he pulled over the other chair and picked up her tennis shoes. Her pale blue socks were banded with a dark line of ash. "Would you like me to get you a clean pair of socks?"

It tugged a smile from her as she wiggled her toes. "No, but thanks for asking."

He picked apart the knots in her laces, slipped on her tennis shoes, and then retied them.

"Jack." He looked up. She leaned forward and rested her right hand against his cheek, holding his gaze. "Thanks."

He leaned his cheek into that touch, surprised she would offer it but charmed by it and the smile. *Cassie, you're making me feel like a heel because this isn't over.* "You're welcome."

She moved her hand to his shoulder and used him as leverage to push to her feet. "Cole is going to be annoyed with you."

The decision already made, Jack could afford to be philosophical about it. "What else is new?"

"Tell him to call me."

"I will."

She laughed at his immediate agreement.

He'd take her home. It might be easier to have the discussion outside of this place.

They walked through the district building and back to the bays. The sound of their footsteps echoed in the empty, cavernous room. Jack grabbed his jacket and a spare one for Cassie. It wasn't quite as large as Cole's but it still swallowed her.

"We'll take my car." He tugged out his own keys. "Do you have someone who can work at the store for you tomorrow so you can sleep in?"

"Linda covers for me fifteen hours a week. She was already planning to open up in the morning."

Jack held his car door for her. There was a high-pitched squeak as she started to sit down and they both froze.

"Sorry." Embarrassed, Jack reached over her for the rubber cat toy he'd meant to give Kate that had fallen between the front seats.

He waited until Cassie was settled and had fastened her seat belt before he circled the car and slid in behind the wheel. He turned up the heat to the point he would bake but where Cassie might be comfortable, then turned on the scanner.

"What happened to J. J.?"

The small, white lifelike mouse had been a practical joke from Bruce. It had traversed the district showing up in various people's sleeping bags until finally taking up residence on Jack's dashboard tucked between the radio and the scanner. "Lisa borrowed it last week to surprise Quinn."

"How is your sister?"

Lisa was still getting over her too-close brush with a man who had killed more people than the authorities would probably ever be able to discover. "Falling in love smoothes over a lot of stress."

U.S. Marshal Quinn Diamond was the last person Jack would have expected Lisa to fall in love with, but it had developed into a great match. Quinn would keep Lisa out of trouble, or at least be there to get her out of it.

Silence descended as he drove Cassie home and Jack didn't try to break it. If he was going to get her to change her mind and realize she had no choice but to trust him and tell him, giving Cassie time to think was to his advantage. Silence forced her to rethink options.

He had such a good evening visiting Cassie at her store. To have the day end like this… Jack hated having friends hurt. She was moving the ice pack around in her hand, searching to find a way to rest her hand to lessen the pain. The painkillers the paramedics had given her were wearing off.

Jack did not like where she lived. It was an impersonal apartment complex, an older group of eight brick buildings. She lived in building number three on the second floor in a corner apartment. The building foyer did not have good security, the carpet needed replacement, and the hallways were well lit but dreary. The only redeeming feature was the fact that her balcony overlooked the playground in the complex.

Jack knew she had chosen the apartment because it was three minutes from the station where she had once worked. He wondered if she would consider moving now that she was no longer bound by residency requirements.

He parked four spaces away from the building door. The sounds of nearby tollway traffic were intrusive. He walked around to open the car door for her.

He knelt down when he realized she wasn't even trying to release the seat belt. "Cassie?" He leaned across her and freed the seat belt clip. In the dim glow of the dome light he could see the tension.

"Jack, it wasn't what I saw." His hand tightened on the door frame as the words were whispered. She surprised him by saying what she had been unwilling to say before. "It was what I thought."

Jack rubbed his thumb across the back of her hand, wishing he could soothe the turmoil he heard.

"He slipped his hands into his pockets and turned. The way he moved…" Her eyes filled with an incredible agony. "Jack, I think I saw Ash."

He stopped breathing.

NINE

Jack used Cassie's keys to unlock her apartment door. He found the light switch inside the door. Boxes were stacked in the entryway. She was moving? Cassie passed him, stepping around the boxes and moving into the first room on the left. Jack turned the lock on the door and followed her.

His gaze swept the living room with its green recliner and ottoman, couch and rolltop desk. If she was moving she hadn't begun to pack this room; pictures were still on the walls, a jigsaw puzzle was spread out across a cardboard table. She'd been folding laundry. The basket was beside the coffee table and mismatched socks were lined up in a neat row from light colors to dark.

Jack helped her off with the jacket. "Sit."

He headed toward the kitchen, flipped the lights on with an impatient hand, and tugged open cabinets until he found drinking glasses. Like his sisters she kept medicines beside the spices. He scanned prescription bottles, found the one for pain, and dumped two tablets in his palm.

He wasn't surprised at the extensive bandages and gauze she had stocked but it was sad she needed to use them again. He took out supplies for her hand.

He was under no illusions that anything he said in the next few minutes would help. She thought it was her partner setting the fires. Few things would cut more than that.

The humor he could normally dredge up to defuse a tense situation wasn't there. And he never needed it more.

She was on that brittle edge of tears. He hated being asked to deal with a woman who was ready to cry. Of all the things he could remember with clarity about his childhood, one of the most vivid was how lousy he was at comforting someone who was crying. He wished liked crazy she hadn't told him. Why couldn't she have waited and told Cole? His friend could deal with this.

She hadn't sat as he instructed. Jack set down what he carried on the mahogany end table next to the lamp, settled his hands on her shoulders, and put her into the recliner. He settled on the ottoman and handed her the glass. "Take the pills. This is going to hurt."

She set aside the ice pack as it had warmed. Jack carefully unwrapped the bandage Neal had put around the blisters. It was damp with more than just water; the blisters were weeping.

He carefully added burn cream and replaced the gauze. This he could do. This was practical and tangible. He did his best to ignore the fact she was occasionally sniffing against the threatening tears. "Tell me why you think it was Ash."

"He lives in that neighborhood."

Jack stopped. He wasn't expecting that. "Where?"

"Quincy Street. He moved there about a month before he disappeared."

"Why?"

"Why did he move?"

Jack nodded.

"Something about storage for a boat. He called it his little rowboat."

"The way he stood, moved, reminded you of Ash. What else?"

"His clothes. Jack, the impression I got was a confident, comfortable, reflective man." She shook her head. "It feels so incredibly disloyal to think this."

"Cassie—it wasn't Ash. He would not have started a fire and let you walk into it. It's impossible."

"But what if he did?" she whispered.

"Then he's become a different man than the one we've known for years."

"I can't get the impression out of my mind. I looked through the arson books for someone who looked like Ash. I'm so ashamed of that. I was wishing I could find someone who looked like him."

"Figuring out who you saw will be Cole's job to solve. Trust him. The description gives him a lot to work with."

"Would you talk to him for me?"

He was going to be talking to Cole all right, pushing his friend hard because this arsonist had just made this very personal. It was one thing to go after him, but when Cassie got hurt— Whoever was setting these fires, whatever his motivation, he had hurt a friend. "I'll talk to him," Jack reassured. It was something else practical he could do for her. He rubbed the tape in place. "This should hold for the night. Soak your hand in the morning."

"I will."

He didn't immediately release her hand. "Cassie—" He paused, trying to find the right words. "I hate to leave you alone tonight. Is there someone I can call for you?"

"Amy is across the hall. Go, Jack. I'll be fine and you've got work to do." She lifted her good hand to touch her hair. "Besides, I need to wash my hair."

"Get some sleep first."

"That would be more logical."

The right answer to that was a smile. "Those pain pills are going to knock you the rest of the way out. Come lock the door after me."

She leveraged herself from the chair and walked with him to the door. "Are you moving?"

She nudged one of the boxes. "My extra inventory of books that are on their way to the bookstore."

She had eight boxes of books in her hallway. "I'll haul them over to the store for you."

"I'd appreciate that. Call me later with what Cole has found?"

"Around noon," Jack promised. He took out his keys as he stepped across the threshold. "Cassie?"

She paused in closing the door.

"Check the batteries in your smoke alarm tomorrow."

It took a moment, but then her smile reached her eyes. "I will. Good night, Jack."

He headed downstairs.

Where did he go next? The fire cleanup would have Cole's attention for the next few hours as he located and secured the evidence. He needed to talk to Cole. This news was going to go over like a lead balloon.

Jack started his car, thought for a moment, and instead drove to Quincy Street. The first fire had happened a week after Ash disappeared. It was too troubling a fact to ignore. Forget what he had said to Cassie. His gut reaction was intense.

Ash setting fires…it was a reach. But Jack could remember the hallway conversations at the hospital. There had been a lot of anger at the cost cutting being made that Ash felt had been a factor in Cassie's getting hurt. The nursing home annual inspection was delayed because the number of inspectors had been cut back. When the drastic cost cutting resulting in fire department consolidations had come down, Ash had been vocal and horrified at what was happening.

He had been so focused on helping Cassie—Jack couldn't see Ash abruptly turning off that emotion and going on a long and sudden vacation. The department consolidations…what if he felt he had no choice but to act? There had to be a reason he disappeared.

Was Ash back?

Dawn was brightening the sky when Rachel shut her car door and started walking, having been forced to park three blocks away from the fire scene.

Engine 81 and Truck 81 were on the scene to deal with cleanup. There were two police squad cars and three news vans. Spectators watching the firemen work were gathered in clusters on the sidewalk across the street. Four of those spectators had brought out lawn chairs to sit and watch the scene in comfort.

The entire scene was sad.

Cole was here somewhere. Finding him was going to be a challenge. Rachel picked her way across a snake's nest of hose lines. Since she came in an official capacity wearing her Red Cross jacket, she was waved across the police lines.

The firefighters were still cooling off what had once been the garage. The water flowing away from the house had cut rivers in the yard. The mud was thick under the men's boots.

She looked for Jack as he had also left her a message but didn't see his distinctive helmet. Jack had painted a yellow smiley face on the back of his helmet and another on the back on his fire coat. He said it was to make it easier when he had to deal with scared kids at a wreck, but Rachel knew the truth. It was Jack's attitude about life. He didn't waste his time worrying about something he couldn't change.

Cole strode through the front door carrying a power saw. He saw her coming up the drive and nodded. She stopped and let him join her.

"Thanks for coming."

She tried to read his face, but the man didn't give much away. "You said it was important." She had been surprised by the request but was not about to show it. She frequently was asked to make assessments about how victims and witnesses were dealing with a trauma, how law enforcement could best get answers about what had happened. But from what she could see of the scene, they didn't appear to need that kind of help here.

"I need your opinion on something." Cole set down the power saw beside the black plastic sheeting at the curbside. Opening the cab door of Engine 81, he reached in back and retrieved a fire coat.

Rachel spotted Gage's partner Jeffrey in an animated conversation with the fire captain. She hoped Gage wasn't here. Hanging up on him hadn't been wise. It would guarantee several pointed questions when he saw her next.

"Rachel."

She took the coat from Cole.

"This stays confidential."

She was annoyed by the reminder. She was bound by professional ethics as well as moral ones. "I'm not going to tell Gage."

"His yappy terrier of a sidekick has been pestering us."

She had to bite her tongue; the description fit Jeffrey perfectly. "You have never liked reporters."

"That's a given."

She struggled into the coat and looked with distaste at the fire hat he held out.

"Quit thinking fashion, woman. No one around here is going to be taking your picture."

"I'm entitled to a little vanity for how my hair looks this early in the morning." To think she had actually lingered in front of the closet this morning debating over what to wear when she met him.

She understood practicality. Her shirt was heavy khaki and the jeans broken in, the shoes near boots. The accessories were anything but practical. The scarf was expensive, the belt braided, the bracelet wide and bold. Cole didn't even notice and now she was annoyed she'd made the effort. "Is Jack around?"

She was surprised at the look of irritation on his face. "Talking to the man who reported the fire." He changed the subject before she could ask what Jack had done now. "When we get in the house, I want you to step where I step."

"There's not someone dead in there, is there?"

"I wouldn't let you near the scene if we had a victim. No one was home."

"This was an arson?"

"Yes."

No hesitation or qualification. "Show me."

Rather than lead the way to the house, Cole pushed his hands into his pockets, took out a roll of lifesavers, and with his thumb offered her the cherry one at the end. "The other night, did you ever find the lost Gage?"

"Yes."

"I wondered. How's he doing?"

"Ask him yourself," she replied, not feeling in a generous mood to talk about a friend. The two men were polite with each other, there was even grudging respect, but Rachel had no intention of stepping between them. Cole did not like reporters probing into ongoing investigations, and she was under no illusions about Gage. The man could irritate a saint.

"You were late getting home."

She raised one eyebrow.

"I called," Cole said simply.

He didn't elaborate and Rachel wasn't comfortable asking. He had a piercing gaze and his brown eyes were warm as they watched her. But she did feel a need to at least offer something. "I shared a piece of pie with Gage and then swung by to see Kate for an hour. Why are you stalling showing me what you asked me here to see?"

"It's disturbing, Rachel."

"I've walked into a fast-food restaurant where a man sprayed an assault rifle and left eight people dead. Disturbing is relative."

"*This* is disturbing."

"Cole."

"Just be prepared. If I didn't need you to see it, I wouldn't ask. If this means what I suspect it does, you and I are going to need to talk."

This wasn't going to be good. She followed Cole up the drive to the house, skirting around worktables made of plywood braced on sawhorses, past sheets of plastic marked with bright yellow criminal evidence tape.

Inside the house the smell of smoke was overpowering. Her eyes immediately started to water. "It was toxic?"

Cole glanced back at her and gave a sympathetic smile. "Onions. A bag of onions in the kitchen pantry burned."

She separated the smells and realized he was right. She wanted to get away from this as soon as possible. "Please tell me we are going upstairs."

"We are. Stay close."

Heavy plastic had been rolled out down the upstairs hallway.

Rachel was surprised at the amount of structural damage. Normally a fire consumed the contents of rooms, the personal items that made fire such a tragedy for people, but left the house itself only scarred. This fire had gutted walls. There were openings torn in the ceiling to get to the attic.

Rachel looked in the rooms as they walked down the hall, getting a sense of the occupants. The bathroom had a melted mermaid shower curtain. "The family had children?"

"A daughter."

Cole stopped at the third doorway. "The fire started in this room." He clicked on his torch flashlight and gingerly skirted the door, hanging half off its hinges, to enter the room. Rachel followed him.

"What do you make of this?" Cole illuminated the message. He'd wiped down the wall to reveal it. Drywall and plaster had fallen away but the letters were huge and the single word was readable. It glowed in a fluorescent red.

Murderer.

She pulled her emotions back, fighting the swamp of reaction that shallowed her breathing. "This is the master bedroom?"

"Yes."

The huge letters were an assault to her senses. She followed the flow of the spray paint, feeling the sensation the man who held the paint can had also felt. Arm straight, fully extended, even reaching, as he walked along the wall. "He moved the furniture before he wrote this."

"Good observation."

The letters tightened and grew smaller, the paint much heavier at the final Rs. It was adrenaline and excitement at the first part of the word and tightly wound anger at the end. The word was huge, the wall a billboard into the arsonist's mind. "How many fires?" she asked, dreading the answer.

"This is number six. Impressions, Rachel."

"He's justifying his actions. He's not just angry, it's become part of who he is. He's working his nerve up to also kill."

She looked over at Cole when he didn't say anything. The intense control the man was exerting over his darkening anger had her taking a step away. "Cole?"

"Rae, I think Jack is in his sights."

TEN

Cassie woke up sweating and sick to her stomach. It was a sensation and a reaction she had unfortunately felt before. She rolled over and carefully put her weight on her elbows, lifting herself up enough so she could hang her head. It had been months since she had to deal with a morning like this. On the worst mornings she had been sick while in bed, in too much pain to risk moving.

When she thought the nausea was at least checked, Cassie slid herself off the edge of the bed and made it to the bathroom. She had changed the fixtures on the sink to long handles so she could turn on the water without having to grip and turn a knob.

She pushed the cold water on full force and lowered her hand into the basin without bothering to remove the gauze. The agonizing pain sharpened and chilled, then eased.

She drew in a shaky breath.

She didn't have the strength to pick up something with her right hand. Her left hand had swollen overnight to the point it was useless. She looked at the phone on the wall beside the light switch. It had been installed as her safety blanket.

The certain knowledge that Jesus was with her wasn't much comfort as she contemplated the odds that in a few minutes she would be sitting on the tile floor in her nightgown, shivering and whimpering and fighting the why-me pity party.

Lord, I hate being alone.

She didn't want to have to call for help. As horrible as this was, the pain was only about a six on her ten-point pain scale. But when she hadn't felt pain above a level of four in several months, it was agonizing.

She laid her head down on her arm as the water continued to lap over her hand. She would just stay here with her head down for a while. If she didn't try to move for the next hour, it would be just fine.

You asked me to go back into another fire. It's haunting me. Please don't let me be sick. I'll cry. I've cried enough these last couple years.

The doorbell rang.

She raised her head too fast and got caught by the dizziness.

Lord, You have a sense of humor in Your timing.

Arranging something like this was just like God—send her help and be polite enough about it to let the doorbell ring ten minutes after she was out of bed instead of while she was still hiding under the covers.

Cassie forced herself to straighten and reach for the robe on the back of the door, whimpering as she lifted her arm higher than it wanted to rise. If help was here, she couldn't ignore the fact she needed it.

She made her way to the front door and looked through the security view hole.

Rachel O'Malley. Cassie had not even had her on the list of possibilities. She was wearing a Red Cross jacket. There was no sign of Jack.

"Just a minute." Cassie worked to release the locks, then eased open the door. "Hi, Rachel."

"Jack called me."

"He didn't need to do that."

"Jack did."

Cassie blinked, then smiled. "Yes, I suppose he did." Ever the protector, Jack had looked more than a little frustrated last night at the idea he was leaving her home alone. Recruiting his sister fit something he would do.

Rachel nodded to the towel and the wet gauze. "It looks like you could use some help."

"I could and thanks." Cassie had learned long ago to set aside her independent streak that made accepting help difficult. She stepped back to give Rachel room in the crowded hall. "Would you do me a favor and start the coffee while I finish getting dressed? I'm dying for a cup."

"Glad to." Rachel locked the door behind her.

Cassie turned back toward her bedroom, already feeling better just knowing someone was around with two good hands. "You saw Jack?"

"Yes. I just left the site of the house fire," Rachel called as she headed to the kitchen. "Both Cole and Jack were there."

Cassie sorted through her closet for something to wear as she listened to Rachel move around the kitchen. She really liked Jack's sister. They met for the first time at a rescue. A trench had collapsed on some utility workers, and Jack had been one of the men working through the night to get the pinned men free. Rachel had been invaluable that night. She'd arranged for sandwiches and coffee to be brought in for both the crews and reporters. She had spent hours talking with the wives of the guys trapped, listening, reassuring.

Cassie had spent most of that night looking at the smiley face painted on back of Jack's fire coat, serving as his eyes for how the ground was shifting as he worked deep inside the trench being shored up. It had put Cassie in a position to be able to relay comments from one of the trapped men to his wife and back. She'd also served as a relay for a very long conversation between Jack and Rachel over baseball games, recent movies, and Jack's habit of leaving stupid jokes on her answering machine. It had been very clear by the end of that conversation that Jack and Rachel were very good friends. She'd envied them that closeness.

❧❧

Cassie finally chose sweats and a loose blouse she could button and slowly dressed. She needed an ice pack for her left hand; it throbbed in time with her heartbeat.

She headed to the kitchen and found Rachel crouched down looking through the refrigerator.

"You've got eggs and cheese. Would you like an omelette?"

Cassie nudged a chair at the table out with her foot. "Fix me toast and your-self an omelette. I want company for the breakfast I'll pretend to have."

Rachel cast her a sympathetic glance. "Would crackers help the queasiness?"

"Please. There may be a box in the pantry." Cassie spread out the towel she carried and reached for the burn cream left out from last night. "Did you ever play Kick the Can when you were a kid?"

Rachel opened a tube of crackers and brought them over. "Sure. Why?"

"Ever miss the can and kick concrete by mistake?"

"Oh my, yes. Feels like that?"

"A lot like it. The kind of hurt that just circles and keeps coming back in waves." Cassie studied the blister on the inside of her thumb. "I'm so glad the house was empty."

"Jack rescued the teddy bear you were gripping when they found you. He asked me to see what could be done to get it cleaned up before it was returned to Tina."

"That was nice of him." Cassie nibbled on a cracker. "It struck me as probably a favorite stuffed animal given where I found it. Could you hand me an ice pack?"

Rachel opened the freezer. "Oh, Cassie."

"I know; I've got a few."

"Seven is more than a few." Rachel retrieved one of the ice packs and brought it over, along with the first cup of coffee. "I can see how your hand is doing, what about your arms?"

"Not bad. Stiff." She carefully settled the ice pack into her aching hand. She sipped the coffee as she watched Rachel fix breakfast for them both. She had to give Rachel credit. The odds she was here for more reasons than the one she had given were high, but she was starting with the practicalities. "Feel free to tell me the rest of it. Cole was there. I've got the feeling Jack wasn't the only one who sug-gested you come by."

Rachel pushed down bread in the toaster. "We need to talk. But we can do it while we eat."

Cassie conceded the inevitable. Cole wanted more information about her suspicions of whom she had seen. Her hope she wouldn't have to think again about the fire last night was unrealistic. At least Cole had sent someone who would ask the questions with some gentleness. "About Ash?"

Rachel looked over, her expression grave. "Jack."

≫≪≫≪≫

"Did you watch this one burn down too?"

Jack turned to face Gage. The insolent tone and the dig at him—there was no attempt to hide it. Jack wished the man would just take a swing at him.

Gage liked to use words and he was very effective with them. He had eviscerated Jack with the article he had written after the fire that had killed Tabitha. Jack figured he had that one coming, but in his world a fight finished the matter. Gage was never going to let it die.

Jack turned his attention back to the hose he was draining. "What do you want, Collier?" Since he decided on his own to see if there was any sign of Ash, Jack was in the doghouse with Cole. There hadn't been, and Cole was annoyed both at his seeking out of a potential suspect and his delay in conveying what Cassie had said. Jack had accepted the rebuke. What he planned to do if Ash had been there was an interesting question that, looking back, Jack was glad he had not faced.

He was now being kept out of the burned-out house for the more serious cleanup. Jack thought it was childish on Cole's part, but he wasn't in a place to complain. It was a crime scene now. He didn't mind the basic tasks of cleanup— the heavy lifting and constant bending—but the wet gloves made him clumsy as he worked, and with an audience Jack found that annoying.

Gage set his foot on the bumper of the rescue squad. "Lincoln Park, Ash Street, the Assley fire…"

Jack forced himself not to react as Gage started naming off the locations of suspicious fires over the last several weeks. He was braced to be asked how many more fires there had been. Cole would kill him if he said anything to a reporter.

"Rachel is worried about you."

Jack rapped his knuckles on the concrete as the wrench he was using to loosen the hose connector slipped. In one short sentence Gage could shake him up.

Rachel, worried about him and talking about it to Gage…. This he did not need. "I'll speak to her."

"I'd appreciate it."

"Getting tired of hearing my name?"

Jack caught a glimmer of a smile as Gage lowered his foot, then turned to leave. "I only use inside sources when I can't find a direct one."

Jack silently apologized for his assumption that Gage had been prying at Rachel to get details about the fires. "Talk to Cole."

"Already have," Gage replied. "He was unusually chatty today too."

Jack narrowed his eyes. Cole had voluntarily spoken with a reporter? That was not like him at all.

Being somewhat out of the loop went with being in the doghouse, but not being shut out of something newsworthy. Rachel had been at the scene. Jack started worrying again about why. He had taken her answer that she had come looking for him at face value, and he should have realized a phone call would have answered his page to her.

Rachel had been here. Now Gage showed up. Something was going on Jack didn't know about.

Gage stopped, then looked back. "By the way, where is Rachel?"

Jack would prefer to keep Cassie's name out of the equation, but Gage could get an answer with just a page to his sister. "Cassie's."

"Really? Brave lady to go into a house fire after what happened at the nursing home."

Jack heard the reality of Gage seeking out Cassie, knew it was inevitable. Other news organizations would have found her by now. Add going into another fire with her history and it was a good human interest story, something reporters craved around the holidays. "Gage, be kind."

Gage took offense at the veiled threat, but then Jack had intended him too. If Gage stung Cassie in a tough interview, Jack was going to return the favor. Someone had to protect her and he'd just elected himself. Jack set aside what he was doing to stand and face the man.

"Something between the two of you?"

Jack went to the heart of the matter. "She's one of us."

Gage finally nodded. "Fair enough."

"The arsonist wrote the word *murderer.*" Cassie felt cold just saying the word.

Across the kitchen table, Rachel circled her coffee mug around her napkin. "Red spray paint. Sweeping letters. He spent some time in the room before he torched it."

Cassie pushed aside the plate that held her toast and reached for the crackers again. The nausea was back with a vengeance.

"Cole thought it was important for you to know."

Not only that, but that he needed to send Rachel over rather than wait until he could come later—it was an extraordinary step. Whoever she had seen at the fire was that angry.... Cassie forced aside the implications. "You said we needed to talk about Jack."

"Have you ever known Cole to be afraid?"

"No."

"He is now." Rachel's hand shook slightly as she lifted her coffee cup.

The arsonist was clearly dangerous, he was escalating, and Jack had fought the six fires.... Cassie froze. "Jack—he's the common factor to the fires."

"Who did you see, Cassie?"

She wished she could answer that question. The truth was painful. "I honestly don't know."

ELEVEN

"Cole, I want back in."

Cassie closed his office door, shutting out the startled looks of the inspectors, arson investigators, and firefighters she'd surprised as she came striding through the building. She had rushed the words before she lost her nerve to say them.

Rachel had driven her over to the fire scene, where they had just missed Cole. Cassie had been forced to follow him here to the fire district offices. She had passed Jack in the equipment bay replacing air tanks aboard Engine 81. She had not stopped to answer his questions, leaving that to Rachel. Cassie was on a mission.

Cole was in the process of taking off his fire boots, had rolled out a thick sheet of plastic to keep the ash off his carpet. He'd been up all night, but other than looking a little more grim than she remembered, he didn't show it.

Eight hours ago she had left this office relieved to get out of it, and now she was closing herself back in. She was crazy to be doing this. The tension in her gut was incredible. If she were smart she would turn around and leave. Cassie planted her feet and refused to let herself turn.

Cole looked at her in that inscrutable fashion of his. "Sit."

"I'm serious."

"So am I." He pointed to the chair.

She complied, staying on the edge of the seat. "You didn't need to send a doctor to make a house call."

"Cassie, if I'm hiring you again, I get to do whatever I like. Your hair's wet."

"Rachel helped me wash it." She scowled at him for the distraction. "I want back in. So what do you need done? Name it. I want to help. You think Jack's a target. We've got to do something."

"Slow down."

She got up to pace. "Your office makes me feel like I'm back in the principal's office."

"Spend a lot of time there, did you?"

"Cole—"

He held up his hand. "I didn't say no. How'd you like the pumpkin pie?"

He took her enough by surprise she stopped to smile. "You made it."

"Yes."

"Not bad."

"I miss having you take turns on KP. You still owe me a raspberry cobbler."

"I'll deliver eventually."

"How's the hand?"

Rachel had done a good job with the new bandage. In a week it would still be sore but would have begun to heal. That didn't help today. "It hurts like crazy. Now can we talk?"

"If we have to."

"We have to."

He set aside his boots. "I sent Rachel because I figured you had a right to know."

"I came close to seeing that spray painted word while it was still cooking into the plaster."

"Be glad you didn't. If you want in, you're welcome. I need a spy."

"No."

"Listen."

"No. It's not Ash. I don't care what I thought. It's not him. And it's not someone else from Company 65."

"You're talking to the former chief of Company 65. Now sit, and quit jumping to conclusions. I am not suspecting your partner...yet," Cole growled.

She sat.

"Two grass fires, two trash fires, two empty houses, this last one with a message. Whoever this man is, he's setting the fires with a great deal of thought. He's got an escalation plan he's implementing. And you may be our best chance of catching him."

"I can't give you a description, Cole. All I've got is an impression."

"I understand that. What I need is someone who can roll out with Gold Shift and look for him. We know this guy is a watcher. Anyone who strikes you as a possibility, you let the police on the scene deal with it. What I need to know is if you can handle going back on shift."

The hours would kill her. Twenty-four hours on, forty-eight off would be exhausting. But she'd do it if that was what had to be done. "Somehow." She rubbed her eyes. *"Murderer*. He's blaming the department for someone who died."

"A car accident, a fire, a medical rollout that wasn't able to make a difference. We know two things: He called the chairman of the fire district a murderer and he's ringing fires around the boundaries of this district. That makes the focus of his anger the bureaucracy in this district."

"And specifically Jack?"

"Gold Shift fought the first five fires. This fire Jack went on duty early and the arsonist hit again. I've got to conclude from that pattern that he's targeting Gold Shift, specifically Jack, and take what precautions I can."

Cole yanked open his desk drawer that had warped and stuck. He found a new roll of Lifesavers. "Maybe it's because he's got a problem with Jack. Maybe it's the opposite. Jack is the best lieutenant we have. If you wanted to set fires and yet not hurt anyone, who would you ask to put them out?"

She was startled at the suggestion. "The man with the safest reputation."

"Exactly."

"He's setting fires, yet you think he doesn't want to hurt anyone."

"I don't know. This man puzzles me. The locations and times of the fires, how they are set—this arsonist is being very careful. That would suggest the guy has something driving him, an objective in mind. It just doesn't ring true as a thrill seeker. The pattern to the fires suggests he will escalate until he finally gets whatever it is he's after."

"What does he want?"

"Rachel thinks he has already told us and is incredibly frustrated that no one is listening, so he's setting fires to get attention. Rachel is also sure that he will start hurting people if he has to, which is why we've got to stop him very soon."

"Jack doesn't have enemies."

"He's got a few, but no one who strikes me as a firebug," Cole corrected. "For a man to be setting fires out of frustration and anger, either he feels he has no voice or that his voice is not getting heard."

"The guy I saw was confident, self-assured."

"He thinks we're not going to do what he wants and is trying to force it."

"There will be another fire."

Cole nodded. "And soon. Likely targeting Gold Shift. The problem is, accidents happen. Ask Jack to face so many fires and it's not a matter of if he gets hurt, it's when. Jack likes you, Cassie. Use it. Watch his back."

She would have qualified his assumption about Jack's interest if something more obvious had not just occurred to her. "You're not going to tell him, are you?"

"Tell him what? About the word *murderer?* The fact this guy will probably strike harder next time? Cassie, you know Jack. Think about it."

"He'd quit a job he loves if he thought he might be responsible for someone getting hurt in one of these fires."

"Exactly." Cole rubbed the back of his neck. "In this case, Jack's habit for doing the noble thing is more of a headache than a help. You and I are going to make sure it doesn't come to him even thinking about making that decision. You saw the guy. You'll recognize him. And when you do, point him out to the cop on the scene and let us handle it."

"How do I explain my presence to the guys on Gold Shift?"

"Since the department consolidation, we're required to file an efficiency report every ninety days during the first year. You just became the captain's scribe."

"Paperwork."

"You always did love it."

"Like a case of the flu. I need to see the fire reports."

"The red folder on the table. I already had the secretary print the reports for the suspicious fires. There are some items being kept silent regarding the arson methodology and signature; they've been blacked out in the reports."

Cassie wasn't surprised at that; ongoing investigations were always restricted. "How does he know when Jack is working?"

"He's at least got inside access to information, which is why you and I are going to keep this low key. I'll put you on the administrative payroll rather than add you to the duty payroll. You'll do it?"

That decision had already been made at her kitchen table looking across at a worried Rachel. "When do I start?"

"A week give you enough time to figure out how to juggle your bookstore? Gold Shift will be on duty on Thursday. Consider yourself on rotation. Shift starts at 8 A.M."

She groaned. He smiled. "Be here early."

TWELVE

Cassie paused the movie when the phone rang that night and struggled to sit up.

"Would you stay put and let me get it?" Jack protested, getting to his feet. He'd shown up after his shift got over, he said to check on her hand, but Cassie suspected it had a lot more to do with trying to figure out why she rushed over to see Cole earlier in the day.

He arrived with three videos and an offer to buy the pizza. Since she had been reading the fire reports Cole had given her, she was more than ready to set aside the work and accept unexpected company. She hadn't realized what that meant. About the only thing Jack had let her do tonight was hold the TV remote—not that that was minor, but still…"It's my phone."

"And you only know everyone in the state. I can say you are fine as well as you can. And you've talked to enough reporters for the day." Jack put his hand on her forehead and pushed her head back on the pillow as he passed the couch. "Stay."

"I'm not a puppy."

"You act like it for all you listen."

"Get me another piece of pizza while you're up."

"I didn't come over to spoil you."

"Sure you did."

He answered the phone in the kitchen. "Cassie's."

It wasn't fair that someone was starting fires and either out of anger or strategy was choosing Jack to put at risk. It must make him miserable to go to work knowing that the odds of a fire being set during his shift were high.

If Cole was right and the fires would likely escalate to put people in danger— In the passion of the moment she knew how high adrenaline surged. No firefighter wanted to back away when someone was trapped in a fire. Jack would take unreasonably high risks to try and rescue someone. Cole had warned her to stay on the sidelines no matter what fire they faced, and she knew that directive was going to be incredibly hard to follow.

Jack reappeared in the doorway. "Luke's Linda. Want to chat?"

She held out her hand for the phone, amused at Jack's way of placing her caller's identity. Luke was the fire department's volunteer chaplain and his wife Linda worked for her at the bookstore. Jack stretched the cord to its limit and handed it to her. She'd talked at length with Linda earlier in the day about the fire.

"Hi, Linda." She glanced over at her guest disappearing back into the kitchen. "Oh yes, he's enjoying himself. He's bossing me around. But since he brought the movies I'm letting him stay. Did we have many customers at the store today?"

An object, which sounded like her phone book, hit the floor in the kitchen.

She covered the phone. "Drop something?"

"Deliberately," Jack called back.

She laughed at that.

She turned her attention back to Linda. "I'll be at the store tomorrow. I wanted to check and see if you could switch schedules with me for this next month."

Jack reappeared a few minutes later in the doorway with a bowl of ice cream. He should be out on his feet from lack of sleep; instead he'd spent the last two hours sprawled on the living room floor laughing over the movie. He said he caught a nap that afternoon, and having worked the twenty-four-hour shifts for years, she knew he probably had. Still, she was surprised to find him so ready to spend an evening with her on the spur of the moment.

When she had her work schedule shuffled around for the coming month, Cassie said good night to her friend and pressed the off button on the phone. "Hang this back up?"

"Sure." Jack took the phone from her.

She nodded to his ice cream. "I'd like some of that too."

"I thought you would. I fixed you a bowl. Do you want this along with or instead of the pizza?"

"I'll wait on the pizza."

"Back in a sec." Jack returned to the kitchen to hang up the phone. He came back with her ice cream.

With chocolate syrup he drew a smiley face on the ice cream and had given it a cherry for a hat. "Nice." And fitting. Jack liked to make people smile.

"Tastes good too."

He dangled a black plastic spider on a string over her face. The things he had in his pockets… She captured it, tugged, and he let go.

"That one is smaller than the one I just killed under your sink. You need to move."

"Don't you start too. Moving is work. I'm not moving." Winter was coming. It meant she had to kill a few more unwanted guests as the building superintendent tried but could only do so much to keep the problem of pests under control.

"How many people owe you favors?" Jack asked.

"More than I can count."

"So collect. This place doesn't have room for a Christmas tree. You definitely need to move."

"It's a waste of time to drag a dying tree up to a second floor apartment, stuff it in the middle of the room, and never be there to see it. Then haul it out three weeks later and spend a few months picking pine needles out of the carpet. I'll do a Christmas tree at the store. That's plenty."

"You need more Christmas spirit."

"Not of the commercialized kind," Cassie countered. "Besides, you know how many fires are started from dried-out Christmas trees overloaded with lights."

"Just because you have to do it smart, doesn't mean you shouldn't enjoy it. What do you want in your Christmas stocking?"

She looked over at him. "I don't have one."

"Cassie."

"Why do I get a feeling I'll have a Christmas stocking this year?"

"J. J. needs a new home."

"Don't give me your mouse."

"I heard you had been missed in his travels." Jack stretched out on the floor again. "Where's the remote? Let's restart the movie."

She shifted around on the couch to dig it out from between the cushions. She hadn't told him yet that she was joining Gold Shift on Thursday. She should tell him. She needed to tell him. It would not be good just to show up. But the man brought funny movies and five-cent plastic spiders. She didn't want to talk about serious subjects tonight. Cole could tell him.

She circled around the smile on the ice cream with her spoon. "Jack?" He leaned back on his elbows, then looked over at her. "Why did you come over tonight? Really?"

"Rachel told me to."

"Oh." She wasn't expecting that. Was really confused by it. She paused the movie again. "Why?"

Jack shrugged. "Who knows? Rachel said go see Cassie, and I'm not one to question my sister. I learned a long time ago she's smarter than I am."

He had come over because Rachel had asked him to. She had thought he had come over to see her.

Jack reached back, picked up one of the pillows he was using, and tossed it at her feet even as he laughed. "Don't look so disappointed. I was planning to come over this weekend. Rae just gave me an excuse to come over tonight. If you were busy when I rang the doorbell, I was going to blame her for the fact I was interrupting."

His laughter as much as his statement he'd been planning to come over made her feel better. "Were you?"

"Hide behind her, or come over?"

She wanted to say come over, but she offered the safer answer. "Using her as an excuse."

"Sure." He pulled over another pillow to replace the one he had thrown. "That's why guys have sisters, to get them out of awkward jams. And if you buy more ice cream I'll probably come over again."

"Really?"

"Yep."

Cassie started the movie. And made a mental note to buy more ice cream. She could use a friend who made her laugh.

"Did you see Cassie?"

Jack looked up from the disassembled snowblower engine spread across the garage floor to see Rachel coming up the drive. She was skirting around the trash barrel and blue recycling crate he temporarily moved to the driveway to make room for this necessary but messy task in preparation of winter.

"I did. What are you doing here? Not that I'm not glad to see you, but I thought you were heading back to Washington." And what was she doing wearing sweats? He had rarely seen his sister not dressed to make an impression, and if it wasn't so hard to imagine, he would say someone also needed to hand her a hairbrush.

"Change of plans. I'm staying. How's Cassie doing?"

"Better. She's at the bookstore today."

"Got a copy of today's paper?"

"You came over for a newspaper?"

"I came over to show you something."

Rushed over appeared to be more accurate. "Try the kitchen counter."

Rachel opened the door from the garage into the house and disappeared inside. She reappeared a few minutes later brushing the rubber band down the rolled up newspaper. "You haven't read it."

"Read what?" He wiped the grease off his hands, then accepted the city section of the paper she tugged out for him.

"Second page."

The photo of the burned-out house clued him in.

Arsonist Targets District. Gage's byline.

"Rachel."

She took a seat on the steps going into the house, her dejection apparent. "I'm sorry. I didn't know he was going to do it."

It was a long article, under the Weekend Focus banner. Jack started reading. Gage had four of the six arson fires identified. Lincoln Park, Ash Street, the Assley fire, this latest one targeting Peter Wallis. Gage didn't have the popcorn signature yet, but he had most of the details for how the fires had started within the walls of the two homes. There was an entire sidebar on Cassie, including her picture, a long recap of the nursing home fire, and her role in this last fire.

The more Jack read, the deeper his fury grew. From somewhere Gage had found a copy of the letter his sister Lisa had written to the newspaper editor a month ago expressing her concerns with the dangers inherent with the fire department consolidations and the added risk it was placing on him. A forensic pathologist, his sister had to deal with those who had died in fires and her letter was both poignant and personal.

For Gage to turn Lisa's letter into the basis for an article was distressing. Gage used the arson fires to show Lisa's worries had come true. He had shown the series of fires, shown Jack had fought them all, then gone on to show how Cassie had been forced to risk entering a burning house because the new hub stations put help too far away. "How did he get all this?"

"I think I told him some of it," Rachel whispered. "We need to call Cassie."

Jack heard the *we*. Rae intended to duck behind him. "Forget Cassie; someone needs to warn Cole." He saw her dismay. "Rae, Cole doesn't yell at ladies."

"I told Gage what Cole had said because I was worried about you. I wanted his help to find the guy responsible for these fires. But I didn't mean for this to happen. For you or Cassie to be pulled into it."

She had meant well; it just hadn't turned out well. Gage was her friend and she trusted him. Jack thought the man was driven first and foremost by the anger and grief he still felt. Gage was going to compromise this investigation if he didn't carefully exercise a reporter's discretion. This was the first article to tell the public about the link. The dominoes had begun to fall and they were going to end up with panic and copycat fires.

Jack got to his feet and settled his hand on Rachel's shoulder. "Come on. Go borrow my comb, clean up. I'll talk to Cole."

"Would you?"

"What are brothers for, if not to hide behind?"

THIRTEEN

Well, at least her life was no longer boring. Cassie struggled to get her shoes on, finally gave up, and kicked her dress shoes across the room. She got up to retrieve the casual flats she had picked up earlier and set aside. She was going to be late to church if she didn't leave soon, but she refused to look like she was falling apart even if it felt like she was.

The phone rang.

"I'm not home," she muttered as she listened to it ring, rejecting the idea of answering it. If she had to tell one more friend the story or duck one more reporter, she was going to scream. That newspaper article had about sunk her.

If she were smart, she would be late to church on purpose just so she could slip into the back row and not have to answer questions. If not for her friend Linda, the last twenty-four hours would have been unbearable. Linda had juggled her schedule and come over to the bookstore Saturday for a few hours just to answer the phone that had never stopped ringing.

Friends called, worried about her after reading the newspaper article. Reporters were leaping all over her actions angling for details to feed further articles. By tomorrow's newspaper, the hype would be unchecked. She'd lived through it once after the nursing home fire. She did not want to live through it again.

Gage had been fair. He kept the quotes he used in context of what she said when they had spoken. But the last thing she needed was a focused sidebar. What she had done was worth a buried sentence late in the article. And the way he had shaped Lisa's letter— Cassie knew Jack would be furious about that. It was way out of bounds to use a letter Lisa had written to further Gage's own purposes.

It didn't help that Cassie was going back on shift. She was nervous. Cole was counting on her. She was going back to work to find an arsonist.

The person she had seen and the impression that it had been Ash continued to haunt her. Time had only strengthened that impression.

Lord, why am I in this position? Who am I supposed to be helping? Protecting? Jack? Ash? Rather than prayer clarifying the issue or bringing a sense of peace, there was an overriding weight coming down on her shoulders. The realization was growing that her first impression may have been the correct one, that she had seen Ash.

I can rationalize him doing it.

Cassie shoved aside items in the bathroom drawer as she searched for her perfume.

Late at night, edge of the district, set to destroy the structure—the fire reports spooked her. She had seen that signature of fires within the walls once before. She had been a rookie still in training. They were conducting a controlled fire as a training exercise at an abandoned house the county was going to tear down. Cassie had watched Ash set the fire using small flowerpots filled with fertilizer set between the joists in the wall. It had created a hot fire similar to an electrical fire beginning in the walls.

The last thing she wanted to do was tell Cole about the flowerpots Ash used ages ago only to find out she had just implicated her partner. The mere thought had the queasiness she was fighting intensify; she reached for the glass of 7-Up she had been sipping through the morning.

Cole had blacked out sections of the reports. She didn't know what the arsonist used as a mechanism for starting the fires. And if it was pottery between joists? Ash had been setting training fires that way for years. How many other rookies going through the academy had seen that signature? A few hundred?

Loyalty to her friend against a suspicion she couldn't prove—figuring out what she should do was impossible. Cole knew her initial impression was Ash. She wasn't hiding it. But without more information to go on, she didn't want to take it further.

Lord, I can't sit idly by while this suspicion lingers, but what can I do?

With no ideas, only churning turmoil, she forced herself to push it aside and start thinking about practical realities.

Where had she stored her extra uniform shirts? It had been a tear-filled spring afternoon after a bad day in physical therapy when she ripped open her dresser drawers, opened the walk-in closet, and sent the evidence of her profession into a pile on her bed. By the time she finished the purge, not only the clothes of her profession but also the specialized tools of the trade she'd acquired over the years had been tossed out. She had no idea where those boxes were stored.

She'd need to find extra socks, sunglasses, and a book to read after the workday portion of the shift ended. It had been so long since she packed to work a department shift she knew she would forget something. And she realized last night that Cole had snuck one in on her with that efficiency report assignment. She'd need to double-check that she had a good briefcase; efficiency reports influenced pay incentives and it would be more than just the reporters who would like to read over her shoulder.

The owl clock over her dresser sounded the half hour. Cassie pulled open the closet and retrieved her long coat. This was not the mood to be in for leaving to go to church.

Lord, forgive me for not being ready to worship. I'm bringing a lot of baggage with me this morning. Calm me down and give me again Your peace that is bigger than these problems. You've gotten me through a lot more uncertain and stressful moments than this, and I should be remembering this last year and relaxing.

She found her purse on the kitchen floor near the pantry beside a case of soda and a plastic grocery sack with cookies and paper plates she had bought for the youth group. A search of the bottom of her purse yielded her store keys but not her house keys. Cassie yanked out her billfold and checked the torn inner lining that seemed to eat her keys every time. Nothing.

She reached for her spare set of house keys in the catchall drawer. There wasn't time to find the missing set. It was frustrating how often it happened when she was in a hurry. With her blistered left hand she reached to tug close the apartment door, which had shut but not latched, and paid for the mistake. The pain rippled. Her hand had settled to a dull throb this morning, so she didn't always stop to think before she acted.

She headed downstairs. A stack of newspaper sales circulars had been delivered to the building and sat on the bottom step. Yesterday her mailbox had been jammed full with Christmas sales flyers. The annual deluge had begun. She opened the building door and shivered as the cold morning air rushed in. She never enjoyed winter and this one had arrived early. When she stepped outside she found her breath was visible.

Jack was leaning against the passenger door of her car. He was dressed for the weather, wearing a leather jacket over a thick black cord sweater and jeans, cradling a Styrofoam cup. Steam rose from the cup, wavering in the cold air. Cassie was stunned to see him.

There must be news about the fire, news either Jack or Cole thought needed to be delivered in person. Ash. Cassie took a deep breath, all the tension she felt coalescing as she braced for the news Ash had returned and it had been him behind the fires. "This is a surprise." Her steps slowed as she approached him.

"I'm here to take you to church. You don't need to be driving until that hand heals."

Church. Cassie struggled to reorient her thoughts.

Jack had protested her driving herself to the bookstore yesterday and she conceded the point, letting Linda give her a lift. But today she could have driven herself. She was surprised that he had not called ahead, only to realize if he had she'd ignored the call. "Did Rachel ask you to do this too?"

"I have a few original thoughts. You look pretty, Cassie."

The compliment delivered with such a lazy smile had her smiling back. She glanced down at the blue pantsuit she was wearing. She'd been after practical and warm. But it was one of her favorites and it did look pretty. "Thanks."

"You're very welcome." His expression turned serious. "I also want to talk to you about the newspaper article."

"Cole called me last night. He said you had been over to see him after reading it."

"You should have told me last night you were coming back to work."

She pushed her right hand deeper into her coat pocket, hating having Jack frown at her. She was worried he would react this way. If he knew part of the reason she was doing it was to try and protect him— "Cole thinks I can help."

"You're going to go out on calls to look for the man you saw."

"I have to do something."

"Not this," he replied grimly.

He was pushing down his anger. It was fascinating to see and realize it was being felt on her behalf. "I appreciate your concern but—"

"He's dangerous."

She had seen a man who was setting escalating fires, who had written the word *murderer*. "I know."

"I don't want you getting involved."

He wanted to protect her. She was grateful, but it left her between a rock and a hard place. "I'm already involved. To do nothing—that's not an option, Jack."

His frustration was obvious, but he glanced away, checked what he was going to say before he looked back at her, then shook his head. "I know, Cassie. But this option is a lousy one." He pushed away from her car and moved over to his. "It's cold. We'll talk as I drive." He opened the passenger door. "How's the hand?"

"Sore." She wrestled to get the seat belt fastened. The heat had been on in his car. And while it had cooled as he waited for her to arrive, it wasn't as cold as her car would've been. She was thankful for that as she settled in.

"You'll have to give me directions."

She thought he'd been to the church the department volunteer chaplain pastored in the past, but that assumption had apparently been wrong. She gave him directions as she shifted her feet to be under the floor heating vent.

Jack backed out of the parking spot. "What time are you coming in to the station Thursday?"

"Cole said the shift starts at 8 A.M. I plan to be in early so I can store gear."

"When there is a rollout you'll ride with Bruce, Nate, and me in Engine 81. We've got room in the jump seat."

Procedure was to roll an engine with a crew of three, then to go with a fourth man if only one engine was responding. It would be crowded on the back U-shaped bench if she was joining a complement of four guys. "I thought I'd be rolling with the captain."

"With the number of calls we respond to he's often moving from scene to scene. And while your stated purpose is to work with him, it's going to take about one shift before the rest of the guys in the company know what you are really doing."

He was right about that. Secrets never lasted very long among a company.

The last thing she wanted to talk about this morning was what she had seen that night, the state of the investigation, and what the upcoming week was going to be like. She tried to change the subject. "Besides chauffeur, do you have other plans for your day off?"

He glanced over at her. "Let's go get a Christmas tree this afternoon for your bookstore."

She was startled by the suggestion. "A Christmas tree."

"Got a better idea?"

"Laundry. Paying bills. Packing for the shift."

"Come on, Cassie." His voice was touched with laughter. "You'd enjoy decorating a Christmas tree more."

"I bet you believed in going out to play before you did your homework too."

"Absolutely."

She knew she was going to need help with the tree; she couldn't move one by herself. Her plans had been to finish pricing books, decorate the front window, then move around furniture to make room for a tree. She could shift that around. "I might be able to find a couple hours if you would like to help haul a tree for me."

"I'd like to help decorate it too."

She smiled at that request. "Are you a tinsel fanatic?"

"Definitely, it's one of my favorite memories from childhood. Life is full of serious people who grew up too soon. I've never been accused of being one of them."

Jack pulled into the parking lot at the grade school where the church met on Sunday mornings.

"Would you like to come to church with me? You know Pastor Luke and his wife Linda. Cole and Bruce both come too. It's a pretty casual crowd since most of the guys help set up the stage and sound and pack it away in the trailer after services each week."

"Thanks, but no. Being a Christmas and Easter churchgoer isn't my style. I'll be back to pick you up after the services."

She was disappointed by that but understood his reluctance. So many people felt unless they attended church regularly it was hypocritical to go. And while her church tried hard to make visitors feel welcome instead of the center of attention, it did happen.

An opportunity to share what she believed was in front of her, and she didn't know how to make it comfortable for Jack to join her. Hearing the truth about Jesus challenged someone to consider what he believed, and it wasn't always a comfortable experience. She could sympathize, but it was reality of the power inherent in the truth.

She stepped out of the car, then leaned down to look back in. "Jack, yes. I would like to get a Christmas tree this afternoon."

His smile made it worth it. "Good. I'll pick you up here at eleven. Tell Luke and Linda hi for me."

"I'll do that."

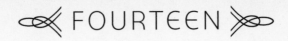

FOURTEEN

"Jack, that tree is huge," Cassie said, trying not to sound too critical.

"I know. Isn't it great?"

He was straining to hold the center trunk of the tree. He shook it and the branches that had been mashed by the fence the tree had been leaning against settled back into their original shape.

"It looks like a tree that needs to be on a diet. Stuff that falls inside these thick branches will disappear and never be seen again. The lights won't show unless they are on the branch tips."

"Have some faith. This tree will hold up for a month. Think about how great it will look with ropes of popcorn and layers of silver tinsel."

Cassie had been trailing him around the nursery looking at Christmas trees for the last two hours. He was like a kid in a candy store, choosing one, only to go to the next one and decide it was even better.

"Spin it around. Let me see the full thing." She sipped at the hot apple cider she held. The afternoon was perfect for this—crisp air and sunny blue skies. Leaves crunched under their feet as they walked around the nursery. There were hundreds of Christmas trees to consider, and the discussion around large or small, fat or thin, wide needle or slim had been debated on merits all afternoon.

Jack was a riot to walk around with.

"Admit it, Cassie. This is the one. You'll have the best Christmas tree in Lincoln Hills."

"Do you really think you can get that tree into Stephen's truck?" He had borrowed his brother's pickup for this adventure.

"Absolutely."

"Along with about ten feet of pine roping, that gargantuan wreath, three poinsettias, and the musical door chime?"

His grin grew as she reeled off the list of items he had already talked her into. "I'll even make sure there is room for you."

It was a beautiful tree. She only had one reservation. "I don't know if we can get it in the front door of the store."

"Trust me."

She gave him an easy smile. "Oh, I trust you. I'm just trying to decide if I want to jump off this particular cliff with you. It will take about a mile of popcorn rope to decorate it." She was tempted to agree if only for the challenge of it.

The pressure of this morning had been replaced by a relaxing afternoon. She was enjoying Jack. So many men were like Cole, everything close to the vest. With Jack she didn't have to wonder what he thought. She had seen everything from amusement to occasions of worry and anger. The best thing about him was his laughter was contagious.

Her left hand stiffened as the blisters had tightened. She had a headache from the restless night's sleep. But the day had improved because of Jack's company. And it looked like by the end of this day she was going to have spent most of it with him.

"This one?"

She looked at the tree best described as a monster. "This one."

"Sit," Jack ordered.

"I'm fine."

"Cassie."

She tugged over a stool, loath to admit he was right. She was tired enough the tangles in the strands of Christmas tree lights had already won, and she just didn't want to admit it. Cassie pulled the entire mess onto her lap.

"I'll finish them."

She stubbornly shook her head. "I'll get them," she muttered. If only her stiff fingers would simply work. The string of lights were plugged in so that she could find and replace burned-out bulbs. It was a sea of red, green, blue, and white flashes every three seconds. When she tried to hold the strand of lights with her left hand to unscrew a bulb with her right, her left hand would spasm. Clenching her fingers was the equivalent of grasping a live wire. She was beginning to think there actually was a short in the light strand somewhere.

"Patience."

"Patience isn't the problem. I just need some wire cutters."

Jack chuckled as he moved down from the step stool he was using, squeezed her shoulder briefly, and crossed over to the table to get another box of ornaments. He'd long ago finished stringing the lights at the top of the tree.

The tree took over the entire center of the bookstore.

The poor front doorway still showed its scars from where it had lost the fight. The tree won. It had literally been pushed inside, not that Cassie was allowed to help. Jack had called Stephen. She stood by and watched as the brothers wrestled it inside.

They tried placing it by the front window and found, as Cassie suspected, that there was no way to have the tree there without blocking either the counter or the doorway. The guys ended up taking two chairs into the storage room, sliding the main table closer to the display of children's books, and moving the history book display in order to give the tree enough space.

It had been worth it. The tree was going to be beautiful. After all this effort, that wasn't optional. It was going to be beautiful, or it was going to be firewood.

The bulbs finally replaced, Cassie plugged the strand of lights into the end of the previous one on the tree and began working to place them.

Jack stepped back up on the step stool. "Do you want me to use all the glitter balls at the top?"

She glanced up at Jack. He was working from the top of the tree downward. His smile— She shook her head and glitter rained around her. "Now I know why you wanted to do the top branches."

"You look cute wearing the glitter."

What she probably looked like was a six-year-old who had gotten into the glitter sticks. She had to smile at that image. She leaned back on the stool to check his progress. "They look good up there near the room spotlight. Use all of them there." She blew glitter off the back of her hand. "Besides, then they can shed on the tree rather than the floor."

"You need packages under this tree."

"The tree practically hugs the floor. No one could see packages under it." It had already proven to be an effective black hole.

Currently somewhere under the tree were his kicked-off tennis shoes, what she was fairly sure had been an orange glow-in-the-dark superball seen briefly as it bounced past after falling out of Jack's coat pocket, and a handful of French fries she dropped when she tripped over the extension cord to the train set.

"A Christmas tree needs packages."

"I'm going to wrap the books I'll use as my Christmas giveaways." As she now had a twist tie held between her lips, she was forced to mumble her answer as she fought a blue light that didn't want to stay where she placed it.

"Any comic books?"

She got the strand wedged into place and used the twist tie to secure it, triumphant that she had subdued another wayward light. "Sorry. If you want to enter the drawing you have to like to read." A small black spider appeared again dangling and she batted it away with the back of her hand before picking up another tie. Jack and his toys…this one was smaller than the one he had offered at her apartment. He'd probably bought them in all sizes in one of those plastic eggs available from a gumball dispenser.

"How about a coloring book?"

She reached for more ties and conveniently clipped him on the back of his knees.

"I take it that was a no."

"How did you ever pass the lieutenant's exam if you don't like to study?"

Jack laughed. "I've got a good memory and I'm a great talker."

"I agree with the great talker part."

"Just to satisfy my curiosity, where do you buy all these books?"

"Estate auctions. Garage sales."

"You're a Saturday sales junkie?"

"Don't laugh."

"I'm trying not to. Want company some time?" Jack offered.

"Will you carry the books for me?"

"As long as you don't buy one for me to read."

She shook her head at him as she smiled. "You're impossible."

"True. Cassie?"

"Hmm?"

"Thanks for today. I'm enjoying it."

The spider reappeared and she batted it away again. "I'd enjoy it more if you'd quit dangling your spider every time I turn around."

"What?"

It dropped into her lap.

And rather than lie there, it moved.

She flung out her injured hand and slapped the spider away, sending it sailing across the room. The stool tipped. She would have landed in the tree had Jack not flung out a hand to stop her. Instead of getting a face full of pine needles, she fell backward and came close to hitting the back of her head on the table leg.

"Kill that thing," she ordered.

Jack went after the spider scurrying away and stepped on it with his foot. Cassie winced, wishing she hadn't seen that. Wearing shoes was one thing, socks was another.

"Did you hurt your hand?"

She was shaking it to take out the sting. "I caught it on the strand of lights." Half of the bottom strand of lights she had just struggled to put in place were pulled free.

Jack strode back over. He set the stool upright for her.

She looked at it with disgust. "I think I'll sit on the floor for a while. I need to fix the bottom row of lights."

Jack obligingly sat down on the floor beside her. "Let me see your hand first."

"It's fine."

"Cassie—let me see."

There was an edge of lieutenant in his voice, and the command was hard to ignore. She held out her hand. Two blisters had broken on her thumb. She was ashamed at the mess her hand was in. The blisters lay over older scars that had turned smooth skin into stiff ridges. "I don't need your pity."

He looked up, his gaze holding hers. The seriousness never left his eyes but a smile appeared. He curled her fingers closed. "Battle scars don't bother me." He tugged at her buttoned shirt cuff. "Any of them. I've got a few of my own. In rather embarrassing places."

He was doing it again, putting a line of humor under what was very serious. "Do you?" she asked, intrigued.

"I sat on a broken bottle once."

"Sat?"

"Considering I was twelve at the time, sat is more appropriate than lost my balance and tumbled off a railroad tie to land on my tuckus."

"Sat does sound better."

He released her hand. "I'll help with the lights."

She hesitated, then offered him the twist ties. "I'm sorry I thought that was you dangling the spider."

"My fault for having done it before."

"Promise me you'll never use a lifelike snake."

Jack leaned his shoulder against hers. "Promise."

And because he had been nice enough not to laugh at her overreaction to the spider, she leaned back, using his shoulder as a support, and dumped the now tangled Christmas lights into his lap. "Fix this, please."

Jack warily picked up one end of the mess. "Interesting…"

"No, we are not going out to buy more lights."

"I just thought it. I didn't say it."

"I'm a mind reader."

"Do I get to help with the popcorn strands?"

"Are you any good with a needle?"

"I'll learn."

Cassie looked over at him, skeptical. "Buy yourself a box of Band-Aids. You'll need them."

"O ye of little faith."

"One of us has to be practical."

"What's this?" He reached across her and plucked a coin from behind her ear.

"Jack." She was amused by the simple magic.

He walked the gold coin between his fingers and offered it to her. "Your first Christmas gift."

It was a gold foil-wrapped piece of chocolate. "I didn't get you anything."

She expected him to laugh and make a joke. Instead, he just smiled and picked up the Christmas lights.

He gave gifts. She fingered the piece of chocolate stamped as a coin. "Jack?"

"Hmm?"

"Thanks." The word didn't have enough impact to convey everything she was feeling, but she didn't know what else to say.

"You're cute when you're at a loss for words." He tugged over the box of decorations. "I'll flip you for the right to put the angel on top of the tree."

She sent the piece of chocolate spinning into the air. "Call it."

"Heads."

She caught it carefully. He leaned over to look. "I won."

She turned over the coin. "It's a two-headed coin."

"Well, what do you know—"

FIFTEEN

Cole had said be early. Cassie was early. According to the clock on her car dash, which was known for its creative timekeeping when the weather was cold—and this Thursday morning certainly qualified—it was just after 6 A.M. She was back on shift work. Wide awake at five o'clock, the choice between killing time at home or going to work had been simple. She'd even rushed through breakfast; the old habit of rolling out of bed, grabbing gear, and heading to the station still was ingrained in her thinking.

Where to park had been a problem. She was missing a department sticker for the car bumper to use the official lot but ran a bigger risk of having her car towed if she parked in the visitors' lot for the duration of the twenty-four-hour shift. She compromised by taking Cole's parking place. There was a good chance he was driving the district vehicle and wouldn't need the assigned parking space anyway. If he did…he could find her.

He would certainly know it was her car. Not only had he driven it from the fire scene for her, but he'd left a Post-it note on the rearview mirror suggesting she might want to rethink listening to Saules Trie at full volume. The local band was making a name for itself, and after months in the hospital she'd unwittingly become a fan because the FM radio station DJ was also a fan.

Cassie unlocked the trunk and shoved a box of books out of the way so she could get hold of her duffel bag. She'd bought it at the army surplus store because the canvas bag could easily be tossed into the wash.

She was starting to get nervous. She tugged the cuffs of her jacket down before picking up the duffel bag. The next twenty-four hours were going to be as tough as the day she had arrived at her first station assignment as a rookie.

She'd tried to brace herself for the reaction her presence would trigger. From the firefighters, she knew there would be an overeager effort to show the burns didn't bother them. From those who had only heard about her, it would be an awkward fascination. Eventually they would work up the courage to ask her to tell them about what had happened.

There would be uncertainty over what to say around the kitchen table. Fire crews joked about what they feared, and the dark jokes about fire were legendary. She'd told a few herself during her years at the table. She knew there would be humor that would miss the mark.

For herself—she was worried about her hearing. It was difficult following conversations when she was in a noisy environment. It was acutely embarrassing to try and have a conversation with someone and have to admit she was only able to make out every other word. Concrete floors, large rooms, a constant level of background noise—the fire station was the definition of a place that would give her problems.

Most of the guys had no idea how poor her hearing had become, especially in her right ear. The first time someone called her name and she didn't hear them— She just hoped she didn't come across as rude if it happened.

She had one goal for this first day back on shift: surviving it.

"Morning, Cassie."

She looked up, startled to see Lieutenant Ben Rohr, the head of Black Shift, appear. "Lieutenant."

His smile was welcoming. "Be glad you came early. There are homemade cinnamon rolls coming out of the oven."

"That sounds wonderful."

He took the two straining garbage bags he carried over to the dumpster. The trash was just one of many housekeeping chores done before the shift change. She wasn't surprised to see him pitching in with the housekeeping. The best lieutenants led by being willing to do every job. She waited for him. Ben had seen the department through years of transitions; she was curious to know what he thought of the arson fires.

"How's the hand?" He offered to take her duffel bag for her.

The swelling had disappeared. The blisters had begun to callus over. It was healing. "Stiff."

"Cole is here somewhere." He held the steel door for her. "Can I get you some coffee?"

"I'd appreciate it."

"We cleared a locker for you. Unpack, get settled in, then come join us for breakfast. I'll introduce you around."

A breakfast conversation would be perfect. Ben was heading off duty with the shift change. "Is everyone already up?" She knew how precious those last hours of sleep were before the eight o'clock shift change. It was rare for a firefighter to get a full night's sleep.

There was no getting around the fact the dorm rooms were near the equipment bays. When those massive doors rose and vehicle lights came on, sleep stopped, at least long enough to notice the time of night. Even at the smaller station where she had worked, at least one or two dispatches a night were a given.

"A car accident shortly after five woke the station."

Cassie hung up her coat on an empty hook in the walkway. A yellow caution sign was out to remind people the hall had been mopped recently.

They passed the kitchen. Two firefighters were debating how crisp to cook the bacon and a small group had taken up station near the coffeepot. The rich smell of baking cinnamon rolls hung in the air. The kitchen was always the center of social life at a fire station, the place to linger and talk. "Thanks, Ben." She accepted her duffel bag and turned toward the women's dorm room.

"Cassie." Cole appeared from the equipment bay. "I saw your car. Dump your bag and come on through. I've got some gear for you to try on. Ben, grab her some coffee? She takes it sweet, but not as sweet as you."

Cassie wanted to laugh as she obediently set down her duffel bag and hurried to catch up with Cole. He had never been a boss to let time slip by.

"I want to get your gear straightened out and then talk through the plan for today with Frank. I'm heading over to the scene of the last fire after roll call, and I want you to come with me and talk me through the report you gave of that night."

Her idea that she'd get a rather leisurely chance to settle in went out the window; it sounded like she would be racing to keep up with Cole today.

She hesitated when she saw the gear Cole was heading toward. Her fire coat had saved her life even if it hadn't been able to prevent all of the burns. There was a new one waiting for her. Her old helmet was there, the Company 65 markings still present, and by the look of it her old fire pants. She'd handled a road crew accident where hot asphalt was being laid and the black tar had permanently adhered to the left pant leg.

She had known Cole would not let her ride along as a spectator. She would be rolling out to fire scenes and for safety's sake would have to be in gear in order to stay with the captain. She thought she was prepared for it, but the emotions came stronger than she was ready for. Difficult rescues, out of control fires, numerous drills—so many years of her life were captured in that gear.

"I wasn't sure about the fire boots. I had several sizes sent over."

"Nines," she said absently, her attention focusing on what she had just seen. Cole had set out the self-contained breathing apparatus. The nightmare flashed by. She hadn't worn a mask since the fire. She'd come close to suffocating because her air tank had run to empty.

Ash had saved her life by risking his own and buddy breathing with her, hoping that help could reach them before he too heard warning chimes. She didn't know if she could handle facing that sensation of breathing on canister air. Using SCBA gear wasn't as simple as the public often thought.

"You need to be able to use it just in case," Cole said quietly. "You're rolling out to fire calls."

"I know."

Faced with picking up the fire coat with her healing left hand or her weaker right arm, she reached for it with her right hand. Heavy, stiff, the nomex cloth feeling like thick rubber, she pulled it on, reaching out of habit for the clips near the collar. Tossing the collar up, she fastened the top button of the coat and worked her way downward. She worked the cinch of the belt tight. When this coat was broken in she wouldn't have to fight the way it lay. Equipment weight would help the material pull and eventually relax.

"Cuffs. Let me." Cole took care to get the best fit possible, adjusting the cuff straps so that with the gloves they would fit tight. Her arms couldn't handle another brush of heat. "Will this coat work?"

"It's a good fit."

Cassie sat down and pulled over the SCBA gear. The best way to fight the nerves was to fall back on training and safety procedures. Cole had set out a sixty-minute cylinder for her.

"Did you bring your recipe box with you?"

She smiled as she turned the tank to check the gauges. "Still thinking about your raspberry cobbler?" She checked the hydrostatic test date and the fill pressure. Eighty-eight cubic feet of air compressed inside the canister should have pushed the pressure up to four thousand five hundred pounds per square inch.

"I'm going to use my informal seniority to put you on kitchen duty sometime in the next few shifts."

"Thanks for the warning." She checked the overpressure plug. The small metal disc was set to rupture if the compressed air refill went past those limits. "If you've got a preference for dessert, what about dinner?"

Ben brought in the coffee. Immersed in the work, she accepted it with a quiet thanks, took a sip, and set it aside.

"Lasagna with Italian sausage, not that bland stuff Bruce prefers."

"An easy request. I was afraid you were going to say fried chicken."

She tightened the cylinder into the harness. The high pressure hose that let air flow from the cylinder to the regulator where it would be lowered to a breathable pressure was finger tight.

Refusing to let her hand tremble, she reached for the face mask. The entire assembly was designed to keep positive air pressure inside the mask to prevent any smoke from entering. A donning switch would shut off the air to the face mask when it was slipped on. She cleared the exhalation valve on the face mask. With the positive pressure it was necessary to forcibly exhale.

The safety checks were done.

She glanced over at Cole. His expression was inscrutable as always. It gave no indication of whether he felt she was stalling or doing the right level of detail.

Calling herself a bit of a coward, she looked back at the gear and let years of training take over.

She grasped the backplate and cylinder with both hands and lifted it above her head, letting the harness straps fall across her shoulders and past her elbows. The harness and air canister slid onto her back in a smooth motion she had done hundreds of times in the past. Only this time the thirty pounds took her to the limits of what her right arm could manage in a controlled way. She secured the straps, pulling them tight to let the weight settle to her shoulder and back muscles.

Fanning the spider straps of the face mask, she took a deep breath and donned it chin first, then straps at the neck, temple, and chin were tightened. She did those moves quickly as her first breathes were now on SCBA.

Breathe in through the mouth, out through the nose. Inhale fast, exhale slow. She heard the litany in her mind and used it to block the surge of adrenaline. She had never felt claustrophobic before, and it hit fast and hard. She locked her attention on the job at hand as a way to fight it, finishing the safety checks.

When she was confident she had missed nothing, she looked toward Cole, a good suspicion on what was coming.

"Your regulator hose just became disconnected."

She scowled at him and quickly moved to execute the emergency procedures. Cole was merciless with the drills. She had to strain to reach straps and hoses. She braced for the possibility he would want to see the movements with a hood plunging her into darkness. The procedures were difficult enough; doing it in the dark as would be the case in a real emergency— She turned her frustration into a focused effort to keep her breathing steady despite the exertion. Cole was going to run her into the ground and she was too stubborn to let that happen.

"Stand down."

With relief that it was close to over, she forced herself to be methodical in how she removed the gear. She lowered the cylinder to the floor with care.

She was drenched in sweat from the nerves and the hot coat.

"Good job. Have breakfast, then come find me." Cole walked away, leaving her to store gear in the empty locker that now bore her name.

Two words. Good job. It had taken her three months as a rookie firefighter to finally earn them. This time—they had never sounded more beautiful.

"Let's get roll call started."

Cassie leaned against the back wall beside Cole as Frank called the shift to order at 8 A.M. The tension that had built over the morning finally broke. This was familiar turf.

Jack raised an eyebrow at her when she didn't choose to cross the room to join the other firefighters from Engine 81. She smiled back and didn't move. There was no way she was going to get sandbagged into a roll-call introduction. She'd been to way too many of these meetings over the years to fall for that tactic.

Get introduced, and end up being the person called on for the remainder of the meeting to answer questions regarding station business. It was an efficient if brutal way to make the point that day one on the job was no excuse for not being fully prepared.

A review of the rollouts for the last forty-eight hours began. Cassie scanned the thick report. Forty percent had been calls for medical assistance. Eight percent had been false alarms. There had been five car accidents, two with injuries.

The only fire had been a kitchen grease fire put out before they arrived. With the upcoming holidays and arrival of winter, those numbers would shift dramatically.

Cassie dreaded the first snow. Winter and fires—the water froze to the ground, to the equipment. The fire scenes became skating rinks. Ladders had to be used with extreme caution. For the firefighters bathed with water mist, frostbite became a serious danger. If there was wind, a fire in the winter could become a life-threatening situation.

"In-house, where are we at? Any vehicle problems? Equipment problems?" Frank queried.

Firefighters around the room called out suspected and confirmed problems with starter cords, pumper valves, hose connectors, vehicle brakes, floodlights. Everything went on the white board with men assigned to each issue. If a problem couldn't be addressed immediately after this meeting, it would go up the chain of command.

Frank turned to the training schedule for the day. It was aggressive. The focus of today's drills was on emergency egress procedures. Cassie was relieved. He was doing everything possible to make sure Gold Shift was prepared for the arson fires. "In the spirit of saving the best news for last: Weight training just became mandatory. I want a minimum of an hour in the gym worked into your daily schedules." The announcement was met with a few good-natured groans.

Roll call ended with an order she had heard many times in the past. "Lieutenants, check your rigs." For every problem known about and assigned to be addressed, there were assumed to be two equipment problems coming. Men were not going to be put at risk because of equipment failure if it could be inspected or tested out.

Cole closed his notebook. "Grab your turnout coat and boots, a notebook, and meet me out back at the SUV. I'll get coffee for us both."

His announcement ended any idea of talking with Jack after roll call. She caught his attention and pointed to Cole, then shrugged. It was a twenty-four-hour shift. There would be a moment they'd both be free before the day was over. Jack nodded, his disappointment clear. She smiled at him for that, glad to know it mattered. Turning, she hustled to grab her gear and get out to the vehicle, determined not to leave Cole waiting on her.

SIXTEEN

"Go away." Cassie didn't even bother to open her eyes. If she had to move short of dispatch declaring a five-alarm fire, she was going to snarl at the cause. The official workday was over, even if the shift wasn't, and she had crashed to try and recover from her first taste of being back on the job.

Cole lifted her left foot out of the bucket of hot water. She sucked in her breath as he firmly rubbed at the muscle cramp along the top of her foot curling her toes back. "It will ease."

"You said the same thing an hour ago."

The day hadn't been heavy work, but she'd been on her feet, constantly up and down, hauling paint cans of evidence, carrying equipment, acting as Cole's gofer. The cramps that had hit late in the day had been unexpected and severe. The weight of the boots and the heat inherent with wearing fire gear had eventually taken its toll. Muscles had cramped. It was embarrassing and painful.

She reluctantly opened her eyes. "Cole, you're a slave driver."

"Guilty. Feels good to be back to work though, right?"

She smiled a little at that. "Ask me in the morning."

They were sitting near the horseshoe pit at the back of the fire station. Sunny skies and moderate temperatures in late November were rare and the firefighters were taking advantage of it. The two grills beside the picnic tables had been fired up. There would be barbecued pork chops for dinner.

"You were a good help today."

"Trying to butter me up?"

"Is it working?"

"Some." She sighed and eased her foot back into the hot water. "How do you do it, your job?" She'd spent the day helping him go through the burned-out house, reconciling reports written by the responding firefighters with the police report, and helping create the critical timeline for how the fire had begun and spread.

Walking the upstairs hallway where the firefighters had found her, it had been obvious how foolish she had been to rush inside the house. That was the inherent problem when someone was thought to be in danger—the first instinct was to help and it overrode any instinct for safety.

The word *murderer* haunted her.

She'd seen Cole looking through a report of everyone who had died in the district since the consolidations began. There was nothing easy about the road he had chosen to go down. And she felt a burden for that, knowing one of the key reasons he had accepted a move to the arson group had been what happened to her.

"Someone has to do it," Cole finally replied.

"Do you think he's going to hit again tonight?"

Cole rolled his shoulder. "Fifty-fifty. Don't take chances, Cassie."

"Do I have permission to walk around the fire scene if we do roll out? This guy is not going to be standing out in the open."

"As long as you remain in sight of a police officer or the captain. I know it's going to be a chaotic scene so that burden will rest with you."

"I'll be careful." She did not want to think about the guy she had returned to work to find. "Is Jack back yet?"

Engine 81 and Rescue 81 had been dispatched to a car accident just over an hour ago as she and Cole were returning to the station. It had been hard on her, seeing the rescue squad roll out with lights and siren and not to be on it.

"Jack's on his way; they've been released from the scene. I heard a report of two injuries, both listed as stable."

"I wanted to be on that rig."

"I know."

"How did you handle the first few times the captain rolled out and it wasn't you?"

Cole smiled. "Badly." From behind them came the sound of the engine returning. Cole got to his feet. "Want me to send Jack out once he gets his gear cleared away?"

"Jack won't need the prompting—he'll follow the smell of food. But you might ask him to grab me a soda on the way."

"Glad to."

"I think I like having you feel guilty."

"Thin ice, Cassie."

She laughed softly as Cole walked away, then reached for the book she'd been reading.

Jack spotted more blood in the seam of his left boot and dunked the steel-tipped boot back into the plastic bucket of soapy water. He switched from scrub brush to toothbrush. It had been a bad wreck: a delivery van swerving through traffic and plowing into the side of a red Toyota.

The lady in the car had stoically insisted she was okay, while her five-year-old son had screamed at the top of his lungs. At the memory of the boy's outrage, Jack gave a rueful smile. Kids weren't afraid to be honest and give their real opinion of a situation. She'd bled, the boy had thrown up, and both had survived. They'd just had to be cut out of what remained of the crumpled car.

Jack couldn't find much sympathy for the driver of the van who had broken his leg. The guy had been doing forty on a downtown street.

The side door into the bay opened. Jack glanced over, hoping to see Cassie. He couldn't believe it was closing in on dinner and the day had passed with no more than a brief chance to say hi to her.

Cole came in. "Good run?" He must be out of Lifesavers, he was eating a piece of red licorice.

"Fine."

"The grill is fired up. Pork chops are coming off soon. Cassie appropriated your chair."

His chair—the metal patio chair he had picked up at an auction was huge and swallowed up whoever sat in it. Jack smiled at the mental picture. He got up to begin storing gear in his locker. "Did she?"

"She looks settled in for the night too. Don't hassle her about the foot cramps. The boots weren't broken in and she's paying for it."

"Cole."

"My error. Her feet are up; she's off them for the night short of us getting a dispatch. And she's sensitive about the entire matter."

Jack got the message. Sympathy wasn't the right response. "Feel guilty enough you want to do paperwork for me?" Jack backtracked with a grin on seeing Cole's expression. "Just checking. I'll take it outside with me."

"Snag her a drink on the way."

"Yes, sir."

Cole headed toward his office, tossing a question over his shoulder. "Is insubordination contagious?"

"I'm going to respectfully not answer that," Jack called back, slamming the locker closed.

"Smart man."

Cassie was lost in a book. Jack slowed as he approached for it was clear she didn't hear him. She had escaped into her favorite pasttime.

A folded newspaper and a spare book were tucked by her side in the big chair. Over the arm of the chair hung a pair of black tube socks. Cassie was soaking her left foot. Muscle cramps were a common problem and he wasn't surprised that a full day wearing fire boots had left her fighting them.

Jack leaned over the chair and dangled the item he carried.

"What?" She caught it, turned to look up at him. "Hi." She glanced at the chain.

"Keys to the station. I meant to get them to you earlier. Sorry about that."

Carrying keys in a pocket when entering a fire scene was a bad move. Most firefighters carried them on a belt clip or a chain that could easily be removed. He'd guessed which she would prefer.

She slid the chain on. "I was rather hoping to get locked out."

He tweaked a curl as he took the seat beside her. "Sorry. You're on call like the rest of us." He offered the soda he carried. "Bruce said you were drinking orange today."

"Thanks."

"You've had an interesting first day."

"An understatement." She cracked open the soda.

"You might want to try and get a nap in after dinner. This guy has been hitting around midnight."

Cassie nodded. "I'll do that." Peter lifted the lid on the grill. "There are some things I really missed about station life and this is one of them."

"Good food?"

She shook her head. "A guy fixing it."

Jack stretched out his legs and crossed his ankles, feeling like the Thursday had been going on forever. It was great to finally have a chance to have her full attention.

"How was this last callout?"

"Routine."

He glanced at her, caught an edge of frustration in her expression, and realized he had made a mistake by not covering the details. It had been routine, but she hadn't been on it.

She changed the subject before he could expand his comments. "I've read the reports of the earlier suspicious fires. It was unclear if there has been any indication of someone watching those fires. Is there reason to think he might be staying around to watch every fire he starts? Or am I going to be rolling out with just a fifty-fifty probability of him being there?"

Jack wasn't surprised that Cole had stricken the popcorn signature from the records. Until an arsonist was apprehended any information that might suggest a way to identify him was restricted so that a news report would not reveal it and the arsonist react by changing his MO. Cole would tell Cassie when she needed to know it. "We think he watches all of them. He's got a couple signatures."

He was still frustrated with the underlying decision that she should roll out with them to try and find the man. It was dangerous. If this conversation continued he'd probably say it again. He changed the subject rather than risk it coming up. "Could you use any help at the bookstore finishing the Christmas decorations? My schedule for the next couple days off is free."

"Sure. I've also been intending to build shelves in the storage room. Would you be interested in swinging a hammer?"

"Will you make me one of those super subs I've heard Cole talk about?"

She reached over and patted his stomach. "I'll make you half of one. You'd never manage a Cole-sized one."

He caught her hand and held it up to study her fingers with interest. "What's this?"

She curled her fingers down into a fist.

"Cassie, have you been working on the popcorn chains without me?" She had Band-Aids on her first fingers and thumb. The needle had to be difficult to handle with her stiff hand.

"Don't go there, Jack."

"You're cute when you're embarrassed." Her hand felt rough as the scars had healed in ridges. She didn't need someone to cry for her, and he tapped down the regret he felt. He soothed his fingers around the back of her fist and set her hand down in her lap. He would have held on to her hand, but Peter was watching. "What kind of shelves do you want built at the store?"

He needed to find a good place to watch this fire that would let him linger without being seen. But where? The fire would be huge, multialarm. And perfect—this destruction would embarrass them.

He didn't need Cassie Ellis getting a better look at him. He'd been keeping periodic checks on her since she'd almost stumbled into him, then had determined after the first week she was no threat to his discovery. She'd seen him, but she didn't know him. He'd even crossed her path, said hello, and there had been no recognition.

He'd get one break in his favor but probably not two. He would go for broke with this fire and push hard. He'd get his point across.

His family wouldn't thank him, but then they didn't have to carry the burden of paying the bills. Thanksgiving had been frustrating, but Christmas…

This time he would make sure the newspapers got the message, even if he had to tip someone off to the signature. There was an arsonist loose, and the fire department wasn't up to the job. There would be changes. One way or another, he would force them.

SEVENTEEN

"Cassie, are you sure you want to do this?"

"I'm doing it, Gage. If Ash wants to complain, he'll have to show up to do it." She pushed against the back door of Ash's home and found it had very little play in the door frame, but it did have some. She pulled out a laminated video store rental card, slid it into the crack, and started working it around the frame.

"You could just ask his cousin for another copy of the key you lost."

"She's in California for the month." She worked the card downward while she kept the doorknob turned. "You are not printing in your paper an allegation of what I said that I can prove to you is wrong."

Gage ran a hand through his hair. "I already said I wouldn't print it. Would you stop? A cop is going to come by."

"Then I'll tell him exactly what I'm doing. That it's my partner's home, I lost my key, and I am doing what I feel the circumstances warrant. There was a natural gas leak two houses down yesterday that caused a dispatch, and this house needs to be checked."

She wasn't taking this step lightly, but she was frustrated with the idea she had seen Ash, and that the fact lingered in her mind. If Gage hadn't gone probing like a pit bull, her suspicion would not have become known to the press. "And you will print it if you think you can find supporting evidence; I know you." She owed it to her partner to kill the idea now. It was Friday and Gage was in the process of writing his next article.

"I'm not going to apologize for a factual story. The Weekend Focus article last Saturday was accurate."

"Then consider this insurance to remove the basis for your assumption Ash was somehow involved." She gave up on the card and looked around the porch for something else to use.

Ash's home had a decidedly neglected look. His cousin collected his mail from the post office, where it was being held, and paid his bills. His neighbor kept the grass mowed, but it showed the evidence of its vacancy in the weeds that grew, the lack of any Christmas decorations, and the closed window blinds.

She picked up a brick.

"Hold on. Put it down." Gage headed back to the car. He came back with a thin metal strip. "I can't believe I'm doing this."

"You owe me."

"You're the one who asked me to run a background check on your partner. You're not exactly showing confidence in your stated position. Either you think you saw him or you didn't."

"I'm worried about his continued absence. That is all that is behind my request," she insisted. At this point she would love to hear Ash had received a speeding ticket somewhere. It was coming up on Christmas, and she needed to find him.

Gage took her place and popped the lock in a matter of moments. He opened the back door. "Rachel is going to have my head for this."

"Then don't tell her."

Cassie stepped over the threshold and entered Ash's house. It smelled musty. She had been braced to smell natural gas or more precisely the chemical added to it to create a sharp odor. The house had been closed up for months. Her need to check the house was real. During the early months of winter, natural gas home explosions happened more often than most people realized as the ground grew cold and froze, stressing buried lines.

She walked through to the kitchen. The counters were clear. Her note to Ash from her last visit was still on the kitchen table. She opened the refrigerator and found it cool and empty. Ash's cousin had cleared it out after four weeks. Cassie checked the living room. The only thing that appeared to have changed was the formal clock on the mantel had stopped at 7:04.

"He's really not here. I believe you. Satisfied?"

"No." She headed to Ash's office.

Sitting down at his desk, she turned on his computer.

The password was *backdraft;* the same one he had used at the office. She suggested it to him years before and he had never changed it. She brought up his e-mail. It took twelve minutes for all the pending messages to transfer from the server. She should have changed his discussion groups to nomail as she watched all the nightly digests flow in.

The fact so many messages flowed over suggested he was not going on-line to check his messages. There was a chance if in his travels he'd visited friends, someone might have dropped him a note. There were several individual messages. She recognized names of his friends.

The message with the subject line FIRE caused her pause. It was anonymously sent. She checked the date. It had been sent over eight weeks ago.

She opened it. Flickering flames appeared, and the word *CHICKEN* emerged from the flames, flashed, then disappeared.

"What was that?"

She closed the message. "A firefighter's joke," she told Gage and resumed her search through the messages.

Had Ash been a target before the first fire had been set?

Where was he?

Nothing else in the e-mail suggested anything. She shut down the machine. "Okay, Gage. We can leave. Now what are you writing about this weekend?"

"I hate to burst your bubble, but a suspicion that a firefighter might be starting fires—read the FBI November 1995 report: 66 firefighters set 182 fires in the brief review of cases they looked at. When I can prove who this arsonist is, that will be news. The Weekend Focus article I'm writing at the moment is a devastating look at the manipulation of gas prices at the start of the winter heating season."

"My bills are going up?"

"I strongly suggest you sit down before you open your next bill."

EIGHTEEN

If the arsonist was going to strike again, he was taking his time about it. And having learned her lesson, Cassie was wisely keeping her nose out of the investigation. It was Saturday, December 9, her fifth shift, and so far she had rolled out only once. Rather than be a suspicious fire as first reported, it turned out to be a chimney fire caused by the home owners' first use of their fireplace this year.

Cole had heard her rather nervous statement about the e-mail message Ash had received, the word *chicken,* and the fact Gage knew about her suspicion. He'd accepted the news with a growing frown, noted down the date she said the e-mail had been sent, and told her not to worry about it. But he had done it with an implicit suggestion that she stop chasing ideas and let him do his job.

Cole believed she had scared off the arsonist. She had seen him, and since then his behavior appeared to have changed. Cassie was quite willing to go along with that supposition if only because it bought her a few weeks to get back into Cole's good graces. No one seemed to think the arsonist would quit setting fires, but as shift after shift passed, there was a growing sense that his MO might change.

Being back on shift work, it was as if she had never left. The twenty-four hour on and forty-eight hour off pace had a rhythm to it, and she adapted back to it much easier than expected.

Cassie opened the oven to check the raspberry cobbler. As promised, Cole had arranged for her to have kitchen duty for the day. He was getting his requested meal. She was fixing lasagna, hot breadsticks, Caesar salad, and raspberry cobbler for the eighteen firefighters on duty. She promised to make enough cobbler so there would be leftovers for the next shift.

"Cassie, do you have a minute?" Cole asked.

She glanced over to the doorway. "Of course."

"I know you're off duty…"

She smiled at the hesitation. He was being unusually deferential because he wanted to keep in her good graces as well. Technically she went off the clock at 5 P.M. "Bring the paperwork. I know you've got a finance meeting on the eighteenth."

She found working with Cole fascinating. Getting involved in the efficiency reports and the budget paperwork had radically opened her eyes to the scope of his job. She'd thought she would find watching him wrestle with the numbers boring, but instead it was a very big challenge.

"I'd like to try changing these budget figures."

"Which ones?" She held the spoon she was using over the sink, so the grease wouldn't drip on the stove top, and leaned over to see the report.

Cole held it steady while using his pen to highlight a line. "Paid oncall class I. Let's shift the increase to salary class III. And I want to cut the administrative budget another 3 percent and move it to training."

"Given the increase in grounds and maintenance, I don't know if there's another 3 percent that can be cut from the admin figures. You can barely afford a box of paper clips as it is."

"We'll have the fire station auxiliary sell cookies, sponsor a car wash, have another chili cook-off…something. I can beg and cajole the community for things; I can't do that for people. And we've got to squeeze another paramedic and firefighter in under the budget caps."

She agreed with him on the hires. After watching five shifts Cassie would consider the need acute. The guys were getting run ragged with the dispatch rate. If they got back from this last rollout by seven o'clock she would be surprised. She was doing her best to slow dinner preparations so they wouldn't have to come back to rubbery lasagna from overcooking. "I'll get as creative as I can."

"Figure out how to do it and I'll owe you a big one."

"Let me roll out to the next car accident."

He leaned over and pinched some of the grated cheese for the lasagna. "No."

"Cole, I know the job, and you just said you needed the help. I know I can't do everything at a scene I once could, but you know how valuable an extra pair of hands would be. And it's not like you're not already paying me." It was killing her to have the dispatch tones sound and at times be the only member of Gold Shift left at the station. It wasn't the first time she had asked. She didn't understand why he wouldn't agree. "If you think it's a liability issue, could I request a finding from the personnel board?"

"It's not my decision," Cole said quietly.

"Should I talk to Frank?"

"It's Jack's decision to make."

Jack was the one choosing to leave her behind. She blinked as that registered. She had worked hard to show him she was not only up to speed with the status of the rig and the equipment, but also to prove she was not a liability to him on Engine 81. Finding out he was the one blocking her request…it felt like she'd been betrayed. How could he hurt her this way?

"I support his decision."

"Cole—" She needed to understand. "Why?"

"Talk to Jack."

It was the only answer she was going to get. She slowly nodded. "Okay." Cole wasn't going to explain, but she heard what sounded suspiciously like sympathy in his voice. She looked back to the dinner she was fixing. Sympathy ran close to pity. She didn't need either.

She pushed away the hurt. Her issue was not with Cole; it was with Jack. "Leave the budget on the table and I'll do some work on it tonight, if you don't mind my using your office."

Cole gave a rueful smile. "You're welcome to it."

The man worked too many hours. She had found him already at the station when she arrived at a quarter to seven this morning. Unlike the guys on shift, Cole was in the office five days a week. On top of that, he was on call for suspicious fires around the county and had a full court docket to manage as arson cases moved through the courts.

He pinched more cheese. She wasn't sure if he'd had lunch. "There are extra raspberries in the refrigerator."

"Really? I'll accept. Do we have any ice cream?"

"French vanilla. I bought it this afternoon."

"Bless you." He opened the cupboard to retrieve a bowl.

"Jack." It was seven-thirty that evening, after dinner and kitchen cleanup were complete before Cassie was able to search out Jack to raise the subject she had been wrestling with ever since Cole's comment.

"Over here."

She pushed her hands deeper into her pockets and picked her way carefully across the parking lot, trying to avoid the puddles that were actually disguised potholes. The rain had come down in a steady drizzle for most of the afternoon, then had finally stopped, but the mess remained. Several car accidents today were attributed to the weather.

Jack was in the county garage. The building next to the fire station was used to store some of the more infrequently used equipment, including a flat bottom boat and a scaffolding system for construction sites. The large doors were rolled up and the overhead lights glared. He was stretched out under the belly of what the guys affectionately called the Blue Beast.

The old pumper engine had been retired when the Quint—a combine engine and truck—had been bought three years before. The Blue Beast was kept serviced so it could be used when access to a scene was constrained. The narrow wheel bed of the old engine made it the only pumper that could get to certain locations or at major fires where it became necessary to stage water from either the lake or a retention pond.

She could see Jack's boots and not much else of him. "Can I talk to you for a minute?"

"Sure."

"Face to face."

What sounded like a wrench struck concrete. "Just a minute," he muttered through gritted teeth.

"Rap your knuckles?"

"About broke my thumb."

When he rolled out from under the engine two minutes later, his face was still grim and he was shaking his hand to take out the sting.

Now wasn't a good time. "We can talk later."

He sat up and tossed two wrenches into the toolbox. "Now is fine." His expression lightened. "Did I mention it was a great dinner?"

"Several times." She perched cautiously on the metal bins used to store salt blocks.

"Cole was wrong about the cobbler. It's not good. It's fabulous."

"I'm glad you liked it." She smiled but it faded rather quickly.

He moved to sit on the running board of the pumper, his curious look turning serious, his mood changing to match hers. "What can I do for you?"

"I'd like to ride along when there's a dispatch to a car accident and help out. Cole said I should talk to you about it."

She searched his face for an indication of his thoughts. She didn't know what she expected but it wasn't the remote expression that appeared. "I'm not asking to go back on full duty, just roll out and be there if you need an extra hand."

"I'm afraid the answer is no."

"I'd like to know why."

His gaze was calm and resigned. "It won't change the decision," he said quietly. She heard in his answer the caution that it might be better if she would accept that.

She hesitated. She didn't want to push him into a corner, but she needed to know. "Do you think I'd be a liability because of my weaker arm?" He was ruling her out and yet there had to be something she could offer that would be acceptable. "Could I do care and comfort?" Under current department policies, even Luke as a volunteer chaplain was trained in emergency medical response and could provide that kind of help at the scene of an accident.

He turned his attention to wiping grease from his palm.

"Jack?"

"I'm sorry, Cassie."

The rejection hurt. "I need to know why."

He looked at her with sadness and regret, and he gave it to her straight. "You're partially deaf."

She'd asked; the answer cut. Her hearing had been compromised, especially on her right side, but it was not as bad as his answer suggested.

"I can't have you working near traffic when that very traffic would mean you may not hear a shouted warning. You have a problem hearing me across the equipment bay when a vehicle is running; you struggle to follow a conversation at dinner when several separate conversations are going on. Too many firefighters and cops have been hit or almost hit by traffic when working a crash scene. I can't let you ride along."

It was a calm, quiet explanation, a definite one.

She got to her feet, feeling lost. Being around the fire station, hearing the dispatches, seeing the rollouts, going through the refresher training classes…she had let herself think she was really coming back in a limited but real way. She'd been seeing what she wanted to be the truth but not the actual truth. She'd started to hope.

"Cassie, I meant it when I said I was sorry."

She paused, not turning back because she was afraid the tears threatening might show. She'd been judged and found wanting, not because he wanted to do it, but because it was reality. "You made the right decision. You've got a crew to think of beyond me."

The paperwork was a haven. She had retreated to it, closing herself into Cole's office, focusing on the numbers. The concentration required allowed her to set aside the emotional turmoil she felt.

She'd seen Cole as she hung up her jacket after coming back in. He hadn't said anything, just squeezed her shoulder. Cole was right. Jack was right. And they'd been forced to intervene and stop her from following down a path that would be a danger not only to herself, but to the other firefighters.

The numbers blurred.

Lord, it hurts.

She set down her pen and pushed back the report. The black three-ring binder she used to collect past drafts slid off the table, hit the arm of the extra chair, and fell open when it crashed on the floor. She looked at the scattered papers. It looked like she felt, cracked open and tumbled out. Stuffing her dreams back together was impossible.

She wiped at the tears. *I let myself hope, and instead of open doors they just slammed shut. Lord, just get me through this day and out of here. I need some place safe to cry.*

She began gathering together the pages. She wondered if she could slip down to the woman's dorm without being intercepted. She didn't want to talk to Jack because she simply wasn't sure yet what to say. Understanding his decision and being able to accept it were different emotions.

Her reason for being here had not changed.

There was still a man out there starting fires.

She would help find him, and she would get on with her life in whatever way that meant. The bookstore business was taking off. She and Linda were struggling to keep up with filling the incoming orders shipping all across the country. Maybe she would implement the plans she had talked over with Linda—hire one more clerk and go forward with plans to expand the business.

Maybe she'd move. The thought had lingered since Jack's comment. Maybe she would do it. She didn't enjoy making changes, but since she had been reacting to those forced by circumstances, maybe she would add one by choice.

She struggled to find something that felt encouraging to hold on to.

She sighed. For the next few weeks she was in limbo. Having agreed to help Cole, she could not easily pull back from that decision. She went back to work on the budget, although the confidence that she could help out Cole and make a difference was gone. It had simply become paperwork to struggle through.

The math worked, but the numbers didn't, a reality she had observed in her own business. The budget could support either a paramedic or a firefighter but not both. By 10 P.M. Cassie had figured out there was no way to get creative to make the numbers work. Disappointing both Cole and Jack on the same day…she wished she had never thought to hope about a new future possibly working with the department.

Cole couldn't afford to hire her, not to be doing this kind of work on an ongoing basis. She understood now why he had placed her on the administrative staff. It was the only way to pay her and justify, by her seniority, hiring her for a few weeks. Cole didn't have the money to pay her into next year. If this arsonist was still out there after January 1, for financial reasons it would be impractical for this arrangement to continue.

The phone rang shortly after ten. It was Cole's public versus private line. She'd been answering phone calls and handling messages for him for the last week. She hesitated to answer it at this time of night. Someone would have paged Cole if it were urgent. Remembering Cole's growl about the voice-mail system's habit of cutting off long messages with its set cutoff time, she reached for the phone. "Hello?"

"I was trying to reach Cole. Is this his assistant or did I dial the wrong number?" The voice was raspy and deep and at first she thought it was being done intentionally, and then she realized why it was also familiar. She sounded much like that during the early days in the hospital. The man was recovering from an injury to his vocal chords.

"This is Cassie. I'm working for Cole, borrowing his office at the moment. Can I take a message for him?"

"Please. Leave him a note that it's Chad returning his call."

Chad. Her pen slowed as she wrote the note, finally placing him and feeling guilty that she hadn't immediately done so. He'd been hurt in the paint factory fire last year. Ben had been by to see Cole early that day to talk about when his nephew Chad could come back from disability, if there would be an opening in the arson group available.

"I'll get him the message," she promised.

"Ask him also to check for an incoming fax."

She tucked the phone against her shoulder and reached for the phone book. "Do you have the fax number or can I get that for you?"

"I have it. You are working late."

"Paperwork," she replied ruefully.

Dispatch tones sounded and jolted her. "I've got to go; we've got a dispatch. I'll be sure he gets the message." She pushed back the chair, still scrawling the note as she stood. She said good-bye and dropped the phone. She rushed through the district offices back into the bays.

Men were suiting up. More tones sounded as additional units were called up. Around her was a controlled rush. The ladder truck, two engines, a rescue squad—dispatch was acting based on a confirmed structure fire, not a report of smoke.

She slid on the pants, stepped into the boots, and reached for her fire coat. She tried to hurry. The men around her were already swinging up into vehicles. The ladder truck kicked on lights to warn traffic on the street they were about to roll out.

The new fire coat fought her as she tried to secure the buttons; she abandoned trying. She'd do it on the way. She grabbed her helmet and gloves.

Nate had Engine 81 running. She moved around to the passenger side.

Jack was there, standing on the running board, one hand on the dash, leaning down to have a hurried conversation with the communications dispatcher. She met his gaze.

The rescue squad to her right moved out.

Jack extended a hand and offered her a hand up.

She stepped up and slid to the back bench next to Bruce.

Jack slid inside and slammed the door. One final sweeping glance around the cab and he nodded to Nate. Sirens and lights came on. Engine 81 rolled out.

NINETEEN

Jack had known the address, but he hoped the dispatcher had been wrong on the street number. As they pulled down the street it was clear there had been no mistake. The fire station closed in the consolidation was burning. Flames showed in the burst windows of the dorm wing and smoke spewed from the back of the building where the ventilation system began. The training tower behind the structure glowed like a spire torch.

"This is adding insult to injury."

Jack agreed with Bruce's shouted observation. Jack was willing to bet this would turn out to be their popcorn arsonist. What wood there was within the concrete structure was limited, and yet it was feeding flames well beyond what the normal load would trigger. The smoke was black to the point of ebony and was rolling down suggesting an incomplete burn. The flames had flickers of blue and green indicative of a fire too hot for simply a wood source.

More than just their company had been dispatched. Company 21 had arrived first, thus would have command and control responsibility. Jack reported in to the scene commander via radio and got their assignment.

"We've got the tower along with Ladder Truck 81," Jack called over to Nate. The tower was in danger of collapse, and by virtue of its height it was spreading embers over the surrounding area. It was going to be a difficult fire to fight as it presented a severe containment problem, but at least they wouldn't have to worry about fighting it from the inside with a roof ready to come down.

Jack looked back at Cassie. Her expression was focused ahead on the scene. He'd hurt her with his decision earlier. It would have been easier to ask Cole to make the decision, but doing so would have abdicated his own responsibility as the lieutenant in charge.

He had to admire how Cassie had accepted and dealt with it. She'd wanted his explanation, and even though she did not agree with it, she had not gone over his head to Frank to try and see if it could be changed.

Nate paused the engine long enough for Bruce to step down and pull the five-inch supply line. Nate then rolled the engine forward to join Truck 81, using the vehicle movement to lay hose behind them.

Jack tightened his gloves and swung down to the ground. The lieutenant of Truck 81 already had the aerial ladder moving. The hose line on that ladder would be able to tackle the height of the fire. Jack picked up the radio and linked up with his fellow lieutenant. The truck crew could manage the structure; it looked like the best place for their resources would be fighting to keep the building from collapsing. "We'll take the east face first," Jack shouted over to Nate, who was bringing down the three-inch hose.

Jack caught Cassie's arm and leaned in close to make sure he was heard. "Stay close to Cole." He was convinced this was one of the arsonist's fires. Cassie was going to be looking for the guy. He did not want her wandering around on her own.

She nodded.

He searched her face, worried about how she was going to proceed. She wanted to be fighting the fire; restricted from that, she would want to do anything she could to find the man responsible. And he was comfortable with her doing neither.

"Trust me."

He squeezed her arm, then released it. He had no choice.

He turned to face the fire. The rain earlier in the day was a saving grace as embers landing on roofs of nearby buildings were quenched in the moisture. This was manageable, but it was going to be a vicious firefight.

Was he here?

Cassie kept her back to the fire as she walked around the scene, for it was a personal assault that a fire station had been torched. It would save so much time if she could just find the man. It would release her from the weight of the obligation she faced. It would end the threat to Jack. Cassie stayed within the circuit of the responding units. The fire lit the area and cast flickering shadows.

The roar of the fire and the rush of water mingled with the sound of the men and women fighting it. The smoke had a sharp smell of varnish within it.

She started when someone grabbed her arm. Cole. She hadn't heard him, his grim expression told her that. "Stay with me."

Subdued, she joined him.

"Have you seen anyone at all you consider suspicious?"

"No."

Cole read his watch in the light from his flashlight. "Thirty minutes since the initial dispatch. If he's still watching he's moved back. I want us to systematically canvass a two-block area."

She'd been thinking about it as she walked, trying to find the place where someone would be able to stand in the shadows and have a line of sight to the scene. "What about the high school football field bleachers? That would be a good place to watch from." It was a block away from the fire, but at night with a hot fire raging...that would be a very good vantage point.

"Good suggestion. We'll start in that direction."

"Cole, did you call me and I didn't hear you?"

He didn't speak until she turned to look at him. "I did. And if you get upset about the fact it happened, I'm going to get upset with you. No one holds being hard of hearing against you. We will accommodate you, not the other way around. And if that means getting your attention before we ask you something, we'll do it."

"I should have never put you in this place when I said I wanted to come back. Jack's right. I can't do the job."

"If there was a way Jack and I could remove the obstacles to your being on active duty, we would make it happen. We just haven't been able to find it. And I seem to remember I opened this conversation five months ago asking you to come work for me. I'm not losing years of valuable training by setting you on a bench if I can convince you to get back in this game. I can't put you back on active duty, but you are well qualified to join my investigation team."

"As much as I have enjoyed doing your paperwork, you can't afford me."

"You haven't seen the budget swap Frank and I would make if you ever did say yes. It's a serious offer, Cassie. You know the job. I'd be honored to have you working for me full time."

She knew he meant it, and there was some reassurance in that. "I'll think about it."

He was sweeping the ground with his light as they walked.

"What are we looking for?"

"Anything out of the ordinary."

They walked away from the fire passing spectators heading toward it.

When they reached the football field they found it deserted.

The mud was thick. Cassie stepped up to the bottom row of the bleachers to walk on it, shining her torch over the bleachers and under it while Cole swept the ground with his. If someone had been watching the fire from the bleachers he would have probably sat up high to get a better view.

Her torch picked up something white trailing down the bleacher seats and on the ground underneath. At first she thought it was someone's band music sheets that had blown away during a halftime presentation. "Popcorn." She whispered it as it registered…and the implications hit her like a tidal wave.

She fell off the bleachers and Cole grabbed her arm.

Why hadn't he told her? Why hadn't Cole told her?

"Sit." He turned her and with a smooth motion put her down on the bottom bleacher seat.

She lowered her head toward her knees as it sunk in what she had found and she shuddered with the memory.

Popcorn had also been left at the scene of the nursing home.

TWENTY

"Why didn't you tell me?" Cassie whispered. "Has there been popcorn left at all of these fire scenes?"

"It's a copycat. I swear it, Cassie. A copycat." Cole rubbed her back, worried at the reaction he had frankly not expected. The information had been concealed, not to keep it from her, but because it was part of the restricted information in the files regarding the arson signature, and he had already determined it was unrelated to her.

"The man who started the nursing home fire died in New Jersey in a car accident two months ago. I've got the proof, and I went back to the New Jersey police to confirm it." His gloved hand tightened on her shoulder. "Someone else is copying that popcorn signature. He's mocking the arson group, Cassie. This isn't personal to you."

"It is personal against me, just like the fires have been set against Jack."

"No. It's not personal to you. He's using the popcorn signature as a taunt, just like he's been using locations at the edge of the fire district as a way to mock us. The popcorn is the symbol of the worst fire on record. It's just cruel luck that you were the one who chanced into seeing him."

"Then are you sure this isn't Ash? He was very hot about the nursing home fire. He left. Then these fires started."

For her to formally blame her partner…the popcorn had really shaken her up. Cole forced her chin up so he could see her face. "It is not Ash," he replied emphatically.

"I'm not so sure."

"I am."

"You know something else I don't?"

She asked it with such hope that he wished he could give her something. "I believe what I know in my gut. There is no way Ash would let you enter a building fire again."

"You said this arsonist didn't want someone to get hurt.…"

Cole had wrestled with the implications of the word *murderer,* of the possibility Ash had been called a chicken. They were taunting words. It was very much like a schoolyard fight. The more he knew about this man, the less he felt he understood.

"He's hitting empty buildings, but he just obviously escalated again."

"Who is he? Do you have any idea?"

Cole rubbed the back of her cheek with his glove, wishing he didn't have to answer. What he had to say he had been trying to avoid concluding for weeks. "I don't think it's Ash, but I'm now convinced it probably is a firefighter." It felt a bit like a death sentence for the department to say it. If he was correct the public implications would resonate for years.

"Then what's the trigger? What set him off this year?"

"I wish I knew. Come on, Cassie. This was one of his. It's going to be a long night." Cole gave her a hand up.

TWENTY-ONE

"Cassie."

She reluctantly opened her eyes as Jack shook her shoulder. As the only thing she was qualified to do now at the scene was to be a well-informed spectator, she'd been trying to get some sleep. The passenger seat of Cole's vehicle had not been the best choice for where to rest. "You're letting the cold air in," she protested.

"Sorry about that."

She stretched and took the kinks out of her back.

"Cole says it's cooled down sufficiently that we can get our first look inside. He'd like you to come."

She pushed up her glasses and rubbed her eyes. "Okay." She looked around him. "It's dawn?"

"Yes. You did get some sleep even though it doesn't feel that way."

She smiled at him for that stipulation as she slid from the vehicle. Jack had been up all night and he looked fresher than she did. She didn't have the endurance she once had.

The landscape had changed. The engines, trucks, rescue squads, and police cars had dwindled down to one engine and one rescue squad from Company 81, one engine from Company 21. Three police cars blocked the adjoining roads and yellow police tape was being put up to keep out spectators.

It was very clear it was now Cole's domain. The arson group technicians dominated the scene, the bright red stripes on their fire uniforms marking them as Cole's team. He stood in the middle of the chaos, the calm center in the hurricane of the crisis, directing the setup of what would be a very large investigation.

Cassie walked across with Jack to join him.

"Somebody get Cassie some coffee."

"I'm okay, Cole."

He looked up from his notepad at her. "Coffee and a bagel. You're working for me, it's an order."

Cassie blinked as she was barked at, then smiled. Cole had definitely been up all night.

"Is that replacement photographer here yet or do I need to send out a search party?"

"Here, sir." The man was struggling to get equipment out of his camera bag.

"Don't rush so much that you drop the camera. Someone get him a helmet and show him how to button that fire coat properly. Have you ever worked an arson case?"

"No, sir."

"Gregory!"

"Boss!"

"Your pupil—and make sure you get me your own Polaroids for reference."

Cole looked at the photographer. "How much film are you carrying?"

"Two spools, five hundred frames."

"Plan to use it all. When is your boss getting here?"

"Within the hour, sir."

"Okay. I'm just going to be looking around. Yours are reference frames, not evidence; we'll leave those to your boss. When Gregory says take a picture take three, one normal and the other two one step overexposed and underexposed. You'll get me what I need that way." Cole looked around. "Now where's my scribe?"

"Right here," his assistant replied. "Get moving, boss; it's freezing out here."

Cole paused long enough to wink at her. "I'm trying to, ma'am."

Cassie smiled at the interplay. Cole's assistant was comfortable pushing him back, and it spoke to the relationship that Cole deferred to her.

Cole pulled back on his work gloves. "Let's go see what we've got."

The building was cinder block and concrete. While the fire damage was extensive, it was also limited to what would burn. The roof would need to be replaced, windows, doors. Any equipment left in the building after the consolidation would definitely be ruined, if not from the fire, then from the water used to fight it.

Cole led the way.

Cassie stayed a step behind walking beside Jack. The smell of the fire scene made the coffee taste terrible. Jack rubbed the back of his neck. He'd scorched the back of his hand. That sight made her wince. "I'm sorry I dropped out on you to get some sleep."

"I'd call it smart. Cole is going to be pushing you hard today."

They entered the dark building. Torches clicked on. Water dripped from above and splashed into the puddles below. Their steps sounded hollow across the wet concrete floor.

The word *cowards* was boldly chiseled across the concrete wall of the engine bay.

TWENTY-TWO

"I hate this guy."

"Let it go, Cassie."

She shoved open the door to her apartment, Jack a step behind her. "There is not a single firefighter in this district who is a coward."

"He pushed a button with you."

"Don't sound so surprised. I've got a right to get mad at what he implied; quit telling me I don't."

"Since the shoe is normally on the other foot and I'm the one people are talking out of being mad, I find it rather interesting to be on the other side," Jack calmly replied. "Where would you like the gear?"

"In the bedroom. I'll unpack it there."

Jack carried it through. Cole had released them at 2 P.M., long after the shift had formally ended, long before Cole himself called it a day. Jack had given her a lift home, carried her duffel bag inside for her.

Cassie moved into the kitchen to check her messages.

"Is Linda picking you up tomorrow morning? Or do you want me to give you a lift in the morning to get your car?" Jack asked as he came back.

"I think we are doing some Christmas shopping. If for some reason I need a ride, I'll give you a call."

"Fair enough. Get some sleep."

"You too." He had been the one up all night.

Jack gave her a tired smile back. "I'm going to shoot for at least eighteen hours," he admitted.

She saw Jack out and locked the door behind him.

Cassie headed back to the bedroom. It was the middle of the afternoon and she was definitely heading to bed. She closed the blinds. She considered just pushing the duffel bag to the floor but forced herself to spend the five minutes necessary to unpack. She separated the laundry that would need to be done from the clothes she would take with her to the next shift.

She set the bag on the floor.

Jack had left his stuffed mouse J. J. on her pillow. She smiled when she saw it. He had promised it would appear and she'd been waiting for it. She reached to pick up the white mouse…and it moved.

Cassie shrieked and hit the floor as she fell back. The mouse disappeared toward her walk-in closet.

She was moving.

And someone else was packing her closet.

TWENTY-THREE

"Rewash this one," Cassie ordered.

Jack quickly stepped back to avoid the splash. It was the third glass Cassie had rejected and dropped back into the hot soapy water in the last twenty minutes. There was nothing wrong with his wash job. He'd been assigned kitchen duty for the day and she had been giving him a hard time since breakfast. Jack scooped up a handful of the soap suds and blew them at her. Cassie laughed and tossed the dishrag she was using into the sink, this time generating a splash that did hit his shirt.

"Next time, please don't volunteer to help."

A towel was lobbed over his shoulder. "Throw it in, Jack."

"No way," Jack called back to Peter. He retrieved the glass, nudged the hot water faucet back on to rinse the glass free of suds. The guys were enjoying having Cassie here and had certainly made her welcome over the last weeks.

Jack glanced over at Cassie and waited until she looked his direction before he spoke. The kitchen was noisy and it was his habit now to notice that factor and wait until he had her attention before speaking to her. "Do you—" His pager went off. Jack set the glass down on the drain rack and glanced at the number.

His sister Jennifer O'Malley; it was her emergency code. Jack paled at the sight of it. He grabbed the towel and dried his hands, then reached for his cell phone. There had been less than a handful of emergency pages from his family over the years.

"Jack—"

He held up his hand and cut off Cassie, punching in numbers with his thumb, having to go off memory for the Houston area code. The large kitchen quieted as the men realized something was wrong, but Jack still headed outside where the transmission would be better. Dusk was falling on the late December day. His wet shirt grew icy in the cold air.

The call was answered on its second ring. "Jennifer, what's wrong?"

"Sorry…make it an emergency."

He could barely hear her. "Easy. Slow down and get your breath."

"I fell." She was crying.

And Jack started panicking half a country away. Fell? Or had her spine collapsed? The cancer around her spine, the radiation treatment— "Where are you? Is help there?"

"I fell."

She was worse than shaken up. Jennifer was a doctor, and he'd never heard this kind of confusion before. Jack took a deep breath and focused on one objective. "Jen, where are you?" She called him looking for help from somewhere half a country away. It petrified him. Cole came outside carrying an extra jacket. Jack pointed at him and urgently whirled his finger in a circle, asking for a communication loop.

Cole tossed him the jacket and immediately turned and yanked back open the door. "Get me two phones. Fast."

Jen had to be either home or at the office. But apparently no one was around.

"Laundry." Jack caught Jennifer's faint whisper.

At her house, in the basement, a concrete floor—she'd fallen, or more likely fallen down the stairs. She lived in Texas but it was still cool at this time of year. The basement would be chilly and not somewhere he wanted her with this kind of growing shock apparent. "Don't try to move, Jennifer. Please. I'm getting Tom." He'd find her husband somehow.

Cole reappeared with phones.

"Rachel," Jack whispered. "Then get Houston, Texas, dispatch."

Cole raised an eyebrow and started dialing. Any other time Jack would have found the realization that Cole knew Rachel's number by heart fascinating; at the moment he was simply relieved.

"Tom's car phone," Jennifer whispered. "Don't remember number. You were a speed dial."

"Really? I appreciate that." Jack was sure her husband Tom was also a speed dial but he had no intention of mentioning it for fear in this confusion Jennifer would hang up and try to call Tom. He hoped her phone battery had been recharged. He needed her to keep talking. "What do you want for Christmas?" he asked, grasping for subjects.

"It's soon."

"I know, Jen. What do you want for a present? You never gave me a list," he coaxed from her.

"Coat."

She was cold. "I can do that. What else? What do you want for your kids?" Her patients were personal to her, and she always thought of them at Christmas.

Cole strode over. "They're patching me to dispatch. I've got Rachel," he passed on quietly. "What do you need first?"

"Find Tom. Jen—" he forced himself to put what he feared into words— "spine injury, shock, concussion. The basement at her house."

Cole absorbed that in one long look. "Okay." Cole shifted phones. "Dispatch? I need an emergency break-in."

And Jack started pacing. He was petrified by the rasp in Jennifer's breathing. "Have you bought Tom's Christmas present yet?"

TWENTY-FOUR

"Jack, it's Tom. I've got her. Spine pain, but she's got mobility." There was calm steadiness in Tom's voice. Jennifer's husband Tom Peterson was also a doctor, and in this enormous upheaval of Jennifer's cancer he had always played it straight on medical information. "She fell down about four stairs, went through the railing, and landed in a tangle of Christmas decoration boxes. I'll call you from the hospital. We're heading there now."

Jack heard the sound of people arriving, and from the volume of the footsteps on the stairs knew Jennifer had been lying near the steps. "She hit her head."

"The confusion is from a recent change in medication. Hold on, Jen wants to talk to you again."

"Jack...he bought me a butterball."

She was talking about a brand of turkey. "Okay, Jen. That's good. Let Tom take you to the hospital now."

"He's so sweet."

Jack had to smile wondering what Tom was thinking of this. "Go to the hospital, Jen."

A bark nearly shattered his eardrum. There was a clatter as she dropped the phone.

What? They didn't have a dog.

Tom was the one who came back on the line. "A puppy, Jack. I was out getting her Christmas present. Jennifer, you can't take the dog with you. Let me have him, honey." The phone got set down, leaving Jack listening to a faint conversation.

"Baby."

"Yes, he's a baby. But he doesn't need to go to the hospital."

"Then I don't want to go."

"I know. Let them fasten the straps, honey."

The phone scratched on concrete. "Jack, I'll call you from the hospital."

"You bought her a dog?"

"Only because it's illegal to import the warm water penguin from Argentina she wanted."

"She's confused."

"A little," Tom conceded. "We're weaning her off this med and back to the prior one. A couple days and I promise she'll be back to normal and embarrassed about this."

"I hear you." Jack knew embarrassed would be an understatement. "I'll call the family and give them a heads-up. What do you want me to say?"

"She's wrenched her back, but she's wiggling her toes and she's not biting her lip to handle the pain, so I think we'll be back home after I get a spine scan as a precaution. I'll call from the hospital and let you know how it's going." Tom shifted the phone. "Jen—" He laughed. "Hold on, Jack. Give me the towel, honey. You really don't want to have your monogrammed towel chewed up. Jack...I'm glad you were near a phone. Jen was sleeping, the housekeeper went to the store, I got delayed by a page on the way back...everything went wrong."

"It was my pleasure. And Tom, when she gets a little more coherent, ask her what she bought you for Christmas. You might have a problem."

There was a deep pause. "Is it alive?"

"To tell you the truth...I'm not sure."

Tom laughed. "I'll check. Thanks for the heads-up. We're heading out now. I'll call when we get there."

The call ended. Jack shifted his phone from hand to hand before folding it closed, feeling lost as all the responsibility for the crisis shifted entirely to Tom.

Jennifer. Jack took a deep breath and let it out slowly, grateful that he was very rarely asked to be the point of first contact for a family crisis. It was one thing when it was a stranger and an entirely different matter when it was family.

Cole walked over. His friend had been listening in via the dispatcher in Houston.

"Thanks for the help."

"Trust Tom. Jennifer is going to be just fine."

"From this."

"Jack, don't give up hope. A lot of people are praying for her."

Jack knew Cole was one of those people. While he didn't understand how they thought prayer could change things, he knew how sincere they were about it. At this point he'd take just about anything that might help. "I appreciate that."

"Is it okay if I tell the guys what's going on?"

Jack was peripherally aware that several of the firefighters had stepped outside in the last half hour to see if there was anything they could do. "Please do. Rachel?"

"She hung up on me when I passed on the news Tom had arrived. My guess is she's going to be here very soon."

"Cole—"

"She's not going to cry all over you."

"So you say." Jack wished with a passion that his brother Marcus was in town. This was the stuff his older brother handled with ease. "Let me know when she arrives. I'm going to try and track down Marcus and Kate."

"I'll do that." Cole headed inside.

Jack turned the phone toward the light that had come on at the back of the building in order to pick out the numbers. He paged his sister Kate to start informing his family of what was going on. As he looked up from dialing, a splash of red caught his attention.

Cassie was sitting at the picnic table. Her head was bowed. She was praying.

And the appreciation Jack felt was incredible.

"Hey, lady." Jack slid onto the bench across from Cassie.

"You're shivering."

Cassie's quiet observation had him realizing she was right. He'd been holding his jacket the entire time, not willing to set down the phone long enough to put it on. He rectified that, pulling on the jacket. The warmth was immediate. He turned his phone so he could see the signal strength and make sure the batteries remained strong. He reached his sister Kate and she was going to track down everyone else so he could leave his phone free for Tom's callback.

Cassie had pulled on a coat and gloves, but she had to be getting chilled just sitting there. Jack would suggest they go inside but it would remove any chance to have a private conversation. It wasn't the most comfortable place to chat— beneath his hands the wood was rough, the paint beginning to curl after a year of exposure—but after this day the discomfort didn't matter as much as the chance to have a moment with her.

She picked up a thermos from the bench beside her and spun open the top. The aroma of hot coffee drew a final shiver from him as she handed him the cup. He curled his hands around it, grateful.

"You never told me your sister had cancer." There was no reproach in the words, just quiet concern.

"I'm sorry about that. I didn't mean to hide it." He circled the coffee mug around a knot in the wood. "It's all happened pretty fast. She didn't tell the family until the weekend after the Fourth of July."

"Protecting the family from bad news."

Jack gave a slight smile. "Temporarily preempting my job."

"Jack, she didn't make a mistake in calling you. Jennifer might have been confused, but she knew exactly who she wanted to intervene. How bad was the fall?"

"Four stairs. Maybe it was an accident, but I'm afraid it's going to prove to be something worse. The cancer is around her spine, touching her liver. She's had a brief remission, but this may be the first indication that has ended." Jack ran his hand through his hair. "If the remission doesn't last through Christmas…" He shook his head.

"I'm sorry."

Her words were a mere whisper. She did understand. Cassie had spent Christmas last year in the hospital. And while she'd had visitors during the day, when Jack had swung by the hospital after he got off shift on Christmas day she'd been alone.

The foot-tall ceramic Christmas tree had looked pitiful, and all the Christmas music in the world hadn't been able to change the fact it was a hospital room. She'd had skin graph surgery on her right arm ten days before. She'd had her arm elevated, resting on a pillow, and any time she tried to shift on the bed she'd paid an excruciating price.

Cole had been there earlier in the day but had been called away by a page. Jack had taken Cole's place, picked up the crossword puzzle he had been reading aloud for her, and teased her into smiling as they debated words.

His Christmas gift to her had been a copy of *How the Grinch Stole Christmas*. She had laughed at it, as she'd laughed at everything else going on. He watched her by force of will refuse to let the pain win, refuse to let the despair take hold.

If Jennifer was in the hospital, he'd deal with it. But creating moments of lightness in such a dark day was not what he wanted for his sister. Not on what might be her last Christmas.

"She was at Johns Hopkins for weeks, then released to go back to Texas. Her wedding was two months ago. She was so happy, Cassie. They've got plans to come here for the Christmas holidays so Jennifer can see old friends from high school. If Tom calls and reports the cancer around her spine has returned and become aggressive, she's likely to be going back in the hospital for the foreseeable future."

"I'd say don't borrow trouble but it's probably best to be prepared."

The phone call had been a shock. He was definitely not prepared and he had to get there fast. "Thank you for praying."

She glanced over, surprised.

"Jennifer believes."

"I'm glad," Cassie replied.

"She needs something to hang on to—she chose the idea of heaven and the practical reality of marrying Tom."

Cassie looked at him, then down at her coffee. She dumped the small amount that remained and had grown cool onto the grass behind her, then reopened the thermos to pour more. "You think heaven is a myth."

"I mean no offense, Cassie, honestly." That was the last impression he wanted to leave with her. "It would be nice to think eternal life did exist. But why should Christianity's claims about heaven be more relevant than the claims of any number of other religions? Christianity rests on the idea a man rose from the dead. That's pretty tough to swallow."

"Not if Jesus was the Son of God. Are you familiar with what the Bible says about Him?"

"Jennifer talks about Him a lot." And frankly confused Jack, not that he'd tell Jennifer.

"You need to get to know Him. Then you'll understand why Jennifer believes. Why I do."

"How?"

"You could try reading the Bible."

It took him a couple seconds to realize the dry humor in her answer, to understand the smile she was trying to stop. He lightly kicked her foot under the table. "How did I know your answer would be to read a book?"

She reached over and tapped his knuckles with hers. "I know you, Jack. A look at the evidence and what Jesus said and you'd get your answers. Jesus is not a myth."

"If you say so."

"It would be easier to handle Christmas with Jennifer if you would look at it again with an open mind. Did you ask Cole to call in a replacement for you? The odds are good we're going to be rolling out again tonight and you're going to be busy for the next few hours. Ben can come in and cover your shift so you can focus on your family."

The arsonist. The reminder was a wrench back to another painful reality. "If I'm not working he probably won't start a fire."

"Jack—"

"Don't tell me that isn't the current theory. I may be slow to put together the pieces, but I get there."

She slowly nodded. "It's a possibility."

He rubbed the back of his neck, surprised she had been willing to put it into words. He didn't know what to do about it. Pull himself off active duty? He'd wanted to be a firefighter since the day as a child he'd seen his first fire. He couldn't imagine being anything else. He had an obligation as well as responsibility to his men, but if that was what it took…. "I'm a firefighter. This is what I do, who I am. If someone does have a beef with me—" He shook his head. "I'll cross that bridge when it's more than a possibility." Tom would be calling back in the next couple hours. "Any more coffee in that thermos? It's going to be a long night."

"I'll go get us a refill." She slid from the bench. "Jack—you're interesting to watch in an emergency. You're the first guy I've seen who likes to pace and kick rocks while you cajole the world around you to get what you want. You did a good job."

"Flattery, Cassie?"

She squeezed his shoulder as she walked behind him. "Truth."

His cellular phone rang.

TWENTY-FIVE

The district offices were dark but for the lights on in Cole's office. The clerical staff, other arson investigators, and building inspectors had gone home. Rachel would either park in the visitors' lot beside the district office or along the street just past the fire station. Cole paced in the conference room where he could see both the lot and the street. Where was she?

He'd scared her with that phone call regarding Jennifer and he hated knowing that.

He interrupted something; Rachel's hello had been distracted. As soon as she heard why he was calling, she practically swallowed her words. She scrambled to get him Tom's car phone number, talking to herself in frustration as she searched for it and couldn't quickly find it.

Cole was going to graciously forget what she had said aloud to herself even while he remembered it as an issue he'd have to soon tackle. Stupid had been the kindest name Rachel had called herself as she'd taken not knowing the number from memory, a misplaced purse, a jammed clasp on her address book, the tumbling out of dozens of business cards all as somehow being her fault.

Under the stress of a family crisis he'd gotten a glimpse beneath the layer of poise Rae normally maintained and learned just how hard she was on herself. He didn't like it, not one bit.

She had to read him the phone number twice as she transposed digits the first time, and he finally had to stop her with a quiet word and remind her to get her reading glasses.

There hadn't been time to reassure her. He was forced to leave the call with her open while he worked with the dispatcher to expedite getting help to Jennifer. And in the time that he had been talking with the dispatcher and waiting for Tom and the rescue squad to get to Jennifer, Rachel had been able to hear only thirdhand what was happening.

He'd passed word to her just as soon as he knew help had arrived. Her response was to abruptly hang up on him. He was afraid she had been crying.

Cole tapped his knuckles on the edge of the table.

She should have been here by now.

The phone in his office rang. With one last long look at the dark street, Cole moved to take the call.

The coordinator for the state crime lab was on the phone. "Hold on, Kevin."

Cole unlocked the secure file cabinet to retrieve his case index log. While he had a great support staff to keep track of case numbers, assigned officers, pending evidentiary tests, and court dates, it made his life easier to keep his own reference log that could go with him. "Okay. Give me the case numbers."

Kevin read a list of six. The last two numbers Cole knew by heart. The popcorn case arson numbers were burned into his memory.

Cole turned and punched in his secure number on the fax, which would enable encryption and provide the requisite date and time log to make his life easier when he inevitably had to testify at trial. "How much paper are you dumping to me tonight?"

"Forty-two pages."

"Oh, joy." Cole checked the paper supply. "Shoot them to me. And thanks for the evening response."

"Thank your administrative assistant. Your paperwork always arrives complete, with tracking numbers and labels preprinted for my convenience. I don't mind expediting requests that only need my signature to prep. She's even started sending the stamps."

Cole smiled. "Before you ask, no, you can't hire her away from me. I'm working on a raise if I have to pay it out of my own pocket." The fax machine by the window came to life. "I see paper. Thanks, Kevin."

"Anytime."

Cole dropped the phone back into the cradle.

Forty-two pages were going to take a while to come through the fax. Cole rubbed his forehead at a rare headache and reached over to the inbox for the top inch of paperwork already waiting there to be read.

The problem with having an efficient staff was that paperwork that needed his attention rarely got delayed. If he initialed or signed something, made the mistake of writing an e-mail, action happened immediately. Inevitably that meant follow-up status reports coming back. His own success with hiring great staff often felt like the making of his own downfall. He could delegate work; he couldn't delegate responsibility.

An official-looking binder with the red stamp budget was on top of the stack. It was a problem that would not go away. Every time Cassie got a draft that would work someone else on, the committee would make more changes.

He set aside the report to take home with him. It was part of the reality of command. He and Frank were fighting the bureaucracy. Between the two of them he had no doubt they would eventually get the aggressive training program they wanted in place, but it was like rolling a boulder uphill—all the pressure was coming from the other direction.

The next item was a blue folder clasp, used for personnel matters to protect confidentiality. Cole opened the folder and slipped out the two pages. The bottom line through the official paperwork: Chad wanted to come to work for him.

A message from his assistant noted Chad had called again that afternoon. Ben had caught him yesterday over lunch to mention the doctor was releasing Chad for light duty.

Telling a firefighter on disability he couldn't come back on shift work was hard, telling him there wasn't even a place for him in the administrative side of the house felt like hitting a brother when he was down.

There wasn't a seniority card he could play. He'd done that with Cassie. She had enough seniority he could authorize paying her out of his own budget. To justify bringing Chad off disability meant having a clear permanent position available he was qualified to take.

Cole found a pen and made a note to his assistant that he would call Chad. He'd find some way to at least give the guy hope at Christmas, even if it meant calling in favors at every other fire company in the surrounding counties until he found someone with an opening. Ben was absolutely right, firefighters had to take care of their own. Cole dropped the paperwork in his out box.

The fax finally went quiet. Cole reached for the stack of pages, then sorted out the reports.

The third report was for him. Lab work was done on the evidence he had expedited from the fire department fire. He started reading.

The first popcorn arson fire had been pinned down to a match dropped with the right wind, humidity, and temperature conditions. In those fires, it had been the popcorn signature linking them.

The structure fires were different.

The fires starting in the walls had a strange burn pattern. They were very hot, with characteristics of a flash fire. That suggested a spark-triggered accelerant. But there were also odd characteristics of a slow, sustained burn.

Cole wasn't surprised when the report pointed to chemical traces of fertilizer. That would explain the heat and flash characteristics of the fire.

The gold mine was found on page 2 of the report.

Tar.

That explained the way the fire clung.

He'd read just about every arson report this district had written in the last decade to strengthen his own understanding of what type of cases he would have to deal with. Tar was an interesting choice. An unusual one.

He reached for the phone book. He was about to get a crash course in how many stores and businesses sold tar.

Car headlights moved across the window. From his office, Cole couldn't tell if the car turned in the visitor lot. There was the faint sound of a door slamming. That had to be Rachel. He locked away the reports and his log book, then grabbed his coat.

When he reached the door he caught a glimpse of Rachel already rushing along the sidewalk. Cole pushed open the door and hurried down the handicap ramp. He darted around the railing and caught her arm as she nearly got by. "Hold on, Rachel."

She stepped on his foot. He was wearing boots, but he still felt it and wasn't entirely sure it had been an accident. She'd been driving while crying. The realization made him mad. She should not have been behind the wheel. "I promised Jack you weren't going to cry all over him. Don't make a liar of me."

"Let me go."

"Not until you get your composure back." He was bigger and broader and he got in her way, refusing to let her past. A sidewalk wasn't the place to have this conversation, but she wasn't in a mind-set to slow down at the moment. "Rae—Jennifer's okay. She's got some pain in her back from the fall, but she's got good mobility; she's alert. Tom's going to call as soon as he has news."

"You don't understand. Where's Jack?"

Her voice wobbled. He wanted to wince when he heard it. Rae normally handled crises so calmly that he was having to scramble to get in sync with where she was at. He hadn't been expecting this, wasn't ready to handle it, and he blamed himself for being the one who had put it in motion. If only he'd handled the situation differently when he called her. "We'll find Jack in a minute." He turned Rae back the way he had come. "Come on. Dry your eyes. You really don't want to cry all over him, do you?"

She wiped her face with the back of her jacket sleeve.

Inside the building she turned to walk on through to the fire station, instead he turned her toward his office. Someone had been raiding his Kleenex box; he found it tucked on the bottom shelf of his bookcase atop a copy of an old edition of the fire science journal.

"You don't understand," she repeated. "I talked to Tom last night. Some preliminary blood panels came back...." Rachel wiped at her eyes and blew her nose.

The fact she didn't care that she'd shown up in an old Northwestern sweatshirt with spaghetti sauce splatters on it, a pair of faded jeans, and running shoes told him more than she realized. "The remission is over."

"Tom—he hasn't told her about the panels until he gets the results from a more sensitive series over the next couple days."

Cole pressed another Kleenex into her hand and guided her into a chair. "That's why he went out to buy a dog today," he murmured, adding another piece to the puzzle of what had happened in Texas. He felt for Tom, having to face the fact Jennifer was taking a turn for the worse so that he needed to move the holiday presents up.

"Yes."

It was serious if Jennifer's remission was indeed showing signs it was over, but it didn't explain this. Rachel was falling apart.

Cole had watched her step into trauma situations on a moment's notice where she faced putting back together the shattered lives of children. He watched her deal with Jennifer's cancer for five months. Rachel had gone through far more difficult crises than the incident tonight without this kind of fight for emotional control.

He wished their relationship was such that he could ask what was wrong and she'd trust him enough to answer. Something was very wrong.

It was not the time to try and pry.

He reached over and squeezed Rachel's hand. "I'll go get Jack."

TWENTY-SIX

"An interesting shift."

"That's an understatement, Cole." Cassie pushed a mug of coffee across the table to him and resumed her seat. It was approaching 1 A.M. The fire station was quiet. The skeleton crew working through the night handling routine paperwork and monitoring dispatches in the various districts had retired to the communications room. "Every moment past midnight has been a relief. I've never watched a clock like this before."

"It's tough to watch and sit on edge."

"Should I take coffee down to Rachel and Jack?"

"Let them be."

She wanted to head to bed as she was so tired she was about to fall asleep in her chair, but it didn't feel right to leave Cole sitting alone at the kitchen table. He showed no sign of leaving even though she knew he had been here before 6 A.M. He had to be exhausted too. She straightened, abruptly realizing the obvious. "Your car keys are in your office."

"Yes."

"Cole."

"Let it go. Rae needs Jack's attention, not an interruption."

"I thought the phone call at eleven was good news. Jennifer's home with only bruises and the need for a heating pad for her back. I know they were going to conference call with the others in the family, but that was some time ago. Do you have any idea what they could still be talking about?"

"I've got a suspicion."

Cassie hesitated. She wasn't in the same position as Cole who had known both Rachel and Jack for years. "Is there something I should know?"

"Stay close to Jack. He's going to need a friend."

"Jennifer's cancer?" Cole didn't answer her. He didn't have to say it. His expression told her what he feared. "Christmas with his sister dying," she whispered.

"It looks that way."

An arsonist targeting him. Jennifer taking a turn for the worse. Jack had a freight train coming toward him. *Jesus, what am I supposed to do to help?*

"Cole," she hesitated. "I was hoping I'd be able to show Jack the real meaning of Christmas this year. He's been asking a few questions." She amended that. "He's been asking hard questions."

Cole smiled at her observation. "Cassie, don't get fooled. I've watched you take Jack at face value over the years and you're making a mistake by doing that."

"What do you mean?"

"His questions don't surprise me and they shouldn't surprise you. He's forthright and transparent in a way I admire. He laughs at life. But under that tapestry—you let his humor and casualness suggest that is how he also thinks. That's a mistake. Watch him around the station. He's a natural leader in his instincts. He listens, probes for details, is not afraid to make a difficult decision and act on it. When Jack talks about faith—he's got a lot of respect for the people making the claims, but he's not comfortable the claims are right. So his response is to respectfully keep listening. That's very revealing. He's trying to understand."

"I'm simplifying, but he seems to think Christianity is nothing more than a myth that grown-ups believe in."

"He's not yet convinced that a baby in a manger and the King of kings should and could logically be the same person—Jesus."

"A hard question to resolve."

"Don't feel like you have to force the questions, or worse, force his conclusions. God has been tugging at him for a long time. Jack will slowly keep working through the claims to decide what he thinks."

"I wish it were easier to start that conversation. I feel like I'm stumbling around sometimes. He hadn't mentioned Jennifer's cancer."

"Cassie—" Cole winced and rubbed his forehead.

"Need more aspirin?"

He shook his head with much more care. "A little less caffeine."

"What were you going to say?"

"How long have we been friends?"

"Long enough probably to handle what you're about to say."

"I wish you and Jack could get on the same page." Cole leaned forward and folded his arms on the table. "I see the frustration he feels at times, but I don't know that you see it."

"Over what?"

"You're honest, but not open. And it has an impact when you try to talk about something like religion and why you believe. In a rush to convince Jack of the truth, you gloss over eighteen painful months. Faith doesn't stand in a vacuum. He knows you're not telling him everything when you talk about other things, so he listens to you talk about God and wonders what it is you're not saying."

"Cole—"

"Just listen, Cassie. You hurt him when you hide the scars. Not just the cosmetic ones, but the deep ones. Jack knows it's been a rough eighteen months, yet you're wanting to tuck it away and downplay it with him on the assumption that it would be a drag on the friendship. Over Thanksgiving it would have helped had you been straightforward that you were fighting the depression of a holiday without Ash."

She winced.

"I don't mean it in a harsh way. I know where you go when you are retreating as a means to cope. I know the things you turn to and hold on to. But Jack doesn't have that history with you. So he gets worried. And he's a man who prefers to act, not worry. He about took my head off for this insane idea of you riding along on the fire calls."

There was a balm for the searing truth of his observation in those last words. "So…Jack's giving you a hard time about me."

"You don't need to sound so amused about it," Cole replied, pushing a napkin toward her to put under the straight pretzel sticks she was stacking into a log cabin square. "Start being more open with him. God can use openness on your part to touch Jack's heart."

"Cole, I understand your point, but I don't know if I can."

"No one ever said witnessing was easy. You've got to step back and get your priorities straight. It's wrong to flirt and mess up Jack's head only to draw back later because you can't marry someone who's not a Christian. Be a true friend and convince him about Jesus."

"I can't change his mind."

"Try."

She made a face at him. "Easier said than done."

"You got through the last eighteen months because the option was to give up and you refused to do it."

"Yes."

"So just decide to do it and don't give up. Jack's got that kind of crisis coming. It would help him if you'd let him learn from what you've been through."

"I'm not wise about how to cope just because I've been forced to do it."

"Yes, you are. You sat outside in the cold because what you most wanted on your own bad days was someone to talk to, so you instinctively gave that to Jack. That's wisdom learned from experience."

Cole reached across the table. "Watch your square of pretzels." He pulled a lower one out. The pretzel wall shifted, then held because the side walls held them in place. "As the pressure builds, Jack's going to be reaching for strong things to brace himself against. And I do expect him to look toward God because that's who Jennifer is resting against."

"The O'Malleys will close ranks. They're doing it with the conference call tonight; they'll do it through the holidays."

"Yes."

"I envy them that."

Cole smiled across the table at her. "Jack would be glad to share. There are times having four sisters drives him absolutely crazy."

"If that's where Jack is at, what about Rachel? How's she handling this?"

Cole pushed aside his coffee mug.

"Cole?"

"Unlike Jack, Rae is impossible to understand."

"She's gracious, thinks about others, helps in practical ways, is there to do whatever she can in a crisis—what's so hard to understand?"

Cole didn't answer her, just looked at her, let her think through what she had said. Cassie knew she was getting tested, but she just didn't see what he did. She shook her head slightly, not understanding.

"What's she leaning against to get herself through this?" Cole asked quietly.

The truth hit like a brick through glass. Rachel was leaning against herself. "Cole—"

He shook his head. "She's my problem." There was a grimness to that statement. "I'll deal with it."

"What are you going to do?"

"I have no idea."

TWENTY-SEVEN

Rachel pushed her car door closed and wiped at the tears that made her eyes burn. The tears would simply not stop. She'd cried all over Cole. Cried all over Jack. Was still crying. She was losing Jennifer, and the grief had grabbed hold and shook her so hard she could not get it subdued. She headed into the apartment building.

The phone call—one simple little trigger and the wall holding back the tears had burst. It wasn't Jennifer's fall that was the entire embarrassing reality of tonight. Jack had even lost his ability to offer a joke to help lighten the moment because she'd so flustered him with her tears. She dealt with too much grief in her life already through the tragedies of others, she simply didn't have the strength to face it on a personal level. Not grief this overwhelming.

She had denied what was happening with Jennifer since July, denied the reality of what it could lead to. She knew it, could clinically see the pattern of denial she so often counseled against in others. She knew this break in the wall holding back the tears was inevitable, and yet when it happened it caught her by surprise.

The entire family had seen her lose it. Five months of bottled-up tears were all getting shed in one night. The conference call had lasted so long because everyone in the family had been trying their best to offer reassurance that Jennifer would be okay. Jennifer was home. Even if the remission was ending, the doctors had not exhausted treatment options.

Rachel had been in Florida early in July when Marcus sent the initial emergency page about Jennifer. She caught the next flight out in the middle of the night, learned the news about the cancer diagnosis very early that next morning, and by that afternoon had been on a plane to Baltimore to join Jennifer at Johns Hopkins.

It had been so easy to simply do what she did professionally. To step into the role of helper. To be there. To do whatever needed done. To not only help Jennifer get through the chemotherapy and radiation, but on Jennifer's behalf to also undertake the complex job of implementing wedding plans in Houston so that Jennifer would have that upcoming day of joy to focus on rather than be forced to delay it. Rachel was grateful there was a way to help; it had been her gift to her sister. To pull it off she spent hours on the phone, had made several round-trip flights between Houston and Baltimore.

The wedding had been a wonderful day. And her relief that it was over had been real.

Jennifer in remission, the wedding over, Rachel had been looking forward to a chance to step away and catch her breath. Instead, she had walked into the situation with Gage and rearranged her plans.

Now this.

She simply did not have anything more to give. She was given out.

And now the tears would not stop. She walked up the stairs in the apartment building, sorting through her keys. She struggled to get the key into the lock.

"Rachel."

She leaned her head against the door. Not this. "Go away, Gage."

Behind her on the stairs going to the next floor, Gage stood. "Cole called me."

Cole had called Gage…no need to wonder what impression she had left with that man. She pushed the key into the lock. "Come on in," she whispered. She was too tired to fight anymore and he'd come in regardless.

Gage caught the door before it could close on him. "You should have called a cab."

She ignored the comment and tossed her keys into the dish on the table in the entryway. Her home was an eclectic place that Gage rarely visited, not because he wasn't welcome but there was barely room to turn around and he hated the lack of space.

The rooms were stuffed with furniture. The hallway was lined with pictures. There were enough pillows tossed on chairs and the couch to outfit a small hotel. She liked it this way. Her apartment in Washington was more functional. This was her nest. Not that she would defend it that way to Gage.

He paced past her into the living room and tossed his jacket on the couch. "What's going on?"

"I'm tired."

He shot her a frustrated look. "Shall I interpret tired or do you want to get a little more expansive on the language?"

She pushed aside his jacket so she could sink into the cushions on the couch. She was very aware Gage would have already grilled Cole for the details. "You're the writer," she muttered. "Tired: as in go away so I can go to bed."

"As if you would. I know you too well, Rachel LeeAnn. You grieve by turning on the TV, curling up on the couch, eating ice cream, and staying up to see the dawn. Where do you keep the aspirin?"

"I already took some."

"I haven't."

It nudged enough sympathy she thought about the question. "Try the bathroom cabinet."

He reappeared minutes later, shirtsleeves shoved up, a glass of ice water in his hand. He tossed pillows to the floor and dropped into the chair across from her. "Tabitha used to say crying her eyes out was incredibly therapeutic."

Rachel opened her burning eyes. "She was lying."

Gage chuckled, albeit forced.

He was studying her with a frown on his face, and she could almost hear him thinking there was so much coiled energy apparent just in how he sat. She was a problem to be solved and he was figuring out where and how to begin. He had a habit of probing everything in a way that would strip a subject bare, although he rarely did it to her. Under the abrupt exterior there was still a softer Gage loath to hurt her feelings.

"You held Jennifer's hand through weeks in the hospital, stepped in and planned her wedding, provided a shoulder to your family for the last five months. Now you've got to find the strength to get through Christmas with Jennifer's health failing. Forgive me for being astonished by your habit of assuming you are strong enough to deal with everything."

She was startled at the amount of raw emotion in his words. "I've got no choice but to deal with it."

"You could have called me; you could have talked to me."

"And say what?"

"How about something honest like, 'Gage, I'm scared'?"

She wiped at tears and didn't answer him.

He let the silence stretch out for minutes. "Did you think I wouldn't understand?" There was so much tenderness in those quiet words.

"I feel like a fool."

"Been there, done that. You live through that one."

She smiled at his prompt reply, knowing he was speaking from experience. There had been days around the anniversary of Tabitha's birthday when she wondered not if he would make it, but if she would, after the all-night sessions on the phone when she refused to hang up because Gage was prowling like a caged lion. Months later he had sent her roses in memory of those evenings. He'd survived. It just didn't always happen without a few scars.

She leaned her head forward into her hands, heavy of heart, weary, and honestly not sure what she should do in the next few minutes, let alone the next day. Just the idea of facing tomorrow was beyond her at the moment.

"Where are the sleeping pills?"

"You know I dumped them," she muttered. It would be so simple to reach for sleeping pills to push away this stress, to smother it. Gage had turned to alcohol to numb his grief; she couldn't afford to go back to using sleeping pills.

They had been a blessing at first, recommended by her doctor. But they had begun to cover the stress of her job and make her think she was dealing with it when in fact she was relying on the pills. And the day had inevitably come last year when she'd scared Gage, scared herself. He'd called in the wee hours of the morning and she answered the phone for all practical purposes incoherent.

Severe jet lag from a delayed flight home from Los Angeles followed by a sleeping pill had been a mistake. She'd spent three weeks dealing with the fallout of a suicide pact among four high school football players and she just wanted to get some sleep. She'd gotten it. She managed to answer the phone, mumble an answer, and drop the phone without hanging it up. She'd gone immediately back to sleep only to be aroused shortly thereafter by Gage pounding on the door.

She'd dumped the pills.

"Go to bed and put in one of your favorite tapes: the ocean waves one that makes you seasick or the one of those crazy loons on a pond."

His description of the relaxation tapes she had once made the mistake of loaning him drew a smile as she knew he had intended. "I'll compromise with the radio station."

"If I leave, you promise to go to bed?"

"Yes."

"You'll call if you can't sleep?" There was no question there was an edge of skepticism in the pointed query.

She pushed herself to her feet. "I will."

He pulled on his jacket. "I want a call when you wake up."

"Gage—"

He hugged her, taking her totally by surprise. She not only was swallowed up with her face pressed into his jacket, her ribs got squeezed until her breath was lost. "Don't scare me again," he whispered. "If you want to cry, do it on my shoulder. Don't ever again do it alone."

Years of friendship boiled down and focused to one point in time. She'd always wondered if he understood her core concern for him. He had; he was mirroring it back to her. "Thank you," she finally whispered.

"Crying alone is a waste of good emotion."

She rubbed her cheek against his jacket and hugged him back. "Go home."

"I'll go home."

She was smiling as she locked the door behind him, the relief of his visit real. She turned out lights, confident she'd be able to sleep.

The bedroom was chilly as the wind had picked up, and she had not yet put up weather stripping to better seal the window frame. Last week she had added extra blankets and changed to flannel sheets. She slid under the weight of the blankets and wrapped her arms around a pillow.

She owed the relief she felt to more than just Gage. A brief battle over that fact ended when she reached for the phone. She punched in a number.

"Yes?"

"Cole...thanks."

"Rae." She'd surprised him but clearly not woken him up.

"Calling Gage was a nice thing to do."

He floundered for a moment. "Better than doing nothing."

She curled her hand under her cheek. She'd embarrassed him. "He handles tears better than you do."

"Oh, really?"

She chuckled. "You want to solve them."

She expected a quick reply and instead he was quiet for so long she was afraid she offended him.

"No. I want to remove the reason for them."

The breathtaking scope of what he reached for—how could she have so misread the man not to have seen that coming? He was not offering it as a casual statement. Their conversations over the years had often revolved around the subject of religion and tragedy as he asked about what crisis she was dealing with at work and how she was approaching it. But the few times he tried to make it personal, she avoided the conversation.

She had a choice to make. Did she want to have such a conversation? One word would step her back, the other… She took as big a risk as he had when she answered. She so desperately wanted the peace Cole had. "There is no remedy for tears when the reason for them is inevitable. Jennifer is dying."

"The despair can be remedied." He spoke to the heart of the matter.

"Only by denying the pain of the loss."

"If death is permanent, despair is the right conclusion. If death is a brief separation, it's merely a reason to be sad," he replied gently.

"Heaven." She'd seen people cling so hard to that conclusion in the face of tragedy. She had known he would base his position there; it was where those who believed anchored themselves.

"The reason for this Christmas season—*Unto you this day a Savior is born.* There's hope, Rae."

They were nice comfortable words that were said so often at this time of season. But she'd heard the words so many times said by others in the face of tragedy that it had become something of a panacea. Cole believed those words; she didn't doubt his sincerity. And because it was him, for the first time she was willing to press the contradiction she saw.

"There's hope, but only if I accept the premise that God loves man so much it rationalizes the fact He would allow His own Son to be killed."

"You think God acted arbitrarily." She'd stunned him.

"Is it rational to do wrong in order to do right? He let His Son be crucified supposedly to save mankind. Where was the love for His Son?"

"Rae—"

"I don't buy loving someone at the expense of someone else."

"Love can't be inclusive? A parent's love for a spouse and a child? Equal and yet unique."

"The Bible says because God loved us He sent His Son. Jesus would later cry from the cross, 'Why have You forsaken Me?' The Bible contradicts itself on God's character."

"Rae—you've got it wrong. Giving His life was Jesus' own choice. He came to save us and the way to do it was to die in our place."

"Maybe."

She was met with silence. An absolute silence. "I can hear the hurt," Cole finally replied. "You've obviously thought about it. Would you be willing to talk about it another time?"

It didn't sound like she'd offended him, but it did sound like she disappointed him. She buried her head in her pillow. "Of course." She'd listen, even if the emotions behind her conclusions ran deep. "Buy me breakfast some morning." She had no idea she was going to make the suggestion until it was made.

"I'd like that a great deal."

She'd offered it, she couldn't easily back out. "Good."

"Sleep well, Rae."

She looked at the clock, which showed most of the night gone. "I'm going to try."

"If you're awake in half an hour, I expect a call and we'll talk about it tonight."

The two guys in her life expecting the same thing…she smiled, hoping she didn't find herself awake and forced to choose between the two of them. "Good night, Cole."

TWENTY-EIGHT

"Jack, I don't want to move to this apartment complex. It's too new and pristine and…well, yuppy. I want a place where rust on the car in the parking lot isn't considered an eyesore to be scorned."

Jack leaned against the side of his car, smiling at Cassie's definition of the apartment complex. It had been built two years ago. There was a swimming pool, two tennis courts, a weight room, and a large community center. The one-and two-bedroom apartments were spacious with high ceilings and large closets. It was the opposite of what she had now. "You haven't even see an apartment here and you don't like it."

"I just know I won't."

She was so sheepish about it that Jack had to bite back a grin. This was the fourth complex they had looked at on Tuesday their day off, and with every stop her excuses got more and more nebulous. They had plenty of time and the full attention of an apartment complex staff eager to rent an open apartment, but Cassie wasn't biting. "Admit it, Cassie. You don't want to move."

"Yes, I do. There is a mouse now living with me who I didn't invite to be my guest."

"You could put out a trap; you could let me find him."

"I'm not going to put out a trap that I'm the one most likely to step on."

He'd expected that to be her answer, although he suspected it was for a far more fundamental underlying reason. He moved away from the car and opened the passenger door. "Come on. Let's go get lunch."

"No. It's okay, we can look at the apartment while we're here. I promise I'll keep an open mind."

"There's no need. I know what you want."

"What's that?"

He chuckled. "To look like you moved without actually moving. That can be done too." He waited for her to get in the car. He closed the door for her and circled around to get behind the wheel. "Paint. Wallpaper. New curtains." He added one more just to tease her. "A cat."

"The building manager would never agree."

"Sure he will. I'll do the asking." If it came down to it he was sure he could find someone who knew someone who knew the owner of the complex to get the approval.

"I don't like wallpaper."

"You need a flowery border for the kitchen. Trust me on this."

"Then I don't need a cat. I don't want a dead mouse. I kind of like my mouse."

"What's his name?"

"Her."

He barely heard her. "What?"

She sighed and spoke up. "It's a her. T. J."

"A cousin of J. J.?" Jack glanced over at Cassie, amused by the choice of name. "I'm jealous. At least your mouse is alive." Despite her protests, he'd suspected she was attached to the unexpected guest. "I promise I'll find and rescue your mouse. We'll build you bookshelves; you can do your spring cleaning early and get everything in your drawers and closets nice and neat and organized. It will be just like you've moved."

"Maybe I had just better move. This sounds like work."

"I'll recruit help."

TWENTY-NINE

Cassie bit the tip of her tongue as she carefully cut the Christmas wrapping paper to give an inch overlap. She set aside the scissors and smoothed the paper, folding the corners of the paper and neatly creasing them. Jack leaned across what she was doing. "Hey—"

"You're hogging all the bows." He selected a huge red one from the plastic storage bin sitting beside the Charlie Brown-size Christmas tree he'd insisted she get for her apartment.

"Well, you're hogging the tape."

"I need it. There are only five days to Christmas and I've got close to a zillion packages to wrap."

He added the bow with a flourish to what had once been an envelope box and was now a colorful if rather interestingly wrapped package. He added the box to a growing mound that was threatening to topple over.

"What was that?"

"A new toothbrush for me."

"Jack—" She laughed.

"Cole said to buy what I want and give him the bill."

"A toothbrush."

"A Wile E. Coyote that will not be mistaken by any other guy at the station in the early hours of the morning."

"I take it back. That's a good gift," Cassie agreed.

"I thought so. What did Cole get you?"

"He's actually buying my gift himself and I have no idea what he's getting. Last year at least he asked for a list of what I wanted. This year—he just gets this grin on his face."

"It's got to be something noisy," Jack speculated.

"Please. Cole has not bought into the idea that color and sound somehow make the gift better. I think, I hope, it's a book."

"You have a truly boring Christmas list. Books, gloves, a new coffee-pot."

Cassie smiled. "I asked for what I want."

"You asked for what you need. Books to you are like food. Is there a second tape dispenser around here somewhere?"

"Try the box you labeled this afternoon: everything-that-has-nowhere-else-to-go."

"That's what you told me the stuff was," Jack protested.

"I meant it in frustration, not to be taken literally."

Jack got up from the floor to head to the hallway and search for the box. If someone had suggested to her at Thanksgiving that Jack would be so intertwined in her life that a day off when she didn't see him would feel like a loss, she would have laughed at the suggestion. Jack had transformed the holidays for her.

Lord, he's wrestling with a simple question. Who You are. If You're a myth or real. I need an opportunity to talk with him. Please show me an opening. Now that I've got my nerve up to try, it's hard to wait for that right moment.

"Cassie, what's this small box marked hot stuff?"

She smiled, having wondered how long it would take him to ask. "Salsa for the department Christmas party. Remind me to take it over to the station tomorrow."

"I see you finished packing the front closet."

"I got it done last night."

At Jack's suggestion she had brought in packing boxes and was doing what he defined as spring cleaning. His method was extreme. It was to empty the drawers so that furniture could be moved away from walls while they painted and so that stuff, as Jack described it, could be put back where it should go instead of where it had been.

It was effective. It felt like she was moving. The good thing was she didn't have to carry boxes outside in mid-December. The bad thing was her apartment hallway had become a floor-to-ceiling stack of boxes.

Jack came back with tape. "Where did you put those books of wallpaper samples?"

"A couple of them are on the kitchen counter, the others in the bedroom."

"Have you thought about wallpaper for the bathroom?"

"Paint."

"Then do something other than white." Jack leaned over to tap the end paint sample strip spread out on the carpet. "What about this blue for the trim?"

"Too dark."

"It would look sharp. You need bold colors."

She shifted the paint strips. "Maybe a soft rose."

"That would look good too."

"As long as it's color."

"Exactly. White is boring." He tore open the plastic wrap on a new package of Christmas wrapping paper. "Have we decided what to get Cole?"

"We?"

"Come on, Cassie, help me out. He's my friend but he's also a boss. It's not easy."

"He wants a copy of the movie *Apollo 13.*"

"Easy enough."

"And a copy of the movie script."

"Where am I supposed to find that?"

She looked at him and smiled.

He sighed. "How much is it going to cost me?"

"I'll be kind."

"Sure you will." He spread out paper, sized a box to wrap, and liberally cut the paper. "You didn't ask what Christmas gift I wanted from you."

"Jack—"

"Ask."

She'd already bought him a game player after meeting with his sister Rachel to find out what he really wanted. "What do you want me to get you for Christmas?"

"See, that wasn't very hard. I want you to come to the O'Malley family gathering with me."

She set aside the scissors rather than cut the paper and make a mistake. "Your family Christmas gathering?" She was enjoying spending time with him, had known she'd see him sometime over the Christmas weekend around the shift on Sunday, but his family gathering— "You're sure?"

"Yes."

"I don't want to crash your family gathering." Maybe he didn't know what that implied, maybe he did. She wanted his friendship because it was going to be hard to spend Christmas without Ash, and she certainly didn't want to spend it alone. But going to Jack's family gathering—

"I want you to come," Jack insisted. "You already told me you don't have other plans."

"Maybe not, but spending Saturday night with your family would be presumptuous."

He leaned over to crowd her space to pick up the scissors. "Jennifer wants to meet you. You have to come or I'm going to be in the doghouse with her. You wouldn't want that, would you?"

"Come because your family wants me to?"

He caught her off guard by sliding his hand along her cheek. His laughter turned serious. "*I* want you to come. Please."

Her gaze held his. The last thing she wanted to do was hurt him. But if she said yes, it would just complicate a friendship. She leaned against his hand, appreciating this man's strength, and tried to calculate the cost of a yes.

The radio on the counter sounded dispatch tones. The conversation stopped as a fire dispatch came across. The address was given.

Cassie paled. "Cole—"

Jack surged to his feet, pushing back wrapping paper and packages. He caught her hand to pull her to her feet. "Get your jacket. A call will find out if he was working late at the office."

The dispatch address was Cole's home.

THIRTY

Smoke was curling up behind his house, and Cole didn't have to see the source to have a good idea of what was burning. As soon as he opened his car door he got confirmation. It smelled like what it was: the stench of burning garbage. Someone had set his trash cans on fire.

He had a big backyard with his garage set to the back of the lot, the trash cans along the side of the garage next to the alley. It wasn't the first time someone had set fire to his trash and it probably wouldn't be the last. At least this time it hadn't dropped sparks and spread to the grass.

Engine Crew 21 had been able to pull into the alley to within fifteen feet of the fire. Under the distant streetlight there was some light to work with, but most light at the scene came from the engine's own halogen spotlights. "There's a garden hose and water hookup on the east corner of the garage," Cole called over to the lieutenant as he reached in the back of his car for his fire coat. Two men had just about suppressed the fire with fire extinguishers, but the area would have to be wet down to handle any smoldering remains.

A car pulled in behind him, headlights briefly lighting the scene. Cole turned and recognized Jack's car. Cassie was with him. Cole wasn't surprised that his address in the dispatch would have caught attention. He was surprised to see them together.

"Cole?" Cassie called, worried.

"Everything is fine. It's a nonevent." He'd have to replace some boards and repaint his garage in the morning, then do some digging at the local school after the Christmas break to find out who had thought tossing a match would be a fun thing to do, but it wasn't a crisis. It was the typical complication that showed up when he least needed another problem on his plate.

Cole slipped his hands into his back pockets and watched the firefighters do their jobs. He was tired enough he was willing to stand back and let others take care of it.

"Who called it in?" Jack asked.

The breeze changed and Cole gave a rueful smile. "I suspect anyone downwind." His pager went off. Cole glanced down and saw the return number for the office. "Come on up to the house if you like. I need to call the office."

Cole walked around the curving stone walkway through the trees up to the house. "Watch your step. There's wandering ivy across the stones."

He dug out his keys.

"Cole." Jack caught his elbow, stopping him. The alarm in Jack's voice would have halted him without the hand reaching to stop him. "Back of the house."

Cole looked up. Jack swept his flashlight over the area.

The back door was hanging at an angle from its hinges, wood from the door frame torn open.

"Cassie—" Cole waited until she looked his direction and held up his keys. He tossed them toward her. "The phone in my car. Get me the arson squad coordinator and the police liaison." It would keep her out of the way, which was nearly as important as the task he gave her. She nodded and turned back toward the cars. "Jack, come with me."

The floor was littered with popcorn.

"Wait for the police," Jack cautioned.

Cole took a careful step around the shattered door. Someone had taken an ax with at least a five-inch blade to it. The door frame had been shattered at the lock and at the top security bolt.

Murderer.

Cowards.

Cole wondered cynically what he was going to get tagged with. *Trash man?* The guy had torched his garbage cans. But why the vandalism? Had there really been a change in MO? The popcorn said it was the same guy. "Jack, get back to Cassie and clamp a hand on her. He may still be in the area. When the cops get here, you two can look around."

He expected Jack to do it. Instead, his hand came down hard on Cole's shoulder. "Outside."

"This may be set to burn. I need to know where and how." He was not letting tar and some spark mechanism send his home up in flames when they were early enough to prevent it.

Jack muscled his way in front of him and got in his face. "Outside. Now. Or so help me, Cole, I will take you out."

Jack was furious.

And it drew Cole up short.

"It's your home…but it's not worth people's lives. Get out, and tell the firefighters coming up the walk to stay out."

And in that moment the man facing him moved from being a friend to being a lieutenant correctly reading the scene and flexing his right to take charge and assume authority. "We'll wait for the cops."

THIRTY-ONE

Cole shone his bright torchlight around the living room walls. Jack swept his light across the floor behind him.

"Somebody doesn't like you," Jack said tersely.

"Now whatever gave you that idea?"

The word *liar* was sprayed repeatedly across the walls. They had waited forty minutes after the cops arrived to make sure the house wasn't going to explode on a timer before entering to begin the arson sweep. The room where he relaxed to watch a football game, read a book, make his regular Sunday afternoon phone call to his aunt in California now looked like a whirlwind had blown through. Bookcases had been dumped, tables overturned.

"He didn't bother to torch your place; he just trashed it."

"He knew if it burned down, I'd get compensated."

"Annoying little man."

Cole silently agreed. *"Liar.* It's an interesting word choice." The man had hit out at him. It could have been worse. He could have lashed out at someone else.

"You're an honest man."

Cole chuckled at the fact Jack felt the need to say it. "Nice to know you think so." He studied the words and the way they were spray painted literally from floor to ceiling. The letters were huge. It wasn't necessary, and thus it probably meant something, but he had no idea what. "Who's going to be next? And what does he want?" Cole murmured, thinking aloud.

"You need to ask Rachel to profile this."

"No." He rejected that suggestion immediately.

"Cole, if you reject what she does, you implicitly reject her."

"She's got enough on her plate."

"Give her a chance to get back on her feet. It will help her to have work to look at over the holidays."

Cole didn't want to add another burden on her. He already felt guilty about seeking Rae's opinion over the word *murderer* and telling her of his suspicion regarding Jack being a target. Had he understood what else was going on in her life, he would have never added that pressure. "I'll think about it," he replied non-committally. "Did you notice that this time Gold Shift was off duty?"

"We're losing the ability to predict his behavior."

"A wonderful thought."

"Cole?" The faint call came from outside.

"Cassie, stay outside. I'll be right there." Cole looked at Jack. "Who's with her?"

"One of the cops. He knows we'll be having words if she gets out of his direct reach."

Cole nodded. Jack and Cassie had spent an hour looking around the area, and Cole was relieved their search had come up blank. If he did continue to allow her to rollout to fires to look for the man, and he hadn't yet decided if he would, there would have to be someone assigned to stay with her. This had moved from just an arsonist they needed to spot, to someone who took an ax to a door. There was too much violence here.

Cole stepped around the men working to get plastic sheeting in place to cover the broken windows and exited the house through the destroyed back door.

Cassie was waiting at the turn in the walkway.

The police officer standing literally a foot behind her cast a nervous glance at Jack. Cole bit back a smile. There had clearly been a rather frank warning given. Cole couldn't blame Jack. Whoever had trashed his place, set a fire, and scrawled the word *liar* was not someone either one of them wanted Cassie ever again coming face to face with.

"Gage is here," Cassie told him.

The press. It was the last thing Cole wanted to hear.

"Do you want me to talk with him?" Jack offered.

Jack and Gage were oil and water. Cole didn't need that tension brought into the situation. He needed the press limiting how much they said. Gage knew how to dig for facts, and the details of this fire and the fire station would be in his sights. "I'll talk to him."

Cole glanced from Jack to Cassie and decided it would be best not to have her seeing what had been done inside the house. She was worried enough about Jack as it was. "Jack, do me a favor. Would you go over to the station and start clearing my calendar for tomorrow? There's a couple court hearings that will need to be postponed. And Cassie, if you can print out another copy of that draft budget for Frank he can cover the finance meeting. It will be several hours here before I'll be able to do anything more constructive beyond watching the investigating officer do his job."

"I'll take care of it," Jack agreed.

Cassie looked troubled at the thought of leaving. "You're sure?"

"Cassie—this is bad, but it's stuff. I'll deal with it. I'm more concerned with who is next."

"How many popcorn arson fires does this make?"

"Eight." Cole followed the investigating officer as the vandalism was cataloged. They had worked cases together many times; Joe was an old friend. It was five in the morning, and at this point Cole wasn't sure he was drawing reasoned conclusions after being up most of the night. To keep some perspective, he was using his friend as a sounding board. "It's strange that he goes from creating a huge fire at the station to now settling for burning trash."

"Any odds this was a copycat?"

"Slim to none. Neither the popcorn nor the words are known signatures to the public." And unless Gage was snowing him, the reporter didn't have either of those facts yet.

"Then it's not the fire that he's impassioned about. It's the message."

A very interesting conclusion. "The words have got to be the key. Murderer. Cowards. Liar—they intersect somehow to make clear who this is." Cole picked up an autographed baseball which now had its seams slit. For the first time he felt sick. It had been a gift from his dad. He rubbed his thumb over the gash in the ball that scored through the autograph. The ball could not be restored. "Do the words suggest someone to you?" he asked Joe.

"Not really. But it does sound like there was an event that occurred."

"I've searched the cases we've worked for the last two years and I'm still drawing a blank."

An officer appeared at the doorway. "Sir, there's someone out here to see you."

"I'll be right there," Cole replied. He looked to his friend. "If there is anything here that would suggest a possible suspect, I could really use something to put my hands around."

"You'll get anything I can find as fast as I can," Joe promised.

"I appreciate it. I'll be on my pager if you need me."

There was nothing he could do here beyond watch. His possessions had been trashed. His home turned into a crime scene. And he was tired enough that it was hard to even get angry. Exhaustion overrode the emotions. Cole left his friend to the task of finding evidence and went to see who needed him. It was setting up to be a very long day.

He ducked under the plastic sheeting put up to stop the snow flurries swirling in through where his back door had once been. His steps slowed when he realized who it was. "Rachel."

She was waiting just inside the police tape.

He wasn't surprised to see her here. For Rachel not to respond when something like this happened to someone she knew would be contrary to her nature.

That said, she'd had a rough few days, and he was distressed to see her here. At this time in the morning she should be asleep, not standing outside his home on a cold late December morning. She wore a long black dress coat and black leather gloves, a deep red scarf setting a bold splash of color. She was dressed up and he wondered briefly if she hadn't also been hit with the unexpected and a call that was going to take her away over the holidays.

She gestured to his house. "How bad is it?"

He pushed his hands into his back pockets as he walked down the path to join her. "It's trashed but he didn't get as far as the kitchen dishes or my closets."

"This is personal."

"Very."

She looked down, shifting her booted feet on the walkway stones. "Can you leave for twenty minutes?"

He could see Rachel was clearly hesitant to ask. "What do you need?"

She glanced up at him. "Breakfast."

Rachel saying she needed something... She was saying he needed something but was suggesting it in such a way that it was her need. He smiled as he dug out his keys. "Let's go to breakfast."

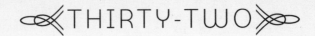

THIRTY-TWO

"Would you relax?" Rachel was still very ill at ease with him and Cole didn't like it. He handed her the sack with breakfast burritos. He wasn't into bacon and eggs for breakfast when he could have something more substantial.

"I don't like eating breakfast in the car."

"Sorry, but I'm not dressed for the public. I'm not planning to share you with a crowd, and at least the car is warm." He was too tired to be anything but frank with his answer. He handed her the carrier with two coffee cups, then turned to get his change from the drive-through clerk.

"I hear echoes of my mother over the propriety of eating in the car."

Cole smiled at the comment. "I grant a waiver. I stop here for breakfast most mornings, and while you can quibble the nutritious value, I can vouch for the fact the food at least tastes excellent."

"I don't mean to criticize the food. This is fine."

"No offense taken. And like I said, please relax. It's not yet 6 A.M. If there was ever a time for going with the flow it's now."

He took them to the community park where he could park and they could watch the dawn come up without the morning rush-hour traffic flowing around them. He occasionally came to the place to have morning devotions, for it was a peaceful place to walk.

Rachel handed him the first breakfast burrito he had ordered. Cole unwrapped it and picked up a napkin. He closed his eyes and took thirty seconds out of a day that had not ended for him. *Lord, I'm exhausted. Rae needs something or she wouldn't have sought me out. I'm hardly equipped to give it at the moment. Later today I have a case to work and a home to try and repair. I could really use some energy.* The emotions of the night flowed out in the quiet words. Cole opened his eyes. He reached for the coffee and considered the odds if adding sugar to the caffeine would keep him awake when he finally found somewhere he could sleep. It wouldn't be his own bed for the foreseeable future. He opened the coffee and drank it black.

Rachel nibbled at her breakfast burrito; he ate his.

Cassie had been right when she said Rachel was gracious. She allowed him to eat in peace, passed him the hash browns when he finished the burrito, and when he was done with them handed him the second burrito.

The food helped. He leaned his head back against the headrest as he wadded up the napkin.

"What do you pray for when you bow your head?"

He was surprised with her opening question. "In one word? Comfort."

"Someone to listen and care."

"Yes."

"I need to ask you something."

He turned his head toward her. "I'll do my best to answer."

"Jennifer is coming to town Saturday. Tell me how I can find the strength to smile and not cry when I see her."

It was very hard to get handed such a question, to know the door was open to the basis of her doubts about Jesus, and yet know he was at his lowest ebb for constructing a coherent answer.

"If Jennifer needed a bone-marrow transplant to heal her cancer and you matched—you'd jump to do it."

Rachel nodded.

"You'd do whatever was in your power to help her because you love her."

"Yes."

"Jesus loves her too."

He waited for that loop to circle, hoping she'd draw the obvious conclusion and make it simpler for her to hear him.

"Rae, unlike us, Jesus can do something about it. He had the power to come and lay down His life for her. He chose to do so. He opened the door and gave Jennifer the opportunity for eternal life. As the Bible says it, He took away the sting of death."

Cole tried to sort out some way to answer the contradiction Rachel had presented him a few days ago.

"I don't see a contradiction in God's actions. People die physically from things like cancer, but we're dying in a more fundamental way from sin and the evil that pervades the world. Jesus knew that. He chose to lay down His life to save us. And God the Father let Jesus make that choice, not because He didn't love His Son, but because He had decided in turn to express His own love for His Son and raise Jesus from the dead. God honored the sacrifice His Son made."

"But Jesus didn't just die," Rachel whispered. "He was crucified and abandoned by His Father."

"Rae—Jesus made a huge sacrifice. But I think God the Father actually made a larger one. He let the one He called His beloved Son be humiliated and murdered. Can you imagine how hard it was to sit on His hands and allow that to happen? He wasn't being contradictory. God was in agony, but He loved us enough to allow it to happen."

"The Bible says that?"

"Look at the anger God feels against anyone who rejects what His Son did. *Hell* is a mild word for the reality. Based on what Revelation says, when God the Father acts at the end of time it is going to be unlike anything mankind has ever seen. Men will beg to be spared that wrath. God loves His Son, and He's going to call the world to account. Every knee in heaven and earth will bow to the fact Jesus is Lord, and if they don't do it by choice, they will do it in judgment."

Cole tried to focus on the emotion he knew Rachel was struggling to cope with as she faced the fact Jennifer might be dying. "Please understand. I'm not saying don't cry. I'm not saying don't be sad. I can't and don't minimize what it is like to face losing someone you love. For the rest of your life that void will be there. I'm saying cling to hope. Grab hold of it and brace yourself against it. It is the only way you are going to get through what is eventually going to come, whether it is months or years away. Jennifer has that hope in Christ. Claim it, Rachel. I don't know how better to package it for you. It's waiting there for you. Christmas is all about hope."

She was crying.

He pressed a napkin into her hand and didn't say anything else as the sun came up.

"He's changing behavior, which suggests new triggers are arising," Rachel offered.

Cole nodded. "The suggestion was made that it's not the fire that he's impassioned about as much as the message in the words he is leaving."

The sun was rising on the horizon and shining through the side windows of the car with a gold cast. Rachel had retreated to talking about the arson cases and Cole had accepted it. She needed time to think about what she had asked him, and he knew the value of time to let questions settle and to let God work on her heart. He was relieved the tears had ended.

He knew she had a headache, but she was doing her best now to turn her focus to what he was dealing with. Rae's sense of fairness wouldn't let her talk about her situation without talking about his.

"Why did he go after you?" Rachel asked.

"If I had some idea of a suspect maybe I could figure it out. *Murderer. Cowards. Liar.* Possibly *chicken* although that's suspect. He's being extremely blunt."

"He's going after authorities."

"Fair conclusion."

"Any idea on why he changed to vandalism?"

"An arson fire in an arson investigator's home—there is not enough sting to it, I imagine." He finished his coffee. "Give me your opinion. He goes after the man responsible for public safety and calls him a murderer. He goes after the men responsible for facing down fires and calls them cowards. Finally, he goes after the man, me, whose essential job is to discover the truth and he calls me a liar."

"Questioning integrity," Rachel concluded.

Cole nodded his agreement.

"You also know he's setting fires at the edge of the district," Rachel added. "He doesn't want you to be able to respond in a timely fashion to what he is doing. You know he's watching the scene. So he feels some responsibility for the results of his actions. You've got a contradiction in front of you. Cassie said she saw a thoughtful man. Trashing your place—that's the action of a man in a rage and out of control. For those to be two sides of the same coin...it's a man who has snapped and is fluctuating like a pendulum between two extremes."

"How do I stop him?"

She didn't give him an immediate answer. He looked over at her.

"Cole, you've got one slim hope. He's escalating. That's being caused by something. Everything revolves around this district so the trigger is probably here as well. If that can be removed you've got a chance to change his behavior, slow down his escalation in time and type of fires. That might give you the time you need for the investigation to give you enough information to identify him."

"How are the holidays going to affect him? Christmas, New Year's?"

"The season is a stressor even for people who otherwise have happy lives—the pace, the financial pressure, the people pressure. And I doubt this is a man with a stable family with whom he spends the holidays. He's probably alone. If you haven't found him by Christmas—" She shook her head. "He'll hurt someone, Cole. There will come a point where he doesn't care."

THIRTY-THREE

Jack paced the terminal waiting for Jennifer and Tom's flight to arrive. The O'Malley family was assembling from all corners of the country and he was the designated chauffeur. For the fifth time he glanced at his watch. This was going to be tight. He had an errand to run after he took Jennifer and Tom to the hotel, and then he had to get back here to meet his brother Marcus and his fiancée Shari.

Since the family gathering had grown from seven to fifteen with the addition of spouses, fiancées, and dates, they had decided to make it easier on Jennifer and arrange the whole event to be at the hotel where she and Tom would be staying. They had been able to reserve a block of hotel rooms and had hired the hotel to cater the gathering.

Jack knew it was the best compromise. They'd hopefully be able to keep Jennifer from overextending her energy and get her to agree to call it an early night if she knew everyone would still be at the hotel and around for breakfast.

The relief that she was able to come was intense. That decision hadn't been made until early yesterday morning, the twenty-second. Jennifer hadn't wanted to leave her puppy behind, but other than that, when he talked to her yesterday she'd been eager to get here.

The family had taken her fall as a warning of what was coming. They were eager to have this weekend as a full family celebration of not only Christmas but also New Year's. All of them realized that the next time the family gathered as a group it might be around a hospital visit. Jennifer was going back on chemotherapy in January. She'd pleaded for the extra week before it began. She had been so wiped out last time that her doctors had agreed a few more days of recovery before she was hit again with toxic drugs would mean she'd have a better chance of success.

Jack checked the wall clock to confirm his wristwatch time was correct. If this flight was late, he would have to track down Stephen and see if he could handle meeting Marcus and Shari. Jack did not want to be late picking up Cassie. She was nervous enough about the idea of coming with him to the family gathering that he didn't want to give her any excuse to back out.

Jack knew Cassie had to be tired. They had spent most of yesterday and part of this Saturday morning at Cole's helping him deal with the mess the vandalism had created. They had rebuilt the back door yesterday, then replaced the last windowpanes this morning. Cole had hired a professional painter to come in because it would take a blackout paint to cover the glowing spray paint and not have it show through the next coat of white paint. Jack knew he'd have to make it an early night for both of them. He didn't want Cassie walking away from tonight with anything but fond memories.

The flight finally arrived. Ten minutes later people began to flow from the gateway. Jennifer and her husband Tom appeared at the end of the first group.

Jack had been braced to see her looking ill, to have lost weight, to look tired, as she had during the hospital stay. Instead she looked wonderful—her color was good and she'd gained a little weight since being released from the hospital. She dropped her bag at Tom's feet and raced toward him. Jack caught her.

"Jennifer." He took care with his hug knowing how injured her back was. "Hi."

She hugged him back. "Oh, it's good to see you." She'd turned into a bubbly blonde with the choice of the wig to deal with the loss of her hair. She caught his tie and tugged it as she laughed. "You dressed up for me?"

"Cassie actually, but you get the benefit of it." A suit jacket and dress slacks were not what he would normally wear to an O'Malley gathering but he knew Cassie. She was going to be dressed up, and he wanted something that at least felt like a comfortable middle ground.

"Did she pick out the tie?"

"An early Christmas gift."

"I thought so."

"I like this tie."

"You hate ties."

"I hate ties, plural. I love this specific tie."

She giggled. "In that case, I'm buying you a tie for Christmas."

"Jen, while I'm not opposed to wearing two ties to this O'Malley family gathering and recreating my clown costume, on basic principle it will look kind of bad if I don't wear just Cassie's tie this time."

"Very good save. So shall I buy you cuff links instead?"

"I really don't want to dress up that much."

"Unless Cassie gives them to you."

He conceded that point with a sheepish nod.

"I can't wait to meet her."

"She's coming. Would you look after her tonight for me? She's not used to large, boisterous families."

"I'd love to." She slid her hand through his arm. "Where are we heading first?"

"How much luggage do we have to deal with?"

Jennifer smiled.

"That bad?"

"I'd hate to ruin my reputation."

He glanced over at her husband Tom. "Let's go to baggage claim. If needed I can bring the car to the lower level. Then I'll take you over to the hotel. The party gets under way at seven."

Jack glanced at his watch and sprinted up the steps. He was late and Cassie was a stickler for punctuality. This was not the impression he wanted to leave with her.

She had buzzed him into the building so he wasn't surprised when she immediately answered his knock on her door. Her coat was over her arm and her keys in her hand.

"Sorry I'm late." And then what she wore registered. "Wow."

Her smile was immediate.

She was wearing a pink cardigan and a black pleated skirt with an explosion of color along the bottom four inches. She looked absolutely gorgeous. He spun his finger.

She swirled to show it off.

"Beautiful."

"Thank you."

She was blushing and her voice wasn't quite steady. He tilted his head, surprised at that. He hadn't expected the nervousness before they got to the party. "Jennifer can't wait to meet you," he offered. He took her coat and held it for her as she slipped it on.

"It's mutual."

He squeezed her shoulders. "You'll have a great time. I promise."

She smiled as she pulled on her gloves. "Nice tie."

He glanced down and ran his finger across it. "It's quite grown-up."

She slipped her hand under his arm and companionably walked the stairs with him. "I also bought you a much less grown-up one." She leaned over against him to admit.

"Did you?"

Jack opened the apartment building door and the snow swirled in. She was wearing flats that looked like they had smooth soles. "The walkway is slick," he cautioned. She clenched his arm as she took the first couple steps, slipped, then got her footing.

"The tie was a joke, you know. Cole dared me to give you one."

"I know. But never let it be said I can't take a gift in the spirit it was intended." He wrapped his arm around her shoulders. "What's this?" A small, gold chain glinted in the cold evening air and tumbled from his hand to dangle by a finger. He lowered it into her palm.

"I do wish you would quit doing that," she said, and then she looked at what he had pressed into her hand. It was a gold heart with the flowing word *Cassie* across it. Jack saw unexpected tears get blinked away. He'd had it made for her thinking it would look good with whatever outfit she chose for tonight.

He tugged her toward him and pressed a kiss against her hair. "Merry Christmas."

Rachel had brought Gage. Jack drew up short when he saw the man across the room talking with his brother Marcus. Rachel stood beside him.

The hotel meeting room was set up with casual, adjoining groups of sofas, a faux fireplace providing a focal point on one wall, and floor to ceiling windows on another wall, giving a spectacular view of the city skyline. From the thirty-fourth floor the skyline was a sparkling set of lights spread out like a blanket. A buffet table was on the east wall.

It looked like he and Cassie were the last to arrive.

Jack was surprised Gage had agreed to come. But knowing how difficult the last few weeks had been on Rachel, Jack suspected the man would have found it next to impossible to tell her no when she made the invitation.

"Call a truce."

Jack glanced at Cassie. "I wasn't the one who started it." He was more than willing to bury the hatchet, but he wasn't the one keeping it alive. Gage had reason to hold on to his anger. Christmas for him without his wife Tabitha had to be unbearable.

"Jack." Cassie pulled on his arm. "We're going over to say Merry Christmas and to shake hands."

"Later, Cassie." Jack didn't want to intensify that grief by interjecting himself into the man's Christmas. But Cassie was heading that way, and it didn't matter that he wanted to wait. There was nothing he could say that would eliminate the unease that the entire group would feel. Beyond Merry Christmas there was little safe territory and Rachel would land all over him later should he say the wrong thing. Cassie had no idea what she was asking of him.

Gage spotted them coming and leaned over to say something to Rachel. Moments later he came across the room to meet them, surprising Jack. "Cassie, Merry Christmas." He leaned down to hug her.

"It's good to see you, Gage."

He looked over at Jack and his smile faded. Jack flinched at the coolness. "Can I talk to you a minute in private?"

Jack glanced at Cassie, loath to leave her before she'd been introduced around. Abandoning her in the midst of his large family was not the way to ease her into meeting them. The O'Malleys as a full group could feel overwhelming; Jack was under no illusions about that. His family was great, but you had a cop, a U.S. Marshal, a paramedic, and a doctor, to name just a few of their jobs, and the conversations were not going to be about the latest television comedy. Shari was here and there was a good chance Marcus's fiancée had the title congresswoman in her future.

Rachel was coming toward them. At Cassie's slight nod toward Gage, Jack reluctantly accepted he had no choice and agreed to Gage's request. "Of course."

"Cassie, I'm so glad you could come." Rachel greeted her with a smile, grasping her hands. "The guys had us outnumbered. Come with me. Let me get you a glass of punch and I'll introduce you around to all of these O'Malleys."

"I've worked with Stephen many times in the past," Cassie offered.

Rachel seized on it as Jack knew she would. Rachel was a natural hostess. She would do what she could to ensure Cassie was comfortable. "Since he was the only one who dared show up alone, we'll start by pestering him about why that happened," Rachel said.

"I told him he should invite someone," Jack protested when Rachel looked pointedly at him. He offered Stephen more than one suggestion about whom to bring. Jack looked to Cassie to back him up.

Cassie glanced up at him once again to offer him a distinctly amused smile. "He tried."

Since Cassie didn't have a big family, Jack had been forced to deal with her laughter at the idea he was working to play matchmaker for his brother. Jack figured it wouldn't take long for her to figure out just how involved the topic was in his family. The questions directed to Cassie regarding him would be subtle but they would come. Before the night was over Cassie would catch the drift.

The ladies headed toward the punch bowl. Gage gestured toward the hallway. With some reluctance, Jack nodded and headed that direction. Gage closed the door behind him, and they walked in silence to where there was an open area near the stairway.

Gage had requested this conversation, so he was the first one to speak. "Popcorn."

Jack waited for the rest of it.

"It's appeared at all of the arson fires."

Since Gage was not a man to allege facts, Jack confirmed it just to find out where this was going. "Yes."

"That signature has leaked. It will hit the papers tomorrow or the next day."

"Who has it?"

"The *Daily Times* and the ABC news affiliate. Do you want to go on record?"

"No."

"Jack, I suggest either you or Cole do so because you've got a problem. I've been sitting on the words used in the fire station arson and at Cole's home, but it's only a matter of time before someone else gets those. Once that happens I'll have no choice but to lay out the connection with all the fires."

"No one else has the words?"

"Not that I've been able to ferret out."

"Gage, we don't need public panic, not over the holidays."

"Reporter's discretion only goes so far. You can duck the news becoming public and react once it does, or you can intervene to shape it before it comes out."

Jack understood the man's position, respected the way in which he worked to get the details confirmed even if Jack didn't often like the specifics of what Gage wrote. "Talk to Cole. And if you can, sit on it a while longer."

"Do you even have an unofficial suspect?"

Jack didn't reply.

"That's what I thought." Gage nodded back down the hall toward the room. "I'm glad you brought Cassie. She needs a good Christmas."

It was a generous statement from a man who understood just what it meant for Cassie to be here. "I'm glad you came with Rachel," Jack replied, meaning it. He looked down and studied the pattern in the carpet. He wanted to say he was sorry for what had happened in the past but didn't know how. Straightforward was still the best approach. He looked up and locked his attention on Gage. "I'm sorry about Tabitha. We tried, Gage. We couldn't get to her."

"My son would be celebrating his first Christmas this year," Gage said softly.

Jack knew how deep that grief went. He'd watched Rachel be the one to reach out to Gage and listen to that pain. Had the situation been reversed, Jack wasn't sure he would have handled it as well. For Gage to face this Christmas without his wife and son had to be a shattering thing to handle. "I know."

"You were late."

"We were late. It wasn't in our control, but it happened." Jack held Gage's gaze. "You want to take another swing at me?" he asked, hopeful. If a black eye would help, he'd give Gage a free shot.

"Yes, but then Rae would take one at me."

The two men looked at each other.

"It's history."

Jack's relief was intense, for he hadn't expected Gage to give at all. "Good. Are you going to date my sister?"

The question rocked Gage back on his heels. "You don't waste any time in shifting to brother mode."

Jack simply held up four fingers.

"I hear you. Marcus already gave me the elder brother look." Gage laughed. "No wonder Rachel wasn't worried about how her family would react to my coming along. She already knew."

"She's an O'Malley."

Gage conceded the point with a nod. "We're friends. And as her brother, you've got a right to know if that changes." He gave a glimmer of a smile. "That said, I might tell Marcus first." Gage gestured down the hall to where the gathering was under way. "Anything else you want to say before we go back in?"

"Not at the moment. But when I do, I know where to find you."

They headed together to the party. And Jack felt like he had managed to put to rest a burden from the past. He knew Rachel would be relieved.

"Cassie, it is a delight to get to meet you. I'm Jennifer."

Cassie was feeling overwhelmed with O'Malleys by the time she was finally introduced to the youngest of the seven. The hug she got from Jennifer was long. The petite lady leaned back, smiling at her, and Cassie smiled back somewhat tentatively.

"I know, you don't know me," Jennifer said, "but the way Jack talks about you I feel like I know you. How's your mouse? Jack said you named her T. J.? And how did you ever get my brother to dress up and wear a tie? He looks great. By the way, I was ordered to make sure you didn't get overwhelmed, but it appears you already are. So would you like to come find a seat with me or get a piece of cake? I'll tell you anything you want to know about Jack."

Cassie grinned, charmed with Jack's sister. "If I could get a refill on the punch and find a seat, I would love to chat with you."

She followed Jennifer, keeping a lookout for Jack's return.

"I hear you are a good firefighter."

Cassie leaned over to hear what Jennifer said, missing a few of the words but getting the heart of the question. "I used to be," she replied. "I got hurt a couple years ago so I'm pretty much on the bench doing paperwork now while I watch Jack do his job. He's pretty good."

"What happened? Jack's only given me the highlights. The doctor in me is intensely curious if you don't mind talking about it."

Cassie was politely smiling. It startled Jack. She wasn't enjoying herself?

It mattered that Cassie enjoy tonight and he felt a sense of panic at the idea she wasn't. The ladies in the gathering had split off and were sitting on the two couches by the fireplace, Cassie sitting in the chair beside Jennifer. Cassie was politely smiling at his sister Lisa, glancing over at Jennifer as she spoke, her head turning back and forth as she followed the conversation.

He'd been able to stay close to her during the first hour of the gathering before the dynamics of the family had split them into groups. For the last hour he had been trying to work his way back to Cassie's side.

No one in his family would want to exclude Cassie, but if the conversation had drifted into issues of only family interest, they might have unintentionally done so. It had been hard to get Cassie to agree to come, and if it turned out to be a mistake...and then he realized the truth.

He'd seen that polite expression on her face before. The background

Christmas music, the half dozen conversations going on in the open room…sound was bouncing. Cassie couldn't understand what was being said.

"I'll catch up with you later, Stephen." He broke off his conversation with his brother midsentence and headed over to intervene.

He was mad at himself for letting this happen. He hadn't warned Jennifer that Cassie would struggle with the noise level; therefore, Jen wouldn't know what to watch for. Cassie was so good at assuming adapting to a problematic situation was her issue and not that of her host. She was wrong. He was her host, and he'd just blown it.

He had wanted one thing more than any other—to give her a good Christmas. Instead he had just reinforced what was the most difficult part of her transition to accepting the limitations imposed by the accident—the feeling that she no longer easily fit in.

Jack maneuvered around the room, his grim look causing a couple conversations to stop as he strode past. He forced himself to shake off that intensity before he joined her. It wasn't Cassie's fault; it was his. Stopping behind her, he smiled over at Rachel and rested his hands lightly on Cassie's shoulders.

She started at his touch.

She looked up at him and he leaned down close to her left ear. "You can't understand a word of what's being said, can you?"

She couldn't hide the chagrin.

He searched her face, rubbing his thumb in small circles along her shoulder blades. She hadn't wanted to rock the boat. He wasn't sure what to do. He wanted to hug her but settled for reaching down and catching Cassie's hand in his. She rarely offered him her hand, as if the scarred skin made it less than perfect to hold. When he wanted to hold her hand he had to reach for it.

There were times someone needed to protect Cassie from herself, and this was one of them. Jack shot Jennifer a smile. "I'm tired of sharing." His remark drew a laugh from the group. He gently tugged Cassie to her feet. "We're heading out. Okay if I join you for breakfast?" he asked Jennifer.

His sister noted their entwined hands and smiled. "Please do."

Jack settled Cassie's coat around her shoulders. "You should have said something."

"It wasn't so bad at first; it just got confusing as the evening wore on."

She pushed her hands in her coat pockets as they walked down the hotel hallway. Jack didn't like the subdued, frankly exhausted impression he got from her. He tried to figure out how to say he was sorry for putting her in this position without making her feel worse. He didn't know the right words.

"You've got a wonderful family."

"I think so."

"Jennifer is a very special lady. You would never know she was ill from casually meeting her."

"She's normally a brunette."

Cassie gave him a small smile. "So she told me."

He pushed the button for the elevator to take them down.

She rubbed her eyes as she leaned against the wall, her slight frown marking her headache. "Did you see Jennifer's pictures of her puppy? The husky is adorable."

"She's in love with him," Jack agreed.

When they reached the lobby, he reached again for her hand. Her hand tensed in his and then relaxed, curling around his. The lobby was crowded with people flowing from the restaurant and a Christmas party going on in the lounge. He was relieved when they stepped outside and out of the noise.

Garland and Christmas lights were wrapped around the streetlight. The night was cold and clear. Cassie shivered with the impact and stamped her feet. She slid her hand into the crook of his arm to keep her balance on the slick pavement.

The silence during the drive told Jack a lot. Cassie's exhaustion was nearly as bad as what he had observed at Thanksgiving.

"I'm sorry you had to leave the family gathering. I didn't expect to have it affect me this way."

"This is not your fault."

She hesitated, started to say something, then stopped herself.

"What?"

"It's not your fault either." She sighed. "I couldn't hear Jennifer very well. Her voice was too soft…and I so wanted to."

He reached out his hand and waited for her to take it. When she finally did, he squeezed it gently and held on to it. "Give me time, Cassie. I didn't intend to put you in such a difficult position tonight. I just didn't think everything through."

"I did enjoy the party."

"My family loved you."

She gave a slight smile. "I envy you them."

He let the rest of the drive pass in silence. The apartment complex where she lived had been dressed up with Christmas lights on the entryway trees. It was at least a small reflection of the season. He parked near her building and came around the car to offer a hand.

He had one hope to redeem this day.

When she unlocked her apartment there was a gift-wrapped basket with a large bow set in the middle of the hall. Jack had arranged for her neighbor to bring the gift over after they left for the party.

Cassie bent down to pick up the basket. She looked at the contents and cast him a puzzled look. "Jack? This is from you?"

"Yes." And he was suddenly very nervous about this being the right gift.

"What do I need cat food for?"

He smiled at the wary tone in her voice and reached past her to turn on the other lights. "Go on through to the living room. Your neighbor helped me out."

There was a large box very carefully gift-wrapped waiting for her. He'd spent a week making the arrangements. "It's the last gift of the season. I promise."

Cassie pulled over the ottoman and lifted off the box lid.

The kitten was incredibly small, heather gray in color, asleep on a bed of monogrammed towels.

"She's not much bigger than your mouse so I don't think she'll be any threat to your other guest. Her name is Benji, B. J. for short."

Cassie reached in the box and the kitten woke to stretch. Cassie carefully picked her up.

"I brought everything you would need for her. Cassie—" he waited for her to look up at him—"don't feel like this is a gift you have to accept. You can borrow her for a couple weeks and then B. J. can move to my place." He smiled. "I don't even know if you're allergic to cats."

She nestled the kitten against her sweater. "I think I'll keep her for a while if you don't mind."

Her voice had gone so soft. Jack breathed a sigh of relief because he really gambled with choosing such a gift. Jennifer had been so overjoyed with her puppy. Cassie's apartment complex only allowed cats.

Cassie glanced up at him. "B. J.'s a good name."

"I thought so." He pointed to the box. "There are extra monogrammed towels with her name on them and the equivalent of a cat bed and several play toys in the second box. The basket should have everything she'll need to eat for a few weeks. There's also more milk in the refrigerator."

"You thought of the details."

"I hope so."

He stepped close and ran a finger along the kitten's back.

He wanted to kiss Cassie good night. He pushed his hands into his pockets instead. "I'd better go so you can get some sleep."

She carefully got to her feet so as not to disturb the kitten.

"I will catch your other guest when I come over to help clean out the closet so we can start painting."

"I'll appreciate both." She looked up at him. "I love the kitten, Jack."

"I'm glad." Relieved was the better word. "Shift starts at 8 A.M. tomorrow. Do you want me to pick you up?"

"If you wouldn't mind. Christmas weekend and snow flurries—there will be a lot of calls."

"But hopefully no fires."

She looked down at the kitten and stroked a small ear. "I'll have to leave B. J."

"I have a feeling she'll sleep most of the time you are gone," he promised.

"Would you do me a favor and call me when you get home? The roads are slick."

It meant a great deal that she would ask. "I will."

"Oh…she's purring. I wish I had bought you a better gift."

He laughed. "Cassie—" He waited until she looked up. "You already gave me the Christmas gift I wanted." He ran a finger along her jawline, leaned down, and swiftly kissed her. "Good night, beautiful."

Someone needed to remind her she was supposed to sleep before she went on shift. Cassie curled her hand up under her cheek as she watched the kitten sleep on the second pillow.

Jack had her tied in knots. No one had kissed her since the accident, and that simple act still had her head spinning. Jack had caught her off guard.

She was in wonder over the fact he would like her that much. That he would consider the fire and its aftermath to be something he could look beyond.

Jesus, I'm in over my head. I don't want to hurt Jack's feelings. This feels awful. He doesn't know You. I've been hesitant at witnessing, but now I need to reach out and find a way to do so.

She reached over and ran her finger over the soft fur of the kitten.

She had faced a fire and been hurt. If she was going to get involved with a firefighter, she would only be able to handle it with someone she didn't have to worry about should the worst happen. *Lord, give me the strength to resist my feelings for him.*

If only Jack believed…

He'd overstepped. He knew it.

Jack tightened his grip on the steering wheel as he headed home. That kiss had been spur of the moment, and as soon as he had done it he knew he'd made a mistake.

The problem with rushing fences was he all too often knocked them over. Hadn't he learned the basics? She'd blinked at him, not exactly frowning but definitely not smiling, and he wisely left before she could react more than that.

The kiss was wonderful. It had just been badly timed.

Two strikes for the night. The noise, the kiss…he certainly hoped the kitten turned out to be considered as nice a gift in the morning as it was tonight or it was going to be three strikes all in one night.

This was not the Christmas weekend he had planned and hoped for.

THIRTY-FOUR

Cole balanced the paintbrush on the edge of the can and stepped down from the ladder to answer the doorbell. He was not going to get the living room done today if the interruptions continued, let alone his hope of also finishing the hallway. The phone had been ringing ever since he got home from church; now he had visitors.

The blackout paint had covered the spray paint but it had dried a chalky white. The quicker he got at least the first new coat of white on it, the better. Right now there wasn't a room on the first floor that wasn't in some state of chaos with furniture moved out of the way or recovered items packed in boxes waiting to go back on shelves.

Cole wanted his house back.

He picked up a towel and wiped at the paint splatters on his hands as he maneuvered around two sawhorses balancing long pieces of trim for the stairway to replace the damaged pieces. He unlocked his new back door.

"Rachel." He was stunned to see her. "Please, come in." He pushed open the door. She'd been over Friday with Jack and Cassie helping him sort out the mess. He hadn't expected her back today.

"I tried to call. Your phone was busy."

"It's been ringing ever since I got home from church."

"You're painting."

He tossed the towel on a box and gave a rueful look at his hands. "Yes."

It didn't look like she'd come over to help. She was dressed to the nines in a blue silk dress. She was absolutely lovely and if she was feeling tired or stressed it was not apparent in her looks. There wasn't a good place to have a conversation where she wouldn't get paint on her dress or snag it on something. So he leaned his shoulder against the wall, deciding where they stood in the hallway was probably the safest place. He was delighted to see her even if he wasn't sure why she had come over.

"I had breakfast with Jennifer and Jack."

"How is Jennifer?"

"Recovered from her fall. She's going back on a new round of chemotherapy after the first of the year."

"How is she handling it?"

"She says she's going to worry about it next year."

"Are you going to wait to worry about it too?"

Rachel gave him a small smile and didn't answer. Instead she looked around. "You're making good progress."

"You want to come shopping with me sometime this next week? The insurance guy took one look around and said it would be cheaper to replace versus repair. He handed me an early Christmas check."

"Can I replace the blue monstrosity you call a recliner?"

He enjoyed that glimmer of a smile she gave him. "Just because you got stuck in the chair and had to have help getting out…"

"It's not a very lady friendly chair."

"You're welcome to help me find another one." He waited a beat until it was clear he knew she was hesitating on saying more. "What's up, Rae?"

She reached into her large bag and drew out a square-wrapped package. "Merry Christmas, Cole."

He accepted it slowly, caught off guard. "Can I open it now?"

She bobbed her head.

Intrigued, he split the tape. "Your gift will be at your place in the morning by the way."

"Really?"

"You'll like it."

Rachel laughed at his confidence.

He had bought her new luggage. An expensive gift, but it had taken only a brief consideration of her job and schedule to know what she needed was something practical and pretty. He checked with her family to make sure he wouldn't be stepping on her independent streak. He'd been assured the gift would be well received. He'd know tomorrow if that were true.

Cole lifted the lid on the box. "Rachel."

"Cassie told me," she said quietly.

He slowly moved aside the tissue paper. "It has been a very long time since someone so surprised me." He lifted out an autographed baseball to replace the one that had been cut open. "Where did you—" He was at a loss of words to know how she had found the same autographed baseball.

"My dad would have liked yours. He followed the same team."

It was one of her few mementos from her own past. And as a gift it was incredibly generous. It was a family heirloom. "Are you sure?"

She smiled. "It's a baseball, Cole. It's important enough for me to hold on to for a lot of years, but I had it in a drawer. You obviously had yours out on a shelf to be enjoyed."

"I'm grateful."

"You're welcome."

"Listen—" he pointed to the kitchen—"would you like to join me? I'll make sure I find a safe place you can sit down."

"Another time. I'm heading over to go shopping with Jennifer."

He tried to bury the disappointment, understanding that higher priority. "Would you please wish her a Merry Christmas for me?"

"I will. I'll let you get back to painting."

"Rae—" he tossed the ball and caught it on the way down—"thanks."

"We should have brought Jack to carry the packages," Rachel said ruefully as she unloaded the department store sacks from the car trunk and prepared to carry them to her apartment. Snow swirled across the open trunk. The wind cut through her wool coat and even with earmuffs, hat, and gloves she found the weather unbearable.

"I've never seen a man more delighted to be able to say he was working than Jack over breakfast when he heard our plans for the day," Jennifer agreed, picking up the shoe boxes and the sweater box.

Rachel wasn't so sure Jack was having a good day, not with holiday traffic, snowy roads, and this cold. She would be surprised if he got time to thaw out between dispatches.

Jennifer nudged the trunk closed. "This has been so much fun. I always love to shop with you."

"I notice it's primarily my wardrobe getting extended again."

"Cole will like the peach sweater."

"Jenny."

"Don't look at me like that. You were the one who had me up until 2 A.M. on the phone while you debated the implications of giving him that baseball."

"I still don't know if it was smart. He acted like I'd given away a priceless heirloom or something." Rachel shivered as she stepped inside the building and the warmth hit her. She held the door for Jennifer and then led the way upstairs.

"After having his place trashed, I suspect having the one item that would be the hardest to replace taken care of first meant a lot." Jennifer retrieved Rachel's keys and unlocked the apartment. "The door wreath is beautiful."

"Thanks. Gage gave it to me." It was a spectacular Christmas wreath with dried white rosebuds woven into the evergreen and a satin red ribbon wrapping it. "Toss the keys in the bowl," she suggested to Jennifer. Rachel maneuvered with her packages through the apartment as best she could without knocking items off the tables.

She had been in a rush this morning. She was able to make the bed, had pushed the dark green comforter up, but her numerous pillows were scattered, some on the bed and others on the floor. Two plastic storage tubs were pushed against the wall near the closet. She'd been exchanging her fall lightweight sweaters for the heavier sweaters for the winter.

Rachel lowered the packages onto the bed.

"How's Gage really doing? Last night he was being his charming self, but it was hard to tell how deep that calm extended."

"Gage is…well, let's put it this way. He's decided to pretend Christmas Day tomorrow doesn't exist on the calendar. It's a decent way to get through the day, I suppose."

Jennifer set her packages down on the floor beside the bed. "Worried about him?"

Ice crystals had formed on the inside of the windowpane. Rachel frowned when she saw it and knew she'd have to check the weather stripping again.

"I'll always be worried about him. But no, I think Gage turned the corner this last month. His grief has less anger in it." She tugged open the closet door and pushed clothes around, sorting through her closet to find empty hangers. "Did you hear Jack bought Cassie a kitten?"

Jennifer piled pillows against the headboard and sat down on the bed, leaning against them. "He told me he was going to. I think Jack likes her."

"Whatever gave you that idea?" Rachel shot her sister a grin as she opened the first box and folded back the tissue paper to retrieve the new amber blouse with pearl buttons. "The fact it's the first time he's ever brought someone to a Christmas family gathering?"

"He cheated and told her to come so I could meet her. I thought that was interesting. I liked her."

"So do I."

Jennifer picked up the book on the nightstand. "Rae, I thought you were going to do light reading for the holidays. *Causes of School Violence?*"

"I'm trying to get ready for the commission next year."

"I wish you had passed on that assignment."

"It's what I do for a living, Jennifer. Someone has to figure out a way to get around the problem. And you know quite well that I was chosen because I'm an unknown and can manage the volume of material so others can be the face of the committee."

"It's a lot of stress."

"Had I known last spring what my new year would be like I would have graciously declined, but I said yes. I gave my word. I have to do it." Rachel knew the concern for her was real, knew Cole would probably think the same thing as Jennifer if he learned what she had volunteered for. It was a prestigious assignment. She hoped she had the reserves to deal with the stress.

"If there is anything I can do to help, you'll ask?"

"Of course."

Jennifer looked over at Rachel. "Without being intrusive, how bad were the burns on Cassie's arms?"

"Severe. I don't think Jack cares," Rachel replied.

"She does."

"You noticed that too?"

Jennifer nodded. "It's more than vanity. She knows the subject often makes people uncomfortable." Jennifer tugged her wig. "She's got great empathy for my no-hair status."

"Jack gets protective around her."

"I thought it was cute."

Rachel started folding up the empty sacks. She'd cut tags off the new purchases later. "I thought I'd fix salad and soup for lunch."

"Sounds wonderful. Want help?"

"Without wanting to say no, at the moment the kitchen only has room for one. I'll call when it's ready."

"Fair enough." Jennifer tossed the pillow to the floor and stretched out. "How long of a nap did you promise Tom I would take?"

"Twenty minutes."

Jennifer looked at the clock on the bedside table. "Then wake me in twenty-one because I am not sleeping away my Christmas vacation."

"Deal. You still want to meet Kate and Lisa for Christmas Eve services?" Rachel was leery about going to church, but she knew it was a big deal for Jennifer and would go along for that reason.

"Absolutely. And Rae?"

"Hmm?"

"I'm going to beat this cancer. Believe it."

Rachel was stunned by the unexpected comment, and by the fact Jennifer had obviously clicked into the subject that had been just off center stage all day as they shopped. Rachel was chagrined at the realization that her agreement with Tom to keep an unintrusive eye on Jennifer had not been so subtle after all. "If optimism can affect it, you will."

"Prayer will," Jennifer said easily. "Wake me in twenty-one minutes."

"I'll do that," Rachel said quietly. She closed the bedroom door and leaned her head against it.

She wished she felt comfortable calling Cole. Jennifer had an assurance inside that she would be okay. Cole was pointing toward that same assurance, encouraging Rachel to reach out and grasp it too. She needed to have someone to talk with who would listen to what she was thinking and just be a sounding board.

She wanted so desperately to believe. She wiped at the tears. She had to talk to someone. Jack. He was a good sounding board, and he'd keep the conversation private. And better yet, he wouldn't try to convince her God's love existed. If anything he'd try to convince her she was wrong.

The reality she feared was Jennifer heading back into the hospital, and Rachel was going to need to find the strength to go along and help her. Not to do so…it wasn't an option.

A decision had to be made. She couldn't carry on like this much longer; the weight of what was going on was too heavy. How many people had she seen break under the weight of impending grief? Too many. She couldn't do that to her family. She had to be strong enough to get through this.

But her sister was dying…and Rachel was dying along with her.

Jack stretched out in Cole's spare office chair, trying to relax while he could because this shift had the markings of a hard one. They'd been out on four calls already. He tried to find a clear spot to set his soda, couldn't, and ended up setting it on the floor under his chair. The piles of file folders, books, and printouts had grown into mountains.

The map on the wall tracking the location of the arson fires was new. Jack studied it. There was no clear clockwise or counter-clockwise to the pattern. "He's going to do something over Christmas."

Cole used both hands to wrestle a file cabinet drawer back on track. "Very likely."

"Who's setting these fires?"

"Not you." Cole shoved the file cabinet drawer one last time, gave up, and propped his foot on it. "I don't know, Jack. It's the same answer as the last five times you landed in that chair to ask me."

"It wasn't Christmas weekend last time. I don't want my men hurt."

"Join the crowd."

"You've got to at least have some suspicions."

"Several."

"Names? Someone I know?"

"None you need to know about, and not when you're going on shift. I don't need you distracted, Jack."

"I'm trying to help here, Cole, and you're not making it easy."

"Live with it."

"I don't want Cassie rolling out with us today."

"Any particular reason?"

"I don't need her getting hurt on Christmas Eve," Jack replied, ready to argue the point.

Cole just held up his hand. "She'll ride with me today. I don't particularly want her in the middle of this either. Did you read that nursing home report I gave you?"

"Yes. I wish you would tell me what you're looking for."

"The words murderer, coward, liar. He's angry. And he's leaving popcorn with a flourish. The nursing home was the fire where popcorn became a calling card. There were other signatures he could have copied: the gas can and red bandanna for a fuse, padlocks on the doors. Why not the fireworks signature that made such a splash in the press last year? He chose popcorn for a reason."

"We've already looked at the people who died in the nursing home fire, their relatives."

"It's time to rethink it. Something is there."

"Ash disappeared," Jack said quietly.

Cole just nodded. "Has Cassie said anything about that fire?"

"No."

"She's a key to this, Jack. Just like you are."

Jack scowled. "I don't know why he's focused on me, this shift. I've racked my brains for names. Does Ben have any ideas?" Tones sounded. Jack pushed himself to his feet.

"Be careful."

"Always, boss."

There was new caulk around the sink in the fire station women's locker room. Cassie added her toothbrush to the blue spin rack, opened the cabinet, and found on the shelf below the towels an empty basket with her name on it nestled between others overflowing with shampoo bottles, makeup, cotton balls, and hair dryers. She tossed her toothpaste and hairbrush into her basket.

She had been on enough shifts she had finally decided to bring enough items to the station to effectively move in. She hadn't wanted to appear presumptuous about her position for she knew it was day to day based on how long it took for them to find the arsonist.

Living at a fire station wasn't all that different from her days living in a college dorm with the exception of a few unique realities—behind her, hung on a shower curtain rod, one of Margaret's uniform shirts dripped dry. It had been soaked to remove blood stains acquired while working at the car accident earlier that morning.

Cassie walked back into the women's dorm room. Bunks were made with precision; rugs covered the concrete floor. The room had been turned into more than just a place to sleep. There wasn't much privacy to be found at a fire station, but an effort had been made here to make it a place to relax. Two comfortable chairs had been moved in along with a small television. Bookshelves had been built along one wall. A desk had been squeezed in.

Cassie picked up the folded yellow T-shirt that had been waiting for her on her bunk. Jack had snuck in a gift. The shirt was one from last year's chili contest, boldly proclaiming Company 81's standing as the hottest company. The Post-it note simply said Jack. He'd begun the effort to shift her loyalty to Company 81.

It was trivial, but she thought it was his way to add something light to counter what had felt like an awkward parting. She had seen him only briefly today, and only long enough to casually pass a few general remarks. He was out on another dispatch.

It was another day where she was stuck at the station while Gold Shift rolled out numerous times to car accidents caused by the snowy day. She hated being stuck in the station.

Lord, is there anything different I could do to help find this man?

She could feel the tension that grew with every shift and the awareness that a fire would come. With the two holidays what was normally a festive time of the year was markedly different this year, almost grim. She was worried about Jack. But there were many other families equally being affected by the threat this arsonist presented.

They needed a different game plan. They had to be able to find him.

Cassie went to find Cole to see what she could do for the rest of the shift. If it was paperwork… She sighed at the idea. She was coming to be proficient at it, and she knew Cole was relying on her and giving her more and more to do. It was a love-hate relationship. When Jack was here at the station, being here to work on paperwork was a nice reason to be in his world. When Jack was out on a dispatch, she found herself watching the clock and paying close attention to anything over the dispatch radio.

Maybe if Cole didn't have anything really urgent for her to do, she could retreat to the kitchen and do some baking. The guys always relished having big, fresh cookies available. They had all the ingredients for Italian beef sandwiches that could be left in the Crock-Pot and kept hot for when the guys returned. It would be great to also get a soup started. The guys coming in and out of the station through the night would be cold and very likely hungry. A bite to eat and some desperately needed shut-eye would be high on their list of priorities.

"Got an extra one of those?"

Cassie looked up from the sandwiches she was cutting to see Ben had paused to lean around the kitchen door. "Sure, Lieutenant. Roast beef, mustard, and hot peppers? Heated?"

"Perfect. Cole around?"

"His office I think."

"Thanks. I'll be back in a few minutes."

Cassie fixed Ben a thick sandwich and turned to take out of the oven the pan of brownies she had left there to keep warm. She wasn't surprised to see Ben, even though it was only eight hours since he'd gone off duty. He'd been home, gotten some sleep, and come back to where he was needed most.

Ben rejoined her as she was peeling apples for a pie.

"Cole's a miracle worker. He may have found Chad a job."

Cassie slid Ben the sandwich. "Not the arson investigator slot he hoped for, but a community safety officer is a pretty good option." She'd helped Cole find a way to get it created. "Think Chad will accept?"

"He should. It's a good job, but will he?" Ben looked uncertain, and in the tightness around his mouth a touch of anger. "If he's ready to accept he won't be able to fight fires any more."

Cassie studied the older man, knowing how hard he'd been trying to help his nephew, understanding also how hard it would be for Chad to adjust to the disability. "He's depressed?"

The man's discomfort increased. "It's the holidays."

"Anything I can do?"

Ben shook his head as he wadded up his napkin. "You adjusted; he's got to do the same. It's time he faced reality and got back to work. Would you do me a favor and make two pies? Black Shift loves your baking."

"Glad to."

The phone rang. Ben motioned for her to stay put and got up to answer it. Cassie wondered if she should point out Chad had been making those steps back—the application to Cole, stopping by to see Cole. Chad was trying, but she knew the job offer that would have him talking about fires instead of fighting them would hurt. It would really hurt.

"Jack!"

He struggled to turn in the ditch where the blue sedan had flipped. He squinted against the blowing snow, holding up his hand to block the wind as best he could. Daylight was dwindling, vehicle headlights were becoming brighter in the fading light. Traffic was rushing by and throwing up dirty snow and ice creating a background of constant noise.

"No joy on the tow," Bruce shouted to be heard over the traffic. "Mark the car to be pulled out later."

Jack waved his hand acknowledging that he heard the message. He struggled to get the top pocket of his winter gear open. He took out a bright red fluorescent seal and unfolded it.

Christmas Eve was proving to be the day that would not end. Jack marked the wreck by putting the red seal on the shattered back window so patrolling cops would know the vehicle had been checked out. This car was trashed, but the driver had walked away once they had been able to get the door pulled open. He was on his way to the area hospital to be checked out as a precaution.

Jack struggled to work his way back up the slick incline. Snow had begun to fall midafternoon and already his boot tops were disappearing as he walked. It wasn't expected to let up for hours. Snow-packed treads, slick roads where salt melted the snow into mush, drivers hurrying to get home—as the temperature fell, the wind picked up, and as the snow got heavier the number of accidents grew exponentially. The spinouts and fender benders were coming faster than dispatch could take the calls.

He was cold and miserable, and the odds were good he was going to be cold and miserable for the next several hours. Jack slipped and jarred his wrist as he stopped the fall. He brushed snow off and tried to get it out of his glove.

Cole had arrived, his SUV parked behind Engine 81, red and blue lights flashing to warn traffic. His friend had come back to work shortly after 4 P.M. to help out Frank with command and control. Prioritizing scenes was crucial when bad weather hit.

He wished traffic would slow down to a moderate speed so they didn't have someone else end up in a ditch before they got done packing up from this one.

Cassie was standing near Cole's vehicle, bundled into winter gear. Jack wasn't thrilled with the idea of her being out in this to help Cole, but he was grateful to see her. The wind felt like blowing ice as he walked over to join her.

She wiped the snow off his face. "The shift is half over."

He leaned against her hand. "I volunteered to work part of tomorrow."

"I know. You'll survive."

He gave a weary smile. "Promise?"

"I brought you a hot roast beef sandwich and the biggest thermos of coffee the station had. They're in the engine cab."

"Bless you. I've forgotten what food was."

"Cole is sending me home at 10 P.M. He doesn't want me rolling out if we have a fire tonight."

Jack heard the unasked question of his role in that decision. "It's Christmas Eve. You need a chance to enjoy it."

"Protecting me, Jack?"

He hoped she would understand. "Trying to."

She squeezed his arm. "Be careful tonight."

"Guaranteed. Want to share my coffee?" The radio broadcast tones for another car accident. He scowled at it as he listened to the mile markers. It was about a mile north.

"Find a few seconds to eat the sandwich before dawn," Cassie sympathized.

"Did you put on hot peppers?" Jack asked, walking backward as he headed toward the engine to join the guys.

"Absolutely."

"Did you save me any of that cake you were baking?"

"I already set a big piece aside with your name on it."

"Enjoy Christmas Eve, Cassie."

"I will."

Cassie drove home very slowly when she left the station; the last thing she wanted to do was add another accident to what the guys already had to deal with. The radio was playing Christmas music with no commercials.

Her windshield wipers struggled to keep up with the falling snow obscuring the window. The car heater still blew cold air. She was glad to get home.

Jack had added bags of sand to her trunk in case she hit ice and spun out. The added weight helped. Plows had come through the apartment complex parking lot, piling the snow into large mountains. The parking lot had been cleared but the sidewalks had not yet been shoveled.

Lord, this is a strange night. I didn't expect to spend it alone.

She envied Jack the fact he was working tonight. He was making a lasting difference in people's lives. People died in car accidents, people were injured every day of the year. But when it happened on a major holiday—the memory of that holiday was destroyed for years to come. For everyone Jack was able to help tonight, someone escaped a painful memory for the future. *Jesus, please keep him safe tonight as he tries to keep others safe.* She hoped the new year brought some clarity to her own future. She desperately needed to find it.

THIRTY-FIVE

Jack considered thumping the snowblower with a wrench on the assumption that action would have as much success at fixing the thing as the last two hours of effort.

He was spending Christmas Day trying to fix it because he didn't want to shovel snow by hand. If he had started shoveling the snow by hand when he got home from the fire station, he would have been done by now. Instead he had yet to begin.

He'd finally gotten off work at 1 P.M. Jack wanted to get the snow cleared so he could go over to Cassie's and talk her into building a snowman or having a friendly snowball fight. He shifted on the carpet remnant he was using to block the cold from the concrete.

The door between the house and garage opened and Rachel came out to join him. She was bundled up in a ski suit that would make a professional skier jealous. Jack was willing to bet Jennifer had been behind that gift. Rachel often ended up working at natural disasters where cold and wet were part of her long days.

"Here. Warm up."

He accepted the hot chocolate. "Thanks. This garage is like ice." His hands were painfully cold even with the palm and half-finger gloves.

"Jack, Jennifer believes in Jesus. I think I finally understand why." Rachel perched herself on the bag of salt he planned to spread on the walk once it was cleared of snow.

"Hold it, Rachel. You walked in, said hi, and now we're talking about religion. Give me two seconds to shift gears."

"It's Christmas."

"And frankly I'm going to be very relieved when this holiday is over." He'd had his fill of snow, car accidents, and drunk drivers. Jack drained the hot chocolate. "Do we really have to talk about this now?"

"I went to church with Jennifer last night."

They *were* going to be talking about it now. "Okay…" He hadn't expected that but wasn't totally surprised by it, not if Jennifer had asked Rachel to go along.

"What if Jennifer is right?"

It sounded like instead of talking about Jennifer's puppy and plans for New Year's Eve, it was going to be the subject of religion. Jack rubbed his eyes, annoyed at the grime on his hands, and tried to give Rachel his full attention, knowing he was about to be left behind in the dust with this conversation. She didn't mean to talk over his head, but Rachel was comfortable talking in-depth about subjects like psychology and law. If she was now adding religion— He figured he could get in one statement that sounded intelligent before he got confused. "You think Jennifer might be right to believe Jesus is alive."

"Yes."

He picked up the wrench and considered stripping apart the carburetor. He had spent hours on this snowblower over Thanksgiving to avoid just this situation. He needed this thing to start. "Why? You've been the one saying for months that it didn't make sense."

"She's happy."

He was expecting a profound answer and instead she surprised him with a very simple one. "I could have told you that." He grimaced as the wrench slipped and he scraped his knuckles against the concrete.

"She's got cancer, her remission is officially over, and she's going to be fighting for every day of her future. In the face of that she's able to be happy. Even being married can't explain that joy."

"You're using an emotional argument to justify why she is right."

"Yes."

He shook his head, confused. Rachel was logical as well as empathetic with people, able to sort out what seemed like contradictory human behavior and shape it back into some order, but there were times he simply could not follow her reasoning. He looked at her and was surprised by the almost pleading expression.

"When you're dying, you can't easily lie to yourself. Jennifer's gut tells her Jesus loves her and has given her eternal life. The fact that the closer she gets to death, the stronger she believes tells me she's right."

Jack didn't feel it wise to point out the contradiction in her statement. She had just said Jennifer was in denial of the fact she was dying. Rachel wanted him to agree with her, and he couldn't do it, but neither could he discourage her. He'd missed that sound of hope in her voice. "What are you going to do?"

"Am I blowing smoke with that conclusion?"

"Sounds reasonable to me."

"Good. Because you need to read the Bible. Jennifer wants to talk to you."

"Rae—" he instinctively protested. He did not want to get into a discussion of religion with Jennifer. The last thing he wanted to do was disappoint her, and he would if they talked about that subject. She wanted him to believe too and he couldn't yet say that he did.

"Tough. You need to wrestle it to the ground. If I do choose to believe, that leaves only you and Stephen on the wrong side of the decision."

He glanced at her, hearing the line being drawn with a smile. "If you're right, everyone has to agree with you."

"About this, yes. I want company on this scary step."

Being told by his sister to read the Bible after being told by Cassie the same thing, he was willing to concede at least the fact he couldn't ignore making a decision any longer. "Is there a large print edition that I don't have to squint at, written in something better than Old King's English?" When she nodded, he sighed. "Get me a Bible for a Christmas gift, then I'll see what I think."

She beamed at him. "I already did. It's the package on your kitchen counter."

"Am I that predictable?"

"You hate to tell family no."

"I'll start working at it."

She laughed. He smiled at her, then looked back at the hunk of metal that was the bane of his existence. "Do you know how to fix a snowblower?"

"I'll kick it for you."

"Doesn't work." He finally grabbed hold of it, tipped it, and shook hard. A screw tumbled to the concrete floor. "Now I wonder where that was supposed to be?" He went back to searching.

He finally leaned over and pulled the cord. The snowblower started.

"It works." She said, surprised, smiling at him.

"Good, because you get to use it on the drive while I use the shovel on the steps."

It was snowing. Cassie hated winter as a rule, but on Christmas Day she made an exception. The snow was building up on the kitchen windowsill. The sun was out, and the reflection off the snow was so bright she had to narrow her eyes as she looked around. Long icicles hung in neat rows along the building gutters. The world outside looked new.

She had given herself the luxury of sleeping in until ten and fixing flavored coffee. The apartment was toasty as the building heat had shifted into its too hot mode. She was wearing sweats, but she could easily be in short sleeves and be comfortable.

"Come on, Benji." She picked up the kitten from the couch. B. J. had curled up on the new leather jacket Cole had given her for Christmas. It was gorgeous. She owed her friend a hug although he'd get embarrassed if she did it.

This was the day she had targeted as her turning point and she had woken in a good mood, was absolutely loving the day. There was no stress, no bookstore to worry about, or shift to go to. It was a day off and totally free. She hummed along with the Christmas music on the radio as she finished unpacking the gifts she brought home from the department party and set on the couch last night.

After all the painting and wallpapering was finished, she'd basically have a new apartment by the end of the week. The bookstore business through the month of December had been wonderful. She planned to catch up on paperwork tomorrow and do the final budget planning for next year. The owner of the bike shop was talking again about moving to a larger store, and that put the option of expanding the bookstore back on the table. She was excited about that possibility.

Jack should be home from his shift by now. She would call him and wish him Merry Christmas, but she was afraid she might wake him up from a much-needed couple hours of sleep. The wind had tapered off around midnight and the brunt of the storm had skirted north. She hoped Jack had an easier end to his shift.

She put Benji down on a pillow she pulled to the center of the bed. The kitten loved to play and equally loved to sleep. As a gift Jack couldn't have found a better one.

Cassie looked around her bedroom. Everything short of the walk-in closet had now been Jack's definition of spring cleaned. She had toyed with the idea of starting the painting on her own, but then decided for simplicity's sake to wait for Jack.

She stepped over the vacuum cleaner and went back to work on the windows. She'd been finishing up the cleaning. When this was done, she was going to look at baking some cookies. Jack hadn't said whom he had recruited as help, but knowing the odds, she figured planning to feed them would be a good idea. She reached to clean the top of the windowpane.

A snowball splattered against the window. Startled, she took two steps backward and then warily returned to the window to see the source. Jack stood on the curb looking up at her window, his hands on his hips. She cracked open the window and shivered at the cold.

"Can Cassie come out and play?"

"You're crazy, you know that?"

"Gloves, woman, and get yourself down here."

"Hold on." With a laugh she closed the window.

She opened her closet, got out her long blue coat, hat, and black gloves, then went to join Jack.

Jack had a girlfriend. He drank hot coffee as he watched the two of them struggle to roll a growing snowball across the hilly ground. They were having a good Christmas. At least someone was. He'd listened to a near suicide threat; the holidays doing what time had not, nearly causing another casualty in his family. Popcorn fell on the car floorboard. He shook the box to spread out the butter better. He was getting tired of it all.

The snowman grew. Acquired eyes and a nose.

Cassie tumbled back in a snowdrift and made a snow angel as Jack stood watching and laughing.

The pressure had to increase and this was the most vulnerable point. He sighed. No one had found his last message, his most elegant message. It was frustrating as he had worked hard at it. But this situation…it had possibilities.

They went in and the lights soon came on in her apartment.

He stepped out of the car to check out the snowman.

Jack stretched out on his back on the living room floor, exhausted but happy. Benji, sitting on his chest, made a tentative swipe with her front paw at the pretzel stick Jack twirled in front of her. The kitten pounced and butted his chin. Jack laughed softly because the fur tickled, and the kitten tumbled, an earthquake rumbling beneath her. Jack nudged Benji back to the center of his chest to prevent her tumbling off.

Jack rubbed his cheek with the back of his hand. Just before they came in Cassie had hit him square in the face with a snowball. He had frozen feet, cold hands, and a wet shirt. And he was happy.

"Cassie, did you get lost?"

"I'm drying out."

"Bring me another towel when you come. I'm melting all over your carpet here."

She reappeared in the doorway, and the towel lobbed his direction caught him upside the head.

"Thanks." She sat on the floor beside him and dropped a monogrammed towel for Benji beside the kitten. "B. J. still has a milk mustache."

"She's getting better at it. At least she didn't tip the bowl this time."

Cassie was towel drying her own hair. She'd made a snow angel and come up looking frosted afterward.

She changed into a gray short sleeve shirt. She'd never done that before with him. Jack noticed it immediately. The burns that scarred her forearms curled back around her forearms to behind her elbows. Her upper right arm muscles looked deformed by the results of the fire, contracted and withered.

A glance at her face told him she knew he had noticed. He didn't say anything, but he did relax. She'd trusted him. That meant a lot. She was also wearing his pendant. And that meant even more.

He carefully started drying off Benji's milk mustache.

"Thank you for her." She reached over to stroke the kitten.

Jack caught her hand, turned it, and kissed the back of her hand where the scars marred her skin.

Startled, her hand curled. "Why did you do that?"

"To kiss it better," he said matter-of-factly. "You hide your hands. Now you don't have to."

"Jack—"

He quirked an eyebrow when she struggled with words. She finally just offered a smile to him. He smiled back and turned his attention to the kitten, now trying to eat a button on his shirt pocket.

"Who do you think is going to be his next target?"

"Our firebug?"

Cassie nodded.

"So far he's gone after the fire board, the arson group, and the fire department. It's pretty obvious he's trying to get us to react, so take your pick at what he strikes at next."

"Cole thinks it's a firefighter."

Jack nodded. It was depressing but given the situation probably accurate. "Do you think it's someone from the old Company 65?"

"No."

"It's no one in Company 81."

"It can't be someone we know," Cassie agreed. She hesitated, and then added, "I'm worried about the next fire."

He heard an undercurrent of something deeper under that general comment. "You're worried about my getting hurt."

She nodded.

"It's a possibility for any firefighter." He reached over and gently traced the scar that ran from the back of her hand across her wrist. "Would you have not gone into the nursing home had you known this would happen?"

"I would have gone in."

"Don't borrow trouble, Cassie. If something happens, we'll deal with it. Until then worry is wasted emotion."

"You're not going to take Ben up on his suggestion that you and he change shifts, Black and Gold, and find out if it's you or Gold Shift itself?"

Jack shook his head. "I would be leaving Nate and Bruce and the guys. I can't do that to them if it's Gold Shift who's the target."

The mood was becoming way too serious, the laughter of the afternoon replaced with a more somber mood. She'd had one Christmas wish, and he was unable to help fulfill it. "I'm sorry you are not able to spend Christmas with Ash."

"So am I. I think something happened to him. I can't imagine him not being here for Christmas if he could."

"Again, please don't borrow trouble."

"He isn't a man to abandon me like this."

"It took you the better part of two years to reach acceptance of what happened. Ash held on to his anger for much longer than you did. He needs the time. Let him have it."

"He felt responsible for what happened."

"That's his right," Jack cautioned her, understanding why Ash would have reacted the way he had.

"I just wish I knew where he was spending this day."

Jack needed to shake her out of this growing melancholy. "Do you want to try and find your mouse tonight?"

"Are you up to it?"

He smiled at her doubt. "I think I can find the energy if you can."

"I tried to sort through some of the boxes, but I found the closet has been used as the place to store everything I didn't want to unpack in the last move so it's a bit chaotic." Cassie stood and offered Jack a hand to pull him to his feet.

Jack set Benji in the small box that had become her bed.

Cassie turned on the lights in the bedroom, opened the closet doors, and turned on the lights in the walk-in closet. "Where do you want to start?"

"I'll hand out the boxes if you want to stack them in the hall."

"There's no room in the hall. What if we stack them between the dresser and the bookcase in here?"

Jack was doubtful that they would fit, but it would mean she had to carry them a shorter distance. "We can try it."

He moved aside the hanging clothes. If he worked clockwise around the closet... "This mouse is white."

"Yes."

"You're sure it lives in here?"

"I've seen it three times."

Had he known there were this many boxes he would have suggested it another night. Maybe if he got them at least shifted away from the walls so the mouse wouldn't have a place to hide... Jack picked up the first box, deciding to first clear out enough space so he could turn around. He made sure Cassie had both her arms under the box and that the heavier part of the box was toward her left arm before he released it.

As he started to move clothes around on the rods to reach boxes below them, he realized she had been wearing only a fraction of her wardrobe since Thanksgiving. It was past time to take her out to a nice dinner. "This box has broken tape on the bottom."

She took it gingerly. "Got it."

"Jennifer wants to talk about religion." Cassie had trusted him; he was going to return the favor. Frankly he needed some advice.

Cassie bobbled the box. "Does she?"

"Where am I supposed to start reading the Bible?"

"Jack, we jumped from a mouse to a discussion about Jesus. Did I miss something?"

He shot her a smile. "I am so glad similar shifts in conversation levels confuse you in the same way it does me. Every time Rachel does it I get lost."

She looked relieved at that. She carefully set down the box atop others. "You want me to tell you where to start reading the Bible."

"It's a thick book."

"Actually, it's sixty-six books put together into one book."

She laughed at his look.

"You've read them all," he guessed.

"Yes, although I admit some of them are easier to read than others. What exactly does Jennifer want to talk about?"

"Jesus."

"Try opening the Bible to the middle, then open the section to the right in the middle again. That will probably put you in the book of Luke or John. Those books are basically biographies of Jesus' life."

"I don't suppose there are CliffsNotes?" he asked, hopeful. He glanced over at her. She was doing her best not to laugh. "I didn't think so."

"Jack, it's not a hard book to figure out. Read it with common sense. When does she want to talk about it?"

"She's heading to Johns Hopkins on January 3 to start the next round of chemotherapy. Sometime before then, I imagine."

"Start with the book of Luke. It's practical. I like it."

"Jen's going to tangle me in word knots like Rachel does."

"Not intentionally," Cassie offered sympathetically.

"They never do it intentionally," Jack countered. He pushed aside shoe boxes, looking to see if any had corners chewed out. He was reaching the last wall of boxes and so far there had been no sign of her uninvited guest.

"What are we going to do for New Year's Eve?"

Jack liked the assumption of we. "Besides cut drunks out of car wrecks?" he asked, remembering last year.

"True. Besides that."

"I'm not big into late night parties."

"Do you want to bring over a movie? We could invite Cole, Rachel, make pizzas."

"Sure, we could do that."

"Your family wouldn't mind?"

"Nothing formal is planned. We're scattering to different parties this year." Jack picked up the next box. "Be careful with this one. I feel something sharp on the right side." He was getting down to the last of the boxes. "I don't think your mouse was home tonight."

"Or he's inside one of these boxes," Cassie offered, worried.

Jack tipped forward the next to last box labeled books. "Get him!"

Cassie scrambled toward the scurrying mouse that darted into the room and headed toward the dresser, trying to cut the mouse off. She was too late. "It's a her," she corrected, using her foot to block the path the mouse had used.

Jack sat on the carpet in the now almost empty walk-in closet and rested his arms across his upraised knees. "She just went behind the boxes we just moved."

"I'm afraid so." Cassie looked at him and she couldn't stop the giggles.

"It's not funny."

"Yes, it is."

She walked over to the closet doorway and leaned against the door frame. "You got beaten by a mouse."

He tossed a wadded up sock at her.

"I could go get Benji and let her try," Cassie offered.

"As you're the one who has to sleep in a room with a mouse, I wouldn't laugh too hard. Do you have some cheese? We can at least try to lure it out of the bedroom."

Cassie pushed her hands deeper into her pockets as she stood on the curb and watched Jack scrape the frosted windows of his car. He had declined to let her help. "Would you call me when you get home?"

"Of course."

"I don't mean to imply you're a bad driver."

Jack laughed. "Just that everyone else is."

"Exactly."

He opened the passenger door and tossed the windshield scraper onto the floorboard. "I had a good Christmas, Cassie."

"So did I."

"I see someone has added a hat to our snowman."

She looked toward the playground. A baseball cap had been pushed down on the snowy white head with a carrot nose and charcoal brick eyes. "He looks dashing." A gust of wind blew snow from the overhang. She shivered and wrapped her arms tighter around her waist. "I'm going to head in before I freeze."

Jack grinned at her. "Good idea, you're turning blue. I'll call."

"Thanks." She hurried back up the walkway.

A car door slammed to her right and she glanced over. Her feet went out from under her and she fell hard on the sidewalk. "Ash."

THIRTY-SIX

She heard someone rushing up the walkway, then realized Jack had seen her fall. Her attention was focused solely on the man standing by an old Plymouth. There was no mistake about who he was. Ash was a ghost of the man she remembered—thinner, a suggestion of hesitancy where there had once been obvious confidence—but he was really here. "Ash."

He started walking toward her, pushing his hands into his pockets. "Hello, Cassie."

Rather than help her up, Jack stood between the two of them. Cassie grabbed the edge of his coat, using the hold to get leverage to sit up. "It's okay, Jack. The man I saw at the fire was not Ash," she murmured, understanding Jack's instinctive move. Ash had grown a beard; his clothes were flannel and denim and his leather jacket looked beat-up.

She caught Jack's hand and forced him to give her his attention. He reached down and helped her up.

"I would have been here earlier but the snowstorm slowed me down. I wanted to spend Christmas with you," Ash said quietly, stopping a few feet away. "Hello, Jack."

"Ash."

Cassie felt like she was dreaming. He was really here. The prayer she had prayed for months had been answered. She hadn't been expecting it and that made her feel ashamed for doubting. "Please, come in," Cassie urged. Months that Ash had been gone…she wanted to know all the details. And she was nervous about those answers. Her hand around Jack's tightened painfully, hoping he'd offer to stay without her needing to ask him.

Jack didn't even give her a choice about it. He took the keys from her and settled his arm around her shoulders, putting himself between Ash and Cassie. "Were you driving into this storm?"

"Skirting along its edge. I was in St. Louis yesterday coming up from the gulf."

"You do look like you've got a bit of a tan," Cassie offered, getting her first good look at her partner in the light from the front door. He'd aged. The man she admired and trusted and followed without question into a fire was different tonight than the man she remembered.

"I was out chasing a sunburn again."

He looked different, but he was starting to sound the same.

Upstairs, Jack unlocked the apartment door and returned her keys.

"You're moving?" Ash asked, on seeing the boxes.

"Cleaning house," Cassie replied, shooting Jack an amused glance.

"You're a brave man. I helped her move in originally," Ash commented to Jack.

Cassie started to slip off her coat and Jack stopped her. His hands on her shoulders tightened and he leaned down. "Go change into something with long sleeves," he whispered.

She shot him a look, saw the sympathy, and understood. "Keep Ash company?"

"I'll host."

Cassie went to the bedroom before she slipped off her coat. She changed, choosing her best sweater, a soft pink cashmere. On their first meeting Ash didn't need to encounter her most vivid scars from the accident. She was relieved Jack had caught her attention before she slipped off the coat. She ran a brush through her hair and went to rejoin them.

The two men were standing by the patio door. Their conversation was pitched too low for her to hear.

Jack turned when he heard her come back in. She smiled as she saw he was holding Benji. He walked over to join her. "I'll leave and let you two have a chance to talk," he said softly. He handed her the kitten.

"Jack." She didn't want him to leave.

He hugged her. "Listen to him, honey," he whispered. "Then call me."

He wasn't giving her a choice; he was pulling on his coat. "I'll call." She reluctantly walked him to the door and locked it behind him.

Ash hadn't moved from his place beside the patio door. "Jack gave me the kitten for Christmas," she commented as she set B. J. down on her towel, suddenly nervous as she didn't know what to say.

"I won't stay long."

"Ash—I've been hoping so long to have you back, but now that you're here, I don't know what to say." She sat on the couch and gestured to the chair. "Why didn't you tell me you were leaving? Where have you been? Why didn't you call? Oh, it's good to see you."

"Cassie." He waited for her to run down. "I got a call from an investigator looking into a fire in Tallahassee. It fit the pattern of the fire we had here, so I decided to go check it out."

"That abruptly? You couldn't tell me you were leaving?"

"I was tired of pacing, of being able to do nothing. I didn't mean to abandon you; I just felt like until I could find something out, I had nothing left to offer you. And I wanted out. I'm not proud of it, but that was where my head was at."

Cassie wished he understood how much he had been doing just by being there for her. She heard so much lingering pain in his voice. "The accident wasn't your fault. And the man who set the nursing home fire died in a car accident in New Jersey."

"I heard about his accident."

"But you still didn't come back."

"It's taken the last couple months to decide if I wanted to have a firefighter's life again."

"What changed your mind?"

He gave her a small smile. "The memory of your determination to get to this day and have your new beginning. I decided I needed one too."

"I'm glad." She leaned her head back against the couch. "I don't think you've changed, Ash. You're still stubborn, impatient. And you would have gotten answers faster had you stayed here instead of taking off on your own."

He smiled at her. "You look well, Cassie." The subject changed abruptly. "What's been going on here that I missed? Besides Jack getting his act together."

The reference to Jack made her smile; the other question really disturbed her. "There's been some fires."

"Arson fires?"

She nodded. She got up and from her desk sorted around to find the file where she had collected the newspaper accounts. She handed him the file but didn't immediately release it. She swallowed hard, feeling incredibly guilty. "I thought I saw you at the scene of the Wallis fire."

He stilled. "Did you? Why?"

Water was dripping. Jack listened hard to the quiet in his house, trying to decide if the sound was coming from inside or outside. It sounded like it was coming from the bathroom. He was going to have to replace the seal on the sink.

Jack shifted around and grabbed one of the extra pillows on the bed beside him and tossed it at the open door to push it closed and block out the sound. In the middle of the night small, unnoticed sounds from the day grew loud and annoying. Water dripping was one of the worst.

He turned the page of the Bible, wondering why they made the pages so incredibly thin. The words might be large type, but it was still a bit like reading a newspaper with its two-column format.

Come on, Cassie, call. He was struggling to stay awake.

Ash was back.

The shock of that was still settling in. Jack had a feeling his life had just gotten more complicated.

Ash felt like part of this. In the same way Cole was part of it, as Jack himself was. Ash was one of those people connected to the department that had this arsonist's attention. Someone, something had triggered the arsonist to start to act. And while it might be coincidence, the calendar said Ash had disappeared; then the fires had begun. Now Ash had reappeared—it was going to create a reaction. That was what Jack uneasily sensed in his gut. Why had the fires begun after Ash disappeared? What had that triggered? And what would happen now that he was back?

Jack was glad Cole was involved to help sort out those questions. They were agonizing ones, and not something that could be talked about with Cassie. She would try to protect her partner. Jack wanted to protect her. And he was afraid their two goals might collide.

He fingered the page of the book, considered closing it, but accepted he couldn't duck this issue as easily as he could the other. Jennifer wanted him to consider this, and Cassie... Religion certainly mattered to her.

He had to find a middle ground on this that showed he respected their position without offending them. He adjusted the bedside light and turned his attention back to what he had been reading for the last two hours. He wasn't calling it a night until he heard from Cassie. And if he didn't hear from her in the next half hour, he was going to call her.

Who was Jesus Christ? This should not be so hard to figure out. Jack ran his hand through his hair, frustrated with how difficult it was to make sense of the book of Luke.

Before reading the book Jack would have said Jesus was a man who was a good teacher who had ended up being martyred, and His followers were so impassioned about what He had taught they insisted He rose from the dead so they could claim they followed someone living rather than dead. It was a rather brutal opinion but common sense said claims of a resurrection had to be a myth.

Luke presented something so much more complex. Jack got hit in the first pages of the book with talk of the angel Gabriel, of how the virgin birth came about. Long sections of Luke dealt with Jesus healing the sick. There were references to Jesus knowing men's thoughts. His teaching was blunt and searing to the heart of the matter. He was called a King, the Son of God. He claimed to be able to forgive sins. It was already an incredible statement of the man before Jack ever reached the chapter that described the Resurrection.

To swallow any part of this, he just about had to swallow the whole. But to reject it because the Resurrection was implausible would do a serious disservice to the whole thing presented. There was so much here. It was a massive package.

Jack was annoyed Jennifer and Rachel had simplified things in the past when they talked about it. It was easier to see a big, deep picture and possibly accept the Resurrection as part of it than to support it as a single stand-alone event. Was this why Jennifer and the other O'Malleys believed? Because of the whole?

The phone rang. Jack glanced at the clock and reached for the phone. "Cassie, I was getting worried about you. It's almost 1 A.M." He shifted the phone to his other side and bunched the comforter as a pillow, closing the Bible he had been reading. "How did it go?"

She didn't say anything. "Cassie?"

"I wish you were here so I could get a hug."

"Honey, go get some Kleenex."

She went away and eventually came back. "Sorry. It was just so good to see him. I'm happy. I cry when I'm happy."

Jack gamely accepted that because he had no choice. "Okay. That's good to know."

She laughed around the tears. "Ash is going to come by the station this week and nag Cole into letting him come back to work."

"I'll enjoy having a chance to talk with him. Cole was relieved when I called to let him know Ash had returned; he'll be eager to talk with him too." Jack was relieved to hear her quieting down. He wanted desperately to change the subject. "I was reading the book of Luke tonight," he offered, hoping to divert her.

"Really?"

There was hope in that one word and he was glad he raised it. "Cassie, is Jesus alive?"

"Yes."

"How do you know for sure?"

She hesitated.

"Tell me."

"In the dark days after the fire, Jack, Jesus understood all of it. The nightmares of being trapped in the fire, the pain, the despair. I could talk to Him and read His Word, and it was talking to someone who was there. He was always there. He answered me in so many profound ways, through events, through people, through His Word. He heard me."

Jack closed his eyes as she spoke. The man she called Jesus had been there to comfort when no one else could. No wonder Jennifer believed if that was what she had also found in the midst of the cancer.

"Do you want to come to church with me next Sunday?" Cassie offered. "Pastor Luke explains things so much better than I do."

"Maybe." He heard a beep on the line. His frustration was immediate. "Hold on, Cassie, I've got a call coming in." He accepted the call. "This is Jack."

"It's Ash. What's Cole's number? I've got a problem at my place."

"Something happen?"

"Does popcorn mean anything to you?"

"I'm on my way."

"No. I've got cobwebs growing on the message. Cole can handle it. If you come, Cassie will hear and have to come. It's not the way I want her ending her Christmas."

"Then I'll call Cole for you."

"I'd appreciate it."

Ash hung up. Jack warned Cassie he would be a minute coming back; then he called Cole, wondering what the message was that Ash had received.

≫≪≫

"This is quite a welcome home, Ash." Cole shone his light on the living room wall revealing a huge mural of a fire. No wonder the arsonist liked big, sweeping letters. He liked to paint murals. It had been here a while for there were cobwebs in the corners of the room.

This had taken several hours if not days to create. Cole walked back into the hallway near the front door where the painting began. He crouched down to study it. There was amateur skill in it and a good understanding for how fire began. The painting began low, just above the floor, as black smoldering impressions. As he walked down the hall it slowly rose on the wall. There was a flash as flames briefly flared for the first time and then it fell back to a steady burn and slowly grew.

Cole traced his light up as the fire moved from the floor to the ceiling. The ceiling fire then dropped burning embers to the floor. There was an incredible burst of fire as the room was shown to reach the flash point. "Any spray paint cans?"

"Not that I've found. Who paints murals?"

"A young man who likes elegant graffiti." Cole replied. It had to be a young man who knew all about fire. This was too accurate for how a fire moved and breathed to be chance. Cole stood back, looking overall at the problem. Ash's home had not been trashed, and that was interesting. "How did he get in?"

"Someone scratched the back door lock."

"That was Cassie breaking in. She lost her key."

"Then no, I don't have any idea."

Cole frowned. After he painted the arsonist had taken the time to move the furniture back to their original spots, had taken the time to rehang pictures. And Cole found it interesting that he didn't see any picture out of order. Why the arsonist had hit him, it made sense. He was part of the district leadership. But Ash—this had been painted when there was no idea when or if Ash might return.

"Did you stay in touch with anyone here? Did you call someone? E-mail anybody?"

"I was planning to leave it all behind and permanently end any idea of being involved with a fire department. I didn't call or write anyone. I came back simply to see Cassie for Christmas."

"I'm tempted to give you a headache for giving Cassie cause to worry about you."

"Let's not and say you did. I didn't hurt her intentionally."

Cole looked at his friend, having understood more than Ash probably realized. "There is a reason they call those nightmares you were having flashbacks."

"They stopped about four weeks ago."

"Admit it, you've been bored without the firefighter job."

"If you think I was safety picky before, you haven't seen anything yet."

Cole nodded and made an offer he'd been hoping he would one day have the opportunity to make. "Frank and I have the budget in shape to increase the training funds. If the board gives us the final approval at their next meeting, we're going to need someone to run it."

"Cole—"

"I want you back on rotation, and I want you teaching at the academy. It's time to get back in the game and help me out."

"I suppose I owe you one."

It was a grudging admission, but Cole would take it. "In a month you'll tell me you love it."

"Rookies? Please. I've done too much training through the years. I know the reality. It's like corralling a bunch of show-offs." Ash stopped by the entryway to his office. "At least he left this room alone."

"He called you chicken in the e-mail message he sent you."

"I wish he'd had the courage to call me that to my face." Ash walked around the room to see if anything else had been touched. "Cassie said you think this is a firefighter."

Cole leaned against the doorjamb, watching Ash prowl around the room. "He's setting fires within the walls using small flowerpots."

Ash stopped, then turned on his heel. "My signature?"

Cole nodded. He knew it would get a rise and he watched, interested in knowing exactly what that reaction would be.

Ash looked grim. "One of my students."

Cole understood the emotion clouding Ash's voice. The idea this was a firefighter bit hard, and the realization it was someone they might have worked with was hard to swallow. "I don't know if borrowing the signature is another way to turn the knife, like he's doing using the popcorn and setting fires at the edge of the district, or because he knows it's the best way to start fires in the wall."

"More than one rookie has washed out because they failed the training."

Cole nodded.

"Getting my address would be easy to do."

Cole let Ash think, hoping he would be able to put a name to the details.

"What's the base he's using?"

"Tar," Cole replied.

From the front of the house came the sound of car doors slamming. Cole walked back to the foyer and turned on the outside light. His friend Joe, the police investigator who had worked the vandalism and garbage fire at his place, was coming up the drive.

Cole held open the door for the man. "Sorry for interrupting your Christmas."

Joe stopped long enough to stamp snow off his feet before coming into the house. "Don't worry about it."

Cole gestured to the living room. The investigator stopped at the door to the room and whistled.

"Tell me about it," Cole agreed.

"No fire at all with this one?"

"None." Cole was worried about that. It was a change in MO and any change was a sign of possible coming trouble.

"I'll pull the same team that worked your place as they'll have a better sense of what to search for. This is going to take a while. Give me a couple days."

"It would help if there was a way to figure out the brand of paint. He's gone through a lot of it recently."

"I'll see what I can do."

"I appreciate it. Come on, Ash, you can spend the night at my place," Cole offered. "I just got the spare bedroom put back together. You and I need to talk."

"I'll take you up on that."

THIRTY-SEVEN

"It can't be Charlie. He's older than the man I saw." Cassie tossed the blue folder into the eight-inch-high cardboard box collecting files of people they had ruled out. She tried to shift around in her chair and nearly kicked over her drink sitting on the floor by the box.

"How many people did you train over the years, Ash?" Beside her on the table was a sliding stack of files to go through, and every hour more of them came from the records archive. Since she had seen the man they thought had started the fire, she was given the job of going through the files first. If she could absolutely rule out the person, it meant one less file for Ash to deal with.

Ash lowered his feet from the corner of Cole's desk so Cole could get back to his chair. "About three hundred, give or take how many you count from the year I was an assistant at the training academy."

Cassie knew he had done a lot of training. Like most firefighters he had a specialty within the district, and his happened to be structure fires. She had not known the extent to which he had trained over the years.

Ash was paging through a roster for a class six years ago. Learning who Cole suspected, Ash had dug out the class material and old rosters from a box in his attic. "Cole, do you remember a Larry Burcell?"

"He's working with the forest service in Montana."

"That's a guy I could see setting a fire."

"Ash, you've gotten cynical in your travels," Cassie protested.

Cole laughed. "You're just now learning your partner was a closet cynic? Where have you been all these years?"

Ash laughed. "It's called loyalty, Cole. I inspire more of it than you. Cassie still thinks I walk on water."

"The muck is getting deep in here." Cole picked up one of the files Ash had quietly passed him to review. The two men were bantering back and forth as they worked, while underneath it was very serious business.

Cassie was feeling a little out of her depth. She and Ash had been partners; they had worked for Cole. And while Cole had been her friend as well as her boss, she had not realized the extent of the friendship between him and Ash. She was hearing for the first time about a shared history.

"Cassie, where's that list you put together of businesses that sell tar?"

She shot Cole an annoyed look at the idea of having to find it. What she knew for sure was that it was buried. Cole just laughed at her look.

Trying to avoid the whole stack of files spilling across the floor, she moved the stack of files from her lap to the floor. The last time she had seen that list it had been somewhere on the round table with notes scrawled by Cole and three Post-its marking corrections. "You could print another copy."

"That's work."

She started searching. "Here's the phone list of attorneys you lost last week." She checked the portfolio and found the page of the minutes from the budget meeting. She scanned a list of restaurant take-out order phone numbers. Cole had to eat better than this. She finally found the printout he requested and passed it over to Cole. "I was able to eliminate a few of them as being irrelevant to what you were looking for."

"Do you remember any of these being art, supply-type companies?"

"Spray paint can be bought at a hardware store as easily as an art supply store."

"The guy has to have a job somewhere. We know he likes art."

"He's an amateur," Ash pointed out. "I would suggest you try frame shops or the like."

Cassie sorted through the files, trying to figure out if there was some way to get them in roughly chronological order for the age of the individual. Jack had been doing that for her, but he disappeared about twenty minutes ago to return a phone call. "I think Jack has gotten lost." She appreciated the help even if Jack had been driving her crazy this morning with his teasing.

"I asked him to see if the conference room schedule could be moved around so we could take all this stuff down there," Cole replied.

"It is a little much for your office," Cassie agreed.

Ash handed Cole another file of a possible suspect. "I still think the words should tell us something," Ash commented, going back to a conversation they had had several times over the course of the day. "Doesn't calling you a liar imply you made a promise to someone?"

"Calling you a chicken probably implies someone ran into your cautious safety streak."

"I want to know how he got my e-mail address."

Cassie reached down to the red milk crate beside her holding temporary file dividers. She found last year's training course catalog that was mailed to all departments in the surrounding counties. She flipped through it, spotted what she remembered on the back of the catalog, and tossed it in Ash's lap. "That's how."

"My picture too? Man, I look like some fugitive from the seventies."

"You still do."

"Ooh…cruel, Cassie. You wound me."

"If you're coming back on shift you have to get a haircut," she pointed out.

She reached to the floor into the bag of chips she had carried back from lunch. Startled, she jerked her hand back up, then looked down. "Jack!"

Cole and Ash broke up laughing.

She very gingerly picked up J. J., the traveling mouse.

THIRTY-EIGHT

"Jack, where are the new curtain rods for the window in Cassie's bathroom?" Rachel asked, coming into the kitchen where Jack was working. He glanced back at her. It was Thursday, and he had recruited most of his family to help with the painting and wall-papering so it could be done in one long day.

"I set them inside the hallway closet so they wouldn't get tripped over." He shifted his paintbrush to his left hand and reached for a rag to wipe paint off the countertop where a break in the masking tape had let paint touch the caulking. "Leave them for me. I don't trust you to get the braces tight enough."

"Didn't I hang all the curtains in my apartment?"

"Didn't I fix all of them?" he countered, smiling.

"Fine." Rachel looked around. "Stephen, I need curtain rods hung. The wallpaper is finished."

"Hey—" Jack protested, looking over at Rachel. "I said I'd do them."

She nudged him aside to reach for a cold soda. "You're busy."

"So am I," Stephen replied, lifting the globe light fixture into place, "but I'm almost done. Jack, what do you think?"

Jack leaned back to see around his oldest brother Marcus. As usual Marcus was ignoring the debate going on between the rest of them. "Looks good to me."

Stephen used the power screwdriver and secured the fixture.

"I'm going to start on the wallpaper in the hall then," Rachel offered.

Jack pointed to the sack on the countertop. "The double rolls are there."

"Stephen, after the curtain rods, I need someone helping me with the wallpaper."

"I nominate Jack."

Jack smiled at Stephen. "You're taller. And I would hate to rob you of the fun."

"You just want to paint the ceiling in the living room."

"It is more fun," Jack agreed.

Laughter from the bedroom interrupted the football game commentary on the radio. Jennifer, Cassie, and Marcus's fiancée, Shari, had taken over painting in the bedroom and were having a great time. He had known Jennifer and Cassie would become friends. He hadn't expected them to shove the guys out of the room so they could have girl talk.

Benji wandered into the kitchen.

Jack nudged the ball of yarn, which had rolled up against the dishwasher, toward the kitten. B. J. pounced on it and tumbled over. In the space of a week the sleepy kitten had disappeared and been replaced with a kitten full of energy.

"Jack, I want a hug."

He barely got the paintbrush out of the way before Cassie invaded his space and wrapped her arms around him.

Bewildered, he looked over her head at Marcus. His brother just rescued the dripping paintbrush, offering no help on this situation at all.

Jack indulged Cassie and wrapped his arms around her, enjoying the chance to hold her.

She leaned against him, didn't say anything, and he got more confused as the moments passed. She rubbed her cheek against his shirt, tightened her arms, then stepped back. "Thanks." She disappeared toward the back bedroom before he could get a good look at her expression.

He turned to Marcus. "Do you understand women?"

"No."

Afraid he'd missed something, Jack was grateful for the clarification. "Okay, then." Since his brain had short circuited, he left it at that. He picked up the brush and slapped paint on the wall.

"You've got a mushy smile on your face."

"She likes me."

Marcus laughed as he punched his shoulder. "Good job, Jack."

Jack used a rubber mallet to tap the paint can lid down. "What was all of that about earlier?" The last of his family had headed home. In one long day Cassie's apartment had been transformed. The place smelled of drying paint and it was enough to give a person a headache. They opened the patio door for a while this afternoon despite the cold in order to air out some of it.

Cassie was rolling up paint-splattered newspapers. Her jeans were speckled by paint and her sweatshirt was marred by wallpaper paste. He was intrigued at the reality she was blushing. Jack reached over and tipped up her chin, amused. "Cassie?"

"Did you really tell Jennifer I was gorgeous?"

It was his turn to get a bit embarrassed. "Maybe." He remembered telling Jennifer Cassie was adorable; gorgeous had probably showed up in the description along the way.

"That was cute."

He grinned. "Worth a hug at least."

Cassie reached for the black garbage bag and shoved the newspapers inside. The plastic sheeting used to protect the furniture had been rolled and folded into the black trash bag.

Jack scanned the room, seeing a few pieces of furniture that were close but not exactly back in place. Once the paint had dried he'd directed Stephen and Marcus as they moved furniture back against the walls. "Do you want to unpack any of the boxes tonight? We could do your desk, or start on the new bookshelves."

"Another day. You might have energy to move but I'm a puddle of mush."

Jack laughed at the image. He gently rubbed her shoulder. "It was a very long day."

"I think it would have been easier to just move." She nodded to the bookshelf. "That was a really nice addition."

"You're welcome. Stephen likes to build stuff."

"The bookshelf should be full in a few weeks."

Jack got up to sort out the wallpaper remnants, deciding what should be kept for repairs and what small pieces should be thrown away. "Would it be okay with you if I just threw away the paintbrushes rather than try to clean them?"

"Sure."

Jack closed the garbage bag. "Your mouse didn't reappear."

"I think my mouse and Benji have been flirting with each other. Lisa looked everywhere to try and find her."

"My sister likes odd pets."

Cassie gathered up catalogs. There had been discussions with Rachel and Jennifer on what kind of new furniture she should consider buying. "Jennifer said you were joining her tomorrow?"

"Planning to." He sighed. "I'm going to get grilled." For the past six months the subject of religion had been a quiet undertone to his conversation with Jennifer. With the end of the cancer remission, conversations she had been willing to pace with time were now being brought forward.

"She just wants to talk. Why are you absorbing so much pressure about this?"

"I don't want to argue with her, Cassie. If the worst happens, Jennifer doesn't have much time. Having a division now—" He shook his head, finding the idea intolerable.

Short of agreeing with Jennifer on the issue of religion, he didn't know how to find the right words. Respectful disagreement was not how he wanted the conversation to end. That would hurt Jennifer. He would do anything he could to protect her. "Can Jesus stop Jennifer's cancer?"

"Yes."

"Will He?"

When she didn't answer, he looked over and found she had stopped what she was doing. "Jesus is not Santa Claus. He's God. There's a huge difference. He does whatever He wants."

"I find it fascinating that you believe in Him so absolutely." How was that possible?

"I know Jesus loves me."

"Even though He let you get burned?" he risked asking her. He had thought about it many times, thought he would offend her with the question, so he hadn't asked it before.

"Do you know what I decided back when I was lying in that hospital bed enduring the slow passage of time until the next shot of painkiller?"

Startled by an answer that again opened a door into what she had been thinking during those days, he stopped what he was doing and gave her his full attention.

Cassie raised her hand, flexed it, and the scars near her thumb tightened, whitened. "God made the ability to feel pain. He didn't have to, you know. He made the ability to feel pain and He also made it possible to feel joy. Should I hate Him for allowing one and praise Him for allowing the other? God knew what He was doing. I may not always agree, but that is part of what respecting His authority means."

She rubbed her thumb across her palm, glanced up at him, and smiled. "Jack, I personally know Jesus. I have no doubts about the fact He loves me. He helped me get through those long hours, sometimes minute by minute. I found out life is tough, but God is tougher."

"No matter how good she looks and tries to act, Jennifer is very sick."

"I know," she whispered.

"I'm supposed to believe Jesus is okay with this?"

"He's got a plan in mind that will maximize her joy. Jack, I know that—" She flung out her hand. "No, Benji!" She caught the kitten but she had already walked through paint. "Oh, Benji. White and blue paint in the same day..." Cassie got to her feet, talking to the kitten as she headed for the kitchen.

The phone rang as Cassie was coming back into the room. She gave Jack a frustrated look and turned to answer it. It was Linda; it quickly became apparent the conversation would go on for a while. The opportunity to talk lost, Jack got his coat, carried the trash downstairs to the dumpster, then carried the paint cans down to the car. *"Maximize her joy."* Cassie's perspective didn't mean Jennifer would necessarily get well. Jack sucked in a deep breath of cold night air. Jennifer had to get well. He couldn't handle losing a sister.

It felt good to be back at the bookstore. Cassie shoved the last box of Christmas decorations across the threshold into the storage room. The shelves Jack had helped her build were now filled with shipping boxes, packing tape, preprinted lists of current inventory specials, and rolls of bubble wrap. Jack had helped her custom build a worktable that could fit in the corner of the room so she didn't have to haul the shipping material into the other room when she filled orders.

Soon, this would once again be her full-time job. The arsonist wasn't going to linger out there for more than a few more weeks before Cole had enough information to locate him.

Cassie turned her attention to the next box of books to be priced. Linda had already entered them into the inventory database.

Jack was meeting with Jennifer today.

Lord, please let that conversation go well. Cassie was worrying about it, about how Jack was dealing with the subject of faith. He was obviously feeling pressured, and that was the wrong way to get anyone to consider such a fundamental question of who Jesus was. She hadn't helped matters.

She glanced at her watch. She was meeting Jack after he saw Jennifer, and she needed to get home in time to change.

Cassie looked around the bookstore.

It no longer felt like an albatross to see herself as a bookstore owner, to see the place where she put her passion. She enjoyed the department work, but she had missed this place. Her days here in the last few weeks had been more focused on filling orders and keeping up with the paperwork than stepping back and dreaming about where she wanted to take the business.

She found she missed that time to dream and it was a good thing to learn about herself. She no longer felt the attachment to the past and clinging to what had been as necessary to be content. There was a future here in the bookstore business.

And Jack would worry less about her.

She knew he was nervous about the job she was doing for Cole, rolling out to look for the arsonist. He didn't like her doing something that had that element of risk. And since she was nervous about him simply fighting fires, she well understood his concern.

"Hello, Jack." Tom let him into the hotel suite on the fourteenth floor.

Jack pushed his hands into his pants' pockets. "How is she?" he asked softly, worried, having received the call changing plans as he was getting ready to leave his apartment. Their lunch plans had been scrapped.

"Jack, I'm fine. Quit whispering to my husband," Jennifer said. She was stretched out on the couch by the large screen TV that had the news on. She set aside the book she was reading. She had received a number of books for Christmas, had been especially thrilled with Cassie's gift of an autographed copy of a T. Emmond mystery.

"She's fine," Tom reassured. "She's just ordered to the couch for the next few hours."

Jack crossed the suite to join Jennifer and leaned down to hug her. "Faking it, are you?"

"I pulled my back. Tom doesn't want me walking because he hates my shoes or some such nonsense."

"I'm going to ignore the fact you're questioning my medical advice," Tom called back to his wife as he picked up his pager.

"You're sure that is all?" Jack whispered to her. No disrespect to Tom, but Jennifer's medical opinion had been the one that always carried the most weight.

There was no hesitation or shades of gray in her reassurance. "Yes."

"Jen, I'm heading over to meet Marcus for lunch. Anything you need before I take off?" Tom asked.

"Tell my brother I want to see him and Shari for dinner before we fly east."

"Will do, honey. See you later, Jack."

"Tom."

Jack sank into the plush chair across from Jennifer, relaxing. She turned down the volume on the television then set aside the remote.

Appearances were deceiving. Her health was precarious. She was in that edge of reality with the remission ending and the next round of chemotherapy beginning. The last round had taken all her energy and left her voice so soft it had been a struggle to hear her. Jack had spent enough time staying with Jennifer during the last hospital stay that he knew the best hotels near the hospital. He wasn't looking forward to that return trip.

"It's going to take me a while to get used to this," Jennifer said.

"What?"

"Your suit and tie."

Jack ran his hand along the tie. It was burgundy and blue to match the dark jacket and wool slacks. "I'm taking Cassie out later." And he was trying his best to make a good impression.

"I like her."

Jack looked at Jennifer, hearing a lot more in those three words than were on the surface. Jennifer's opinion in this family carried a lot of weight. "What's the family grapevine opinion?"

"Very positive. She's upbeat in her outlook despite everything that happened. She surprised me a bit with that dry sense of humor. Lisa really enjoyed talking with her."

"Cassie was equally complimentary. She enjoyed herself." Jack stretched out in the chair, studying his sister. "I've got the rest of the afternoon free, so what would you like to talk about first?"

"Oh, I think I've got a few more dozen questions about Cassie to start with…"

He laughed. "You're so predictable."

"You're not. You surprised us with that invitation to bring Cassie to the party. I want to hear how you met her."

⚛

"You look a bit shell-shocked." Cassie leaned against Jack's arm to get his attention, worried about him. She wasn't used to Jack not joking and laughing, smiling at life. Dinner out had been enjoyable, but she'd felt like he was struggling to keep up with even the general conversation he offered. He had been subdued ever since he picked her up.

"What?"

She handed him the bowl of ice cream. She added chocolate and two cherries to the vanilla ice cream; the smiley face she had drawn was rather lopsided. They had come back to watch a movie after dinner but she didn't think his heart was in it. She curled up on the couch beside him, tucking her feet underneath her and tugging down the afghan. "What did you and Jennifer talk about?"

Jack smiled. "You." Then his smile disappeared. "Family history, her cancer. God. A lot about God."

Lord, what's wrong? This is a man who looks like he's been hit by a two-by-four. She rubbed his arm. "You've missed what I've said a few times. Do you want to just pass on tonight? You've got a lot on your mind."

"I'm sorry. I don't mean to be so scattered."

"Don't worry about it. I've been there many times."

He set aside the ice cream and pushed his hands through his hair. "Yes, it's probably best I head home."

"Call me later?"

"Sure."

She put her hand on his arm and squeezed it. "If you don't call me, I'm calling you."

"I'll call."

She pushed aside the afghan, then got up to fetch his coat from the hall closet. She waited by the door as he pulled it on. "Don't forget your gloves."

He tugged them out and slid them on, smiling at her as he did so.

"Want a hug?" she asked softly.

She'd taken a risk asking the question, but his expression of relief was deep and it confirmed she'd made the right decision. He opened his arms and she stepped into them, his arms wrapped tight around her. He sighed and she could feel the exhaustion in him. "It will be okay, Jack. All of it."

"Pray for me," he whispered.

Her throat closed. She hugged him tighter, fighting the tears. "Sure," she choked out.

When he finally stepped back, she searched his face, looking for anything that would help her know how to help. "She's dying, Cassie."

He was reeling from it. It was coming home to him emotionally, and he was walking the tightrope of figuring out how to accept it. For all the benefits of knowing Jennifer was sick, the extra time just made each step along the journey a roller coaster for her family.

"Love her, Jack. That's what she needs from you most," she whispered.

Jack gave a sad smile. "I'm sorry to ruin tonight."

"You didn't ruin anything. Go home, get some sleep, then call me."

He nodded. "Good night."

"G'night, Jack." She locked the door behind him. And she leaned her head against the door. *Lord, Jack needs hope.*

She rubbed the back of her neck, no longer afraid of the hard conversation, no longer afraid of how vulnerable it might make her. She wanted to help Jack more than she wanted to make it easier on herself. She hoped he'd call. She needed him to call.

The phone call woke Cole up. He pushed aside pillows and saw on the bedside television that Jay Leno was talking with an actor. Cole waited for Ash to get the phone; his houseguest was the one receiving most calls tonight as plans for the department New Year's Eve celebration were being put together.

At the third ring Cole forced himself to reach toward the phone. Only then did he see the clock and realize that rather than ten o'clock it was 1 A.M. and it was a replay of the *Tonight Show* on TV. He braced for news of another fire, a big one this time. "This is Cole."

"It's Rachel."

"Rae—" He sat up and turned on the bedside light. "What's wrong?" Had something happened to Jennifer? She rarely called him, and she'd never called before at this time of night.

"Your arsonist."

Cole blinked, surprised at the topic. "Did something happen?" he asked sharply, fear leaping inside at the very idea that she had also been touched by the events going on.

"No, nothing like that. I couldn't sleep, I was thinking about the cases."

She couldn't sleep…his voice softened. "You should have called me rather than lie there awake."

"What do you think I'm doing now?"

"Don't get annoyed. Tell me what you've been thinking about."

"It's just an idea."

Cole reached for the pad of paper on the nightstand, knowing with Rachel she didn't have what-if ideas, she had well-formulated suggestions. And her voice told him she thought this idea was significant.

"It's hyperbole, Cole. The mural, it's more than just a paint form he likes to use. It's a grandiose painting with things made larger than life. The words he chooses—he's doing the same thing. He's overblowing facts in the same way."

Cole started to click into what she had realized. She was on to something. He knew it as soon as she said it. And the implications were startling. He clicked on his pen and pushed the notebook to a blank page. The paper curled on him and he fought the spiral binding. Cole started offering specifics to Rachel, interested to get her reaction. "The word *murderer.*"

"Think smaller," she offered. "Someone might have come close to dying. He may have transformed what came close to happening into the conclusion of what it would mean had that death occurred."

A near fatal accident… Cole winced as he mentally thought through the size of a report listing injuries that had happened in the district over the last year. He'd have to have help to even get that report categorized. "Cowards."

"It's an extremely personal remark, again, a conclusion he reached. He probably knows the men who worked at that fire station or at least knows of something they did. They probably exercised normal caution and he saw it as timidity."

He was taking notes as fast as he could. "Liar."

"The most personal of all. Look for something you tried to accomplish that didn't happen. It would have affected him or someone he cared deeply about."

"Any suggestion for that one? Are we talking about an arson investigation that didn't get closure? A personal decision? A financial one?"

"I'm not sure, Cole. It does imply that you are a known figure to him, not just a name. I find it interesting that he set your trash on fire. That suggests he knew it had been done to your house before."

"Popcorn."

"Contrary to your assumption, I don't think it's a reflection of the nursing home fire in the sense of being a jab at what happened. The man who set that nursing home fire was a professional arsonist. Instead, I think the popcorn reflects an admiration of the man who set the fire and the reaction he got. Think about the popcorn as a way for him to suggest he's got the capability to be like that other arsonist."

"That man did arson jobs for profit motives."

"I think it's a good assumption that this man does have financial problems. You don't lash out without it being a reflection of intolerable stress."

Cole thought about that image she was drawing. The profile they had of this man was becoming more and more specific. Cassie had given him the rough age and appearance; the location and type of fires being started were good indications of his background; Rachel's suggestion was a very good look at how the man thought. He needed to find this man before someone got hurt. "Anything else strike you? This is good, Rachel."

Silence met his question. He twirled his pen, giving her time to think. He was surprised that she had spent her time unable to sleep thinking about this, but it was obvious her thoughts were more than casual. "Anything," he urged. "I'm not looking for professional conclusions here."

"The mural with no word."

Cole flipped some more notebook pages.

Rachel clearly hesitated over her choice of words. "That one is very serious, Cole. He went mute."

"He assumes he will no longer be heard," Cole concluded, understanding what she feared. And if he was done talking, it meant there would be an explosion coming.

"What's it mean that that message was left at Ash's home?"

"It means he knew Ash was gone and not likely to return for a while. A mural has to be painted in layers and allowed to dry between each one so the paint won't mix. Even spray paint takes a few hours to set. And it takes planning. I think he had visited Ash's home before because that trail of fire motif implies he thought long and hard about actually torching the house, then decided instead to leave just his signature."

His house had been trashed, Ash's just painted...the arsonist didn't want to burn a fireman's home? Cole wondered, and wrote himself a note to think about that some more. "What is the probability he also knows Ash?"

"Very high."

"The e-mail word *chicken?*"

"One of those cruel taunts, like a school yard pushing match."

Cole hesitated but had to ask. "And Jack?"

"It has always revolved around Jack and Gold Shift."

"Will he be targeted?"

"When is his next shift?"

"Today."

"Can you take him off the shift?"

"Rae—"

"Please."

"I can't."

"You have to."

"Rae—I can't." He had accepted the reality weeks before. He could protect Jack, but not at the price of robbing Jack of his job. "I'll talk with him," he struggled to reassure her. "I'll do everything I can short of taking away his job."

"Don't do this, Cole. Take him off duty before he gets hurt."

She would never forgive him if something happened. "I'm sorry."

She hung up on him.

Cassie struggled to follow Ash through the smoke-filled corridors of the nursing home. She'd helped eight nursing home residents get out, and there were more waiting to be rescued. There was no way to hurry now as the heat and smoke built. Over the radio came the terse messages of rescue crews as rooms were cleared throughout the building.

She swung her light along the room numbers: 1613, 1614, 1615. All rooms they had helped clear. The fire was above them, in corridors to the east. As soon as the last rooms were checked she would be glad to get out of here.

Ash's torchlight shot upward, and his hand shoved her hard. She hit the wall, an instant before something struck a glancing blow on her shoulder and she went down, training tucking her toward the wall with hands to protect her neck.

Something struck her air tanks, and then the world exploded with flames and weight, burying her, pinning her.

She was burning. She screamed as she realized she couldn't move. The debris was crushing her. The burns touched nerves and she coiled into her mind against the agonizing pain.

She was dying. She fought the panic and the pain. She wanted to live. Oh, she wanted so badly to live. She strained to try and move.

"Cassie!"

The yell was the most blessed sound she had ever heard. "Ash…" She couldn't think against the pain. "Get me out."

"Hold on. I'm coming, Cassie." Debris began to move from near her face. Ash strained against the beam pinning her.

Agonizing time passed. He couldn't move it. She desperately struck her free hand against anything she could reach. She couldn't wiggle out of the debris and he couldn't move it.

"I've got a fulcrum."

There was a moment in time when she felt the weight move and then it settled back. She was going to die here. She gasped against her air. Her partner was going to die here too because he wouldn't leave her, because she didn't have the strength to get free.

Her air tank began to chime. She was running out of air.

Ash started kicking the beam pinning her.

A good life, and she hadn't enjoyed it nearly as much as she should have. She'd been too busy trying to get ahead.

Her air ran out. Her ability to move her hand dropped, consciousness was fading.

Her mask was pulled off, the smoke and heat hit her face, and Ash desperately pushed his mask against her face. "Breathe, Cassie. Breathe," he ordered, choking to say the words as he got as low to the floor as he could.

She breathed, revived. Ash removed the mask and grabbed a breath. Then his mask was tight against her face again.

They were both going to die here. His air canisters had only a few more minutes of air than hers. She wanted so desperately to at least be able to tell him good-bye. The tears were choking her so hard she couldn't get the words out. Jesus, don't let me die.…

Her partner grabbed her free hand. She used what strength she had to squeeze it.

The shrill ringing phone woke her up. Cassie leaned her head over the side of the bed and heaved at the remembered tears, struggling to breathe. *Lord, the fire…* She fought to get away from the remembered panic. The memory was alive, in her memory, in her emotions, the panic so real she could taste the bitterness of the smoke.

She groped for the phone. "Hello," she choked out.

Silence, and then, "Cassie, what's wrong?"

"Jack, don't go to hell. Please don't go to hell. It's awful." She struggled to hold the phone, shivering, closing her eyes against the remembered flames.

"The fire."

She gasped a desperate half laugh. "The fire."

"Oh, honey."

"Promise me you won't go to hell."

"Cassie—"

"Come over and take me for a walk. We've got to talk."

His hesitation was brief. "I'm on my way."

Cassie had on her coat and gloves, her keys in her pocket, and was waiting in the downstairs landing when she saw Jack's car come into the lot. She went out to greet him and leaned into the hug he offered, wrapping her arms around him and resting against the solid comfort of the man.

His jacket was cold against her cheek and his arms strong around her. "Shh, it's okay." He rubbed her back as he whispered the words.

"I wanted to be a hero that day. I nearly became a victim."

"Fire doesn't respect a person, good or evil; it will grab and kill whomever it can reach."

"Satan is just like that, Jack."

He went still and she tipped back her head to look at him. "Jesus is alive. And unless you trust Him, someday you are going to be caught in a fire like hell that never ends."

He tightened his arm around her shoulders and pointed her to the walkway. "Come on. Let's walk."

There was no finesse to her approach tonight, only a heartfelt passion. If she offended him, she'd accept that. The hesitation to force the conversation had disappeared under the weight of her fear. If something happened to Jack during this arson investigation, she'd never be able to live with herself.

"When we found you and Ash in the nursing home, you were barely conscious. Do you remember what you were saying?"

She shook her head, puzzled. She'd avoided talking about that day, not wanting to relive the details any more than she had to.

"I was cushioning your head while we moved you to a backboard. You were whispering from a psalm the phrase 'The Lord is my shepherd' over and over again."

"I reached for Him that night and He was there."

"Jennifer said essentially the same thing, when she described the night she met Jesus."

She tightened her hand around his. "Don't wait for tragedy to strike like I did, Jack."

"Did you ever hate God over what happened, when you saw the burns?"

"A man I knew kissed them better," she whispered.

He dashed a glove across his eyes. "I've got so much on my mind it's hard to sort it out, Cassie. Heaven and hell, the Resurrection—it's a huge step to accept it all."

"Trust Jesus. Trust what you do understand. The rest will come. I'm scared for you, Jack."

He rubbed his gloved thumb across the back of her hand. "I appreciate that, Cassie. And I promise, I am thinking about it."

She searched his face, longing to find he meant it. She saw a reassurance there. She squeezed his hand. "Thank you."

"I'm so sorry you dream about the nursing home fire. I dream about the fires too, and it's hard to wake to those memories."

"The fear. And the sound of the fire…"

"The awareness that it's going to happen and there is no way to stop it," he finished for her.

"Yeah."

"They'll go away with time."

"Oh, I hope so."

He slowed her as they walked up the sidewalk. The apartment building lobby door had been propped open.

She tightened her hand on his. "Jack."

"Stay here."

She didn't listen but followed him instead.

Popcorn littered the hall.

"He was watching us, watching her," Jack said to Cole, feeling the fury and the helplessness. This was becoming so personal it was like living a real nightmare. He didn't know what to do with the fear. If he hadn't come back tonight, would it be a fire here matching the popcorn? He watched Cassie sitting in his car to keep warm, and he was terrified for her.

Police officers were sweeping the grounds, but they had found nothing so far.

"Go in for shift early, take her with you, sleep at the firehouse, and let me sort this place out."

"Cole…" Jack did not want to say the words but he had to. "If I go in to work, he'll strike. The man is escalating. Maybe it's better if I don't report in, if we change our plans."

His friend squeezed his shoulder. "I don't think it's going to matter to him anymore whether you're there or not."

"I can't live with someone getting hurt."

"The best thing to do is accept it's a foregone conclusion and be ready to respond when he next strikes. In case you didn't notice, he just acted close to the firehouse rather than at the edge of the fire district. Odds are good we're not going to have a long time to wait before he acts again. Get Cassie to the station. I'll join you once the canvass is done here."

FORTY

"Gage, couldn't you have at least tempered the article a bit?" Rachel scowled at her friend as her headache throbbed. She tossed the folded paper down on the table. "You waved a red flag in front of the guy." Gage had reported the mural, the words, the popcorn, and the sequence of eight fires in his Weekend Focus article. There was more information in the article than she had known.

She'd joined him for breakfast in order to talk about plans for New Year's Eve. She'd borrowed his newspaper. Now she wished she hadn't.

"Rachel, you can't have it both ways. You asked me to help you out. He's a serial arsonist, and that mural painting is a signature someone who knows him will recognize. This article is a public service. Someone knows the man and this will generate the leads Cole needs."

"Couldn't you have at least warned Cole?"

"I asked him for a quote. He knows. Quit scowling at me. I'm doing my job."

"You should have told me."

"Rae—"

She shoved back her chair "I'm going home."

"You just got here."

"And now I'm leaving."

"Sit down."

His quiet order caught her off guard. She looked back at him. "Sit down."

She sat.

"Jack knew this was running. Cole. Ash."

She sank back as what he said registered. "Jack is planning to use his presence on the shift to draw the arsonist out," she whispered.

Gage just looked at her.

She underestimated Jack so many times in the past; she'd done it again. "If he isn't on shift, the arsonist just goes underground to strike out another way."

"Jack's not going to take unnecessary chances. Cole won't let him. But they've got to do something."

She didn't want a noble brother; she wanted one who was selfish and thought of himself first. She rubbed at the headache. It was going to be a very long day and night until he came off shift.

"Finish breakfast. Stay for the day. I'd like the company."

"You just don't want to come to my place in order to hold my hand."

Gage smiled at her and nudged her orange juice toward her. "You can help me dust."

"Can I now tell you I told you so? You shouldn't have fired the housekeeper."

There was ice in the rain. Cassie leaned against the engine bay door watching the pellets bounce when they hit the pavement. She was scared. And the longer the day went, the more scared she got. The arsonist had been at the apartment building last night. Why? Following her, or worse, following Jack? Jack had just given her a hug this morning when she tried to raise the concerns and she understood why. He couldn't offer anything more definite but that silent reassurance. He'd protect her. That was what worried her the most. *Lord, protect Jack.* With night would come the odds of another fire. On top of that, there was this incoming weather disaster.

The weather station was on in the lounge. They had spent the day watching the ice storm come their direction. The front edge had arrived. The day before New Year's Eve, one of the busiest travel days of the year, and they had an ice storm coming through. Somehow Cassie didn't think people were going to be wise enough to stay off the roads. Mandatory callbacks of all shifts had begun forty minutes ago.

"Cassie, you're riding tonight on Engine 81. Check your gear."

She turned to look at Cole as he strode by, stunned. "Who, me?"

"You're drafted. And if I can get the blasted fax machine to work so I can get a waiver issued for Ash, he's drafted too. As soon as he gets here find him gear."

"Yes, sir."

"Has Ben reported in yet?"

"I haven't seen him."

"Holler when you do."

She nodded.

She was on active duty on Engine 81. It took her a moment for that to sink in. There was no question they would be rolling out nearly continuously during the next hours. If Cole was drafting her and Ash, he considered this to be an emergency shift requiring all manpower available. She hurried to her locker and started checking out her gear. She knew it was ready, but it wouldn't hurt to check it again.

"Cassie."

"Jack, don't protest to me. Cole said I was rolling out with you. Take it up with him."

His hand came down on her shoulder and she paused long enough to look around. "A face mask. You're going to need it to avoid frostbite," he said, handing her the blue cap. "And I asked for you."

"Oh, thanks."

"Thank me after you spend a few hours trying to walk on a skating rink. Ash was going through some gear a couple days ago. Do you know where he stored it?"

"The unassigned locker next to Frank's. Ash had checked out everything but the boots. I think some came from the warehouse earlier today."

"Your partner is riding with us in Engine 81 as well. Stay beside Ash throughout the night, understood?"

"Not a problem." She was willing to accept any conditions he set just so she wouldn't have to sit here at the station while they went out.

"Medical runs; I want you on the cardiac kit. If we hit a wreck and have to do an extraction, you're my mouse. Be prepared with the blankets to go under or into the wreck if necessary. Any signs you've acquired a taste of being claustrophobic?"

"Not a bit."

"Good. Where's Cole? We need a plow assigned full time to work with us tonight."

"Heading back to his office. He was working that problem earlier," she offered.

"Toss extra gloves and socks into the Engine 81 cabinet. You'll need them."

"Yes, lieutenant," she said, and meant it with absolute respect.

He grinned at her and tossed her a bright orange packet. "For your coat pocket." It was an instant hot pack; break the seal and it heated to 105 degrees. Jack glanced around the bay. "Bruce, find us at least one extra thermos of coffee. Ash takes it sweet like Cassie."

FORTY-ONE

"Can you get in there?" Jack leaned in near Cassie to be heard above traffic.

She shone her light on the crumpled metal of the van tailgate. She had to squint as stinging pieces of ice were striking her face. "I can get in there." The van had been broadsided by a sedan and then hit from behind by a taxi. It was the third accident of the night she had worked.

"In the passenger side door of Engine 81, there's a canvas bag with a Velcro tab on top. You'll find a handheld tape player, a pair of child sized earphones, and a bunch of *Sesame Street* tapes. Get them and a thermal blanket. Try to hold the boy still. He's going to react when we take the Jaws of Life to the roof, and I don't want him moving that leg. I'm certain it's fractured."

Cassie nodded.

She struggled the ten feet back to the engine, the scene lit by its flashing lights and halogen strobe. Walking on ice was impossible and more than one firefighter had fallen. As tough as the job was, she loved being back on the job. It was good to be useful again. She was getting proficient at how Jack liked to work.

Even with gloves her fingers were frozen. She struggled to get the door open. *Sesame Street* tapes: It shouldn't have surprised her knowing what she did about Jack and his habit of being prepared, but it did. She was grateful he had them available.

With the blanket and the cassette tapes, Cassie worked her way to the boy, her world closing down to the size of the air pocket inside the crumpled vehicle. She was able to use Ash's help to get leverage.

"Hi, Peter." The boy was screaming and for once she was glad she was partially deaf. "I'm Cassie." She shoved aside the coloring books that had tumbled out of a child's backpack and winced when her knee landed on a metal Matchbox car.

The boy was buckled into a car seat, but when the impact had happened the entire bench seat had been thrown off its tracks and had crunched into the driver's seat. The boy's left foot had been caught. The paramedic had been able to work an air splint around his lower leg and inflate it. Now they just had to get a way to move the boy out. If they tried to bring him out the way she had wrestled her way in, his leg would have to turn. Cassie strained to get the blanket across him.

She clicked on the cassette player and the sound of the familiar music startled the boy into stopping midcry to look around at her. "This is for you," she reassured, adjusting the volume and then slipping the headphones on him. She used the blanket to wipe his wet face and running nose. The screams had become broken sobs. She put her arm across him and silently gestured to Jack for him to get started.

Exhausted, feeling a crick in her neck that refused to ease, Cassie stood back as the ambulance pulled away. The boy had been whimpering rather than crying, clearly relieved to be out of the van, clutching the bear the paramedic had offered him. His mom had already been transported to the hospital. Both were stable. It was the way the accidents were supposed to end.

"Good job."

She looked over at Jack and offered a weary smile. "Thanks."

The sleet had temporarily ended but the wind had picked up. She adjusted the face mask, knowing exactly how Jack had felt on Christmas working in the snow.

"Climb up in the engine and thaw out while we finish the cleanup. Ash and I need another ten minutes," Jack recommended. Behind him the whine of a tow truck winch started.

Cassie nodded, more than willing to accept the offer. "Deal."

She was grateful for Bruce's help up into the engine cab. She gave a relieved sigh as she stripped away the frozen face mask and the cold gloves.

"Coffee, drinkable hot."

"Thanks, Bruce." She warmed her hands around the cup as she drank the coffee.

Cole's vehicle was parked immediately in front of Engine 81, its lights flashing. She watched Cole walk cautiously from the wreckage back to his vehicle.

Jack and Cole made a good team.

Tones sounded. It was for Company 81 but served as a heads up for Cole. She saw him duck into his vehicle and knew he was talking to dispatch. He got out of the vehicle and called something over at Jack. Moments later tones for the engine and truck crews sounded.

She opened the door and braved the wind to hear Cole.

"We've got a report of smoke at an apartment complex. We're pulling out from here to check it out. Rescue 81 will finish up with the taxi driver and join us."

Cassie could feel the fear and dread building. It was a fire call. She was glad she was not responsible for driving the rig. A million dollar rig on icy roads was not a job for the faint of heart. She leaned forward from the back bench to hear Jack as she worked the buttons on her fire coat and turned up her collar. "Make sure you keep an eye on where the hose teams are to try and keep out of the water mist."

She nodded. She'd worked many fires during the winter and the advice was something she knew well. Bathed in water and moving into the wind was a prescription for frostbite.

"Do you think it's him?" she asked, worried.

"Maybe. If conditions are such you are able to look around the scene, you have to stay with Cole or Ash. No exceptions."

Wandering around on her own was the last thing she wanted to consider. She had no desire to meet him alone. "Will do." She was grateful Ash was with her. Her partner was checking his gear beside her as if nothing unusual was going on. He was a good man to have around in a crisis.

Cassie leaned forward and peered into the night. She recognized the red and white light display on a white house with pillars. She had been in this area recently, and they were heading to an apartment complex— "Jack, this street. There's only one apartment complex out this way."

He nodded, his expression turning grim as he picked up the radio to call Cole.

The smoke wasn't heavy, there was no sign of flames, but it was definitely not a false alarm. The smoke curled into the night sky lazily, not sure of its movements, with the exception of the east end of the building where the rise of smoke was stronger, indicating more heat was present.

It was either good luck or bad that they had approached the one building she and Jack had visited when viewing one of the apartments to rent. Had she wanted to move, this complex had the best layout of those she had looked at. Engine 81 pulled to the front of the building, as close as they could get given the cars in the handicapped spots.

Cassie hurried to join Cole as they did a fast planning powwow. "Jack and I were in this building less than two weeks ago to look at an apartment."

"Where exactly?"

"East wing, one of the end apartments."

"Jack—you, Ash, and Cassie check the east wing. Bruce and Nate, handle the west. This is defensive only, so take no undue risks. I'll start generating a head count out here. Feed me temperature and smoke data, and I'll have the next arriving units laying hose. But dispatch just warned it's going to be a few minutes. They've got a pileup on the tollway slowing them down."

Cassie looked to Jack for directions. "We go in carrying air. Be ready to don it at a moment's notice."

She walked carefully across the slick pavement. Ash was already bringing out the self-contained breathing apparatus canisters. Cassie accepted one. The weight helped, making it easier to walk on the slick sidewalks. Cassie held on to that truth as she tightened the harness and clipped the face mask to the harness within immediate reach. She refused to consider the fact that this time she was wearing SCBA with a good likelihood she would need to use it. "Relax, Ash."

"Stay between Jack and me." He was worried about her and not bothering to hide it.

She smiled and clamped her hand on his forearm, dislodging a thin film of ice from his coat as she did so. "Fine with me. You carry the ax, I'll handle the extra torchlight."

The number of people coming from the building had slowed. Cassie winced at the realization two of the ladies had taken enough time to retrieve not only purses and coats, but one was carrying a photo album and the other wall pictures.

Bruce jammed a wedge-shaped piece of wood under the front door as a doorstop. He followed Nate into the building.

Building fire alarms were piercing.

Cassie followed Jack inside. She got hit with a wave of warm air. The lights were on in the building, the hallways wide and empty of people. It smelled smoky but no smoke was visible. It was a smell not much different than a grill in a neighbor's backyard, a lingering whiff of something close to lighter fluid.

"We've got dormant water," Jack indicated, using his torchlight to point out the sprinkler head on the ceiling. "Watch for heat spots that may suddenly trigger it."

Ash used the fire department master key to unlock the steel box where building master keys were kept. He handed keys to Bruce and Nate. Cassie closed her glove around hers. It was an odd key, *T* shaped for grip, master fit to open every door in the building. She nodded and pushed the strap around her glove.

Jack led down the east hallway.

"I bet it's a Christmas tree fire. I'm smelling whiffs of pine," Ash said.

"There's something sharper underneath it." Jack paused. "What's that?"

Ash used the handle of the ax to turn over the package. "Someone dropped a Christmas present as they rushed out."

Cassie nudged the box to the side with her foot so it wouldn't be trampled as she left.

From behind them came the sound of voices as Bruce encouraged someone to go outside, insisting it was necessary even if no smoke was visible and it was bad weather out there.

They reached the turn in the hallway into the east wing proper. Smoke lingered in the hallway, hovering around the ceiling and surrounding the hall lights, creating an impression of a fog coming down.

The hall was warm and edging toward hot, but still no flames were visible. Cassie watched the walls and the ceiling for any clue of the source.

Jack pointed her to the first apartment door to the left, Ash to the first one on the right. The three of them moved down the hallway checking doorways. They opened one apartment after the next, checking to confirm everyone was out.

The fourth apartment on the right had small wisps of smoke coming from under the door. The smoke burned her eyes.

Jack tentatively closed his glove around the doorknob and tried to turn it. The door was locked.

"Go to air. Cassie, stay within arm's reach of me."

She nodded, slipped off her helmet, and donned the mask. Her breath hissed inside the mask and her hands grew clammy at the thought of what she was doing.

Jack reached over and rested his hand heavily on her shoulder, setting the maximum distance. "Ash, open it. We search clockwise."

Ash nodded and popped the lock open.

There was a quiet whoosh and an inward flowing breeze as the room drew in air. It was an eerie feeling. The apartment was dark.

Cassie felt her fear level leap. The movement of air was a good indication the fire had found itself a flume for the heat.

Cassie shone her torchlight inside and saw only thicker smoke. It was hard to tell if it was coming from a ceiling or a floor fire; the smoke simply hovered.

She looked toward Jack, letting him make the critical decision. He nodded and gestured for Ash to watch the ceiling. Jack led them inside single file. Cassie was grateful to be between Jack and Ash.

A cat darted out between their feet, startling Cassie and causing Ash to trip a step back. It was an occupied apartment. And most residents rushing outside would probably have stopped to grab their pets. Odds had just increased to fifty-fifty that someone was still in here.

It was the same layout as the apartment she had looked at briefly during her short consideration of moving. Jack led the way through the smoke toward the bedrooms.

She could hear the fire.

FORTY-TWO

The apartment was laid out with the bedrooms to the left and the kitchen and living room to the right. Jack made the turn toward the bedrooms, hating the way the hallway narrowed down. Two bedrooms on the left, bathroom straight ahead, Jack moved forward from memory.

He stopped at the doorway to the master bedroom, feeling incredible heat. He put his hand back to pause Cassie, not sure what they were facing. His light disappeared in the smoke, touching what might be the edge of a bed but unable to pierce the smoke. His light crisscrossed the floor, then stopped. Someone had tried to reach the door and gone down about three feet inside the room.

"Cassie, with me. Ash, see if you can break out a window."

He moved toward the victim. An adult male. Cassie's light joined his and together they turned him over. "Chad." Jack was horrified to see someone he knew. He had been expecting smoke inhalation, ready to grab and carry to get him out, but it took a moment for the realization to set in that there was blood staining the man's chest. What had been a dark blue shirt had a huge stain.

"No."

Jack tightened his hand on Cassie's arm to steady her. The man's stiffness was rigor mortis setting in. His light picked up the gun the man had been lying on. Self-inflicted? Murder? He couldn't tell.

Glass shattered. Ash took out both windowpanes and the room exhaled, smoke and heat rushing toward the new vent as a warm wind. All the panes had been in the window, the front door had been locked, the apartment hadn't shown an obvious source of entry. Jack mentally cataloged it as he tried to decide if they could stop the fire so as not to disturb the scene. That suggested suicide. The fire, something much more sinister. Ash moved back toward them, his torchlight now able to pierce through the clearing smoke.

Jack saw something that frightened him, and he grabbed his torch and swept it up. He lifted his light to the wall behind the large headboard.

There was a mural on the bedroom wall. A mural of flames. Big, bold, red flames. It shocked him.

Cassie got to her feet, locked her hand onto his shoulder, and aligned her light with his.

The word atop the mural of fire was huge. *Burn.*

Fear rippled through Jack's muscles from his toes up to his back.

The huge word flickered.

The paint peeled back.

He shoved Cassie toward the open windows. "Get out!"

The wall exploded toward them.

"I've got five trapped. Go to three alarms," Cole ordered the dispatcher coolly, not having time for emotions. Around him people were screaming and trying to run backward, falling on the slick pavement. Rescue crews were not going to get here in time. He needed help. Unfortunately he only had himself.

The dispatcher was swift to put out tones.

Natural gas, that was his first hunch. The explosion had ripped through the back of the east wing of the building. He couldn't see the wall that had collapsed at the back of the building, but he saw the effects the instant it blew out. The crown of the roof snapped and the second floor shifted backward.

Lord, have mercy. Cole was depending on the truth of that mercy. He dropped air on his back. Five people. He didn't have the wisdom of Solomon, but he now needed it. He had two in the west wing hopefully only trapped; he had three in the east wing who were likely injured. And he could only go one direction.

The police officer working to keep residents back got a terse message from Cole. "When firefighters arrive, tell them three are down in the left wing and two in the right. Do whatever you must to keep other people out. Untrained help won't be a help, no matter how good the intentions." He looked at the man hard to make sure that message was received. "This building is going to collapse at any time." Unsaid was the simple reality that five firefighters might give their lives if that happened, but he'd allow no one else to join them.

The cop grimly nodded.

Cole headed into the building to try to reach Bruce and Nate. It would take more than one to have a chance to reach the others.

FORTY-THREE

"Nate, pass him across." Cole braced his feet to take Bruce's weight. It made more sense to go out a window than try and work back through the hallway. The shock wave of the explosion had taken out almost all the windows.

Considering what might have happened, Cole was relieved Bruce only had broken ribs to deal with. He lowered the injured man as carefully as he could to the ground. Nate dropped to the ground beside them.

"Leave me here. You two go get the others out," Bruce bit out, his hand fighting the straps to remove the air pack.

"You can walk if you have to?" Cole asked.

"Yes…go."

Additional help still had not arrived. Cole looked at Nate. "Let's try to get in through the back of the building."

Cassie was looking up at Ben. He hovered over her, blocking the worst of the stinging sleet. She was outside, the shattered wall lying around her dotting the snow. She'd been blown through it. She struggled to think as adrenaline surged, as the agonizing impression formed that he was the man she'd seen watching the Wallis house fire. "Ash. Jack—"

"They're in there?"

She struggled to nod, her ears ringing with a white noise that surrounded and swallowed her. She fought the nausea to turn her head.

It had exploded. The outside wall of the apartment had blown out. Part of the second floor had collapsed into the void. It was a blackened shell with a glowing red flame flickering in the heart of the destruction. The fire was beginning to spread.

She was left lying in the snow as Ben headed into the building.

Cassie rolled onto her stomach, gagging. She fought the waves of pain as she struggled to try and get to her feet.

She had to get inside.

She had to find a way inside.

Lord… She fell again, hard.

"Cassie!"

Cole caught her. She wanted to cry at not having seen it. No fires on Black Shift— "Ben. It's him. He's the arsonist."

Gloved hands caught her face and helped lift it. "You're sure?"

She nodded, and she felt betrayal so deep it hurt to breathe. Not Ben. Not someone she admired.

"Nate, get her farther back," Cole ordered. He headed into the building.

Jack fought to keep focused. The pain in his shoulder was not yet a broken bone, but it was agonizing to be alert and trapped. He was facedown, the only thing visible the flickering light of flames and the edges of something wooden. Where was Cassie? Jack fought against the panic and the fact he couldn't move. He was going to die here, and it wasn't nearly as ugly a thought as knowing Cassie was somewhere in this exploded rubble.

He listened to the hiss of his air exhalation valve. The heat was building. His air was running down. He hoped they went after Cassie first.

Jesus.

The awareness of someone coming back from the dead now rippled as something more than a myth. The desire to live was incredible. If Jesus truly was the author of life and had overcome death…

He was crying inside the mask. He remembered the words the thief said to Jesus as he hung on the cross beside Him: *"Remember me when you come into your kingdom."* Jack desperately wanted Jesus to remember him too. *Jesus, I'm a sinner. Save me. I don't want to die.*

He struggled to get air into his lungs. He was at the mercy of someone he couldn't see, could only believe in. A calm replaced the fear. Lie still, conserve energy. When his air tank ran dry, push off the mask and hold on.…

Cole yanked Ash from under burning carpet. Cole's elbow struck a walnut dresser lying on its side and his hand momentarily went numb. The owner of the apartment above had loved walnut furniture, and all of it was in the way now that the floor above had collapsed. "Hold on, Ash."

The man had broken his leg but the time for finesse was later. Where was Jack? Where was Ben? He had to prove Cassie wrong. It couldn't be Ben. Not a friend, not a man who had spent his life fighting fires.

"Cassie forgot to say getting buried in rubble was like being landed on by an elephant," Ash bit out, able to help some by protecting his leg as Cole finally pulled him clear. "Did you get her out?"

Cole paused long enough to grab a breath and get a firmer grip. "She's got a concussion." He was guessing on that but it fit her total disorientation and unco-ordinated movements trying to get up.

"Jack?"

"Not yet. Let me get you to Nate, then I'll find him," Cole gasped out. This was a job that needed several people; instead he had Nate and himself.

"Chad's dead."

Cole felt like he'd been kicked in the gut. "Chad?"

"We found him just before the inferno ripped through. Gunshot to the chest, maybe self-inflicted. He was lying on the gun."

Cole tightened his grip on the back of Ash's coat and hefted him into a fireman's hold. Ice hit Cole and a sharp wind bit as he got out of the protection of the building.

"Cassie, knock it off!" Cole ordered. She was fighting Nate, trying to get up. The sight scared him to death, for her movements were uncoordinated and would increase injuries she was too adrenaline blocked to feel.

"Dump me beside her," Ash ordered. "I'll deal with her."

Cole lowered him down as carefully as he could, grateful it looked like Ash had a simple fracture. Cassie looked horrible. Her face wasn't white as much as it had a grayish cast. The only thing keeping her moving had to be adrenaline. And it was obvious by her actions that she was not thinking clearly.

Ash stripped off his gloves and started unbuckling Cassie's fire coat. "Both of you go get Jack," Ash ordered. Ash turned Cassie toward him and gingerly cupped her face. "What did you do to yourself, partner?"

Confident Ash would be able to help her, Cole headed back inside the building with Nate.

Cole worked his way back into the destroyed apartment, knowing where Ash had been found. He made a guess that if Jack had been with him, he would be buried somewhere nearby.

There was a gas line feeding the flames, and the fire was growing in intensity. As more and more material and carpet ignited, the smoke became denser.

The only thing working in their favor was the way the structure had settled. There was a wind tunnel effect coming through, pushing the smoke back into the structure and keeping the air near the floor clear, if freezing cold. It created an odd explosion of sparks upward as the dampness in the air snapped and popped as it was blown into superheated air.

Nate grabbed his arm and pointed.

Cole added his torchlight to Nate's. In the wavering light Cole spotted Jack by the smiley face on the back of his fire coat.

Seeing his position was almost a dagger in itself.

The fire was close. Getting from here to there…even if they could get to him, digging him out was going to be nearly impossible before the fire swept the area.

"Nate, we need new sixty-minute cylinders, an extra one for Jack, and a cutting torch to deal with that ductwork. On the second trip be thinking about how to suppress that gas line fire."

Nate nodded and immediately headed out for the gear.

Cole shoved aside furniture and ducked down to get under the door tilted on its side now holding up part of the ceiling.

He tested if an overturned bookshelf would take his weight. He didn't have room to move it aside. He climbed over it and winced when the back panel gave way and his booted foot crashed through. The heat started to make him feel like he was getting a sunburn.

"Jack." He slapped the man's leg when he got near, looking for a way to get him free.

"About time."

"Get on air," Cole growled.

"Get this thing off my shoulder and I can move. It's hot."

"That thing is a personal safe and it's wedged under what looks like the central ductwork for the furnace."

Cole heard his response but decided to ignore it. He had no choice but to wait for Nate. He started moving away anything he could that would burn. The mural would have been interesting to see as a whole. Cole tossed chunks of plaster out of the way, the red flames in the paint mirroring the reality of what was around him.

"It was a good painting. My gift to Chad when he used to dream about being a fireman as a child. It's been a long time since I painted, but the skill returns." The voice rasped from the wrong side of the room.

Cole froze.

He looked across Jack and into the dark building where the only light came from reflected flames.

The man clicked on a torch.

He stood in the apex of the wind tunnel, the hot air and sparks blowing toward and swirling around him. Ben. Cole took a deep breath and suppressed the emotion that surged as the horrible reality was confirmed. He had suspected it might be Chad, but never Ben. Cole ignored the danger obvious in Ben standing there and kept moving debris.

"The painting haunted Chad after the accident. He wanted to paint over it, but I wouldn't let him. I kept promising him he'd come back to work. But I couldn't give him back the job he wanted, being a firefighter. He shot himself, Cole."

Cole wanted to reply and couldn't afford to get drawn into the pain the man was feeling. He heard a shrill hiss and knew the gas line was building toward another explosion. He was not going to let Jack be caught in it.

"The department destroyed us. My marriage. My nephew. And they'll destroy the community if they don't reopen the fire stations they closed."

"Why Jack? What did he ever do to you?"

Jack had stopped moving, hearing the conversation.

"I sleep during Red Shift. Jack was the one on duty when I was awake. Awful, isn't it, the randomness of who gets to be a victim?"

Cole squeezed Jack's leg to apologize for what he was about to do. He put his strength into shifting the safe, knowing that because of how it was resting, moving it would actually cause the corner to dig harder into Jack's shoulder. If he could get two inches, Jack had a chance of sliding back....

The best Cole could do was raise it a fraction of that distance. He was forced to let it settle.

"Use this. I went into the fire to get it." There was irony under the words. Ben tossed him a crowbar.

Cole picked it up.

Ben grabbed the ductwork from his side and put his weight on it, shifting it back. "All they had to do was restore the stations they closed, Cole. Rehire the men they let go. That's all they had to do."

"Shut up," Cole said coldly. The safe slid up ever so slightly. "Move," Cole ordered Jack, as he fought to keep the safe from slipping back.

Jack's hand grabbed hold of Cole's boot to use it as a leverage. Jack pulled himself back. The rubble shifted and Cole got his feet knocked out from under him. He landed hard atop Jack and rolled.

The dragon lashed out.

Cole felt agonizing heat brush his face.

Jack grabbed the back of Cole's coat and yanked him back. "Move!"

Cole struggled to his feet. He pushed Jack ahead of him. As soon as Cole saw Jack was able to get out under his own power, he turned back toward Ben. They were divided by the ductwork that had come down. He reached out his hand. "Come on."

"Not this time."

Cole heard his tank begin to chime.

"Ben—"

The man turned back into the burning apartment.

Cole wanted to dive after the man. Ben was making his decision, and it was agonizing to realize Cole didn't have the time to change it. He prayed for words but none came. He closed his eyes, turned, and struggled to get across the rubble. Twenty seconds later he was breathing icy night air.

A second explosion ripped through the building.

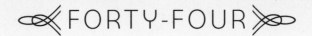

FORTY-FOUR

"You look horrible."

Cole struggled to open his eyes. The emergency room was not the place to try and overcome a headache. He ached. He licked lips that were cracked. "Rae."

"You got a fire sunburn."

He gave a painful smile. Her hand touching his was so tentative it felt like a feather. "Some," he whispered. Most of the flash burns from the second explosion were at worst first degree; they'd heal. "How's Jack?"

"Pacing until he can see Cassie. Jennifer is keeping him company."

The relief was incredible.

"Thanks for getting him out."

There was a lot he could say. About duty, about friendship, about feeling responsible for what Ben had done. He passed it all by to say what he wanted to most. "You're welcome," he whispered.

Cole struggled with his memories of the man he had known and the man he had changed into. It was senseless. Ben had been pushing him on the budget, for more personnel, to get at least one of the closed stations reopened, but Cole had missed the desperation Ben felt.

Ben felt he had to force change to happen—setting the fires, focusing on Jack and on department officers to get across the point they were stretched too thin to fight the arson fires. Using popcorn and vicious words to make his actions something the public would react to with alarm. Making it personal, raising the stakes by threatening a former victim— Cassie being in trouble had gotten Cole a call from the fire chief and a push to find a solution. Eventually what Ben had been after would have happened. Only Chad had cut it short by taking his own life. Had Chad read the paper that morning and realized the arsonist was Ben? The young man had been smart; the mural information Gage presented would have been enough to convince Chad it was Ben.

Cole had failed them both. Rae's hand slid under his. "Can I stay a while?" She spent her career trying to heal trauma from events like this.

She was doing that for him, being here right now, trying to heal his trauma. His hand closed around hers. "I'd like that." He took a shallow breath feeling the pain in his ribs. "No jokes."

Her smile was worth the attempt at humor. "No jokes," she promised.

⊰⧓⊱

"Jack, sit down."

Jack paced the ER waiting room and ignored Jennifer. "I should have seen the warnings when I went toward the master bedroom. I let Ash and Cassie stand there as the wall blew up."

Jennifer grabbed his hand, caught him by surprise, and pulled him down to the chair beside her. "Great, blame yourself for what Ben caused. Just because he's dead and you can't be mad at him does not mean the answer is to be mad at yourself."

He rubbed his sore shoulder that had been so bruised he could not lift his arm without agony. "Ash busted his leg, Cassie's got a concussion—" Jack shook his head.

"Would you quit changing the diagnosis? She does not have a concussion. The doctor said a bad headache and a disoriented inner ear impact with her balance."

"What's the difference?"

"She'll want to go home in the morning is the difference."

Jack pushed his hand through his hair. "How long before they are going to let me see her?" he muttered.

"You asked me that three minutes ago. Soon."

He got up to pace again. Cassie had been his responsibility. Instead of protecting her, he'd come close to killing her.

"I know what Cassie must have felt when she got hurt. Trapped, desperately worried about friends, hoping for help to arrive, dependent on others. It was awful."

Jennifer didn't say anything. He looked over at her.

"Cassie needs someone who understands her. God gave you a chance to taste what she went through. I'd consider it a gift."

He smiled. "One I would have been glad to pass on. But it did get me off the fence to make a decision."

"You chose to believe," she whispered.

He simply nodded.

"I'm glad."

He leaned over and hugged her. "Between you, Rachel, Cassie...the three of you are pretty persuasive. Hell is a scary place if tonight was any glimpse of what it will be like."

"It will be much worse."

"Will Jesus heal you, Jen?"

"He's the I Am. He doesn't explain Himself. But I trust Him. If He heals me, it will be a gift I'll treasure. If He doesn't...there's something gracious still in His plans for me, something that will bring Him glory. He loves me, Jack. I trust Him."

The doctor came into the waiting room, interrupting them.

"Cassie, can I see her?" Jack demanded.

"She's being admitted for the night for observation. You can go with her as she's transferred to a room if you like."

"Definitely."

"Do you want the lights off, not just dimmed?"

"They're okay," Cassie reassured Jack. She was relieved to finally be done with the moving around and the doctors prodding her.

Her headache had become a throbbing reality. The world still had the nasty habit of spinning when she moved her head. The explosion had set her left inner ear ringing, and as a result, messed up her sense of balance.

Jack had pulled over a chair but it was obvious he was having to force himself to stay sitting. She could see the tension in him, or rather inferred it from her impression of him. Even with her glasses, which she'd begged him to find for her since she hated a fuzzy world, at the moment nothing was very clear given this headache.

Jesus, thank You for keeping him safe. Jack could so easily have been killed.

"Tell me what happened," she whispered. "I remember your hand coming back and propelling me toward Ash. Then the next thing I know I'm looking up at the night sky with Ben standing there."

"He had been setting the fire to cover up Chad's suicide. He wanted a fire that would crawl through the walls and floors. I got a glimpse of the holes between joists in the drywall at the base of the walls just before the paint began to peel back. The way the wall came back at us, something explosive ignited."

"He disabled the building sprinklers?"

"Either that or they never worked."

"Please don't blame yourself," she whispered.

He touched the back of her hand. "Is this going to bring back all the memories of the nursing home?"

It was a worried question and it brought a lot of comfort that he would ask. "If it does, it will fade. How's Cole?"

"He got caught by the second explosion and has some flash burns. He'll recover."

Jack walked back to the window.

Cassie watched him and sensed there was a lot more here than what he had said so far. "Are you going to tell me?" she asked softly.

He was prowling around the hospital room struggling to push down emotions. She'd seen it before.

He sank back down in the chair beside her bed and buried his head in his hands, raking his fingers through his hair. "Jennifer's here. It's so hard, Cassie. I don't want to accept she is dying. I have no choice but to accept it."

Her heart hurt at that broken admission from him. She knew how tight Jack held to his family, how close he was to Jennifer. He would do anything to protect her. "If you don't accept it, you're just going to hurt yourself," she whispered.

"Jesus loves her as much as I do?"

Tears filled Cassie's eyes. She felt the depth of those quiet words. "More."

"I know Jesus is alive; I got past that hurdle tonight while I lay there helpless. It's finally more plausible that He is who He claimed to be than not. I just resent not being the one in charge when it's Jennifer we're talking about."

Tears welled up in her eyes, of relief that he had finally wrestled through the question of who Jesus was, of sadness that he was so deeply hurting. Cassie shifted her hand to his shoulder. "Being a follower isn't so bad. Jack—" she waited until he looked at her—"when it's time for Jennifer to go to heaven, let her go with grace. That's the gift you most need to give her."

He looked at her and in the silence Cassie finally saw if not peace, then at least acceptance.

"Jesus loves her," Cassie whispered. "Really loves her."

His hand brushed back her hair. She closed her eyes and relaxed into the touch. She was so thankful he believed. Where this was going now… He leaned over and kissed her forehead. "Get some sleep."

The one good thing about a hospital on a holiday weekend was that dawn came and lightened the room before a nurse appeared to interrupt the peaceful stillness. Cole could see the edge of pink in the dawn and could tell the coldness outside by the occasional brush of wind against the windowpanes. Cole heard footsteps in the hall and turned to look as the door was slowly pushed open.

"Cole?"

He raised his hand to warn Jack.

Rachel was asleep. He'd been watching her for the last hour. She was asleep in one of the hospital chairs, curled sideways, her legs drawn up, her head resting against the curve in the high back of the chair. It had to be the most awkward place to sleep. It was a tribute to her fatigue that she slept without any sign of movement.

Cole saw Jack's expression soften and shared that reaction. Rachel had come up last night when they transferred him from the ER to a room, had helped in so many small ways to make the transition easier to accept. Just having her available to make calls for him had been invaluable. The burns weren't too serious, but the smoke inhalation was enough to make him glad he was flat on his back. He thought they talked about her getting a lift home with Frank, but now that he thought about it, she'd just nodded as he gave her options.

"I'm going to take Cassie home," Jack whispered. "She's getting stircrazy at the idea of staying."

"Good. Thanks. You'll keep her company tonight for New Year's Eve? I don't want her even thinking about going to the department party."

"I will."

Cole nodded toward Jack's arm. "How's the shoulder?" Cole still hated the memory of what he'd been forced to do to get Jack out.

Jack stopped at the side of the bed. "It aches but I'll live."

Cole raised his hand to his chin and looked at Jack enquiringly. "How bad's my sunburn?"

"Enough Rachel will want to sympathize but not enough Jennifer will do more than suggest you swallow aspirin."

"That's what I thought." He glanced at Rachel. "She stayed the night."

"She likes you."

"Yeah. I think so. It feels nice."

"Do you want a lift home later today? I can plan to come back in."

"I'll call if I do. Before I make plans I want to hang around and see when Ash is going to get released." He didn't want to ask but he needed to. "Is Gage here?"

"Working on his follow-up piece," Jack confirmed.

"If you see him, please ask him to come up." Cole knew he needed to talk to the man professionally but also for much more personal reasons.

"I'll ask him to come up." Jack nodded to Rachel. "Take care of her."

"I plan to," Cole reassured, feeling it as a promise.

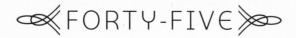

FORTY-FIVE

"Are you falling asleep before midnight?" Cassie leaned over the edge of the couch to look down at Jack. He was stretched out on the floor, his head resting against a pillow near the center of the couch, his eyes closed. She was now wide awake and headache free. He wasn't in so good a shape. "The new year is eighteen minutes away."

"Come kiss me awake in seventeen minutes."

She blinked at that lazy suggestion, gave a quick grin, and dropped Benji on his chest.

He opened one eye to look up at her as he settled his hand lightly on the kitten. "That's a no?"

She smiled. She was looking forward to dating him, but she was smart enough to know he'd value more what he had to work at.

He sighed. "That was a no. How much longer am I going to be on the fence with you?"

"Is that a rhetorical question or do you want an answer?" If this was the right relationship God had for her future, time taken now would improve it, not hurt it. She was ready to admit she was tired of being alone.

He scratched Benji under the chin and the kitten curled up on his chest and batted a paw at his hand. "Rhetorical. I'd hate to get my hopes up."

She leaned her chin against her hand, looking down at him. "I like you, Jack."

"You just figured that out?"

"I'll like you more when you catch my mouse."

"The only way we are going to catch T. J. is to turn this place into a cheese factory and help her get so fat and slow she can no longer run and hide."

"Or you could move your left hand about three inches to the right and catch her."

Jack opened one eye and glanced toward his left. The white mouse was sitting motionless beside the plate he had set down earlier. Jack closed his eye again. "Let her have the cheeseburger. You put mustard on it."

"You're horrible."

He smiled. "I'm serious."

"So am I."

Jack leaned over, caught Cassie's foot, and tumbled her to the floor. "Oops."

"That wasn't fair. You scared my mouse."

Jack set the kitten down on the floor. "Benji, go get her mouse."

The kitten took off after it.

"You're teaching her to be a mouser."

"Working on it. Come here. You owe me a kiss for the new year."

"Do I?" She reached over to the bowl of chocolates on the table and unwrapped a kiss. She popped the chocolate kiss in his mouth. "I called your bluff."

He smiled and rubbed his hand across her forearm braced against his chest. "That will last me until next year."

She glanced at the muted television. "That's two minutes away."

"Two minutes to put this year behind us." He slid one arm behind his head, adjusting the pillow.

She patted his chest with her hand. "That shouldn't take long." She felt him laugh. "It ended up being a very good year," she offered.

"Next year will be even better."

"Really? Promise?"

"Absolutely." He reached behind her ear and a gold coin reappeared. "What do you think? Heads you say yes when I ask you out, tails you say no?"

She grinned at the idea. "Are you cheating again?" She took the coin. "This one isn't edible," she realized, disappointed. And then she turned it over. "A real two-headed coin?"

"A rare find." He smiled. "Like you."

"That sounds like a bit of honey."

"I'm good at being mushy."

"Oh, really?"

He glanced over her shoulder. "Turn up the TV. There's the countdown."

She grabbed for the remote and hit the wrong button. The television came on full volume just as the fireworks went off. Benji went racing past them spooked by the noise to dive under the collar of the jacket Jack had tossed on the floor. The white mouse scurried to run into the jacket sleeve.

"Tell me I didn't see what I think I just did."

"I won't tell you," Jack agreed, amused. He watched the jacket move and raised an eyebrow. "Am I supposed to rescue the kitten or the mouse?"

Dear Reader,

Thanks for reading this book. I deeply appreciate it.

Fire has always fascinated me, even more the men and women who fight them and why. It's a special person who stands guard to protect the public. I've had the honor of knowing such men and they are guys you can count on when trouble comes. In Jack and Cassie's story, I hope I captured a slice of their lives and was able to convey the deep friendship that ties them together.

Jack's story also offered an opportunity to ask a profound question: Who is Jesus? Cassie Ellis has found the real meaning of Christmas and Jack is still searching to understand. To Jack, Jesus seemed to be the serious myth that people believed in at Christmas, Santa Claus the childish one. Watching Jack with Cassie, with Jennifer and Rachel, as he searched for an answer, was a chance to see a man honestly asking why and not shying away from making a life-changing decision.

By the way, about Rachel…Cole and Rachel were an added bonus. I had no idea this man existed until I wrote the opening chapter of this book. I'm looking forward to telling Rachel and Cole's story in *The Healer*.

As always, I love to hear from my readers. Feel free to write me at:

Dee Henderson
c/o Multnomah Fiction
P.O. Box 1720
Sisters, Oregon 97759
E-mail: dee@deehenderson.com
or on-line: http://www.deehenderson.com

Thanks again for letting me share Jack and Cassie's story.
Sincerely,

Dee Henderson

book five

THE
HEALER

To my mom,
who is the best friend an author could have.

⤫⤫⤫

"I am the LORD, your healer."
EXODUS 15:26B

Carol Iles pulled on tennis shoes to replace the heels she'd worn at work and tossed her shoes down the hall toward her bedroom.

"So where are we going for dinner?" Her friend Amy asked, digging through her cosmetic bag for a lipstick tube. She had come over directly from work, bringing a change of clothes to replace her suit with jeans and a sweater. Amy stepped into the bathroom to use the mirror.

Carol looked at the clock on her kitchen wall. "I was thinking Charlie's Grill at the mall; then we can walk off dinner and spend some of your vacation money before you leave." She opened the refrigerator to see what she had available to offer her guest. "I've got Sprite, Pepsi, and several sports drinks."

She had bought the sports drinks for her son when she went grocery shopping last night, and it looked like he'd managed to gulp down two before his father picked him up tonight. She should have suggested he take them with him. It would be two weeks before her son would be here again. His absence was a painful reminder of what hadn't worked out in her life. Divorce left everyone struggling to make new routines work.

Carol touched one of the bottles. It was one of the few traces of her son's presence left in the house. He insisted on bringing his things in a duffel bag and leaving with everything, as if to put roots down here in her house through his clutter would be to admit that he too had been split apart by the divorce. He lived with his father; he was always quick to point that out.

"A Sprite is fine."

Carol forced aside the melancholy. She set the can on the counter for Amy and got a Pepsi for herself. Amy was making a special point to stay in town on Friday night just to cheer her up when Amy could've made an early start on her vacation. Carol was determined to make the effort to enjoy tonight.

She took the soda with her to the dining room and flipped through the day's mail. Amy rejoined her and put her lipstick and hairbrush away in her cosmetic bag. Carol offered Amy three catalogs that had come the day before. "I found that blouse in one of these."

"Thanks." Amy carried them over to the kitchen counter and opened her soda. "I'm hoping they have it in a soft peach." She dug through her purse for a pen. "Oh, I found the card I had told you about." She held up a blue business card.

"Brian would blow his top if I asked him to let us get professional help for our son."

"You have to think about what is best for Mark. It's normal for divorce to be hard on kids, but Mark is taking this rougher than most," Amy replied.

"Brian keeps insisting it's a family problem."

"Carol, I know your son hates my guts for convincing you to leave Brian. And if he knew I was the one suggesting this, he'd dig in his heels, but I really do think it would be good for him to see someone. It's been over a year. He's not getting better on his own. Would you at least talk to Rachel O'Malley? She's very good at what she does."

Carol felt exhausted at the idea of bringing yet another person into this trauma, of having to once again explain. Amy was so hopeful this could get better. Carol smiled. "Leave the card. I'll think about it."

"You won't regret it."

The doorbell rang. Carol wasn't expecting anyone. "Just a minute." She went to get it.

Carol opened the door only to stop, surprised. "Was the basketball game canceled?" She stepped back to let her visitor in. She hoped Amy would be smart enough to stay in the kitchen when she heard his voice so they could avoid a confrontation.

"Not exactly." The gunshot hit her in the chest. She went crashing back into the living room table.

ONE

"We need to go, Mrs. Sands." Rachel O'Malley stopped the elderly lady from turning toward her living room and instead steered her toward the front door and the waiting Red Cross volunteer. Shutters rattled and a misty rain blew in the open door, dampening the hallway. The Des Plaines River was surging through the levee; and getting people to safety was the priority. It was Tuesday, March 13, and rains across Chicago had triggered rapid flooding along six miles of the river.

"I need my pictures."

"Yes, ma'am. But I'm afraid there isn't time." Rachel shifted the birdcage and medicine bag she carried to help Mrs. Sands with her raincoat. "This wind is strong, so let Nora and the officer help you."

With twenty minutes warning to leave their homes, residents were able to grab a few clothes and personal items but that was it. Nora took Mrs. Sands's arm and helped her walk to the waiting rescue vehicle. Rachel handed her personal items to the officer.

In the twilight, torchlights bobbed like fireflies along the block as three police officers and two other Red Cross workers took part in the evacuation search. Rachel worked disasters for a living, but she would never get used to floods. Little could be done once the flooding took ground. Rachel placed a red fluorescent square on the garage door of 58 Governor Street to mark it as confirmed empty. Cold, muddy water swirled over her boots and reached to her jeans as she waded into the water to cut across the yard.

The next house was set back from the road, with sloping, landscaped grounds. Located closer to the river, the house was suffering the most damage of any so far as water poured in through the backyard and rushed around the house to flow down Governor Street. Rachel fought against the water to walk up the driveway. It took her feet out from under her. She instinctively threw her arms up to protect her head as she was swept downhill toward the street. It was her second dunking of the day.

She slammed up against fire boots.

"Got you." The reassuring words came moments before hands slid around her jacket and hauled her to her feet. Captain Cole Parker stood in the rushing water with his feet braced apart and let the current break around him. He'd been buttoning his fire coat.

"Thanks, Cole." Everything on her was wet. She leaned forward and dried her face on his shirt. It was rough blue denim and she could see the white T-shirt beneath it. He had planned for the reality of this weather better than she had, with layers to fight the chill. The breadth of muscles on the man stretched the fabric taut.

"My pleasure, Rae." His hands pushed back her dripping hair as he laughed. "You are really wet. The water bang you up any?"

"I'm okay." She was embarrassed and annoyed that he'd seen her fall, but she couldn't do much about any of it. Her short haircut was new, and when it was wet it lost any definition and simply became straggles of hair. She blinked water out of her eyes and sniffed, then reached for his hand and dried her eyes on the back of his cuff.

"I wish I'd brought at least a hand towel."

She tilted her head to dislodge the water in her ear. "You're enjoying this."

"I'd love to have a camera right now," Cole confirmed, his smile widening. He put his hands on her shoulders and helped her turn against the rushing waters. "Go with Jack. I'll check the last house."

Her brother was crossing the street toward her. He was a lieutenant in the same fire company where Cole was a captain. Cole said his premature gray hair was at least partially Jack's fault. Jack was a careful, safety-conscious firefighter but invariably led his men in a firefight from the front lines, especially when there was someone at risk. Jack was here, and Cole, so Company 81 must have been dispatched to the scene. "I didn't know firemen fought floods."

Cole tugged straight the now sopping Red Cross jacket from being bunched around her back. "It looks like we're going to learn how. The Corps of Engineers guys are stretched thin. The bridge is ours to defend."

She raised startled eyes to meet his. "Whose blacklist are you on?"

Cole laughed. "I hope it only looks impossible. Jack said it sounds like fun. You have a change of clothes at the shelter?"

"If I don't it's going to be a miserable couple hours drying out." The water was inching up around them. She glanced at the house that had been her original destination. "You'd better go check the house while you can still get to it. But please, be careful."

"Always," Cole promised. "Can you get me a head count at the emergency shelter and ask around about pets? I'll be pulling my guys back from this street in about twenty minutes."

"Will do." Rachel grabbed Jack's hand to keep her balance in the fast-moving waters and headed up the street toward the truck, which was on higher ground. Cole was defending the bridge. She smiled. Well at least she knew where to find him in the foreseeable future. The idea of working at the nearby shelter suddenly had more appeal.

❧❧❧

By Friday the rushing waters were a roar in the night that grew louder the closer Cole got to the Des Plaines River. One of the residents of Governor Street forced out by the floodwaters had raised an American flag to fly over the sandbag levee that workers had named "the Alamo line." The flag waved in the night breeze, backlit by the emergency lights that enabled workers to keep an eye on the bridge, which was now cut off and surrounded by water. It was a defiant symbol. It fit the attitude of those dealing with the disaster over the last three days.

Today had been rough. When he hadn't been hauling sandbags or fixing pump equipment, he'd been working with the guys who were doing the dangerous job of breaking up and hauling out debris that had gotten stuck and piled up beneath the bridge. As he made his evening rounds, Cole felt a bit like a general inspecting the state of his troops. Fighting water was far from his specialty—he led the arson group—but his men had met the challenge. They'd fought the river to a draw today, and it felt great.

Cole kept a lookout for Rachel as he walked. She'd been supplying them with hot coffee and sports scores. Her caramel-colored hair had dried with a flyaway curl to it, and when he happened to catch her during the rare moments she had her reading glasses on, Rae reminded him of a studious college student, years younger than her real age.

She was thirty-five if her brother Jack was to be believed, and given the intensity of Rachel's job working disaster scenes nationwide, Cole wasn't surprised her hair had begun to show signs of gray. She was aging elegantly. If he couldn't have the pleasure of her company on a date tonight, he'd settle for a few minutes to talk with her and enjoy that smile that lingered in his memory.

Cole didn't see her and hoped that meant she was finally tucked away somewhere getting a few hour's sleep. She had been staying at the emergency shelter rather than returning to her home a few miles south, her sleeping bag and duffel bag well used. She carried odd things in that duffel bag she considered her emergency kit. He'd seen fingernail polish and stickers and all kinds of colorful hair ribbons alongside aspirin and envelopes and postage stamps. He had slipped in a funny Hallmark card he'd picked up at one of the few businesses in the area determined to stay open. He wanted her thinking about him with a smile and a laugh tonight.

Spotting the yellow smiley face on the back of Jack O'Malley's fire coat, Cole changed directions and headed toward the blue pump engine. The engine had been retired and replaced by more modern equipment years ago, but in a fight like this one, anything that could pump water had been called out.

Jack was working on the top of the levee, pushing thirty-pound bags around. Beside him a six-inch-main fire hose was taut, stretched up and over the wall of sandbags, dumping water into the river as fast as the pumps could throw it back.

Cole stopped by the front bumper of the pump engine, curious as to what was going on, cracking open another peanut while he waited for Jack to finish what he was doing. His pocketful of peanuts was turning out to be dinner tonight.

His friend hauled the hose into the new cradle he had made. The shoot of water became a water fountain with spotlights illuminating the flood area. Jack reached down and lifted a flat cardboard box onto the sandbags. Moments later a yellow rubber duck with black sunglasses dropped into the shooting water and reappeared in the middle of the river.

Jack was playing.

The swift-moving water carried the yellow duck downriver and under the bridge, where it disappeared.

"Nice shot."

Jack turned on his perch. "We've got ten thousand of them. I figure they won't miss a couple dozen." He dropped another one and the water shot it into the river where it bobbed upside down, righted itself, and got slaughtered by a tree branch it slammed into.

The local chamber of commerce had been planning a duck race as its opening event in a charity fund-raising drive. They had ten thousand ducks stored in the fire department's maintenance garage. It looked like they would be stuck with them for a good long time—the event had been canceled.

"Hold on to a box for Adam tomorrow. He'll love them," Cole said.

"That's what I was thinking."

The boy's home was visible through the trees during the day, the water now up to the middle of the living room windows, the mailbox at the roadside underwater. Adam was down here every day, helping them. He had to watch the river destroy his home. They were all trying to make the situation a little easier on him.

"Does the river look like it's picking up speed?"

Jack reached for his inside pocket and pulled out a stopwatch. He timed the next duck as it raced between two poles they'd marked with red flags. "Eight-point-two seconds. It's really moving now."

"The crest should hit in another forty-eight hours."

"I saw what looked like a small propane tank go by that was rolling like a cork. Someone's backyard grill probably got ripped apart."

"The cemetery off Rosecrans Road flooded this evening. That ground was as much loose sand as dirt. I bet this river current is eating it up like mulch," Cole said.

"You know about the most ugly things."

"I work at it." Cole didn't mention that Jack's sister Lisa had stopped by to drop off two body bags. Lisa's boss, the medical examiner, remembered the last time he'd received a body pulled from the river. It was wrapped in a curtain for want of a better covering. He'd sent out his central staff today to make sure rescue crews were prepared. It was inevitable that someone would attempt to drive across a flooded street, try to reach a flooded home, or otherwise act before they thought. The river would have no mercy.

Cole gestured toward the pump engine. "How's it holding up?"

"Beautifully. This baby could pump the whole river if we asked her to."

Jack was wet and tired. The hyperbole was getting a bit thick, but he had cause. He'd been keeping the old pump engine in top shape through scraped knuckles and frustrating part replacements. This was her moment to shine. And so far she was holding her own against the heavy seepage.

The sandbags were slowing down the river and forcing it to soak rather than slam through the levee. The pumps still had to keep up with the fact that unless the water working its way through was repelled, the river would flood the city sewers.

"I'm laying a new line of bags around the bank just in case. It's going to rise at least another six inches before the crest. Anything you need?" Cole asked.

"Coffee. Dry socks. Cassie."

"Interesting order you put those in. I won't tell Cassie you made her third." Cassie Ellis and Jack had been dating since last fall, and Cole was looking forward to seeing them married someday. A former firefighter, Cassie had been badly burned in a nursing-home fire. Cole admired the way she'd dealt with that tragedy and rebuilt her life.

"Coffee and socks are not a problem. I've got Cassie supervising the hauling out of the library historical documents. If it can't be replaced, there's no use taking chances." Cole glanced at the ducks. "But I'll send her down later if you want to put her name on one of those." He dug out a black waterproof marker from his coat pocket and tossed it to Jack. "She'll get a kick out of it."

"Thanks, boss."

"Don't fall in."

Jack laughed and picked up a duck to start his artwork.

Cole moved on to check the rest of the guys working the front line.

Rachel's legs were numb and her left arm ached. She would not have moved for the world. Nathan Noles was finally asleep, hiccup-sob-sighs still occasionally shaking his small frame. Tear-drenched lashes covered his big, brown, break-her-heart eyes. Life was rough when you were three and your favorite blanket was missing, swallowed up in the fast moving waters that had swirled into his home on Governor Street.

Rachel rubbed her thumb in small circles on his back. They were buddies. The teddy bear she had offered him to take the place of his blanket was now muddy in spots and still clutched under one arm. Nathan had latched on to it and refused to let go.

She didn't have a family of her own, but she had her dreams. A lump rose in her throat as she looked at the sleeping child. She wanted a son like him. She kissed his forehead and smoothed out the wrinkles in the warm pajama top, then tucked the blanket around his shoulders.

Nathan's family had arrived at the emergency shelter while Rachel was setting up tables for the Red Cross help desk. She found her duffel bag, which she had tossed in a corner, and pushed aside her blue sweatshirt to retrieve the bear tucked in the corner. "This is Joseph. He's old and kind of beat up, but would you like him, Nathan? He's a friendly bear."

The boy's eyes glanced from her to the bear. Nathan sniffed and reached out to wrap his hand around the bear's arm. He tucked Joseph close and sighed, then leaned his head back down against his mom's shoulder.

A shared smile with Nathan's mom and Rachel had made her first friend of this tragedy. Ann Noles was a single mom who worked emergency dispatch for the 911 center. She was staying optimistic that something in her house could be salvaged. Rachel found in Ann a kindred spirit.

Nathan's brother Adam was asleep now, his sleeping bag spread on top of one of the gym mats. Rachel reached over and picked up the paperback he'd been reading with the help of a small flashlight, marked the page he was on, and slid it in his backpack. A teddy bear had helped Nathan; she was still working on something for Adam. The flooding had destroyed a four-year collection of comic books he had mowed yards and run errands to be able to buy.

Ann would be moving her family from the shelter to stay with friends tomorrow, for it would be some time before they could get back into their home to start the cleanup. Adam wasn't thrilled with the idea of going back to school on Monday. The guys working on the levees had made him welcome. It was much more exciting than school.

Rachel leaned her head against Nathan's, closed her eyes, and sought a few moments of rest. Her days began before dawn. Floods were harder to work than tornadoes because they first exhausted people with a fight against the water and then presented them with nothing but devastation. The tragedy would strike home anew when people could see the loss—chairs punched through ceilings, furniture smashed and piled up by the water, plaster collapsed, appliances destroyed. Exhaustion and dashed hopes would overwhelm people.

Rachel had built her life around helping hurting people, but she just wasn't as young as she used to be, and the pace wore at her. Being a trauma psychologist for the Red Cross was a young person's profession. Not everyone was able to remain as optimistic as Ann, and keeping other people's spirits up inevitably drained her own.

How is Jennifer doing?

Whenever Rachel paused in the midst of her day, her thoughts returned to her sister. Jennifer's cancer had gone through a brief remission, then came back more aggressive than before. It was around her spine and had moved into her liver. This return stay at Johns Hopkins was lasting longer than her first admission a year ago. The news wasn't good. Rachel had to get back to Baltimore to see her.

Having a close family was one of those dreams that had come true with the O'Malleys, and the idea of losing her sister to this cancer… The thought was enough to make tears return. Jennifer was the most precious friend she had.

"He's in love."

Rachel opened her eyes and blinked away the moisture before turning her head and offering a smile. She hadn't heard Cole come into the gym. "So am I."

He sat down on the mat to her left. Mud had stained the shirt he put on this morning. She was tempted to reach over and try to brush some of it off. It would dry stiff and be uncomfortable, but she knew he wasn't done for the evening. He'd be walking the sandbag levee several times through the night.

He opened the duffel bag he'd left near hers and found dry socks. "Did you get some dinner?"

"They brought in chicken tonight."

"I'll buy you a real dinner when this is over."

"It's a deal."

He paused to look over. "Really?"

She chuckled at his reaction. "How many times have I pleaded work as an excuse lately?"

He smiled at her. "Three, but who's counting?"

She'd spent enough time with Cole since Christmas to know that she more than just enjoyed his company. She was looking at a guy she could spend the rest of her life with. And as hopeful and joyous as that idea was, as much as she wanted to explore what their relationship might become, she just didn't have much time or energy to offer at the moment.

She knew the other O'Malleys would catch wind of their relationship soon. She had done her best not to mention Cole too often around them to avoid the speculation. But in trying to save herself and Cole from some of that family attention, she'd probably been more cautious with him than warranted. "Let's not do Mexican."

"How about Chinese?"

"Sounds good."

"I'll look forward to it." His gaze shifted to the boy she held. He reached over and tucked Nathan's teddy bear closer. "He looks comfortable."

"I like kids."

"Me too."

She smiled and rested her head against Nathan, choosing to let the comment pass.

"Ann is just finishing up at dispatch," Cole mentioned. "Are you okay with the boys for another twenty minutes?"

"Yes."

Cole leaned his head back against the wall, folded his arms across his chest, and closed his eyes. "Wake me when she gets back."

Rachel hesitated for a moment, doubt creeping in just for an instant that she was reading Cole's interest in Ann correctly. "Sure."

He didn't open his eyes but he did smile. "She's a friend, Rae. I like her boys. But it's your brother who has his eyes on their mom."

"Stephen?" She had only one brother not involved in a serious relationship at the moment. Her surprise woke Nathan.

"Hmm. Only reason I can think of for why a paramedic hangs around dispatch on a Friday night."

She could think of another, but still... "He offered to help them move to her friend's tomorrow."

"I heard that too."

Ann had mentioned that she'd met Stephen, but she hadn't asked anything beyond a couple of general questions. Rachel thought about it as she rocked Nathan back to sleep. "Stephen?"

Cole chuckled and reached over to pat her shoulder. "You've been busy."

Rachel saw a sliver of light appear as the door to the gym opened and the person entering the room paused to let her eyes adjust to the dim light inside. Ann crossed the room with care and eased down on the air mattress beside her.

"Nathan woke and realized you were gone," Rachel whispered. She waited until Ann was settled, then eased Nathan onto his mom's lap, immediately missing the weight and comfort of holding him. Rachel tugged a tissue from her jean's pocket and wiped away a tear trace from the boy's cheek. "How was work?"

"Hectic." Ann lowered her head against her son's and closed her eyes. "I'm so tired the air mattress will feel like a featherbed tonight."

"I put your ice pack in the freezer. Want to use it for twenty minutes before you crash?" Ann had waded into the flooding to help a neighbor and had unfortunately taken a hard shot from a floating tree limb.

Ann nodded. "I could use it. Thanks."

Rachel went to get the ice pack. She snagged two tapioca pudding cups and spoons on the way back. It was nice having a friend to share the quiet moments with at the shelter. Pausing inside the doorway, she searched among the three-by-five cards on the corkboard with her penlight. She found five messages for Ann and took them with her across the gym. Ann was cuddling with Nathan.

"A few messages were left for you today. And Cole said he needed to talk to you." The man slept so soundly he hadn't stirred at their quiet conversation. After three days of fighting the river, his exhaustion had to be complete. Every time Rachel had seen him he was in the middle of the work.

"Let him sleep. He was passing on a message from my cousin, and I got it just before I left work." Ann leaned around Nathan and settled the ice on her knee. She sucked in a breath at the cold.

Rachel winced in sympathy. "You need to see a doctor."

"It's just bruised. I should have gotten up and walked more today. Sitting just made it stiffen." Ann relaxed and opened the pudding cup.

Rachel offered the Hallmark card Cole had left for her. Ann laughed as she read it, glancing at the sleeping Cole, then back at Rachel. "He's sweet on you." She handed back the card.

"I hope so." Rachel tucked it in her bag to make sure it got home with her. "I'm thinking about being gone for a couple days," she said, testing out the idea.

"Going out East to see your sister?"

"Trying to figure out the logistics of making it happen."

"You should go."

The kids needed her. Her sister Jennifer needed her. Rachel was stuck with the reality that she couldn't be two places at once. "I'll be back before the water recedes."

Ann smiled. "Trust me, the water will still be here." She laid Nathan down and stretched out beside him. "I heard a rumor today."

"What's that?"

Ann reached over and rubbed Adam's back. "Jack was behind my son's desire to toss a ship in a bottle into the river."

Rachel licked the lid of her pudding cup. "My brother is a kid at a heart."

"I noticed that. Adam talks about him all the time. Jack's a good man."

"All my brothers are. Stephen is the responsible one." Rachel bunched her pillow behind her head and stretched out on her own sleeping bag.

"I've noticed. He brought me flowers tonight."

"Did he?"

"Hmm," Ann murmured.

Rachel hesitated, wondering if Ann would say more. "If you'd like to go out, I'll baby-sit for you."

"He didn't ask me."

Rachel pushed herself up on her elbow. "Why not?"

"Good question. Will you ask him for me?"

Rachel reached for her jacket and her phone.

Ann stayed her hand as she smiled. "Tomorrow is soon enough."

"You're ruining my fun."

Ann chuckled. "Thanks, Rae."

"For what?"

"Telling Stephen to bring me flowers."

She'd been found out. "You're welcome. I kind of figured you needed something to brighten your day."

"Don't apologize. A nice guy bringing me flowers and flirting fits the bill beautifully."

"I didn't tell him to flirt."

Ann smiled. "Exactly. It was nice for morale. I'll take you up on the baby-sitting. Tell Stephen I like a good steak and salad."

"Done." Rachel had never met a crisis that flowers couldn't help. It sounded like sending Stephen on that errand had turned out to be a good move. Rachel tucked her arm under her head and closed her eyes. It was after eleven, and in six hours she would be starting another long day.

Rachel woke to the sensation of someone tickling her wrist. She moved her hand, smiling. "Cole, that—" she murmured, opening her eyes. No one was there. Her pager was going off. She had clipped it to a sweatband on her wrist to ensure that she would wake if it went off. She tugged it free and looked at the number. Her heart broke at the special number, suspecting what the page meant. She slipped from the sleeping bag, left the gym, and returned the page in the quiet hall.

"Rachel, he didn't come tonight."

Marissa was crying.

"Oh, honey, I'm so sorry." Rachel walked outside and sat down on the steps, hearing the hurt and wishing Mr. Collins could see past his own grief to understand what he was doing to his daughter. Marissa was a junior in high school, and her music competition had been tonight, the top awards included scholarships to college. Tonight had mattered.

"I got your message. Mom said I should call you back in the morning."

"I asked you to call," Rachel said. "Trust me, friends don't care about the time. How did you do?"

"Second."

"I'm proud of you, Marissa."

"Linda took first. Her solo was wonderful."

"There's always next year."

"I wanted Dad to be there."

"I know, honey. He gave his word. He should have been there." Marissa had lost her leg in a car accident two years ago. Traumatic enough for a young girl, but her dad had been driving and he'd never been able to get past his own grief. He had walked out last year. Broken promises hurt when you're an adult, but when you're a child and it's done by family— Rachel had been there, and even decades later the hurt didn't entirely fade. The only thing she could do at this point was be a friend and listen.

"Mom took me out to eat afterward. I was too nervous before then."

"What did you have?"

"She talked me into trying the scampi. It was pretty good." The girl's tears were fading. "I just thought he might come."

"Love always hopes," Rachel said softly. "He's still hurting over the fact that he was driving."

"Yeah."

Marissa had fought for two years to get her life back. But family wounds hurt so much deeper than physical ones.

"Am I doing something wrong?" Marissa whispered.

Rachel closed her eyes. "No. Your dad always wanted to protect you. Now he feels a need to protect you from himself. It will eventually get better, Marissa. Remember when we talked about how time changes people? Keep giving him opportunities into your life. There will be a day when he'll feel able to come. When he does, just start with 'I love you.'"

Silence lingered. "Thanks."

"Time, M. It will help."

Rachel leaned over to pick up two jacks a child had missed.

"Greg Sanford asked me to the prom."

"Did he?" Rachel was pleased to hear the news, for she knew how much Marissa had hoped to be invited. "I've got to meet this gentleman. I already like him. What did you say?"

"I said yes, as long as he wouldn't ask me to dance. We'd just go."

"Greg has been there for you this last year. Trust me, you'll have a wonderful time."

"I wish he didn't graduate and leave in four months. I'm going to miss him."

"Did he receive his acceptance papers yet?" Rachel asked, feeling out the changes coming for her friend.

"From the Air Force academy. He wants to become a pilot like his dad." Marissa hesitated. "Do you think we could maybe have a soda next time you're in town?"

"I'm nearby," Rachel said. "I can meet you tomorrow, or we can do something next week when I get back from visiting Jennifer."

"After school next week would be nice."

"It's a date." Rachel wrote a note on the palm of her hand until she could update her day planner for the month of March. This kind of fatigue shot holes in her memory. "Anything you need or want me to tell your mom?"

"Everything there is okay."

"Anything you're not telling me that I should know?"

Marissa paused to think about it. "I'm okay there too."

"Then I'll see you next week. If you want to talk before then, promise to call me?"

"Yes. Thanks, Rae."

"Honey, I'm proud of you." Her pager went off again. "I'll call your mom tomorrow to confirm arrangements for next week," Rachel said as she got to her feet. It was a page from Jack, and that meant trouble at the levee.

"Cole." Rachel shook him gently, wishing she didn't have to wake him. He'd fallen asleep sitting against the wall with his chin tucked against his chest, arms folded. She admired his ability to close his eyes and drop off. If he worried about things, she'd never been able to figure out when. They certainly didn't affect his sleep.

Cole opened his eyes, blinked, and focused on her.

"Jack paged. They need you at the levee."

He took a deep breath and sighed. "Okay, I'm awake."

"It's 1 A.M."

"I didn't ask."

She let her hand settle on his forearm as she smiled back at him. "I know, but your watch stopped. It's blinking this strange pattern of red and white numbers. Nathan thought it was your night-light."

"Water and watches do not mix. It's never going to dry out."

She stepped back as Cole rose to his feet.

"What's going on?"

"Jack said something about too much mud in the water—it's clogging the pumps."

Cole reached forward and rested his hand on her shoulder. "You were up?"

"I had another call."

"If you need a place to hide so you can get some sleep, try the front seat of one of the fire department vehicles. No one will find you."

He was taking care of her in the same way he took care of his men. It was nice. "Thanks."

"Take me up on it. And bring Adam down to the levee later this morning. Jack's got something he should see."

"I'll do that."

"You really said yes to finding time for dinner?" His thumb rubbed her shoulder blade. "I would hate to think I had been dreaming."

She chuckled. "Chinese. And hopefully an evening with no interruptions."

He was stalling, not wanting to break this moment. She didn't either. He was so good-looking half asleep—she wanted to give him a hug and get swallowed in one in return. "Go to work, Cole."

"Yes, ma'am." He smiled at her and headed toward the door.

Rachel watched him leave and then settled back on her sleeping bag. She reset her pager and wrapped her arm around her pillow. When she closed her eyes, she was still smiling. A smile from Cole and an invitation to dinner was nearly as nice as getting flowers.

⟫⟨⟩⟪

"What's happening, Jack?"

Cole found Rachel's brother in the parking lot where they had the flat-bottom fire rescue boat parked testing brake lights on the trailer. "I didn't want to worry Rae. Lisa needs us. She said to bring a body bag."

"Where is she?"

"Rosecrans Road."

Cole squeezed the bridge of his nose and tried to get past the fact that it was 1 A.M. "Please tell me she knew I was joking with her earlier. Is the body embalmed?"

"Lisa's first words when I returned her page were, 'the water is destroying my crime scene!' Then she got testy. It sounds real to me."

"You've got interesting sisters."

"Tell me about it."

Cole pulled out his keys. "I'll drive. Do we need more than the two of us?"

"It sounds like she needs us for transport. Company 42 is working in the area."

"Okay. Let's go see what she's gotten herself into."

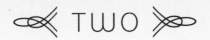

TWO

The intersection of Rosecrans Road and Clover Street had become a parking lot for emergency vehicles. A hundred yards further east, Rosecrans disappeared into standing water. Men were wading through the water around a brick house three blocks down, visible in the improvised lighting set along the edge of the roof. The house was on a slight rise, but the front yard and the driveway had disappeared underwater. Cole saw a man leaving the garage lose his balance. "Another few minutes and those men are going to find themselves unable to get back here to safe ground."

Jack swung down from the truck. "Cops are just like civilians when it comes to underestimating rising water. How are we going to float the boat?"

Cole walked into the water until it reached his bootlaces. The roadway flooding appeared to be backwater with the current coming toward him. "I'll back up the truck."

Jack buckled on his life vest. "I was afraid you were going to say carry it." He released the straps across the boat, climbed up on the hitch, removing the locking pin on the winch. "Okay, let's do it."

Cole backed up along the road until Jack was able to shove the boat off the trailer and float it. Cole returned the truck to a safe distance, parked it, and picked up the body bag they'd brought along in the truck bed. He waded back to where Jack was idling the boat. The water quickly deepened.

Jack steered the boat right up the driveway of the house in question and gently beached the flat bottom of the boat on the concrete. Cole stepped off the front of the boat and tied the rope to a brick planter by the garage. Men were working to build a break wall across the front steps with bags of dirt, birdseed, and anything else they could find in the garage.

"Who's in charge?"

"Detective Brad Wilson, inside."

Cole knew the name. "Wait here, Jack." He stepped over the improvised wall to enter the house. Four men were in the hallway, and he could see another two in what looked like the dining room. With the power out, the lighting inside was established by bright flashlights.

"Cole, good timing." Detective Wilson came to meet him, picking his way around evidence markers. "This situation is getting away from us. I didn't want men walking back through the water in the dark."

"Jack can take five at a time."

"You know this river better than I do. Can you handle the water battle and arrange the evacuation? I need what time is left to work the crime scene."

"Sure." Cole stepped into the living room. Halogen flashlights had been set around to provide basic lighting. He dealt with fire deaths, but murder was something else. A woman, probably in her thirties, who appeared to have been shot once in the chest, was lying on her side near the coffee table. It was a sight that made Cole feel nauseous. He couldn't see her face and he had no desire to. This memory would already be hard enough to shake. Lisa O'Malley was bending over the body, slipping paper bags around the lady's hands to protect evidence.

"I've got your body bag."

Lisa looked over and rose to cross the room and get it. "Thanks, Cole. I went through the three I had with me at a car accident." Her shoes squished. "Would someone please stop this water? Sandbag the doorways or something."

"It's coming up through the flooded basement," one of the officers working the problem called.

"Then block the basement doorway. Start a bucket brigade and haul it out. I need more time."

Cole stepped around the man dusting for fingerprints and went to see the problem. Two inches of water stood in the kitchen and had made it across the dining room floor. The water was beginning to soak the living room rug. He tagged the two nearest men. "Check under the kitchen sink and in the utility room. Garbage bags, freezer bags—grab whatever there is. Fill the bags with water and stack them—create a barrier at the basement doorway, another at the kitchen doorway, and a third at the dining room doorway. If you can't stop it, try to control it. Lisa, prioritize. You've got ten minutes max."

"Make it fifteen."

"Ten, and your time is running."

"You're killing me here." She had the body bag open. "Wilson, let's get her out of here."

Cole sent five men to the boat and then turned his attention to helping create the final barrier into the living room. The cushions from the dining room chairs worked as a fast sponge to stop the water from crossing the boundary. One of the officers tossed him some of the empty plastic bags they'd found.

"Does anyone have a name for her yet?" Lisa asked the room at large.

"I just found her purse," an officer said. "Carol Iles. 32. Her driver's license expires in July."

"What else does she have in her billfold?"

"Seventy-nine dollars in cash, credit cards, library card, and what looks like an electronic key card—to the federal court building no less."

"Great. Marcus is going to love to hear that." Lisa's brother was a U.S. Marshal, a job that involved protecting the federal courts and those who worked in them. Lisa pointed to an officer. "An address book, bills, files from her desk—shove them in a box and get it out of this water. Find me as much as you can about Carol's life."

"I'm on it."

"Do we have pictures of the blood splatters on the wall?" Lisa asked the crime lab photographer.

"Got 'em."

"I need as many pictures of this room as you can take, then get the hallway and doorways. And if you can get out there, I need photos of the garage and her car." She pivoted on her heel to look around. "Someone start bagging these couch cushions and throw pillows. If it's fabric and it moves, I want it sealed and out of here."

"What about the bloody lamp shade?"

"Take it."

Lisa rose and with Detective Wilson's help lifted the body bag. They carried the woman to the hall.

Lisa came back to examine the scene afresh, shining her light around the living room walls and floor. "She was shot, but where's the gun? Where's the shell casing?"

"This room is a hiding place for small objects," Wilson said.

"Then let's start moving furniture. We need that shell casing."

One of the officers working to keep the water away from the front door stepped inside. "The boat is coming back."

Cole sent two cops and two of the coroner technicians transporting the victim out to the boat, along with all the bagged evidence they could carry.

"Lisa." Cole waited until she turned. "We can take the living room rug if you want it. But we've got to do it now."

"Yes, I want it. See if she has clean sheets in the hall closet. I want something as a control barrier before we roll it. Who checked her bedroom?"

"I did," a technician called out.

"Have sheets been gathered to take, toothbrush and hairbrush, medicine bottles?"

"Bagged and ready to go."

Cole helped Wilson move the couch into the dining room to free the floor rug. "Four minutes, Lisa." The house was groaning. He could hear the water gurgling up into the floorboards under their feet. It would be pouring out of the heating ducts any moment.

Lisa spread out the sheets. Cole had done some unusual things in his job, but rolling up a bloody rug by flashlight was a first. Wilson helped him lift it. "Let's set it on chairs until the boat gets back." Water began cascading into the room from the floorboard ducts. Lisa jumped back as it swept across her feet.

He heard Jack's call. "There's the boat. Everyone is leaving this trip."

Cole let the technician and Detective Wilson take the carpet out. He helped Lisa gather up the last of the evidence bags.

"So much stuff I didn't get…"

"There's no choice, Lisa. We've got to go."

Cole waded to the boat, unloaded the items he carried, and came back for Lisa as she stepped outside. He grabbed her as the floodwaters hit her feet and tried to knock her over. "We stayed too long." He carried her down the flooded drive to the boat. Jack helped her over the side. Cole heaved himself into the boat and took a seat on the bench beside Lisa.

"Someone is getting away with murder because of a flood."

Cole leaned around Lisa and got them both towels. "Who found her?"

"A cop checking on the mandatory evacuation. From the rigor mortis, it happened probably three to four hours ago."

"As bad as the scene was, it could have been worse. She might not have been found until after the floodwaters subsided."

"I know." Lisa tried to wring water out of her denim pant legs. "Man, I hate wet socks. Wilson, do you have any ideas?"

"The mail on the dining room table was in two stacks, one opened and one unopened, with one envelope dropped on top half-opened. There was an open soda can on the counter, still cool enough that the can was sweating. I didn't see signs of forced entry. Her purse still had cash in it."

"She opened the front door and someone shot her," Lisa offered.

"Could be that simple."

"I saw nothing in her home that suggested two people lived there—milk was bought in a half gallon; the shoes I saw were the same size; the sink had one cereal bowl and one glass. There were no pictures of her with someone, not even one that looked like a family picture. Did you see anything in the house that suggested otherwise?"

"No." Wilson braced the rolled carpet as Jack swerved the boat to miss a floating tree limb. "She lived alone; she was shot for a reason other than robbery. It's probably domestic trouble."

"Maybe." Lisa shook her head. "Her car was in the middle of her two-car garage. The soda was on the counter, not at the table where she was opening the mail. A second person could have been there and tried to get outside. There may be another victim we didn't find. Until the water recedes we're guessing." Lisa leaned over and tapped her forehead against Cole's shoulder.

He smiled and squeezed the back of her neck, understanding well how an O'Malley reacted to being stymied. "Time will tell."

She sat back with a sigh. "I want the murder weapon found."

"Cole." Jack pointed to the north.

A dog was swimming in the water, trying to make it to dry ground, his eyes the first thing visible as the torchlight reflected on the dark water.

Cole leaned over the side of the boat and called the dog. The mutt changed course toward them but the current impeded his progress. Jack steered to meet the animal. Cole hauled the animal aboard. He got a lap full of wet, exhausted dog. The animal was shivering, his fur wet and plastered to his body, appearing to be nothing but skin and bones. There was no sign of a collar.

"What are we going to do with him?" Lisa asked.

Cole stroked the mutt's tattered ears. He had room for a dog at his place, and he wouldn't mind keeping him if no owner could be found. The animal could also use some immediate help. "For tonight, take him to Rae."

THREE

Rachel snapped her fingers to get the dog's attention. She offered him a breakfast biscuit one of the children had dropped by the picnic table. It was taken carefully from her fingers. He looked like part sheepdog for the curly coat, part basset hound for the ears, and part German shepherd for the nose.

Cole had been like a little boy in his delight, lugging the wet animal up the stairs of the community shelter last night. It had been a labor of love to try to clean the dog up. She'd sacrificed some of her no-tears shampoo and a blanket taken from her car trunk. She banished the animal from staying inside but had made a bed for it in a box that she set in a sheltered spot of the breezeway.

The animal slapped his tail against her jeans. "I know; you love whoever feeds you."

The dog took off to rejoin Adam. It'd been sticking like a shaggy shadow to Adam's side this morning, for the boys were lavishing the mutt with attention.

Rachel watched Stephen shift boxes in the back of his truck, helping Ann pack the few belongings she had been able to get out of the house and bring to the shelter. He was giving them a lift to their temporary home. Nathan was standing in the bed of the truck, peering over the side at his brother Adam, who was lobbying to ride in the truck with Stephen.

Ann paused beside Stephen, crowding his space, her comment making him laugh. Rachel had already seen at least one wink from Stephen to Ann's boys. Cole was right. Something was going on between Stephen and Ann. If her brother hadn't already corrected that lapse of a missing dinner invitation, she knew he likely would before he dropped them off.

Rachel rested her chin on her fist, a rush of emotion leaving an ache of sadness in its wake. She was glad for Stephen, but if he found someone special, she'd be the last of the O'Malleys officially unattached. She didn't want that distinction.

"That frown is going to stick."

She glanced over. Gage Collier took a seat across from her at the picnic table. He was hanging around because he was a reporter and smelled a story in the flooding, but also because he knew she was here. The last two years had refined their friendship into gold. He would have been celebrating his son's first birthday this year if his pregnant wife hadn't died in a fire. It had been a hard couple years, for his wife had been one of her best friends.

Gage didn't mean to miss her sadness now and incorrectly assume it was the thousand details of this flood getting her down. He would probably even understand if she explained. "Did you bring a newspaper?" Rachel asked.

"Hello, Gage. It's nice to see you, Gage. You're here early…"

She heard the gentleness under his teasing. The care she remembered him taking with Tabitha was now being directed toward her. He knew how hard the last few months of Jennifer's illness had been on her. She smiled back. "Hello, Gage. It's nice to see you, Gage. I haven't seen a newspaper. What did you write about this week?"

"The proposed tollway fare increase. You're not into politics so you would just read it and ask me, 'what?' I did bring you an early mock-up of tomorrow's comics."

"Bless you."

He handed over the folder. "You're so easy to please."

She opened it, drew out the pages, and started reading the comics. Gage tugged out the notebook that went everywhere with him and flipped to a back page. "I checked your apartment and put the mail on the kitchen counter. Nothing urgent there, but your neighbor asked me to tell you, 'Kathy said six on the third and bring Crock-Pot potatoes,' whatever that means."

She glanced up. "A birthday party for a five-year-old, want to come?"

He made a face at her and drew a laugh in response. "Your fern was dying. I probably drowned it."

"It's the thought that counts."

"I'm a thoughtful kind of guy."

She tugged over his plate and speared his pineapple slice. They had shared breakfast many times over the years. He thought yellow fruit should be banned. He only got pineapple because he knew she liked it.

"Eat your eggs," he suggested.

"They're cold. I was on my way to reheat them."

He pushed his plate over and offered his fork. "Eat. I'll go get another tray."

He left his notepad and crossed over to the serving table. The Red Cross had made arrangements with a local restaurant to set up and serve food on picnic tables outside under the breezeway. It gave parents a chance to relax and not worry if a child dropped something, and it let crews working on the levees come and go. The menu this morning was cereal or fruit, scrambled eggs, toast, and hot blueberry muffins. She'd made the rounds of picnic tables earlier, pouring coffee and asking questions, listening. Breakfast was a good time to stop and talk with people, pass on news of progress, and note new problems that needed to be solved.

With little warning of the evacuation, most people had been able to get out with only their children, pets, cars, and what they could carry. Rachel had been able to solve the hot shower and toothbrush problems. Prescription refills. Shoes.

She was working now on the more complex items: where to go for temporary housing—friends, family, or a hotel—photo IDs so some people could pick up their mail at the post office, temporary checks, replacement credit cards, insurance agent contacts. Small steps but they mattered.

The loss of little things amplified the sense of having lost control of their lives and was often the point when the stress overwhelmed. A mom would break down in tears because she didn't have her fingernail file. A dad would lose it when he wanted his change and didn't have pennies. A child would cry because shoelaces on borrowed tennis shoes were not tied right. Rachel couldn't restore to people the valuable things they had lost—pictures and keepsakes and memories—but the other items she could help replace. And by solving the small things, a reservoir of trust was built that the bigger obstacles coming could also be solved.

Gage returned, jelly-smothered toast stacked beside his eggs.

"Did you know they think this flooding could have been prevented?"

"Don't ruin my breakfast." She looked up from the comics. Gage was predictable: he was either seeking news or passing on news. "You're serious."

"Yes."

She glanced around. "Keep your voice down. What did you hear?"

"When they built the bridge, they narrowed the river to save some money. But because that speeds up the water flow, they were supposed to extend the concrete along the riverbank to the original river width. They took it only half that distance. It was the dirt around the ends of the concrete that gave way and brought down the levee. Who lives in the house nearest the river? There may have been some warning."

"Don't make it worse, Gage. They just lost everything."

"It's a story. It's breaking. If not by me, it will be someone else. I'm just going to ask a few questions. What did you see that night? That kind of thing."

She could steer him or let him go out on his own, but she couldn't get him off the story. "Mrs. Sands will talk with you. She lives in the brick house with the ivy on the chimney, two houses down from the bridge crossing. Nice lady, in her seventies, still sharp. She has lived in that house for thirty years. The house one closer to the bridge—the owner is out of town. He's coming home to a mess."

"Where can I find Mrs. Sands?"

"She's staying with her sister Eva Grant in Mount Prospect. I've got her address in my reference book."

"You're sending me an hour away and you're enjoying this."

She just smiled and finished the fruit.

Gage closed his notebook. "What did you hear about the murder Lisa was working last night?"

"Just that Jack and Cole took the boat down to help her out with transportation." She tried not to dwell on what her sisters did for a living. Lisa was a forensic pathologist, Kate a hostage negotiator. The aftereffects of tragedies were hard enough to deal with.

"It was one of three shootings overnight. Someone shot an off-duty cop as he was leaving a restaurant, and a taxi driver was robbed and killed."

"You're full of good news today."

"Which is why I left mentioning them until after you ate breakfast." Gage got to his feet. "Cassie Ellis sent you a package. It's in the backseat of the car. Do you want me to get it before I chase down this lead?"

"Please. Cassie was looking for a rare comic book to be the linchpin of a new collection for Adam. Did she say which one it was?"

"Just that he should like it."

Rachel shoved keys and cash into her pocket on the off chance she'd have time to stop and buy Cole a Hallmark card in return. She picked up the package for Adam and headed toward the levee where she'd last seen the boy. She found Adam with Cole saying good-bye to the firefighters. Cole's new dog climbed over a mound of sandbags, chasing the smells.

"How fast is it going?"

Adam scrambled down from his perch on the levee carrying a clipboard. He came to join her and show her. "Cole showed me how to graph the river's speed based on how many seconds it took for the duck to travel between the poles. It's slowing down today. See? This was early this morning; this is now."

She looked at the careful graphs made on a grid. "Excellent job." Adam beamed at the praise and she ruffled his hair. He was a bit shy, careful, and eager to get things right. She was going to miss him. "I got you something to take with you." She held out a hand towel she'd thought to grab from the general resource box. "You'll want to dry your hands first."

After he did so thoroughly, Rachel handed him the sack.

Adam opened it with care. "Wow."

She'd seen Cassie get that same fascinated look on her face when she held a hundred-year-old book. He held the old comic book reverently, careful not to bend the pages as he turned them. "Mom said it was okay?"

The hope in his voice made her smile. "She was the one who gave me the issue and date."

He hugged Rachel, catching her around the waist while holding the comic to the side. "Thanks."

She circled his shoulder and hugged him back. "My brother Jack, the fireman who has that smiley face on the back of his fire coat? His girlfriend Cassie owns a bookstore with rare books. She said she'd help you find some more comics so you can rebuild your collection."

"I've got to go show my mom."

"One more thing." She held out a blue business card. "For you. Since you're going to stay with friends, I might not see you for a couple days. If you have a question or just want to tell me about your day, your mom said you could call me anytime. All you have to do is punch in the special numbers on the back, and I'll know it's you."

"I've heard about your cards."

"You have?" She squeezed his shoulder. "I only give them to special people. If you need anything or if Nathan or your mom need anything, I'll help. That's a promise."

He carefully put the card in his back pocket.

"Adam." He turned at his mom's call. "Ready to go? We're packed."

Rachel nodded. "Better join them."

Adam walked backward two steps, holding the comic book. "I'll treasure this forever."

"You're very welcome. I'll see you soon."

The boy raced to where his mom was waiting. "Mom, she got me a comic. A rare one."

Cole stopped beside her. "Nice of you, Rae."

"It might help when he actually sees what he lost. Thanks for letting him come down here and help out."

"He's a good kid. I've met some of his friends at the middle school. It will be good for him to get back into his routine."

"Anything I need to know about in Adam's network of friends?" She knew Cole was often in the schools teaching fire safety classes. Arsonists tended to get started early.

"A couple pranksters, but nothing to worry about."

"He'll take some ribbing about his stuff being underwater and about sleeping on a gym floor for a few days."

"Sure. He'll also be a hero among his real friends because he's got cool stuff to talk about, not to mention making friends with a rescued dog. This hit him hard, but he's bouncing back fine."

"Did you guys make him an honorary member of Company 81?"

"Who, us?" Cole smiled at her. He nudged a LifeSaver from the roll he held, offering her the orange one at the end.

"How are you doing after last night?" She studied his face, looking for the signs of strain around his eyes that she had begun to recognize when he'd had a lot on his mind. Helping Lisa couldn't have been easy.

"It was a bloody tragedy. I frankly don't know how Lisa handles walking into scenes like that." He shook his head. "Your sister is intense at a crime scene. Trying to collect evidence before the water surged inside made it chaotic."

"Did the water ruin any chance of solving the case?"

"It didn't help. As much as we got out before the water forced us to abandon the scene—it probably wasn't enough. But knowing Lisa, she'll figure it out."

"Lisa will take it personally if she can't. She'll do her best." Lisa was known for her ability to think outside the box and find connections in the evidence that could make a difference. "Thanks for not sending the dog to the pound."

"You're not the only one with a soft heart. He needs to stumble into a few soup bones and see a vet." Cole tossed a dry pair of gloves to a man joining the levee crew. "You were the one who suggested I needed a dog."

"You picked an interesting one. That big three-bedroom house all to yourself, a backyard with shade trees—you could probably use more than one. Have you named him yet?"

He rebuttoned his fire coat, getting ready to rejoin the men resetting the pump lines. "I have to come up with something better than Dog?"

She laughed. "Yes."

One of the pump lines being moved hit the pavement with a sharp crack, and the dog disappeared under the blue pump engine. Cole kneeled to coax him out. "He spooks at sudden noises and darts under the nearest vehicle as if his world was coming apart."

"I've seen it before. A tornado goes through a farming community and the next storm that comes, the animals will crash through fences to find shelter. The poor thing must have been swept into the water."

Cole rose as the dog crept out. "Why don't you name him?"

"Me? I don't know good dog names. I've never had one."

"Think about it for a few days."

"He'll end up with a name like Spot."

The dog barked. Cole laughed and ruffled the mutt's ears. "Sounds like he approves."

"No. You can't name him Spot."

"Naming isn't easy. Can you imagine Adam from the Bible being asked to name every animal on earth? No wonder we ended up with *aardvark*. God probably asked Adam how to spell it and Adam replied two *a*'s."

She smiled because it was funny. And she knew she'd find that fact in the Bible when she looked, for Cole was comfortable with the book she was just beginning to learn. "I can come up with a name somewhere between Spot and aardvark. Give me some time to think about it." Rachel took a step back and slipped her hands in her back pockets. "I'm going to be gone for a few days. Can I take you up on that dinner when I get back?"

"Going East to see Jennifer?"

She nodded.

He searched her face, and she tried to keep the worry under control. "Wish her well," he said gently. "We'll have dinner when you get back. You have my number?"

"Memorized."

"Call collect if you want to talk, okay? It won't be an easy trip."

"Thanks."

"Do me a favor and take me up on it."

The offer helped. "Would you pray for her?" Rachel was a new Christian, and she knew she had so much yet to learn about prayer. She didn't want anything she might not understand to hinder an answer.

"You know I will," Cole said. "Remember, God cares about the small things as well as the large, okay? I know the prayers that Jennifer be healed haven't been answered so far, but if the big prayers don't seem to be getting answered, try the small ones. God really is in the midst of this."

She rested her hand on his arm. Cole was helping her bear this burden in so many ways. The steady, dependable calm he had about life headed the list. There weren't words to say thanks. "I'll call you when I arrive."

Rachel had no idea what the temperature was like in Baltimore. Mid-March, turning into spring…she added two summer-weight shirts and a sweater to her bag. Her bedroom was in chaos as she tried to pack. She pulled more tissues from the box, slipped most in the suitcase, and used the last one to blow her nose as she fought tears. She had been with Jennifer through chemotherapy and radiation treatments and had stepped in to help with arrangements for Jennifer's wedding. One remission had come and gone. Her options were shrinking. The idea of seeing Jennifer and having to find something rosy and positive to say… She simply had nothing left to draw from inside, and the last thing Jennifer needed was more sadness. Her brother was on the speakerphone. "Marcus, I'm bringing the family scrapbooks. What else?"

She was so grateful her brother was already out East with Jennifer. "Just you, honey. I'll meet you at the airport."

She picked up her tickets to check the flight number and time. "It's a 9 P.M. flight, but it'll probably be delayed."

"I'll have a book with me. It's not a problem."

Rachel sank down on the bed, holding the package that had been waiting for her, brought in by Gage with the mail. The return address was from Jennifer. "You can tell Jen I'm obeying her note, but it's killing me to wait to open it."

"It's for the flight out here."

Rachel placed it with her purse. In her job when a crisis erupted and she could do something, her coping skills were pretty good. But when unable to help, her defense mechanism was to freeze. She was doing it now, finding it hard to put one step in front of the next. Marcus was reading her correctly and doing what he could to help her out. It was the second time he'd called this afternoon.

Lord, Jennifer has to get better. Please. There has to be some way for that to come true.

Marcus hadn't called in the entire O'Malley family, and he would have done so if things had changed seriously in the last ten days. Rachel had some hope in that. They were a unique family. All seven of them were orphans. They had met decades earlier at Trevor House and later legally changed their last names. They were a family related not by blood but by choice. The O'Malleys thrived as a group by depending on and being there for one other.

Rachel transferred what work she had to take with her to her briefcase. She added the composition book she'd been using as her log for the flood so she could update her notes during the plane trip. Six months from now a glance at the book and she'd be able to see a person's network of friends and neighbors, see in her notes the small things that would matter the most—birthdays and anniversaries—days when this tragedy would really sting.

"How's Jack doing?" Marcus asked.

She smiled. "Working around the clock and playing in the water. Stephen snapped a few pictures at the levee of what is going on. I'll bring them with me."

"Shari arranged a room for you at the private bed-and-breakfast near the hospital. If you want the company, we brought Jennifer's puppy in for a visit."

Another dog in her life... "I'd like that. Thanks."

"Thank me after he hides your shoes. I'll see you in a few hours. I'll be by a phone if you have any problems."

"I'll see you soon, Marcus." Rachel disconnected the call.

She added the Bible she'd started to read in the last few months to her briefcase. *Jesus, I want so badly not to face this.* She had been tugged toward belief by Jennifer, who had such a joy in her life these days even as she fought the cancer. *I can't figure out how to have that joy in suffering that Jennifer describes. I just wish doctors would call and say the cancer is back in remission and heading toward nonexistence. Having her healed would be such a celebration.* The Bible had numerous accounts of people who were very ill being healed by Jesus. She read those passages and had so much hope that maybe Jesus would heal Jennifer too. Her sister believed He would.

Believing in but not seeing that improvement come—Rachel was accustomed to accepting hard things, but this open question of what Jennifer's future held haunted her. When Jennifer smiled and said it was okay, it was going to be so hard to smile back.

Rachel was afraid she was going to Baltimore to help her sister die.

FOUR

Rachel waited until the flight east was at its cruising altitude and the flight attendant had brought refreshments before she reached for the package Jennifer had sent with a note that said: 'Open on the way here.' With hesitant hands she tore open the wrapping paper. The box was old and inside it, nestled in tissue paper, was a fabric-bound book whose plaid colors had faded. The words stamped in gold were still readable: *Diary* and a date. It was Jennifer's diary from the year she had come to Trevor House. Rachel picked it up with care. She remembered the day she'd given the gift to Jennifer.

TREVOR HOUSE

Two Decades Earlier

The group assembled in the third-floor library. The room was musty, the few books on the shelves worn, curled, and warped from heat and humidity. It was a forgotten place, the encyclopedia set even several decades old. Rachel was late to the gathering. She found a seat beside Kate as she offered an apology. Jack and Stephen sat in front of the window taking advantage of the only breeze available. Lisa perched on the edge of an old table. The room was a quiet place to gather, and they had made it their own assembling point when they preferred not to have others listen to their discussions.

"There's a new arrival today," Marcus said, explaining the reason for the meeting. "What do we know about her?"

"A drunk driver hit her parents' car, killing them both," Kate replied. The others winced, for a family with two parents was itself rather rare, and losing both at once was a tragic loss.

"No one wants her?" Stephen asked, his quiet question reflecting what they all felt at the idea.

Kate shook her head. "No family. Not even a distant cousin. She's been staying with neighbors. The court heard the case last week, and no one offering to be her guardian came forward."

Marcus looked around the room. "Do we want a seventh person in our group?"

Rachel tried not to catch his eye, not wanting to be the first one asked to offer an opinion. They must have had a meeting like this to decide on her. It felt selfish to suggest that they had to limit the group size at some point if they wanted to keep it special. Marcus and Kate had led the group for years, and Stephen, Jack, and Lisa were settled in. Rachel was still trying to feel her way. They liked her—why she wasn't quite sure—but they liked her. She wanted to help the group as her thank-you, and if they kept adding numbers, it would be tough to fulfill her role.

Lisa leaned over and tapped Kate's shoulder, whispering something. Kate nodded. "Is she a whiner?" Lisa asked. "We don't need to add a whiner to the group."

Rachel smiled at her roommate. She had never had a more loyal friend in her life, and they had known each other only a few months.

"If she is, I'm sure she'll grow out of it around you," Marcus replied to laughter around the room. "Do we want a seventh person?" he asked again, then looked at her. "Rachel?"

She wasn't sure why he had known she was ambivalent about it, but he was making her decide. "Yes."

"Are you sure?"

She nodded.

"Is that a group consensus?"

There were more nods around the room.

"Then the question becomes, do we want *her* as the seventh?"

"It would make it four to three, gals to guys. I suppose they deserve the advantage in the basketball games," Jack offered.

Kate turned in her chair to smile at him. "You just need another excuse for when we beat you."

"Let's add her," Lisa said. "She'll be the youngest of the group. If she has to endure several years here at Trevor House, we ought to at least make it less hard on her than it was on us coming in."

"She can be our group project."

More laughter met Jack's pronouncement. "Don't get too carried away, Jack," Marcus said. "We're still working on getting you to grow up. Who does she bunk with?"

"Put her with Kate," Lisa suggested. "Kate needs practice at being a mommy."

Kate threw a wadded-up page of notes at Lisa.

"Good idea." Marcus nodded to Kate. "I'll handle talking the office into putting her with you. We need to assemble a welcoming kit. Don't be stingy on items from your stashes."

"Rachel," Kate said, "we need a gift."

She nodded. "Something pretty but useful. I'll find it. And I've still got wrapping paper left."

Marcus stood up. "Let's meet downstairs at one-thirty to greet her."

≈≈≈

Rachel had given Jennifer the new diary as her welcoming gift. She opened the small card Jennifer had put in the box.

Rachel,
 On a day that was one of the hardest and loneliest in my life, you met me midway up the outside steps before I even reached the front door of Trevor House and asked one question: 'What's your favorite flower?' And by the time I reached the third floor bedroom I had been assigned to, the vases were full of carnations. Kate was sitting on her bed reading a magazine. She glanced up and said hi, then pretended to ignore me so I could wipe tears without being noticed. Lisa stopped by to show off a new gerbil she was searching for a place to hide. Pretty jewelry in a box was on the dresser and a stash of cookies were in the nightstand drawer. Stephen brought artwork for the walls, and Marcus—he came with a VCR so I could watch the videotapes I had of my parents. I got swallowed up and made welcome. And the fact that you sat with me on the stairs that first night and just listened to my story—I have never forgotten what it was like to be loved like that. Remember that as you read this diary and share some memories.
 Jennifer

Rachel found her reading glasses, slipped them on, adjusted the reading light, and opened the diary and began to read.

The flight attendant came down the aisle one last time before touchdown, checking trays and seat backs and that people had seat belts buckled. Rachel stowed her items into her briefcase. No matter how much she flew, she would never get accustomed to the disorientation it caused. She had brought one bag and a briefcase, having long ago learned that it was easier to buy what she needed if she ended up staying longer than planned. The plane landed and taxied to a gate. She followed passengers from the plane, Jennifer's gift protected against her chest.
 Marcus met her by the gate and took her bag. She leaned into her brother's hug. "She sent me her diary from her first year at Trevor House."
 "I know."
 "I think I cried and laughed the entire flight here."
 "The headache has your eyes practically crossed."
 "Add to that I'm hungry."
 Marcus stood still, holding her, letting people flow around them. He led the family and there was a reason all of them turned to him: Marcus was a U.S.

Marshal. He could handle any trouble that came his way. She hugged him, grateful that he was in her life.

"Kate called. She swung by to see Lisa and the guys. All is quiet on the home front."

"Good. I brought pictures of Jack's ducks."

"I'd ask, but you said Jack's name. They weren't alive, were they?"

She giggled. "Rubber ducks. But I'm sure if someone had suggested the real thing, he would have located them somewhere." She stepped back. "Let's get to this bed-and-breakfast. What time is Jennifer expecting me tomorrow?"

"She asked if I'd bring you over to the hospital about ten. She's got something planned, but she's keeping it a secret."

"How's she doing?"

"Jennifer? Trust me. She hasn't changed. She talked me into wearing a tux and tails and taking a special dinner to her friends in the pediatrics cancer ward."

"I bet you looked...spiffy."

"Shari laughed. Putting my fiancée and Jen together is trouble," Marcus replied, his voice softening at the mention of his fiancée's name. Rachel was glad he had found Shari as his partner for life. Someday she was going to have that too. She thought about Cole and wondered what Marcus would say about him. His opinion mattered to her, more than he knew.

The airport was busy but the parking lots had cleared out. Once seated in the car Rachel opened her briefcase and removed her composition folder for the flood. She clicked on her penlight to make sure she had her to-do list for tomorrow in order. She had a list of calls to make in the morning. She understood the bureaucracies involved in emergency assistance, and just getting people status updates could eliminate a lot of stress.

"What's coming up on your calendar?"

Rachel reached for her day planner. The latch had given way, so she had used sturdy rubber bands to hold it together. "Pretty light. I've got a commission meeting in Washington on May 10. Clayton, Georgia, is dedicating a memorial on May 6 to the five who died in the tornado last year. I'm planning to go. On the come-if-possible list are—" she counted—"twelve graduation and three birthday parties. Denver, Chicago, and Miami. I'll make most of them."

"When's the commission report being released?"

"July. We're already passing around drafts." The Presidential Commission on School Violence had held two public hearings this year and had another two scheduled. She'd been serving on it since December. Kids killed kids. She knew it. She'd counseled kids forced to live through it. But she wished she hadn't said yes when the president of the Red Cross asked her to serve. It was a tough assignment.

"The bottom line?"

"The chain of events leading to a shooting can be broken at a thousand places. But parents, adults, or friends have to intercede. The signs of trouble are there—kids are poor at hiding that kind of pain and anger—but adults and friends often don't step in for just as many reasons. Shootings will keep happening. A report isn't going to change that."

"Not an easy fact to live with."

"No, it's not."

He took her hand and squeezed gently. "Let it go. You've only got time to fight one battle at a time."

"That from a man whose pager goes off more often than mine." Rachel returned the notebooks to her briefcase. "I'm wearing out."

"And I worry about you. Anything I can do?"

She rested her head on the headrest. She wished there were. "A vacation would help. A few days of solid sleep. I'll be able to get both next month."

"You said that last month too."

"I mean it this time."

Marcus slipped a card from his pocket. "I got you something."

She took the plastic card he offered her.

"It's a guarantee of a room at any hotel in their chain, anytime you need one. The bills come to me, so order room service."

She turned it over and laughed at the sticker on the back. There was a badger sticking its nose out of a hole. "I like your gift."

"You better use it."

Marcus had a way of offering just what she needed when she needed it. "I will. Thanks."

Rachel knew hospitals in a way few others outside of staff could. As a trauma psychologist she spent about a third of her life in them—visiting with patients, sitting with relatives, talking with doctors and rescue personnel. When on the job it wasn't uncommon for her to be the one getting direct updates from the hospital personnel to convey to the families involved. She'd learned what to expect and the questions to ask, but it didn't make her any more comfortable spending time in one. She carried the family scrapbooks and wondered what Jennifer had planned for their Sunday.

"Marcus, go ahead and make your call." His partner Quinn Diamond had paged him as they were coming inside.

"You sure?"

"Room 3212. I can find it."

"I'll be up in five minutes."

Rachel was relieved to be able to go up on her own. It was one thing to keep a steady expression for Jennifer, another to fool Marcus who saw her just before she entered the room. She knew how critical it was to keep her composure during the first few minutes.

She found 3212 and leaned around the doorway.

"Rae!" Jennifer beamed at her and waved her into the room. She was sitting up in bed, a newspaper spread across the blanket.

It wasn't the loss of hair covered by a colorful scarf, the jaundice, or the thinness that threatened to freeze Rachel in the doorway. Jennifer looked so incredibly young. Rachel crossed the room to the bedside and hugged her sister, in no hurry to let go. "Hi." She leaned back, relieved to find Jen's blue eyes clear of pain. There was joy there. "Marriage looks like it suits you."

Jennifer grinned at her. "Tom just went to check on something for me. Sit, Rae, sit. Marcus didn't tell me a fraction of it." Rachel eased down on the side of the bed. Jen laid her hands lightly on either side of Rachel's face and studied her. "The stress is showing. The missing sleep shadows are growing and we need to get some hair color. You've got gray hair appearing."

"I've been working around Jack recently."

Jennifer laughed. "That would do it."

Rachel tugged a strand. "I've been hoping it would come in as a nice white."

"Just gray, I'm afraid." A quiet moment lingered as Jen still held her face. "Don't worry about something you can't change. Do that for me?"

Rachel didn't have a good answer to that request. "I like to worry." She was struggling with a new faith that said it wasn't necessary. It felt so foreign not to worry.

"I know." Jen smiled at her. "I love you for it, even though I want you to stop." She rubbed Rachel's arms, then nodded toward what Rachel held. "What did you bring me?"

"Photo albums."

"Oh, excellent! The old ones too?"

Rachel nodded. "I thought Shari might like to see the ones of Marcus as a teenager."

"She'll love it."

The door opened. "I found a blanket, but they only had pink, I'm afraid, so we're going to stand out for a mile." Tom came into the room pushing a wheelchair. "I had greater success on the pillows and beach towels though. Hey, Rae."

"Tom." Rachel smiled as she turned. She was enveloped in a hug by him.

"You ready to bolt from this place for the day?"

Rachel looked over at Jen. "What do you have planned?"

"An adventure. Bring the albums."

"Marcus is on the way up," Rachel commented.

"Good. He's going to get my puppy for me. Shari is bringing lunch."

Tom pushed the wheelchair next to the bed. Jennifer rested her head against her husband's shoulder, wrapped her arms around his neck, and he carefully lifted her from the bed to the wheelchair.

Rachel blinked away tears. Jen was no longer walking. It might not be official, but Tom made the move with an ease that said he had done it many times.

Blanket, pillow, beach towels…Rachel was glad they were getting out of the hospital for a while. She already found herself at her limits and the day had only just begun.

Rachel had forgotten how relaxing it was to be with her sister. For the afternoon Rachel's attention barely went beyond the fact that it was a comfortable temperature, sunny, and she was in love with the puppy scampering around her feet. For the first time in months there was peace inside. "He's wonderful."

"You need a dog of your own," Jennifer said.

Rachel was already coming to that conclusion. If she couldn't have kids in the forseeable future, at least she could have a dog.

Jennifer reclined on a blanket to enjoy the day outside. The Johns Hopkins complex was behind them, this grassy park area held for future expansion. They were just a few of those who had come out to enjoy the day. It was a place of normalcy for those otherwise having to fight against serious illness.

"My Washington apartment doesn't allow pets, and the Chicago one—I'm not home enough."

"Then it's time to move."

"You make that sound so simple. Maybe next year." Rachel struggled to stop a yawn. Lunch followed by the warmth of the day was making her sleepy. Marcus's fiancée Shari was already dozing lightly, a book resting open on the blanket beside her.

Jennifer's attention turned to Tom hustling over the grass tossing a Frisbee back and forth with Marcus. "Is my husband good-looking or what?"

Rachel laughed. "You don't want me to answer that. You get jealous."

"I love being married."

"I've figured that out. Tom spoils you rotten."

"He tries to." Jennifer tossed the sunscreen she used out of habit to the side. "How's Cole?"

"Jen."

"I'm not the only one who would like you to be married."

Cole was one of the most intriguing guys she knew, but Rachel didn't want to mislead her sister. "He's Jack's boss. He's a friend. Let's leave it at that." She had so many knots in her past, and her present would never fit a definition of orderly. As much as she hoped something might work out with Cole, she knew better than to assume anything. Her past wasn't as tough as Kate's or as tragic as Jennifer's, but it had still left scars.

Jennifer dropped the towel over her face. "Where'd I go?"

A bark, and the puppy set to joyfully digging with his front paws at the towel. He lifted the edge and shoved his nose underneath to pull it off Jennifer. The little guy gave her face a bath as she giggled. "I taught him this game."

"So I see."

The puppy tried to climb over Jennifer and got stuck. She helped him with a push. "He is so much fun."

Rachel held out her hand and the puppy came to climb all over her. "He still looks a bit like a butterball." He settled across her lap, panting.

"Butterball is his unofficial name since my lapse in speech with Jack." Suffering from a bad fall and confused by medicinal side effects, when Jennifer had first seen the golden fur and a very round puppy, she told their brother that Tom had bought her a butterball for Christmas. Amid the laughter, it had stuck.

Jennifer returned to studying the album and the loose pictures Rachel had slipped in the front. "Who's this?" Jen held up a picture.

"Adam Noles. Jack was teaching him the finer points of skipping rocks in the river."

"One of yours?"

"He got a card," Rachel confirmed.

"I thought so. Think anything from their home will be salvageable?"

"Not much. If it was just rising water in the house, it would be one thing, but there's a strong current through the floodwaters doing a lot of damage. His mom Ann is hopeful, but it's going to be a mess."

"How long before you know?"

"Once the water recedes they have to get the structural engineers in to look at the homes. It will be at least a week before cleanup can start. Have you found the pictures of Jack and his rubber ducks yet?"

"I just did. These are priceless."

Rachel looked at the picture Jen held up. "That duck was his tribute to Cassie." She settled her hands behind her head and closed her eyes against the sun. "Summer is going to be here before we know it. And this sun is going to give me freckles."

"You look good with freckles. You know what we need this summer? An O'Malley ladies only weekend. A hotel, pool, girl talk."

"What a wonderful idea," Rachel agreed.

"Maybe we can talk Kate into setting a wedding date."

"She wants to elope."

"It takes two. Dave's sister Sara would kill him."

"Very true." Rachel wasn't sure which O'Malley wedding would come next. Lisa and Quinn's probably, but Lisa wanted to wait on Marcus, and he and Shari didn't want to set a date while Jennifer was in the hospital. Everyone was trying not to make plans so as not to complicate things for Jennifer.

"Ouch."

Rachel turned sharply, for it wasn't a soft sound. "What's wrong?" She had watched Jennifer closely enough through the day to know that the pain was constant and her energy didn't last long. Her health was precarious at best, all the upbeat talk notwithstanding.

"Just a twinge. I moved wrong." Jen was leaning back on her elbows, cautiously moving her toes.

"Tom!"

"Did you have to—?"

"I had to."

"Here, Jen, lean back against this." Shari offered her pillow.

Tom came hustling over. "Good plan. Lay back, hon."

"The meds are wearing off. That's all."

"Any numbness?" Tom asked.

"Just that all-too-familiar pinch followed by a case of the tingles."

"Since we've been out here for three hours and I've been run ragged by your brother, it's just as well." Tom leaned down and kissed Jen's forehead. "Let's go, darling." He scooped her up and settled her carefully in the wheelchair.

Rachel hurriedly gathered up the blanket and pictures.

"It's no big deal, Rae," Jen tried to reassure. "The meds wear off and it's like an adrenaline letdown. It caught me by surprise is all. I just need a nap."

Rachel smiled at Jen because her sister didn't want this to be a problem. "We both could do with an afternoon nap."

"Who's got the puppy?"

"I do, Jen," Marcus said. "Go with them, Rae. Shari and I will bring the stuff."

Rachel paced in the lounge down the hall from Jennifer's room, feeling like the walls were closing in on her. By the time Jen was settled back in bed, she was no longer trying to insist that it was no big deal. She was in severe pain and the numbness had spread.

Rachel drew in a deep breath, fighting the fear. *Jesus, I can't do this.* How many people had she sat beside who were having to accept losing a loved one? She knew what it would be like toward the end and what the aftermath would do to the O'Malleys. *I see so many lives cut short—by illness, natural disasters, tragedies caused by men. I don't have it in me to lose family. Please, Lord, be merciful.*

Tom stopped beside her and rested his hand on the window glass.

"Is she going to die here?" Rachel whispered.

"They'll tell her to go home first."

"How long does she have?"

"She won't die in a hospital, Rae. I've promised her that."

She leaned against Tom and hugged him. Jennifer had married such a good man. The fact he hadn't even offered a guess for how much time was left... "How can I help you?"

He drew in a deep breath. "Pray. She's still got the heart to win. She doesn't want to talk yet about that not happening."

"She's a realist under that optimism."

"She's not talking about that reality because she knows I can't handle it."

Rachel tightened her grip. She was hurting, but for Tom…this must be agony to daily watch Jen's decline.

"Rae, she's getting better in some ways. Her blood work is finally improving. Another remission is possible."

"But is it likely?"

"No."

The silence lingered. With a child she knew the words to help, with a woman she understood how to communicate with the silence, but for a doctor watching his wife die… "Jen mentioned she was craving peanut butter cookies."

Tom kissed her forehead. "I know why she loves you so much." He tucked a tissue in her hand. "She'll sleep for the rest of the afternoon. Marcus will take you back to the bed-and-breakfast if you'd also like to get a nap. Why don't you join us for dinner around six? Bring the photo albums. It was good to hear her laugh today."

"My pleasure." She hugged him. "Six o'clock."

Rachel was glad Marcus was driving. She wiped her eyes, grateful she didn't have to hide tears from him but doing her best to stop them. There was a place deep in her heart where an ocean of tears was waiting to fall if she let them start.

"You want to talk?" Marcus asked.

They were almost to the bed-and-breakfast. Rachel shook her head and quieted the puppy she held.

"You need to."

"Is it going to get worse than this in the next week? Do we need to get everyone here?"

Marcus rubbed the back of his neck. "No. Jen is stable. Not doing great, but stable."

"Then I think today I just want to sleep."

Marcus reached over and squeezed her hand. "Kate's coming in on Wednesday for a quick day visit. Jen doesn't have the energy for a bunch of us. We'll have one of us with her at all times, with Tom."

"He needs that support."

"It's there." Marcus glanced over. "You heard about Lisa's tough task during the flood, but did you hear about Kate's evening last night?"

"No."

"She got called out on a domestic squabble, a guy threatening to shoot his elderly mom. It goes on a couple hours; she isn't getting anywhere negotiating with the guy, so she has the SWAT team guys dig up the cable line going into the house and cut it. She got the man so mad at her for making him miss the ending of the ballgame that he came out of the house to go after her. They cuffed him while he yelled at her."

"It sounds just like Kate."

"She called me when she got home and wanted to know if I had heard the game's final score. She'd been following the game while negotiating with the guy and wanted to know how it ended." Marcus shook his head. "I trust her instincts—she can figure out a way to end a standoff short of a tactical response in more creative ways than I have ever seen—but every time she gets one of those calls…"

"She'll never change that take-control attitude when a hostage is involved." Rachel agreed. "The best thing you can do is just keep close contact."

"Anything I can do for you when I get back to Chicago? I know you were rushed to get out here." Now that they were both engaged men, Marcus and his partner Quinn had arranged to split their time fifty-fifty between Washington, D.C. and Chicago, where their respective fiancée's Shari and Lisa worked.

"I think I'm covered," Rachel replied. "Jack's going to call if the river gets away from them. And Gage is keeping an eye on my place for me; he'll handle mail and the rest."

"If Jennifer needs anything, just let Kate know and she can bring it out with her on Wednesday."

"Will do."

"We'll get through this, Rae."

She wondered if he was saying it for her benefit or his own. They had no choice.

The puppy disappeared under the bed with Rachel's tennis shoe. "It won't fit under there." She gave up and held out her favorite belt. The end was taken, shaken, and the belt disappeared after the shoes. "And those were new shoes, just for your information."

She couldn't sleep and she was talking to a dog. Rachel tugged the pillow over. Grief was hitting so hard it was difficult to breathe.

Jesus, what do I do? I need to sleep. I really need to sleep.

Was she going to be facing a family funeral this summer? The thought was terrifying. *Why don't You heal her? Why are the prayers answered with silence? Am I doing something wrong?*

She could counsel Marissa through that question, but she didn't know how to answer it for herself. Through the past year Jennifer had shown a joy and confidence that didn't waver. Rachel would have pegged it as denial—the safe place that people went to when the tragedy was this huge—but now she knew it wasn't denial as much as it was hope.

What am I going to do when Jennifer's hope wavers?

She wasn't ready for this.

Rachel thought about Cole and the way he so easily fell asleep. She wished she was more like him. Did years of believing lead to that calm trust, or was she missing something more profound? Rachel thought about calling him, but he'd likely be at the levee and busy. Besides, she couldn't think of anything to ask him; she'd be calling just to hear the comfort of his voice.

The comfort of his voice… She buried her face in her pillow. Cole had slipped through her defenses over the last year. He'd shown himself to be a man able to help her carry the weight of nights like this one.

Her relationship with Cole was so different than most in her life. He didn't need her for anything, not really. It was disquieting to realize she consciously tried to keep the scales balanced in most of her relationships. With Gage it was a balance of helping him with his grief and her getting back in return someone she could absolutely trust. With the O'Malleys it was helping them with anything they needed as a thank-you for the deep family loyalty she had that survived any pressure.

With Cole…he might seek out her company, enjoy it, but his life was pretty complete as it was. He was ready to settle down, and he needed someone to love who would love him back. If she missed fulfilling that, then there weren't many other things he needed to take up the slack.

Jesus, this is scary. An unbalanced scale with Cole—I need him more than he needs me. Does he realize that? Does it matter to him? Or is my desire to have a balanced scale part of my own habit of trying to stay safe in a relationship? To ensure that I am needed and thus not going to be abandoned? It's old territory, Lord, and I wish I were past this. It complicates my life and my relationship with Cole. I trust You. I know Cole is Your man. Help me figure out how to trust You for my security without attaching that emotional weight to Cole.

Rachel looked at the clock and didn't know if Cole was working the day shift or still working nights. She'd feel awful if she woke him up when he most needed his rest, but she needed to talk about Jennifer and this grief.

She leaned over and picked up her Bible, seeking a deeper source of comfort available tonight. There was a slip of paper in the front where she'd been collecting verses on suffering and comfort and prayer. Jennifer understood the subjects as did Cole, but Rachel couldn't share this with Jennifer unless she understood not only the words but also what they meant.

> *"After you have suffered a little while, the God of all grace, who has called you to his eternal glory in Christ, will himself restore, establish, and strengthen you"* (1 Peter 5:10).

> *"These things I have spoken to you, that my joy may be in you, and that your joy may be full"* (John 15:11).

"Is any one among you suffering? Let him pray. Is any cheerful? Let him sing praise" (James 5:13).

She loved the first verse and was puzzled by the second. The verse in James was clear, but what was she supposed to pray for regarding suffering? Relief from it? The verse in 1 Peter suggested that God would step in when the time was right.

Jennifer had often said that prayer was simply the honest expression of what was on your heart. Cole said to pray for the small things when the big things didn't seem to be answered.

Jesus, I'm thankful that I have so many incredible people around me—Jennifer, Marcus, Kate, Cole, even Gage, who has taught me that anything can be endured if necessary. I'm suffering because I love Jennifer and the cancer is taking her from me. I know heaven is real and a day is coming when all of this will go away, and there will be no more illness or evil or suffering in our lives. Heaven sounds so gloriously peaceful. But I don't want heaven to come yet. I want more time with my sister. Please, don't let her die.

The puppy started pushing his bed around the room. Rachel held down her hand and snapped her fingers. He scampered over to join her. "Are you going to wear out soon?"

He rolled over to have his tummy rubbed.

"That's what I thought."

She obliged. It was comforting to have him around.

"Lisa? It's Cole." It had taken him more than two hours to track her down on a Sunday night. "Sorry to interrupt." His secretary had gone to Post-it notes with messages across the back of his chair because his desk was overflowing with incoming mail. Arson investigations didn't stop just because he was wading through water for a few days. Cole pulled them off, read them, and either deep-sixed them for later in the week or added them to his list of calls to make tonight.

"Don't worry about it," Lisa replied. "I'm between trips to the lab. It's been a busy night for people dying. What's happening?"

"Your murder at the house that was flooding out—"

"Hold on." She shifted the phone. "No, I need that blood panel tonight. Her kid is in the hospital with the same symptoms!" she hollered back in answer to another question. "Sorry, Cole. Carol Iles. Okay. I'm with you now."

"I knew her." It hadn't clicked until he read the obituary in the newspaper this afternoon, and forty minutes of hunting through archived files had confirmed it.

"How?"

"Five years ago, a house fire. Her son was playing with matches. Her name was Carol Rice then, which is why it didn't click."

"That fits. Detective Wilson's been looking at her background. She'd been divorced less than a year with joint custody of one son. Wilson jotted a note that the boy lives with his father."

"Her son—that would be Mark."

"Was it an accidental fire, or the first signs of future trouble?"

"My notes show that he was playing with matches in her closet. He had all her expensive shoes piled together in a mound with one of her silk blouses balled up under them."

"He'd have been what, eight, nine? This kid is trouble."

"Home had been a battleground and the fire was just the latest round. I'm not surprised to hear the marriage came apart in divorce. His dad dismissed the fire as 'boys will be boys.'"

"Has Mark started any other fires lately?" Lisa asked.

"He got through middle school with a lot of stuff I suspect but can't prove— a trash can fire, bottle rockets, pulling the fire alarm. I'm more worried now that he's a freshman in high school. He's hanging out with a bad crowd. The boy strikes me as an insecure kid, a bully, looking for attention even if it's for being a troublemaker."

"Would he be violent enough to kill his mom?"

"I'm no expert on what a kid might do. But no, I think this info is just background noise," Cole said.

"I'll pass it along to Wilson."

"Making any progress with other leads?"

"Not much. No luck matching the bullet to a gun."

"The river will crest soon. Let me know if you need a lift back to the crime scene."

"I'll do that. Thanks, Cole."

"Talk to you soon, Lisa." He cradled the phone with one hand and closed the Mark Rice file with the other. He'd have to get by the high school Monday and talk to the counselor. It was hard to tell how Mark would react to Carol's death. Cole didn't want to deal with another arson fire set by an angry boy.

Cole dialed home and checked for messages. If Rachel had called, she hadn't left a message. He hoped she was handling today okay. She had called from Baltimore to let him know she'd arrived, but he hadn't heard from her since. He wished she would call. He could do so little from here. The next trip Rachel took East to see Jennifer, he would figure out a way to go with her.

FIVE

"Did you ever plan to become a doctor? Or did we just decide you'd make a good one?" Rachel asked Jennifer, idly paging through one of the photo albums. The lights were dim and Tom was sound asleep in the hospital chair by the window. Rachel was keeping one eye on the clock. She had moved her flight to nine o'clock Tuesday night, and she didn't want to leave one moment before she had to. It was getting close to that time.

"The way I remember it was I wanted to be a surgeon and you and Lisa kept taking me by the hospital nursery to see the babies."

"I remember now. That was around when Lisa got fascinated with what they did with dead people."

"I did not enjoy that visit to the morgue."

Rachel didn't think she would ever forget her glance into the autopsy room. "Don't tell Lisa, but I nearly threw up." She held up the list they had written over twenty years ago when they were meeting to decide on a last name for their new family. "I forgot we had the name Lewis on the list."

"Who suggested that?"

Rachel held the list close to see the handwriting. "Lisa."

"She wanted matching initials."

Rachel read to the bottom of the list and laughed. "Jack suggested Magnificent."

"Jack Magnificent." Jen let that draw out. "What a fantastic name. Who suggested O'Malley?"

"I don't know. It's not on the list. There is a list of nationalities. I wanted an Australian connection. Ireland is not on the list though."

"You need one of the later lists. That sounds like our first meeting on the topic."

Rachel studied the list. "I think you're right. If you find the last list, set it aside. It would be a good memento."

"I'll keep an eye out." Jen slid over the pad of paper she held. "That's everything I can think of that I could use sent out here. The pistachio nuts are the most important item. They are Tom's favorites and he needs something to munch on."

Rachel scanned Jennifer's list. Most items could easily be bought here, but that wasn't the point. Jen knew it helped if there was anything tangible she could let family do for her. "I'll send the stuff out with Kate." Rachel closed the photo album and looked over at Tom. "Do you think I should wake him up before I go? He's got to be uncomfortable in that chair."

"Let him sleep."

Rachel reluctantly got up from her chair and gave Jennifer a long hug. Rachel leaned back, searching her sister's face, very aware of the fact that it might be the last time she saw her alive. She didn't want to forget so much as a curl of an eyelash, and she was afraid that over time this memory might dim. "I'll call you when I get back to Chicago."

"Please do. No matter what the time."

"God bless, Jen."

Her sister hugged her back tightly. "He already has. He gave me you for a sister." Jen leaned back. "And I want to hear about this dinner with Cole."

She should have never mentioned it. "It's not that big a deal."

"Right. You'll tell me everything?"

Rachel smiled. "Maybe not *every*thing."

It would have been cheaper just to buy a new picnic table. The sander jammed and kicked back at him. Cole shut it off, wiped the sweat from his hands, and reached for the ringing phone. "Cole." The bugs around the garage light swarmed in a hum. His second chance to get a few hours at home, and he'd felt like taking out some of his weariness on wood. Ann's patio furniture had likely been washed away, and this table would at least be a start in replacing it.

"Hello, Cole."

The voice was faint but just hearing it filled him with pleasure. He settled on the bench he had been sanding and pressed the phone close. "Jennifer O'Malley. This is a surprise."

"A good one I hope?"

"You're now the bright spot of my day."

"That bad?"

He laughed. "It's been a long one."

"I've only got a minute, I'm afraid. Could you do me a favor?"

"Done."

"You're a trusting man."

"I just know you."

"Rachel is on her way to Chicago. She's trying to sneak back into town."

His smile disappeared. "Jen—"

"I can't call family. I gave her my word."

The bonds between the O'Malleys went deep. If Jennifer had given her word, she wouldn't break it. But she couldn't leave a problem alone either.

"Rachel just left the hospital. I'm worried about her. I was trying not to cry on her shoulder too much, but she's so good about being empathetic that I probably did more than I realized. They stuck me in a wheelchair for good."

Cole wanted to help, but for all the time that he and Rae had spent together, she had yet to call him when she was in trouble. And he knew he wasn't the one she would necessarily turn to when the pain hit this hard. "Call Gage."

"I did," Jennifer said softly. "He's not home."

So much for hoping Jennifer would say he was wrong about the way the wind blew. Gage had several years of history with Rachel, and in the past Cole had himself called Gage on Rae's behalf. For Rae trust was the hardest emotion to extend, and she trusted Gage with her tears. Cole wanted that role in her life, but he was very aware that he would have to earn it.

In the last few months Rachel had let him into a lot of her life, but the relationship was still progressing slower than he'd like. He understood part of it. Rachel didn't take major risks in relationships; she inched her way to find out if the ground was safe before stepping forward. He wanted forever with someone; he had chosen her; and he was trying to proceed at her pace. She had heavy burdens to carry right now with Jennifer's illness and her own work. He'd tried not to step into the time and energy Rae had left and take it for himself when she really needed some breathing space. "What time's her flight getting in?"

"After midnight. Northwest flight 712."

"It's not a problem. I'll meet her."

"I appreciate that."

"I'm sorry about the wheelchair," Cole offered, at a loss for better words to express how sorry he was for what it represented.

"So am I. Tom wants to get me one of those horns they put on kids' bicycle handlebars so I can warn people I'm coming through. I've got to work on left turns. You'll help Rae, Cole? With whatever she needs?"

There was more going on than what she was saying. "You know I will, Jen. I'm glad you called."

"So am I. Thanks, Cole."

"Anytime, Jennifer." Cole said and hung up the phone. Rae had so much on her plate right now. She wouldn't want company tonight. Not when she had just left her sister, not if the news there was bad. He had observed Rachel long enough to know she was a hider by nature, wanting to curl up with her own thoughts until she gathered perspective on what to do. But Jennifer wouldn't have asked if she wasn't concerned.

Lord, what should I do?

Rachel might not want the company, but she needed it. Giving her twenty-four hours would leave the situation twenty-four hours older, but it wouldn't heal the hurt on its own. Cole went to call the airline for the exact flight arrival time.

〜〜〜

Rachel glanced up from her book as the seat belt light chimed and flashed off for the fourth time during this return flight to Chicago. Given the repeated turbulence, adults ignored the freedom because they knew the seat belt light would be back on soon for landing.

There was a scramble behind her. "We're going to crash."

She turned to look at the young girl pulling on the back of her seat, peering over the headrest. "If we do, I'll get you out." Rachel was sitting in the emergency exit aisle. She'd worked too many plane crash aftermath's to voluntarily sit anywhere else.

"And Mommy?"

"And Mommy."

"What are you doing?"

She half closed the book to show the cover. "Reading a teenage girl's diary that was published."

"She's pretty."

"Yes, she is." She was also dead. The Columbine High School shooting had been memorialized in several ways, *The Journals of Rachel Scott* one of the more poignant. Rachel's namesake had been murdered, and all the dreams written in the diary would remain just dreams.

Setting aside the book, she reached for the sack in the empty seat beside her and offered a gummy bear to her new friend.

"What do you say, Kelly?" the girl's mom said.

"Th'k you."

Rachel shared a smile with Kelly's mom. Traveling with an infant and a bored, bright young girl who was not interested in sleeping was a challenge. "Is someone meeting you at the airport?"

"My father," Kelly's mom said.

"I'll give you a hand getting down the causeway if you'd like. I'm traveling light; I checked my bag."

"I'd appreciate that. I worry about Kelly getting away from me in the crowd."

"I stay close, Mom."

"You try to, honey."

The infant went from sleep to scowl to tears. Rachel winced, knowing painful pressure in the ears was an unpleasant way to wake up. "We're descending."

The offered pacifier eased the infant's pain. "Buckle your seat belt, Kelly."

The girl scrambled to fasten her seat belt again and then looked out the window. "That's Chicago?"

It was hard to see the city lights through the haze and light rain, but there were glimmering twinkles down there.

"That's home," Rachel agreed, stowing her book in her briefcase. If she could slip into town unnoticed, she just might get twenty-four hours to herself before she returned to the site of the flooding. She had plans to curl up on her couch in a nest of pillows with a homemade milkshake and watch reruns of *Quincy* she had on tape until her mind was numb and she fell asleep.

"Grandpa."

Rachel released Kelly's hand to let her join the gray-haired man getting up from the first seat in the waiting area.

"It looks like we're not the only one being met." Kelly's mom nodded toward the concourse.

Rachel turned to look. Cole stood a few feet away blocking traffic, people flowing around him like he was a rock in the middle of a river. She held his gaze for a long, searching moment, then looked away. "So it appears. That's Cole." Her rock. Immovable. And not supposed to be here.

Kelly tugged on Rachel's jeans. "He's a fireman?"

Surprised at Kelly's question, Rachel glanced back. He wore his old jacket, wet at the shoulders, faded jeans, and then she saw the boots. Only Cole would think nothing about wearing steel-tipped black boots with yellow stripes on the sides outside of an arson scene. "Either that or a sewer repairman."

Cole heard her and chuckled.

Rachel touched the child's shoulder. "Have fun with your grandparents, Kelly."

"We're going to go see the big fish aquarium this week."

"That's a good plan."

Rachel said farewell to Kelly's mom and moved to join Cole. "I didn't realize you knew I was coming back to Chicago tonight."

"Jennifer called me. Gage apparently wasn't home."

And her sister didn't have time to be subtle—she was matchmaking from a hospital bed. *Oh, Jennifer, did you have to call Cole?* Rachel knew that Jennifer's focus on seeing the O'Malleys settled could come across as pushy if presented wrong. "I could have caught a taxi." She never knew how long she might be gone on a trip, so she had a habit of taxiing back and forth to the airport.

"Nonsense. You want to spend the next hour in a smoky taxi with a stranger? Tollway traffic is always a mess when it rains," he said easily.

Cole had a point, but she struggled to offer him a smile and thanks. She wanted this man to see her at her best, and right now she was far from it. If exhaustion was not written across her face, the sadness probably was. She was ready for the anonymity of strangers.

"Not that pleased to see me?"

"It's not that, Cole. I'm just overwhelmed right now," she apologized. "I'm afraid I'm not adjusting well to even good surprises today."

"That I can understand." Cole held out his hand for her briefcase. "Why don't we see if we can't make life a little less overwhelming."

She stepped forward, gave him the briefcase, and wrapped her arms around him in a hug. "I missed you."

She heard her briefcase hit the floor beside him as his arms came around her. He was such a solid, steady man, and it felt good to close her eyes for a moment and just enjoy the comfort he offered. He cared so much about making this better, and she leaned into that strength and emotion, using it to let go of the trip and the weight it had pressed into her soul.

"Forget my phone number?" he asked softly.

"I thought about calling just to hear your voice."

"Why didn't you?"

She was wondering the same thing and sighed. "I didn't want to interrupt your work."

Cole rested his head on hers. "Work I get 365 days a year. It doesn't hold a candle to you."

She smiled as those words reassured that they were okay. "I'm sorry I didn't call," she whispered.

"You're forgiven." He stepped back and tipped up her chin. "How's Jennifer really doing? She dodged my question." She held his gaze as his searched hers, seeing in his eyes the same sympathy she heard in his voice.

"Jaundiced. On morphine. Spending what time she's out of bed in a wheelchair. We cruised the pediatric cancer wing at Johns Hopkins last night reading bedtime stories and hearing 'bless my mommy and my daddy and my kitten' prayers. The kids giggled at the fact that their visiting doctor had no hair."

His hands soothed hers. "I'm sorry you couldn't stay longer."

"Three days was enough. You could tell Jennifer was trying to be up for me."

Cole reached down and picked up her briefcase. He turned her toward the concourse. "Feel like eating?"

"Another time perhaps."

He rubbed the spot on the back of her shoulders where her headaches were born. "Let it go."

"It's not that easy."

"You can sleep in, watch cartoons in the morning."

The man had passed forty and stopped apologizing for liking Road Runner and Wile E. Coyote. "I appreciate the suggestion. I'll stick to my newspaper, coffee, and a morning walk."

They had to wait for the luggage to appear on the carousel. Since Cole had bought her the luggage for Christmas, she let him retrieve the bag. He was a practical man. Gage bought her a Christmas wreath; Cole bought her luggage. She thought he spent too much, but a quiet word from her brother Jack had stopped her from mentioning that. She hadn't known the autographed baseball she gave Cole for Christmas to replace one destroyed by a vandal had been worth a small fortune. She'd had it in a drawer. She hadn't looked at the value of the gift and neither had Cole.

"You're doing it again, Rae."

"What?"

"Worrying a problem in circles."

She slipped her hand under his arm, squeezed his forearm, and offered a smile. "A bad habit of mine." She really was trying to take those worries to God and then let them go. "Take me home."

"Home it is."

Cole led the way through the tunnel to the parking garage. He unlocked the passenger door for her and the faint smell of charred wood filtered out. His fire coat had been tossed on the backseat. "You came here from a fire scene?"

"Left over from this afternoon."

"Was it serious?"

"No injuries, moderate damage. Repairs to an attic fan sparked and caused an insulation fire." He pulled out into traffic.

"I came up with a name for your dog," Rachel offered.

"You did? I've been waiting with great expectation."

"Hank."

Cole laughed.

"Have you ever met someone named Hank?"

"Besides a famous pitcher and singer? No."

Rachel swatted his arm. "I like it."

"Hank. Okay, I suppose the mutt can grow into it. It's an old dog name."

The rain was intensifying. Rachel watched the wet darkness. She had missed Cole, and his calm presence. Just seeing him was enough to help her relax. It meant a lot that he had set aside his plans for the night to come and meet her. "I changed my mind. Think you can find carryout at this time of night? I need to talk."

"This storm is drifting east over the lake. If you don't mind eating in the car, I'll find us Chinese carryout and a place to park and watch the storm."

"Please."

Lightning hit the water. The blinding flash destroyed Cole's night vision.

"Wow."

Rae had disappeared into the darkness, but the awe in her voice told Cole she'd seen it too. She emerged from the shadows as his eyes adjusted again to the night. She had folded her jacket into a temporary pillow behind her against the window and turned in the seat to angle toward him. She'd finished her sweet and sour chicken. It wasn't the elegant Chinese dinner he'd hoped for, but it was hot and she'd been hungry. He was pleased to see her relaxing.

Cole set his shrimp-fried rice carton on the dash. "It's a good show tonight." Lake Michigan was spread out in a vast expanse from this parking lot at the south end of Illinois Beach State Park. Rae said she'd nearly called just to hear his voice—he let that one linger, pleased to realize she'd been thinking about him. And his new dog had been on her mind. *Hank.* He was not letting her name their first child.

"The storm is scary."

"Powerful."

He let the silence return. He had no desire to push, not about her family. But it was late, and after what Jennifer had said when she called, Cole felt he didn't have the option to take a pass on this one. He rested his left arm across the steering wheel, picked up the special issue North Carolina quarter he'd received in change, and walked it through his fingers. "What's going on, Rae? You told Jennifer not to call family. You don't hide like a turtle from them unless the pressure is fierce."

She sighed. "It's easier to have these conversations over the phone than in person."

"Then I'll take you home and you can call me."

It earned him a brief smile. She pushed the remnants of her meal into the sack. "Jennifer still thinks God is going to heal her."

He paused the quarter between his third and fourth finger. They had talked about this problem too many times before for him to have a new answer for her tonight. "Don't do this, Rae. Don't search to understand what can't be understood." She'd only been a Christian a few months. He'd been one for over thirty years, and he didn't have an answer for why Jennifer was still dying from cancer despite their prayers. There was just a God to trust.

"I doubt that God means what He says," she whispered.

Cole tossed the coin back with the other change. He wasn't surprised at her words, but he wished he could take away this moment that most new Christians experienced. Doubt was like smoke—it found cracks and worried its way inside until it clouded the joy that was there before. A little could fill a big volume of space. "Christianity isn't what you thought it would be like. Okay. So change your expectations."

"You said there would be peace; Jennifer says there's joy."

"There is both," he promised, trying to reach through her turmoil. "What Jesus actually said was, 'These things I have spoken to you, that my joy may be in you, and that your joy may be full.'"

"I've read that verse several times, but I don't understand it, Cole."

What were the right words to explain it? Cole had never felt more challenged in his own faith than when he tried to help her see some of what had taken him years to grasp. "A few verses earlier He said, 'Peace I leave with you; my peace I give to you.' Jesus said *My* joy, *My* peace, Rae. He said that even though He hardly had an easy life. Crowds pressed in on Him; the authorities hated Him; Jesus had no place to call His home. He died on the cross, but He had a joy and a peace in life that was absolute. At its heart, the concept is simple—Jesus trusted His Father. He didn't doubt God's goodness, His control of the situation, or the fact that His plan would lead to everlasting glory. That's what Jesus is asking you to do too. Trust God, even in this."

He wished he had the wisdom of Solomon to give her an answer. "You can see only one answer to Jennifer's cancer—a cure. God may see another. A verse in Psalms says, 'The LORD will fulfill his purpose for me.' If God has to choose between His purpose for our lives and a long life, I believe He'll go with the purpose every time. Jesus died when He was thirty-three."

"Jennifer's a pediatrician. She has a life ahead of her helping children. What purpose could God have in not curing her?"

"When you choose to trust despite the circumstances—it's called faith, Rae. And sometimes it's so hard that you wonder why God demands it. Think about this: Is a promise made that's not yet delivered on any less of a promise? God is trustworthy. It isn't easy to take that on faith when circumstances are tough, but that's what He asks of you." Cole went to the heart of it. "You love Jennifer, and her suffering is pressing hard. Leave the questions for later. You can't fix this. It will break you to try. And Jennifer is worried about you."

She rubbed her eyes. "You had to add that last point."

He covered her hand with his. The bond between the sisters was so great that he knew to Rachel this felt like it was happening to her. "Were you going to call Jen when you got in?"

She nodded.

"Then let me take you home so you can call her." He started the car. "Tell her we talked. She'll worry less."

"You mean she'll just ask me about you."

Cole smiled, hoping that would be the case. "You can tell her I still owe you dinner. Eating in the car doesn't count."

"This dinner is becoming like the event of the year. Don't set your expectations too high. It's likely going to be our typical meal grabbed in spite of a busy day."

"Rae, it's time with you that makes it special, not the circumstances. I'll make sure it's Chinese—not in a carton this time."

SIX

Rachel leaned against the wall of sandbags. The stagnant water stank, the current gone. The sun was out on Saturday morning, reflecting off the muddy water. The floodwaters had crested and receded in the last two weeks and were down to a mere foot. The workers were repairing the initial breach in the retaining wall, hauling rock and sand out to the now visible break. Cole was out there in one of the boats, helping Jack move heavy bags that rocked the boat as they dropped them into the water.

Her brother Stephen stopped beside her. "Another day and the break will be repaired. It will then just be a case of pumping out the last of the water."

It was better progress than she had hoped. Governor Street had been drying out for the last week. Structural engineers were in the houses now, finishing their inspections. People were lingering at the community center, waiting for word that they could return to their homes for the first time.

"It's going to be a mess," she observed. The emergency shelter had transformed itself into the headquarters for the cleanup, the Red Cross giving way to the local Emergency Services Agency. Plywood sheets were already piled and waiting. Six large dumpsters were lined up, ready to be taken in and placed near driveways to allow for expedited removal of destroyed belongings.

"The damage isn't as bad as it could have been. Rather than be a trash pit for the floodwaters, the moving water kept the worst of the debris from building up here. About three miles south is apparently a real mess. Twenty minutes, Rae, and the chief inspector said they'll be letting residents in. I've heard Ann's house is bad but recoverable."

"Thanks, Stephen."

Having worked numerous flood cleanups, Rachel had dressed in old jeans and a bleach-stained shirt, thick socks, and heavy boots. She wore an unbuttoned long sleeve shirt over it to protect her arms. She was already hot. She retrieved the water bottle she'd let chill in the freezer for an hour and tossed it into her bag.

She'd checked at the command center to make sure there were plenty of volunteers for the block. It was well organized. Since other needs were covered, Rachel put herself down to help Ann. With Cole, Jack, and Stephen already on the list to help Ann, someone needed to keep them in line.

"Hi, Rachel." Adam was the first to reach her, racing ahead with a friend he had brought with him, Cole's dog running alongside.

"Hi, Adam." Rachel knelt to pet the dog. The boy with Adam looked to be about the same age as Adam, but shorter, stocky, with red hair and freckles. A healing scrape on the boy's chin suggested a recent collision with pavement. "Who's your friend?"

"This is Tim Sanford."

"Hi, Tim." She offered her hand.

"Hi."

Rachel offered the boys pieces of gum from a new pack she had tucked in her pocket that morning.

"Tim goes to my school," Adam said, dancing around the dog as Hank tried to knock him over. "He's staying with me today, and next weekend I get to go stay over at his house."

"Fun."

"Are they still pumping water?"

"I think so. Why don't you join the guys at the blue engine."

"Come on, Tim. Let's go see."

With a smile Rachel watched them go. She tucked the gum back into her pocket and unwrapped a cough drop for herself.

Ann joined her. "The idea of staying at the sitter's with Nathan was the worst idea Adam had ever heard of, so I let him come. I told him he couldn't enter the house until we called him so if it's real bad I can warn him."

"Good plan. As was letting him bring a friend along." Rachel looked at Ann. "Are you ready to do this?"

"I don't think reality could be any worse than what I've been imagining."

Rachel offered her one of the licorice hard candy drops. "The taste is sharp enough it will at least help counteract the odors."

"Thanks for the warning. I brought buckets, mops, bleach, and lots of garbage bags."

"Let's haul the supplies down to the checkpoint, and the guys can carry them the rest of the way."

Cole, Jack, and Stephen joined them as they brought the last items from the car. The inspectors opened Governor Street to residents, and in small groups people began to see what was left of their homes.

The walk up Ann's driveway was an adventure. It was covered in a muddy river flowing down to the street. Rachel walked beside Cole, ready to grab his arm if necessary to keep from falling. A demarcation line of dirt, wrapped around the house's siding, displayed the crest of the water. The sun had been working at it for days as the water receded, and the residue looked baked on. Grass remained in the yard but it poked up through a muddy swamp. The ground had acquired rocks, stray branches, and odd-looking leaves now wilting in the sun.

The front door had been propped open by the inspectors and windows around the house opened. Rachel followed Ann inside. The living room carpet was under two inches of standing muddy water. Furniture had floated. The sofa and television and heaviest items had not moved, but it was as if a powerful hand had shoved everything else to the east side of the room. Books had swollen and now lay curling as the pages dried. The smell was of mold and humid mustiness.

"Is the house still structurally sound?" Ann asked softly.

Stephen came up behind them and settled his hand on Ann's shoulder. "Yes. Once we dry things out, the inspectors want to look again at wiring before they restore the power. We'll be able to run off generators for now, start fans blowing to assist with the drying out."

Cole walked through to look into the kitchen, then turned to look at the guys. "It's best if we divide and conquer. I'll take care of hauling out the spoiled food. Stephen, if you can start with the clothes, take them out to the truck, we'll take them to the cleaners. Jack, why don't you tackle the generator and get fans blowing, and then hose down the drive. We'll carry out furniture and wash it off there. The sun will help things dry, help us figure out what we can recover first."

"I'll also see about cleaning off the back patio," Jack offered. "We can bring in the picnic table you sanded and fixed up so there is a clean place to sit and take a break."

"Good idea."

"Ann." Rachel could see that her friend was fighting tears, for this devastation was huge. "I brought lots of boxes. We can start in the kitchen and take the dishes and pans out today. The restaurant next to the bank offered to let us run items through their industrial-sized washer. We can at least have them washed and ready to unpack once the kitchen cleanup is done."

Ann nodded.

Stephen hugged her. "We'll get your house back together."

"Can we start with Adam's clothes? He needs options for school," Ann said.

"Sure."

Rachel picked up a bucket and a bottle of bleach. "Jack, when you can get to it, will you thread a hose into the house? It will make it easier to clean walls than if we have to haul water in."

"Glad to."

"Someone find a good radio station with music, something peppy," Ann requested. She headed toward the kitchen, and Rachel followed after her friend. This would discourage even the most optimistic lady.

Rachel worked from the top of the cabinets down, washing the wood with the bleach water twice, letting it dry, and then coming back a third time with soap and water. She turned her head and wiped her eyes on her sleeve as the smell overwhelmed her. The open windows and fans were not keeping up with the fumes. Smelling bleach was going to ruin her sense of taste for days.

Cole had the stove tugged out and was working on removing the side panels. It was comforting to work with him, for he was a man who assessed the job and then dug in to do the work.

"Rachel, look what we found." Adam came in the back door with Tim. She leaned over to see. In his hands were three silver dollars, still crusted with dirt. "They were in the mud out in the flower bed." The boys were having a great time discovering all the strange things left by the water.

"Excellent finds, guys."

"Would you keep them for us?"

"Sure. Put them in my burlap satchel. I'll get them cleaned up and put in coin sleeves for you."

"Thanks."

Ann came into the kitchen and Adam hurried to show his mom their treasures. "We'll be with Jack, okay? He's going to start washing the siding."

"As long as you don't get in his way."

"We're helping, Mom."

Ann smiled at her son. "Have fun."

The boys rushed out as fast as they had come in.

Rachel hauled another bucket of soapy water to the corner cabinet. "It's a treasure hunt out there."

"Boys and mud. They are having fun," Ann agreed. "It's looking good in here."

Rachel wet a new rag and started on the next cabinet. "How is Adam's room?"

"Most of his clothes can be recovered, probably his chest of drawers. Stephen is hauling out the mattress and is looking at pulling up the carpet and padding. If you're okay in here, I thought I'd start cleaning some of the furniture they've carried out."

"I'm fine."

"Cole, can I get you anything?"

"I'm good. Thanks, Ann."

Rachel watched her friend as she left the kitchen. "She's handling this better than I would."

"You handle what you have to," Cole replied. He got the second panel off the stove.

Someone turned the radio up. Rachel hummed along with a song as she tried to distract herself from the aches. She finished the final cabinet.

There was so much to do. She sat down on a stool to begin sorting out items under the sink.

Rachel jolted as a hand touched her shoulder. Cole leaned down. "Call it a day. I'll help the guys finish hauling items to the dumpster and move furniture to the garage, and we'll start again tomorrow."

"I'm okay. I want to do one more round on the cupboards in the kitchen."

"It's five o'clock. If you don't leave, Ann won't think of leaving. She needs to take Adam home."

Rachel had had too much on her mind to realize the time. "Good point." She got to her feet and stretched to take the ache out of her back. "I need to take a walk around the block anyway, see how others are doing."

"In that case—" he offered the full roll of LifeSavers from his pocket—"got tissue with you?"

She tapped her pocket.

He smiled. "Go walk the block. I'll make my own walk-around of the levees and bridge and catch up with you."

Cole would never fail to be surprised by what the floodwaters left behind.

"How did a golf cart get under there?" Gage asked.

"Great question." Cole leaned against the bridge railing next to Gage. They were both spectators. Four guys from City Services were down there wrestling to get it out of the weeds. Cole kept a close eye on the men's safety lines but otherwise left them alone to figure out the problem. "It doesn't look like much of a golf cart anymore."

Gage leaned too far over the edge for Cole's comfort. He tugged the man back. "Let's not have a casualty." The river was rushing by within its banks, but it was still violent.

"Is the bridge going to reopen soon?" Rachel called out.

Cole turned around to see Rae coming across the improvised walkway made from sheets of metal. The flooding had washed away and collapsed sections of the roadway. Cole went to meet her. "Another two weeks at the earliest for repairs to get finished."

"Hey, Rachel LeeAnn. Come give us your opinion. What does that look like on the bank to you?" Gage asked.

Cole reached over, grasped her by the waist, and swung her over the last few feet to more firm ground. He wiped a spot off her chin with a grin. "Chocolate?"

"I was sharing cupcakes with the kids."

"So I see. Hold still." He tipped up her chin with a finger and wiped away the evidence, thinking seriously about kissing her. Their first kiss was going to be a forever memory for both of them, and he liked the idea of it being on a day they worked together. He'd been looking for that perfect moment—one that had both their undivided attentions but not so obvious for the kiss to be expected.

A soft blush tinged her cheeks as she caught the direction of his thoughts. Her eyelashes dropped and then swept up again. "Not here," she whispered.

He settled for tightening his hands on her waist and leaning down to rest his forehead briefly against hers. "Later," he promised. "How was the walk-around?"

"Most are relieved just to be able to get in and do something."

He stepped back and when he did, she slipped her hand in his and stayed in his space leaning against his arm. "Tell us what you think," he asked. "The riverbank, just beyond where the breach has been repaired."

She reluctantly turned to look where he pointed.

"Does that look like car tracks to you?" Gage asked.

"Gage, you can't look at anything without seeing a mystery. It's two deep valleys cut into the muddy bank. Are you sure it's not just the results of one of those boulders that got shoved around by the water? Or for that matter, the first landing of the golf cart?"

"That's what I told him," Cole replied.

"What's on your plan for the evening?" Gage asked. "If I buy the steaks, Cole offered to fire up the grill. Want to join us?"

Rachel looked between the two men, her surprise that they were getting together showing. "Sure."

Cole understood her reaction. He and Gage respected each other, but their jobs had often put them working on opposite sides with his job in investigating arson fires and Gage's to find news. It was slowly becoming a friendship. They both recognized that for Rachel's sake it was important that the tension end. Gage had a story running this weekend about the flooding, and Cole was in the mood to be generous when asked to comment. "How do you like your steak?"

"Medium. Not too charred on the edges. With a baked potato that is falling-apart done."

"Can do. Eight fit your schedule?"

"I'll make it fit."

Cole cut the French bread in thick slices. He could get used to this. Rachel sat at his kitchen table occasionally spearing a strawberry with a toothpick, keeping him company as he fixed Texas Toast to go with the steak and potatoes. The steaks on the grill were coming along to perfection under the watchful eyes of Gage and Hank. It was the kind of night that made memories.

"You have a quart of 1 percent milk in the refrigerator, oatmeal in the cupboard, and enough vegetables to start a market, but we're eating steaks and potatoes. I sense a contradiction. Now I wonder which one is really you?"

He could get used to her teasing. She'd relaxed with him. "It's called balance."

"I'd say you were trying to impress me with your discipline but you forgot to take down your shopping list, and it's more of the same."

"One of the realities of a desk job is to adapt or pay the price. I don't mind working the weights, but I'd rather not have to add another session to my workout schedule."

"I handle it by never being home to buy groceries." She rested her head on her arms.

"You're falling asleep."

"You should feel flattered. I no longer feel like a guest. The days when I could handle the pace of keeping up with kids and doing a flood cleanup are long gone."

"Age teaches you to think more and act smarter. It's good for you." He set a glass of iced tea beside her.

"Why didn't you get married a decade or two ago?"

She didn't censor her questions when she got tired. He tucked away the observation, knowing it would be useful. "I was too young to realize what I was missing, too busy to make time, too stupid to take my mom's advice. You would have liked her Rachel LeeAnn."

"I was hoping you didn't hear Gage call me that."

"It's not a bad middle name."

"What's yours?"

Cole chuckled. "Something worse." He slid the toast under the broiler.

"I'll be nice and not ask."

He got out the fixings for the salad. She was idly moving her glass of iced tea on the table, watching the moisture form a circle.

"What?"

She shook her head.

"You're biting your lower lip. What's the question?"

She glanced over and gave an apologetic smile. "Your middle name isn't Clarence is it?"

He burst out laughing. "Clarence? No, it's not anything that bad. It's Joseph." He stepped back to the table, leaned down, and kissed her. He was smiling as he did so, intending it to be a casual kiss. He knew she'd been waiting for him to keep his promise from that afternoon, and he didn't want the first kiss to become such a huge deal she got tense expecting it. Casual didn't last, though. He wanted to linger in that kiss and deepen it. He let himself do so briefly. She was sitting at his kitchen table where he would love to have a chance to greet her with a kiss every morning. He reluctantly opened his eyes to find hers still closed.

She curled her hand in his shirt rather than let him move back. "What was that for?"

"You need a reason?" He had several, not the least of which was the fact that she was adorable and he fully intended to win her heart in the coming months.

She blinked at him, and he loved the fact her eyes still weren't quite focused. She shook her head slightly. "Come here." She slid her hand around his neck, pulled him back down, and returned his kiss. The memory of their first kiss got swamped by the emotional wave from the second. "One to dream about," she whispered. She smiled at him and slid her hand around to touch his jaw, her hand soft against the end-of-day roughness of his face. "Breathe, Cole. You want me to help fix the salad?"

He took a deep breath. "Okay, sure, whatever you like." Her smile was incredible when there was laughter behind it. He chuckled and pulled her from the chair. "You're precious, Rae." He wrapped an arm around her and hugged her, then stepped back and let her go. He held out the paring knife. "Not too many radishes."

SEVEN

"Lisa."

Hearing her name and having nowhere to set down the blood-stained shirt, she carried it with her to the door of the conference room. "Back here, Marcus."

So much evidence had been collected from the Carol Iles murder scene that Lisa had taken over the room to manage the processing of it all. She returned the bloody blouse Carol had been wearing to its plastic evidence bag.

Her brother came to the doorway where he paused, looking around. "Detective Wilson called and said you needed to see me. How's it coming?"

She rubbed her forehead with the back of her arm trying to eliminate an itch, avoiding using her hand still in the rubber glove. "Since I haven't seen much daylight because of this case, I suppose it's relative. Wet stuff molds and my allergies have been going crazy. I hate mysteries."

"You've got one."

She nodded and walked over to the wall of enlarged photos she'd been using to try and recreate the crime scene from the evidence. "Tests are finally coming back on some of this stuff. It's like a Chinese puzzle. You checked the federal court building and the office where she worked?"

"I ran down the information for Wilson. Carol didn't have access to anything classified, didn't work on any profiled cases. Just routine paperwork in the criminal division. I sent over the box of personal stuff we found in her office. There wasn't much."

"Wilson brought it over," Lisa confirmed. "Thanks for sending over the fingerprints from her file."

"No problem. I figured it would save you some time. Any ideas at this point?"

"Carol's murder was either domestic, work related, or random. I'm ready to rule out random. It's too neat of a scene and there are no signs of burglary or other violence. Wilson is getting nowhere on domestic. She'd been divorced about a year, shares joint custody of her son who primarily lives with his father. Her ex-husband and son were at a high school basketball game that night. I don't have a good time line yet, but so far their alibis hold. And there is no indication Carol was dating anyone. That leaves work related, and you've pretty much ruled that out."

"Anything coming from the evidence?"

"That's why I wanted you to stop by. The bullet that killed Carol is in pretty good shape. No shell casings, so I'm limited in info, but it's typing as a Smith & Wesson .38 caliber." Lisa tapped two of the photos. "And my puzzle: I think someone else was there. This mail being opened at the dining room table had Carol's prints on it. But this soda can on the kitchen counter? The prints are unknown."

"Her husband or son?"

"They both offered prints and neither matched. One other thing." She crossed to the table and lifted a plastic evidence bag. "This cosmetic bag? One of the officers cleared everything on the dining room table into a box, and this was in that set of items. You can see it on the table in that photo." She lifted out the brush. "Long, blond hair. Carol was a brunette with a pageboy haircut."

"You're looking for a woman shooter?" Marcus asked, obviously intrigued at the idea.

"Someone brought over a cosmetic bag, had a drink, and then shot Carol? No. I think Carol and another woman were going out that evening, shopping, dinner, something. Her guest brought in the bag to retouch her makeup and hair, and while she was there someone knocked on the door and shot Carol."

"Then there's a second victim."

"We never explored the basement. It was flooded." Lisa leaned against the table and tugged off her gloves. "Want to go play detective with me?"

"I'm federal not state, remember?"

"Wilson won't be free for another three hours. He said I could draft you. And technically I don't need company to go back to a crime scene, but even I have a bit of a problem walking down into a flooded basement with just a flashlight."

"I'll go along, but I'm calling Quinn. If you're going to get spooked by a ghost, I want him there to see it."

Lisa smiled at the idea of her fiancé going along. "Call him. But you two are going down into the basement first."

"This is creepy," Quinn protested. The stairs creaked as he walked down them, his halogen flashlight peering into the darkness.

Lisa tugged the back of her fiancé's collar. "There's creepy and really creepy. It doesn't smell like a decomposing body's down there," Lisa mentioned, keeping her hand on his shoulder for extra balance as she came down behind him. "Let's just get down there and get it over with."

Marcus went down ahead of them and hung the lantern he'd brought along on the staircase banister. It dimly illuminated the room. "We've still got some standing water down here. The pump lines dropped in those basement windows to pump out the water weren't weighted to reach the floor. Walk carefully."

Quinn paused near the bottom of the stairs. "What is that?"

Lisa leaned her head against his shoulder to see around the rafters and follow his flashlight. "A dead rat."

Quinn stepped off the last step and shone his light around. "Why don't you stay right there, Lisa?"

"And miss all this fun? How do you want to do this, Marcus?" It was her crime scene, but by asking the question, she knew Marcus would select the toughest part of the task for himself.

"You two work clockwise from the steps; I'll work counterclockwise," he decided, taking the deepest segment of water. "Let's get this done."

Lisa circled with Quinn, looking for anything that suggested evidence. They found a workbench, boxes of stored Christmas decorations, and a couple pieces of furniture Carol had moved downstairs that she didn't need. Items that had floated ended up on the floor in strange places. Lisa knew from the lack of the distinct smell of decomposition that this idea hadn't panned out. They finally met up at the other side of the room.

"Ready to call this search done?" Marcus asked.

She reluctantly nodded. Their search had been thorough. She led the way upstairs.

The kitchen and living room still showed the rapid recovery of items they had made the night of the flooding. She looked out the kitchen window. "The body could have ended up in the river, but it's going to take a lot of convincing before Wilson agrees to dredge."

"The river doesn't hold things forever," Quinn reassured. "You want to look around some more while we're here?"

"Let's assume Carol's company is in the kitchen when the gunshot goes off in the living room." Lisa looked around. "She only has two options of escape: the garage or the back patio door. I want to walk the grounds."

She pushed back the vertical blinds on the patio door. It was unlocked, but she had to wrestle it open. Draining water had left a place mat, candle ring, salt-shaker, and several pages of a wall calendar plastered against the glass. She pushed the items away with her foot. "See if you can find me a garbage bag, Quinn. If it looks interesting, let's take it." She stepped outside. "I bet the shooter threw the gun into the river as well. It's close and it washes everything away."

"We'll start walking the riverbanks," Quinn offered.

"We may have to." Lisa rubbed the back of her neck. She wanted this case solved, but she had a bad feeling about it. So much evidence had been lost in the floodwaters.

Marcus stopped beside her. "Let's walk."

Lisa nodded and led the way into the yard.

EIGHT

"Adam, listen to Rachel and help with Nathan. You're a guest in her home so be helpful. Don't just watch TV."

"Mom…"

Rachel smiled at Ann and shifted Nathan against her hip. She was going to have a great time baby-sitting. "We'll start with Battleship and then play Scrabble."

"We're just going to pick out carpet and paint. We won't be long."

It was Friday night. It had taken days, but the cleanup had finally turned the corner, and it was time to start restoring rooms. The electricians had been in; the furnace and ductwork had been cleaned out. Drywall had been replaced and new subflooring put in where needed. Stephen thought they could start painting Saturday and lay carpet down midweek. Ann's home would feel new although rather sparse, as most of the furniture would have to be replaced. "Stay out as long as you like," Rachel said. "I'll page Stephen if I need you."

Stephen set down the backpack with things for the boys, Nathan's now worn teddy bear poking out of the top. "Expect us about eight, Rae."

She nodded to her brother.

"I appreciate this," Ann said.

Nathan reached for Rachel's necklace, and she caught his hand, kissing it. "I'm glad you took me up on the offer. Say bye, Nathan."

The boy waved to his mom. "Go. Wanna play."

With a laugh Ann kissed her boys and said a final good-bye.

Rachel closed the door behind Ann and Stephen and from years of baby-sitting experience immediately offered a distraction. "Adam, I've got a question for you."

The boy was looking around her apartment in a curious kind of way. Nathan could get into all kinds of things, and she could imagine Adam wondering if he would constantly have to stop his younger brother. Her apartment wasn't very kid-proof. Knowing that, she held Nathan rather than setting him down. Adam turned to look at her.

"Cassie brought over a box of stuff she found at an auction. She needs it sorted and items put into those plastic sleeves. She said if you wanted to do it for her, she'd pay you for your time—you can choose an item for yourself. There are a few comic books in the box."

"I'd love to."

"Help me clear off the table and we'll lay everything out. Does pizza sound good for an early dinner?"

Nathan leaned back. "Pizza, yes!"

"Can we come stay more often?" Adam asked.

Rachel laughed. "I'd like that. Come on, let's get this evening started."

The sounds outside the hospital room carried through the closed door. Evening rounds were being finished, medicines given. The hospital corridor was bustling. Jennifer reached to take hold of her husband's hand. He interlaced his fingers with hers. She found such comfort in his strength. "I love you. Have I told you that lately?"

"Yes, but you can keep saying it. I'm storing them up." He smiled at her, the gorgeous smile that still turned her heart to mush. The first time she met him had been in an emergency room over a screaming two-year-old. Tom glanced up and gave her that smile, then returned his attention to her patient. She'd remembered him for that smile.

Tom used the cuff of his sleeve to wipe her chin. "Cookie crumbs and icing."

"It's pretty awful when homemade cookies don't have much taste."

"Do you want me to call your family for you?"

Jennifer felt like her heart was breaking. "It's going to kill them. You saw how hard it was on Rachel and Kate to see me like this. If I call now and tell them this…"

"Marcus is coming in on Tuesday. He'll take one look at you and tell the others to come. If you want to make the decision, you'll have to make it soon. We're out of time, honey."

"The doctors were wrong before. Why do they have to be right this time?" She so desperately wanted them to be wrong.

"All they said was that your body needs a rest from the treatments." He kissed the back of her hand where the morphine line had been removed. They had put her on a constant pump she now wore on her belt.

"I don't want them to be done." She loved this man, loved her family, and she wanted something that could help her fight this cancer. Having her primary oncologist say that they recommended a break in treatment was terrifying. She didn't want Tom to have to watch her die.

"We're not done yet, hon."

"Spontaneous remission is another name for a miracle," she whispered.

"So we'll pray for a miracle."

"I'm losing faith that there will be one." She'd been trying so hard to trust God through this. She knew God had a plan. The O'Malleys had turned to Him because of this cancer; only Stephen was left to make that decision. Time had been her ally, but now it was going against her.

Tom turned her wedding ring around. "Does God love you more or less than I do?"

"He gave me you."

"Good answer. God will give you all the faith you need. You don't need to wish harder or do more."

"I trust Him. I just don't want to die. And I'm dying."

He leaned over and kissed her. "Don't cry, Jen. He hasn't forgotten you." Tom rubbed his thumb across the back of her hand. "Good-bye is still a long way away. I have today with you, and I plan to enjoy it. You want to sneak out tonight down to pediatrics and see a movie with your buddies?"

She struggled to smile. "I'd love that."

"And the next days? We can do whatever you want, Jen."

"I could use some better scenery."

"Then let's leave. This hospital is a lousy place for getting rest, and you're just surrounded by germs. There are better places to spend our time."

"Maybe Chicago?"

"Let's do that. I like your family, and they need time with you. Who do you want to talk to first tonight?"

"Rachel. She can handle me crying while I try to talk."

He kissed her again. "You're my wife. You don't even get out of that by dying, remember? We struck the *till death do us part* phrase from the wedding vows. Trust me, Jen. We are far from finished with this fight."

She could rest against the determination she heard in his voice. He wouldn't let this fight end. And just hearing that made it easier for her to breathe and think about tomorrow. There was one bright spot in this change—not having to spend hours focusing on the medical treatments and side effects of medications, she would have more time to focus on her family. It mattered now more than ever. "Try Rachel at home. I'd rather not have to page her."

Nathan was asleep. Rachel moved pillows on the couch so he would settle back farther in the cushions. The game of Twister they had squeezed into the living room had probably been a little much, although the laughter had been worth it. The two boys had made up rules that all too often put her at the bottom of a pile of giggling boys.

She picked up the plate beside Adam. "Very nice." He was carefully writing tags for the items he had put into plastic sleeves.

"These comics are really old. Are you sure Cassie meant me to have one?"

"Yes, she did. You can choose the one you'd like."

"If I take it with me before shelves get rebuilt in my bedroom, it might get damaged. Could I leave it with you?"

"Sure, sweetie."

"I made Cassie a thank-you card."

"She'll love it." Rachel hugged him. "I'm so glad you came over." She heard the outside door close and footsteps on the stairs. "I think that's your mom now."

"We were good tonight?"

Rachel laughed. "Yes. And you've got a standing invitation to come over anytime. Let's get your stuff together. Now where did Nathan hide his bear?"

"Behind the couch."

"Of course."

Rachel leaned against the car window. Nathan had already gone back to sleep in his car seat. "I'll be over to help paint tomorrow, Ann. You want to start about ten?"

"Yes. I'll bring lunch for us."

"I'll bring the ice chest with drinks and dessert," Rachel offered. "I'll see you then. Good night guys." Rachel headed back to her apartment.

The phone was ringing as she unlocked the door. She hurried to answer it, hoping it was Cole. "Hello?"

"Hi, Rae."

"Jennifer." Rachel carried the phone into the living room, reached for the notepad of messages she had for her sister, and then she slowly paused. Her sister's voice was soft, heavy, like she had been crying. Rachel settled on the couch and tugged a big pillow over into her lap, leaning back against the cushions. "How are you doing tonight?"

"The doctor recommended I go home."

No. Not this. Rachel closed her eyes and felt blackness deeper than any disaster tragedy swallow her. "Come home to Chicago, Jen," she whispered. "If it wouldn't be too hard on Tom, come here."

"Yes. I need to." Jen stopped.

Rachel waited while Jen fought for composure, wishing she had stayed out East rather than come back here. Her sister needed her. "What did the doctors say?"

"That my body needs a rest from the treatment."

"How bad is the pain?"

"It's under control."

"You can rest here. I'll share my mountains of pillows, and we can pull out that box of videos from under my bed and have a Cary Grant movie night." She was reaching for anything that Jennifer could still look forward to.

"I'd like that." Jennifer went quiet for several moments. "It isn't fair, Rae. Why is God allowing this?"

Jesus, please. I'm failing her. How do I help her?

"Come home," Rachel whispered again. She struggled to keep her voice level.

"We were thinking about maybe flying back on Wednesday night. I'll call you tomorrow with travel plans."

"I'll meet you at the airport," Rachel said.

"I've got to call the others."

"We love you."

"I love you too," Jennifer whispered and drew in a deep breath. "Tomorrow, Rae. I'll call you early."

"It's going to be okay."

"I know. Good night."

"'Night, Jen."

Rachel hung up the phone. Her hand shook. She lowered her head and her body shook. She would have to be breathing to make a sound. The only thing more devastating than this call would be the one saying Jennifer had died. She lifted the pillow and pressed it against her face. *Jesus, it hurts.* The sobs came hard and lasted a long time.

She didn't want to talk, but she didn't want to be alone either. Gage would walk with her. Cole. She needed someone other than family while she waited for Jen to make the other calls. She'd known this day was coming and yet it was shattering. Rachel picked up the phone and her hands shook again as she dialed.

Cole pulled into the drive and drove around his house to the detached garage. He reached in the back for his briefcase. He had to testify in an arson case next week and had preparations to do. He locked the car and walked up the path to the house.

Rachel was sitting on the back steps. Cole slowed. He would have to leave one of his lawn chairs out so she'd be comfortable when she waited, since she wouldn't accept a key. Something was wrong. One of her kids had paged, work… He walked up the path but didn't ask. It was enough that she had come.

"Jennifer called."

There was such sadness in her eyes. He brushed a finger along her cheek. "Will it help to talk?"

She lifted a shoulder in a shrug. Cole saw in her gesture what he had feared was coming. How much could Rae carry before it overwhelmed her? Jennifer's illness was the one weight that would break her. He clicked off the back door light to stop the gathering bugs and settled beside her on the steps to share the silence and the night. He would invite her in, fix her a cup of coffee, but he was afraid she'd shift to guest mode and feel a need to ask about his day.

"Jennifer's coming back to Chicago."

He blinked back tears that came when he heard the news. "When?"

"Probably Wednesday. Details will come tomorrow."

"I'm so sorry, honey."

"I need a hug," she whispered.

And she chose to come see him. Cole wrapped his arms around her. Under the pain he felt at the news she had to share, he knew they'd just crossed a point in their relationship that would change it forever. Suffering the deepest level of hurt, she'd chosen to trust him.

She felt fragile in his arms. He shifted positions to tuck her closer. Her head rested against his shoulder, and she began to shake as she silently began to cry. In another setting having her in his arms would be a memory to treasure. Now he simply wished there was some way to help her through the hurt. Jennifer's dying…this tore at the heart of the O'Malley family.

He sat holding her for a long time—his leg went to sleep, his back ached. He was lousy at dealing with tears. There was nothing he could fix. He wanted to say something profound, but the reality was tougher than that. There were no words he could offer that would take away this hurt.

He settled for silence, grateful she had come. There was strength in this woman that went deep enough to handle this. Faith would get her through when she had to face tomorrow, but her grief needed the tears to fall. There was healing in those tears.

She took two final shuddering breaths, lifted her head from his shoulder, and eased back. "So, what's happening in your life?"

If she could still smile like that…she'd found the strength to get to tomorrow. Sometimes that was all that could be done. "I'm dating this really nice woman."

"Cole."

He tucked her hair behind her ear. "I'm thinking about asking her to go for a walk if she's interested." He gently wiped her eyes.

Her hand lifted to his and sought comfort in the contact. She offered a watery smile. "Let's walk. That's what I came over to ask anyway."

"Really?"

"Yeah."

"What, Gage wasn't home?" he teased, trying to lighten the emotions of the moment.

She lightly punched his arm. "I called you first, then decided to just come over."

He wasn't sure what to say.

She smiled at him. "That's sweet."

"What?"

"Your assuming you might be my second choice."

He rose to let his dog out of the house. "I've found that life goes smoother if I don't make assumptions where a woman is concerned." Hank threatened to knock him over in his excitement at company. It was good to hear Rae's laughter. "I don't know about sweet."

"Unexpected. Nice. Charming."

"I can go for charming." He snapped the leash onto Hank's collar and offered it to Rachel. Hank danced around Rachel's feet as she knelt to greet him.

They set out for an ambling walk. When they reached the sidewalk, Cole pointed north. "You and Gage have been close for a long time."

She nodded. "Gage is the man I call at 2 A.M. when I'm mad at the world and want someone to tell me I'm right. He has a dry sense of humor, a black-and-white right-versus-wrong mentality. And he's the only one I let get away with calling me by my middle name. Since Tabitha's death…he's become a cross between a cynic and a realist."

Cole knew some of that history, for the fire that killed Tabitha had been one his department worked. "He's a friend."

"A good one," she said quietly. "But that's all, Cole. And that's all he was ever destined to be."

He squeezed her hand.

The silence lingered past the point either had something else to say, and it became a comfortable silence, broken only occasionally as Rae corrected Hank's enthusiasm, which threatened to tangle his leash into a knot.

"Would you come with me to the airport to pick up Jennifer and Tom?" Rachel asked.

Cole rubbed his thumb along the back of her hand. "You know I will, but your family will be there."

"I know."

He heard something under the question and tipped up her chin. "What is going through that pretty head of yours?"

"I like the word *pretty.*"

"Rae—"

"Jennifer doesn't have much time left."

"Maybe not," he said gently.

"Probably not."

He nodded, conceding.

"Jennifer has had two dreams driving her the last few months. First, that all the O'Malleys would come to believe in Jesus like she does and would understand heaven and the hope she feels. Only Stephen is left to make that decision, and there isn't much I can do for that beyond what she's doing."

"And second—"

"She wants all of us to be happy, wants to see our dreams come true. It would help if Jen knew you and I…" She stopped and closed her eyes.

"What, Rachel?" He thought about her words. "That we're seeing each other? That you're special to me? Trust me, your family already knows that." He rubbed her hands, trying to reassure her.

"Jennifer's been my best friend for so long; she knows all my childhood dreams."

"I'd like to know them too."

She smiled at him but didn't take the tangent. "Would you be comfortable being part of the family gathering over the next few weeks, let Jennifer get to know you better? I'm happy around you, and I want her to know that. Regardless of what the future holds, I want her to know she doesn't need to worry about me. That's the only gift I have left to give her."

"Rachel, I already like your sister, and I would certainly enjoy getting to know her better." He searched for words. "I want to be part of your life, all of it. Trust me with this part too, the weight you carry regarding your family. This isn't going to be an easy time for any of you."

"It's not such a little thing, being part of the O'Malley clan."

"Spending time with you the last few months has begun to make that obvious. You've got an interesting family, Rae."

She hugged him. "I appreciate this, Cole."

He tipped up her chin and kissed her. Her lips tasted salty from the earlier tears. He took his time with the kiss, letting it soften and comfort. It was as much for him as it was for Rachel; there was so much emotion inside. His hands soothed hers. "I know what the next months are going to be like, how hard it will be to have both intense grief over Jennifer's situation and also let yourself build new joy with me, but you need to trust me and try. Life is going on."

"Cole—"

"Are you crying again?" he asked, struggling with that.

She wiped her eyes as she tried to smile. "You don't know what you're walking into."

"I think I do." He wished he knew how to convince her. "I'm a safe gamble, Rae. I promise not to break your heart."

"Oh, now you've done it. Hold on. I need a Kleenex." She searched her pockets and found one. "I don't deserve you."

"Probably not," he agreed, relieved her tears were only threatening this time. "But I don't deserve you either."

She smiled at him and he felt his heart skip a beat. He was definitely falling in love with that smile...with her.

He rested his arm around her shoulder and turned them around to start the walk home. It was time to lighten this conversation. "So you think Jennifer might be interested in telling me stories about you? She must know a few."

Rachel laughed. "Knowing Jennifer, probably."

He couldn't resist. "Any embarrassing ones?"

Rae pushed him off the sidewalk.

NINE

Rachel woke early, her eyes still puffy from the tears of the night before, but her heart was unexpectedly light. She hugged a pillow close. *Jesus, is this going to work out with Cole?*

Their relationship was so different from most she had ever had. There was a steadiness about him that gave her hope they could indeed work out this relationship even while the rest of her life remained chaotic.

Cole was right about the struggle it would be to balance the heavy heart that came from accepting Jennifer's cancer, while at the same time trying to build a long-term relationship. Rachel was glad he was willing to take the lead: To her it was a scary undertaking, while he seemed comfortable with the challenge. She should have sought him out for a hug and poured out her tears a long time ago.

Did Cole understand how huge her dream was to be married and have children? He was great with kids; she only had to watch him with Adam and Nathan to see it in action. He'd more than once made a point of mentioning he looked forward to having a family someday. It was a wealth of little things that said he wanted to be a husband and father.

Marriage was her deepest dream, and yet she had held off on it the longest. She'd lived through her own parents' bitter marriage and been abandoned by so many people that she trusted through the years, she'd put work ahead of settling down. The odds of seven O'Malleys succeeding in strong marriages were long. She couldn't afford to be the one who made a mistake.

Rachel pressed the pillow tightly against her face, then tossed it aside. As much as she wanted to daydream about what the future would be like, it was time to get moving. She rose and got dressed.

Rachel was reading the newspaper when the doorbell rang. She carried her coffee with her and went to get the door, expecting one of the O'Malleys to come to talk about Jennifer. Marcus had already said both he and Quinn had made arrangements to work in Chicago indefinitely while Jennifer was here. Sometime this weekend they were sure to assemble somewhere to make plans for the coming week.

"Gage, hi."

"I got your message." When she got home she'd called him with news about Jennifer. He handed her a copy of his newspaper. He knew she did the unthinkable and subscribed to the rival city paper. She leaned into his hug and peeked into the sack he held. "You brought me a chocolate-covered donut."

"Only because I wanted to make sure my muffin was safe. I'm fixing breakfast. What do you want in your omelette? I brought the eggs and my brand of coffee."

"Whatever you can find. You may have to settle for scrambled eggs."

He headed toward the kitchen and opened her refrigerator. "A vegetarian omelette it is. I can live with that."

"The peppers are going mushy."

"So are the tomatoes."

Saturday morning breakfast was something of a tradition. She normally met him at a restaurant somewhere. He liked to hear her reaction to the piece he wrote. She settled back at the table as he began working and opened the paper he had brought. There wasn't room in her kitchen for two people. "The flood is almost over and now you write about it?"

"You haven't been down to the really bad section. About three miles south, by the bend of the river, homes are still underwater. It's becoming the trash pit of the floodwaters. One house has already collapsed, and they think another one is about ready to fall down. It's dangerous enough that they haven't even let engineers go in by boat to look at what's going on. Some think the ground has collapsed in a huge sinkhole under the homes. It was new construction too, the expensive homes."

"I'm glad I haven't been down there. Governor Street was a big enough disaster."

He brought over breakfast plates. "You want to talk about Jennifer?"

"She's coming home."

"So you said in your message."

"I don't know, Gage. I swing from relief that she'll at least be here with family to fear over what each day will be like. Will her energy hold up? Will she be bedridden soon? The situation has too many unknowns to be able to do much planning."

"How can I help?"

She knew he would offer; it was one of the things she loved most about him. "She mentioned wanting to do a ladies' night out. I may need some help with logistics. Swap cars possibly. Yours has more room."

"Whatever you need."

"I appreciate it."

They ate breakfast sharing the paper.

"Gage, do you ever think about getting married again?"

He set down his fork. "Since we normally have these conversations late at night over the phone when you want to hide what you're thinking, I'll assume this is a hypothetical question?"

She lightly kicked him under the table.

"Oh, one of *those* conversations." He leaned back in his chair, holding his coffee, smiling at her. "Tabitha used to start these with her famous 'what would you do if…' questions that drove me crazy. She once asked me what would be easier: having to spend a year living with the in-laws or a year apart from her. As if there was a safe answer to that question. Sure, I think about getting remarried. Every time I get up and have to face a morning alone. I've even turned on that classical music Tabitha loved to listen to in the morning even though I can't stand it. Life is boring without a need to constantly compromise with someone. Always getting my preference is no fun." He set his coffee back on the table. "Rae, I'm still married in my heart. It doesn't matter that I haven't heard Tabitha's voice in two years. She's still a huge part of me. I don't know when that will change, or if it ever will."

"Your marriage to Tabitha was the first truly happy marriage I ever saw."

"Considering the competition I was up against in O'Malley history, I don't think it was such a huge target to hit. It's not like we didn't have problems."

"Yeah. I heard about some of those too. But you gave me hope again that a great marriage wasn't a myth."

"It didn't last as long as I would have liked."

She was careful with her next comment. "Cole and I—it's getting serious."

He didn't give her a quick answer, just looked at her, and then he smiled. "Rae, there is no one I know who deserves to be happy more than you. Dress up, turn on that megawatt smile, and go spin his head around."

"Somehow I don't see that being Cole's reaction. But it's a nice compliment."

"You don't see the guys who turn to watch you cross the room."

She gave a slight smile. "I see them." She looked at him and her smile faded.

"Going to tell me the rest of it?" he asked gently.

"The grief is heavy, facing this with Jennifer. Cole is…helping balance the other side of the scales."

He thought about that. "How long have we been friends?" Gage asked.

"Please, don't remind me of my age."

"Exactly. I know you, better than even your family in some ways. Tabitha didn't have many secrets either. If you two talked about something, chances are I heard about it. You're doing the right thing."

"I don't know."

"Cole's got a reputation for honesty, hard work, and loyalty. He's got a house. Now he's even got a dog. He's a settled type of guy. Give yourself a chance, Rae. And I say this to my own detriment here."

"It's noted. Thanks, Gage."

"I haven't had the fun of kidding you about a date in what? Three years?"

"Larry was a nice guy."

He laughed. "Sure. Which is why you never let the O'Malleys meet him." He rose from the table and picked up his plate.

The phone rang, saving her from further conversation. She went to take it in the living room. "Hello?"

"Hi, Rae."

"Jennifer."

Gage stepped into the room on hearing the name.

Her sister sounded in good spirits; Rachel gave Gage a relieved okay sign with her fingers. "I'll head out and let you two talk," Gage whispered. "Call me later."

"Thank you," she replied quietly.

Gage let himself out.

Rachel settled on the couch with the phone.

"I'm sorry it was a tearful call last night," Jennifer said.

"It was probably good for both of us. It gave me an excuse to bawl for you."

"I hope you weren't crying alone. Tom was mopping my tears for me."

"Cole did a pretty good job last night, and Gage came over to fix breakfast this morning."

"We have very nice guys in our lives."

"Very nice."

They had been sisters for a long time. The silence was peaceful.

Jennifer broke it. "God is my doctor, Rae. It's not like He doesn't know what He's doing—He created this body. If He wants to heal me, He knows how. I'm going to quit having a pity party now. I've got some living to do. And since getting released from the hospital is actually a pretty nice change, I'm going to enjoy it."

"Good for you." Rachel knew her sister; she had known today would bring that optimism back to the forefront. "It was hard to believe in miracles before today, Jen. But I believe in them now. Because we're at the point we need one; it's the only thing left. God is good. His answer to this will be good."

"I don't want to be the trendsetter, to be the first O'Malley to enter heaven. I'm sure it will be better than here, but I'm just not ready to go."

"How did the others take the news?"

"A lot of quiet. No one sounded surprised. And it helped when I said I was coming back to Chicago."

"We all want your company."

"Kate asked if I wanted to go back through old haunts—Trevor House and the rest."

It wasn't an easy question to think about. "What did you say?"

"Let's leave the past in the past."

Rachel found herself relieved at that. She didn't want to go back either. "Jen, do you really think God will cure you?"

"It's a feeling, Rae. A confidence inside that He's got more people for me to help. I'm a doctor; it's how I answer who I am. And I'm convinced I'm not done yet."

"Then that's what we will pray for. That you get well enough to go back to work."

"So you went to see Cole last night."

Rachel settled deeper in the cushions. "How did I know you would pick up that fact in this conversation? He's a nice guy, Jen. You'll like him."

"Something going on I should know about?"

Rachel hugged the pillow. "Cole kisses great."

Jennifer laughed. "Tell me about last night."

TEN

Cole drove Rachel to the airport to meet Jennifer and Tom Wednesday night. He kept one eye on traffic and the other on her, not quite sure how to read her retreat into silence. They had spent the afternoon helping Ann paint and were invited to stay for dinner. Rachel had been keeping her spirits up during the afternoon, but now… Cole knew how tough this evening would be for her. He was still having to guess a bit on how best to help her. "Are you ready for this?"

Rachel had roses for Jennifer balanced on her lap and her head resting against the headrest. She didn't open her eyes. "Did I really eat hot dogs and purple Jell-O for dinner?"

"I wondered how many times you were going to nod when Nathan asked 'more?'" Nathan was attached to Rachel, and the evening had shown in vivid ways that it was mutual.

"I thought he was asking 's'more?' The chocolate graham cracker things Adam was fixing for dessert."

Cole reached over and rubbed her knee, appreciating more than ever the way she opened her heart to kids. He was sure over the years she had said yes to more than one odd dinner because a child asked for her company. "I picked up a soda for you if you'd like it."

"When we get to the airport I'll gladly accept it." She took hold of his hand and looked at it. "How's your thumb?"

The bruise under his nail from the accident while hanging shelves was turning black. "Nathan swings harder than Adam."

"It will ache for days."

"He's not the first boy I've taught the hard way. It will heal." He reluctantly turned the conversation back to the coming evening. "Marcus said Jennifer and Tom had decided to stay at the hotel across from the hospital."

"It's a hard decision because we all want them to stay with one of us rather than in an impersonal hotel, but it makes the best sense. Her doctors would like her to continue with the daily pool therapy so that she keeps as much muscle strength as possible, and they have mutual friends on staff at the hospital. As it turns out, Kate's fiancé Dave's family owns a major part of the hotel. The best suite is theirs for as long as they like."

Rachel sighed. "I'm beginning to accept the fact that a month ago I still thought in terms of having months if not years with Jennifer. Now I'm adjusting to thinking about the next ten days. I know she's going to be limited in what she is able to do, and I don't want to add to her stress by showing the sadness I feel. There will be time for sadness later."

Cole squeezed her hand. "A day at a time."

She squeezed back.

"Have you talked about plans for the next few days?"

"We'll give her a day to sleep. The rest of the weekend—it will depend on Jennifer's energy. We'll probably have an O'Malley gathering. You're invited."

"I'll be there." He reached the airport exit. "At which gate are they arriving?"

"You'll want to circle around to the private terminal. Dave is flying them in."

"You meet him in a suit and tie, a badge and a gun, and you forget the fact that the man is rich enough to live comfortably."

Cole parked and paused Rachel with a hand on her arm. "Stay put. I'll come around and get the door so you don't tip those flowers."

They walked toward the terminal together. "Do you want to make an impression on Jennifer tonight or let her draw a few conclusions over the weekend? Say the word and I'll not let you get a step away from me tonight," he offered, smiling.

"The suit and tie already make a pretty big statement," she teased.

"You noticed?"

"I did. You dress up very nice, Cole."

He rested his hand on the small of her back. "There's the rest of your family."

Then he spotted Jennifer. And any question he had about Rachel's sense of urgency disappeared. Jennifer was a shadow of who she had been just months ago. His heart broke at the sight. "There they are." Tom was pushing Jennifer's wheelchair.

Rachel's grip on his hand tightened, and then she released it and hurried forward.

Cole relaxed in the lawn chair in his backyard later that evening while he waited for Rachel to finish a phone call. She was twenty minutes into a conversation that sounded like it would continue for another twenty. His dog had given up on the walk starting and had stretched out to sleep sprawled across Rae's feet. Cole tossed the baseball into the air and caught it on the way down, the feel of the ball comfortable. He had dug it out of a storage box to give to Adam next time he saw him. Cole's love of baseball went back to his childhood, and he enjoyed sharing it with Adam.

He knew Rachel had a gift for helping people; he had experienced it himself. But tonight he observed something he hadn't anticipated. He'd watched Rachel open her heart and literally pour it out. With her family, she held nothing back. It was there in the quiet words with Marcus, the laughter with Jack, the private moments with Kate, the questions for Lisa and Stephen. She had eased each of them over the pain inherent in Jennifer's homecoming, and they'd trusted her enough to let her take that burden.

It had cost her in energy. After seeing Jennifer and Tom settled at the hotel, Rae had barely said two words on the drive back. If she ever opened her heart like that toward him… He wasn't sure he deserved something that precious.

Rachel was talking to Marissa. Rae had seemed relieved to have the page come in, and as he watched and listened, he understood why. For Rachel work was a distraction. One of Marissa's school friends had gotten into trouble and Marissa needed a sounding board. Rae listened with her full attention, and when she did speak it was most often to ask a question. She had a nice blend of calmness and realistic advice. She cared. Rae would do everything she could to help, but she could compartmentalize the needs. With family she never released the weight, and Jennifer's cancer had continued as a building burden for a year now. The strain was telling on her.

She reached for her day planner and confirmed a date for next week. The call finally ended and she leaned her head back against the lawn chair. "Sorry, Cole."

"First rule of couples—no need to apologize for your job."

She half smiled. "Are we going to be making these up as we go along?"

"Very likely."

"Then you'll let me replace this lawn chair. It's got a hole in the webbing that is tickling the back of my arm."

"I'll even let you put your name on it so Jack won't stretch it out," Cole offered.

"Can we just sit here awhile before we walk? I don't think I've got the energy to get up at the moment."

"As long as you like." She was far from ready to go home. And he was in no hurry to have the day end.

"How did Jennifer look to you?"

There was no good gained by ducking the honest answer. "Like someone alive by strength of will."

Rachel let that reply sink in. "I'm not ready to say good-bye."

"How can I help you, Rae?"

"You already are."

"Seriously. How can I help *you*?"

She turned her head toward him and thought about it.

"I don't want to be alone," she whispered.

"You won't be, through any of this."

"It feels very alone. Death is like a cloud coming near that shadows and blocks the color from life."

"I'll be here, Rae. Whatever you need. And God promised He would never leave you. He meant it. For the rest of eternity you will never be alone."

"How am I supposed to be praying? Death is the one thing everyone fears: dying alone, afraid, before we are ready, leaving things undone. It feels like a betrayal to pray for God both to heal Jennifer and to give her a peaceful death with people she loves around her."

"Do you think God doesn't understand that duality? Loving Jennifer means you pray for a long, healthy life. Loving Jennifer means you pray for a peaceful death when the time does come. Rae—" he waited until she met his gaze—"if there is one person it's safe to share what's inside your heart with, it's God. All of it. His love is steadfast and He describes it as stretching to the heavens. He cares. And He knows what tonight took out of you."

"Stephen has taken it on the chin losing patients in accidents, and tonight hit him like that. He was struggling not to cry when he saw Jennifer. It's not fair, Cole. This family can't handle a funeral."

There was nothing he could say that would help. He knew Rachel couldn't handle it either.

She reached for Hank's leash. "Let's walk. I need to set this aside if I'm going to be able to sleep tonight. And I'm a long way from learning your habit of setting stuff aside."

Cole offered her a hand up. "You'll get there."

"Thanks for being there tonight."

He hugged her, taking the moment to reassure himself as well as her that they would get through this. "My pleasure."

"Would you keep Saturday morning free? It sounds like the O'Malleys are getting together about ten."

"I'll be there."

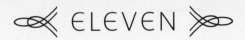

ELEVEN

If Cole had known why Rachel had asked him to keep Saturday morning free, he would have made a point to get more sleep first. He was playing baseball, although the rules appeared to be creative. Someone should put warning signs around that woman. Cole bent down and picked up the baseball that had dropped like a rock and stopped in front of the pitcher's mound as Rachel took her place on first base with a flourish. A shout of delight from the bleachers rose as Lisa and Cassie scored another two runs for the O'Malley women.

The catcher came jogging out to the mound. Marcus shot a look at Rachel on first base, now pausing to adjust the folds on her socks to be even over her brand-new tennis shoes. Marcus took the baseball from Cole and made a point of checking it for smudges. "She hasn't officially started dating you yet. It's okay to get her out."

"The sun got in my eyes."

"Sure it did." Marcus nodded toward Gage playing third. "*He* wouldn't let a little thing like a wink work on him."

"She wasn't winking at him."

Marcus dropped the ball back into Cole's glove, his smile growing. "I noticed that too. One more out and we can take them to lunch. They have a tradition of folding after five innings so neither side has to admit defeat."

"Good point. Besides, you just told me to get your fiancée out."

Marcus glanced toward Shari stepping up to home plate. "No, I just told you to walk her. You can strike Kate out."

"Come on, guys, give me a pitch. I'm ready to add the icing to the cake."

Marcus grinned. "If she doesn't get on base this game, she'll want to spend this weekend practicing in a batter's cage. A walk is purely self-preservation."

It was an elaborate baseball game being played for one person. It was worth it to hear Jennifer's laughter. Tom had transferred her from the wheelchair to the bleachers and swallowed her in a blanket to prevent her from getting chilled. They were all stretching themselves, and the humor of this game was to give Jennifer a day of laughter.

Cole pitched Shari a soft lob way outside of the box, and she still went after it. She swung like a girl and spun all the way around with a clear miss. She pouted, laughed, and stepped back into the hitter's box to try again.

Kate rushed out from the women's bench and showed Shari how to choke up on the bat. She whispered something that made Shari laugh. The next pitch Shari hit and it dribbled six inches in front of home plate.

Shari looked at the ball and then back at her fiancé. "I'm not getting it," Marcus assured her. Shari took off for first base with a delighted hop and a run.

Cole looked at the ball, then at Shari, and decided it was better not to move.

A glance around and Gage decided it was time to dust off third base. When Shari rounded first and the bleacher seats were screaming for her to keep going, Jack playing right field loped in from the outfield to get the ball. A tag-team race ensued between home plate and third as he tried to tag Shari out. He finally caught her in a hug and a fit of laughter. "Out. That's the inning." He picked her up to carry her toward home plate. "I caught a Shari."

"Toss her back," Marcus called.

Shari blew him a kiss over Jack's shoulder. "I nearly stole home."

"Nearly."

"I'm hungry, guys, let's call the game and go eat," Jennifer called.

The guys made a production of showing their disappointment, but they turned their attention to packing up gear.

The pizza shop was busy on a Saturday afternoon, crowded with families and kids. Cole slid in beside Rachel on the bench. She was toying with her straw while watching Tom and Jennifer play an arcade game together. He replaced her empty glass with a full one. "I like your family."

"The guys made you pitcher. You should feel honored."

"They didn't want to strike out their girlfriends."

"I noticed I was on base more often today than ever before." Rachel gave a small nod toward Jennifer. "She's happy."

Cole looked at Jennifer, leaning back in her wheelchair to share a laugh with her husband. "She's getting rest and a lot of laughter. Without the medicinal side effects her body is getting a chance to rally. This is a good week for her."

Rachel tucked her straw into his pocket. "Got any change? I want to play some pinball."

"I've got a pocketful of quarters just for us. Couple play, a flipper each?"

"How are your reflexes?"

"Better than yours."

She grinned at him. "Your age tends to regress around my family."

The carefree morning had lifted a burden from her. Rae was happy. Cole leaned over and kissed her, capturing the moment.

"What was that for?" Rae whispered.

"Because you make me happy." And he wanted to make a memory of this day for both of them.

"Half my family was watching."

"Only half? Remind me later to make up for that lapse."

She laughed softly. "I'll do that."

"I still owe you dinner out; Chinese I think it was. Want to go out this Friday?" he asked. "Just the two of us? Good food, movie, take Hank for a walk to end the evening?"

"I would love to."

He slid off the end of the bench and caught her hand. "Let's beat Jack and Cassie's score."

"It's impossible. I watched them play for four hours one afternoon on one quarter."

Cole rested his arm around her shoulders and steered her around the kids. They joined Jennifer and Tom. With her wheelchair angled to the side of the game she was handling the spinner and timing it perfectly. "The points are racking up."

"A lot of practice with video games in the hospital," Jen mentioned. "You should see me slaughter Pac-man."

"They still make that game?" Rachel asked.

"The version I play is the one they have on the children's ward. It has cancer cells and big, happy red blood cells eating them up."

"I hope you maxed out the counter."

"Twice," Jen replied, amused.

Rachel took the quarter Cole offered. "That one," she pointed out an open game.

TWELVE

Rachel met Marissa Tuesday at the ice cream shop down the street from the high school. Arriving a few minutes early, she chose an outside table and worked on a chocolate malt. The Franklin High School complex was new and had over seven hundred students. When the bell sounded and the exodus began, the teens merged into a sea of backpacks, jeans, and small groups of friends holding together in the moving crowd.

Minutes later, bells rang at Quincy Middle School across the street. Parents were lined up along the sidewalk and the edge of the parking lot to meet the younger kids. Adam was somewhere over there with his friends. Rachel had plans to meet him after soccer practice.

Marissa appeared from the crowds of high school students, walking with a rocking gait as her prosthesis threw off her stride. Her friend Janie carried her backpack for her.

"Hi, M."

"I knew you'd be early."

"An excuse to sit and remember my own high school days. Hi, Janie."

"Miss O'Malley."

"Would you like to stay and join us for a soda?"

"I have to get home. I watch my brother in the afternoons." Janie glanced inside toward the counter. "Greg is working today."

Marissa pulled the chair out and carefully sat down. "I saw him." Rachel saw the hint of a blush along with the fact that Marissa did not turn to look for herself. Without having to turn more than a fraction, Rachel took a glance at the boy now moving behind the counter, talking with the manager who had made her malt. A nice-looking young man, a senior from what Marissa had said. They'd make a good couple at the prom.

"I'll meet you in the morning at the corner?" Janie asked Marissa.

"Early? I've got a council committee meeting."

"Early. Bye, Miss O'Malley."

"Bye, Janie."

Marissa's friend headed home. Marissa tucked her backpack under the table.

"I love your earrings," Rachel mentioned.

"I made them."

"Really?"

Marissa slipped one off and offered it to Rachel.

"I'm impressed. You could go into jewelry making if you wanted to."

"It's a hobby Janie is teaching me."

Rachel handed it back. "You should make your mom a pair for her birthday."

"Really?"

"Trust me, she's still young at heart." Rachel picked up her heavy glass. "I'm going to get another malt. I forgot how much I love these. What's your pleasure?"

"A cherry Coke with a scoop of vanilla ice cream."

"Coming up."

The ice cream shop was a popular stopping point after school. Rachel took a place in line. She watched Marissa as she waited. The girl called a couple hellos to friends passing by, picked up and absently twirled the paper from a straw. Twice teens left the sidewalk to cross over and talk. Rachel smiled when she heard Marissa's laughter. If there were problems at school, they were not the major ones of not being accepted.

Rachel reached the counter.

"Yes, ma'am. What can I get you?"

Greg had blue eyes. He was lanky, tall, and had a smile that compelled a smile back. "Another chocolate malt, and for my friend, a cherry Coke with a scoop of vanilla ice cream." He glanced outside to where she nodded.

She caught the smile when he saw Marissa. "Coming up."

He was fast, efficient, and generous with the ice cream for both of them. Greg told her the total with tax before he rang it up, and she wasn't surprised to see it ring up to the penny he quoted. She paid with exact change.

Rachel nodded her thanks, took the drinks, and saw Greg's attention get caught by someone behind her.

"I got a gold star."

"Good for you, squirt. Grab your stool and I'll fix your reward." His smile told her it was family.

The girl was maybe six. "I want a swirly today."

"Do you?" Greg nodded his thanks to the lady who had walked the child to the shop.

The girl rounded the counter and climbed up on the stool by the small counter with the phone and the order pad. "Mom said she'd pick me up at four."

"I get you for almost an hour?" Greg asked in mock horror. "Guess I'll have to put you to work then."

Rachel said a quiet thanks to the teen who held the door for her and carried the glasses outside. She could see why Marissa blushed when Greg was mentioned. The choice of the ice cream shop on Marissa's part had not been an accident.

Rachel set down the glasses and took her seat. "I like him, M. How did you two meet?"

"I baby-sit for his sister sometimes."

"She's cute too."

"Clare is a gem." Marissa ate the cherry atop her ice cream. "It's sad. Their parents split up last year. Clare lives with their mom, and Greg and his younger brother live with their dad two blocks away. Greg's been kind of the go-between, looking out for Clare and Tim."

"It must be hard on Greg, thinking about leaving them in order to go to the academy."

Marissa nodded and dropped her eyes.

Rachel worked on her malt.

"Mom wants me to go to college for a music degree."

"I know."

"But I don't want to."

Rachel hadn't seen that coming. "Go to college or major in music?"

"Both. Mom won't understand."

"She knows your singing could take you places. She knows that's been your dream for most of your life."

"I can't walk across a stage like I used to. People feel pity before they even hear the singing."

Rachel wished she had been at the concert, wished she had asked Marissa's mom more questions when they had spoken. Something had been said, done, that had touched a raw memory for the girl. "It's not an obstacle to your dream of recording music." She knew that was the real dream Marissa had, to make records of her songs.

Marissa nodded. "I know."

"What are you thinking?"

"If I leave town, it's going to be very hard on Mom. And Dad might leave town entirely if I'm not around. I know he keeps this job because it lets him provide health insurance for me."

Rachel nodded.

"I'm known at the high school. No one asks what happened to me because everyone knows. I don't want to go to a four-year college and start over."

"It's not easy to go into new territory, to face people who don't know you, who notice your leg first."

"I'm not afraid of that."

"M, I would be more surprised if you weren't scared."

"I'm just not ready to go away to college yet."

"That's a good place to know you're at."

"I want to help people like you do. Only in my own way. I could get a job at the medical clinic as a receptionist and go to the local college here for two years to get my basic course work."

"Have you talked to your mom about doing that?"

"She'll be disappointed with me."

Rachel smiled. "Trust me; she's working hard to be able to send you to college in another year without crying all over you when she sees you leave. If you want to stay local for two years of college, maybe you could transition to your own apartment after you graduate. You could get in the habit of going home for dinner twice a week and calling her early on Saturday mornings to wake her up and say let's go shopping. I can tell how you're going to make your mom miserable by staying here."

"That sounds fun. That's what I want. A couple years of not having to push so hard. I just want to relax after the last two years before I dive into something huge like a competitive college music degree. I'd have to start the scholarship work this summer, and I'm just not ready."

Rachel would have been concerned had Marissa been changing a long-term dream without that kind of thought behind the decision. But what she was hearing was an honest assessment of what Marissa wanted and why. She'd had two years dealing with the amputation, her dad's grief, and a struggle to catch up on schooling to be able to still graduate with her class. Deciding she wanted a couple years without major life changes was a very grown-up decision. "That sounds reasonable." Rachel turned her glass, thinking about it. "Most of your friends will be going away to college."

"I'm okay with that."

"Marissa—" The door to the ice cream shop pushed open. Clare struggled to hold it. "Can I show you my drawing?"

Marissa turned in her seat. "*May* I. Sure, Clare." She waved at Greg, he nodded, and Clare came out to join them.

"Mom's hair curls at the bottom. I don't think I got it right." The child automatically came around to Marissa's good side and climbed up on her lap with an ease that said she had done it many times in the past. "I'm doing the picture for Greg so he has one of Mom at Dad's house."

"It's a good picture. I can help with her hair." Marissa took the brown crayon.

The child leaned across the table. "Hi, I'm Clare."

Rachel took the offered hand. "Hi, Miss Clare. I'm Rachel."

"You're pretty."

"Thank you."

The child smiled back. "Welcome." Clare leaned back against Marissa. "I wanted to draw your picture for Greg, but he said he already had your picture."

"Did he?"

"He showed me. You were at his football game. With Janie."

"Oh."

Rachel relaxed. Marissa had a pretty full life back. A boyfriend. Her own ideas of what she wanted for the future. The progress was good. And if in another couple years her father got past his own sense of guilt—the hope was there. It was good to see. Marissa was nearing the end of her process of healing.

Rachel finished her malt as she watched Clare and Marissa. From one case nearing its end she'd change to one still in process. Adam was still working through the losses he'd suffered in the flood.

When Clare took the picture to show Greg, Rachel shifted the conversation. "Marissa, would you happen to have some earrings I could borrow that would go with a jade dress for Friday night?" Cole was taking her out to the dinner. She needed something to make a better impression than the jeans and sweatshirt she'd been wearing the last few times she'd seen him.

"Spinners or maybe hoops?"

"I was thinking I'd pull back my hair and have wisps around my face."

"Something long, gold, with a hint of jade. I've got just the thing. You could use a matching hair barrette with a fine ribbon woven into it. Do I get to hear details of your date?"

Rachel smiled. "Maybe. You don't know him."

"Your reporter friend?"

She shook her head. "Cole—he's with the fire department."

Marissa rested her chin on her fist. "A nice guy?"

"Very nice guy."

"You'll have a good time."

"I hope so."

Marissa grinned. "You're nervous."

Rachel laughed. She was, for she'd never set out to turn Cole's head as she hoped to for this date. "Absolutely."

"Kate, if I knew you were going to stress out over this, I would never have mentioned it." Rachel shifted the towel over her wet hair to look back at her sister. Her sister's bathroom was small, and the exhaust fan in the ceiling was out of balance and whining. Rachel shifted her feet carefully. Kate's cat was rubbing her ankles and making her sneeze, had already sunk its claws in her socks twice trying to force attention to his desire to be fed.

"You are going on a date," Kate replied. "We're doing this."

"It's hair color. You put on those plastic gloves and use the stuff."

"Quiet. I'm reading."

"I'm getting tired of staring at sink fixtures that have toothpaste specks on them."

"That's soap specks, thank you, I cleaned in your honor. Okay, we're going to try this. Close your eyes."

Rachel squeezed them tight. "Did you turn off your pager? You get paged in the middle of this and we've got a problem."

"We've already got a problem. The directions look like Greek to me."

"I trust you."

Kate gently pushed Rachel's head farther forward. "Loyalty was never a prob-lem. Common sense, yes. Tell me about this date. Have you chosen the dress?"

"The jade one," Rachel mumbled through the towel, trying not to breathe in the awful smell.

"It's gorgeous. Want to borrow my bracelet and pearls?"

"Just the pearls. Marissa had the perfect earrings." Rachel wiped liquid away from her forehead with the corner of the towel. She turned her attention to the real reason for this visit. "How did Jennifer seem to you?"

Kate's movements didn't slow, but her words were sad. "She'll be bedridden soon."

"Is there anything we can do for her we're not already doing?"

"I can't figure out what it might be."

"It feels awful."

"I know. We do whatever we can to make her happy. She needs time with Tom—that's the most important thing now."

Rachel jerked as Kate's cat tried to bite her toe. "Marvel, I'm going to bring Cole's dog with me next time I come. Kate, you feed the cat too much; he weighs a ton. What's his problem?"

"You're in his bed. He's taken to curling up in a ball inside the sink for some strange reason."

"Your cat is dumber than a rock."

"About as hardheaded as one too."

"Then you'd better get married and let Dave teach him some manners."

"Soon."

"You've been saying that for months."

"Hold your breath. I have to do your bangs."

Rachel held her breath. If she didn't know Kate loved Dave an incredible amount, she would suspect that her sister had cold feet about getting married. Kate wanted to be married; she just didn't want to go through the headache of getting married. She figured if she stalled long enough for Marcus to marry Shari and Lisa to marry Quinn, she could talk Dave into eloping. It would never hap-pen. But Kate was as stubborn as her cat.

THIRTEEN

It had been a hot house fire. Even the caulking around the windowpanes had coiled up. The windowsill wood gave under the force of the crowbar. Cole jolted back as a cooked cockroach tumbled out. Arson and bugs. It made for a memorable Friday.

"Cole?"

"Back here."

Cole poked a pair of grill tongs down into the wall between the joists to fish out the evidence he was after. He had to give this homeowner credit for originality. He had spliced a string of fireworks into the outlet to start the fire. The explosions had sent the strand dancing around within the wall and dropped the evidence into a crevice out of the way of the resulting flames.

"So this is your idea of a date."

He turned his head to look back toward the door. Rachel crossed the scarred flooring where the burnt carpet had been ripped back.

Rae was the classic beauty in the O'Malley family with an innate sense of how to dress well to make an impression when she chose. She was making one. She'd chosen ivory and jade, and the vibrant color looked gorgeous on her. He could look for hours and simply enjoy the sight. Even if it did leave him with a permanent crick in his neck.

She smiled. "You should have said you needed to cancel."

"An evening out with you—I'm not canceling. You look gorgeous."

"Thank you, sir."

"I'll be about ten more minutes."

"Take your time."

He reluctantly looked back to the task at hand. "I wasn't comfortable the tarps would hold for tonight."

"Cole…you stood me up for work, not another woman. We're fine."

"Sure?" He didn't know which he appreciated more, Rachel's looks or her common sense.

"It will cost you the larger cannoli."

"Italian? I thought we had settled on Chinese."

"I changed my mind."

"Then it's a good thing I happen to love Italian."

She laughed and started to wander around the room. "What happened here?"

Cole finished gathering the outlet wiring. "My initial guess, the owner got behind on his bills and wanted to collect the insurance."

"So he burned it down."

"Tried to." Cole sealed and initialed the last evidence bag. He'd seen just about everything in his years leading the arson squad. This fire had been an obvious arson attempt, interesting but obvious.

Cole picked up the box with sealed evidence bags. "Want to follow me to the fire department while I drop this off, or head to my place? I'll change and you can leave your car there."

"I'll meet you at the house."

Cole took Rachel to Antonio's. The Italian restaurant was tucked into a hard-to-find circle drive near Sterling Lake and the owner was a friend. He watched Rae in the candlelight toy with her salad. She could push away the weight of what was going on in her life up until the point she paused, then the details rushed back to take her attention. "How did your meeting with Marissa go?"

"Good. I always enjoy seeing her. She's wrestling with college plans."

"And Adam?" He wasn't sure where to take the conversation tonight. He wanted her to have a relaxing evening. But until he got her out of silence mode, it wasn't easy to know how to accomplish that.

"Adam wants to know when the bridge will be reopened so he can watch the water up close."

"Another week at least. I'm thankful. Kids on the bridge would not be a good idea with all the interesting things still floating in the river just begging to be grabbed."

The waiter brought their dinner and another basket of hot bread. Rachel tore in half a piece of the bread and buttered it. "I'm fading on you already. I'm sorry; Friday night was probably not the best day to suggest."

"On the contrary, this is the perfect time. A good meal, a walk afterward, a chance to sleep in tomorrow—" He raised an eyebrow.

"My schedule is clear," she confirmed.

"Then consider this the start of a chance to relax. That's the definition of a good date." Her smile made the evening worthwhile.

"Your mother taught you wonderful manners, Cole."

"Thank you, ma'am." An idea occurred that might lift her spirits. "Hey, I've got a question for you."

"Sure."

"You helped Jennifer make the arrangements for her wedding. Do you still have your notes?"

"Two notebooks of them. Why? Do you know someone who's getting married?"

"I heard from Marcus that Kate wants to elope."

"He's working the problem now?"

Cole nodded.

"Then it has become more than a rumbling rumor that she might just talk Dave into it."

"I was thinking it would do Jennifer good to be part of planning a surprise wedding."

She blinked, and then her smile bloomed. As tired as she might be at the end of a week, Rachel still blossomed at a suggestion of something she could dive into. "Dave would have to like the idea."

"A given." Cole watched her as the idea developed. He found it fascinating the way her fatigue disappeared.

"Kate's been avoiding setting the date, but the problem is simple—she doesn't want to plan a big wedding, doesn't want to face a day fighting tears trying to keep her smile in place. If it was just her preference, she would have eloped back in November." Rachel thought some more and nodded. "You know, it might work. I've got a pretty good idea what Kate wants at her wedding. We've been sounding her out for months about it. And if she arrived and found Dave had made all the arrangements for them to essentially elope without leaving—" She grinned. "Jennifer will love this, and it will give her something fun to focus on. Thanks, Cole."

"Put those candy mints on your list. I like them."

"Glad to. I wish I had Dave's home number memorized. If he likes the idea, I could call Jennifer."

"Is your phone in your purse?"

She nodded.

Cole slipped out his address book and thumbed through it, looking for the card Dave had given him. "Try this." He gave her Dave's unlisted phone number scrawled on the back.

"You're helpful to have around."

He grinned at her. "Sure am."

"I owe you one." She turned her attention to the phone call. "Dave? Got a minute? Kate's not there is she?"

Lisa had the crime lab to herself as most people in the building had already gone home. She shifted the phone against her shoulder. Rachel and Cole were going out tonight; it was the best news she had heard in days. "Really, Jen? Where was Rachel at when she called?"

"She was just meeting up with Cole. I hear it's going to be Italian tonight."

Lisa brought down the next photograph from the Carol Iles murder scene from the wall and slid it under a magnifying glass and bright light. She was looking for anything that might help give her another clue to work on this case. "Italian sounds wonderful. I think Cole's perfect for her."

"I know she's perfect for him," Jennifer replied. "Rae lights up when she talks about Cole."

"Very much like you do when Tom comes into the room." Lisa spotted something in the photo of the kitchen counter that puzzled her. "Jen, let me call you back."

"Sure. I'll be here."

Lisa called Marcus and asked him to come over with Quinn.

She took the photo with her and went to locate the negative. She took it with her to the image lab. Twenty minutes later she had a twenty-by-twenty blowup of the kitchen counter. She pinned it to the board. Her eyes hadn't been fooling her.

She started looking through the evidence for the box collected from the counter.

"What do you have, Lisa?"

She turned as Marcus and Quinn joined her. "The blown-up photo on the board," she indicated, letting them see for themselves.

She found the right box and pulled off the lid. She pushed aside two pot holders, a napkin holder, salt and pepper shakers. The cop that had cleared the kitchen counter had swept his arm across it to put everything into a box. "This box has already been sorted once already, but the photo said it was here."

"Find it?" Marcus asked, joining her.

She started pulling out each napkin from the holder. "Got it." She gingerly held up a blue business card by the edges. "Carol had one of Rachel's cards."

FOURTEEN

Rachel finished off her list of Kate's favorite foods. "Timing is going to be a challenge. If we wait too long, Kate will get wind that something is being planned." She ate another bite of her dinner and nodded to the waiter who had come to refill their coffees.

Cole leaned over and added strawberries to her list. "Three to four weeks max," he agreed, "especially since you're going to want all the O'Malleys involved in pulling it off."

"It will be tight. Dave's going to ask his brother-in-law Adam Black to be his best man, and the two of them will come up with a good cover story for us." She stirred cream in her coffee.

Cole smiled at her. "What?"

"I need a date for the wedding." She had a feeling Cole would look really sharp in a tux.

"You've got one. I wouldn't miss this for anything." Cole looked beyond her and set down his coffee. "We've got company." He leaned back, his words and actions catching her by surprise.

She turned and was stunned to see her brother Marcus coming toward them. She nodded to her brother and met the gaze of his partner. "Quinn."

"Ma'am."

She loved the way he said ma'am with his Western drawl.

Marcus pushed his hands into the pockets of his slacks. He looked ill at ease. "Can we talk for a minute, Rae, outside?"

She slowly set down the pen and closed the pad of paper. "Of course." She glanced across the table. "I'll be back in a minute, Cole." She followed her brother, confused by what was going on. Lisa, waiting by their car, raised her hand. Rachel nodded to her and looked back at her brother.

"Lisa's got a murder case. And your name came up."

"How?"

"The victim had one of your cards."

Marcus offered her the card encased in a plastic sleeve.

Rachel took it and turned it over. The ink was faint but readable. "Yes, it's one of my cards. But the number—it's very old. 930710. It's my original numbering sequence. It was the seventh event in 1993, the tenth card I gave out there."

"Remember back that far?" Marcus asked.

She held up her hand and walked away, looking at the card and thinking back to that year in her life. She remembered incidents and children in detail, but putting a number with an event took more thought. She circled back. "9307 was a shooting at a federal park in Colorado. A man walked into a gift shop carrying a handgun, looking for his wife." She had it now, clear in her mind. "It was early May, a sunny day, but cool. A group of school kids were at the park on their way to see the sulfur springs. Police coming in to surround the building were forced to get the kids out one at a time from where they hid behind the counter." She remembered the children's fear of what they had gone through and their fear that their friends wouldn't get out safe.

"Anybody hurt?"

She shook her head. She thought about the event and she could see those kids. "It ended peacefully. But the kids were badly shaken up. Since they got trapped together, the fear one felt transmitted to all of them. They collectively started to be afraid of the outdoors and the strangers who might be out there watching."

"Carol Iles. She's thirty-two," Marcus offered.

"The shooting murder during the early days of the flooding?" Rachel thought about the name. "No. The name is wrong, and the age. I gave this card to Amy Dartman. She'd be in her early twenties now."

"You're sure."

Her memory tag for names was vivid. "Dean, his friend John, Paul and Brad, Cheryl, Emily, Leah and Lucy. The teacher was Nicole. The tenth card went to Amy Dartman." She felt silly explaining it. "A DJ eating a peanut butter sandwich while talking on his cell phone saying awesome deal: DJ, PB, CELL, AD. Those were the cards."

"Any idea how Carol got this one?" Quinn asked.

"It's not unusual for kids to still have the card years later. But why Amy would have dug it out and passed it on? I have no idea."

"When did you last talk with Amy?"

Rachel shook her head. "A long time ago. It will be in my log book back at my apartment."

"I hate to interrupt a night out, but it would help if you could get the book. Amy must have given Carol the card, and it's not something that would be passed on for no reason. I'd like to locate her if possible," Marcus said.

Rachel looked back at the restaurant. "Let me go tell Cole. I left my car at his place."

"We'll take you by the apartment and then over to get your car."

"No. I came with Cole; I'll leave with him." She patted Marcus's arm. "Give me a few minutes." She nodded farewell to Quinn and smiled at Lisa, and walked back into the restaurant trying to figure out how she was going to explain this to Cole.

He was still at their table, but both plates had disappeared. He rose when she returned. "The plates are being kept warm. Trouble?"

"Remember Lisa's murder case the night of the flooding? One of my blue cards turned up among the victim's things."

"Rae, you live an interesting life," Cole murmured. "How can I help?"

She appreciated the man more every time she was with him. "Take me home? They need my old files."

"Of course."

"I'm sorry about dinner."

Cole smiled at her and spoke briefly to the waiter who had come over. Their dinner became to-go. "Don't worry about it, Rae. We'll try this again next week." He offered her one of the chocolate mints left with the credit card receipt. "How old was the card?"

"From '93. I'm amazed the ink was still readable."

"Your place to get the log book, and then stop for ice cream on the way to get your car?"

"I'd like that a great deal. I am sorry. This wasn't what I thought the night would be like."

"Don't worry about it. Interesting dates are much more enjoyable than boring ones. Besides, the evening isn't over yet."

"I don't like this, Marcus," Quinn remarked, turning over the card. "Amy Dartman. We've heard that name before."

"Criminal division, down the hall from Carol, mentioned as one of Carol's friends. She was on vacation the day we were there," Marcus confirmed.

"My missing blond?" Lisa asked.

"Maybe," Marcus replied. "Let's get Rachel's file and check out Amy. I'd rather not tell Rae more than we have to until we understand this. She doesn't know one of her special kids from years ago is missing and may be dead. She was having a good evening with Cole. Let's try not to totally ruin that."

"Agreed," Lisa replied.

Rachel unlocked the door to her apartment and turned on the lights, hoping she hadn't been in such a rush this morning she had left her housecoat in the living room and her cereal bowl on the desk. She didn't want Cole getting a bad impression.

Her home was cozy, filled with furniture, the walls crowded with pictures of kids she had helped, and pillows dominating the couch and chairs. It was her haven. She loved every inch of it. And with four guests crowding into her living room, it got distinctly small. The material she had been reading in preparation for the upcoming commission hearing was spread out on the floor by the couch.

One wall of the living room was solid bookcases. Rachel crossed over to them. She kept the composition books in chronological order. She searched the bottom left shelf, tugging out books and reading the front labels. "Here it is. 9307."

She opened the book. Over time it had developed into a detailed log. There were factual accounts of the events in the words of those who had lived through it—the children and adults caught up in it, spectators, officers on the scene. Accounts had been underlined to show unique facts brought out by each individual. Spider webs of circled names and interconnections showed relationships among those present. There were neat pages of addresses and phone numbers for family members and friends, records of her follow-up calls with detailed notes. And inside the cover, an index listing of cards given out. "930710 was Amy." She handed the log to Marcus.

"Is this phone number beside her card number Amy's parents?" Marcus asked.

"Yes. Check the center of the book for names and address. Would you like me to call them?"

"Let us check the address, make sure they still live there. Thanks, Rachel."

"I hope it helps."

Marcus smiled at her. "It's a lead. There have been few. I'll let you know what we find."

"How *did* you know where we had gone for dinner?"

Marcus smiled. "You called to talk with Jennifer while you waited for Cole. She happened to mention it to Lisa."

Rachel glanced at her sister. "I hate being on this end of the grapevine."

"Give me interesting news to share—"

Rachel laughed because Lisa was stating the obvious. "Turn the locks on your way out. Cole and I are going to get dessert and then my car. And Marcus, if you've got a minute. The kitchen window is stuck. Could you elbow it down again?"

"What broke when it jammed?"

"I knocked over two flowerpots and broke the string on my sun catcher."

"Ouch. Sorry about that. I'll see if I can fix it permanently this time."

Cole held the door open for her. "How many events are recorded in those books?"

"Forty, sixty, something in that range."

"Amy held on to your blue card for years. When she was scared, she called you." Cole looked over at her.

She nodded. "The incident really shook her up. Amy was scared of the dark and sounds in the night for years."

"Maybe Carol had a reason to be scared about something. Amy gave her your card and told her to call you."

"She never did."

He unlocked the car door for her. "What would you have done if a stranger had called you out of the blue?"

Rachel wasn't sure how to answer that.

"Would you have called your family first? Or just gone?" He started the car.

"If it was a woman, I would have just gone."

"You work with kids. Marcus and Lisa and Kate deal with the crime. Remember that, okay? Call your family before answering a page like that."

The protective words touched her. "Thanks, Cole."

Her pager sounded. Rachel glanced at the numbers. "Okay if I make a call? It's family."

"Sure." He turned down the radio.

She knew the number by heart. "Jennifer. Hi."

"Tell Cole I'm sorry to interrupt tonight of all nights."

"You can tell him yourself in a minute," she offered. Jennifer's voice was soft, but she sounded good. They had spoken a couple hours ago about planning Kate's wedding. Jen should be asleep at this time of night.

"I need a favor."

"Anything."

"I just talked to Stephen. He worked a tollway accident this afternoon. A child wasn't buckled into a safety seat. He sounded pretty down."

She hadn't heard the news yet. "I'll stop by," Rachel said quietly, knowing how hard the day would hit her brother. For a paramedic, a child dying from what may have been preventable was the call they dreaded the most. Stephen talked at times about moving from Chicago to a small town where he would get calls to treat bee stings and broken arms more often than tragic deaths. The years were wearing on him.

"Thanks, Rae. Enjoy tonight with Cole."

"I plan to. You want to say hi?"

"Maybe another time."

"Good night then. Sleep well." Rachel put away her phone and double-checked that her pager was reset. She changed the radio station to the all news station to see if she could get a name for the family involved in the accident.

"Do you need to go directly to get your car?"

She turned to Cole. "This will wait until the morning."

"You're sure?"

She knew Stephen. The first hours after such a death, he wouldn't want to talk about it. Tomorrow would be better. "It will wait."

"Then if you don't mind a suggestion—plan what you will do, and then set it aside until tomorrow," Cole said. "You tend to worry things in circles. Try to worry in a straight line."

"You make that sound so simple."

"Actually it's just the opposite. But it's worth learning how. You'll sleep better."

"I'm trying to pray and let go, but it's hard. Who taught you the wisdom of how to do it?"

"My dad."

"He sounds like a good man."

"Dad was a civil engineer; he built roads. He called it permanent job security because a good road got used the most and always had to eventually be rebuilt. You would have liked him, Rae."

"I'm glad you have that memory."

"What do you remember of your parents?" Cole asked.

"I didn't have a good home, Cole. You don't end up at Trevor House because life has gone smoothly."

"Were there good memories in that mix?"

Rachel had tried over a lifetime to sort out the emotions. "Mom was a good cook. Dad could fix a car no matter what was wrong. They just weren't a couple; you know what I mean? They would rather fight with each other than work together to find a solution. And I was all too often caught in the middle." They'd divorced, and Rachel had gone with her father, but it hadn't worked out. She ended up at Trevor House. "Trevor House wasn't so bad. It was lonely, but I was already that. And the O'Malleys solved that problem."

"Is that past what made you go into the profession you did?"

She took a risk no matter how she answered that. "Kate says my childhood was such a crash course in how to survive a crisis that I now spend my days teaching others who don't have the skills. The reality is much more basic. I work in disasters because I learned how to be good at cleaning up a mess. That's all people really need, a helping hand to get started and a reminder that they did survive."

"You have to admit, not many people can hear news that a tornado came through town and rather than freeze, have a prioritized list in mind for what needs to be found, starting with blood supply, doctors, generators, and water."

"I'm a gofer, Cole. I know enough about what has to be done to be able to plug in where they are shorthanded."

"You fill the need, no matter how big it is or how huge the commitment on your part."

"You exaggerate that a bit."

"Rae, you would do your job even if no one paid you."

She smiled. "It's my own version of job insurance. A disaster will always be around to work."

"Let's hope not for a few months. I've enjoyed having you in town."

She reached over and squeezed his hand. "I'm enjoying it too."

⧓

Marcus pulled up to the federal court building, leaned across the seat, and opened the car door for Quinn. His partner was juggling a cardboard box and a laptop. "You were persuasive."

"Judges are a tight group when it comes right down to it. Judge Holland called Judge Reece, and the order was issued. Security unlocked Amy Dartman's office and I collected everything that looks personal," Quinn replied.

"Amy's seventy-two hours late getting back from her vacation; if she actually made it to her vacation. We can't even prove she's missing." Marcus checked traffic and pulled back onto the road.

"We can prove she was at Carol's that day. It's Amy's prints on both the soda can and the blue card. Amy hasn't called anyone lately that we can find, including her parents. She had a vacation plan that comprised a full tank of gas and a map, but sometime in the last few weeks she would have had to use a credit card. I don't buy a coincidence, not when they both worked in the criminal division."

"How does a twenty-three-year-old manage several weeks leave for an unpaid vacation?"

"Call it work for a master's degree," Quinn replied. "I want to see her apartment."

"The warrant came through. Wilson and Lisa are already on their way. I told them we'd meet them there." Marcus looked at his partner. "What do you think?"

Quinn held up a picture of Amy. "Blond. Nice smile. Twenty-three. She's probably dead."

Marcus opened the refrigerator at Amy's apartment, studying the near empty contents. She had tossed anything that might spoil during her vacation. "What are we missing, Quinn?" He wasn't sure what he was looking for that would suggest a lead, but this was the place Amy had called home. Looking around should at least tell them more about her.

His partner turned on lights in the living room. "What's the first thing you do when you return from a trip?"

Marcus thought about it as he opened kitchen drawers. "Park the car, bring in the luggage, toss my jacket, and probably kick off my shoes. Get something to drink. Listen to any messages. Turn on the TV while I look through mail to see what's urgent."

"I don't see evidence that she did any of those things."

"Confirming the suspicion that she never got back from her vacation." Amy was neat to an extreme. There wasn't anything approaching a junk drawer. The phone book was in the drawer near the microwave with a blank pad of paper, one pen, and one pencil in the drawer. There were no coupons for restaurants in the area, no pack of matches, a rubber band, a garbage bag tie—the inevitable items discarded in such drawers. Had she moved in recently? Marcus made a mental note to check that out.

"You know what else would be here if she had gotten home?" Quinn wandered around the living room, turning over cushions on the couch, the chairs. "Pictures, souvenirs. The first trip upstairs to the apartment she would have probably been carrying at least one or two valuables with her that she wanted to take extra care with and not leave downstairs unattended."

"If she never got back from her vacation, we're now at the more critical question: Did she ever leave for vacation? The refrigerator has been cleaned out."

Quinn turned on lights in Amy's bedroom. "Her closet is noticeably missing clothes." A few minutes later he added, "There isn't a toothbrush or hairbrush in her bathroom. That cosmetic bag recovered at Carol's is going to prove to be Amy's."

The small second bedroom had been turned into an office. Marcus pulled out the desk chair. Starting clockwise, he started checking drawers.

Lisa entered the apartment. "In the morning I'd like to walk around the block."

"See something?"

"Just curious. Her car is missing from the apartment garage. Wilson is checking to see if security tapes are left from that day that might tell us when she was here, if someone was with her."

Marcus uncovered a card from someone named Diana and a bill from a hair salon. Amy had probably gone to get her hair done before she left for vacation. Women talked while they got their hair done. It would be worth tracking down.

"Marcus, come look at this," Lisa called.

Straining to read the date on the receipt, he went to join them.

"This was on her nightstand." Quinn opened a folded plain white envelope. "Do you know anyone who keeps old movie ticket stubs?"

Lisa leaned against him. "I'm planning to hold on to the stubs from the movies we see."

Quinn bent down and kissed her.

"Break it up, you two." Marcus wasn't sure if he was ready to see them married. He took the envelope from his partner and looked through it. There were about fifty movie ticket stubs. "Amy's got a boyfriend."

Quinn reluctantly leaned back. "Any idea who?"

"Someone she trusts. You're talking a couple years' worth of movies."

"So if Amy has truly disappeared, there might be another person out there with motive than whoever shot Carol."

"First, are we in agreement that she was indeed planning to go away on vacation?"

"Everything here says she was," Quinn said. "Even her mail had been stopped."

"Second, we're agreed that she was at Carol's the night of the murder?" Marcus asked.

"Yes. She might be my missing body tossed in the river," Lisa added.

"Maybe. If we can track Amy's movements that Friday, we can firm up the time line for the earliest Carol could have been murdered."

"Let's go find Wilson," Lisa recommended. "Maybe there are also security tapes for the elevators. We can find a boyfriend a lot easier with a picture."

FIFTEEN

Marcus covered the phone as Lisa joined him at the marshal's office Monday night. "Quinn wants to know if you'd like to do a midnight movie with him."

"Absolutely. You can afford to give him a few hours off?"

"It's the only way *I'm* going to get a few hours off," Marcus replied.

Lisa laughed and took a perch on the corner of his desk.

"She said yes, Quinn."

Lisa took the phone from Marcus. "Not a murder mystery, Quinn. Make it funny." She laughed. "I'll hold you to it. I love you too." She hung up the phone.

"Hey, I wasn't done talking with him."

"You can call him back." Lisa handed him a folder she had brought. "For you. Morgue reports. This is every Jane Doe that was found since the day Carol was murdered that was roughly Amy's age, in this and the surrounding states. Two are slim maybes, but I looked at the dental work. I'm no forensic dentist, but they don't come close. You'll have that officially in a couple days."

He scanned the list.

"Amy's in the river somewhere," Lisa offered again her most likely guess.

"And her luggage? Her car? We should have found something by now."

"There are a couple stretches of lowland still to be searched where the flooding is at best contained by sandbags. And for all we know, the car was buried in a mud bank somewhere with a foot of water now running over it."

"True." Marcus held up the list. "Can I keep this?" Lisa nodded. He added it to his briefcase. "For what it's worth, at least you have a body to work with. I can't even prove I've got a crime. For all we know maybe it was Amy who shot Carol."

"No motive."

"But at least we've got the two of them placed at the scene of the crime. Any luck breaking the ex-husband's alibi?"

"Wilson reinterviewed people, but with his son Mark saying Brian was with him, and with others who were at the basketball game confirming they saw Brian there, it appears solid." Lisa spun the pen on the desk. "What about this being work related? Someone watched the house or followed them and intentionally murdered both Carol and Amy?"

"We're burning the midnight oil to see if we can find something. Any luck on finding the gun?"

"None. We need to talk to Rachel some more about Amy."

"Not yet. She's having her first break in weeks, and I don't want to interrupt that."

"It has been nice seeing her with Cole."

"Exactly."

Lisa slid off the desk. "I've got a car wreck to go look at, and then I'm heading over to the hotel to see Jennifer. Tell Quinn to meet me there later?"

"Will do."

Laughter filled the hotel suite Jennifer had made home Monday night. Lisa had brought a movie with her called *Down Periscope,* and it played in the background as they made secret wedding plans for Kate and Dave. Tom had met them at the door. He kissed his wife, and with amusement told her to behave, and then he had disappeared to join Marcus for a few hours to give them the run of the suite. Jennifer was dutifully lying down on the couch as promised.

"I think we should go with these napkins."

Rachel leaned over to see Jennifer's choice. The floor by the hotel couch was crowded with open books of cards and napkin samples. Between Lisa's ideas, Rachel's notebooks, and Jennifer's lists, they were actually trying to do the impossible and plan the wedding in one evening. "Those would be great."

"Which ones?" Lisa called from the suite's kitchenette.

"Medium size, white, with a red ribbon border, and a heart in the center."

"Yes, great choice. Get matching tablecloths."

"Do they have tablecloths?" Jennifer asked.

"Got it." Rachel found the page and added the stock numbers to their master list.

Jennifer found the wedding cake book. "Did you hear, are we on for the ladies night this weekend?"

Rachel added streamers to her list. "Lisa and I will be over with Kate about 2 P.M. Friday, so make sure the wedding stuff is hidden. Shari and Cassie are going to meet us here about five. We've got dinner reservations at the restaurant downstairs, and Kate is in charge of the movie selection. She promised to get something that was dramatic and romantic, but her taste has been pretty interesting recently, so I may slip one into my bag as a backup. I hear the guys are going to have a night out of their own to occupy Tom."

"I think they are starting with basketball," Lisa added.

"He'll come home with a black eye and look sheepish about it." Jennifer held out the book. "What about this cake?"

"That is beautiful." Rachel looked closer. "It's the cake you had at your wedding."

"I knew it looked gorgeous."

"Kate would go for something with even more roses. She likes frosting."

Jennifer turned pages. "How about this one?"

"Nice. Lisa, what do you think?"

Lisa set down the coffee tray. "Excellent. Did Dave say what he was thinking about for a honeymoon? He's got to make a decision soon."

"He's going to take Kate somewhere her pager won't work. Beyond that he hasn't given much away," Rachel replied, curious about it herself. She had no idea where she would like to go if she were planning her own. "Have you and Quinn decided about yours?"

"We'll go back to Quinn's ranch." Lisa sat on the floor beside the couch and reached for sugar for her coffee. "We need another cake."

"Another sheet cake beside this one?"

"A second wedding cake."

Rachel glanced at Jennifer and both looked at Lisa.

"I want to get married too," Lisa said simply. "We'll have a double wedding. This way if Kate stumbles on some plans, we can just tell her they're for Quinn and me. He and I talked, and we don't want to wait anymore."

Jennifer leaned over, wrapped her arms around her sister, and squeezed until Lisa giggled. "A double. This will be so much fun."

"This way we get a Chicago wedding in and Marcus and Shari won't feel so guilty about having theirs in Virginia where it will be more convenient for Shari's family," Lisa offered.

"And then Jack and Cassie's," Rachel said.

"They get the huge public wedding with all of Company 81 there to help them celebrate," Lisa said.

Jennifer looked over at Rachel. "Let's find two great cakes."

SIXTEEN

Rachel could barely remember what it felt like not to have aching feet. She shifted shopping bags between her feet trying to get comfortable as Kate pulled around to the restaurant drive-thru window to pick up their order. The Tuesday afternoon shopping trip that had begun as a quick trip by Rachel and Jennifer to the local department store had mushroomed into the four O'Malley sisters going to the mall. Jennifer's brief stretch of renewed energy wasn't likely to last, and they were determined to make the most of it. They had shuffled work schedules to get the afternoon of April 24 off.

The four of them shopping together was an adventure. There was barely room in the car for them on the return trip because of all the packages. Rachel turned in the front seat to check on Jennifer. "Comfortable back there?" Lisa had as many pillows as Jennifer did. The two doctors were having a good time together.

"Just fine." Jennifer looked at Lisa and the two of them cracked up laughing. Lisa had taken charge of Jennifer while they explored the mall, pushing her wheelchair through stores and often stopping to compare ideas on clothes with Rachel. Four times she had found herself being sent to the dressing room to model something they had found for her. Several of the packages she now carried were gifts from her sisters.

"Who ordered the coffee that looks like fudge sauce?" Kate asked.

"Back here," Lisa replied.

"That stuff will kill you."

"As long as someone else has to do the autopsy," Lisa said cheerfully.

Rachel handed the coffee to Lisa and the cold soda to Jennifer.

Rachel's pager went off.

"We're off duty. All of us," Kate reminded her.

Rachel tugged the pager free to see the number. "It's Adam."

Kate turned down the radio as Rachel reached for her phone. She had wondered if Adam would ever use the card. She was surprised—it was at two-thirty on a school day. He should be in class. "Hi, Adam."

"You called me back." He was breathing hard like he had been running, but he didn't sound like he was crying or scared.

"Always." Rachel took the large iced tea Kate handed her and slipped the extra sugar packets into her pocket so she could squeeze the lemon slice.

"The nurse let me call you after I called Mom."

"The nurse's office, huh?"

"I got a black eye."

"Ouch. Did you get a bloody nose too?"

"Huge." He sounded proud of it.

"Did the nurse give you an ice pack?" He'd gotten hurt somehow and called her after calling his mom for a reason. She was picking up the sounds of a nervous boy.

"It's freezing. Would you tell Tim it's not his fault? He kind of did it. We were playing volleyball in gym class, and the kids were laughing at him. He got mad. He didn't mean to hit me when he threw the ball." Adam was rushing his words, trying to protect his friend.

"Accidents happen all the time. I'll be glad to talk to Tim. I bet he feels awful about what happened. Would you like me to come by when school gets out?"

She looked over the seat at Jennifer as she made the offer, trying to decide if she was going to be getting a cab to keep this promise.

"Please. Mom is coming to get me. Could you kind of smooth things out with her too?"

"I would be glad to. Why don't I meet you by the bike rack?"

"Okay. Tim and I will be there."

Rachel hung up the phone.

"Trouble?" Jennifer asked.

Rachel put away the phone. "I need to swing by the school. Let me call a cab. I'll catch up with you guys back at the hotel."

"The school is on the way to the hotel. We'll wait for you," Jennifer said.

"Are you sure? You need to get some rest before dinner."

Jennifer nodded to Lisa. "I'm resting. Ask my doctor."

Lisa smiled at her. "You need to listen to your doctor more."

"You need to work on your bedside manner," Jennifer suggested with laughter.

"We'll stop at the school," Kate decided, the driver settling the matter. Kate's milk shake arrived. She put it in the cup holder and pulled to the street exit. "Are the streets still one way around the school?" she asked Rachel.

"Yes. Take Buckley Street to Converse. You'll avoid the traffic."

Rachel shifted her sacks, looking for the one with the gift for Marissa. She'd found the perfect beaded clutch purse for her to take to the prom. "Does anyone see the sack with the wrapping paper?"

"Back here. Which one is your pleasure?"

"The gold foil. And a white bow. And somewhere back there is a roll of tape."

"Found it."

Rachel had small scissors on her keychain. She tugged them out and cut off the tags from the gift. "What do you think?" She held the purse out for Kate to see.

"Marissa will love it."

Rachel slipped it into the tissue paper and back into the small box. "She deserves a great prom." Rachel wrapped the gift and added a bow. "Park at the ice cream shop. You won't get stuck in traffic since you can exit with the light."

They were a few minutes early. Rachel checked that she had her phone and her pager as Kate parked. "If you see Marissa while I'm over at the middle school, will you get her attention? I won't be long."

"We will."

"Do you want to sit out at a table, Jen, or stay in the car?"

As that question was debated, Rachel got out of the car and leaned against the side, watching the gathering parents. She could see the bike rack at the middle school from here; it was one of the reasons she had suggested that meeting place. She didn't want to head over too early for the shade wasn't great and kids had a way of being late coming out, given there were lockers to get to, gym things to collect, and friends to find.

Kate came around the car to join her. "Remember when you were in high school?"

"I'm doing my best to forget."

Lisa opened the car door and shifted pillows around so Jennifer could stretch out. The high school bell rang. Kids began streaming out. Rachel kept an eye out for Marissa as the high school parking lot became crowded. Then the middle school bell sounded. Rachel watched the growing crowd of kids meeting up with parents until she saw girls from Adam's class appear. "If I'm going to be more than twenty minutes, I'll call you," she told Kate.

"Tell Adam hi for me."

Rachel lifted a hand in acknowledgment and headed toward the middle school.

Gunshots erupted.

SEVENTEEN

Cole listened in on a conference call with family services and the district attorney regarding an arson fire last week while he worked on the department budget. It felt odd to be back at his desk, but he was trying to clear the paperwork.

"He set his tree house on fire the first time; this time he started a fire in the trash bin behind his apartment building. You can call them accidents as much as you like, but if we don't pursue charges, we're going to be unable to stop him before someone gets hurt," the lawyer with the district attorney's office weighed in.

"He's eight. He needs counseling," the family services officer protested.

This was the third call concerning Rusty Vale in the last year. It wouldn't be the last. Cole revised budget numbers trying to squeeze in another set of wet gear. The flooding had demonstrated they didn't have as many guys trained as they needed.

Outside the fire station the long ladder truck warned with tones that it was backing up. It was Tuesday, and on Tuesdays that rig got a full checkout. A sticking valve had been reported, and four guys led by Jack were working the problem. It sounded like they had it resolved.

"The family refuses to discuss it and I can't sit by and do nothing."

"Captain, do you have an opinion?" The family services officer was looking for help.

Cole agreed the boy needed help, but he wasn't sure the counseling she had in mind would be enough. "You said he's been having trouble at school. He's going to run afoul of the zero tolerance policy and face expulsion. His parents may be more willing to agree to counseling if faced with the headache of finding a new school."

The prosecutor and counselor began discussing the school counselor's report. Cole leaned back and reached for the fax coming in from the lab on evidence collected Friday.

"We'll go back to the parents one more time," the prosecutor agreed.

Tones sounded.

"I've got to go, folks. Let's touch base next week."

Cole cut off the call. He reached for his fire coat. They were short handed today as men who had been on full-time flood relief finally got a few days off. Cole was backing up Frank, the other captain on this shift, on the fire runs. He walked into the equipment bay as the huge doors rose.

"We've got a fire alarm at the middle school," Jack called over.

Cole swung up on the newly polished ladder truck, praying this was another in a string of false alarms. If Rusty was behind this, the discussion Cole had just listened to was moot. Hundreds of kids, panicked, with smoke filling the halls of the buildings… A fire at a school was something they all dreaded. It was policy to always roll a full response for a school alarm. "We'll take the east side; you take the west."

Jack nodded and Engine 81 rolled out.

⚛ EIGHTEEN ⚛

"Get down!"

Pain flared through the center of Rachel's back as Kate shoved her down, knocking them behind a nearby car. Gravel tore into Rachel's palms and glass bottle fragments on the pavement ripped into the knees of her jeans. Kate landed beside her and reached over to push her head down. Lisa slammed the open doors of their car to hide Jennifer and dove to the ground near them. The screams were terrifying as teenagers in the parking lot tried to get to cover and horrified parents across the street pulled their children to safety.

"Jen, keep your head down," Kate ordered, all cop, as she tugged out her sidearm. "Where's it coming from?" she shouted to Lisa who had better visibility in the other direction.

A car window in the school parking lot shattered with an explosion of glass. Someone was shooting in the midst of the kids. Rachel wanted to cry.

"Two o'clock," Lisa yelled back.

"Call this in!" Kate ran toward the high school parking lot.

"I'm calling," Lisa shouted back.

Rachel scrambled to the front of the car. Her heart broke as she saw the faces of the terrified kids. Incredible fear was frozen on their faces as they didn't know which way to run to get out of the way. She recognized the shock. They thought they were invincible, and someone had just ripped away that sense of safety.

"Marissa!" Rachel saw her stumble as she tried to hurry down the stairs, lose her balance, and tumble down the final six concrete stairs to the ground off the side of the stairs. Rachel wanted so badly to go help her friend.

The gunshots stopped. For good, for the moment… Rachel couldn't breathe. Beside Marissa she could see kids in the parking lot on the ground not moving. *Oh, God, what do I do?*

Jennifer pushed open the car side door. "Jen, close the door," Rachel pleaded.

"Kids are hurt. Get me to the kids." There was determination in her face and she wasn't thinking about the danger to herself, just the need. "Lisa, get someone to help carry me. We can both help them."

"Not yet," Rachel urged, "not until Kate has stopped this." She knew the counsel of the experts on this critical moment. *Think about your own safety. Realize if you get hurt, you can't help and will in fact slow down help getting to victims by becoming one yourself.* She couldn't stand to follow the advice. More gunshots erupted, and this time it sounded like shots and returned shots. Kate would get hurt trying to stop this and they wouldn't know. Rachel looked back at Lisa. "Stay with Jen. I'm going." She headed after Kate.

She could feel herself exposed to the danger, could feel the slowness in her movements as she struggled to hurry. She could feel her heart pounding and her breath coming in short gasps. Kate spent her life doing this, running into danger. She understood why Kate did it, but not how she lived with these moments of fear.

Rachel passed a blue Chevy with its back passenger door open. A gray Ford had backed into a white Honda and stood abandoned. Under her tennis shoes she could feel the sharp edges of glass from the shattered car windows. Backpacks lay where they had been dropped, spilled books and papers fluttering in the wind. Rachel passed kids crouched down and hiding behind vehicles and memories flashed back to the Colorado holdup years before. The kids were afraid to move for fear they would attract gunfire. She silently pointed back the way she had come.

Rachel caught up with Kate crouched behind a van.

"I told you to stay put," Kate whispered angrily.

"I couldn't."

Her sister peered around the front of the van again, trying to sort out the scene and find the shooter. "There! Past the blue Lincoln. A school jacket, black jeans. The kid has a crew cut. That's the first gunman, but there are at least two. Stay here. I mean it."

Rachel leaned against the side of the van and struggled to catch her breath. She was halfway to Marissa. Her friend had landed in an awkward angle and it looked as if her leg was broken. She was exposed, and the shooter appeared to be moving in Marissa's direction. Rachel crept from behind the safety of the van to the sedan in the next row.

She bit her lip to keep from crying out.

A boy had been shot in the thigh and lay where he had fallen across a white parking space stripe. He was using his elbows to edge himself toward safety. Before she could move, two of the boy's friends rushed back toward him to grab and carry him behind the cars. "Pressure," she called urgently, "put pressure on the wound to stop the bleeding."

She hurried back the way she had come. "Lisa! Over here." Rachel waved to attract their attention. Jennifer was out of the car with Lisa and the manager of the ice cream shop helping her. Lisa waved back.

Rachel caught up with Kate as she crouched behind the car in the handicap parking place.

Kate looked at her and there was dread in her voice. "The two boys are heading *into* the high school."

Rachel recoiled at what that might mean. They had to stop this, now. "I'm coming with you. I've been in the school. I know the layout."

NINETEEN

The school building was brick and rough against her back as Rachel leaned against the wall to the east of the front doors. Behind them in the parking lot the screams had been replaced with soft calls for help. Kate was on her phone, trying to raise through dispatch any security officer that might have been assigned to the school.

Kate pushed her phone into her pocket and looked over at her. "They can't raise anyone. The wise thing is to wait." The blare of fire engines and police sirens were coming from all directions through the subdivision as help rushed toward the scene. They were coming to help, but they weren't here yet.

Rachel already knew Kate's decision. "There are innocent kids in there," she replied softly.

"Two shooters entered."

Kate didn't want her going in, and yet to stay here would be nearly impossible. "It's all the more reason to have someone watching your back." They had to stop the shooters so they could safely help the injured, and it was worth the price that had to be paid. She could help after a tragedy, but for the first time she was in a position to prevent one. Rachel had spent a lifetime desiring to be able to stop some of the pain rather than just help people recover from it. "I'm coming with you, Kate."

Her sister looked back at the glass doors. Alarms going off inside the building were making the glass vibrate. "Describe the layout."

"The school cafeteria is the center of a large square of hallways. Around the outside of the buildings are classrooms, and lining most of the hallways are rows of lockers. Behind the cafeteria is the kitchen and then the music room."

"Stairs?" Kate asked.

"Immediately on your left and at the middle of the building on your right. Locker rooms and access to the gymnasium complex is on the far left."

"Okay." Kate thought about her plans. "I'm going to open the door and prop it open with a backpack. When I signal, you come through fast. I want you keeping an eye on the stairs. Any kids I point out, your job is to get them out these doors."

Rachel prayed she didn't freeze under fire. It wasn't the first time she had walked into a shooting, but this time it would be deliberate. Kate was showing her trust by not even objecting.

Kate reached for one of the numerous abandoned backpacks. She ducked and rushed forward, yanking open the door, dropping the backpack, and darting to the right. When Kate signaled, Rachel rushed after her, the glass door heavy as she squeezed through.

She flattened herself against the wall beside Kate. The sound of the fire alarm was deafening. The hallway was deserted. Rachel had not been expecting that. Only several dozen open locker doors swinging back and forth suggested this had not been a normal exit of students. Books had spilled out of a couple lockers, a wastebasket had been overturned, and there were a couple sodas that had been dropped, the liquid running slowly down the hallway to the lowest point.

Kate checked the staircase and peered around the first hallway. She pointed Rachel to the first doorway between lockers where there was a little protection. Rachel hurried that way. She passed beneath one of the alarm horns and her ears hurt. School had just been letting out. There had to have been hundreds of people still in this building when the shooting started. It was eerie the way they had vanished.

Kate tried the doorknobs one by one as they passed rooms. They were locked. Teachers had barricaded themselves and students inside the classrooms.

Kate pointed across to the cafeteria where a door was still swinging. Rachel nodded. She stayed behind Kate as they crossed the hallway to the doors.

"Mark, where are you? Come out here, you jerk." A door slammed. A gunshot hit something metal.

She gasped. Kate silenced her with a hand across her mouth.

Rachel leaned against her sister. "I know that voice," Rachel whispered, horrified. "That's Greg Sanford."

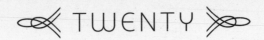

TWENTY

Kate could feel a piece of glass that had worked its way inside her tennis shoe cutting through her sock as she shifted her weight. She grasped Rae's shoulder, feeling her sister's tension in the damp shirt. She leaned in so she could be heard. "You recognize the boy speaking?"

"Greg is Marissa's prom date. Kate, he's a good kid."

"Who's got a gun in his hand. Describe him."

"Tall, lanky. Blue eyes. Brown hair, wavy. He's not the crew cut kid you saw in the parking lot. Kate, he fits none of the profiles of a school shooter. He's been helping take care of his younger brother Tim and little sister Clare; he's been there for Marissa. You've got to figure out a way to negotiate a peaceful ending to this."

Kate wished there was some way she could promise that. "Do you know who Greg is yelling at?"

"No. Marissa never mentioned anyone named Mark."

Kate pointed to the recessed doorway to the chemistry lab. "Stay over there, away from these doorways. No matter what you hear, Rae, stay out here."

Rachel nodded and reluctantly moved away. Kate took a deep breath. Her hand was sweating. The shouting inside the cafeteria grew louder but was indistinguishable. Shots rang out again inside, the overlapping staccato of gunfire and return fire. She was walking into a beef between two kids being solved by bullets.

Movement at the end of the hall caught Kate's attention. Another cop was in the building. Kate held up her badge, knowing he couldn't read it but would at least understand the meaning. She pointed at the cop and the far doors, then pointed at herself and the near doors. He nodded. They would have to get into the cafeteria and sort it out under fire.

Kate eased open the doorway a crack and saw an overturned table and chairs. She pushed the door open and slipped inside as fast as she could. Kate looked fast around the large room and dashed toward the serving counter. The floor was tile and her tennis shoes squeaked. It was the end of the school day rather than the lunch hour. Most chairs had been stacked and put away on the side of the room so that the floors could be mopped. Two rows of tables had been in use. The floor was sticky from spilled drinks around a few of the overturned tables.

The shouting was coming from the kitchen area.

She made it ten feet inside the cafeteria and found her first victim. A girl had been struck in the head, the open book in her hand suggesting she died where she had been surprised when the gunmen burst in.

Shots slapped into the metal supply carts near the salad line. "Police! Drop it!" The cop coming in the other end of the cafeteria took incoming fire and returned it.

Kate rushed to the end of the counter to help him. "Police! Put it down!"

The tall lanky kid went crashing over the counter. Kate moved toward him and barely ducked in time as the crew cut boy crashed atop her. A shot went off so close her ears rang. And then the pain registered. "Rachel!"

TWENTY-ONE

Jennifer struggled to remember her residency days in the ER. She wasn't used to this degree of trauma, but she knew how to keep the girl shot in the side from bleeding to death. She worked as a one-person trauma team trying to assess and treat the injury, knowing she was in a fight against time even as she listened to the shouts of firemen and paramedics and police surging into the area. She needed a medevac flight and a good surgeon.

Jesus, I could use Your healing touch right now. It was a desperate prayer as she packed off the injury with the lining torn from a school jacket. "Hold on, Kim."

"It hurts."

The girl was crying and moving her legs against the agony. Both were blessings. Her lungs were clear and she had good mobility. Jennifer could feel the exit wound. This was a clean gunshot that had gone straight through and had luckily missed her liver.

"Were you planning to ride the bus home? Was your mom coming to meet you?"

"Ride with Theresa," she gasped. "She lives on my block."

"Theresa Wallis, she's over there by the oak tree," the baseball player who had been helping her pointed out. There were heroes in this group of high school students, those who had rushed back to help despite the risks. Jennifer had seen adults doing the same thing, shielding students as they helped them get away.

Jennifer turned. "Light green blouse and jeans?"

"Yes."

"Go get her. If asked, tell the cops she's coming to help me."

The boy nodded and took off at a sprint.

Across the high school parking lot paramedics and firemen were rushing to help kids, the first arriving officers covering them. They were working toward the school as fast as they could, getting the kids who could be moved back to where they could be treated. Jen was relieved to see her brothers. Jack and Stephen were both working the front lines. Kate and Rachel had disappeared inside that building too long ago for comfort. A few teachers had broken out windows and were getting kids out of first floor classrooms, trying to avoid the school hallways.

The boy came running back with Theresa beside him.

Jennifer added another layer to the bandage covering the injury. She had the bleeding under control. That was rule one. "Kim, Theresa's here." She smiled at the friend and nodded to Kim's other side. "I'm Jennifer. Can you hold her hand and relay messages to Kim's mom? I've got my phone here you can use."

Theresa gladly complied, her relief at seeing her friend alive obvious. "Hi, Kim."

"Mom…the community pool. She teaches the tadpole class."

Her friend dialed the number information gave her.

A police officer reached them. "Can she be transported by ambulance? General Hospital has a trauma center; it's a six-minute drive with escort. Air is still minutes away."

"As long as she goes now."

He nodded and got on the radio. The logistics of containing a site that encompassed two schools and several hundred students that had yet to be secured was huge, as the number of responding police and ambulance grew each moment and already in the mix were parents trying to reach their children.

"Doc. We need you over here!" an officer yelled.

"I've got my hands full, Jennifer," Lisa called. "Can you—"

Jennifer turned and looked. "Yes." They were working like a MASH unit doing fast triage and trying to keep students alive until more help could get here, and right now there was a desperate need for more doctors. Jen could see the ambulance coming. She reached for the hands of the boy. "Keep pressure here, steady and firm. Don't lighten up until the paramedic takes over. Can you handle that?"

The boy nodded.

The owner of the ice cream shop was working alongside her. "Get me over there please."

Jennifer clenched her teeth against the pain of moving as she was lifted to the wheelchair. She wished Tom were here. They not only needed another doctor but she needed her husband. She hoped he didn't get himself killed running red lights rushing here from the hotel. She'd promised him to take it easy this afternoon. The pain was growing as she tried to get her body to bear up under the strain.

Jack and Stephen were both in the group helping the girl, which was the first clue of what Jennifer was getting into. She eased to the ground beside the girl lying facedown on the concrete beside the stairs. Jennifer battled tears as she saw who was injured.

"Marissa, this is my sister Jennifer." Jack eased a blood pressure cuff around the girl's arm, trying to rapidly get an assessment of how severe the shock was hitting her.

"Bad," Stephen mouthed, shifting the bandage on her leg.

Her leg had an open compound fracture below the knee. Stephen was working to stop the bleeding from the long gash while trying not to make the break worse. Jennifer could see the intensity in Stephen's face as he worked: He knew the reality—he was trying hard to insure Marissa did not face amputation in order to save her life. Jennifer checked the tourniquet and nodded to Stephen then checked the other leg. When Marissa had tumbled on the stairs, her prosthesis had twisted around and broken at the ankle. Jennifer leaned down so the girl could see her. "Hi, Marissa."

The girl's face was pasty white and she was sweating, both bad signs. Jennifer ran her hand lightly along Marissa's arm, reassuring that the worst was over. A splint on her hand protected fingers broken in the fall. Jack had been able to lift her head just enough to put a soft cloth beneath her face, and it was absorbing the blood from the scrapes that had marred her face during the fall.

"You're the doctor. Rachel's sister."

"Yes. You broke your leg pretty badly," Jen said, at least able to reassure the girl she hadn't been one of the unlucky ones shot. Caught in the rush to get out of the way of the shooters, badly hurt, and forced to lay and watch her friends in the parking lot fall to the shootings, Marissa was fighting to overcome the shock now absorbing her. Stephen held up a note. Jennifer nodded agreement. Stephen filled a syringe and provided the first shot of pain relief.

"Both of them, I didn't think it was possible." Marissa tried to smile. "No more dreaded leg exercises to improve my gait. No more trying to carry my backpack and not tip over as I walk. It's okay. It's just a few months of sitting down. I can do this."

Marissa's words were slurring and her breathing grew more labored. "Don't you hate that they make most wheelchairs gray instead of in a rainbow of colors?" Jennifer asked, reading the latest vital readings from Stephen's clipboard. The teenager had spirit. Jennifer could see her sister's influence in the calm responses and optimistic attitude. Marissa would have to endure months in plaster, but she'd be able to do it with humor. They had to get her stabilized or she wouldn't make it that far.

Jack and Stephen carefully placed an air splint around the leg break.

"We're going to turn you over, Marissa. You'll feel a little dizzy as we do. I just want you to relax into the pain. It's going to pass."

Stephen pointed to the guys helping him to make sure they did this smoothly. "On three." They turned her with care.

There was a scramble of hands as they realized the lower front of her shirt was bloody. Jack ripped material. She had a penetrating wound from something she had fallen on. They struggled to stop the bleeding.

While they worked, Jennifer carefully wiped the blood from Marissa's split lip, then ran her hand gently across the facial injuries making sure they weren't covering broken bones. "You got yourself a couple nice bruises. How does it feel?"

"Not bad." Marissa breathed out in relief as the pain subsided.

Stephen was checking vitals. Jennifer knew the numbers were stabilizing. She could see the relaxation of stress on Marissa's face and the return of some color. Her breathing began to ease.

"Does your mom carry a phone with her?"

"Most of the time," Marissa whispered.

"She's probably on her way here. Let's give her the good news and a chance to hear your voice before we give her the bad news."

"What's a phone number to try?" Stephen asked Marissa, being passed a phone by the one of the officers. He was able to get through to her mom, and the conversation began with a calm reassurance that Marissa was with him and able to talk with her. He held the phone for the girl.

"Mom, I love you." The words came accompanied by tears. Jennifer gently wiped them away so the salt wouldn't burn her scrapes.

Jack helped her tuck a blanket around Marissa. They had to get her to the hospital, but for the moment giving her vitals a chance to come up and stabilize mattered more than moving her. Jennifer would prefer to take her to the hospital by air so that jarring movement during the trip would be minimized. She wasn't sure where the air ambulances would land but guessed they would use the football field. The leg break would have to be dealt with by a great surgeon.

"How are you doing, Jen?" Jack asked.

"I can last until more doctors get here." She could feel an incredible exhaustion now taking over, her hands quivering at times, and a deep burning pain in her back. The agonizing pain building in her side nearly doubled her over. Jennifer looked toward the school, wishing Rachel and Kate were out here. It would do Marissa good to see Rachel before she left for the hospital. "Jack, they've been in there a long time."

"I put out a family emergency page. Marcus and Quinn will be here soon."

"Where's Cole?" She had seen him earlier with Stephen. Rachel would need someone to hold her when this was over, and Cole was the perfect choice.

Jack looked over at her and he shook his head. "You don't want to know."

TWENTY-TWO

Rachel walked out of the high school cafeteria stunned. The blood on her hands was Kate's, and her hands trembled as she tried to wipe it off but couldn't feel it through the rush of adrenaline. Kate had screamed her name, and Rachel had risked entering the cafeteria. The image wasn't going to fade. *Jesus, I need…* She reached for the wall to steady herself.

"Easy." Gloved hands caught her and steadied her. Cole wrapped his arms around her. She was enveloped deep in a fireman's coat and broad chest. She collapsed into the breadth of the man, knowing it was a safe place to hide.

"Cole…" She struggled to form the words. "Kate needs a doctor. Her arm is ripped up and bleeding. And Greg—" her hands coiled into the stiff fabric—"is dead."

She shuddered at the images seared into her memory. Greg had been on the floor near Kate with two bullets in his chest and a gun in his hand. Her sister had been feeling for signs of a pulse. Rachel tried to help, only to have Kate gently take her hands and stop her, shaking her head.

Reaching for a towel, Kate wrapped it tightly around her arm to staunch the bleeding and rose to check on the other boy. Lying facedown, he'd been hit in the head and there had been no hope, but Kate still checked. From there Kate headed over to the other officer, who had been hit in the shoulder. He'd already been struggling to his feet. They began a sweeping of the school cafeteria to make sure no trapped students were still inside.

What had happened here?

Cole moved Rachel back against the wall to keep her upright, his hands rubbing her back.

"Greg and another boy are dead. They were shooting at each other," she whispered. She couldn't get the image of the girl who had been caught by surprise and killed with a book in her hand out of her mind. It was senseless. It was a school day, and there were kids dead in the cafeteria.

Kids.

She struggled to get beyond that horrifying thought. Rachel looked up at Cole's face, and a chill settled across her heart at his expression. "How bad is it out there?"

His hands tightened. The man she cared about had faced arson fires and car deaths, and the calm she depended on had been replaced with incredible distress.

"Tell me."

"Rae, it started at the middle school."

TWENTY-THREE

"Adam is dead," Rachel whispered, terrified. There was a scene like this at the middle school. Tears began to flow as the shock reached unbearable levels.

Cole's hands shook as he cupped her face. "No."

She braced herself for the words coming.

"It's his friend, Tim. He was shot once in the chest. We found him in the boys locker room."

"Adam's best friend? Greg's brother?" Rachel struggled to get her thoughts around the information. How was she going to tell Clare the news that both her brothers were dead? That precious little girl with a smile that beamed and who had so adored her older brother… And the boys' parents—this news was going to further tear apart their lives already damaged by the divorce.

Rachel leaned against Cole, feeling sick. She rubbed numb hands on her jeans, trying to get sensation back. "What about Adam? Was he hurt?"

Cole slid his hand around the back of her neck and tenderly cradled her against him. She could feel him trying to absorb the pain she was in, and she didn't know how to release it to him. "I didn't see him, but it's chaotic out there."

"I was supposed to meet Tim and Adam at the bike rack. Maybe if I had been over there—"

"Don't," Cole interrupted her. "We don't know what happened yet to cause this. Don't start the if-onlys yet."

She forced herself to face reality. "How many others are hurt?"

He hesitated before answering her. "There were six high school students injured in the parking lot. How about inside the building?"

She eased back and struggled to get a deep breath. "I know of one girl killed. The two shooters. I haven't heard about the building sweep." Someone finally killed the building alarm and the school became eerily silent. Rachel rested her hands against Cole's chest and felt it rise and fall with his breathing. He was here, alive, well. She was going to hold on tightly to that reassurance. "You got called."

"Someone pulled the fire alarm at the middle school and a short time later the high school."

She was grateful for whoever had thought to do so, for it had triggered the emergency units to come even before phone calls could reach 911. "Marissa was among those hurt."

"She broke her leg, Rae. It's bad, but she wasn't one of the shooting victims."

The cafeteria doors opened behind them and Kate stepped out. Her sister was furious. Rachel could see it in the tight control and contained expression with her jaw clenched. Kate's impassive distance in a crisis had given way to the reality of this one. It was kids. Her sister would be haunted by the deaths. Her arm was already bleeding through the next towel. Rachel wrapped her in a hug. "I am so sorry."

Kate hugged her back. "Are you okay?"

"Shaky."

Kate ran her hands across Rachel's arms, trying to reassure. "It's over, Rae. Keep telling yourself that."

"You need Jennifer to look at that arm."

"Two minutes," Kate said. "We're sealing the cafeteria and then they'll start clearing classrooms. They'll need a full debriefing at some point tonight," she said softly. "I'll come find you."

Rachel nodded.

Kate looked over at Cole. "Would you tell Lisa I need her inside as soon as she can break free?"

"I will."

"Take Rae out of here."

Rachel wasn't sure she could walk that far.

Cole's arm around her waist tightened. "Come with me, Rae."

She had met one of the shooters in Greg. She knew one of the casualties in Tim. And she knew one of the victims in Marissa. Outside there were hundreds of students who had just gone through the most traumatic moment of their lives, who needed to be held, and she wasn't sure she had it in her to cope with her own experience and also theirs. She wasn't ready to face the questions.

"Trust me, honey," Cole said gently.

She let him lead her outside, her muscles still quivering just to walk straight. The sunlight made her blink.

"I want you to sit in my vehicle until Stephen can check you out."

"I need to get to work." She had to get past the incredible shock of what happened and work was something that would force that distance.

"You're walking wounded at the moment. Others can do your job for a short while."

"I need to see Marissa and Adam. Then I'll sit down." She tightened her grip around his arm. "Please." She had to see for herself that they were safe.

He studied her face, and then he nodded. "This way."

She spotted Jack amid a small group near one of the ambulances. "Marissa?"

"They're transporting her to the air ambulance."

Rachel headed that direction. She took a deep breath and forced herself to smile as the group parted to let her through. If ever she was going to help someone, it had to be here, now. She saw Jennifer first. Her sister looked much better than Rachel had expected. Jennifer was in pain, that was clear in the white tenseness in her face, but her sister was focused on the job at hand.

"Hi, M. How are you doing?" Rachel knelt beside the stretcher.

Marissa tried to smile. "You bought me a purse for the prom."

"A pretty one." Rachel brushed back her hair. It was wet. Marissa was alert, but she was in a lot of pain.

"Do you think Greg will mind if I spend it sitting down?"

Rachel held back her tears. Marissa didn't know about Greg's death, and Rachel wasn't about to tell her in these circumstances. "He won't mind." Her friend had already endured so much, and asking her to endure this as well was heartbreaking.

"Jack helped me talk to Mom."

"I'm glad. Hearing your voice is the thing that matters the most in this situation."

"Can you come with me to the hospital?"

Rachel sent a pleading look to Jennifer and then looked back to her friend. "It may be a while before I can come. I'll send Jennifer with you until I can get there."

"It's okay. The orthopedic doctor will have to get creative. I don't know which leg will take longer to fix. My artificial foot broke off."

"You've been down this road successfully before. Remember to take it one hour at a time today."

"Our ride has arrived. Ready to go take your first helicopter ride?" Jack asked.

Marissa nodded. Rachel moved back out of the way as Marissa was lifted into the ambulance. Jack lifted Jennifer into the ambulance to sit on the bench. "Page me?" Rachel asked Jennifer.

"I will."

Jack closed the ambulance doors. Rachel watched it pull out.

A crowd of kids stood on the other side of the yellow police tape. Weeping kids, some watching in silence, some standing defensively with arms crossed and trying not to show the emotion, but none of the kids were able to walk away. Rachel was overwhelmed at the numbers, knowing all of them needed someone to help them deal with this. She could see the Red Cross jackets of those on the response team already mingling with the crowd of students and parents. This school district was like others in the country; there was a folder with a plan for how to respond to an unthinkable event like this. It was being implemented.

The sun was still shining, and outside the five-mile radius that comprised this school district the afternoon was proceeding as normal. It was hard to put normal and chaos together. What had just happened would have to be integrated into the fabric of this community and into the lives of those present. They were still alive, she was still alive, and there would be a week anniversary, a year and five-year anniversary.

She wanted to sit down and cry. She'd been part of this tragedy, not just a witness to it. Who would be putting her name in a composition book to check back with her and ask how she was doing? Who would listen to her painful memories of what it had been like to sit by the chemistry lab and watch doors through which her sister had gone? To listen to multiple gunshots ring out from behind those doors? To hear Kate scream her name?

Cole's hand tightened on her shoulder. "Let's go see Adam."

She wiped the back of her hand across her eyes.

He left his hand on her shoulder in a firm grip until she nodded, and then he slid his hand down to grip her hand. "Come on, honey."

She tried not to look at the destruction in the parking lot as she walked, the damaged cars and the shattered windows. She tried hard not to look at the bloodstains on the pavement. She saw people in those reflections and kids' faces as they ran.

Cole led her across the blocked-off street to the middle school.

Yellow police tape was up now around the building and across part of the parking lot. On the other side of the tape parents were clustered in groups, talking about what had happened, and holding tight to their children. Word had spread that a child was dead; she could tell by the way parents talked in hushed tones. They were feeling relief that it wasn't their child and guilt for thinking that.

Rachel saw her sister Lisa enter the middle school. "They've gone through the school? Was Tim the only victim?"

"I was part of the two walk-throughs. The tragedy here was contained to the boys' locker room and Tim," Cole said.

Rachel looked around for Ann, Adam and Nathan. How was she going to tell Adam about Tim? The two boys had a tight friendship with sleepovers and scavenger hunts and shared secrets. The news would be devastating.

"Cole—" She stopped him when she spotted Ann. Rachel had seen a lot of distraught parents in her days. She released Cole's hand and ran toward Ann.

"Where's Adam?" Ann was panicked. "Rae, I can't find Adam."

TWENTY-FOUR

"Ann." Rachel rested her hands on the sides of Ann's face, knowing the contact would serve not only to reassure but also to block out much of the chaos around them. Her own terror dropped away in the face of a friend she had to help at all costs. "They've been through the school and they haven't found him hurt. We'll find Adam. He's just lost in the crowd. You can help us by describing what he was wearing today at school." Nathan was crying, holding on tight as Ann held him equally tight. Rachel didn't offer to take him to help Ann, for the boy desperately needed the reassurance of his mom's embrace. This had terrified the little boy. He would have been here when the students ran screaming from the school.

"Adam had on his short sleeve blue-and-white baseball shirt, with...jeans. His black tennis shoes. He was carrying a dark green backpack and a blue lunch bag."

"Tell me the five best friends he has."

Ann's eyes filled with tears. "Tim."

Rachel was fighting the tears too. "I know. Who else?"

Ann struggled to think. "His soccer friends, Scott and Jay. Mike from his homeroom. Our neighbor, Mrs. Sands."

"Let's talk with his homeroom teacher, his friends, find out where Adam was when the bell rang. He knew to get out of the building when the fire alarm rang. He must have gotten outside and wasn't sure where to go. What did you teach him to do if he got lost?"

Ann's panic was fading. "To sit down. To wait for me to find him."

"That's what he did then," Rachel said.

She looked around and spotted Nora from the local Red Cross office. Rachel waved her over. "Do you remember Nora? She was helping out at the flood scene."

Ann gave a shaky nod.

"I want you to walk with Nora through the parking lot. Check every row, look around the cars. Ask every parent you know to be on the lookout for Adam. Cole and I will search the school building one more time. We'll find him."

Ann nodded, looking relieved to have a plan.

"Nora, do you have a radio? Add Adam's description to the lost list. They'll canvas four blocks around the school for us, Ann." They were looking for a scared little boy whose best friend had died. They had to find him quickly before he heard rumors and misinformation about what had happened. The truth was awful enough. "Either Cole or I will check in with you every fifteen minutes."

Ann took a deep breath and nodded. "Okay."

Rachel waited until Ann and Nora had begun their walk before she looked at Cole. She took a painful breath. "I need to see what happened. I need to see Tim."

"It's a crime scene, Rae."

"If I'm going to find Adam, I have to see the scene. The boys were coming to meet me at the bike rack after school. Both of them."

"We don't know Adam was with Tim. They may not have met up yet."

"It's best to assume the worst."

She was relieved he didn't try further to dissuade her. "Come on."

They entered the school.

The hallway bulletin boards were covered with pictures from art class. Children had dropped backpacks and fled when the fire alarm went off. The hallway leading to the gym and locker rooms had been limited to personnel from the state crime lab. Lisa came back to meet them. The boys' locker room was at one end of the hall, the girls at the other, with the PE teacher's office in the middle. Large boards on the hallway walls were posted with information and schedules for basketball, soccer, and baseball. Rachel spotted Wilson talking with the fire captain and was grateful he was one of the homicide officers working the case.

The window in the PE teacher's office was open, adding fresh air to what was otherwise a stale and sweaty hall. The office was cramped with a desk and a line of chairs, but it was well lit with sunlight and cheery in its colorful posters and neat desk. The line of chairs inside the office was disrupted, but it was hard to tell if the teacher had shifted them when the chaos started or if it was the result of the normal visits of children to her office during the day.

There was no indication of how many children might have been back in this area when the shooting happened.

Rachel followed Cole into the boys locker room.

She flinched.

Tim had yet to be moved.

Cole tightened his grip on her arm. The boy lay between one of the benches and a row of lockers. He was slumped on his back, his face still showed his surprise even in death. He'd been shot in the center of the chest. Death must have been instantaneous. The way he lay suggested he had been standing by one of the lockers and had fallen backward when he was hit. There was an open gym bag with a towel half out the top resting on the bench near him.

Remembering the boy as he had been with Adam and now seeing him still and lifeless was crushing. She scanned the locker room but saw no obvious evidence of a fight. Lockers were dented, but from this event or simply wear and tear from use could not be determined. The photographer was still documenting the scene. The technicians working with Lisa were using bright lights to search the room for any signs of another bullet.

"Cole, if Adam saw this happen—his reactions are going to be intense. Even if he's hurt, his instinct would be to hide. You'll pass by calling his name and he won't answer. We need to go through this area again searching for him—this locker room, the girls locker room, and the classrooms outside this hallway."

"Lisa?"

"We'll get a third search underway," Lisa promised, "including the gym itself. A few minutes delay won't matter for Tim."

"Where would Adam go if he ran?" Cole asked. "If he was here or he simply heard the shooting, where would he likely go?"

"Outside. The parking lot. His mom's car. A friend's house. He'll seek familiar things and familiar places that give him a sense of distance and safety."

"Let's start outside. It's the most likely place he would be. There are people who may have seen him that we can talk with, and they may not be here in an hour."

He wanted her out of here and she wanted to leave. His suggestion made sense. Rachel nodded.

Cole walked with her out of the boys locker room, down the hall, and back into the school's main corridor. He stopped her. "Give yourself a chance to absorb this before you add another layer."

She stepped into the hug he offered and squeezed him hard, knowing how hopeless this felt. He was fighting tears himself. "A little boy is dead. Across the street his brother is dead. What do you tell a mom in this situation? A dad?" she asked.

"A heartfelt 'I am so sorry for your loss.'"

"And tonight, when the police go through Greg's room looking for a motive? When the press starts hounding? How do parents get through it then?" She hurt just thinking about it, for she had been through many such media spectacles after tragedies. The grief would be aggravated by the search for someone to blame, the simplistic analysis of news reporters, and the extended focus on the most sensational images of the scene.

She forced herself to focus on the task on hand and eased back from Cole. "We need to check the soccer field. It's one of Adam's favorite places to go."

"We'll start there and work our way around the building."

He led her outside.

Jesus, it didn't occur to me to pray. It didn't occur to me that Cole would be with one of the units responding. I didn't even think to put out an emergency page to the O'Malleys to alert them to come. In the midst of a crisis when I think myself organized and ready to be there for people, I wasn't even thinking about the obvious steps I could take. Her steps slowed and stopped.

Cole's hand warmed between her shoulders. "Worry the problem in a straight line, honey."

"I didn't think of you. I didn't pray. I didn't even think to page family."

"You were focused on keeping yourself and Kate alive."

"I watched her go into a room where two shooters were exchanging gunfire."

Cole rubbed the back of her neck and, when her tension didn't fade, settled his arms around her in a hug and kissed her forehead. "Let it go. I thought of you, I prayed, and God knew you were busy."

She wanted to absorb Cole's steady assurance and wear it like a cloak around herself. "I saw Marissa fall. And they tried to shoot Kate."

"I know." He turned her hand and brushed his fingers across her palm where the gravel had torn the skin. "It looks like you took a tumble too."

She looked at the injury and found it odd she hadn't even realized it had happened. "Kate tackles hard."

"I'm giving her a hug when I see her next."

"Give her a long one. This has devastated her." She took a deep breath and started walking again. The soccer field was beside the ball diamond and beyond it the groundskeeper's equipment shed. They walked toward the ball diamond.

Rachel stopped. "Over there."

Adam was beneath the bleachers by the ball field. She squeezed Cole's hand. "Go get Ann," she whispered. She crossed the field to the bleachers and looked for how he had gotten under there and crouched to crawl in after Adam. His face was streaked with tears, his clothes dirty.

Adam's eye still needed ice, and the nurse hadn't been able to totally wash out the drops of blood on his shirt from the nosebleed. The bruise on his arm looked recent, like someone had grabbed his arm to hurry him along during the rush to get kids from the school building. She wasn't worried about the things that would heal; she was worried about the pain she could see simply in how he sat, hunched over his knees.

"Tim was supposed to see the PE teacher after school," Adam said. "He got a detention for throwing the volleyball." She sat down beside him, having to crouch not to hit her head on the bench. "I was coming to sit with him, but the teacher wouldn't let me. Tim still thought I was mad at him because he hit me with the ball." The boy's heart was breaking. Rachel mopped his eyes with her shirtsleeve cuff and then solved the distance by swallowing him in a hug.

Adam cried, his bony arms wrapped around her.

"Where were you when the shooting happened?" she asked as the tears slowed.

"I was waiting for Tim." Adam wiped the back of his hand across his eyes. "Greg had heard about the detention. He stopped me in the hall to ask if my eye was okay. He wanted to see it and told me to get another ice bag when I got home." Adam paused for a long time. "I waited. The fire alarm went off. The art teacher said I had to leave." Adam turned his face into her shoulder and his small body shook. "I should have waited for him. I didn't, and Tim is dead."

TWENTY-FIVE

Marcus felt like he was looking over a war zone as he walked the path the shooters had taken, following the destruction with Quinn and Lisa.

Lisa knelt by one of the white evidence markers and picked up a shell casing. "This one is a .45."

"Two guns and a lot of ammunition in the midst of hundreds of kids—it's a wonder the number of injured and dead aren't higher." Overhead the sounds of helicopters signaled the arrival of more media.

Lisa rose to her feet. "We were there when it started—" she pointed—"standing by our car. I heard the first shot. A pause. Then several more shots. That's when I saw the first boy running toward the high school. Moments later, I saw another boy run into the school after him."

Marcus listened intently, seeing it, and dreading what they had lived through. He had to get over to the hospital to see Jennifer as soon as he could. Quinn looked angry and in his partner that visible emotion was rare. Quinn hadn't handled that emergency page they'd received any better than he had.

Marcus rubbed his sister's shoulders, finding comfort in the contact. "Lisa, I need to know what happened here. It started in the middle school and spilled this way. Who shot Tim? Give me the fundamentals as soon as you can." Rachel was going to need the information, and Detective Wilson was already on scene heading the investigation. Marcus knew he'd be open to a couple days of outside help. It wouldn't be the first time Marcus had joined Wilson on a case that touched the O'Malleys.

"You'll have it. I'm putting a priority on tracing the guns."

Marcus saw Kate walk down the steps from the high school, her hands shoved in her pockets, her head bent. From behind the police tape came a chorus of reporters' voices trying to get her to come over and answer questions. Kate ignored the reporters, spotted their group, and came to join them. He was relieved she'd finally stopped long enough to have her arm dressed properly. She met his gaze, and it was the beaten-up Kate he saw, the one who appeared when she felt she had failed and was struggling to get her perspective back. He'd talk to her later when he could get her away from this, but nothing would be able to take that weight off her. It was the price she paid for being a cop.

"We've got a problem. Where's Rachel?" Kate asked.

Marcus turned and looked back toward the middle school. He spotted Rachel sitting on a bench beside Ann, deep in conversation. Adam was sitting on Stephen's lap. While he watched, Nathan walked over to Rae and leaned against her knees. She boosted him onto her lap, hugging him. It looked like she had been able to turn the emotion and find that focus on work. It was good to see. "She's over with Ann."

"Jack." Kate waved their brother over. "I need you to hear this." She led the way to Rachel.

Adam's eye had swollen with the tears and the black eye was coming in colorfully. Rachel accepted the new ice pack Cole brought them with a quiet thanks. She offered it to the boy, smiling at him, even as she wondered what Adam had really seen and heard this afternoon. He was already trying to protect his mom—Adam hadn't mentioned to her that he had seen Greg in the hallway. And when Adam had first seen Nathan, Adam hugged his brother long enough Nathan started to squirm.

Adam was already showing the early signs of detachment. At his age his emotions wouldn't be able to absorb the impact of his best friend's death, so as a natural defense his mind shoved the details and the emotions of the experience to the side and cut them off until he was better able to cope.

Rachel reached over and brushed the hair back from his forehead. One of her tasks was to help him cope with what had happened. She could feel the desire to be holding a notebook and pen again and was relieved to find her own reaction to the incident wearing off. Her thoughts had been drifting, her concentration poor. Crying with Adam had probably saved her own sanity. She'd helped him from under the bleachers feeling heavy at heart but at least ready to engage in the work she spent her life training to do. To do that, she needed to find a lot more answers to what had really happened here.

Stephen helped the boy adjust the ice pack. "I know it's cold. Just relax against it and it will get better."

"Did you ever get a black eye?" Adam asked, his voice finally coming back to normal pitch.

"Several," Stephen said, "most of them when Jack and I went after the basketball at the same moment."

"Tim didn't mean to give me this one."

"Accidents happen. I spend my days at work helping people after accidents. I'm sorry about this, buddy. Tim was a good kid. The guys at the station liked him. We're all going to miss him."

Adam leaned back against Stephen, finding comfort.

"Rachel."

She looked over and saw her family coming to meet them. Their expressions were enough to warn her. She hugged Nathan and shifted him to Ann. "I'll be back in a moment."

She looked at Cole and her hand motioned him to join her. They met her family at the sidewalk.

Kate looked around to make sure she would not be overheard and then around the group. "They've identified the second shooter. It's Mark Rice."

The news stunned the group. "Carol Iles's son?" Lisa asked.

"A lady is murdered during the flood and today her son is in school with a gun. Anyone here want to speculate on the odds that this is a coincidence?"

TWENTY-SIX

Rachel tucked the phone against her shoulder as she scrawled another note in her composition book and ducked beneath the yellow police tape. "Nora, I've got nine kids who were in the school cafeteria when Mark and Greg ran in. Who do we have that can talk to them tonight?"

She read off the names. They were trying to make sure everyone who had been caught in the path of the two boys had someone debrief them before they had to try to sleep tonight.

Rachel felt like she had been working this scene for days, but a glance at her watch showed that it had been just over three hours. Most of the parents and children had already left for home. Spectators from the community were beginning to disperse, leaving the scene to the investigators under the watch of the media.

Rachel had made Lisa's car her temporary command center. She tugged out the rough sketch of the school buildings' layout and penciled in the information on where the boy shot in the thigh had fallen. She had just spoken with the boy's two friends. The fact that they had rushed back to help him was making it easier for them to adjust to what happened.

She was asking every student she spoke with three questions: "Where were you when the shooting started? What did you see? Who was around you?" From dozens of answers she was piecing together a mosaic. She underlined in red three names on her sketch. She hadn't spoken with them yet, and from the information she had, they would have been standing next to a girl who had been one of those shot. That kind of grief—*why her and not me?*—would be hard to manage without someone to share it with who understood what it was like.

The goal of the first eight hours was to make sure the kids did not feel like they were alone to cope with the experience and to identify anyone who was at immediate risk. Teens who had already spent the hours since getting home calling friends to talk about what had happened were not the ones who had her worried. It was the teens who had just lost their best friends and were having trouble doing anything but crying who needed immediate intervention. Finding those kids among the hundreds at the middle and high schools wasn't a simple task, for their instinct was to withdraw from people under the weight of that grief.

"Nora, I'm heading out now to start the hospital rounds. Would you ask the police chaplain to page me when he leaves Greg and Tim's mom?" She wanted to have positive news about Marissa to take with her when she met Mrs. Sanford and hopefully got a chance to see Clare again. The boys' father was flying today, the Boston to Chicago route, and someone was now at the airport to meet the return flight. The death of his sons was not something they wanted to tell him while he was in the air piloting a plane with two hundred passengers aboard. "I'll check in again in an hour."

She closed the phone. "Cole, I'm ready to go. At which hospitals are the kids?"

He was helping Jack pack up the last of the equipment Engine 81 had used in treating the injured. "Lutheran has three, Mercy has one, and General has two."

"I need to be back here at nine. There's a coordinators' meeting at the church down the street."

He glanced at his watch. "Not a problem." He stowed the medical kit. "Jack, I've got the incident paperwork with me to finish up. Anything you need before I go?"

"We're set, boss. They've released us. We'll head back to the station."

"Page me before you go off shift?"

"Will do."

"Rachel, let's take my car." Cole pointed it out on the street. "Frank brought it over."

She nodded and gathered up her growing collection of paperwork. The school counselor had brought her a recent yearbook and current class rosters.

"Need a hand?"

She passed Cole the folder of sketches she had collected. Most students found it easier to draw a sketch to show her where they had been and who had been near them, and she encouraged it. Anything with pen and paper and an analytical question to answer helped them start thinking like students again.

Cole held open the passenger door for her. And then she saw Gage. He was standing by the grassy knoll near the soccer field overlooking the school grounds. He wasn't working—he was simply standing there with his hands in his back pockets, watching the investigators. "Cole, go on ahead. I'll catch a lift later."

He had seen the man too. "There's work here. I'll wait." Rachel reached for her notebook and a pen and picked up two cold sodas from the cooler one of the students had brought over to her an hour ago, one of the many gestures from students who wanted to do anything they could to help out.

Gage saw her coming but he didn't speak, just watched as she joined him. She loved this man, and she had a good idea what was going on behind that solemn expression. She sat down on the grass beside where he stood and set aside the composition book. She opened one of the sodas.

He sat down without care for the dress slacks and grass stains and picked up the other soda. "I can't handle kids killing kids."

She let her silence be her agreement. They had already shared a sadness so overwhelming they needed no words to convey the depth of this new one. The weeks after Tabitha's death and that of his unborn son had already plowed this ground. She rested her head against his shoulder for a moment and sighed. "Today was the stuff of nightmares."

He rubbed her back.

"Where were you when you heard?" she finally asked.

"Doing the stuff in life that is irrelevant now. I was talking with the mayor's press secretary about a rumor the mayor is going to try to move the parking for the new stadium. You?"

"Enjoying a rare day shopping with Jennifer. We stopped by the school on the way back so I could see Adam and Tim."

She watched the fireman who was hosing down the areas where there were bloodstains. It was a fine balancing line. The men wanted to erase the physical evidence of the day and support students to give them time to heal. While at the same time they had to also slow down their own rush to forget and move on. She watched the man work and wondered what would erase her memories of the four deaths she had seen up close.

"I know you had to go in with Kate, but I wish you hadn't."

"I'm jumping when a door slams or a book drops."

"Give yourself a lot of room in the midst of this to recover. You took it on the chin."

"I hear an echo of my own advice coming back."

He smiled. "So I actually listened over the last two years." Gage nudged the sack beside him over to her. "I brought you some things."

There was a clean shirt, a wrapped toothbrush, a small tube of toothpaste, and a hairbrush. Her emergency duffel bag was still at her apartment. She knew she wouldn't be home for the next twenty-four hours, if not the next forty-eight. She'd been planning to hit the hospital gift shop if she could get there before it closed. Rachel hugged him.

"Call me early in the morning and let me know where you're heading? I'll bring you breakfast and the latest news update."

"Deal."

He nodded toward Cole. "Go on. I know the next twelve hours will be very hard. He'll take good care of you."

She studied her friend. "Will you be okay?"

"Will you?"

"Maybe in six months."

He smiled. "Give me a couple years."

She rubbed his arm and got to her feet. She left him there and crossed the field to join Cole.

He opened the car door for her again and then circled around to take the driver's seat.

"Who do you want to see first?"

"Marissa."

She flipped open the composition book and went back through what Janie had told her as Cole drove. She wanted to stay with Gage and grieve, but she couldn't. Her job was now beginning in its most intense way.

She understood what was coming. Unexpected, sudden violence had frozen a moment in time. Now time would speed up. In the days to come the rush of events would overwhelm: the investigation, the media, the funerals, the reopening of the schools. An emotional roller coaster had begun: denial, anger, despair, and acceptance. How she and the other counselors approached this mattered, for others would take cues from them. And on a day when she most needed to be strong, she had never felt so weak.

Jesus, I treasure those words you proclaimed in Exodus, "I am the LORD your Healer." Remember us today. It is Your healing touch we now desperately need. There was comfort in her new faith. No matter how great the need, she was finally learning to lean against someone who could meet it in full. And on days such as this, that awareness was what kept her going.

"Is your system settled enough you could handle a bite to eat?" Cole asked.

"I'll pass on food, but I'd love another drink." Her voice was already hoarse.

Cole stopped on the way to the hospital and pulled into a drive-thru. He bought her a large iced tea and a small fry. "Try to eat something anyway. It's going to be a long night."

Rachel took a long drink. "Forget sleep tonight. Once the media plays this for twenty-four hours, I'm going to have two schools full of students struggling to adjust to what happened. What they didn't see today, they'll unfortunately have seen by tomorrow."

She searched the radio stations to find one of the news stations so she could listen to how the local reporters were covering the shooting. "How are your guys handling it?"

"I was fortunate. Most of them only dealt with the injured. Once the lead guys saw Tim, they checked the locker room for injured and then sealed off the area."

"How are you handling it?"

Cole looked over at her, then back at the road. "How about you?"

Rachel understood exactly what he meant. "Better a discussion for tomorrow?"

"I think so."

She rubbed her forehead. "What are the odds you have aspirin available?"

"Try the glove box."

She dug around for the packets. "You know, batteries go bad when they get hot."

"Considering I tossed them in there two years ago, they're already goners."

She found the aspirin.

"Hand me two please. My headache is a bear too."

She shook out two for him and passed him her drink.

"Eat some of these." She offered the fries.

She pulled out another stack of blue cards and began marking the back with numbers. She had already handed out dozens. Her pager went off. She slipped it off and read the number, then immediately reached for her phone. "Marcus, how did the walk-through go?" She tucked the phone against her shoulder and reached for the composition book.

"There was a bullet in the chemistry lab room door. Someone was shooting at you, Rae, and you failed to mention it?"

She really didn't want to know. "It must have been before I got there." She'd tell herself that and hope it was true.

"Good. That was my update; the rest I'll give you when I see you at nine," Marcus said. "What do you have for me?"

She flipped back in her composition book to the summary pages. She scanned the information, trying to limit what she had learned to only what Marcus would need in order to resolve the shooting. "Tim was a kid who got picked on. That's the consensus of the kids who knew him. There was genuine surprise when I asked if Tim ever talked about a gun or showed a fascination with guns. If he had any interest that way, it's not showing among those who knew him. I'll talk more with Adam about it tomorrow."

She read her notes. "Did Tim have enemies? Yes and no. He was getting harassed by some freshman kids who were neighbors of his, but it was the *you're fat, have freckles, and you can't even catch a ball* type taunting. Tim would have been the one to retaliate to such taunting, but all I've got so far is the fact that he was looking forward to going to a private school next year."

Rachel hated her final conclusion. "Marcus, for now I'm leaning toward Tim being in the wrong place at the wrong time."

"The wrong place at the wrong time—how many obituaries do we see that should include that statement?" Marcus asked grimly.

"I know," Rachel replied, hearing and sharing the ache in his heart. A child had died and it looked to be an unfortunate chance.

"Regarding Mark Rice." She turned to the center section of the book. "He's the classic school shooter, Marcus. Cole already has him down as a budding arsonist who was a significant contributor to his parents' divorce. The murder of his mom—we'll set aside the question of whether he had anything to do with that—it was a definite trigger in his life. I've got two teachers and the vice principal describing his behavior in the last month as unpredictable with a hair-trigger temper. A notebook in his backpack had doodles of dead people; he's been talking to other kids about guns; and he's angry at authorities and cops in particular. Guns appear to be a long-term fascination of his. Mark's best friend is Chuck

Holden. Three boys who knew Mark have volunteered that same name. The boys hung out together. Maybe he knows something or heard Mark say something."

"I'll get someone to track down Chuck," Marcus promised.

"Good. Let me know what you find."

"What do you have on Greg?"

Rachel read her notes and sighed. "Confusion. Kids are stunned at the idea of Greg shooting someone. He's the one kids describe as law and order, follow the rules, right versus wrong. They joke about the fact that he was careful to round his time card at work down five minutes in favor of his boss. He's a classic caretaker, Marcus. He looked after his brother and sister and got a job after his parents' divorce so he could help pay his way to college. He's an A student with an occasional B. For temperament most people say he's patient, especially with his little sister Clare. If Greg knew Mark, it was in passing in the halls. They had no classes in common. They don't appear to have friends in common."

"Your best guess?" Marcus probed.

"I don't like it."

"Tell me anyway."

Rachel chewed on the end of her pen. "Okay. I heard Greg shout at Mark inside the cafeteria. He was furious. Not just angry, but furious. Like Kate going after someone who caused her to lose a hostage type furious. Greg was out of control. Adam said he saw Greg at the middle school, that Greg had heard about Tim's detention and come over to get his brother. Marcus, I'm thinking it's something as simple as Greg was nearby when Tim was shot. For whatever reason Greg blamed Mark, and he took out after Mark to make him pay for it. The chase went from the middle school back to the high school and ended in the cafeteria with both Greg and Mark dead."

"How did Greg get a gun?"

"Greg wasn't the type to carry one. I'm sure of that. But I could see Mark bringing one to school. Why do kids most often bring guns to school? To show them off to friends, to trade or sell them. I think Mark was trading guns with someone at the middle school, and they were in the locker room. Tim would have been at the PE teacher's office, which puts him right there too, and as a result Tim was in the wrong place at the wrong time. He got killed."

"If Mark handled both guns, we should be able to prove it from prints. Lisa's got the guns as a top lab priority," Marcus said.

"How many shots did each boy fire? Did Greg shoot at anyone other than Mark?" It was awful to think she was trying to put all the blame on Mark and make him the villain when Greg had clearly been carrying a gun and was chasing Mark. But Rachel couldn't get past the fact she had met Greg and her heart was torn up at the fact he'd been involved.

"We all want those answers, Rae. It's going to take time to figure out. I'll see you at nine, and hopefully I'll have something by then. Would you keep an eye on Kate tonight? Make sure she gets something to eat?"

"I already have. She groused because I ordered mustard on her cheeseburger." Rachel smiled at the memory.

"She has to give you grief about something."

"She's bouncing back just fine. I'll see you at nine."

Rachel closed the phone. Kate was bouncing back. Rachel wished she was doing as well. She cautioned every victim not to get stuck on the question: What could I have done to change what happened? And she was getting stuck.

"So you think Greg was avenging his brother."

Cole broke into her thoughts and she tried to refocus. "It's the only logical answer. He was a caretaker. His job was to protect Tim and he failed."

"Kids don't pick up guns and just go after someone without a reason."

Rachel had seen kids react this way before, if not taken to the extreme of killing someone. "Maybe Greg thought Mark would get away with it, and he wasn't going to let that happen."

Cole reached over and squeezed her hand. "Let it go, Rae. The boys made their choices. You can't undo their decisions." He turned into the hospital parking garage past a row of satellite television trucks.

"How many reporters are now covering this shooting?" Rachel turned in her seat to see if she could catch station initials.

"Two schools involved, brothers among the dead, a slow news day otherwise—they'll make this story the headlines for the week."

"Which means copycats," Rachel observed, knowing it was inevitable. "I don't want to end up in the middle of the media tonight."

Cole parked on the fourth floor of the garage. "We'll go through the geriatrics ward. That wing still has its own elevators."

"I like the sound of that plan. Where will we find Jennifer and Tom?"

"She said the hospital had set aside a waiting room near the ICU for the families of the students brought here."

Rachel checked her watch and gathered the items she needed to take in with her. "Marissa went into surgery forty-eight minutes ago. There should be news by now."

"It was a bad fracture. Don't expect her to be in recovery yet."

Cole escorted her through the hospital. They were directed to the private waiting room. She was relieved to see Jennifer in her wheelchair over by the window, not trying to be in the middle helping the families. Rachel crossed to her sister and knelt beside her wheelchair. Jennifer was pale and in pain, her exhaustion apparent, but her smile when she saw Rachel was still there. Rachel leaned over and gently hugged her. "Marissa?"

"The surgeon is excellent, Rae. She should be in recovery shortly."

"I didn't see her mom."

"She just went to meet Marissa's grandmother downstairs."

Rachel rubbed Jennifer's arm. She had been holding back the emotions until a safe moment and looking at Jennifer the tears returned. "Thank you for being there at the school. For saving so many lives. You and Lisa—"

Jennifer smiled. "God knew," she said softly. "He knew I needed to be back in Chicago. I've been watching the coverage. It's been rough."

"Yes." Rachel had been dodging the media, well aware that the scene was being transmitted live to the city.

"How are the kids doing who saw it?"

"Divided between those who felt they were able to help and those who felt like they froze. Between those who were in the parking lot and saw someone get hurt and those who only heard the shooting and were trapped not knowing what was going on."

"You need to make sure to get some sleep tonight."

"I'll try." Rachel held her sister's gaze. "Would you let Tom take you back to the hotel? I'm going to need you as a sounding board this week."

"I've learned my limits, Rae. We'll leave just as soon as Marissa gets to recovery. Have you seen Kate?"

"She's mad about someone shooting her, about all of us being there when it started. Give her a day to get past that. Lisa is busy at the scene tonight, and she promised to keep an eye on Kate for me too. I did nag her into eating since the painkillers were making her queasy." Rachel looked around the room. "Tell me who's here. I need to start making the rounds."

A movement at the door caught her attention. Marissa's mom came in, accompanied by her grandmother. Following them was a man Rachel was overjoyed to see. "Marissa's dad came."

"I was talking with Marissa's mom when he called. He was in Milwaukee when he heard the news."

"Marissa will be so relieved to see him."

"Go talk with them; I'll be a phone call away when you want to talk later."

"Thanks, Jen." Rachel leaned over and hugged her. "I love you."

"I love you too. Go to work. And feel free to call tonight if I can help."

TWENTY-SEVEN

Marcus parked the car down the block from Mark's home Tuesday evening. "This is going to be interesting." Brian Rice stood in his front yard having a heated exchange with a police officer, all of it happening under the view of the reporters across the street. Two officers were standing back a few feet ready to step in if needed.

Lisa stepped out of the car. "His son is dead at school, and we're executing a search warrant on his home. We already know from Carol's murder investigation that this guy has a bad temper. The warrant covered the entire grounds?"

"Yes," Quinn confirmed.

"Let's make sure more than a couple officers search that utility shed and the backyard," Lisa noted, glancing into the backyard.

"Also the attic and the utility room," Quinn added.

They ignored the verbal shouting match going on as they walked up the drive. Marcus held up his badge and led the way inside the house. It was well lit up as officers conducting the search worked room to room. "Mark's bedroom?"

The nearest officer pointed. "Down the hallway, second door on the left."

The photographer was just finishing up his work.

Marcus expected an angry kid with rock music posters, video games, a huge collection of music, and an emphasis on sports. "This is a dichotomy." Mark Rice was into rock collecting. The bookshelf in his bedroom had two handbooks on rocks, and the rest of the shelves contained samples, neatly collected and labeled, some on display, others stored in clear plastic cubes. Quartz, graphite, pieces of fool's gold.

"Don't change your impressions too quickly." Quinn picked up one of the rocks and blew off the dust. "Some of these boxes have labels from before Mark was born."

Marcus watched over the technician's shoulder as the computer was turned on. "Strike out here. He's got it password protected. We'll have to take it in." He pushed around the books and loose papers on Mark's desk. "Restaurant delivery menus, school papers, most of it out of date."

Lisa pulled a box from beneath the bed. "His more current reading." She pushed aside the magazines the boy wasn't old enough to own. "Quinn." She picked up a thin rod and a rag and sniffed the cloth. "He was cleaning something that smells of gunpowder."

She handed it to a technician to bag as evidence.

Marcus opened the closet. "Do you think Mark shot his mom?" he asked Lisa, sorting through T-shirts and jeans, checking pockets.

"He proved today he would carry and use a gun," Lisa replied. "His alibi for the night of Carol's murder is that he was playing at a high school basketball game and his dad was with him. We're still trying to get a time line that tells us if that's airtight."

"Carol was shot with a .38. Neither gun recovered at the school was a .38."

"Which means if the gun turns up in this house, I would be very interested."

Marcus found nothing in the closet beyond clothes and shoes. "This place was cleaned up. How many kids have closets where you can see the floor?"

"I'm getting that same feeling." Lisa flipped through the boy's music tapes. "We didn't get here in time."

"Let's go see what the other search warrants turn up among Tim and Greg's things," Marcus said.

Cole walked out to the parking lot after the 9 P.M. update meeting. This Tuesday felt like a very long year. He was accustomed to disasters where he could do something, but he could do so little here. His work was over, and Rachel's was just beginning.

What he understood about her job had been transformed in the last few hours. She walked among the teenagers and they instinctively turned to her. They clustered around her in groups, seeking reassurance and a chance to share what they had experienced. She took the terror and the pain they felt and absorbed it. And when she wrapped her arm around the shoulders of a teenager, her empathy got through the pain and touched the sorrow. Her calm reassurance that the moment was over made it safe to grieve. She loved them and they knew it. She pointed the way to how to recover.

Lord, Rae's going to need Your strength. She's carrying a difficult burden, and it's not going to end anytime soon.

She was one of many counselors but a vital one. She had worked the aftermath of other school shootings, but the realization of the expertise she had developed was just becoming clear. He'd watched her at the coordinators' meeting. When the National Crisis Response Team began the briefing only six hours after the shooting, they sought Rachel's advice for such questions as how best to reopen the school and when, based on her assessment of which grades and students were most affected.

He knew how to fight a fire; Rachel knew how to heal a school—let students talk about it, grieve, and then help them get back to normal life. On big things and small she had practical advice. She recommended against the school using the normal bell to signal class changes during the first week, but to instead have a woman's voice on the intercom; for security to be in uniform walking the halls to create a solid presence; that a memorial wall be set up in the cafeteria for students to share their memories; that updates be posted on the bulletin boards twice a day for how the injured students were doing. Information, consolation, and for the anger, direction for how to release it.

Cole was grateful Rachel had her family intimately involved in this crisis. He'd left her talking with Marcus. Cole spotted Gage in the parking lot and headed over to see him. A press conference was scheduled after the meeting, and the parking lot had become a gathering place. "How are you doing, Gage?"

Gage considered him. "About as well as you."

"That bad, huh?" Cole gave a rough smile. He leaned against Gage's car and ran a hand through his hair. "I feel a bit like I got kicked by a mule."

"Marcus thinks a bullet missed Rachel by a matter of about three inches."

Cole nodded. "I heard. That kind of news ages a man."

"Tell me about it." Gage tossed him a soda. "The O'Malley ladies took it on the chin. I was there when Kate finally sat down to let someone look at her arm. And Lisa paused to pass word that Jennifer may have to be admitted back to the hospital tonight to try to get the pain under control. She's at the hotel now, but it's not going well."

"I hadn't heard about Jennifer."

"I spoke with her about an hour ago. She's hurting." Gage opened a soda for himself. "Any truth to the rumor you were the first one inside the boys locker room?"

"I was there," Cole replied. He didn't want to ever again see something that tragic.

"Want to trade information?"

Cole broke a long-standing practice of avoiding the press without a qualm. "Deal."

Gage studied him. "It's going to be that ugly of a case."

"Those boys got the guns from somewhere. This isn't over, Gage."

"You want to meet tomorrow and exchange news?"

"Page me. I'm going to try to get by the station house to move what I can from my calendar. Come by. If there are homemade cinnamon rolls, I'll set a couple back for you."

"I'll take you up on that." Gage reached into his briefcase and pulled out a folder. He handed it to Cole. "Show these to Rae. On-line versions of the newspapers are a pretty good indication of what will be running in the papers tomorrow morning. The coverage looks to be over the top. The kids being interviewed are calling this a shooting gallery."

"From what I've seen that's a pretty good description."

Gage nodded toward the church. "Rae's going to have a long night."

"She wants to head back to the hospitals from here."

"Her kids are hurt. She couldn't be anywhere else. If you get a fire call and need someone to relieve you, call me. I can spend a couple hours playing double solitaire with her in the hospital waiting room while she keeps students and their parents company."

"Thanks, Gage."

"It's one thing for Rachel to work a natural disaster; it's another to have her deal with kids killing kids."

"I hear you."

TWENTY-EIGHT

Stephen tapped on Jennifer's hotel suite door at 1 A.M. Wednesday. He'd been awake when her page came, unable to sleep, still trying to cope with the memories of having treated students who were shot. The suite door opened. He was met by Tom still wearing yesterday's shirt and jeans, carrying a cup of coffee. "Is she still awake, Tom?"

"Unlike me, Jen is wide awake. She's starting a late night movie. The pain pills have finally kicked in but not the rest of it." Tom stepped back to let him into the suite. "She has taken over the living room." He turned. "We've got company, Jen."

"Company as in many?" Jen called.

Tom looked over at him and Stephen just smiled. "What's she need, ice packs?"

"And the next meds in...twenty minutes."

"Go find a pillow and a bed. I can handle it for an hour." Stephen walked into the living room. "Hi, precious." He had expected to see her an emotional basket case, but there wasn't a tissue box in sight. She looked a bit like she had the night as a resident when she had delivered her first baby. She had saved lives today. "Or should I say, Doctor Precious?"

She smiled. "What's that you're carrying?"

He set down the squirming jacket. "Your puppy sleeps in the strangest places."

Delighted, Jennifer picked up the puppy and cuddled. "I found him curled up around my cactus once, using the sticky points to scratch his head." She nodded to the TV. "Sit and watch *Godzilla versus Mothra* with me."

"Let's not and say we did. How are you faring?"

She rubbed the puppy's head. She glanced up, then back at the puppy. "I'm dying, Stephen."

There was no good way to answer that matter-of-fact statement. He leaned over and kissed her forehead. "Tom showed me your last blood work panels. I'm not burying you yet." He didn't want to have a serious discussion tonight if he could avoid it. Too much had happened today.

He settled down on the floor beside her and picked up a pretzel.

"How are you doing?"

He shrugged. "I was awake when you called." He smiled at her. "You were the one who paged. What's on your mind?"

"I want you happy. Why don't you get serious about seeing Ann? I like her."

He blinked and then laughed. "This is one of those middle-of-the-night pages." He leaned over and tucked another pillow behind her so she wouldn't wince as she turned her head. The entire O'Malley family felt the freedom to meddle, and they inevitably did it for the best of reasons. Jennifer had always been one of them who liked to meddle for a purpose. "I'm not interested in settling down, Jen, but your suggestion is noted. And Ann says she already has two guys in her life. Sorry. I like her and the boys, but getting serious? She's more than an acquaintance but not nearly what you hope for. Anything else on your mind?"

"I've got a list," she admitted with a laugh. "But it's just because I love you and you've got me curious. Why haven't you moved yet? You've been talking about it for so long."

"Find my place in the country where I'm more likely to treat broken arms and heart attacks than gunshot wounds?"

Jennifer nodded.

He thought about it. "Someone else would have to watch out for Kate and the inevitable trouble she gets into. I've patched her up too many times this last year to want to move very far away. I think I'll hold off on any decision until she's settled."

"She'll be settled soon with Dave. You should think about it some more. Go find yourself a small town somewhere and find out if the peaceful life you dream about is out there, or if what you're really searching for is something spiritual."

Stephen sighed. "How many times have we talked about God?"

"Apparently not enough."

"I know who He is, Jen. I just want to live my own life." He understood the price religion demanded of a man, and he was honest enough to know he didn't want to pay it. But he knew well how badly she wanted him to say yes. "It's my choice. That doesn't mean I don't appreciate the thought." Her gaze held his and there was sadness there, and pity, neither of which settled well with him.

"I'm not giving up on you."

He made himself smile. "Which is one of the reasons I love you. You always were the stubborn one in the family. And quite persuasive. Is that it?"

She dug out a piece of paper she had tucked in the cushions of the couch. She read it, refolded it, and offered it to him. "When I die. Tom doesn't need to worry about the funeral. I planned it."

He took it but scowled. "Don't get morbid on me."

"Stephen."

He looked from the note back at her.

"I've watched many people die during my lifetime. This energy—it isn't natural," she said softly. "I'm dying. Soon."

He wrapped his hand around hers. "It's also likely adrenaline," he said gently. "You saved lives today. It's a high like no other."

She studied him in silence and then smiled. "Yes. I can see why you do it."

Jen nestled down into the cushions with the puppy. "Get me another ice pack and then let's play some Scrabble."

"Only if medical words aren't allowed. It's too easy for you to use the hard letters." He got up to get the ice pack.

"*Latex* is not a hard word."

"You and your *X*s. You want the lumpy ice pack or the thick one?"

"Whatever hits the center of my back the best."

He got the ice pack and retrieved cold sodas.

"How's Rae?"

"I saw her a couple hours ago making a hospital cafeteria table her temporary office," Stephen replied. "The girl who died in the cafeteria? She was the oldest in a family of immigrants. Rae's Spanish has improved in the last year. She's nearly fluent."

"How traumatically is it hitting the students?"

"She's got five girls red slipped. Given the number of students, I'm surprised there aren't more." He found more pretzels. "I saw card number sixty-eight get passed out to one of the injured students. Her pager was definitely getting a workout. Try this ice pack."

Stephen handed it to her and sat back down. He tugged over the table so she could play Scrabble without having to reach too far. He dumped the letters from the board back into the draw bag. "Low letter goes first?"

"Sure." Jennifer drew out an A. "I go first."

"I hope that doesn't represent your luck for the night." They selected letters.

"Stephen, I want a favor." She played the word *TITAN*.

"On top of your list? This *is* an interesting evening. What's the favor?"

"You were a fireman and it wasn't enough to make you content, so you became a paramedic. You're still restless. Go be a carpenter. Go prove to yourself the restlessness won't go away until you finally listen to the truth."

"Run away to find myself?"

"You're smart enough to know I'm right."

"I'm smart enough to know *TITAN* to *TITANIUM* is worth a small fortune in points." He laid down the three tiles and tallied his score.

She laughed and played the word *CHEATING*.

Stephen looked at her empty rack of letters and at 2 A.M. wouldn't put it past her to have palmed a letter. She just smiled at him. He played *HEXAGON*. A brother would let a sister win at only so many things, but Scrabble wasn't one of them. "Do you want me to call the others?" he asked. All the O'Malleys should be here tonight.

She squeezed his shoulder. "Your company is just fine."

Stephen didn't know how to take that.

"I don't plan to die alone. Other than that, it's not that scary, Stephen. I'm on earth one moment and walking around heaven the next. I'm sure it will be a captivating enough place that I won't have more than just a thought or two about the fact it means I just died. You're here so you can assure the others that my death was peaceful."

"Don't talk like this, Jen."

"You're afraid because you don't believe."

"I'm not the one you should ask for this."

"Who better to ask? Lisa? Rachel? Marcus?"

He looked from his letters over to her.

"You've got the strength to deal with death. You've seen that moment of death so many times, when an accident victim stops living. I want you to have one good memory to replace all those horrible ones. I want you to know what it's like to die peacefully when Jesus is waiting to meet you."

Man, she really thinks she is dying. "I thought I had days with you to say good-bye, and now you're telling me there may not be a tomorrow."

"Today, this week, this month," she answered gently. "It's soon, Stephen." She squeezed his chilly hand. "Hand me the remains of Tom's hamburger, will you? Butterball is hungry."

Stephen was relieved to have her change the subject. "Thirsty maybe. That mutt shared my dinner on the drive over here." If she so much as sneezed wrong tonight, he was going to page the family. She hadn't told Tom; otherwise the man would be sitting in the chair beside him talking with her. Jen was a doctor, Tom was a doctor, and there was a hospital across the street. In a pinch, Stephen would call 911, but he was the one they would send to respond. "It's your turn."

"Now we're playing proper names." She laid down *OMALLEY*.

She had boxed him in on the board so he could only play a two letter *ME*. "I wish Marcus had suggested a different name."

Jen switched around her letters, looking for ideas. "Was he the one who first mentioned O'Malley? Rachel and I found one of the earlier lists, but we didn't find the one with that name."

"Remember the St. Patrick's Day party where Jack made the 7UP vivid green?"

"How could I forget?" Jen asked. "Jack ate clam chowder later that night and got sick."

"It was a midnight meeting in the hallway where we drew short straws to see who had to check on him. Marcus made that statement, 'O'Malleys take care of their own' and it stuck."

"I thought he said, 'Men take care of their own' and you were supposed to take the short straw. Everyone knew it was the toothpick with the red on the end."

"You're kidding."

Jennifer laughed. "All these years and you didn't know? You drew the short straw."

"Purely by accident. Jack is not fun when he's sick."

"I know what you mean," Jen agreed. "I think O'Malley came up at the meeting that next weekend. Maybe you suggested it."

"I've no idea. It's your play."

"I'm thinking." Butterball knocked over her rack of letters.

"Puppies can't help. I plan to win this one."

She played *XEROX.* "Triple points." She reached for more letters. "I'm very glad you were there yesterday. It was a relief to look up and see you and Jack heading into the fray."

He leaned over and hugged her. "The next crisis, I'll try to be there even earlier."

TWENTY-NINE

Rachel had trouble reading her own writing. She unwrapped another cough drop, hoarse from hours talking on the phone with kids. She was updating Nora on what she had learned about the network of friends so the other counselors could sort out the follow-up plans. Rachel had on her short list for this Wednesday morning to visit Marissa and Adam and then get some much needed sleep.

"Lisa's back," Nora noted as they finished work.

Rachel turned. She hadn't realized her sister was planning to come back to the command center this morning. She glanced back at Nora as her friend got up from the table. "Do you need help with the morning briefing?"

"I'm ready."

"I'll be over to help with the hotline in a minute."

"It's covered for now," Nora said. "Protect what remains of your voice."

"And eat. You look awful," Lisa encouraged. Rachel took the ham croissant Lisa offered and watched her sister take a seat on the edge of the table.

"It's been a long night." She had spent it moving from one hospital to the other with Cole, for two students were still on the critical list.

"Let me make it a more interesting day."

"Wait a minute." Rachel waved over Cole. "I want him to hear the update."

"Your new-couple side is showing."

"I don't know how I ever worked a disaster without him. Last night—I'm talking with Greg and Tim's mom and Clare is flirting with Cole. It wasn't how I expected that session to go, but Cole making Clare laugh was a delight to see."

"Sandy is a nice lady. I met her when they were executing the search warrant."

"She's convinced if she had never divorced, her boys would still be alive. I'm worried about her, but at least she has Clare as a reason to get up every day. Their father Peter is a bigger concern. He's feeling enormous guilt and facing an indefinite leave at work. No one is going to put him behind the cockpit of a plane with two hundred passengers while he's facing this."

"It's going to get rougher before it gets better," Lisa said.

"I know. The funerals are being scheduled for this weekend. The girl killed in the cafeteria will be buried on Saturday. Greg and Tim will be buried together in a Sunday morning service, and Mark will be laid to rest later in the afternoon."

The boys' funerals were being kept private to limit the media pressure on the family.

The counselors were gearing up to be ready for those tough days. The command center was in full operation. Her friends on the National Crisis Team were here. The relationships among the group had been forged through hurricanes, plane crashes, and wildfires. Her friends stopped by to squeeze her shoulder and share wordless sympathy that she'd seen this one up close, and then they settled in to learn the kids, the parents, to handle the media, and assist with the restoration of the crime scene back to a school.

The two schools would be cleaned up, painted, and reopened for classes on Friday. Rachel had recommended it. Parents and students alike needed to get back into the schools before the memories became bigger than they had to be. The hotline was already lit up with calls from kids who had struggled to cope overnight.

Cole joined them. He offered Lisa a cup of coffee. "Thanks for coming this way."

"I need to walk through the scene again."

Rachel studied her sister. "You've got news."

"Very bad news."

What could be worse than what they already had?

"We recovered two guns from the boys in the cafeteria, both .45s. Tim was killed with a .38." Lisa let that sink in. "We never found that gun. Someone else was there. And ballistics say the .38 is the same gun used to murder Carol Iles."

Rachel walked with Cole up the driveway to Ann's home. The recovery from the flood was still going on in the more subtle changes. New bushes had been planted along the walkway and new gutters to replace those torn away by the waters had arrived and were being installed. Nathan's tricycle was out on the driveway and the flag was flying by the doorway. A yellow-ribbon wreath was on the door. Rachel and Cole had taken a chance and just come over. They had a gun missing.

Jesus, I can't afford to make a mistake. There were kids making rash decisions to bring guns to school, to use them, and somewhere out there was a missing gun and another kid who had to be an emotional mess right now. She had to get control of this situation. She should have seen the shooting coming; she knew Marissa, and through her Greg, and had met Tim. She had known something about Mark and his history and his parents' divorce but still she hadn't realized there was trouble coming within the group. She was desperately afraid she wouldn't be able to figure out what other students had been involved in this event before another shooting occurred.

Cole squeezed her hand. "Adam would have said something to his mom if he knew details."

"Maybe." But she hadn't needed to convince Cole to bring her straight here, and that told her Cole was worried about the possibilities too.

Cole rang the doorbell. Rather than a scurry of feet inside, which was the norm; Ann came to the door. "Rae, Cole. Hi. Please, come in."

Rachel hugged her friend. "How are you this morning?" She knew it wasn't just Adam's reaction weighing on her, but the fact that Ann had been working at the dispatch center when the emergency calls had come in about a shooting at the school. Ann didn't look like she had slept much last night.

"I was just going to ask you the same question," Ann said.

"You get through an event like this one day at a time."

"I know the feeling. I found myself baking this morning at five o'clock."

Nathan tugged Rachel's pant leg and held up his arms. She hoisted him up and hugged him. "Hi, sweetie."

Nathan offered her a bite of his cookie.

"Thank you."

He grinned at her and shoved the rest of it in his mouth with his fist.

"You are priceless, you know that."

Ann laughed and ruffled her son's hair. "He's been helping me."

Rachel was grateful Ann had been able to keep her equilibrium. She was going to need it when they talked about the status of what happened. "How's Adam?"

"He's in his room drawing. I think it helped that Stephen came over last night. Adam slept pretty well. Feel free to pop in and say hi. Can I get you two some breakfast?"

"You've been baking bread."

Ann smiled at Cole. "Rolls actually. Come on back to the kitchen. They are best eaten hot."

Rachel set down Nathan. "Go with your mom. I want to say hi to Adam. And save me one of those cookies," she told Nathan, hugging him and getting in a tickle, sending the boy into a fit of laughter.

Rachel walked back to Adam's room. Whatever he knew, he hadn't said anything to his mom or Stephen.

The bedroom had been transformed into the hideout of a little boy. Adam's comic collection was proudly displayed on the shelves, there were posters of soccer players on the walls, and his schoolbooks were piled beside the desk. Shoes peeked out from beneath the bed and gum wrappers had missed the wastebasket. A shirt had slid off its hanger in the closet and Scrabble game letters had become roadways for Matchbox cars. She tapped softly on the open door. "Hi."

He looked up from his drawing. His face looked solemn, old.

"May I come in?"

He nodded.

"What are you drawing?"

"Just a picture."

She looked over his shoulder. "You draw very well." She rubbed his back. "You like baseball?" He had a baseball set on a cup coaster and was trying to capture what the seams looked like.

"Cole brought me over the baseball and a glove."

"He's nice that way." She sat down on the made bed and kicked off her shoes so she could pull up her feet.

"How's your friend Marissa?"

"Doing better. I saw her after she came out of surgery last night. They were able to set her broken leg."

"I wanted to call Tim's mom, but Mom said I should wait."

"What would you like to talk to her about?"

"Tim's funeral. Will I be able to go?"

"Yes," she reassured softly. "I saw Sandy last night. She would be glad to talk with and see you, Adam. The police just needed her time last night. She wanted to know if you would come over and help her choose items for Tim's memorial chest. You know what he loved the most."

"Do you think I could contribute one of my comic books?"

"I'm sure she'd appreciate it." Rachel rested her chin on her drawn-up knees. "Could we talk about yesterday, Adam?"

He looked back at his drawing.

"It's important." She understood the pain in those memories. From the black eye in gym class to the painful terror of the shooting, he was overwhelmed. He was retreating. It had begun yesterday when he limited what he told his mom about the events so he wouldn't have to talk about them. It showed itself today by his solitary occupation and the care in his drawings. Rather than be with his mom and brother in the kitchen baking cookies, he had chosen to be alone. She had learned enough about Adam since the flood to know a few basics of his personality. It wasn't a bad way to cope. Solitude was a positive for him, as was a tight circle of friends. He had lost his best friend in Tim, and she wasn't surprised he wanted time on his own to come to terms with it. Adam's sadness was deep.

He reluctantly nodded.

"Where were you when the fire alarm went off?"

"On my way to meet Tim. I met Greg in the hall, and he stopped me to ask about my eye."

"Did you go in and see what had happened to Tim? Were you there?"

"I just heard about it."

The boy wouldn't meet her eyes. But he sounded tired, resigned, rather than anxious as if he had lied. "You wish you had been there."

Adam looked up and nodded. "If I had been, I could have helped Tim."

She was grateful he hadn't been there. The thought of a little boy trying to stop his friend from bleeding to death from a gunshot wound… That reality was hard enough on a doctor accustomed to working on trauma victims. "You were not responsible for Tim's death," she said softly.

"He was my friend and he died alone." Adam started to cry.

She reached for the tissue box and offered it to him.

"I know it hurts. I promise he wasn't really alone; God was with him." She waited for him to gain his composure. "I need to ask you something that's hard. Okay?"

He wiped his eyes.

"A gun is missing that was used at the school. Did you take it? Did you bring it home?"

His head jerked up. "No! I wouldn't do that. Nathan plays with anything he finds."

She watched Adam—the flush of anger that showed with his words and the way he dropped his eyes and bit his lip for having yelled at her.

"If you hear anything about it, will you tell me?" She waited but he didn't look at her.

He finally nodded.

She could tell he was upset by the questions. "I need to know and I had to ask."

"It's okay."

His voice said it was anything but. "Not if you feel like I don't trust you. I know how hard you try to do the right thing. I'm just scared because I can't find the gun. I don't want anyone else to get hurt."

Adam looked up as she spoke. "It's okay." He sounded like he meant it this time. He wiped his eyes again. He was nearly breaking the pencil he had picked up. The stress this boy was under was intense. Rachel moved him up to the top of her watch list.

"I'm so sad that this happened to you and your friend. Is there anything you need or want me to tell your mom for you?"

He thought about it then shook his head.

"Is there anything you're not telling me I should know?"

He bit his lip. "Could I ask you something?"

"Sure."

"Why did you go into the high school with Kate?"

"Because she's my sister and I wanted to do anything I could to protect her."

"Were you scared?"

"Very." She paused to see if he wanted to ask anything else. "You know you can page me if you need me, right?"

He pulled her card from his pocket. "Mom laminated it for me."

"I'm glad." Rachel got up and hugged him. "It's going to be okay, Adam."

"I want my friend back."

"I know." She tightened her hug. "Cole came with me. Would you like to come say hi?" She wasn't sure if he would want to, but he nodded.

They joined Ann and Cole in the kitchen. Cole came over and knelt down to greet him. Rachel was relieved to see Adam rebound and start to smile under Cole's attention. It was a tough call to make, but Rachel decided to talk to Ann later that afternoon when it could be a private conversation. Rachel sampled enough cookies Nathan had helped bake that she edged toward queasiness with the sugar and lack of sleep. After half an hour, Rachel hugged the boys farewell.

Cole walked with her outside.

"Does Adam know anything?"

She was still struggling to figure out the answer to that. "He says no, but I'm not sure. I think he knows more about what happened than he's willing to say. If he thought he was protecting Tim by taking the gun, he might have hidden it. I do know it's not in the house. He wouldn't want Nathan to get hurt."

"Who else may have it?"

"Mark's friend Chuck is still a possibility. Wilson was going to talk to him. Do you have time to take me by the hospital to see Marissa?"

"I'll drop you off and go check in with my office, then come back for you."

"Thanks."

He lifted her hand to his lips and kissed it. "We'll find the gun and the student who has it, Rae."

"Before someone else takes a rash action?"

The .38 had already been used in a murder and a school shooting. They needed a lead. And she felt like she was missing it. *Jesus, I'm going to fail without Your help. We need to find who has this gun.*

THIRTY

Rachel eased the door open to Marissa's hospital room. She'd been given a private room on the orthopedics floor. Marissa's mom said she had had a peaceful night and was resting. The fever she had begun to run after surgery had come down. Marissa's mom and dad had spent the night here but had stepped down to the private waiting room to have a cup of coffee.

"Hi, M," Rachel whispered.

"Rae." She opened her eyes, still drifting in and out and smiled.

"How are you?"

"They gave me something to help me to sleep last night. It worked."

Rachel sat down in the chair next to the bedside and slipped her hand under Marissa's. "You look better than the last time I saw you." Her pallor had eased. Around the room were numerous gifts of flowers and dozens of get-well cards. Rachel could hear the sound of the automated pressure cuff around Marissa's ankle inflate and deflate every few minutes to keep a blood clot from forming.

"Tomorrow I'll look even better. Janie was by. She brought me makeup and a pair of wonderful earrings."

"I'll bring fingernail polish. What color?"

"Peach."

Rachel reached for a glass of water and held the straw for Marissa.

"Thanks," Marissa said. "Janie said the press was asking about me. All I did was fall down some stairs. But because I only have one leg, the press thinks I'm a better story than one of the kids who got shot."

"Trust me, they are interested in everybody," Rachel said. "You can decide when and if you want to talk to them."

"Maybe after my leg is in a cast and it's covered with signatures. Did you see my dad? He's here. He helped me with breakfast."

"I talked with him for a few minutes. He's coping, M."

"He promised to be the first one to autograph my cast."

"I'm glad." Rachel squeezed her friend's hand. "I have some hard news for you."

Marissa nodded. "I thought you might. Mom and Dad were doing a good job of not answering my questions directly."

Rachel hurt for the news she had to share. "Greg is dead. And Tim."

The monitor behind Marissa captured the shock as her heart rate jumped.

There was a moment of disbelief, and then tears filled her eyes. "Both of them."

"I'm so sorry, M," Rae said, her own eyes filling with tears.

"Were they shot?"

"Yes."

"What happened?" Marissa wailed.

Rachel rubbed her arm. "We're not sure yet," she said softly. "Tim died in the boys' locker room at his school. People saw Greg chasing Mark Rice. There were gunshots exchanged. They both died at the high school."

"No." Marissa's voice trembled.

Rachel leaned across the bed and hugged her. "I know, honey. I know." She would feel the same way if something had happened to Jennifer. Rachel got Marissa tissues and sat quietly, letting her friend absorb the news.

"I told Greg he should go to the principal."

Rachel stilled at the mention of his name. "Was something going on?"

"Mark picked on Tim. Greg and Mark got into a fight once about it. It just got worse. I know Greg talked to Mark's mom about it."

"Carol Iles?"

Marissa nodded. "It was after Tim came home with skinned knees. He'd been skateboarding at the park and Mark and one of his friends hassled him."

"When was this?"

"A couple months ago. I thought it was getting better. Tim hadn't said anything lately, and Greg hadn't mentioned it." Marissa's hand tightened on hers. "Greg promised his mom he would look after Tim. Did Greg die because of that?"

Rachel brushed back Marissa's hair. "I don't know. But we'll find out." She could offer so little comfort but her presence. Marissa's mom and dad would be the ones to help her through this loss, but there was one part of the shock she could help alleviate. "When did you last see Greg?" Rachel tried to pull out the happy memories, knowing there was comfort in them.

"Greg was teasing me over lunch that he was going to get me to dance with him at the prom, even if he had to hire the band to stay around after everyone else went home."

Rachel shared a smile with Marissa and leaned against the bed railing. She rested her chin on her hand. "I'll tell you about my first date with Cole if you share your first one with Greg."

"Greg took me to a movie."

Rachel reached forward and gently wiped away a tear slipping down Marissa's cheek. "Romance or adventure?"

Marissa smiled. "Romantic comedy. He was pulling out all the stops."

The fire station was humming with activity Wednesday. It had become the staging area for the extra police who were assigned to patrol the community and deal with the intense media and community interest in the schools. The scene yesterday had taken its toll, for more than one member of the department had children attending those schools.

Cole set down his coffee and moved the stack of phone messages on his chair so he could sit down. He wasn't staying long, but he needed to get a feel for what else had happened in the last twenty-four hours. "Did you get any sleep?" Jack asked. His friend leaned against the office door.

"A catnap or two. I'll cut out later this afternoon. I dropped Rae off at the hospital to visit with Marissa, and I'll pick her up in an hour to give her a lift home."

"What can I handle for you?"

Cole appreciated the offer. He handed Jack the top folder. "That diner fire last Saturday? I heard the lab reports came in. They're somewhere on Terry's desk. Would you see what's there?"

"Glad to."

His assistant poked her head in the doorway and leaned around Jack. "Cole, line 5. The district attorney."

"I'm not here."

She smiled back at him. "I already tried that one."

Cole reached for the phone. "Jeffrey, what can I do for you?"

Jack followed Terry out of the room.

Life didn't stop because a school shooting happened. Cole moved as much paper as he could as he talked about an arson case coming up on appeal. No wonder Rachel was so often exhausted. He'd been working the school shooting for twenty-some hours, and the idea of going another five days through the funerals before the first break came felt impossible. He had to make sure Rachel got at least six hours of solid sleep this afternoon.

He wished the rest of her team would get here soon so someone better at debriefing could help her talk through what she had seen. What Rachel had been through was more than just traumatic, and he worried about the after-effects. She had pulled herself together to focus on the job at hand. But when her pager went off and the next crisis came? He dreaded the day she got word of another disaster. She wasn't nearly as far from danger in her job as he would like.

He hung up with the district attorney and then started returning phone calls.

He was hanging up the phone after his ninth call when he heard his assistant say in surprise, "Rachel. Hi." It gave him time to turn toward the door just as Rae appeared.

"I told...Marissa said..." She was crying in such deep sobs her breath was missing. His first thought as her grief sucked him in was that she'd been driving while she cried. He had to break her of that habit. Whoever had brought her a car when she was this tired hadn't been thinking. Since his guest chair was stacked with books, he caught her hand and led her to sit on the credenza so he could mop her tears. "What did Marissa say?"

"Everything okay in here—" Jack froze in the doorway.

Cole met Jack's gaze over Rachel's bent head. "Go away." Cole kicked the door closed.

He wiped Rae's tears. She was losing it. He tilted up her chin and held her gaze, awash in the depths of what she was feeling.

"It could have been prevented."

"I know."

"Earlier. Greg talked to Mark's mom. It's linked somehow, Cole. Carol's death and the blowup at the school. There is history there going back months."

He'd been expecting a wave of emotion from her, but this... "Oh, honey." He pulled her onto his lap and held her tight as she sobbed, resting his chin against her hair. One person should only have to be asked to carry so much, and Rachel... "Shh, it's going to be okay."

Her hands curled into his shirt. "Why, Cole? Why do kids have to be the victims?"

He rubbed her back. "I don't know, precious." How he wished he did.

Cole eased her to her feet. He picked up the keys he'd tossed beside his dying cactus. "Come on; I'll take you home."

"I need to talk with Lisa and Marcus. I'm sorry I'm crying all over you."

"We will. And I don't mind." He wrapped an arm around her shoulders and opened the door. She had hit the wall, and the best hope he could offer was some desperately needed sleep. "Would you like to guess what Jack was doing this morning?"

Rachel leaned against the door of her apartment after saying good-bye to Cole. *Lord, thank You for sending me a man who understands the comfort found in a hug.* She would have asked Cole to stay a while, but she desperately needed some sleep. She was turning to Cole in ways she'd never asked of someone other than family before, trusting him to take this explosive grief and carry her. Even with family she had tried not to lean too hard. With Cole she was dumping it all and hoping he could bear it. She loved him and trusted him even with her breaking heart.

She loved him...

The words were welling up from a place in her heart where dreams were born. For the first time she trusted someone with everything, and she was finding in Cole that the trust was well placed. It felt right.

Lord, thank You.

The peace in her thoughts lasted until she looked down and saw the faint remnant of blood on her shoes. She stepped out of them where she stood and left them there.

Rachel went straight to bed, so tired it felt like a weight was pressing on every inch of her body. She buried herself between the pillows and closed her eyes. Instead of the relief of sleep, she felt a fierce tension build. She couldn't shut off the images or the sounds. She could hear the school alarm blare and Kate scream her name. The harder Rachel tried to forget, the more the memories sped up—of Kate shoving her, of the agonizing images of an injured boy trying to pull himself to safety, and of the girl lying dead where she had fallen.

Rachel stumbled out of the bed and went into the living room to curl up on the couch. She'd left the apartment Tuesday morning expecting a laughter-filled day with Jennifer and her sisters, and thirty hours later she couldn't remember how to smile. She needed to sleep, but she was scared of what it would be like to dream.

God, would You please take away this panic? Death came and it was unexpected and it was random and this time I witnessed it firsthand. She wiped at tears. *I'm not even sure what it is I'm afraid of. I just can't stop the memories.*

It helped knowing at this moment she wasn't alone. In the last hours the only peace she'd been able to offer many of the students and their parents was that God was strong enough to handle this. She was doing her best to lean hard against that strength.

She reached for the phone and placed a page. *Please, Kate, be somewhere you can answer.*

The phone rang back in less than a minute.

"Rae, what's wrong?"

She closed her eyes and exhaled. "I just needed to hear your voice."

Kate's voice gentled. "That bad, huh?"

"I'm trembling."

"I've had the shakes today too. Where are you?" Kate asked.

"Home. Cole brought me about an hour ago."

"Want me to get him back for you? He can hold your hand until it passes."

"I don't want him to worry about me any more than he already is."

"Guys are in our lives to worry about us."

Rachel hugged one of the couch pillows against her, her favorite huge lavender one that had a soft center. "Maybe if it doesn't pass. Are you doing okay?" She hadn't stopped long enough to do the follow-up with her family that was normally her role. Everyone had been there and was affected in various ways, but she didn't know other than generally how they were doing today.

"Dave brought me roses and dinner late last night, and he gift wrapped a bulletproof vest for me."

Kate had the ability to get shot and a day later chuckle about getting a bulletproof vest as a gift. For Kate the school shooting was only one of many incidents she would deal with this month. Rachel was grateful Dave was there to help Kate in a way that best supported but didn't limit her. "Dave's good for you."

"Three weeks and the stitches will be gone. I'll recover, Rae."

Rachel felt herself relaxing as Kate's calmness became hers. "What did I interrupt?"

"I'm at my desk looking at ballistics reports. Those .45s that were recovered at the school have a long history. At least this time they'll be melted down."

"Thankfully. Have you talked to Jennifer today?"

"I spoke to Tom at about noon. Jennifer is really worn out. He's hoping she'll sleep the majority of the next few days."

"Is she going to bounce back from this?"

"She saved lives. She's jazzed, Rae. More than I've seen since she had to quit seeing patients last year when the chemotherapy began. She'll find a way to recover from the exhaustion."

Rachel leaned her head back against the couch cushions and looked toward the ceiling. "I hope so."

"Go to sleep, Rae. Think about Cole. There should be enough good memories to take the place of the tough ones."

She had some wonderful memories and was holding on tight to them. "Please tell me the shakes go away."

"They do. I promise you that."

"I hope you get a boring day stuck at your desk."

"I appreciate the wish. I'll talk to you later, Rae."

Rachel said good-bye to her sister. She had hoped to avoid this backlash of emotions until after the funerals were past. She was going through her own decompression at the same time the kids were. When they described having been in the parking lot when the shooting was going on, she heard and saw those same memories. She had to stop this reaction. She had so much she needed to do in the hours ahead.

She took a deep breath and hugged the pillow against her chest. *God, life is so hard.* She had to see Jennifer. Rachel knew how rough this crisis had been on her sister's health, and yet Rachel had never been so relieved to have someone with her. Jennifer and Lisa had saved lives.

Rachel went to take a long hot shower, for the chill had reached into her bones. She took time to dry her hair and brush it out, then went back to her bedroom. After some thought, she reached for the phone beside the bed and made a second call.

"Cole?" She'd taken a chance that he would be home. She needed the reassurance of hearing his voice.

"Hi, honey." He sounded like he had been dozing.

"You know that verse Kate likes to quote: *'The Lord is my helper, I will not be afraid; what can man do to me?'*"

"You're making me think on twenty minutes of sleep." He was quiet for a moment. "I think it's in the last chapter of Hebrews."

"What can man do to me? One thing he can do is shoot at me. It's scary."

"Bad dreams, huh?"

"I haven't gotten that far. I wasn't ready for yesterday, and I'm a basket case just trying to sleep because I keep thinking about it. My hands are trembling."

"You have to let yourself feel the emotion, accept it's a justified reaction, and then let it go."

"I wish you could make this go away," she whispered.

"Rae, you'll never be able to stop the evil people do, any more than Lisa can stop the murders. But what you do does matter. Kids are coping today because you have been there for them."

She wiped her eyes. "I can't do this anymore. It hurts too bad."

He didn't answer her for a long time. She wasn't sure what she wanted from him. But it mattered, what he said. She was looking hard for a way out of this pain. There had been too many tragedies coming too close together and they were burying her under their weight.

"Rae, another wise thing my dad taught me was don't make decisions when you are tired or upset."

Tears flowed. She was both. She blew her nose. "It's good advice."

"You want me to come over and bring a video? We can eat popcorn and you can pretend to be interested in my choice of movie."

She laughed, appreciating the soft offer more than he knew. "I need to sleep. And so do you."

She shifted pillows around.

"You're exhausted, honey. What do you tell your kids when they're struggling to sleep like this?"

It was hard to remember. "Sometimes the memories start to repeat less once they are written down."

"Want to try that? Or better yet, when they start to race on you, call me back and tell me about them. I'll share it with you, Rae."

She was comforted just by the offer. "I'm going to try to sleep now."

"I'll be a phone call away. Always. Call me when you wake up later? Let me get you dinner?"

"Your optimism is showing."

"Yeah. Sleep well, beautiful."

"Good night, Cole," Rachel whispered. She hung up the phone and put her head down on the pillow.

God, I'm so grateful You put Cole in my life.

She sighed and closed her eyes, her thoughts on the man she had let inside her heart. She finally slept.

Cole pulled his arm back, faked a throw, and then tossed the tennis ball toward the garage. Hank raced after it.

"He has to go crashing through that bush rather than around it," Rachel remarked.

"What he lacks in smarts, he makes up for with enthusiasm," Cole replied, smiling. Rachel had slept through the afternoon and early evening, and he was relieved to see the calmness, even laughter, in her expression. Her phone call hadn't come until after 8 P.M. It hadn't been that hard to talk her into coming over for a bite to eat.

The dog loped back. Cole leaned down and tugged the tennis ball free from Hank's jaws. "Were you intending to feed Hank your sandwich?"

Rachel looked down at the paper plate she'd set on the ground. "Sorry." The ham sandwich had disappeared.

Cole had seen her eat the cookies but not the sandwich. "I'll fix you another if you like."

Her pager went off. She glanced at it but didn't reach for the phone. "This one can wait."

Hank tried to climb onto her lap.

"You're supposed to throw the tennis ball," Cole pointed out.

"It's icky."

She tossed it toward the garage, and this time Hank got stuck when he tried to plow through the bush. "You're going to have to replant that somewhere else to give him a clear path. It's like leaving a piece of furniture in the middle of a hallway—it's not fair."

"Move the bush and the dog is going to crash full speed into the side of the garage. It's like his eyesight is myopic. He's got a lousy sense of distance."

Hank came back with the tennis ball. "Poor boy." Rachel picked twigs and leaves out of his coat.

"What's on your plate for tomorrow?" Cole asked, working on how he could best help her in the next couple days.

"Work the pager and the phone primarily. Join a walk-through at the school. After that, a day spent visiting kids. They are going to try to have the school open in the afternoon for students to collect belongings, so they can have a regular school day on Friday."

"Will you be working at the schools the first day?"

"Probably not in a formal way. There are other counselors who are better at mass debriefing and reassurance. My list for the day will include talking with the students we know are going to need extra help. I'm hoping the missing .38 is recovered by then. I'm terrified of holding school classes again without us having found who has that gun. I've got dread in the pit of my stomach over there being another school shooting just as kids come back."

"The police will do everything they can to find it, but it's not the only gun out there."

Her pager went off. She glanced at the number. "I need to answer this one."

"I'll fix you another sandwich."

"Can you make it to go? I want to stop by and see Marissa on my way home."

"Sure. You'll get through this, Rae."

"I wonder sometimes." She returned the page.

THIRTY-ONE

The middle school smelled of fresh paint Thursday afternoon. The hallways were being repainted white with a blue stripe to match the school colors. Rachel walked around the painters, drop cloths, and ladders. She could think of a lot of places she would rather be at the moment. She had a sketch of the school grounds with a hundred stories to go with it—students terrified by what had happened when the fire alarm sounded and then realizing there was someone shooting in the parking lot.

She hadn't been focused on the investigation, but it was clear seeing Wilson, Lisa, Marcus, and Quinn that it had been proceeding full force. This walk-through was an attempt to take a final look at the time line of the shooting before the children returned.

"The answers to what happened start here." Lisa led the way into the boys locker room. "An unknown number of boys were present. Tim was killed with a .38. Coincident to that someone pulled the alarm."

"Cole, which fire alarm was pulled?" Marcus asked.

"Interesting question. Hold on." Cole searched his reports. "Number 18, which is…the alarm by the PE teacher's office."

"So someone yanked this alarm after the shooting."

"Or before the shooting," Rachel offered, shoving her hands in her pockets.

"Or maybe someone pulled the alarm, and a kid with a gun jerked at the sound and pulled the trigger," Quinn suggested.

"An ugly possibility." Lisa walked the hall from the PE teacher's office to the boys locker room. "Tim is in the locker room with someone who eventually shot him. We know some shoving was going on because Tim has bruises that had just begun to form no more than a few minutes before his death. Someone else came into the locker room, realized what was going on, and pulled the fire alarm trying to break up the fight. Then the gun goes off."

"Someone pulled the alarm, someone took the gun. But who was it?" Marcus asked.

"Adam?"

They looked to Rachel. "He's heartbroken over Tim's death," she replied. "He's not a hider by nature. If he saw something more than just Greg in the hallway, if he saw the boys who hurt Tim, I think he would have told me."

"What about Greg taking the .38?"

"If he did, we would have found it somewhere at the scene."

"Maybe someone else was here with Mark."

"How about Mark's best friend, Chuck Holden?" Rachel suggested. "If Mark brought a gun with him to school, Chuck would know about it."

"We talked with him," Marcus replied. "He denied any knowledge of it or of a problem between Mark and Tim."

"Do you believe him?"

"Not entirely. Are we confident we would have found the .38 if it's still here?"

"We've turned this place upside down," Lisa replied.

"Then we need to go back and figure out what kids were doing in that half hour before the shooting. Someone had to have seen the boys come over here from the high school." Marcus looked at his watch. "It's about time for the afternoon briefing. The press will know soon that a gun is missing."

"If we don't have a lead on it by morning, we may have to put the word out ourselves. We can't reopen the schools and not alert the public. Rachel, are there enough counselors to cover both schools tomorrow?" Wilson asked.

"We'll be as ready as we can." Rachel looked with longing back at the hall door. This place was making her claustrophobic. Cole reached for her hand.

She held on tight.

Rachel used the trunk of her car as a worktable Thursday afternoon and held down the corners of her map with a flashlight, two decks of cards, and her soda can. She bit into the cheeseburger she'd been handed. "Gage, you forgot the onions again."

"But I remembered the mustard this time." He tossed a couple yellow packets to her. They had gotten into the habit of catching a meal together whenever they were in the same vicinity. "Where are you heading next?"

"I have no idea. I've got nine more house calls to make and rush hour traffic is starting." Her street map was wearing out. School resumed tomorrow morning, and Rachel was making an effort to talk to the girls she had identified as the natural leaders among the teenagers.

The teenagers had latched on to the idea of doing something special in memory of the girl who had died in the cafeteria. They wanted to hold the charity rubber duck float that had been canceled due to the flooding, and they had already contacted the chamber of commerce to see if it would be possible. It was a great idea. There were enough rubber ducks that every student at the middle school and the high school could participate.

She swiped some of Gage's french fries. "In your article this weekend would you mention the duck memorial?"

"Sure. Do you have a date arranged?"

"Saturday, May 5. The girls are putting it together so I should have details later tonight."

He pulled out his notebook to jot down the date and information. "Have you even read a newspaper this week?"

"I'm avoiding the press whenever I can." She glanced over at him and smiled. "No offense."

"None taken, LeeAnn."

She wrinkled her nose at him for shortening it to just her middle name. "I need you at the school tomorrow morning when they reopen the doors. Can you come?"

"What do you need?"

"A reporter to work with the five teenagers who put out the school newspaper to help them create an issue that can be kept as a memorial of the event." She knew the student body needed closure and a way to express themselves as a group. The school paper was the most important collective voice they had. It needed the touch of someone who understood how to pull together the event and the memories and to also point the way forward. Gage was the right man to help those kids.

"Me, going back to high school?"

She smiled at him. "Please?"

He finished the fries. "You would have to say that magic word. I'll be there. Did you remember to get gas in your car?"

"You are never going to let me forget last month are you?"

He smiled back.

"I'm set." She folded up her map. "Thanks for dinner. I've got to get going."

"Drive carefully, Rae."

She gave him a hug.

The hotel suite Jennifer called home was quiet. Cole relaxed in a chair and watched her sleep on the couch. She rested on her side, hands tucked under her cheek. Cole hurt just watching her. She'd saved lives, but at what cost to her own health? Did those students know the gift she had given them, the full price that had been paid?

Tom rejoined him and handed him one of the glasses he carried.

"She's running a fever. You should admit her to the hospital, Tom."

"It's 100.6 and responding to medication. She's stubborn. And there are too many germs for her to catch if I did admit her." Tom shifted the ice pack against her back and checked the time. "I can give her more pain meds in twenty minutes. That will help."

Jennifer slept through pain that had tears sliding down her cheeks. It was a hard thing to face. If only the O'Malley's hadn't been caught right in the middle of the shooting… The stress of that moment had taken so much from her.

"She got a chance to be a doctor again in a critical role, Cole. She considers this price minor to that joy."

"Do you?"

Tom looked at the ice in his glass but didn't answer.

Cole finished his drink. "Rachel is coming by as soon as she can."

"There's no imminent crisis to this flare-up," Tom said. "If there was I'd call Rae. Jennifer understands well the time pressure her sister's under. She's frankly more worried about Rae than she is about her own situation."

Cole shared that concern. "Rae copes by keeping busy."

Jennifer stirred. Tom rose and helped her. He changed the ice and she took the medication he offered gratefully.

"Cole," her voice was soft, almost inaudible, "I'm glad you came." Her smile was still the breathtaking one he remembered.

"I'm glad you called."

She lifted her head and Tom shifted the pillow to support her head. "Better, thanks." She relaxed into the new position, her breaths slow and even as she absorbed the pain. "The bedroom gets so boring," she offered. "It's easier to rest here."

"You're sleeping; that's good."

She smiled. "Dozing. You worry about me as much as Tom does." Her eyes closed and she fought to reopen them. "I'm drifting on the meds. Sorry."

"Don't be." Cole waited as she rallied. "How can I help you, Jen?" She'd called him for a reason. He would help and get out of here. She needed that sleep she was fighting.

"I didn't need anything. I just wanted your company."

He blinked and then chuckled. "Did you?"

"I thought we might talk about Rae."

Cole relaxed in his chair, smiling back at her. "One of my favorite subjects."

"I just need a distraction from the pain," Jennifer whispered. "Tom's running out of stories."

"I'd be glad to help," Cole replied, following her rationale and touched that she'd called him instead of one of the other O'Malleys. "Why don't you start at the beginning about Rae? When did you two meet?"

"I really like you." Jen tucked her hands under her chin. "At Trevor House. She headed the welcoming committee."

Thursday evening, Rachel leaned back against the lawn chair that now had her name taped to the back webbing and worked on updating her composition notebook by penlight while she waited for Cole to return from work. He had been out on a fire run when she called the station. She hoped it wasn't a severe fire. The guys had already had a tough few days, and a deadly fire would layer hurt on hurt.

Faced with the choice of returning home or stopping by to see Cole, there hadn't been much need for thought. She was attached to his company, wanted to be with him.

The breeze ruffled the pages and Hank got up to plop two big feet on her knees. "Your breath is bad," Rachel offered as she reached out and scratched under his chin. She picked up the tennis ball and tossed it, and he took off after it.

"You look comfortable."

She leaned her head back as Cole joined her. She hadn't heard his car, but since the driveway had a stack of lumber on it at the moment, he'd parked on the street. "I wanted to watch the full moon."

"It's a beautiful night." He bent down and softly kissed her. She slipped her hand around the back of his neck and leaned against him, absorbing the fact the man was a rock in the middle of a chaotic day.

"You need a shower."

He shook his head and ash fell on her notebook. "Yep, I guess I do. We had a hot fire in a restaurant kitchen."

"Arson?"

"An accident. It took about ten minutes of searching to confirm it had started on the stovetop where a gas feeder line had a pinhole break. Come on in. I'll get cleaned up."

"Why don't you clean up and come back out. It's nice to just sit and enjoy the calm night."

His thumb soothed her shoulder blade. "Ten minutes," he promised and headed into the house.

She returned to the work in her notebook updating observations and contacts made throughout the day. She would have to go to volume two tomorrow, for this notebook was almost full.

Her pager went off. It was from the National Crisis Response Team. She returned the call. The first vandalism of the crisis had been a threat against the high school principal spray-painted on the back of the gym. It was inevitable that some of the anger against what had happened would manifest itself in vandalism and threats. The big problem would be the inevitable bomb threats. The counselors already had the school staff prepared.

Cole slid his arm across her shoulders as she spoke with Nora, and Rachel lifted her hand to grip his. It had been a twenty-hour day, but she wouldn't have missed coming here for anything.

She closed the phone, and he offered her a lemon drop. "You've almost lost your voice."

"Close to it."

She relaxed. She didn't feel a need to put into words the simple fact that she hadn't wanted to be alone. Cole already understood.

He broke the comfortable silence. "Jennifer called me today."

Rachel stiffened. She knew she should have figured out how to make it to the hotel today. "What's wrong?"

"Relax." He eased her back into the chair. "Her recovery is still pretty iffy on the pain levels. Tom wanted you to know they might admit her to the hospital for a couple days, but if they did, it would just be a precaution. A couple weeks recovering and Jen should be okay. She just wanted company between catnaps."

She warily looked at him. "What did you talk about?"

He tucked a wisp of hair behind her ear. "Besides her dog, Stephen, and what Boston is like in the winter?" He smiled. "She loves you."

"Well…" She'd been expecting to hear some comment about her past, and his answer threw her. "That's good. Fine. Okay."

He laughed and hugged her.

On Friday morning, Rachel walked into the hotel where Jennifer and Tom were staying, relieved they hadn't had to admit Jennifer overnight. Tom met her at the suite door. "It's good to see you, Rae."

"I should have been here yesterday."

"Don't. I know what your day was like. I would have called if it was urgent." He tipped up her chin. "I'd prescribe about ten hours of sleep and some good news."

She smiled at his comforting words. "School started today with over 70 percent attendance. I've had several hundred hugs this morning. That was pretty great. Can I borrow your wife for a minute?"

"She's in the bedroom. Can I get you some hot tea for that sore throat?"

"I'd love some."

Rachel walked through the suite to the bedroom and leaned around the doorway to see if Jennifer was awake.

"Hi," Jen whispered. "I heard you come in."

"Can I get a hug?"

"You can get one for as long as you like."

Rachel sat down on the bedside and leaned over for a very, very long hug. She finally sat back. "You look horrible," Rachel said softly. The jaundice had grown worse in the last twenty-four hours. There was no benefit to ignoring the reality they had to deal with.

"I don't feel so hot today," Jen admitted. "Doctoring takes a lot of energy." Jen closed her eyes and rallied. She smiled and reached up to brush a lock of Rachel's hair aside. "You've got gray hair coming back."

"It's going to come in white this time." Rachel kicked off her shoes and stretched out beside Jennifer on the bed. She reached for one of the huge extra pillows. Jennifer had a stack of pillows behind her to support her and three ice packs against the worst of the pain in her back. "Are you numb?"

"It comes and goes in my legs," Jen admitted. "It doesn't take much swelling for it to press against a nerve."

"Is there anything else we can do?" Rachel asked.

"Tom can go to even stronger pain meds if I need them." Jennifer smiled. "I'll get past this one. It just makes me feel kind of mushy, like my hands aren't quite sure they want to move."

Rachel wished she could hide out here with Jennifer for the rest of the day. "The funerals start tomorrow."

Jennifer rubbed her shoulder. "You'll get through them, Rae."

She wished she had that kind of confidence. "The one tomorrow is for the girl killed in the cafeteria. Practically the entire school body is going to be there, as well as the community. It will be televised."

"Was she a Christian?" Jennifer asked.

"Yes."

"How are her parents doing?"

Rachel sighed and wrapped her arm tighter around the pillow. "Better than I expected. The grief is... Remember what it was like when we were fourteen and Shelly got adopted? How awful it felt that she was gone and yet how overjoyed we were that she had gotten her wish for a home?"

"I remember."

"Those are the dual emotions her parents are feeling. They miss her terribly. She's okay in heaven, but they are having to realign their entire lives without her."

Jen nodded. "When you have kids, you expect them to outlive you."

"Yeah. Are you doing okay with what you saw?" Rachel asked.

"No."

She reached for Jennifer's hand. "I thought that might be the case."

"I wish I had been able to do more. Kim is still heavy on my mind."

"The surgery went well, and she's listed in good condition. She's got a very close family. I visited with them last night."

"She was terrified. You really think she'll be okay?"

"I've got many kids on my list having a harder time coping than Kim."

They rested in quiet. Rachel leaned her chin against her hands. "Do you want to go ahead with the wedding date of May 19? We can move it if you'd like."

"This family needs something positive to look forward to. I know I do."

"Do we need to move it forward?" Rachel whispered.

Jennifer held her gaze and squeezed her hand. "The nineteenth should be okay. I want to celebrate their weddings, but Lisa and Kate need time to solve this case. It should give me a chance to get my strength back." Jen reached over to wipe one of Rachel's tears away. "I'm ready, Rae. If God says now is the time, I'm okay with that. I haven't given up on a miracle, but my trust has returned that God is indeed good. He knows what's best. I saved kids, Rae." Her smile grew. "They've got names and faces and it felt really great."

"Is Tom prepared?"

"My husband is my hero. Tom has more courage about this than I do. He asked me to marry him knowing it would take a miracle to avoid a funeral. He's ready because he has to be. That's the best kind of love."

"He's wading into the deep waters with you."

"He is." Jennifer studied her, then smiled. "Cole is a lot like Tom."

"Trouble flows around him, never breaking his calm. It's reassuring."

"You're falling in love."

Rachel smiled back as she nodded. "And in the midst of this pressure, I'm finding out just how much of a blessing it is."

Rachel studied the picture Stephen was hanging for Ann Friday afternoon. "A little higher on the right. There. Good." She was waiting for Adam to get home from school to see how his first day had gone. She had stayed at school this morning helping students, but she didn't want to get in Adam's space this afternoon unless he paged her.

Assuming he would be okay was part of what made it possible for him to be okay. Treat him as overwhelmed and he would stay overwhelmed. Adam needed his routine back, his sense of life moving on.

"Jennifer planned her own funeral," Stephen said, returning to the tough discussion of the afternoon.

"Ann wants the next picture hung over there." Rachel pointed to the spot on the wall. "What did you think Jennifer was doing with her spare time?"

"Something better than being morbid."

"I've got my funeral planned."

"But you think that way. Jen thinks about what wrapping paper will look color coordinated with the gift she bought."

"Stephen, she's got terminal cancer. The doctors told her to go home. Without a miracle she doesn't have much time left."

"Preparing for death is wishing that it would come."

"Denial isn't going to make it go away."

He looked away and didn't comment. Rachel squeezed his shoulder.

"What time did Nathan go down for a nap?" Stephen asked.

"A little over an hour ago." She was keeping an ear open for sounds over the intercom that he was waking up. She'd offered to watch him while Ann went to get Adam from school.

Car doors slammed.

"It looks like there might have been some trouble," Stephen said, getting the first look as Ann and Adam got out of the car. "Adam added another shiner to go with the one he already had."

Rachel set down the picture and caught up with Stephen as he headed outside to the driveway.

"What happened, buddy?" Stephen knelt in front of Adam.

"He called Tim a coward, so I hit him."

The defiance in Adam's tone said he didn't care if it was wrong. He was glad he'd done it.

"And he hit you back."

"He's the coward."

Stephen took a good look at the eye. "Nice shiner. Remember where you put the ice pack?"

Adam nodded.

"Go get it. You earned it. Then you'd better head to your room so Nathan doesn't see you and start to cry."

Adam's defiance faded a bit.

"Nathan's a little sensitive to you getting hurt right now," Stephen said softly. "You might want to think about that next time. Protecting him is probably more important than getting people who don't know better to think well of Tim."

"I'm sorry."

Stephen hugged him. "Just get cleaned up before Nathan sees it."

Adam headed to the kitchen to get the ice.

"Thanks, Stephen," Ann said. "He didn't want to talk with me."

"I should have warned him about the comments. They were inevitable. Mind if we stay for dinner?"

"You're welcome to. It's—"

"Hot dogs and Jell-O," Stephen finished for her. "You let Adam decide since it was a hard day."

She gave a small smile. "But on the grill outside tonight." Ann led the way back inside. "Thanks for hanging the pictures. It's impossible to do by yourself."

"Rae helped." Stephen put away his tools. "I'll go find charcoal and start the grill."

Rachel helped Ann in the kitchen get out items for dinner. "Adam will get through this, Ann."

"He isn't sleeping well. He's restless. I find him up in the middle of the night getting himself a drink or sitting in the living room in the dark. I've seen him check on Nathan at night. It's odd. Rae, it sounds crazy, but it's like he just became twenty. He's solemn, calm, protective. He needs to know where people are."

"He's got a tender heart, Ann. He wants to make it better; he wants people around him to be okay. His world as it existed has taken a huge blow too. The sadness is a good sign, for it shows he's admitting it hurt; the trouble sleeping— part of that is the depression he's feeling. He went back to school without his best friend. The anger today was probably a good thing, considering. He just needs to get through it."

"I don't know what I should be doing."

Rachel wrapped an arm around her friend's waist and squeezed. "Just give him lots of love." The sounds over the monitor signaled that Nathan was awake. He was talking to himself. "What is he saying?"

Ann smiled. "Sounds like *hot*. Nathan wakes up talking to the world. Unlike Adam who doesn't say much, Nathan doesn't have that problem." Ann went to get him.

They took dinner outside to the patio table. Rachel was glad Stephen was here, for he gave Ann and the boys one more piece of assurance that everything would work out. Adam brought out his baseball and glove so he could play catch with Stephen after they ate.

"What do you like on your hot dog, Adam?" Rachel asked, opening the bun.

"Everything."

"A big everything like Stephen, or a small everything like Cole?"

"A kid's everything. No peppers."

"Got it."

She handed him a paper plate.

He carried it over to sit with Stephen. Her brother made room for him and said something that made Adam laugh. Rachel relaxed. Adam would be okay. She glanced at her pager. It was time for her to start her evening rounds visiting kids. She made her hot dog to go. Nathan just about strangled her as the two of them exchanged a giggling good night.

THIRTY-TWO

Nearly the entire school population had turned out for the funeral of the girl killed in the cafeteria. Cole couldn't find Rachel. It took a while to search the crowds. Cole walked the sidewalk in front of the memorial wall. The students needed a way to express their grief, and it had appeared in the spontaneous memorial of flowers and cards and stuffed animals at the high school track, where she had been a member of the track and field team. Rachel never made it into the large auditorium where the funeral service was held. She had spent the time walking the halls of the church and the parking lot, talking with those who came but had been unable to get through the service.

Unable to locate Rachel among those lingering at the memorial wall, he returned back to the church. Rachel had driven herself over early this morning, and it was possible a situation had arisen where she had left to help one of the students. She'd parked on a side street to leave the parking lot for guests. One more walk-through of the building and he would head over to check for her car. Several of those hospitalized had been able to come by ambulance for the hour-long service, and he paused as the last ambulance pulled from the parking lot for the return trip to the hospital.

Marcus joined Cole as he made his way into the auditorium. "Rachel left about twenty minutes ago. She got a page."

"One of the students?"

"Kate," Marcus replied. "Rachel just said it was urgent."

"Any idea where she went?"

"No. But given that Kate called her, it's probably someone struggling to get through the televised funeral."

Cole glanced at his watch. "Marissa called. She was watching the funeral on TV. I was planning to stop by the hospital and see her. She's having a rough afternoon."

"I suggest you go on. When I hear what's going on, I'll give you a call."

Cole didn't particularly want to leave; the odds were good that Rachel would be back to walk the memorial wall again. She'd been gearing up all week to handle this day, and he'd gotten a sense in the first half hour of how intense the day would be for her. The funeral was hard on those who attended, but it was even harder on those unable to handle entering the auditorium. "Call me just as soon as you hear."

Marcus squeezed Cole's shoulder. "She's been through many days like this."

It wasn't the reassurance Marcus meant it to be. Cole was still learning how to support a lady whose job required her to shoulder the weight of grief from events like this on an ongoing basis.

"Peter, think what this will do to Clare. She loves you." Kate leaned against the door between the garage and the house. It was getting hot in the garage. The deck of cards she was using to keep herself alert was starting to stick together. She could hear the TV through the door. Her partner had line of sight through the patio doors into the kitchen, and so far Greg and Tim's father had shown no willingness to back away from the threat of using the gun he held on himself.

Rachel was brought into the garage by one of the undercover cops. They were trying hard to make this look routine without squad cars in the drive and street. Two men stood in the front yard talking, idly walking the sidewalk keeping media from the house. One was walking around the backyard. If asked, they were simply there to make sure something didn't happen after the funeral as emotions among the students ran high.

Kate pointed to the stool against the wall. Rachel took a seat. "What's going on?"

"Greg and Tim's father has a gun, and he's having a very bad day."

"Is it the missing .38?"

Kate raised one eyebrow at the question. "Oh, that would be just wonderful. Three deaths from one gun." Kate unwrapped a piece of gum and offered one to Rachel. She accepted it and Kate saw her sister's tension begin to fade.

"Who called it in?"

"His ex-wife Sandy. She was over this morning to talk to Peter about the funeral arrangements for tomorrow. She called me when she left because she was worried about him. By the time I got here, Peter had already acquired the gun."

"The man is grieving."

"Tell me about it. He watched the funeral of that girl on TV, and he's crying his eyes out."

"I thought you searched his house."

"Trust me, we did." Kate already had the same discussion with the officer on the scene. "Wherever that gun was, it was very well hidden."

It was quiet inside the house, too quiet. Kate turned toward the doorway. "Peter, Rachel is here. You said you wanted to talk with her about Clare."

Silence met her call. Kate cut the deck of cards, the rhythm of the movement helping with the passage of time. She eventually hoped to get an answer to one of her statements. She kept the comments coming at regular intervals. She wanted to reassure him that he was not alone. He'd lost two sons, and the house was a silent reminder as he mourned.

"Can we talk face-to-face?" The question came from Peter, tired and slow.

"If you set down the gun and open the door, we can sit right here and talk for as long as you like," Kate replied calmly. The odds were slim that he'd do so, but she'd take any step she could get. She moved on the stairs from leaning against the door to instead lean against the upright deep freezer.

Her partner was on the radio seconds later. "He's moving. He left the gun on the counter."

"Stand easy, people." He wasn't a violent man, and she wasn't planning to treat him as such. There was a sharpshooter who had line of sight to the doorway.

The doorknob turned.

A glance up from the deck of cards she was cutting confirmed the man had had very little sleep in the last week and looked as though he had aged a few years. "Peter, I'm Kate O'Malley. You remember my sister Rachel." She gave him a moment to look over and see Rae. "There are cold sodas if you happen to like orange."

"Those are Clare's favorites."

"I know," Kate replied. "She brought them over."

The man sat down heavily on the tile inside the doorway. He'd cried himself out. It was hard to see on a proud man, who from everything she had been able to learn had tried to be a good father. Kate handed him a soda. "I'm sorry about your sons."

"Greg did not kill Tim."

"The ballistics prove that," Kate reassured again as she had done many times. "You need to let someone help you."

"I'm tired." He looked at Rachel. "I can't go to the funeral tomorrow. And I can't tell Clare that."

"She understands when you have to fly and are often gone," Rachel replied. "Call her and let her know when you will be over to see her and then keep your word. That's what she needs. To know that you and Sandy are still there for her."

"Sandy doesn't blame me, but she should."

"I met your sons, Peter. Would you remember the fact that your boys loved you? The fact that Greg helped Marissa get through this last year? That Tim was Adam's best friend? They were good kids."

"There's nothing left. My boys are gone, my job."

Kate handed him a note. "Sandy asked if you would stay with her and Clare for the coming week. I think you should take her up on it."

"I can't do that."

"Peter, you said you've got nothing left. What do you have to lose? I don't know what caused the divorce, but Sandy was your wife for eighteen years, and it takes about three minutes in her company to realize she still cares about you a great deal. Spend a week with her and your daughter. Clare would find your presence when she came home from the funeral a great help."

He rubbed his swollen eyes. "What about all this?"

"I don't know about the other guys, but I'm on my day off." Kate cut the deck of cards and turned up a four of hearts. "You take Rachel's card and promise to call her if the grief gets bad. You allow me to take that gun, show me where you had it hidden, and give me your word that there are no others in this house. We don't need to make something of today beyond what it is."

He nodded. "I need a shave."

Kate offered a smile. "Eat something first. I don't know about you, but orange soda isn't the same as what I remember from childhood."

Peter chuckled. "I thought it was just my sense of taste dying."

"You like pizza?" Kate asked. "The guys say the pizza place on the corner is good. They bought a large hamburger and sausage."

Rachel got to her feet. "Is that what I've been smelling? If he's not hungry, I am. I'll get it."

Kate slid her cards into her pocket. "Peter, where did you have the gun hidden?"

"There's a safe in the floor in my office. When Sandy last moved furniture she had covered it with the couch."

Kate walked into the kitchen first and over to the counter. The gun was a .22 caliber. She unloaded it and secured the weapon. "Show me where that safe is."

Rachel handed Kate a bottle of ice water and opened the passenger door for her sister. "You did a great job."

Kate took a seat and reached for the seat belt. She buckled in. Rachel could tell Kate's arm was bothering her as she cradled it against her chest. "I owed his boys." Kate lowered her head and wiped at the dust that had stuck to the back of her neck with a wet tissue. It left a streak of grime.

"We've got a ton of pages to return, starting with Marcus," Rachel mentioned as she started the car.

"You want to do the talking for both of us?" Kate asked.

"I'm the one losing my voice."

"They can find us later." Kate picked up her phone and turned it off. "I stopped by and saw Jennifer this morning."

Rachel looked over at her sister to share a look. "What did you think?"

"I wish I'd taken that vacation two years ago and gone snorkeling with her in the Gulf."

"I've got a few of those moments I wish I had taken too," Rachel replied.

"When did we stop praying for a miracle?" Kate asked quietly.

"I felt it start to change when it became clear that God had a plan in mind for Jennifer much more complex than just healing her cancer."

"I've found myself praying more for us than Jennifer, for those staying behind."

"This is going to be a much harder transition than I think any of us are ready for," Rachel said. "Are you ready for this, Kate?"

"I'm glad I believe in heaven."

"I worry about Stephen." Rachel knew he was already finding it hard to adjust to the fact the rest of them believed and he did not. He was left out of something that gave them hope, and he had no one to relate to who felt the kind of grief he did—believing that life ended at death.

"So do I. We'll keep praying for him."

Rachel drew to a stop beside the building where Kate was meeting Dave.

"Are you heading home next?" Kate asked.

Rachel held up the hotel card Marcus had given her months before. "I'm going to do follow-up with those students visiting the memorial wall, answer the pages that have come in, and then I'm going to disappear for a few hours. I need some sleep before Tim and Greg's funeral in the morning. Reporters found my home."

Rachel checked into the hotel. As much as she wanted to be in her own home tonight, Gage's warning that reporters were waiting for her there had made her decision. She wanted privacy more than she did her own pillow.

She had spent much of her life in hotels and there was a routine for making them comfortable. She hung up her garment bag in the closet as she continued her fifth phone conversation of the evening. "Marissa, did Janie bring by the needlepoint?"

"It was exactly what I was looking for," her friend said. "I want to add something to the memorial wall. Someone needs to remember Greg."

Rachel knew how hard it was going to be on Marissa not to be at the funerals in the morning. "I have your memorial gift for Sandy. It will make a difference, Marissa, for both Sandy and Clare."

"I hope so. Cole came by this afternoon."

"Did he?" Rachel had seen him only briefly this morning before the funeral and wasn't sure what his plans for the day were.

"He talked with my parents for several hours. I like him, Rae."

"So do I." Rachel sat on the side of the bed. "Is there anything I can do to help you with tomorrow?"

"Mom and Dad are both going to be here. I'm glad in many ways that their funeral is being kept private. I don't know that I could handle watching another one on TV."

Rachel understood exactly what she meant. "It's draining." She checked numbers queued on her pager. "I'll call you in the morning, M. Don't hesitate to page me if there is anything I can do for you or one of your friends."

"I will. I'm grateful you are a phone call away."

"You've been making a big difference just calling and talking with your friends, reassuring them. Keep it up, honey. You're a huge help to me."

"And you're sweet. Cole said I could tell you that."

Rachel smiled. "Really? I'm keeping him. Good night, Marissa."

"Night, Rae."

She hung up the phone, paused to open the carton of orange juice she had bought, and then dialed the next number on her list. The calls now were the second and third follow-up calls after the shooting, most of them simply a reassuring contact to see how the students had handled the funeral this afternoon. Only one student was still on Rachel's high-concern list, and one of the other counselors, who had worked with her the day of the shooting, was following up in person daily.

Rachel opened her diary and her Bible, looking for the notes she had made the evening before. In finding reassurance for Adam about heaven, Rachel had found reassurance for herself as well. Heaven was as real as earth. She also made a note to spend some time with Nathan. He was young, but he knew something was wrong and that his brother was sad. Nathan needed the reassurance too.

Her pager vibrated and she checked the number. Other calls could wait a few more minutes; she dialed back. "Hello, Cole."

"Where are you, darling?"

The endearment made her feel so special. She pushed pillows into a backrest and leaned against the headboard. "Hiding."

"I figured that out two hours ago," he replied, amused.

"It's kind of nice seeing your numbers come across my pager." She could no longer imagine her life without Cole in it; his presence had so profoundly changed things. There was comfort just in hearing his voice.

"You're not going to tell me."

"I'm hardly hiding if someone knows where I am," she teased. "I've got two dozen calls to return over the next few hours." She wanted to be able to give him her full attention when she next saw him. She wanted another one of those long hugs.

"Are you holding up?"

"I took your suggestion on the orange juice. I'll make it. What about you?" Rachel asked.

"I had a good visit with Marissa and her parents. I can tell why you enjoy her company so much."

"I've made some great friends over the years. I appreciate you going over to spend time with them."

"Kate told me where you were this afternoon," Cole said.

"She handled the problem with her usual skill." Rachel looked at her watch. "Can I attend the funeral with you tomorrow?"

"Sure. Come over for breakfast if you like and we can go from here."

"I appreciate it."

"Anything else I can help you with?" Cole asked.

"I want a hug tomorrow."

"A long one," Cole promised.

Another page came in. "I'll see you in twelve hours." Rachel said good-bye and took a deep breath. She began working the network of friends, arranging the pages so that one after the other she could talk to a cluster of students who knew each other. It allowed her to gather information even as she gave it out. From her discussions with students at the memorial wall, she had known that this would be a busy night. She hadn't been ready for this.

THIRTY-THREE

The private funeral service for Greg and Tim was scheduled to begin at 10 A.M. Sunday. Rachel was grateful she was with Cole as they entered the cemetery grounds. She came to help ease a family through the grief of saying good-bye. She had to do it when her own heart was incredibly heavy. The funeral service was held in the small chapel on the cemetery grounds so it could be kept out of the range of the media. Cole parked, and they walked over to join Stephen, who had brought Ann and Adam.

The chapel held about a hundred guests and it had begun to fill. As they entered and Adam saw the flowers and the closed caskets, he stopped. Ann knelt and whispered to him and he gripped her hand. They moved to seats reserved for them at the front right of the chapel. Rachel helped them get settled, asked Cole to save her a seat, and moved back outside to meet the arriving family.

Four cars came in together. Sandy and Clare were accompanied by Sandy's sister and husband. Rachel met the group and hugged the boys' mom. "I'm so sorry, Sandy."

"Thank you for sending friends to be with Peter this morning."

"Whatever I can do," Rachel promised from the depth of her heart. She took from her pocket a red-white-and-blue ribbon formed into a heart. "Marissa wanted very much to be here. She sent this for you."

Sandy teared up when she saw it and pinned it to her lapel. "Greg was so happy to have her in his life. Please tell her that."

"I will." Rachel knelt down. "Hi, Clare." She offered the white stuffed rabbit she had brought.

"It's sad without my brothers."

"I know, honey," Rae whispered. "Adam is here. You said you wanted to sit with him?"

The girl solemnly nodded.

Rachel offered her hand. And the small hand gripped hers.

Rachel escorted Sandy and Clare and their family into the chapel and to the front row. Clare was clearly relieved to see Adam and sit with him. Rachel had attended many funerals over the years. It was hard for a child to absorb the emotions of such a day and the feeling of anxiousness about what was coming. Adam was feeling the same. He leaned over to talk to Clare and smile at the rabbit she held. Clare smiled back. Sandy settled her arm around her daughter to try to reassure her.

Rachel slid into her seat beside Cole and was embraced with the comfortable weight of his arm around her shoulders. He was a safe harbor in the midst of this emotional storm. Two caskets, two brothers. The sea of flowers around them and the pictures that remembered the boys as they had been just made the loss heavier. Greg had died with a gun in his hand, angry. No one could go back and give him another chance to make a different decision. Yesterday's funeral had been tragic, but this one was weighted with a deeper grief.

The chaplain rose to start the service.

Sandy did not try to speak during the program. Her sister, brother-in-law, and pastor spoke for her. It was a beautiful service in its music and its words, remembering the love of both a mother and a father for their sons. That Sandy had been able to gather herself to plan it while trying to help her ex-husband through his own crushing grief was all the more a tribute to her sons. For Clare's sake, Sandy was dealing with it. And Rachel knew that no matter how many people were here to offer support, for Sandy the loneliness of the moment was stark. She leaned forward to rest a hand against Sandy's shoulder.

When the service concluded, friends of the family joined together to carry the coffins from the chapel to begin the short trip to the graveside. A solemn procession gathered to follow.

Chairs had been set up under the canopy where the boys would be laid to rest. Rachel watched Clare cross to take Adam's hand. He leaned over and whispered something, touching the rabbit she clutched, and for a moment Clare smiled. The two children were leaning on each other and bonding together through this morning.

The graveside service was mercifully brief.

When the pastor said the final prayer, silence descended as Sandy lifted Clare in her arms and they walked forward to the side of the caskets to say a final goodbye. As they stepped back, Clare wrapped her arm around her mom's neck and laid her head down against Sandy's shoulder.

In small groups, guests came forward to say private condolences.

Rachel walked around the chairs to join Ann and Adam.

"Can I go up to the grave?" Adam whispered to his mom.

"Go ahead, honey." Rachel stood with Ann and watched as Adam walked to Tim's coffin to say his own farewell to his friend. It was painful to watch—Rachel wiped her eyes with her fingers, and Ann offered her a tissue.

"You have a son to be very proud of."

"I am."

Adam walked back, and Rachel could see in his entire body the sadness that gripped him. He was no longer trying to bravely hold back the tears; he wiped his eyes. "Mom, can I come back and see Tim tomorrow? He's going to be so lonely here."

The question broke Rachel's heart and everyone else's who heard it. Ann hugged her son. "I'll bring you."

Adam wrapped his arms around her. "I left Tim my good comic book in his memorial box. I still owed him for the baseball card he gave me after the flood."

"That was nice of you."

Stephen knelt beside them and rubbed Adam's back. "Come on, buddy. Let's go home." He picked up the boy.

Rachel struggled to stop her tears. Cole hugged her. "I know, honey. I know."

Cole stopped Rachel from returning to the chapel after the cars carrying Sandy and her family pulled out of the parking lot. "Stop for a moment. Catch your breath."

She leaned against him. "I'm okay."

Cole wrapped his arms around her and just held her.

"Jennifer has planned her funeral."

He rubbed her back. "She told me." It had been a heartbreaking phone call as he called to hear how Jennifer was doing and she passed on the news in her quiet, calm way.

"I like the music Sandy chose. It wasn't trying to pick you up or lead you somewhere. It was just peaceful and let you remember the music."

Cole blinked away tears. "Anything you need to tell Jennifer you haven't already told her?"

"Good-bye has been said many times and in many ways. But the day that comes when Jennifer isn't a phone call away… It's going to hurt so bad."

"I know, Rae."

He loved this woman. And if he could take away the pain of the moment, he would do so in an instant. How did you tell someone you loved good-bye? It just wasn't something you were ever prepared to do. Over twenty years of history would be broken if Rachel lost Jennifer.

"I've got to shift focus and get ready for Mark's funeral. I'm working the hot-line for the afternoon."

He loved her enough to release her to go do that job. "God will give you the strength you'll need," he whispered. Rachel had been given the gift of knowing what and how to reach out to touch a heart. She had given Adam and Marissa the gift that she'd be just a page away as long as they needed help. Rae had handed her cards to numerous students. She had to go. "Come over tonight. Let me fix dinner, and we'll sit outside and watch the stars."

"I love you, Cole."

He'd been hoping to hear those words for so long. They were the most precious gift she could give him, and today, when her heart was full with so many emotions, he knew she trusted him with her heart. Cole hugged her tight. "I love you too." He wasn't sure when his emotions had fully turned to that reality, but there was no distance anymore between his dreams for his future and his feelings for her. She was the one person he had been praying to find. He loved her smile, and the way she gave without reservation, the way she loved him enough to trust him with everything going on. He brushed back her hair and kissed her. He wasn't going to let her down.

Cole fixed Rachel dinner around seven Sunday night, keeping it to basic spaghetti, salad, and hot bread. He ate quietly and watched her nibble at a salad she was too tired to eat.

She eventually just set down her fork. "I appreciate this, your quietness. Gage pushes."

Cole thought about that. "Gage likes to listen to himself talk."

She paused in lifting her glass and laughed. "You're right. He does."

"He's also worried about you."

"Join the crowd." She rested her chin on her hand and circled her glass, pushing the moisture around. "I'm tired, Cole, deep inside bone tired."

He leaned over and rubbed her back. "You've been doing a great job. And try to remember that God designed us to sleep for a third of our existence, and you are woefully behind." A few hours at a time over the last week were not enough to keep her going.

"I'm getting a crash course in how to lean hard against His strength," Rachel said. She shifted away her plates and lowered her head onto her arms. "I'm just going to rest here a while before I go back to the hotel for the night. Wake me when the brownies are done?"

He glanced at the timer he had set. "You've got fourteen more minutes."

"I'll take it."

He rose to get the teapot as it began to whistle. Rachel had stressed her voice to the limit today. Hank barked once and Cole went to let his dog in. He turned on the backdoor light. The weight Rachel had to carry wasn't over, for the coming week would be uniquely stressful. With the funerals over and school back in session, it would be a struggle for the students to accept normalcy in life. They still felt overwhelming grief and had to return to the schools where the violence had occurred.

Cole shut off the timer and pulled out the brownies to cool.

"Rachel."

She didn't stir.

Cole brushed her hair back and realized she had already fallen asleep. He thought about moving her but in the end decided to simply let her rest where she was. He kissed her forehead. "Sleep well."

He quietly put dinner away.

The lights shining across the window warned him. He moved to the back door to meet the unexpected company.

"Can I come in, Cole?"

"Sure, Lisa."

She knelt to greet his dog. "Where's Rachel?"

He nodded to the kitchen. "She came over for dinner, laid her head down on her arms, and fell asleep."

"She's exhausted."

"Past it. You've got news."

Lisa pushed her hands into her back pocket. "More of the inevitable, we're back to looking at the evidence that Brian Rice murdered his ex-wife and that probably started this rolling crisis of events."

"I hate to wake her up."

"I'm awake," Rachel said, reluctantly stirring. "It's going to be hard to prove since Brian's alibi for the night was his son, and Mark is dead. He's not around to admit he lied."

Lisa tugged out a chair beside Rae. "We've had harder challenges. If you can handle it, Marcus would like to meet tomorrow afternoon to go over what we've found."

"I'll be there."

Lisa looked at him.

"We both will," Cole agreed.

Cole had sent brownies with her to the hotel. Rachel let herself into the room she had made her home, balancing the package, grateful for the freedom that came with being anonymous. Now that the funerals were over and the schools were reopened, the reporters had probably moved on from her apartment, but she was too tired to go check. Marcus's gift of the hotel voucher had become a source of refuge for her.

She pushed off her shoes and left them at the end of the bed. She laid her pager and phone on the dresser. She only had a few calls to return and they could wait a few minutes.

Her hardest work of this crisis was coming up in the next week. She had to walk the fine line to teach how it was possible to continue to grieve while at the same time you went on with life. One action did not contradict the other. But for students stuck on either side of that line, it was hard to understand those on the other.

In a sea of people wanting to move on, there were many who weren't ready yet. Rachel had cried herself out during the day, sharing tears with students struggling with the fact that their lives were torn apart and yet a new week was coming and it was time for them to get back to the routine of being a student. The sympathy of last week would give way to encouragement, which would appear like pushing to those who needed to move more slowly.

Rachel turned on the television for the first time in a week and listened to the late news as she got ready to turn in.

She picked up her diary from the bedside. She tried to keep a diary during a crisis if only because it was a safe place to process her own emotions. She turned to a blank page.

Day 6.

The last funeral was today.

Jesus, I am so glad I saw the verse in the Bible when You saw Lazarus's tomb. It said, *"Jesus wept."*

I cried today.

My heart breaks for the four children who were lost.

Every night I have come to You for strength for the next day.

I come tonight to ask for sleep, renewal, and strength.

Send Your healing, dear Lord. You understand what is happening here much more profoundly than I.

R.

She closed the diary. News about the funerals came on the television and Rachel reached for the remote to turn it off. She couldn't handle any more sadness today. Instead of hitting the off button, she accidentally changed the channel. The laughter on the show stopped her and she watched for a moment, smiling. She moved pillows around and settled down to watch the old comedy. Her emotions lifted as she listened to the soundtrack of laughter.

Rachel wasn't setting aside the sadness as she normally did. It remained heavy on her heart, a burden that was difficult to lift. In the nearby hotels there were other counselors from the National Crisis Team similarly ending their evenings. Only they were carrying the weight of this crisis not knowing beforehand the community and students they had come to help. They came because of the need. There were days it was easier not to know the community you were trying to help.

Rachel reluctantly reached over to the side table and picked up the composition book that recorded this crisis. Over time, every crisis brought a change to her life, and this one was bringing a change to her focus and a reexamination of where she was heading. For the first time a tragedy was teaching her that maybe she was at her limit of what she could absorb for a while.

Life was short. Sometimes cut shorter. She traced the names in the book. So many kids had been impacted by this event.

She knew what drove her desire to help. She saw a child hurting and couldn't stop herself from putting her arm around that child. In the midst of her own personal tragedy as a child, she'd been chosen by the O'Malleys. For years she had been giving back by choosing children from within a tragedy she would give her card to with a promise to help no matter what the cost, what the duration, what the need.

She had found that same kind of lifeline with God. No matter what the need or when she called for help, He was there with everything she required. There was never any lack either in His love or His provision.

She had returned to the cemetery before going over to see Cole. She sat by the gravesides of Greg and Tim, and she began to face the hardest question: Did she have it in her to sit beside the graveside that was coming, one for Jennifer, for the first O'Malley to die? This family would need her then in a very big way, and she wasn't sure if she could meet that need.

Jesus, it's a lonely time tonight.

The phone rang as Rachel dozed watching TV. She reached for it and offered a sleepy "hello," knowing only a few people had this number.

"Rae, I'll be by to pick you up in ten minutes," Cole said, his voice tense, a total change from when she had last seen him.

She swung her legs over the edge of the bed. "What's going on?"

"They found the missing Amy Dartman."

All the implications of that news settled in. She'd known since last week that Amy was missing and that Marcus and Quinn were part of the investigation. She'd known then that the answer would be terrible news when it came. A missing person had been found, and they had contacted Cole. She didn't ask questions. There would be time for those soon. "I'll be waiting by the lobby door when you get here." She glanced out the window and changed to jeans and a sweatshirt, adding a windbreaker. She pushed keys and cash into her jeans pocket and tucked her phone and pager in her jacket pocket. She headed downstairs.

Cole pulled to a stop before her building eight minutes later, driving a fire department SUV. He leaned over and opened the passenger door as the vehicle was left running. She was hit with the strong smell of pine air freshener. The attempt to kill the smoke smell had been a bit overdone. Cole waited until she was buckled in and then picked up the radio and called in to dispatch.

"Where are we going?"

"Carillon Estates. The river finally abated enough to get into the cut-off homes that had taken the brunt of the flood damage."

The expensive homes. She'd been meaning to get down there to see the situation but never had. Another team had been working that subdivision. "Who called you?"

"Lisa. She asked that I pick you up."

Rachel huddled in her jacket. They had found Amy Dartman. Rachel had hoped it would be alive, that Amy had somehow been gone by choice, but with Lisa involved, that clearly wasn't the case. "Do you know why Lisa asked for me?"

"No."

It was a quiet drive that took twenty minutes. The area was crowded with vehicles: police, the coroner's office, rescue personnel, and the media. Cole flipped on his blue light and a cop waved him through toward the center of the scene.

The river had not given up its turf without a fight. The stretch of homes on this block was badly damaged. Near the river four homes had been destroyed, the walls knocked out and roofs caved in. The water was receding, but it remained several feet deep in homes at the end of the block. The devastation had left a river of mud and piled debris.

Rachel got out and stood by the vehicle, scanning the area. She saw Marcus and Quinn talking with a cop and eventually spotted Lisa and Jack. The fire department rescue boat had been brought in. "Stay here for the moment," Cole requested.

She nodded and leaned against the vehicle, watching as Cole crossed over to the assembled group. It was a long conversation, but eventually Cole broke free to rejoin her.

"The collapsed house on the far left—a car crashed through the windows and ended up in the living room. The driver is unidentifiable as the vehicle has been underwater three weeks, but the ID on her is for Amy Dartman. They need the car hauled out of there."

"How?"

Cole opened the back door of his vehicle and took out his heavy gear. "We're going to haul a chain in there by boat, attach it to the car, and pull the wreck out. At this point the river has beaten the car to pieces. Dragging it out isn't going to change the evidence much."

She held his coat and helmet as he pulled on boots. "Do you ever get asked to do simple jobs?"

"I was asked to rescue a cat once," Cole offered. "Lisa's going to have another tough case to solve."

"No wonder they couldn't find Amy. The car was inside a collapsed house."

"Not something they considered," Cole agreed. He slipped on the coat.

"Be careful out there."

His gloved hand touched her cheek. "Always. Lisa needs to talk with you about Amy's parents before she calls them. It may be a few minutes though before she's free to come over."

"I'll wait here."

Cole joined Jack at the boat. Rachel watched them push off for their grim task.

They worked their way to the destroyed home and Cole slipped from the boat. He waded in to attach the chains. Cole came back and signaled the tow truck. The winch started. They hauled the car out of the destroyed house.

The river had beaten the car into a hunk of metal.

When it was pulled clear of the water, Lisa and her team moved in. Quinn and Marcus joined the group. Rachel watched as a photographer came in, the car door was forced open, and a body bag was brought in. When the body was removed, a preliminary search of the vehicle began.

How could Lisa do this job? It was one thing when someone had just died and looked very much as if they were asleep, but when they had been underwater for so many days…

Quinn was the first one to break free and come to join her.

"Is it Amy?"

"Yes. Her seat belt was half off like she was trying to get out of the car," Quinn said. "I can see how it happened. Carol's murder happened late on a Friday night; it's raining; Amy witnessed the murder; and she's driving on roads at high speed trying to get away from the killer chasing her. We know Rosecrans Road was flooded that night, as were several others. She drove into water and thought she could get across, not realizing how deep it was or how powerful, and got swept into the river."

Quinn pointed to the wreckage. "See how the back fender and trunk is crushed in? Something hit that car hard, or the car hit something hard. That impact jammed the doorframe so even if she could get leverage against the force of the water, she couldn't get the door open. It looks like she was trying to get out the window but she drowned before she succeeded."

"Does this help solve what happened that night?"

"It only explains the mystery of what happened to Amy. The real work will happen at the lab to see if there are any clues that can still be found in all this water-soaked evidence."

The drive back to the hotel was quiet. "Would you like a dry towel? I've got a couple in my emergency bag," Rachel asked Cole as he pulled to a stop in front of her building.

"I'll clean up at the fire station. I'm getting accustomed to being wet and uncomfortable."

He had to be miserable. "It has been an unusual couple weeks for water. Oh—" she dug in her pocket—"for you." She held out his new watch. "I kept it nice and dry." She'd had it in her hand most of the night and the metal still felt warm.

Cole slipped it back on. "I appreciate it."

"I hope you get a chance to go home before dawn." She didn't want to say good night, but it was very late. He needed time to decompress from this.

"I'll help Jack get the boat cleaned up and then call it a day."

She slipped from the vehicle so he could get going. "Good night."

"If it's not too late when I get home, I'll give you a call and let you say good night to Hank."

She closed the door and leaned against the window so she could smile over at him. "Do that."

They looked at each other, neither one ready to close the evening with action. "Want to talk about the weather awhile so we don't have to call it a night?" he asked, hopeful.

She stepped back with a laugh. "Go to work, Cole."

"Yes, ma'am."

THIRTY-FOUR

"Lisa, take the whiteboard." Marcus pitched her a marker as more people came into the conference room to join them Monday afternoon. "I want to go back as far as we have leads on the missing gun, and that starts with the murder of Carol Iles."

Cole looked around the assembling group. From the breadth of people Marcus had pulled together Cole could see how rapidly the school shooting was rolling together with the other investigations into one very broad case.

"Just a sec, Marcus." Lisa leaned over to confer with Detective Wilson and then moved to the board. "I'm going to give a brief summary of the time line and then come back to discuss the details within each. Hold the questions for a moment." She pushed a pad of paper down the table. "Dave, scribe this for me. Some of this information has been coming in over the last hour."

Lisa wrote the date March 16. "Carol Iles was shot with a .38 that Friday night. That same night Amy Dartman disappeared. The lab evaluation on her vehicle came in last night—Amy's car was probably run off the road. You can see where her vehicle was hit from behind. Her death is also considered a homicide."

Lisa drew a line connecting the two names. "We have placed Amy at Carol's house that night. We believe she was there when Carol was murdered and tried to run from the scene. We assume the same man who shot Carol also ran Amy off the road. We know Carol was shot in her living room, by someone who stood a few feet inside the front door. The floodwaters have limited what we've been able to recover about that shooter."

Lisa drew a line on the board.

"From there we have nothing on the .38 until it is used again on April 24 to kill Tim at the middle school. Where was it in between those times? Where did it go after the twenty-fourth? Those remain central questions to resolve."

She connected with an arrow the school shooting back to the murder. "We're coming back to the original theory that Carol's murder was a domestic case—Brian Rice killed his ex-wife. His son is just too strong a link to ignore. Brian's alibi for the night of her murder is his son Mark. We have them confirmed at a basketball game at the high school, but the coach said Mark was ejected from the game and sent back to the locker room early in the first quarter. While parents report Brian did take Mark home after the game, Brian left the gym when his son was ejected, and we've not been able to confirm where he was for a period of time during the game. We know he wasn't with his son in the locker room when the coach got back there after the game. Wilson is not ready to say Brian's alibi has been broken, but he's close."

Cole watched Rachel's head nod down against her chest as she fell asleep. He gently pushed Rachel's chair. She jerked awake and shook her head, then tipped her chair back on two legs to rock and keep moving. She'd been returning pages throughout the night and her sleep had been sporadic.

"Can you break his alibi through tracing the guns?" Marcus asked.

Lisa looked to Wilson. "The most likely theory is that Brian killed his ex-wife Carol with the .38, and he kept the gun. Mark lifted the guns from his dad and he brought the .38 to school along with the two .45s."

"What do the prints show on the two .45s that were recovered?" Marcus asked.

"Mark handled the guns and loaded the clips of both. Greg's prints were found only on the grip of the .45 caliber gun he had picked up."

"But what set off the school shooting? There had to be a triggering event, and Tim, Mark, and Greg aren't around to tell us what it was." Quinn nodded to the board. "What's between March 16 and April 10? A river and a flood. No one who murdered Carol is going to hold on to the weapon used in the crime. It got pitched in the river. Only the floodwaters left items behind when it receded."

Rachel's chair fell back to four legs with a small crash. "At Adam's sleepover with Tim, he said they were taking Greg's metal detector to search the riverbanks. Adam was excited about the chance to go exploring again. They had already found three silver dollars."

Marcus turned toward her. "If Tim found that .38, Adam would know about it."

She rubbed her eyes. "He wouldn't want to darken the memory of his friend by saying Tim had taken the handgun to school. In an awful way this makes sense. Tim was getting bullied by Mark. What does a boy getting bullied do? He boasts, 'Back off, I've got a gun.' That might be the trigger that led to the school shooting. We've got two boys goading each other to prove it."

"What time does school get out? Talk to Adam and find out if that .38 was in Tim's possession."

Rachel looked at her watch. "Ann will be picking him up in forty minutes."

"Quinn, Cole, as soon as we finish the general update go with Rachel to meet them at the school. We need to know."

Rachel nodded. Cole reached under the table and squeezed her hand.

Quinn set down the report he'd been scanning. "Was it a truck that hit Amy's car?"

"The car trunk was crushed downward when it crumpled and you can see the height of the bumper on the other vehicle," Lisa confirmed. "They're working on a warrant for Brian's truck now."

"I want to turn to the time line of what happened at the school. Are there any general questions before we do so?" Marcus asked the room at large. Quinn closed his folder and nodded toward the door. Cole and Rachel joined him to head to see Adam.

"I can't read my notes." Rachel struggled to make out the information in her composition book as Cole drove them to the school. "My handwriting wasn't even legible through a few of the days last week."

"Relax, Rae."

"I misread Adam. I asked him my standard follow-up question, and rather than answer me, Adam asked about Kate and why I had gone into the school with her. I should have seen it."

"We've known ever since Lisa figured out the gun was missing that someone had taken it. In an odd way, I hope it was Adam who took it. He's not someone who would use it. If he took it, at least Adam will have the smarts to hide it well."

Rachel looked over at the man she loved and took a deep breath. "Thank you. I appreciate your optimism."

"As bad as the school shooting was, it could have been much worse." Cole reached for her hand. "This is coming to an end, Rae. You'll get a chance to breathe again."

Rachel's pager went off. She looked at the number and tensed. It was an emergency code, and there had been only a handful of them over the years. "Not for a while. There's trouble."

THIRTY-FIVE

Rachel flipped to a blank page in the composition book as she returned the call. "I'm here, Kate."

"Are you driving?"

A chill traveled up her spine. "Cole is."

"I was at the high school when the middle school reported a problem with a number of backpacks left behind after school was let out. With everyone a bit spooked, I've been helping clear them. I found Adam's and gave his mom a call to let her know it had been left behind. Rae, Adam is missing. He called his mom and asked to go home early, that he wasn't feeling well. Ann said when they got home Adam asked her if she would fix some macaroni and cheese and then he went to lie down. When she went to check on him ten minutes later, she found his bedroom window wide open and he was gone. Stephen's on his way to Ann's now, and I'm pulling together a search group."

Rachel reached out and touched Cole's arm. "Hit the car horn and warn Quinn. I need you to divert to Ann's home."

"What's wrong?"

"Adam's missing."

She didn't have time to explain beyond that as she dropped the call with Kate and turned her attention to the composition book she had been assembling. She traced back the web of notes she had for Adam's friends and began placing calls, looking for anyone who might know his plans.

But as she spoke with each friend, it became obvious that Adam had told no one. He would have shared his secret with his best friend Tim, but his best friend was dead. And in trying to protect Tim, Adam was trying to take an adult-sized problem on his own shoulders.

She closed the phone, feeling lost, not knowing what else to do.

"Rachel, what do you need?"

"Wisdom. Where does a little boy go when he's overwhelmed?"

"We'll find him."

"We need to check Tim's grave site."

Cole reached over and squeezed her hand. "We'll start at his neighborhood first."

They turned onto Governor Street. "Cole." Rachel pointed toward the bridge. "I thought the bridge was still closed."

"It is." He slowed to look down the street. "Is that Adam?"

"I think so." The boy was trying to climb under the railing.

Rachel spotted Stephen and Ann running toward the bridge from the opposite direction.

Adam lost his balance and disappeared from the bridge. "No!"

Cole threw the car in park and was out and running along the riverbank before she got her door open. Moments later he went into the river after the boy.

Rachel ran down the riverbank and joined Ann, trying to keep up with Stephen as he raced ahead to help Cole. Rachel saw Cole grab the boy in the swift-moving current.

Cole angled himself and Adam toward the shore. Dirt crumbled beneath Rachel as she slid down the bank to the river's edge. Her feet slipped into the water as she stopped her descent. She reached for Adam as Cole dragged him close to the bank. She pulled Adam from the water, turned, and passed him up to his mom. He coughed up water.

"Go on, help Ann," Stephen urged as he pulled Cole ashore. Rachel left them and scrambled back up the riverbank.

Adam was crying in his mom's arms. Rachel ran her hand across his wet hair and dried his face with her shirtsleeve. "Adam, please, what's going on? What were you trying to do? Where were you going?"

"I didn't want Tim blamed for bringing the gun to school." His voice quivered. "I was going to put it back where Tim had first found it." Adam looked at his mom, pleading for her to understand.

"You took the gun after the shooting?" Rachel asked softly.

"I told Tim I'd meet him in the gym after he got out of his detention. I was bouncing a ball, practicing. Mark came in the back gym doors and went through to the locker room. I heard Tim and I went to see what was going on. I heard the shot and saw Mark run out, being chased by Greg. Mark dropped the gun in the hall as he ran by."

"Where is it now?"

Adam pointed back toward the bridge. "Under the bridge span. I was trying to reach it."

Stephen had joined them. "Come and show me, buddy." Stephen reached down and picked up the boy. In that simple gesture, Adam got the first assurance that the grown-ups had arrived to take over.

Ann offered Rachel a hand up.

"I'm sorry, Ann. I should have been able to help sooner."

Ann patted her shoulder. "Adam left a note on his desk. It said: '*Don't worry, Mom. I have Rachel's card.*' He knew he could count on you even if he was hiding what had happened."

Rachel wiped away tears. "You have a wonderful son, Ann. Two of them."

Ann wrapped her arm around Rachel and hugged tight. "And I've got a great friend."

"You better go join Stephen and Adam. Get Adam a hot shower and then feed him macaroni and cheese. I'll wait down here until Lisa arrives to take the weapon to the lab, and then I'll come talk to him."

Ann nodded. "Take care of Cole."

Rachel smiled. "I'll try."

Cole brushed mud from his jeans. Climbing up that riverbank had left him a mess.

"You're dripping."

"Quit laughing, Rae. I'll lean over and hug you, then you'll be dripping too," Cole threatened, even as he smiled. The river water stank. He slipped off his watch with a sigh. Water dripped from it. This one hadn't even survived a month.

Rachel offered the napkins she had found in the car. With her shirtsleeve she reached up and rubbed his cheek. "That looks like slimy mud."

"You're really finding this amusing."

"Relief. Pure relief. You did great. I want to give you a hug, but I don't want to get that wet."

"Adam's going to be fine, Rae. He's a smart kid. If you want to stay with Ann and Adam for a while, I'll head back to the fire station and get a shower."

"It might be best. Why don't we meet for dinner later?"

"I'd like that."

Tones sounded on the radio he'd left on the front seat of his car. "Get that for me please," he requested as he mopped mud and water away.

She retrieved the radio and Cole listened to the traffic. "I'm sorry, Rae. I may be gone for a while."

"What is it?"

He opened the driver's door and pulled out his keys. "A house fire. I'll call you." He gave a rueful laugh. "At least the heat will dry me out."

THIRTY-SIX

The address of the fire was one Cole knew well, and there were some things he didn't want to tell Rachel. Carol Iles's house was burning.

The intersection of Rosecrans Road and Clover Street was closed to traffic. Cole could see in the blackness of the rising smoke and the height of the flames that the house would likely be a total loss. He parked out of the way and walked down to the scene, annoyed by the wet clothes. The house was brick, but the major parts of the structure in the roof and rooms were wood, and as they burned through they collapsed onto the bricks, bringing down part of the outside walls.

There were enough firemen trying to drown the fire it was creating another miniflood as the water that didn't turn into steam drenched the fire and ran back into the yard. Cole picked his way across the mud, seeing remnants of the police tape that had marked the home as a crime scene. "What do you know?" Cole asked the commander on the scene, shouting to be heard over the noise.

"We got here and the front of the house was fully involved with the roof of the garage smoking," he yelled back. "By the time we got hoses laid, the fire had jumped to the back. It's been burning dark smoke the entire time. Two small explosions ripped through the kitchen area. Gas pockets possibly. They both blew out as much as up."

Cole studied the blaze. "One problem—gas to the house was turned off." The black smoke told him more than even how fast the fire spread that he was likely looking at arson. The carbon particles not burning but rather turning into black smoke told him gasoline probably wasn't used as the accelerant. "Tell your guys as they come off the fight that I'll need descriptions of what they saw. This was a crime scene, and now it's likely also an arson case."

Cole set out to circle the scene. He already knew the suspect he had in mind. Carol's ex-husband Brian Rice. Proving it wouldn't be so simple. A house known to be empty, set a distance away from neighbors, a house floor plan Brian knew: It would require coming prepared, but he could have been on scene mere minutes to set up the arson if he knew what he wanted to do. And the ignition source could be on any kind of timer, making it possible to be long gone before the house went up.

Cole walked back to his vehicle to get his gear. He had to check the chemical composition of the smoke to give him a clue of what he wanted to look for.

"Wilson, I thought you might be this way."

The detective stepped out of his car. "Arson?"

"Looks like it to me, and smells like it."

"We went to serve the material search warrant for Brian's truck and found that apparently he hadn't been home in the last three days. The newspapers and mail were piled up."

"He's at the top of my suspect list for this," Cole said.

"It's one way to destroy evidence, whatever might have been left at the house—burn it down. He's running," Wilson said.

"If he's guilty, he murdered Carol, ran Amy off the road, his son died in a school shooting, and now he's burned down Carol's home. I wouldn't stay around either. He shot his wife and threw the gun into the river. Tim found the gun and thought he could use it to get Mark to back off. Only Mark was already angry and ready to react to such a threat. He brought a gun to school too. Whether Mark ever thought he would fire the gun or not, no one will ever know, but it was a recipe for tragedy from the time Brian shot his wife. Mark was as much of a casualty as Tim."

They walked down the street to the house together. As the garage crashed in, a vehicle appeared in the wreckage. "What do you want to bet that's the truck I'm trying to serve a warrant on?"

"Tires are melted, paint is burnt off, it's crushed under the weight of rubble. Your evidence just got destroyed."

"This guy is annoying me. How long before you can sort through this?" Wilson asked.

"Tomorrow morning at the earliest. We'll cordon off the scene and let it cool for the night."

Cole walked across his backyard, carrying iced tea for himself and Rachel. She had moved her lawn chair to the side of the yard where she could watch the evergreens in the neighbor's yard. She had seen two rabbits there shortly before sundown, and for once Hank had listened to her soft admonition not to give chase. Cole had a pretty good idea his dog hadn't been able to see them.

The moon was huge as it rose in the sky tonight. He paused to enjoy the sight.

It had taken him some weeks to realize why she preferred to sit outside rather than inside during an evening. She worked so many disasters she was braced for unexpected events even when she relaxed. She preferred not to have something over her head that could fall on her. Firemen had similar learned behavior in the routines they maintained.

Cole offered her the drink. "Here you go."

"Thanks."

She was tired but relaxed to the point that she was melting into the lawn chair. Cole moved his chair over beside Rachel's and leaned down to greet Hank. The dog was flourishing under the attention.

"He's growing into his name."

Cole smiled. "He's working on it. How's Adam?"

"I spent an hour walking with him along the river, talking about Tim. He's got a few hard months coming, but he'll get through this. Can you tell me about the fire?"

He'd considered what to say during the drive home, not wanting to add this to her day, but it would be public knowledge with the morning papers. "There was an arson fire at Carol Iles's home. And Wilson recovered the truck Brian drives. Both were destroyed."

"Brian is trying to run."

"I somehow don't think he'll get far."

"While he runs, a thousand people try to cope with the chain of events he began." Rae leaned her head back and sighed. "The right answer to this is to try to let it go?"

"There's not much you can do tonight about any of it," Cole agreed.

She nodded. "The memorial rubber duck float is coming together for Saturday the fifth. Will you be able to come?"

"I've already rearranged my schedule," Cole said.

A comfortable silence stretched between them.

The dog took off barking only to get stuck in a bush. Rachel snapped her fingers at him, laughing. "Hank, leave my bunny rabbits alone."

Cole caught the dog's collar as he raced back. "Yes, I know this is your turf. But you have to learn to share."

"I'd like to take him with us next time we visit Adam and Nathan."

"He'd like that," Cole agreed. One hand holding his dog still, Cole leaned over and kissed Rachel.

Her hand tightened around his wrist to keep him close. She kissed him back. "Thanks. I've been thinking about that for days. I've missed you."

"Same here."

Her pager went off.

He laughed at her expression. "Answer it."

She reluctantly released his wrist. She picked up the pager and her phone and tugged Cole over to listen in to the call. "You'll want to hear this."

"Hi, Jen."

"Tom is on board."

Rachel picked up her notebook and flipped to the short list of wedding plans. "That just leaves the puzzle of getting Kate there. She's already getting a bit suspicious."

"Lisa wants to handle it."

"Tell her not to make assumptions. Surprising a cop can elicit an interesting reaction."

Jennifer laughed. "I'll warn her. Let me talk to Cole a minute."

Rachel raised an eyebrow.

"Give me the phone," Cole said, chuckling. He walked toward the house so the conversation would remain private.

When he rejoined Rachel a few minutes later, he handed her the closed phone.

"I'm like Kate," she mentioned. "I don't like surprises."

Cole smiled. "You'll like this one."

Marcus followed Kate into her apartment. He bent to scoop up her tabby cat and ruffled his ears as Marvel waffled between hissing back and purring. Kate was still talking on the phone with Wilson about the nationwide search for Brian Rice. Marcus bet he'd be picked up within twenty-four hours. The system was designed to find murderers trying to flee.

Since Kate's conversation sounded like it would take a while, Marcus stepped into the kitchen and raided the cupboards. The smell of tuna fish turned the ambivalent cat into his new best friend. Marcus admired the rascal. This family had a habit of adopting pets that were...interesting. He fixed himself a peanut butter and jelly sandwich and made a mental note to get Kate a new calendar. She was still on last year.

"Bring me something to eat, will you?" Kate called from the living room.

Marcus fixed her a sandwich and himself a second one. He carried the plate and two glasses of milk into the living room and set them on the end table.

She had collapsed facedown on her couch. He tickled the bottom of her foot. "Who else is coming over tonight?"

Kate leveraged herself up to reach for the late dinner. "Stephen was going to come by after his shift. Jack and Lisa are working. I didn't want to bother Rachel. She desperately needs a night off."

Marcus sprawled in the corner chair. "What decisions need to be made?"

Kate reached for her Bible and retrieved the envelope inside the cover. She handed over a small slip of paper. "Jennifer found it in the old scrapbooks." Marcus read the list and was smiling as he got to the bottom.

Lisa had been scribing during the family meeting where they chose a last name. Her handwriting had been legible in those days. They had settled on the name O'Malley, and in the margins she had scrawled a note about their twenty-fifth family anniversary.

"We should move up the anniversary celebration."

Marcus looked at Kate. He folded the note and handed it back.

"She's not going to get another remission, Marcus."

"I would not bet against Jennifer. She's been beating what her own doctors thought was possible time and time again."

"I want us to have one final celebration as a family before we face losing her. This would be perfect. I'm worried about how everyone is going to react to her death, and a gathering like this would be a good thing."

"Stephen is the wild card," Marcus agreed.

Kate picked up her cat and Marvel sprawled on the couch, taking a full cushion. "Stephen has nowhere to put the pain he feels. It's bottling up in him."

"He's going to retreat emotionally," Marcus predicted.

"I think so."

"He doesn't want to accept Jesus, and with the rest of us having made that commitment, he's feeling pretty alone through this. He doesn't have the same confidence we do that Jesus will carry this. Kate, we don't need to have a celebration for Jennifer's sake. She is already comfortable with the day-to-day time she has left with us. We do need something to look forward to as a family for after her death. You and I have to make sure this family sees a future together and that twenty-fifth anniversary will be well timed. Far enough in the future to make it a place to be our turning point."

"I don't want to look that far out."

"I know." He had guarded this family for years, and his toughest challenge was coming. "The same thing that holds us so close together is the one thing that will threaten to tear us apart. Will we still risk loving each other this much after we take the pain of losing Jennifer? Or will we start to hold back a little just because it hurts so badly to take the loss?"

Kate didn't answer him for a long time. "I don't know what we will do."

Marcus finished his drink. "In that honesty is a scary reality."

"Remember those first days at Trevor House?"

Marcus nodded. "A common enemy. Loneliness."

"We'll rise to this occasion."

"The O'Malley spirit?"

She smiled. "We're a stubborn group."

"I'll grant you the stubborn." He reached into his pocket and pulled out an item. He tossed it to her.

By reflex, she caught the bullet.

"You came a hair's breadth away from being the first O'Malley we buried."

"Where did you find this?"

"We dug it out of your pager."

Kate paled. He was perversely pleased to see it. "Dave wasn't too happy with you."

"He knows?"

"Why do you think he bought you the bulletproof vest?"

She buried her head under a pillow.

Marcus smiled. They were a family of survivors. He was depending on that.

⊰⊱

Ann had made her final decorating decision to do the living room in bold blue and white, with red accents in the fabrics. Rachel had come over Tuesday to see Adam to reassure herself he was getting over his dunking in the river, but it wasn't long before she had picked up a paintbrush to help out. Rachel thought the color combination was excellent, and she found painting therapeutic. She edged the door frame in blue. Not for the first time she considered taking it up as a hobby. Cole had baseball; she needed a hobby too.

Nathan peeked around the doorway. Rachel held up her paintbrush to keep from dripping on his hair. He put his hand over his mouth in an exaggerated motion for silence. Rachel smiled. The boy was adorable. She pointed toward Ann who was painting the window frame. The boy tiptoed across the room. Small hands reached around to cover Ann's eyes.

"Who is it?"

Nathan giggled.

"Adam, you've shrunk. Oh, no."

Ann reached behind her to Nathan and tickled him. He broke into peals of laughter as he was pulled around onto her lap. "You've had chocolate milk."

"Come play."

Ann hugged him. "In five minutes, sweetie. Turn on the egg timer."

"Go see the river?"

Ann looked over at Rachel.

"Yes, it's important they both be comfortable down there and know how to be there safely."

"Okay, we'll walk down to see the river. Tell Adam."

Nathan ran to find his brother.

"Adam will be fine with it. I intentionally walked with Adam down by the river yesterday."

Ann smiled. "It's Nathan who will be the challenge. He thinks his big brother got a special treat by being able to swim in the river."

"Then we definitely want to take the boys to the river and remind Nathan how muddy it is," Rachel agreed.

Ann closed her paint can. "Thanks for coming over today. It helped, just to remind Adam even after the crisis at the bridge that the day after really is normal and he's getting treated the same as before."

Rachel knew exactly what she meant; it was one of the reasons she had come. "You're very welcome, Ann."

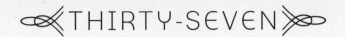

THIRTY-SEVEN

The Saturday of the rubber duck charity memorial was sunny and bright, with a steady breeze from the west. Rachel was proud of the students. From an idea to an event, they had drawn together to plan something that was an honor to the students who had been hurt and killed. They had drawn together in unity. The streets by Governor Bridge had been closed off and lawn chairs and blankets lined the riverbanks. The proceeds of this event were being dedicated to fund the arts and sports programs at the schools. It was fitting that Brian Rice had been arrested that morning in Ohio. There was finally truly closure to the events of the last month.

Rachel uncapped her black waterproof marker. She had decorated her yellow rubber duck with a bright red ribbon.

Nathan landed against her knees. "Look at mine."

He had added a big black stripe down the back of his yellow duck. "What's his name?" she asked, smiling at him.

"Skunk. The river is icky."

"Muddy," Rachel agreed. She added her name to the bottom of her duck. "Okay, Adam, you can add mine to the truck." The boy took it and headed toward the collection site. The huge truck set at the center of the bridge was filling up with thousands of ducks. It would soon lift and dump its load into the water and the race would be on. Adam had already dedicated one for Tim.

Cole was still working on his duck. She leaned against him. "What did you put on your rubber duck?"

Cole turned it over. "Cole & Rachel" was inscribed inside a heart.

"Oh."

He laughed and leaned over to kiss her. There was a point of stability in her daily life now and it centered on Cole. Up until this point the stability in her life had been her family, but now Cole was also there as a solid wall to lean on. She loved him so much.

"Yuck."

Rachel leaned down and tickled Nathan for that comment.

Cole offered his duck to Adam to take to the truck. "Here's another one." A cheer went up across the street as the school band began the school song. "They did a great job organizing this. How many ducks were bought?"

"Over nine thousand, I think."

He picked up another duck to decorate.

"How many did you buy?"

Cole smiled. "A few." He dedicated a duck to each of the students who had been injured and then started on one for each guy at the fire station. Adam took handfuls of ducks to the truck, slowing his steps on his last trip so Nathan could keep up carrying the final duck Cole had decorated.

The program began at noon. Rachel kept an eye on the crowd of students. They had come out in school colors to show a unified spirit, and for the first time she saw more smiles than tears in the clusters of students. They were turning the corner two weeks after the shooting, coming together to help each other move on.

Adam took Nathan's hand and led the way down to join Stephen and Ann. They had set out a blanket on the riverbank where there would be a good view.

Cole took Rachel's hand and pointed to the fire truck behind them. "Let's get higher." The department had brought the boxes of ducks over, and a crew was staying at the event on the off chance there was need for a medical presence. Cole gave her a boost up onto the fire truck. Sitting up on the hose bed they had a great view. Jack joined them.

On the bridge a long solemn whistle blew. The truck raised its bed and the rubber ducks slid out into the river. A huge cheer erupted. A river of rubber ducks with black sunglasses began their journey.

"There's mine." Jack pointed. His had been spray-painted fluorescent blue.

"Trust you to get colorful." Rachel watched the ducks drift in the water, bounce off each other, swirl together in eddies, and then continue their journey downstream.

Rachel picked up her program. She was going to be adding it to her memory box.

"Did you read Gage's tribute this morning?" Cole asked, unfolding his newspaper to show her.

Rachel nodded. "He did a magnificent job." She had expected nothing less from her friend.

She looked around the crowd of students one last time. They were turning the corner today in a corporate way, giving each other permission to go on with their lives. It was the right memorial and at the right time.

Rachel looked down at her pager. For the first time in weeks it was quiet.

Rachel was asleep on a gym bleacher at the community center. Cole paused beside her to read her sweatshirt. Something about honey and cream. Rachel's arms were folded across her chest and she was holding a towel even in her sleep.

Stephen shot a basket from near the half-court line. It hit the rim, and he went after the rebound to grab it and put up another shot. "Come on, Cole. Let's play some one-on-one."

"Is she going to fall off that bench?"

"Doubtful. It's her spot. She's gotten lots of practice ignoring a basketball game. She comes to hold the towels."

Cole set down his gym bag. "I can see that."

He slipped off his watch and added it to the towel Rachel was guarding. He let a finger brush her cheek as he smiled, and then he crossed to join Stephen on the court. "What are we playing to?"

"Whoever is ahead in half an hour."

Cole nodded and caught the basketball. He shot a few practice hoops. "No one else is coming?"

"The guys will dribble in over the next hour if they're free."

Cole tossed Stephen the ball and settled in to play the game. It felt good to be back on the court.

As she awoke, Rachel was aware that a rather intense basketball game was going on. She could hear Jack and Stephen doing their floor chatter as they tried to figure out how to get the ball around their opponents and to the basket. It was a familiar sound, for basketball was an O'Malley family tradition. She opened an eye at the sound of bodies making contact and got a good look at her brother Marcus as he crashed into the wall a short distance away from her perch. The basketball bounced from the rim toward the far wall and got scooped up by Cole. Shirts were plastered by sweat and the guys were breathing hard.

She'd been tired enough to sleep through it.

Rachel sat up, realizing she had become the guardian of two towels, a watch, and someone's sunglasses. Lisa on a bleacher above her handed down a water bottle. "Thanks."

Stephen noticed. "Hey, sleeping beauty is waking up."

Quinn ran past. Rachel slipped on the glasses and found there was no corrective prescription. "Who's winning?"

Jack laughed. "Depends on which scorekeeper you listen to."

Cole used the fact Jack was distracted to score from the baseline.

"I see I'm bringing you good luck," she called as Cole ran back the other way on defense.

"Just sit there and keep smiling, honey."

The *honey* paused Marcus in his tracks and Cole stole the ball.

Lisa laughed. "You are good luck."

"Why aren't you playing?" Rachel asked her sister.

"Too much sweat on the court. You were exhausted."

"It's catching up with me," Rachel admitted. "This is a nice place to hide." She settled her elbows back on the bleacher behind her and watched the guys run the court. "I wish Jennifer were here to see this."

Lisa held up the camcorder on the bench beside her. "I caught about twenty minutes of it for her."

Rachel held out the water bottle the next time Cole ran by, and he took it with a grateful smile. He had a moment to grab a drink and toss it back to her before Jack invaded his corner of the court.

Cole had been accepted into her family. It was comforting not to just know it but to see it.

Lisa moved down to sit beside her. "Are we ready?"

"The wedding dresses arrived," Rachel replied. "My list is complete. We're ready."

THIRTY-EIGHT

Rachel circled the hotel suite, mingling. It felt good to laugh with family. The double wedding they had been planning for weeks was an hour away, and the party had already started. It had begun as something the O'Malleys could look forward to with joy and had become a powerful healing moment for them all. In their own way they were allowing each other permission to enjoy the day even as they corporately worked to accept the fact Jennifer's days were numbered.

Jennifer had been in charge of the guest list and she had cast a wide net. "Marissa, can I get you anything?" Rachel stopped beside her friend.

"I'm fine. Clare is helping me out with the decorations." Marissa smiled at the girl drawing a heart on her cast below the knee.

"See?" Clare asked, pausing to show off the artwork.

"Absolutely gorgeous."

The little girl beamed at her.

Marissa nodded around the suite. "Do you think Kate will be surprised?"

Rachel looked around the transformed hotel suite. "She's going to be overwhelmed." Roses were everywhere. The wedding plans had been cut back in light of how Jennifer was feeling—they had set aside original plans from a dinner together to a large reception. But even so it was going to be a wonderful evening. There would be a beautiful double wedding ceremony with two great wedding cakes. The kids had been awed at the wedding cakes.

Gage was perched on the arm of the couch, sharing a moment with Nathan that had both the man and boy smiling at each other. Nathan could wrap anyone around his finger, and Gage already had an incredibly soft spot in his heart for little boys. Ann was talking with Marcus's fiancée Shari. Rachel saw Adam tugging at his tie and Stephen knelt to help him straighten it.

Jennifer had rallied for this day and was now sitting comfortably in a plush chair set strategically to allow her to be fully involved in the coming evening events without having to move. She was talking with Dave's sister Sara and her husband Adam Black, Jack and Tom both nearby.

Cole joined her. He held out a handful of the mints he had asked her to add to the list. "I think you have managed to pull it off."

She smiled at him. She'd been dragging him all over the city in the last couple days getting the last details figured out. He'd been an incredibly good sport about it. She had so enjoyed the time with him, a chance to decompress from the stress of the last month with a man who had become so important to her. "Come here," she whispered. He kissed her and he tasted like mint. There was a time and a place for everything, and tonight she was enjoying Cole's company.

She accepted some of the mints and wished she had paused to eat dinner during the racing around to get the final details finished. "Now if the brides would just arrive." Lisa was responsible to bring Kate without letting her know what was coming. It was a tough assignment, but so far keeping this a surprise appeared to have been successful. And if Kate for some reason truly got cold feet and couldn't handle the surprise, it would simply be Lisa and Quinn getting married tonight. No one wanted to back Kate into a corner she really wasn't ready for.

"Relax. She's going to love it," Cole assured her.

"I hope so."

The grooms were pacing by the windows. Dave and Quinn were handsome men in their matching tuxes and tails. Rachel smiled as she watched them. Quinn still had on his cowboy boots.

The suite phone rang once and stopped. It was Lisa's signal that they were arriving at the hotel. Kids scurried to their planned greeting positions.

The door to the suite opened. "Surprise!" A number of flashbulbs went off to capture the moment, and only because Lisa had her arm around Kate's shoulders did the initial reaction of a surprised cop not result in something more than Kate instinctively taking a step backward out of the doorway.

Lisa laughed and hugged her. "Welcome to my wedding."

Kate looked around the suite and her smile bloomed. "Really?"

"I'm getting married tonight. And if you would like to join me, Dave has it all planned."

Kate turned a startled gaze toward Dave, who had crossed to join them.

"Kate O'Malley, will you marry me tonight?" Dave asked softly.

Her jaw didn't drop but it quivered. She threw her arms around his neck. He picked her up, holding her tight. "I love you," he whispered.

"Yes, I would love to marry you tonight." She leaned back. "Lisa didn't give away a clue. You really planned a double wedding?"

Dave kissed her. "With a lot of help." He reluctantly lowered her to her feet. He slipped off her pager. "You won't need this for a week."

"Really?"

He slipped it into his pocket. "Really."

Lisa took Kate's hand. "Come on, Kate. You've got to see the dresses. Go cool your heels guys; we'll be half an hour." With a lot of laughter Kate was pulled toward the bedroom. Rachel joined them. The dresses were center stage, laid out on the bed. White intricate lace and silk, flowing skirts, and long sleeves—they were exquisite.

Kate lifted hers up, overwhelmed. "You found it."

Rachel handed her sister a tissue. It had taken a series of long phone calls, but they had found the designer of the wedding dress she had marked in the bride's book. "Dave hasn't seen it yet. He just gave us a blank check."

"How long have you been planning this?"

"Weeks," Rachel replied, sharing a smile. "And it has been so much fun. Jennifer loved it."

Lisa turned Kate toward the mirror. "Hair first. Marissa is going to do our makeup."

They got ready, laughing as they tried to move around the bedroom in their wedding dresses. Rachel helped Marissa move around in her wheelchair and helped her as she did a beautiful job on their makeup.

"Aren't we supposed to have a rehearsal or something?" Kate asked as she studied her image in the mirror.

"Sure." Lisa stepped into white slippers. "Join Dave and say yes."

Kate laughed and picked up her bouquet.

Rachel stepped out of the bedroom to alert the guests that they were ready.

Marcus was waiting at the door to escort them. He was giving away the brides. Rachel gave the sign to Adam and he pushed the button on the tape deck. The wedding march filled the room.

It was hard to tell who was more proud, Dave or Quinn, as they came to meet their brides. The group gathered around the two couples. Rachel joined Jennifer, sitting beside her and just holding her hand, sharing the joy. The ceremony began.

Rachel had never seen Kate so emotional. Kate struggled not to cry through most of the ceremony even as her smile grew wide. Twice Kate turned and buried her face against Dave's shoulder. He rested his head against hers, whispering something that drew a silent laugh. For Kate this was a day that would transform her life forever.

Lisa's gaze rarely left Quinn's as they shared a private conversation of their own without needing to say a word.

Wedding vows were spoken. The O'Malley family expanded. They had been seven, and with Tom they had become eight. Now they were formally ten. Rachel blinked away her tears.

The couples kissed and on cue Adam started the music and Nathan cheered, a happy little boy that made them all laugh.

They moved to cut the wedding cakes amid a lot of laughter and photographs.

Rachel watched Jennifer. She had set her heart on reaching this day. Jennifer was having to conserve her energy, but she was enjoying the evening enormously.

Cole slipped his arm around Rachel's shoulders. "Good job, honey."

"I'm closing my wedding planning book for a while," she said. She was incredibly relieved to have this event successfully over.

The O'Malleys and their guests lingered and laughed and eventually by silent agreement began to disperse. Lisa and Quinn came over to say good night to Jennifer, exchanging a long hug. They were heading to Montana tonight. Dave and Kate came to say farewell and then left for a destination unknown. The other guests followed soon after, with Marcus and Shari taking Marissa and Clare home and Stephen walking down with Ann and her boys.

Jennifer wisely allowed Tom to help her turn in.

With Cole's help Rachel restored the suite to normal. She called the hotel coordinator, who had offered to refrigerate the wedding cakes and transport the wedding dresses. Rachel made arrangements for help to come up in twenty minutes. Only the multitude of roses remained to mark the weddings.

"They were gorgeous brides," Rachel remarked, kicking off her shoes.

Cole draped his tie across the arm of her chair and settled on the couch as she returned the family photo albums to their boxes. "Very. And it was an evening that filled Jennifer with joy."

"Part of this is your credit. You suggested the idea."

"I enjoy weddings," he replied, smiling. He reached in his jacket pocket and offered her a small box. "For you."

She set aside the photo album and took the small box, surprised. She opened it. There was a gorgeous bracelet inside. She lifted it from the box. On the inside was an inscription: '*A time to love*' and today's date. She leaned over and wrapped her arm around his neck. "Thank you," she whispered, overwhelmed.

"Come here." Cole tugged her from the chair to the couch beside him. He took the bracelet and fastened it around her wrist. "This day needed a memory marker."

"It's a beautiful one."

His hands cupped her face. "I love you, in my mind where my thoughts reside, in my heart where my emotions live, and in my soul where my dreams are born. I love you."

Her smile quivered. She held his gaze, absorbing his expression. He meant it. And part of her began to hope as she never had before in her life. The tears began to fall as her smile grew even wider. "Oh, Cole… I love you too."

He wiped her tears for her, his hands gentle.

She laughed and helped him. "I'm sorry. All I've done is cry on you lately."

"You're smiling this time," he said tenderly, smiling back. "It's a nice improvement."

Cole settled his hands on her shoulders and rubbed his thumbs along her shoulder blades. "I'm old-fashioned, Rae. I want a family with you, and nights watching the stars, and quiet moments like this one at the end of long days."

"I've longed for such a future."

"We're going to make it together, and it's going to be special."

"I like that word *special*. A lot." She kissed him. "My brothers are going to meddle. Or have they already?"

He chuckled but he didn't deny it. "I like your brothers. I always have."

"You're going to fit in quite well. I think of them as the chivalrous sort, my brothers. They didn't have an example; they just had an idea of what a brother was supposed to be. And they have never believed in doing something partway."

"Honey, I understand family. I may not have a big one of my own, but I've got the big picture down." He brushed her hair behind her ear. "I like your friends. I like your family. It's a pretty good beginning."

"Where is Gage in that list?"

"Unique." Cole smiled. "Rae, I understand Gage. He's already been hit hard by life. As a result, he's solid. You can't intimidate him. You can't budge him. That's a man who isn't going to move from what he decides is right. I like him."

"I was afraid you wouldn't understand."

"You have a friend there that is a lifelong friend. But he can still irritate a saint when he's working on a story."

"True."

Cole interlaced his fingers with hers. "Are you ready for the next weeks? The next few days?" he asked softly.

"I have to be." She tried to capture in words what had filled her heart in the last days. "We're a strong family Cole, but if Jennifer dies… You can't replace the links that will be lost. The scar in this family will be deep and lasting. I don't know how we rebuild around such a tear."

"You'll adapt."

"Eventually. But I worry about how hard that will be and how long it will take."

"Rachel, have you ever given up on someone you gave a card to?"

She looked at him, puzzled. "No."

"The very first cards you gave out were to your family. They've got your pager number in red. You'll get your family through this."

"It feels like an incredible task."

"You'll get through it."

THIRTY-NINE

The roses had begun to droop. Rachel made a circle of the hotel suite removing those roses that would not last another day. She'd bring new ones tomorrow. She did her work with care, taking her time on each decision. In the month since the wedding, Jennifer had become bedridden. And with that change, there had been a shift in priorities. Rachel's pager was somewhere at home, her phone turned off, the rest of her life blocked off from today. She stayed at the hotel now, having taken a room next door to the suite.

She had been joined at the hotel by all the O'Malley's. Jennifer refused to let it be a sad gathering. The honeymooners were back, and Jennifer loved listening to the stories they had to tell.

Tom joined Rachel. He rested his hand on her shoulder and she covered it with her own. She loved this man who loved her sister. He had not slept much in the last week. "The guys said they'd meet you in the coffee shop," she passed on. Tom had begun the practice of giving Jennifer a gift each night to mark the day. The gifts were lined up on Jennifer's bedside table, small markers of victory, things to make her smile and laugh and give her joy. He wanted to buy his wife a good piece of jewelry for today, and the guys in the family had offered to keep him company for the excursion. Rachel had a pretty good idea that Tom would not be the only one opening his wallet.

"I won't be long."

"I brought a book. Don't feel like you need to hurry."

She finished the flowers and straightened pillows, then sorted magazines. Rachel stepped into Jennifer's room, moving quietly in case her sister was asleep.

"I'm awake."

"I just wanted to see if you needed anything else tonight."

Jennifer patted the bed. "Your company," she whispered.

Rachel stretched out on the bed beside her sister, tugging over one of the big throw pillows to wrap her arms around. "What are you reading?" Jennifer had her Bible open, resting against her chest.

"Ephesians. It's a wonderful book."

Jennifer was drifting in and out of sleep, the medication to stop the pain now powerful enough it wasn't uncommon to have her drift off midsentence. Rachel straightened the edge of the blanket spread over Jennifer, pink and soft, one of her sister's favorite colors.

"I was thinking…"

Rachel waited as Jennifer drifted between asleep and awake.

"…that heaven will probably be colorful."

Rachel rested her chin against her hand. "God likes colors: deep green grass, bright blue sky, vibrant red roses. I bet He made heaven beautiful like that."

"I'm ready to go, Rae," Jennifer said softly.

Rachel interlaced her fingers with Jennifer's. Her sister's hand was chilly. Rachel warmed it with hers. "Tom appreciates every day he has with you."

Jennifer smiled. "It's mutual." She touched the bracelet Rachel now wore. "Cole is a good man."

Rachel knew how blessed she was. "A veteran in a profession of heroes. I love him so much. And the best part is that he loves me too. Do you know how long I've waited to be able to say those words?"

"It makes your heart go mushy," Jennifer agreed. "You'll make a wonderful mom someday."

Rachel struggled to keep her voice steady. "I wish you were going to be here."

Jen's hand tightened on hers with what little strength she had left. "Tom promised to take very good care of you when you do someday have children; he'll be your doc a phone call away in my place. I think Cole will be a wonderful father." Jen's hand slackened around hers. "Tomorrow, would you ask Stephen to bring over my puppy…" Jen drifted to sleep.

Rachel stayed holding her hand until the clock on the dresser moved to the top of the hour. She kissed the back of Jennifer's hand and settled it below the covers, making her sister as comfortable as she could. Rachel moved the Bible and letter Jennifer had been writing to the bedside table. The tears were close but she didn't let them fall.

Jesus, give her another night of peaceful sleep, and in the morning a beautiful dawn.

This family would share her life until her last breath. And there was peace in that for both Jennifer and for them. Peace, and if not acceptance yet, at least peace.

Tom,

My dear husband, I love you with every fiber of my being. I've told you that a few times and basked in the light of your smile as I do so, but I haven't written it nearly as much as I should have. I know the lasting value of words. Your letters to me are of priceless value, sentimental and rich in shared memories. The honor of being your wife is hard to convey. There is a picture of life as it was before I met you and a picture of life as it is with you now. The cancer cannot mar what is obvious to all. I'm blessed. In your love I have found joy beyond words.

Every night you hold my hand to share a prayer with me, and every morning I watch you pray alone. When this pattern began in our marriage, why, I do not remember. But I know an evening is coming when you must pray alone because I will not be there.

I felt it important to leave with you one last prayer for when that moment comes.

It's hard to be alone. I tasted it when my parents died, and as deeply as I grieved for them, I grieved for myself even more. I was alone and I knew it. My knees shook at the idea of facing the world alone. I stiffened my spine and tried, not because I thought I could do it, but because I had no choice.

God knew. He knew that loneliness.

"Surely he has borne our grief and carried our sorrows."

I walked into Trevor House on the most terrifying morning of my life, and I ended that day still in the same place but with the O'Malley's for comfort. I didn't know God until you introduced me to Him, but I understood years later when I met Him just how much He loved me. He acted on my behalf when I didn't even know He was there. He placed me with the O'Malleys. For years they have been the source of my strength. In years to come, they will be yours.

I wish I knew what God had planned for the evening of your hardest day. I know it is coming. I am afraid I will be the cause of that deep, dark night.

My prayer on that night you must pray alone is very simple: I pray for the return of your joy.

All my love, my beloved,
Jennifer

Jennifer woke early Friday with an odd feeling in her chest. The pain that coiled around her back and numbed her legs had not changed, but something else had. *Jesus, You woke me early. Why?* It was odd to awake with an urgency and yet not have a sense that it was to pray for someone. It was for herself.

"Tom," Jennifer called softly.

He was asleep, the heavy sleep of exhaustion. Jennifer reached over and brushed her hand lightly along his jaw, loving him. He'd been holding her family together even as this day came close. She settled her hand on his pillow. "Tom."

He awoke and kissed her palm.

She loved him so very, very much. He'd filled up her life with so much joy that it brimmed over. She wore the ring he had bought her last night, a simple gold band that was beautiful. "I'd like to go outside."

He turned his head and looked at her. She loved him too much not to let him see the truth. Tears filled his eyes. She gently wiped them away.

He leaned over and kissed her. "I love you."

She slid her arms around his neck and returned his kiss. She held him, resting in the depth of that love.

"I'll get dressed," he said softly.

He took his time with the simple steps of buttoning his shirt, sitting to slip on socks and shoes. Tom wrapped her in a blanket and lifted her from the bed.

Dawn cracked the sky.

Tom took her down to the bench near the rose gardens in the park beside the hotel and sat with her in his lap. Jennifer rested her head against his shoulder. "You kept your promise. I cherished every day of our marriage."

He laid his head against hers. "Life is too short. You never got to see Paris."

"I did through your memories."

They sat in quiet, sharing without needing words. She loved this man and knew how his heart beat and what this day would be like for him. "Would you do something for me?"

"Sure." She could feel him wrestling with the emotions.

"There's a package with my diary. Give it to Stephen a year from now?"

"My promise."

She worried about her brother. She wanted so badly to see him in heaven one day. She had done what she could. The rest would have to be left to God and the other O'Malleys.

The sun appeared over the hillside. "I'm tired, Tom."

"It's okay to go home," he choked.

"Hold my hand?"

His arms tightened around her and his fingers interlaced with hers.

She closed her eyes against the brightness. "I love you."

"I love you too," he whispered.

Jennifer died feeling the warmth of the rising sun.

FORTY

"I am the resurrection and the life; he who believes in me, though he die, yet shall he live.'" The sun broke through the afternoon clouds as the graveside service concluded. Tom turned the pages in Jennifer's Bible, reading the Scriptures she had chosen, the pink fabric-covered book looking odd in his hand.

"'If any one serves me, he must follow me; and where I am, there shall my servant be also; if any one serves me, the Father will honor him. In my Father's house are many rooms; if it were not so, would I have told you that I go to prepare a place for you? And when I go and prepare a place for you, I will come again and will take you to myself, that where I am you may be also. For this perishable nature must put on the imperishable, and this mortal nature must put on immortality.'"

Rachel reached for Cole's hand as the final words were spoken. She wiped her eyes as "Amazing Grace" began to play. Jennifer had chosen the words as much for her husband as for them. Just listening to Tom's solemn voice as he laid his wife to rest was enough to bring the grief she had long borne back to the surface. Cole's free hand slid behind her neck and turned her face into his shoulder. How she would have survived today without him…she couldn't imagine it. She took a deep breath and turned back to listen to the service.

Jennifer was being buried next to her parents. Marcus and Stephen lifted the bouquet of roses from atop the casket and moved it to the family headstone. Jennifer had requested carnations, roses, and a simple, very private service. She had chosen the verses, the songs, keeping it short. It was a beautiful service.

Tom stepped to the casket to make his private good-byes.

Her family didn't want to stay to see the coffin lowered into the hole in the ground. But no one wanted to say the service was over either.

Stephen was the first to walk forward, touch the casket, and then walk away, back toward the chapel where the service had been held. Rachel watched him go. Stephen had already lost his younger birth sister, and now he was burying the youngest O'Malley. Even Nathan last night strangling him in a sticky hug good night had not been able to get more than a brief smile from him. Her brother was suffering the deepest of them all, for the words of hope they heard in the Scriptures he wasn't able to share.

Marcus and Shari joined Tom as he moved to place flowers in front of the inscription already added to the headstone. *Wife, friend, and beloved sister.* For

Tom's sake Rachel was grateful that this long weekend journey of farewell was now concluded. Tom had accepted as much sadness and grief as he could absorb.

Lisa lifted one of the white carnations from the basket to have as a keepsake. She broke the silence among their group. "I don't know about the rest of you, but cemeteries give me the creeps."

Rachel blinked and then smiled, for Lisa was right. They had all lost and buried family and when it was personal, a cemetery was a depressing place. Too many memories were pulled back to the present.

"I thought I was the only one feeling it," Kate said. She glanced at her husband. "Shall we gather at our place for dinner?"

Dave nodded. "It would be best. Tom needs a place to relax."

"Why don't you all go, catch up with Stephen. Cole and I will be there in a minute."

"You'll give Ann a call?" Kate asked.

Rachel nodded. Stephen was the one who suggested it was best if they didn't come to the funeral today, for Adam didn't need to experience a second one in such a brief period of time.

Lisa and Quinn, Kate and Dave, walked back toward the chapel's parking lot.

Rachel released Cole's hand and walked to the side of the casket, struggling to find the final words to let Jen go. Everything she could have said had already been said while Jennifer was alive. She rested her hand against the coffin, enormously comforted that God had already given her the opportunity to say the words. *Jen, I miss you already. The O'Malleys will get through this. And we'll take good care of Tom for you, I promise you that. You led us to a hope that will endure even in this grief.* She wiped away a tear. *I love you.*

Cole rested his hands on her shoulders as she began to cry. She leaned back against him and lifted her face to the sky. He'd absorbed enough of her tears in the last month; she wasn't going to break down again, not here.

"Good-byes are hard."

Rachel rested her hand over his. He'd buried firefighters, friends killed on the job, in accidents, and even a friend who had turned to the dark side of arson. He didn't need to say words to empathize; he just had to be with her. "I've said them all. Let's catch up with the others," Rachel said, looking after where Stephen had gone.

The empty chair was haunting him. Stephen shifted his chair so the chair where Jennifer should be sitting was no longer in his line of sight. If she were here right now, she'd be kicking him under the table, trying to get him to smile. She'd taken being his little sister as a serious role. Nathan sitting on his lap bounced and pointed. "M&M?" he asked, hopefully.

Stephen tugged over the dish. He'd made the wooden candy dish for Kate as a wedding gift and the candleholders. "Which color this time?"

"Blue."

"I should have guessed that." Stephen had to dig to find one. Nathan loved the blues.

Stephen could see why Rachel loved working with kids. They were good for making sure even miserable days at least stayed on an even keel.

The family was lingering over coffee: Marcus and Shari, Kate and Dave, Lisa and Quinn, Jack and Cassie, Rachel and Cole. He could hear Tom and Ann laughing in the kitchen. They were fixing homemade milk shakes that Tom swore turned little boys into angels. They had asked Adam to help with the cherries and vanilla and flavorings. Stephen was grateful they had come. Adam was sensitive to the sadness of another funeral, but Tom and Ann were doing a good job distracting him.

Stephen wasn't sure how Tom had handled this last weekend with the equilibrium he had. *Jennifer, you married a good man.* Tom planned to return to Houston next week and the pediatrics practice he and Jennifer had shared. He'd married Jennifer knowing this day might come, and Tom had still let himself love her completely until the very end. He'd never drawn back to separate himself from the pain of this day. How Tom had found the focus to be able to read the Scripture passages and say the final amen… Stephen knew he couldn't have done it. Tom's last act of love for his wife had been to help her take care of them.

Stephen watched his family, and he struggled to make a decision.

Stay, or go.

He'd been wrestling with the decision all night. The arrangements were made; they just awaited his action. And as he hugged Nathan it became simple. He couldn't handle seeing someone else die, not another man-made tragedy like the shooting, not an accident, not even another death from illness. He'd promised Jennifer, and he was going to keep his word. There was no better time than now.

Stephen hugged Nathan again and moved his chair back. "Go to Rachel, buddy. She's got the cookies."

His sister turned in her chair and accepted Nathan onto her lap. The boy mashed her in a hug and peals of laughter ensued as she tickled him. Stephen caught Cole's gaze and shared a smile with him. Rachel had found a good man too. All his sisters had.

Stephen rose and stepped into the kitchen to say good-bye to Ann.

"Does this taste okay?" Adam asked, offering a long spoon and a chance to sample the just completed milk shake.

Stephen tried it. "Great."

"Not too much vanilla?"

He took a second spoonful to taste and shook his head. "Perfect."

Tom helped the boy pour the milk shakes. Adam had a long line of glasses waiting and a cup with a lid for his brother Nathan.

Ann put away the ice cream and stepped over to join him. "You're heading out?" she asked softly. They'd driven over separately.

"Yes."

Ann hugged him, not asking how he was doing, not pushing. Stephen relaxed into the hug, appreciating her comfort. She'd been there for him this month. That friendship had helped more than he could explain. "When you get home, check the back patio," he said softly. He'd made a set of bar stools for her kitchen counter.

"You finished them?"

He smiled. "The paint finally dried. The pattern choice was Jennifer's." The rose and ivy pattern had taken days to paint. He stepped back, absorbing the memory of her face, then simply nodded his good-bye.

In the dining room, Stephen paused at the head of the table by his eldest brother. "Marcus, I'm heading out."

"You want to join us for a basketball game later? Jack wants to run off dinner."

"I'll take a pass. I promised the guys at work I'd swing by and sign off some paperwork."

Marcus's gaze held his and Stephen wondered what the odds were Marcus knew he was lying. Probably pretty good. Marcus slowly nodded. "You need me, call."

"Will do." The last thing he wanted to do was give this man something else to worry about. His brother had carried the weight of arrangements for the last few days and made it possible for all of them to get through today.

With rapt attention Nathan was listening to one of Rachel's made-up stories. Stephen pointed to Jack and got a thumbs-up back. He wasn't saying good-bye. Everyone he said good-bye to died. His parents, his little sister, now Jennifer. As close as this group was, as powerful as it was to be an O'Malley, he still walked out of here knowing he was alone.

He walked out the front door, not letting himself slow or glance back. The clouds had rolled back in and a spitting rain was in the air. There would inevitably be car accidents tonight as the weather changed and people didn't slow down enough to make adequate allowances for the changing road conditions. He couldn't handle the idea of going back to work, not now, not anytime he could see in the next weeks. He tugged on the baseball cap, which was his concession to the weather.

"Stephen."

He turned as Kate called his name. She came running down the stairs to catch up with him. "You're leaving early."

"Some." He shifted his car keys in his hand. He didn't want her prying into his plans for the night, so he smiled at her and reached out to catch her hand and hold up the ring he was still getting used to seeing on her hand. "You never mentioned: What do you think of being married?"

"Marriage suits me just fine," she replied, smiling. She looked at the keys in his hand. "Are you sure you won't join us later at the gym? We'll be there quite a while."

"I'm sure."

"Where are you going?"

"For a drive," he said, telling her the truth.

He was nearly toppled by her hug. "Hey."

"Don't go."

She hadn't cried at the funeral and now Kate was threatening to bawl on him. He tried to pat her back and ease her away at the same time. "It's not forever, I promise," he said, desperate to stop the emotions and get this back to the teasing, which was about the only thing he could take tonight.

"You'll need a navigator."

He had to laugh. He'd never been able to keep a secret from her. He took off his hat and dropped it on her head, tugging the bill straight. "You're a lousy navigator."

"When will you be back?" she asked. "You haven't quit a job in my lifetime. Your boss called this morning," she explained. "He was worried."

"It's just a leave of absence." There wasn't a good explanation for his actions, and given the turmoil of the last month, he didn't feel a need to figure out a good one. "I made a promise to Jennifer; it's time I keep it. I want to drive awhile, see some of the country, think. I'll be gone until I get the answers I'm looking for."

"You'll call more than just occasionally?"

"You know I will," he reassured. "I'll have to call just to make sure you're not getting yourself in trouble, something that happens with regularity."

"Ann's going to miss you, the boys too."

"Rachel and Cole will be there for them." He glanced up at the deteriorating weather. Kate was trying to stall him and talk him out of this. He'd been on the other end of her negotiating skills too many times to miss the subtle signals. "I've got to go."

"Don't drive too far tonight."

"You've been a rock for this family since it first formed. Keep them together and strong."

"We'll be waiting for you to come back." She framed his face with her hands. "And if you're gone too long, we'll come find you."

He loved her for having become his family.

She hugged him. "Find your answers, Stephen."

He hugged her back. "Later, Kate," he whispered.

He walked to his car. His bags were in the trunk. On the seat beside him were a map and a very old note from Jennifer. "Stephen, this spot has to be seen to be appreciated. Remember the church in the southwest with the spiral staircase, built without a single nail? I met a man who built a modern day one like it. You'll need your sketch book." The note was over ten years old, and he could still hear Jennifer's joy even in her written words.

Jennifer had given him a place to begin his wandering. The O'Malleys would be fine. They had found others to share their lives with. He was the last with a restlessness inside that would not settle. He'd spent his life, first as a fireman and then as a paramedic, pouring his efforts into rescuing people. *I'm the one who needs rescuing now.* He wanted a job as far away from life-and-death decisions as he could get. He'd never figured out what it was he was after. It was time to find out.

He drove north.

The publisher would love to hear your
comments about this book. *Please contact us at:*
www.deefiction.com

Dear Reader,

Thank you for reading this story. Rachel O'Malley has been my partner throughout the O'Malley series, helping me understand her family that she loves and knows so well. Cole is the man I instinctively knew had the depth and patience for Rachel and the burdens she carries for others. They were a wonderful couple to get to know through the two books *The Protector* and *The Healer*. It was a pleasure to write their love story.

Disasters happen all around us each year, and the first responders that arrive to help—firemen, police, paramedics, and Red Cross volunteers—make the critical difference in how people recover. I'm pleased to know there are many like Rachel setting aside creature comforts and sleep to be there for others in need.

This was also by far the hardest O'Malley book to write. Jennifer is the special O'Malley, the youngest, and her death hit not only this family, but also the author, hard. I believe God heals. I've seen many examples during my lifetime. For those fighting cancer today I offer the hope of James chapter 5—prayer has great power. I know the story with Jennifer getting well would have been very powerful. But I chose instead to let her die, for death is the one thing everyone fears: dying alone, afraid, before we are ready, leaving things undone. I wanted to let Jennifer show us how to handle those last days, to be an example of living life so you do not have regrets at the end. I know firsthand that Jesus is able to carry us through floodwaters and tragedies, unbearable pain and overpowering grief. He's trustworthy with the deepest hurts of our lives. It's a bittersweet parting as she enters heaven for a joyful eternity and the other O'Malleys now must adapt to the loss.

I hope you'll join me for Stephen's story in *The Rescuer*. He already lost a birth sister to death, now Jennifer is gone, and he's feeling bereft inside. The O'Malleys have stuck together for years, but Stephen is running now…from the pain, from the grief, from himself. The other O'Malleys are going to have to find him, for he isn't sure he ever wants to come back. He's looking for anonymity and space. Only he's about to run into Meghan.

As always, I love to hear from my readers. Feel free to write me at:

Dee Henderson
c/o Multnomah Fiction • P.O. Box 1720 • Sisters, Oregon 97759
e-mail: dee@deehenderson.com
or on-line: http://www.deehenderson.com

Thanks again for letting me share Rachel and Cole's story.
God Bless,

Dee Henderson

book six

THE
RESCUER

"I came that they may have life,
and have it abundantly."

John 10:10

⚍⚍⚍

Paramedic Stephen O'Malley drove north from Chicago the night of June 25, leaving behind life as he knew it. The wipers pushed rain off the windshield, but even on high they gave a clear view of the road for only a few seconds. Cars ahead were visible as red diffuse taillights that occasionally brightened as drivers touched their brakes.

A semi with a trailer rolled past him, throwing water up in a sheet across his windshield. For several seconds he was effectively blind as the wipers struggled to shove the water off. As the deluge cleared, the semi pulled over into his lane. The trailer crossed too far and went into the edge of the roadside. Gravel peppered his car. Stephen immediately slowed, trying to avoid an accident.

He didn't want to die on a stretch of highway tonight. One funeral in a day was enough. It had been overcast at his sister's graveside this morning. By the time the O'Malley family dinner broke up, a heavy drizzle hung in the air. He should have known the weather would turn into a thunderstorm during his drive.

Stephen reached down and changed the radio station, looking for talk radio and a distraction. The oak casket he'd helped carry from the church to the waiting hearse and then to the graveside had been too light. Even with the weight of the casket, it was impossible to hide the fact Jennifer died a shadow of herself. She'd lost a hard fought battle with cancer, convinced until the final weeks that God would work a miracle and heal her. A senseless faith. Stephen shoved a button on the radio to change to a different station. He wasn't going to think about Jennifer. He'd just start fighting tears again.

Wind gusts struck the driver's side of the car. Stephen spotted a blue exit sign advertising gas, food, and hotels and hit the turn signal. He needed a break. If he planned to drive all night, at some point he would need a full tank of gas and something cold to drink. It might as well be now.

He chose a gas station with a canopy over the pumps and a general store for supplies. He topped off the gas tank, checked the oil and fluids, then went inside to pay. The place was deserted but for one other person paying at the register and the sound of a radio announcer listing sports scores.

He wasn't hungry, but food would help keep him awake. He stopped at the self-serve counter in the center of the store under a sign advertising chili by the pint. He could hear Jennifer reminding him about the inevitable heartburn. He shook his head and moved past the kettle.

He had a choice between a Polish sausage spinning on a heat rack that looked as if it had been there for hours or a cold deli sandwich that he couldn't identify. He slid open the cover, used tongs to pick up the Polish, and stuffed it in a hot-dog bun. Onions, pickles, and hot mustard made the meat disappear. A store special offered the drink for an extra fifty cents. He tugged a large blue cup from the stack, set it under the dispenser, and was generous with the ice. The Diet Pepsi was sputtering with air so he added regular Pepsi to fill the cup. At least the plastic lid fit. He tucked a straw in his pocket.

The clerk rang up the items. Stephen added a newspaper to the stack.

"It's a bad night for driving. They're saying this rain will get worse before it gets better."

Stephen pulled bills from his wallet. "At least there's less traffic." He pulled change from his shirt pocket, and as he did so green M&M's tumbled into his hand. For a moment Stephen simply looked at them. He rubbed his thumb across the chocolates, turning two of them over. Ann's son Nathan had been sitting on his lap after dinner, having M&M's for dessert. The child provided a welcome distraction from the solemnity of the funeral meal. Nathan had picked out the blue ones for himself and shared the green. Stephen hadn't even realized. *You're so precious, little man.*

Stephen slipped the M&M's back in his pocket. Jennifer would have been pleased to know that Ann had brought her two children to join the dinner. It was a meal where the boys had to be on their best behavior, but they didn't grasp—nor should they—the reality of death and the loss it brought. That empty chair at the table where Jennifer had once sat haunted Stephen through the meal. The boys' presence had indeed been a welcome distraction.

Life went on.

He took the receipt and nodded his thanks.

Wind whipped the bag as he stepped outside. He turned his shoulder into it and walked to his car. He tossed a roll of paper towels on his jacket in the backseat. The Emergency Medical Services patch on the left sleeve had come up in one corner, and the EMS logo on the back of the jacket was encircled with fluorescent orange tape rubbed nearly through in spots.

He had grabbed the jacket out of habit rather than need. The leave of absence from his paramedic job was open-ended. His boss avoided accepting his resignation, and Stephen had conceded the theoretical possibility that he would change his mind.

He had spent a lifetime rescuing people. The last few months had left him with the certain knowledge that he couldn't carry the weight anymore. He didn't want his pager going off. He didn't want to face another person injured, bleeding, and trying not to die. Stephen was done with it. The profession that had been his career for the last decade no longer appealed to him.

He parked near the exit so he could note down the gas, mileage, and date.

Where was he going? He picked up the map, studying it in the dim overhead light. He was driving north, with no particular plan except to be out of the state by morning. He just wanted—no, needed—some space. The decision had been coming for years.

What would his family be saying right now? "He's hurting...give him space...let's call him tomorrow." Kate had nearly strangled him when she asked him not to go, or to at least let her come along as navigator. As if she could navigate any better than he could. Outside the city she was notorious for getting lost. He smiled as he chose the road he'd take, then folded the map. If it wasn't for the fact she was married, he would have said yes just for the pleasure of her company.

The bond between the seven O'Malleys went deep. At the orphanage where they had first met, family was nonexistent. They had chosen to become their own family and decided on the last name O'Malley. Now with Jennifer's death there was an undercurrent of fear that the bond between them would change in unpredictable ways, would not hold.

Maybe he was the first sign that it was breaking.

He was thirty minutes away from family and already wondered what he was doing. He rubbed the back of his neck. He could turn around and go back. His family wouldn't pry that much. They'd just swallow him back into their fold and do everything they could to try to help him.

He couldn't go back. He loved the O'Malleys. He just didn't think he could handle being around them for the next few months. He was the odd man out. They were all couples now and he was still unattached. They had all recently come to believe in God, and he didn't want to explore the matter. They said Jennifer was in a better place, talking about heaven as if it was real. Maybe it was, but it didn't change the fact that his sister was gone.

For all his discussions with Jennifer about the subject before she died, the reality of her absence overrode any comfort that nebulous concept of heaven gave.

He pulled back onto the highway. He was going to drive and see the country until he found a sense of peace, and if it took a year, then so be it.

The flashing lights in the rearview mirror caught his attention—the blue and red medley bright in the rain—and then the sound of emergency sirens reached him. Stephen pulled to the right lane. The word *ambulance* on the front of the vehicle grew larger as it approached.

The vehicle rushed past.

Ten minutes later highway traffic began to slow, and then both lanes of cars ground to a halt. Stephen eventually reached the spot where a cop was directing traffic to the far left lane. The ambulance, lights still flashing, was angled in ahead of a fire engine crowding the right lane.

A trailer that had broken free from a semi lay overturned in the road and a smashed-in car had taken a nosedive into the ditch. Through the rain he could see the firefighters working to extract a passenger from the car. *Remove the window before you force that door.* The frame was crumpled to the B-Pillar that went from the undercarriage to the roof and provided structural support for the door frames. If the firefighter popped that door before he took care of the window, they would be working on an extraction while kneeling in shattered glass.

He should stop and offer to help. Stephen didn't act on the fleeting thought. He knew what to do—they probably did too—and if they didn't, they had to learn somehow. Most rescue skills came from hard-won experience. He couldn't rescue everyone in the world who got into trouble. He had tried and it about killed him.

The cop finally signaled his lane of traffic forward. Stephen made one last assessment of the wreck as he slowly passed by. In another lifetime he'd written the book on vehicle extraction. The paramedics were bringing in the backboard and just about had the victim free.

He turned his attention back to the road.

He owed Jennifer. She had asked that he be happy, settled, and at peace with life. She had pushed her version of a solution—encouraging him to settle down with Ann and to come to church, but he wasn't able to believe as she longed for, and she hadn't lived long enough to see him settled down, even if he'd been inclined to do so. He had let her down. And it hurt.

Jenny, I already miss you something terrible. Why did you have to die?

Silent tears slid down his cheeks, and he wiped them away.

He pulled out a bottle of aspirin from the glove box and dumped two tablets into his left hand. He popped them in his mouth, grimaced at the taste, and picked up his soda. The sides of the cup were sweating and the paper was getting soft. He took two long draws on the straw to wash down the tablets.

His phone rang for the fourth time. Stephen looked over at it. He had a feeling the caller wouldn't give up, so he flipped the phone open with one hand. "Yes?"

"Stephen?"

Meghan Delhart's voice was like the brush of angel's wings over a bruise, a tender balm to a painful hurt. His hand tightened on the steering wheel and he glanced in the rearview mirror to make sure he could slow down without causing problems for someone driving too close to his car. He dropped his speed another five miles per hour. "Hey there, beautiful." Meghan had been at Jennifer's visitation last night.

"You were on my mind and I took a chance you'd still be up. It sounds like you're on the road somewhere."

"Just driving, thinking." She would understand what he didn't say. There had been nights when she walked out of a shift as an ER nurse not sure whether she wanted to go home, let alone back to work. He'd often played checkers with her on the ambulance gurney while he followed up on the patients he'd brought in.

If anyone had a right to complain about life, it was Meghan. She'd run away for a year in her own way after her car accident and its aftermath. She retreated to live with her parents and told friends not to visit. She went away to lick her wounds, and when the year was over, she came back at peace, with no signs of how hard the transition had been. He envied her strength. If Meghan could adapt to the tragedies that came in life, so could he. Jennifer was gone. He had to live with it.

"How far are you planning to drive?"

"Until sleep says find a hotel." He changed the radio station he was listening to. "I took a leave of absence from work."

She let that sink in. "That might be good."

He rolled his right shoulder. Good, bad, it just was. He didn't have the emotional energy to handle the job right now.

"Are you driving through rain? The storm is getting close here."

"Wind driven rain," he confirmed. "Where are you staying?" She'd come into town for the funeral, so she must still be in the area.

"I borrowed the keys to my grandparents' vacation place in Whitfield."

Whitfield…he finally placed it on his mental map. She was about twenty minutes northwest of his position. The storm must be tracking her direction.

"I have a love-hate relationship with storms."

He heard the tension in her voice. "I know," he said gently. About all she remembered of the night of her accident was the lightning and the thunder. The majority of her prior week—and most of the following several days—had been wiped out of her memory and never returned.

"You okay, Meghan?" He was reluctant to get pulled into it tonight, but the fact that she wasn't asking drew the words out.

At twelve she had worn reading glasses, her nose often in a book, and had a habit of mixing up her *r*s and *w*s when she tried to speak fast. She was one of his first friends from the neighborhood around the orphanage, an endearing one in an embarrassing kind of way for a preteen boy teased about hanging out with a girl by his friends. He hadn't realized until he spotted her across the room last night just how much he missed her.

"I'll be okay when this storm blows over." She turned her radio to match his station. "I'm going back to Silverton tomorrow. Dad is coming in to pick me up."

"Do you want to go tonight? I'll give you a lift if you like."

"I don't need rescuing, Stephen."

He smiled. "Maybe I do."

She was quiet a moment. "You wouldn't mind?"

"I wouldn't mind."

And as she hesitated, he hoped she would say yes. Meghan was one of few outside his family who he fully trusted to understand his mood on a night like tonight.

"Yes, I'd appreciate a lift. I'm already packed, and I won't be able to sleep with this storm overhead."

"Then I'm on the way." Stephen picked up the map to figure out how to get off this highway and over to her area.

"Would you like coffee or tea?" Meghan asked.

"I'd love a cup of your tea with honey and cinnamon."

"It will be waiting. I'll turn on the driveway lights and leave the back door unlocked. Come on in so you don't get drenched."

"I'll be there soon."

He set down the phone. Meghan had talked him out of running away once before. He doubted she could do it again, but he at least wanted to say how much he appreciated her coming to town for the visitation. They were friends, and destined to always be just friends given he hadn't been smart enough to settle down with her when he had the chance—and life rarely gave second chances.

His life was littered with *if onlys*.

He would give Meghan a lift home and then continue with his drive. If he let himself start grieving the past, the pain would never end. One of those *if onlys* had nearly cost Meghan her life.

ONE

FIVE YEARS EARLIER

CHICAGO
Friday, August 16

Stephen parked the ambulance next to a police squad car in the parking lot across from the county building and confirmed his location with dispatch. He'd dropped off his partner Ryan at the gym down the street to take a much needed shower. A happy drunk staggering home at 6 A.M. had lost most of his last beer across Ryan's shirt. It already had the makings of an interesting Friday shift.

The heat hit him as he stepped from the vehicle. It was a day that would send tempers flaring somewhere in the city, and his squad would be sent to patch up the results of the inevitable fights. Stephen hoped they didn't get a DOA run: He'd had enough dead-on-arrival calls to last the year. He spent his days dealing with car accidents, heart attacks, gunshot victims, and drug overdoses. He didn't need some rookie cop trying to comfort the family calling him out to a victim with no pulse whose body was cold and stiff. This job wore at him enough without adding the strain of having to tell people they were looking at a corpse.

Stephen shoved his hands into his pockets and tried to force himself out of the morbid mood. Last night's dispatch to a man who had died hours before lingered in his mind like some dark dangerous cloud. Being a paramedic might be a noble profession, but it didn't run to being a chaplain. He didn't need crying kids and angry spouses shouting at him to do something when it was obvious there was nothing he could do. The voices had haunted his dreams last night.

What he really needed was a vacation, a nice long pedestrian vacation where no one paged him or, for that matter, knew him. The decision resonated, and he made a mental note to force some time off into his schedule. He loved his job, but there were days he wanted to walk away from it.

Stephen entered the restaurant on the corner and paused in front of the display of pastries and donuts to glance around the tables for his sister Kate. Cops hung out here. He eliminated those in police blues and looked at the remaining ladies. Kate rarely looked like the cop she was. As a hostage negotiator, she tried to downplay any sense of being a threat to the person she was trying to convince to surrender. He didn't see her and was surprised that he had arrived first.

Stephen waved good morning to the owner and walked to Kate's favorite table in the back of the restaurant. She preferred to sit with her back to the wall so no one could come up behind her.

He ordered a sunrise special for himself and, since Kate was a creature of habit, ordered blueberry pancakes and coffee for her. He'd learned to eat early and well as time for lunch in his job was never a given. He turned up the sound on his radio. Kate was rarely late unless she was out on an assignment somewhere. There had been too many close calls with her lately. The last thing he needed was his sister getting herself shot.

He was on his second cup of coffee when she arrived. Kate wore jeans and a pale blue shirt and carried a folded newspaper under her arm. He rose and pulled out the chair for her. She had been out in the sun this morning—the beginning of a sunburn was showing on her face and she had the glow of sweat on her skin. Since she hated early mornings, he guessed she'd been on a call somewhere in the city.

He could feel the heat coming from her back as she took her seat, and the sun had lightened a few more strands of her hair. He was constantly tugging a baseball cap on her to keep her from getting sunstroke on the job. She tossed her newspaper onto the table. "Thanks."

"I'm glad you could make it." Stephen sat back down. "I already ordered for you."

"Great. I needed this break." Kate dipped a napkin in her glass of water and used the wet corner to clean her sunglasses. "The heat is getting to people. We had an incident at a manufacturing plant this morning, and I spent two hours leaning in a window to have a conversation with a guy."

He pushed five sugar packets across the table for her coffee. "Did it end okay?"

She glanced up and smiled at his question; he had to smile back.

"It was the usual supervisor-employee fight that just kept building until they threw a few punches and then the employee pulled a gun." She set down the sunglasses. "He talked with his kids and apologized for a fight with them the night before, released his supervisor, then gave himself up. The gun turned out not to be loaded. I would have resolved it in an hour, but the supervisor wouldn't keep his mouth shut. Even *I* felt like hitting the guy at one point, so I can understand how the fight got started."

She dumped four packets of sugar in her coffee, tasted it, and added a fifth.

"You're going to make yourself hyper drinking that."

"Sugar is my one vice and I'm sticking to it." She propped her elbows on the table, steepled her fingers, and pointed at him. "Your call this morning was a surprise. What's happening, Stephen?"

"I need a favor."

She tilted her head to the side. "I'm always good for one."

"It's not difficult—I need you to meet Lisa at the airport for me tonight. She's carrying bones back with her and needs an extra hand." Their sister Lisa was a forensic pathologist for the city coroner's office. She'd been working for weeks to figure out how a Jane Doe had died and decided it was time to consult the experts at the Smithsonian. It got a little complex explaining to airport personnel and taxi drivers why she was hauling around boxes of bones.

"Sure, I'll meet her. Have you got other plans?"

"A date."

Kate's expression shifted from amusement to interest. "A good thing to have on a Friday night. Do I know her?"

"Maybe...Paula Lewis. I've had to cancel on her twice when a dispatch held me up, and it hasn't been easy to get her to say yes again. I'm going to make it up to her tonight."

"Paula's a nice lady, if you like doctors."

He smiled at the qualification. "Very nice." Their sister Jennifer was a pediatrician and therefore an exception, but beyond that Kate did her best to avoid those in the medical profession and their inevitable work-related conversations.

The restaurant owner brought their breakfasts and paused to chat with Kate. News affecting the city in general and the police department specifically was debated here long before it reached the watercooler at the precinct.

Stephen spread jelly on his toast and listened to his sister's intense talk about work. Kate was the heart, soul, and passion of the O'Malleys. When someone in the family needed an advocate, she was the one they turned to.

He couldn't imagine life without Kate in it. Having lost his little sister Peg in a drowning accident and his parents in a car accident by the time he was eleven, he'd been convinced at an early age that he was destined to lose people he cared about. He'd been feeling pretty grim at Trevor House until Kate came crashing into his life. She had practically dared him to try to get rid of her. Her tenacious leading with her chin, her I'm-in-your-life, deal-with-it attitude had slipped under his guard like nothing else ever could. He loved her for it.

The conversation broke up and Kate turned her attention to her breakfast. "So what have you been up to lately besides convincing Paula to give you another chance?"

He opened his shirt pocket and tugged out a checker piece he had carved. "Another one for your collection." They would have enough to play a game soon.

She studied both sides of the checker. "You're getting really good at the detail work."

"The whittling is a challenge. It's certainly tougher than hanging drywall." On his days off he gutted and remodeled old homes. He enjoyed the carpentry work. It didn't wear at his emotions the way being a paramedic did.

She tucked the piece in her pocket. Kate's eyes narrowed as she looked over his shoulder.

He knew better than to turn and look. Her face turned impassive. At her simple shift-to-work mode, Stephen slid his plate aside. The more impassive she got, the more dangerous she was. "Cool off, Kate."

Her gaze met his and the anger in her eyes had him leaning back. "That cop nearly cost me a child's life."

"You look like you're ready to deck him."

"Maybe serve him my breakfast in his lap." She picked up her water glass. "We had a custody blowup last week. A dad took his daughter from school during recess and holed up at his place, threatening to kill her rather than let his wife have custody. I got called in. That patrol officer nearly gave away the SWAT team position when he decided to get some media airtime and describe what had happened and his role in it."

"Not everyone avoids media like you do."

"He's not a rookie; he knows better."

Stephen reached over and loosened her fist. Whoever made the mistake of thinking Kate was not a cop down to her marrow didn't understand what drove her. Justice for her was very black and white. "Let it go."

Peg's drowning had driven him to be a paramedic, and Kate had also made the decision to be a cop at an early age.

"You're right. He's not worth it." Her tension turned to a hard smile. "He's a little out of his normal patrol area. He probably has a meeting with my boss to discuss the incident. He won't feel like stopping to eat afterward."

Stephen smiled. "That's better. Your optimism is back."

"It's going to be one of those Fridays. I can feel it."

"I hope you're wrong."

His radio sounded. Stephen pushed back his chair and stood. He set money on the table and leaned over to kiss Kate's cheek. "I've gotta go. See you around this weekend."

"I want to hear about this date, Stephen."

Knowing the O'Malley family grapevine, it would be common knowledge soon after it was over. "As if I could keep it from you. Stay safe, Kate."

"I'll do my best."

Stephen headed back to the ambulance. He stayed in Chicago because of Kate. He didn't bother to tell her that, but she probably already knew. Someone needed to watch her back, and their oldest brother Marcus who normally filled that role was working in the U.S. Marshal's office in Washington, D.C. After Kate was married and had someone else around to watch her back, he'd think more seriously about moving on. He would find a small town with a lake where he could cultivate his love of fishing and find an EMS job where he'd treat more bee stings and heart attacks than gunshot wounds. He liked the certainty of having that dream even if he didn't have a plan to act on yet.

His partner Ryan was towel drying his hair. The ambulance passenger door was open but Ryan stood outside. The heat built up inside the metal box fast.

"I'll drive," Stephen said. His new partner was still learning Chicago's streets. Ryan tossed his towel across the hot leather seat. "Fine with me."

Dispatch assigned them to a code three run—a transport from Memorial Hospital to Lutheran General—so Stephen didn't bother with the lights and sirens. It was probably a high-risk pregnancy being moved to the specialized maternity unit. He'd almost rather deal with a gunshot victim than a woman in labor. They averaged two pregnancy runs a month where a lady mis-timed the pace of her contractions and left going to the hospital a little too late. Infants were hard to handle in a moving vehicle that was never designed to be a delivery room. At least with pregnancy runs, one of the nurses from the maternity ward rode along to be safe.

Stephen pulled in to Memorial Hospital and looked around at the vehicles. He didn't see Meghan's jeep. There was family, there were girlfriends, and then there was Meghan. The ER nurse was in a class by herself.

"She must still be on night shifts," Ryan commented.

Stephen glanced over, his right eyebrow raised a fraction.

"Meghan. That *is* who you're looking for, isn't it?"

"She's just an old friend."

Ryan laughed. "If you say so, O'Malley." He tugged run sheets from the folder under the seat. "Let's go find our pregnant lady. I'm guessing triplets."

"Lunch says it's twins trying to come early."

"You're on. And if I'm right, I'm driving and you can ride the back bench with her."

SILVERTON, ILLINOIS

Craig Fulton opened the door to Neil Coffer's jewelry store Friday afternoon and heard familiar chimes signal his entrance. He walked through the store past the display counters and the spin racks of postcards of famous jewelry to the door in the back of the store marked employees only. Ignoring the restriction, he walked through to the repair shop.

In a tourist town the size of Silverton, the jewelry Neil sold attracted more look-ers than buyers. Not many farmers and small business owners could afford an antique bracelet that started in the thousands or a modern necklace that cost five figures. Fortunately, Neil also had a thriving jewelry repair business that paid the bills. Orders to jewelry stores around the state were stacked on the side counter, already prepared for Fed-Ex to pick up.

Craig waited until Neil looked up from the large magnifying glass and the piece he was working on. Neil hated to be interrupted while a repair was underway, and Craig had no desire to get on his bad side today. Hunched over the workbench the man looked more like ninety than seventy-five. He was a chain smoker and time had not been kind. How the man ever sold any jewelry was a mystery. He hadn't smiled since the Nixon era. When he did unwillingly part with a piece, he hardly offered much of a bargain.

Neil lifted the diamond from the ring with tweezers and placed it in a small ceramic dish inside a box labeled: Mrs. Heather Teal. Only one customer's piece was allowed on the repair bench at a time, and the smooth metal work area was lined with a ridge to prevent a stone from rolling off onto the floor. Rumors circulated that Neil had been a forger for the army during the cold war, making documents to allow soldiers to move around behind enemy lines, and Craig tended to believe it.

Neil finished his task and closed the box holding Mrs. Teal's work order. He walked to the east wall of the room and opened the door to the walk-in safe. When Neil had bought the old bank building, he turned its massive walk-in vault into a storage place for his jewelry.

Someone had robbed Neil two years ago, taking the pieces in the front room display cases. During the trial a year later, it had come out that the pieces in the display cases were actually excellent fakes of the real pieces Neil kept stored in the safe. When he went back to box a sold item, he retrieved the actual piece.

Some of the town residents had been impressed that he didn't leave out valuable pieces to be taken; others were embarrassed over raving about a fake diamond's size and clarity. The defense counsel had tried to argue that Neil was actually selling fakes and his client was wrongly charged. But the few pieces sold over the years to townspeople had all proven to be real diamonds, emeralds, and rubies, so the accusations didn't stick.

Craig had thought more than once about stealing Neil's real gems as a way to finance leaving town for good. He gave up that idea when he realized Neil kept the vault locked when he wasn't using it, had a loaded handgun under the counter, and had mirrors and cameras set around the rooms to let him see what went on at all times.

Neil brought back a small black box from the safe. Craig set his briefcase on the counter, opened it, then Neil put the box inside.

"You have Jonathan's directions?" Neil pulled an envelope from under the counter and added it to the briefcase.

Craig nodded. "I meet him at his hotel room in downtown Chicago at midnight. I'll be back here no later than 5 A.M."

Neil stared at him, and Craig felt sweat trickle down his back.

"The back door will be unlocked. I'll be waiting for you."

Craig nodded and closed the briefcase. He would consider double-crossing a lot of people, but Neil was not one of them. The man was just crazy enough to be unpredictable.

CHICAGO

The ambulance smelled like disinfectant by midafternoon. Stephen wiped down the gurney with warm water. It never failed to amaze him where blood ended up. The last transport had been a simple nosebleed, but neither ice nor pressure had stopped it. The doctors would have to pack it off. Now the ambulance was parked in Memorial Hospital's side parking lot while they cleaned the rig and restocked supplies.

Ryan closed drawers and locked the drug cabinet that held the morphine and Valium. Including those vials in the red medical case they carried with them to a scene just meant someone would inevitably grab the case and run. "We're in pretty good shape." Ryan passed over the clipboard. "Sign on page four and six and initial nine."

Stephen tugged a pen from his pocket, read the pages, then scrawled his signature. "Add another O_2 cylinder and a replacement nebulizer, and see about a dozen more biohazard bags. We've got a persistent sharps problem by the end of the shift." He'd nearly stuck himself with a used needle that had been slid into a discarded IV tubing for lack of something proper to encapsulate it.

Ryan nodded and took the pad. "I'll go sweet-talk Supply for us." He stepped down from the ambulance and headed toward the hospital.

Stephen wiped down the storage cabinets under the bench, then rubbed sweat off his face with the back of his sleeve.

"Maybe this will help."

He glanced to the back of the ambulance and set down the rag to take the large glass of ice water. "Thanks, Meghan." He wondered if she was working today. He leaned over to touch the sleeve of her uniform. The white fabric still had a pressed crease in it. "Air-conditioning. I'm jealous."

She laughed and perched on the bumper. "It's actually a bit chilly inside. Guys have an advantage—you look good sweaty."

He drained the entire glass then removed a piece of ice to rub on the back of his neck. She definitely did not look wilted. He flipped water from the melting ice at her and then set aside the glass.

It was nice having her back in his life. Her family had moved away from the Trevor House neighborhood when he was fifteen, and it wasn't until she was in nursing school that they'd been able to catch up on their old friendship.

She leaned into the ambulance to look at the roof, getting in his way and nearly dragging her hair in the dirty water. "Where is this bullet hole I heard about?"

He shifted her away from trouble and pointed toward the front of the ambulance. "The guys on last night's shift had an interesting time." They had been trying to treat a gunshot victim and had come under fire from shooters on the roof of a building across the street. It was a sad day when an ambulance wasn't considered an out-of-bounds target.

"If it rains tonight it's going to drip in here."

"Ryan is getting us some patching material. You think it's going to rain and break this heat?"

"Ken thinks so. He's predicting four inches of rain, with heavy winds and unusually strong lightning."

Stephen hoped her cousin was at least partially right. They needed rain.

"According to his forecasts, it will probably blow in around 7 P.M. and last well into the night." Meghan reached for the lotion he kept in the cleaning supply case and rubbed it liberally into her hands. "I'm going storm chasing with him tomorrow. I want a tornado picture for my wall and am determined to get it this year."

"Quit wishing for trouble, Meghan, and drive carefully tonight. You'll be heading right into the rain."

"I get off at six. I'll either go before the rain arrives or wait until the worst of it passes."

"Just don't chase lightning when you can't find your tornado. I want you coming back as you are, not with lightning curled hair."

She laughed and tugged over the supply case to help him out.

Stephen was beginning to suspect she had a boyfriend in Silverton given how many trips home she made, but he drew the line at probing the subject. If he knew a name then he'd have to go check the guy out to make sure he was good enough for her, and that would cross the line into meddling. At least she was smart enough not to say yes to some of the doctors around here who asked her out. Meghan wasn't a city girl at heart, and it would do her good to find someone back in Silverton, move home, and work in her father's medical practice. She talked about it often enough. A house, babies, and working with her dad. The girl had good dreams.

His phone rang in his shirt pocket. He'd just plunged his hand into the bucket of water. He looked around for his towel and scowled when he saw it already pitched in the laundry bag.

Meghan solved the problem by reaching over and tugging out his phone. "Hi, you've reached Stephen's secretary." She grinned and leaned against the bench, lifting one foot up onto the bumper. "Hi there, Jennifer. Your brother is cleaning up the rig at the moment and making faces at me."

It was unusual to hear from Jennifer in the middle of the day. Stephen opened a new roll of paper towels. Meghan covered the phone. "Are you interested in a twenty-one-inch painting of a fish?"

He held out his hand. "Jack will love it for his birthday."

"Oh, that's awful and so perfect." Meghan passed him the phone.

"Hi, Jen. Yes, buy and ship it."

"It comes close to matching that set of painted eggshell salt and pepper shakers he gave you last year. I saw this and thought of you," Jennifer said.

"You're flea market shopping?"

"I'm making a house call on a fourteen-year-old who likes to paint. She's actually pretty good. The fish painting, however, was a joke for her brother, and in the end she couldn't go through with wrapping it."

"I love this kid. Trust me; I'll have no problem giving it to Jack."

The radio up front sounded dispatch tones. "Jen, I've gotta go."

Meghan scrambled off the bumper and grabbed the bucket of water. "I'll dump this for you."

"Thanks, Meg." Stephen shoved back supply cases and slammed doors. He piled into the driver's seat while Ryan ran out the ER doors and scrambled into the passenger seat.

Ryan called up the address and details. "A fire on Lexington Street. Better rush it. They've already gone to a second alarm so it must be big."

Stephen punched on the lights.

Meghan stood holding the bucket and watched the ambulance pull out. The man needed a haircut. She had to think of *something* that could be improved on, for the bottom line was when Stephen smiled at her, her day turned over. That smile made it impossible to look away. Then he'd notice she was looking at him that way and his eyes would fill with laughter. He'd inevitably tease her about it.

He didn't see her as anything but a friend. It was for the best: Stephen wasn't interested in settling down. As far as she knew he had never set foot inside a church, and she couldn't imagine him ever being content to live in a small town that only had a volunteer EMS crew. She'd watched him grow into a tall strong handsome guy who inspired confidence by his presence. His years as a fireman had forged his muscles into an impressive build, and the last years as a paramedic had added a touch of gray now streaking through his brown hair. She watched him play basketball with his brothers and thought he was the best looking of the O'Malley guys. She was probably a bit prejudiced there.

Meghan washed out the bucket with the garden hose hidden by the planters and flipped it upside down to dry. She lifted a hand to the cop car pulling into the circular drive. She hoped Stephen's date with Paula Lewis fell through again. The doctor was nice and likely to turn Stephen's head, but she was heading to California in a couple months to take a position with a university medical group. Meghan didn't want to listen to Stephen's inevitable, "I miss her" remarks.

The guy was lonely. She knew him too well not to know that. He always kept dating relationships casual and short. Her mom said he wasn't yet ready to risk his heart—with people or with God. Maybe Mom was right and it was time to let go of her teenage crush. It just felt like a failure to give up on him.

"You know he likes you."

Meghan glanced at Kate O'Malley who was strolling over from the hospital side entrance. "I saw the ambulance heading out," Kate explained.

Meghan grimaced. "Stephen still sees me as a twelve-year-old."

"Not entirely. He just doesn't think about dating old friends." Kate draped an arm around her shoulders in a show of sympathy. "He notices when you're not at work, keeps tabs on your travels, comments when you are happy or sad. You're in a class by yourself. Think of Stephen as a tree that is inevitably going to fall hard someday. He's looking for something without realizing it's right in front of him."

"Right now I just want him to notice me so I can turn him down."

Kate laughed. "That's my Meg."

"How's the hand?"

Kate moved her bruised fingers. "The ice helped. Next time a kid slams my hand in a door, I'm asking for hazard pay. Come on, let's get a late lunch."

Meghan took one last look at where the ambulance had disappeared and nodded. Stephen would be back after he rescued someone. He just didn't seem to realize how much he needed rescuing himself.

SILVERTON

Ken hung up the phone in his home office and jotted down Friday's temperature and humidity numbers called in from the barge floating down the Mississippi. The captain was a fellow amateur weatherman. The weather map on Ken's table showed isometric lines coming close together at Davenport. The coming storm tonight would be big. He had to get out there. His phone rang as he packed his camera bag. The name on the caller ID urged him to answer. "Are we on, hon?"

"Two weeks in the Bahamas." His wife bubbled with the news. "Mom loved the idea of coming back to work for a couple weeks. I told you she was bored," JoAnne said. "She'll handle the store. You want me to call and confirm the tickets?"

"Absolutely. Neil said he'd buy the brooch himself if he couldn't find an immediate buyer for it. Book the tickets and I'll stop by to see Neil this afternoon then make the bank deposit."

"I'm so excited about this."

Ken folded the latest weather map and slid it in his case. "You found the locket and brooch, hon. You should get the vacation of your dreams as a reward. That and a new dishwasher."

"We might get more for the pieces if we waited a while to sell them."

"We weren't expecting to find real jewelry in that music box in the attic. There's no use being greedy. We'll keep the locket, sell the brooch, and enjoy the honeymoon we never had."

"Okay, I'm calling. Are you going storm chasing?"

"Just for an hour. I'll be back before you get home from work."

"Is Meghan coming home or should I call to tell her the news?"

"She's driving down tonight." His cousin and wife had been best friends since high school.

"I get her for shopping tomorrow. You'll have to take her storm chasing another day."

"How about a trip to Davenport to shop, then we can keep going to get some pictures?"

"If the sky looks interesting," JoAnne compromised. "I'll see you in a couple hours."

"Love ya, JoAnne. Drive careful."

Some things were too valuable to trust to the jewelry store vault. Neil returned the workbench to its original position and carried the hidden ledger over to his desk.

A brooch and a locket… He had to turn the pages back to 1982 to find the pieces. They had been stolen from a couple at the Wilshire hotel in Chicago during a false fire alarm, and excellent fakes were substituted for the genuine pieces. He vaguely remembered the theft…it had been so very long ago. There was no star by the line to indicate the theft had ever been discovered and a police report filed. The lady or her heirs probably still thought they had the real stones. It was rare for one of his substitute pieces to hold up for twenty years, but it was possible if they were in an unopened jewelry box or a safe deposit box.

He never sold the originals until the thefts were at least a decade cold and never in the same state as they were taken from. Stashing the brooch and locket in the music box as a place to let them cool off had been a bad move. He didn't know when his wife gave away the music box, or to whom, but it eventually ended up in Ken and JoAnne's attic.

It was only the fourth time in years he'd had to buy back a piece he had originally stolen. He would have to do something about that locket. If JoAnne had taken a fancy to wearing it— He had best make another fake piece and recover the original from her. She wasn't the kind of woman to stay in a small town like Silverton when a few hours' drive could have her shopping in Chicago or in Davenport. Someone who knew jewelry would find the piece fascinating, and that locket was in a jewelry catalog as an interesting piece of work by a French artisan. He didn't want a chance question raised.

Neil flipped past pages of entries and wrote a new line for this purchase. Someday he would have to create a list of where exactly he had stashed all the pieces he had cooling off. It was getting rather hard to remember. For security reasons, he had never written down that information. It was one thing to record all he knew about a piece that had been stolen, another to admit he still possessed it. He refused to hide pieces at his store, and safe deposit boxes weren't worth the questions. Everyone in town knew he owned his own vault.

As friends in the business died off, he sold fewer and fewer pieces when they reached their decade cold mark. The new generation of young men willing to move a valuable piece such as those he acquired had no honor, and Neil refused to deal with a man whose word wasn't good for something. He was too old to spend a day in jail, and his wife needed someone around to take care of her.

He sold enough that they never lacked money, and he had enough pieces to last him through a comfortable retirement. But a man had to keep his hand in the game, and occasionally a collection was worth acquiring.

Tonight would be profitable.

He took the ledger back to its resting place. Where should he hide the pieces Craig was bringing back? He needed somewhere special for a special collection.

TWO

CHICAGO

The house on Lexington collapsed on itself, flames raging against multiple streams of water from fire companies fighting it. Stephen watched the fire crews from the comfort of the ambulance left running to keep the air-conditioning on. He was a fireman before training as a paramedic. He knew the risks the guys were in from the flames, steam, and heatstroke. He watched for trouble but was content to be bored. Firemen rescued people; paramedics kept them alive. The profession change gave him the greater challenge.

When the fire was suppressed and they were finally released from the scene, rush hour traffic was well underway. Stephen and Ryan took up station in a grocery store parking lot on the south end of the district waiting for the next call. Stephen remembered why he hated the ambulance passenger seat. His knees were crammed against the dashboard, and he was ready to get out and yank the gray leather seat out of the vehicle to find the broken latch that wouldn't give him another two inches of legroom. Ken had been right about the storm. Heavy rain splattered against the windshield, the noise on the roof like crickets slamming into tin.

Stephen ate a burrito, trying not to mess up his new tie. His dinner with Paula was in two hours, and he was still trying to decide on what to wear. Ryan thought the tie he'd picked up was too upscale for the jeans. A 10-55 dispatch—car wreck with injuries—came as Stephen finished his late lunch. "There's construction on Cline. You'd better come in from the north on Lewis," Stephen recommended, picking up the radio to confirm their ETA with dispatch. "Unit 59, Roger code one to Cline and Lewis."

Ryan punched on the lights and siren and pulled out of the lot. By the time he parked behind cop cars and a fire engine blocking off the accident scene, Stephen's knuckles were white on the dash. His partner did not understand Chicago drivers and actually assumed they would get out of the way for an emergency vehicle. "Nice driving, ace."

Ryan grabbed his slicker. "I learned it from you."

Stephen barked out a laugh, set down his drink, which miraculously hadn't spilled all over his lap, and grabbed his own rain slicker.

A red Honda rested thirty feet across the interchange accordioned into a blue Toyota. A white van with Flowers and Finery painted on the side had come to a violent stop across the concrete median. Broken glass and a debris trail of headlight fragments and muffler parts marked the point of the three-vehicle collision. Stephen spotted two air bags in the Toyota still inflated from their explosive deployment.

Firefighters were clustered around the crushed red Honda and two EMTs were working at the van. Not enough ambulance crews had been dispatched. Stephen got on the radio to request two more.

Ryan opened the rear cabinet and grabbed the blue go-case with the airway supplies and trauma dressings. Stephen pulled out the red case packed with drug and IV supplies. The fire and rescue guys would already have collars, splints, and backboards out.

The fire captain met them. "The van driver had a rack of flower vases crash forward and he's covered in glass. We've got a mother and her young daughter trapped in the Honda—the mom is critical; the girl is stable. The Toyota driver walked away a bit dazed."

Stephen absorbed the information. No fatalities; that was a relief. "Two more ambulances are on the way."

"I'll make sure the cops clear a route out of here."

Stephen nodded and headed toward the crumpled Honda.

The fireman helping the driver made room for him. Thick black rubber mats had been draped over the jagged metal edges to make it possible to reach inside without being cut. As Stephen assessed the unconscious driver's condition, he tried to mentally re-create what would have happened to her during the accident.

Her car had been hit hard from the side. That impact would have caused her to hit the window and then would have flung her to her left. While she was in motion to her left, her car hit the Toyota head-on. He winced. That meant the lady's left side and rib cage would have been exposed when the steering column came back. He felt carefully where he predicted the worst impact. Broken ribs, internal bleeding, and from the sound of her breathing a partially collapsed lung. She was bleeding from a deep gash on her lower abdomen. She didn't respond to his touch—the most dangerous sign of all.

He looked over at the lady's daughter. She was maybe ten, terrified, and because of the way she was pinned, unable to turn her head away from her mom. He smiled, hoping to reassure the child. "My name is Stephen, and my partner Ryan is behind you. We're going to get you out of this car very soon."

"Mom's really hurt."

"And I'm a really good paramedic." He took a few precious seconds to reach across and touch her cheek. "Promise."

〜〜〜

The first car accident victim arrived in the ER at 8:12 P.M., the stretcher pushed in by a paramedic wearing a rain slicker, her partner jogging alongside holding an IV bag up with one hand and steadying their small patient with his other. The sounds and smells from outside rushed in with them: An ambulance pulled out with sirens whooping like a huge bird to warn traffic, rain pounded, and a sweet oily smell hung in the air from the asphalt getting washed for the first time in weeks.

Meghan reached them first, taking the IV bag and scanning the ten-year-old girl's face. They had been warned she was coming in. She smiled at the child who didn't have much left of her hair because a rescue worker had been forced to cut it to extract her from the wreck. The remains of the braid rested like a crushed cord an inch above her left shoulder, the sliced golden strands working their way apart in a frayed mat. The girl had been crying, but she was silent now, her eyes wide, her fear growing.

Meghan leaned in close in order to be heard as they rushed toward exam area two. "Tracy, your mom is coming in the next ambulance. Relax and just listen to the doctor; he's nice. You're going to be fine." There was no time for anything more as the trauma team surrounded the girl.

By the time the lead paramedic was done giving his report, the little one was on oxygen, a warm blanket lay across her chest, and two doctors worked on the right leg splint placed at the scene, a portable X-ray machine moved in to capture an image of the shattered bone.

Another doctor worked on the child's facial lacerations and bruises, talking with her as he did so, the only man in the medley of people who seemed unhurried. The child wasn't dying on him, and Jim had a refined sense of when to expend extra energy. Meghan watched the doctor work and wished she understood how to duplicate that stillness. Her ER shifts felt like twelve hours on adrenaline.

She turned away from the group and shoved back the curtain on exam area four. From the early radioed warnings Tracy's mom had been driving without a seat belt, and it had cost her dearly. Ryan's voice on the call had been shaken. Paramedics saw *everything* in their job. It wouldn't be good. She doubled the amount of gauze set out.

Her shift had ended two hours ago but with the heavy rain she'd stayed where she could do some good. Now she was glad that she had. She heard the sound of the arriving ambulance moments before the doors crashed open. Ryan was pushing the gurney and Stephen was at its side. The water dripping from their jackets trailed back to the door, tinged red with blood. The resident took one look and hollered for Jim to join them.

Meghan pulled on fresh gloves and took up position a step behind Jim's right shoulder as Ryan swiftly gave details. Jim moved the packing to see what Ryan was describing. "Push that blood." His lead trauma nurse was a step ahead of him, already hanging another unit. He looked over at the chief resident. "How's her oxygen?"

"Horrible. Her lungs are collapsed on the left. I'm opening it up." The resident readied a deep needle to pull out the misplaced air. Meghan accepted handfuls of bloody pressure bandages from Jim as he worked, and fed him back clean packing.

A movement of blue caught her attention and Meghan glanced up. Stephen was leaning against the back wall watching them. The front of his shirt was covered with blood and he was still breathing hard. His hands were the only thing clean, for he'd stripped off his gloves. The man looked exhausted. Blue eyes met hers and held a moment, and she saw the depths of what he had seen at the scene.

The wall looked as though it was holding him up; he'd given everything he had. At times Stephen cared too much for his own good. She wished she had a free moment to give him a hug just to ease that look of hurt darkening his eyes.

She turned back to what Jim was doing, focusing on staying a step ahead of him. The odds that Tracy's mom would make it were already improving. Her heartbeat had steadied, her blood pressure was low but stable, and the oxygen in her blood was rising. Stabilize her, get her to surgery, and the specialists in ICU would keep her alive and give her a good chance to heal.

"Let's get her upstairs."

The nurse disconnected cardiac leads and transferred the IV to the hanging stand at the head of the stretcher. Stephen pushed away from the wall and touched a hand to the woman's bare foot as she was pushed by. "Where's her daughter?"

"Exam area two." Meghan bent to pick up one of the many bloody gauze squares that had fallen to the floor. Stephen nodded and walked down to see the child.

Meghan watched him go and hoped he remembered the blood on his shirt before he got there. He paused by a biohazard bag and the blue shirt came off, leaving a gray T-shirt that was wet with rainwater, sweat, or both. He tossed the bloody shirt into the bag and then turned into exam area two.

"He was the one who cut Tracy's hair," she murmured to Ryan.

"Yes. She was pinned looking at her mom. It was the only fast solution we had."

Most paramedics she had figured out pretty early on. They were white knights riding to the rescue, who enjoyed the adrenaline rush of a crisis. Stephen O'Malley was still a mystery. He was emotionally invested in rescuing people yet he was one of the best at the job she had ever met. But for all their history together, his past was at best opaque to her. Sometimes she thought he didn't want to do the job as much as he felt he *had* to do the job.

She tossed another bloody towel into a laundry hamper. Get this cleanup finished, get early word on how the woman's surgery was going, then she could head out. Right now more than anything she wanted to be sharing coffee at the kitchen table with her parents and be back in a world that was normal.

At least there she had the illusion of being safe.

A tap on the dressing room door interrupted his music. "Five minutes, Mr. Peters."

Jonathan didn't bother to answer. The music he would perform tonight was already playing in his mind, and in a brief time he would stride onto the stage and sit at the grand piano and let it spill out before the intimate audience of hundreds. He would prefer thousands but not every orchestra hall was perfect.

He smoothed his tux. The Chicago music critics were out there. He played like a genius and everyone knew it. They would write rave reviews. And tonight after the concert he would put on a world-class performance that no one would see.

He tucked a red rose into his lapel. The lady who had sent the huge bouquet would understand the message. She'd slip away to join him at his suite tonight. And he would do his best to ensure it was a night of romance worthy of good memories. It was the least he could do for one of his admirers.

He couldn't live on love alone and genius wasn't yet paying the bills. Before he left for Europe in the morning, he would acquire the jewels Marie wore. Neil had been pressing lately for a major theft and Jonathan would accommodate him. His cut for the stolen diamonds and emeralds would pay his expenses for the upcoming year. He stole a few gems each year to keep himself in the lifestyle he was accustomed to, and if he had to have a partner, Neil was the right choice. One didn't become an old thief without being smart about details.

If Marie realized the gems she put on tomorrow morning were exquisite fakes, she'd never admit the jewels had been taken at the hotel and by him. Her husband was an angry man and he most certainly would not approve.

"Two minutes, Mr. Peters."

He smiled at himself in the mirror. Yes, tonight would be a golden performance. He could hear the music clearly, and the anticipation of and adrenaline for a night of crime was rising. It was time. He strode down the hall for the stage and toward the welcoming applause.

The surgical waiting room was a quiet place on a Friday night. Stephen nudged a sliver of wood from the disk he was whittling, adding ridges to the outside of the piece.

"You are going to be late for your date," Ryan commented, joining him.

Stephen glanced up from his work. "We're going to meet for a late coffee instead."

Ryan set the folder on the bench. "I handed the keys off to the next shift and the paperwork is filed."

Stephen nodded his thanks. "No need for you to stick around. Say hi to your wife for me."

Ryan settled on the bench. "It's Friday. I'll wait a bit."

Stephen looked at the clock. Tracy's mom wasn't going to make it, not if the surgery lasted much longer. She hadn't been that strong going in.

"Meghan is pacing the ER waiting room watching the clock too. You could wander down that way."

"Meghan once told me she paces and prays—the harder she's pacing, the harder she prays. There's no need to interrupt. At this point I'd even rub a rabbit's foot if I thought it might help." He wasn't one to place much faith in a God who supposedly controlled things. From what he could see, life was hardly being controlled. But he wasn't going to tell Meghan her faith wasn't important. To her it was.

"Accidents happen."

"Yes." Stephen flipped the checker and caught it on the way down. Eagle she gets better. He looked at the image. An eagle. He turned over the disk. He'd carved two eagles in this one. He slipped it in his pocket and got to his feet. "I'm going to go say hi to Tracy for a minute." He'd carved the piece for her.

THREE

Meghan walked out of the hospital shortly before eleven, shivering at the wind gusts. She slipped on her lavender windbreaker as she hurried across the parking lot to her white jeep. She didn't carry a purse and her cash and keys were in her jeans pockets. Tracy's mom was finally in the recovery room.

She saw Stephen's car still in the lot—she shouldn't have wished his date with Paula would fall through. He needed the distraction of a date tonight. She hesitated. Should she go find him? No. He knew where she was all evening if he wanted to talk.

She unlocked her jeep and used the towel from the passenger seat to dry her face. The rain was easing up, but it would still be an interesting trip. She headed to the highway.

She had the drive perfected so that she could listen to two audio books, stop at the truck stop on Route 39 for her midpoint fill-up, and in four hours be pulling into her parents' driveway.

Meghan drummed her hand on the wheel as she crept along at twenty miles per hour. What construction was snarling traffic this time? Getting out of Chicago was the longest part of the drive. She finally spotted an exit ramp and got off the highway. Even if the back roads added thirty miles to her trip, at least she would be going somewhere rather than sitting. She could cut through the forest preserve and over to the old two-lane county road that followed the railroad tracks across the state. It would eventually take her directly into Silverton.

The tall oak trees in the forest preserve were casting strange shadows across the hood of Craig's car as he sat in the public parking lot. It was posted as closed after six o'clock but had no gate or security to enforce the curfew. Craig studied the clock on the dashboard and listened to the rain on the roof. He had a little cocaine left, just enough for one more lift. He calculated the time and forced himself to seal up the drugs. He couldn't get too high before his meeting, or Jonathan would notice and not go through with the exchange.

Helping steal jewelry was the easiest money he'd ever made, and he didn't want Jonathan to know what he was spending his extra income on. He was the courier, that was all, but it was steady income and someday… He had plans.

Someday he would walk away with a few stones from what he transported and make himself a fortune.

Craig reached over and opened his briefcase then lifted the lid on the box inside. The jewels glittered even in the dim interior light. He ran his fingers across the stones. They were the fake ones, but he would have the real ones soon. And when he delivered them to Neil tonight, he would have enough money to party for a full month.

He closed the briefcase and looked up at the flash of lightning. He jolted as eyes looked back at him from outside. A deer. Craig giggled. He raised his hand to cover his mouth. It wouldn't do to show that giggle tonight; no, it really wouldn't do to show that. Getting high was his secret.

Oh, life is good.

He worked at his old man's general store and pharmacy during the week, and while his father inventoried the pharmacy drugs each week, suspecting something but never able to prove it, Craig borrowed the car on weekends and drove to Chicago to get away from the small town suffocating blanket of people who thought they had a right to know what he did every minute. Someday he would have enough cash to walk away from that "productive" and "honorable" job, and he didn't plan to give notice.

Craig started his car and gunned the engine, backing up and turning toward the exit. He loved the quiet solitude of this place. He could hear traffic but not see it, hear the sounds of the community around him but not have to show himself. His wheels spun on the wet pavement as he nearly plowed into the entrance sign and overcorrected back to the road. He thought hard. Go left to cross the bridge and head downtown? Jonathan would be annoyed if he was late.

Red lights flashed at him, but there wasn't a railroad crossing here. More construction? It would slow him down. The road began a rising incline and he relaxed, remembering the bridge. Cross the bridge and half a mile down the road he'd be back at the freeway.

White lights blinded him.

His foot slammed down on the accelerator as he tried to get out of the way. The white jeep already on the bridge nearly clipped him as it careened over the south side of the bridge and plunged into the gully below. The sound of the crash sobered him and Craig stopped his car, heart pounding. He looked back but didn't see anything.

It hadn't been real. No, it hadn't been real—he'd inhaled too much powder. His hand shook as he turned up the music. Lights in front of his eyes—the highs always made lights dance in front of his eyes. He drove on.

Jonathan was waiting for the soft knock on the hotel room door that came precisely at midnight. He opened it and stepped back to let Craig slip into the suite, frowning at the nervous way his friend rocked on his feet and looked behind him. "Something wrong?"

"I just heard the elevator."

"It's a hotel, Craig." Jonathan led the way into the sitting room. "Keep your voice down; she's asleep." He turned on a dim light. The jewelry was lined up on the side table: emerald earrings, a square-cut diamond ring, a bracelet and necklace with diamonds and emeralds set in gold. He had taken instant photographs of where Marie left the pieces around the suite so the replacements could be positioned where she remembered them. "Give me the stones."

Craig opened the briefcase and removed a box.

Jonathan laid the fakes beside the originals, comparing the pieces. Neil had made them in the last three months from photos Jonathan had sent him. Neil had a great cover owning and running a profitable jewelry shop. He could do all kinds of custom work quietly on the side. "These will work. I couldn't find her brooch, so you'll have to take that piece back." He returned the fake brooch to the case, then put the real gems into velvet pouches. "Tell Neil that taking all the pieces from a lady like this isn't worth the risk. She might not notice, but someone else bought them for her and *he* will eventually notice." If it had been his decision, he would have replaced only half the pieces with good quality fakes and left the others to help cover the theft.

"Neil wants to move to bigger but more infrequent thefts."

Jonathan looked at his friend. How could he be so naïve? "Neil will have me staking out marks in Europe and you flying over with replacement pieces, figuring if he steals in one country he can sell them sooner in another." The idea wasn't entirely unappealing. He'd like the income, but they just needed to take more care in what they stole. Jonathan closed the box. "Where's my first payment?"

Craig handed over an envelope. "Ten thousand."

"Stay here." Jonathan took the fake pieces and picked up the pictures. He left the earrings on the end table next to Marie's glass with its still-melting ice and carried the other pieces to the bedroom. He placed the ring on the bathroom counter next to the soap dish, the bracelet went on the bedside table, and the necklace inside the still-open hotel room safe.

He had ensured that she was too occupied to spin the dial on the safe last night. Jonathan walked back into the living room with the pictures and gave them to Craig. "Burn them."

"I know the drill." Craig stored the photographs in the briefcase.

"Don't even think about disappearing with those stones and reselling them." Craig's gaze shot up to his. Jonathan had gone to high school with Craig and he knew just how sticky his friend's fingers were.

"Five thousand to be a courier is fine. I'll be in Silverton by morning. These stones— The last thing I want to do is hold hot rocks one second longer than I have to."

Jonathan glanced back to the bedroom. "She does come from a rather interesting family... Get going."

Stephen drove on the edge of what was safe for the current road conditions as he headed to the restaurant. He had missed dinner; now he was late for midnight coffee. Paula understood about his job, but standing her up twice on the same night would stretch her patience too far.

The restaurant was one she had chosen near her home where apparently they had live music until 2 A.M. on weekends. He picked up his street map again. He didn't know this area and had already gotten lost twice. *"Go through the forest preserve and cross the one-way bridge. The restaurant is exactly one mile west on the left."* Her directions could use some help. *Go through the forest preserve*—she didn't mention four miles of forest preserve snaked through this area.

He'd stumbled into a stretch of trees so thick that at times they blocked all light. Homes in this area must run half a million dollars. If the restaurant was priced for its address, this was going to be expensive coffee. He finally found a road going west and saw a sign marking the upcoming scenic bridge. He had to squint to read the words. It really was one-way traffic. How old was this bridge? He waited for the flashing red lights to change and give him the right of way. He crossed the bridge as lightning cracked directly overhead.

A flash of white caught his eye.

He was done rescuing things. He was done... Stephen applied the brakes and backed up, peering through the rain. He'd seen something. Probably an animal. That was all he needed—a hurt animal putting him on pet patrol for the night. He lowered the window to see better.

It was the rear fender of a jeep. The vehicle was so far down into the gully it was visible only with the lightning.

He turned on his hazard lights and stepped out into the downpour.

The muddy bank crumbled under Stephen as he worked his way down, grasping tree trunks to help stay upright. There was the sound of rushing water down below and a squishing sound as he picked up his feet. His car headlights didn't shine much light downward leaving this area in dark shadows. He didn't dare risk using his flashlight until he reached the jeep for fear of dropping it.

Something had sent the jeep into the gully. Maybe a blown tire? So far he saw no signs that it had been struck from behind. His hand touched the bumper and Stephen leaned against the vehicle for balance, relieved to find it wedged into the ground so it wouldn't shift.

The jeep had been down here awhile. Leaves coated the vehicle and rainwater had filled the depressions on the roof. Stephen struggled the last few feet so he could lean in to see inside. His feet went out from under him and he grabbed the side mirror.

Meghan, what are you doing out here? He shoved the passenger door partially open and squeezed himself into the seat to reach her. This road at this time of night— She must have been taking the back roads home.

She was leaning forward against the steering wheel and her seat belt was pulled tight.

"Meghan, can you hear me?"

Her answer was slurred and unintelligible. He probed carefully but didn't find signs she had sustained an impact chest injury. The seat belt had done its job. He pushed aside part of a tree branch that had punctured the side window of the jeep and then snapped off. The blood in her hair had dried.

He spotted her cell phone near her feet and retrieved it, then saw her keys also on the floor near the gas pedal. She'd been conscious long enough to shut off the vehicle and pull out her phone. He started to reach for the keys, but his hand trembled too much to close around them. She'd been here long enough that conscious thought had turned to unintelligible sound. While he got himself lost trying to read a map, Meghan had been resting here slowly dying. The phone had a weak signal but he lost it as he dialed. He tried again and the call dropped a second time. He slid the phone into his shirt pocket.

"Meghan, try to wake up."

He carefully turned her head and shone his penlight in her eyes. Though her pupils reacted there was no indication in her blinking that she noticed the light. She showed all the signs of brain trauma with an intense and deadly result. The rest of her body just hadn't caught up with that fact yet. "I'm sorry I wasn't here earlier, Meghan. I got lost on my drive a couple times," he whispered, sliding his jacket around her, preparing to abandon her and head back up to the road to try to get a phone signal. He'd worked so hard to make sure no one died on him today. The bile in his throat threatened to come up.

He turned toward the open passenger door and got partway out before pausing there with his head down. Not this. The darkness grew for a few seconds until he pushed it away by strength of will. He took a deep breath. Meghan only had him right now. He couldn't afford the emotions.

He pulled the phone out to try again. He punched the redial button and this time the weak signal held. "Dispatch, this is Stephen O'Malley of Unit 59. I need a code one dispatch, and if they can get airborne in this weather, a med-life flight."

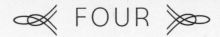

FOUR

"Keep her steady!" Stephen struggled against the mud and wet leaves as he and the other rescuers carried the stretcher up the bank to the road. The bank had turned into a mudslide under the foot traffic of so many people. A helicopter was nearby; he could hear the rotors. Vehicles crowded the road. He'd gotten the response he needed but feared it was too late.

Kate shoved people out of the way to reach his side as they carried the stretcher to the waiting ambulance that would take Meghan the short distance to the med-life flight. He'd put out an emergency page to the family. "She's alive, but it's going to be a fight! Find out what happened here, Kate."

She leaned in close to be heard above the noise. "I will. Jack's meeting you at the hospital."

"Meghan's parents?"

"On the way! Silverton's sheriff is driving them in."

Stephen pulled himself up into the ambulance. The doors slammed behind him and they were moving.

"You kept her alive." Aaron pushed up the oxygen flow. Stephen was glad this man was here to help him. Aaron had been his training officer years before.

Stephen swiftly slipped an IV line into a vein on Meghan's left arm. "It looks like her watch broke at 11:12 P.M. She is well over that critical hour." The survival stats for trauma victims dropped alarmingly after the first hour.

Meghan's face was darkening with bruises. Stephen wiped away mud that had splashed on her pale skin and wished she would open her eyes. If he thought it would help, he'd even pray to her God. Tears burned the back of his eyes but he refused to let them fall. *Hold on, Meghan.* Her breathing was so shallow.

The ambulance pulled near the waiting helicopter. Stephen shoved open the doors the instant they stopped. The helicopter had set down in the parking lot, the open spot in the midst of the trees barely large enough to give the rotors minimal clearance.

"It's a twelve-minute flight. She's heading to the best trauma unit in the state." Aaron grabbed the end of the stretcher and helped Stephen ease it down. They carried her to the helicopter and fit the gurney onto the track that pulled it in and locked it down.

"Do you have room for one more? I know her," Stephen pleaded.

"He's one of mine," Aaron added.

The trauma flight medic pointed to the jump seat. "Monitor her breathing and keep talking to her."

Stephen surged inside before the guy could change his mind, took the seat indicated, and clipped on the six-point restraint harness. Rotors began to spin.

"How's she doing?"

Stephen glanced up from the floor tiles to see his brother striding from the elevators. Jack must have come from a fire scene—his shirt was streaked with the stain of wet charcoal nearly inevitable during a fire cleanup. Stephen rested his head against the wall behind him. "The same. Alive." He was too tired to expand further. In a desperate attempt to keep Meghan alive, the doctors had lowered her body temperature and put her into an intentional coma. Her heart was beating. Everything else was an unknown. They wouldn't remove the respirator that was breathing for her until after the brain swelling came down. He'd been sitting in this chair since she arrived. If he left, he was afraid she'd die on him.

Jack dropped a sack on the seat beside him. "A change of clothes and a razor. Go clean up some of that face fuzz she teases you about. I'll pace for you while you change, see if I can wear a few more millimeters into your path on the floor."

Stephen smiled. Jack was the right kind of brother to have in a crisis, just enough humor to keep a situation in perspective and stop the drowning in despair. Stephen rose and picked up the sack. "Her parents are down in the cafeteria sharing a cup of coffee."

Jack squeezed his shoulder. "I'll find everyone if there's any change."

Stephen nodded and went to clean up. He'd changed shirts earlier, but there were still mud and bloodstains on his jeans, and it wouldn't do Meghan's mom any good to see it.

From the pocket of his jeans he pulled out the new checker he had been working on for Meghan. The quiet conversations between her mom and dad were beginning, *"If she's only blind…"* The other possibilities were too terrifying to plan for. No one knew what was coming, but the blow to her head worried those who saw the early CT scans. At least she would be able to feel checkers and tell by touch which ones were different.

Meghan had been alert for at least a few minutes after the crash. The doctors said that was promising. Stephen's hand tightened around the checker. She had to get better. In an undeclared way Meghan had joined the group of people he would always have in his life. He couldn't lose her.

She'd had a crush on him growing up; he wasn't so blind he missed that. Encouraging her then had seemed the wrong step when he knew he was averse to letting anyone be closer than a friend for the long haul. He'd been protecting her, but he could have been more kind about it. And later when she had come back for nursing school, worked at the hospital—what had he been waiting for?

She'd been the best kind of friend, pleased to see him and kind with her words when he did great but also when he blew it. He should have seized the opportunity. In waiting, he had irreversibly lost.

Please, give me another chance. That's all I want. Another chance. Don't die on me, Meghan. I can't handle it.

Stephen pounded nails through the drywall, each blow a strike against time. They were slowly warming Meghan up and easing her from the drugs. He couldn't take the waiting at the hospital anymore. He was too afraid. Her eyes were open, her hands were twitching, and she was responding to pain. But until the drugs were out of her system, they didn't know how far she was coming back. It had been four days since the accident. She might wake up and talk in an hour, tomorrow, a month from now...or never. It was terrifying.

When Stephen's dark emotions built, the best cure was work. He was remodeling this home, already having an idea of the couple who would best be the new owners. He rebuilt the kitchen with Sandy in mind. She loved to cook.

A knock on the back door interrupted him. He took three steps back, turned the lock without looking, and went back to hauling the next piece of drywall to the table to measure out the cut for the exhaust ductwork.

"You want help?"

He pointed Jack to the counter where extra gloves lay.

Jack grabbed the drywall and held it steady as Stephen started the saw. The noise stopped any conversation. The sawdust felt rough against his skin as it stuck to sweat-covered arms. Stephen shut off the saw and put it in a safety box so he didn't step on it.

"You know it's 2 A.M."

"I know."

Jack rolled up his sleeves and settled in for a few hours of work. It wouldn't be the first time they had spent a night waiting together. "Kate can't sleep either. She's on the way to the hospital."

Stephen hesitated. "Did she find out anything else at the scene?" He knew Kate had spent another day out there.

"She paced every inch of it with the investigating officers and came up with the same answer as before. Besides skid marks left by the other car, which show that the other driver likely accelerated onto the bridge, there's little to work with. So far no one has reported seeing anything. There is some evidence that the very end of the bridge railing might have been clipped, suggesting the other car has some damage, but rain washed away any trace of paint scrapes. Security tapes from the two gas stations in the area have fourteen cars on that road during the twenty minutes before 11:15, just in case Meghan's watch was fast. The cops are looking for them."

"Someone did this and left her there."

"They'll find him."

Stephen nearly drove the nail through the wall. "They better."

"What's next?"

Stephen pointed behind him. "Flooring in the living room. I decided it should all come up."

Jack folded the two lawn chairs Stephen called his living room furniture and moved the two barrels he used as tables. "Meghan's a fighter, Stephen."

"I know."

The phone rang as they were losing the battle to force up a piece of flooring that had been nailed down forty-three years ago. Jack reached for the phone and Stephen waved him off. If this was bad news, he wouldn't ask Jack to take the call.

Mrs. Delhart was on the phone and she was crying. "Meghan's asking for you, Stephen."

FIVE

Meghan turned her head trying to find relief from the headache, but no matter which direction she looked the darkness was the same. She reached a shaky hand up to touch her left eye and felt the brush of eyelashes to reassure herself that her eyelid was open. It was so strange living in this world of darkness. It had no dimensions, no objects, no people…it was just a black hole where she had to feel her way around.

She jerked to the left as a squeaky wheel on a cart moved outside the hospital room door. She longed for earplugs. The sounds were overwhelming. There was never any warning of what was coming. *Jesus, it's like living in a body that is now just one raw nerve. How do I live trapped like this?*

She knew it was night. Her mom had tucked her in and her dad had kissed her good-night. She'd smiled as visiting hours ended and convinced them she was tired so they wouldn't worry so much about her. At least the confusion of voices had ceased with the coming of the night shift. This room was too near the nursing station. She spent her days listening to rushing feet and the sound of overlapping, urgent voices. All too often someone was beside her before he spoke to warn her he was nearby. *I want my privacy back. I hate living in a fishbowl.*

She struggled to sit up under the numerous blankets. The doctors said she would eventually get back her ability to regulate her body temperature, but it wasn't happening yet. Her mind was also doing its own thing with its sense of time. She was wide-awake. She swung her legs to the side of the bed and reached to the left to orient herself with the furnishings.

Mom left her clothes folded in the top drawer of the dresser. Meghan dressed, wishing she knew what color the clothes were. She felt for the chair beside the window, and once she found it, tugged over the blanket from the bed for her lap. It was such a small room. At least she didn't have to walk in the darkness but could move from point to point by touch.

She felt around the chair looking for the television remote. She found the water pitcher, a bowl of jelly beans, a stack of get-well cards, a folded newspaper, and two books. She turned and checked on the radiator, moving carefully so as not to knock over one of the flower vases. It smelled like she was living in a florist shop. She found the television remote and clicked on the late night news. It wasn't too bad, listening to the commentary. She tried to pretend she was doing something else and had the news on in the background so she wouldn't just sit here thinking about how she couldn't see it.

She picked up one of the books. From the weight and the raised lettering on the cover it felt like the book on John Adams she had bought her father last month. Tears welled in her eyes. Being blind was a miserable existence. She wanted to see the pages, to read for herself again. Having someone read to her was such a painful compromise.

She couldn't take her parents down with her into this sadness; it wasn't fair to them. *It's so hard to be brave, Lord. I just want a doctor to work a miracle and let me see again.* She slid the book back on the table. She'd find a way to read again, find a way to live her life. She had no choice.

A soft tap on the door was followed by the sound of it opening. The shoes sounded hard on the tile floor and that suggested it wasn't staff. She swiped at her eyes.

"Hi, Meghan."

Stephen. She desperately wanted to tell him to go away, but instead she jerkily nodded and heard him enter the room. He came by at least twice a day. She carefully touched her face and felt the soreness across her cheek and swelling around her jaw. Mom had told her that the bruises on her face had come in black and purple and were now fading to leave her skin with a yellow leathery tinge. She must look horrible. She lowered her hands, took a deep breath, and smiled toward where she thought he stood.

Stephen would be her friend, be generous with his time, help her cope. She had only to ask—no, she probably didn't even have to ask. He *wanted* to rescue her.

She wanted so badly to lean against him, to let him take that role. But she wasn't sure he was up to it. And she couldn't put that burden on him.

He was a good man, just not someone who could lead the way on the journey she faced. Learning to walk with a cane was the easy part; what she needed was someone who could help her accept. At best Stephen could only be temporary comfort. She was physically blind, but Stephen was spiritually blind. If she pitched forward and had to count on a friend to catch her, she knew her choice—it had to be Jesus.

She heard Stephen cross toward the bed and the springs give as he sat down. She tugged her sweater tighter and then lifted one hand to wipe her eyes again. She hated it when Stephen saw her tears. She purposely lightened her voice. "Just getting off your shift?"

"Yes. I have something for you."

He was always bringing her something. The feel of what he placed in her hand caught her interest. It was fuzzy, small, and the bottom was smooth and warm. She tried to figure it out by touch and when it hummed she smiled. "A Furby thing?"

"They call it a muffin. Your hand warms it up and the heat causes it to hum and then vibrate."

"It's cute." She held it in her palm until the vibration started. She carefully set it on the table and it went quiet.

The silence lengthened and became awkward, but she didn't know how to fill it.

"Meghan, I'm sorry—"

She nearly picked up the book and tossed it at him. "Don't! Don't apologize. I'm sick of people apologizing." Even the cops said they were sorry. They couldn't find the driver who caused this. It wasn't Stephen's fault he hadn't traveled that road thirty minutes earlier. It wasn't her fault for being on that road instead of the highway—it just was. She couldn't handle another apology. She looked down after the outburst and in frustration tugged at the blanket to get it around her cold feet.

Stephen sighed. "Here." His hand slid behind her ankles and lifted her feet, the blanket pulled under them to protect her from the cold floor. He squeezed her knee as he resumed his seat. "I was just going to say I was sorry for coming by so late. I got held up doing paperwork." She heard pillows thump against the headboard. "There's a good TV movie on tonight if you want a reason to fall asleep against me again like a bundled-up snail."

She knew he wasn't intending to say he was sorry for that, but at least he hadn't pursued the subject. A movie would be good. As long as it was a classic she could remember most of the scenes. She didn't want to have a conversation where she had to dance around avoiding answers to how she was feeling and what the doctors said.

"If you can get around here," she shifted back in the chair and pulled over the table, "let's play a game of checkers." He had whittled her a full set: red ones had ridged edges, black ones smooth. The checkerboard brought up from rehab therapy had slim wooden ridges marking off the squares so the checkers could be touched yet not moved out of their square. She'd played endless games with her father just to pass the time.

"Sure." Stephen moved over another chair.

He caught her hand as she set out her pieces, gently turned her wrist, and lifted her hand to his nose. "JoAnne has been by. Nice perfume."

"It's kind of soft. I liked yesterday's better. You smell a bit like soap and a lot like that cologne of Jack's."

"I grabbed a shower. I didn't figure you'd appreciate road oil and skunk."

"Really? What happened?"

"A car wreck when the driver swerved to avoid hitting the animal. It was a big, fat, old-timer of a skunk and the car ran over it. Guys were putting Vicks under their noses and wearing face masks if they had to spend any time near the vehicle."

Meghan laughed for the first time in days. "Oh my, that must have been a sight." She settled her hand on the checkerboard, selected a piece, and made her first move. Stephen took her hand and showed her his.

A game that would have normally taken twenty minutes to play took them an hour. She was grateful Stephen didn't interrupt her concentration. She lost, but at least she'd been able to get a few pieces crowned this time.

"You're improving."

"It's still hard to hold more than two moves in my memory at a time." She picked up one of the pieces. "You did a really nice job with these. I can tell this is an eagle." She handed him her pieces.

He stacked them in the box. "Your dad said they're going to release you this weekend."

She tilted her head, wishing she knew what was behind the quiet statement. It was his work voice: calm and a bit detached. "They're talking about it. Dad can watch for any problems from the headaches."

"You're thinking about moving back to Silverton instead of staying in town for therapy?"

She had guessed right; he didn't like the idea. "I'll stay with my parents. Dad plans to hire someone so I won't feel like I'm imposing on them while I learn my way around." Back home everything from the post office to the church was familiar to her. It was time to go home. She needed desperately to be home.

Stephen caught her hand and squeezed it. "I'm going to miss you, Meghan."

"I'll miss you too." She blinked tears back and started as Stephen reached past her.

"Kleenex."

"I'm sorry. It doesn't take much to make me cry anymore."

"The tears are good for you." He tugged the blanket on her lap tighter. "Your hands are still like ice."

His voice was husky behind the rough assertion and she laughed to try and lighten the mood. "Dad's been calling me his little iceberg." She leaned back in her chair, shredded the Kleenex, and her smile faded. "Stephen, do me a favor. Let this go, okay? You couldn't have changed things. I'll go home, get a Seeing Eye dog, and go on with my life. I need to know you will too. I'm going to be okay with Jesus' help."

She heard the subtle shift of his weight. Just the mention of Jesus' name made him uncomfortable. She'd been trying for years to get him to listen to the truth; and now…Jesus had to make this work or else her faith was misplaced. Maybe then Stephen would understand.

"I'll be fine, Meghan."

"Will you?"

He rubbed her wrist. "Now have I ever told you a fib?"

"I didn't look pretty yesterday."

"You did to me. Is it okay if I come to Silverton to see you occasionally?"

It really mattered that she show him she was okay, and that was not going to be a simple step. "You can call. But give me some time before you come by."

"I don't mind you being blind, Meghan. Please don't push me away."

She reached over and settled her hands against his face, her thumb finding the cleft in his chin and her palms the hard bone of his jaw. Her fingers lifted as a smile played at his mouth, her touch embarrassing him. "We've been friends for a lifetime. We'll always be friends." If she let him come, she'd lean against him, fall in love, and walk herself into a broken heart. "You can come visit in a year and buy me lunch."

His hands covered hers, callused and rough against her skin. "I'm going to hold you to that."

"I'm counting on it." She patted his cheeks. "I'll be fine. I promise."

His fingers entwined with hers. "Yes, you will be. You're stubborn that way."

SIX

PRESENT DAY

WHITFIELD, ILLINOS
Monday, June 25

Meghan fixed tea for Stephen. His offer to come by and give her a lift back to Silverton surprised and pleased her. She was making a deliberate attempt during this trip to Chicago for Jennifer's visitation to renew old friendships. The teapot whistled. She turned off the burner and picked up the kettle with a hot pad. She hadn't wanted to intrude on the O'Malleys' grief, but it would be good to spend some time with Stephen rather than just talk on the phone, as they had done occasionally over the last few years.

The power went out with a snap—the TV she was listening to went dead and the appliances jolted to silence. Meghan froze. She was carrying a teapot full of hot water. The darkness didn't change for her, but she left the room lights on for her dog, and she had to figure out where he was before she moved. Blackie could lead her safely across a street with heavy traffic or around a crowded mall, but he couldn't handle cats, the smell of onions, which made him sneeze, or thunder.

She tried not to tease him about his weaknesses, at least not too much. He was okay with all three when he was in the harness working. Her collie gave her priceless freedom. "Where are you, Blackie?" The animal's tail slapped against her leg. "Why don't you go under the table for a minute, okay? I don't want to step on your tail."

She waited until she heard the sound of his movement before she carried the teapot to the counter to finish fixing the tea. Her grandparents were such creatures of habit that Meghan was able to find the cinnamon by first finding the glass jar of lemon drops and turning the spinning rack two items to the left. It had been that way when she could see, and years later it was still that way. Whoever said *new* was better was badly missing the value of predictability. She would like to strike new from her vocabulary now that she couldn't see.

The TV came back on as abruptly as it had gone off, the appliances resuming operation with a hum. She stirred honey in her tea.

Stephen had taken a leave of absence. She tossed her spoon toward the sink and heard the satisfying sound of metal striking stainless steel. If she were smart she would get over the anger before he got here, but then again maybe not. Maybe it would be better to just give him both barrels of her emotion so at least he'd have to deal with it. Running away. Repeating history. She thought she'd broken him of the habit when they were children.

She pulled out a chair, stopping her hand at the last moment to move the chair slowly until she figured out she wasn't going to give her dog a headache. Did Stephen really think leaving was going to help? She was an expert on running from unattractive realities in life, and it just meant he would inevitably crash into a wall and do it far from home and everybody who cared for him.

Meghan rested her elbows on the table and turned her cup around to grasp the handle. This was a lot more serious than the whispered words from Kate last night had made it out to be. Meghan adored family members that had the nerve to meddle, but had Kate whispered in the right person's ear? It had been over a year since she last talked to Stephen for more than a casual, "Hi, how are you?" and she was supposed to rescue him tonight?

Jesus, I'm no rescuer. Stephen has that title locked up in spades. As do You.

Thunder crashed overhead and she flinched. For years she had chased lightning and hail and tornadoes with Ken and laughed at nature's fury. Now thunder cracked without warning and her nerves couldn't handle it. The storm sounded as if it were directly overhead.

Jennifer's funeral had been this morning. Stephen needed to go out in this storm somewhere and cry his eyes out, release the emotions. But he wouldn't do it. Instead he'd run. And she knew for certain that if he ran, he would come to regret it. But she wouldn't push, not if his family had already decided to back off and let him go.

Lord, please help me figure out what to say tonight. At least blindness had clarified her sight in other ways. All of life was a spiritual battle on one level or another—acceptance, endurance, peace, joy. Trying to find those things without Christ was an exercise in futility. If he kept avoiding the subject of Jesus, Stephen wouldn't find the peace he sought.

Maybe she would have a chance to talk with him about serious things during the drive. Her bags were by the front door, the bed was already stripped, the sheets washed and now in the dryer. She'd been planning to crash on the couch for the few hours before her father arrived. Since sleep wasn't going to happen in this storm, she'd much rather be on the road.

Meghan set down her cup of tea and stood. She walked through her grandparents' vacation home to turn on the outdoor lights.

Stephen needs to find some comfort tonight, Lord. Since he doesn't know You, I'll have to reflect to him how much You care about him. The sadness he's feeling about Jennifer must be incredible. I wish he understood that You're there for him. The man needs to find You. She knew it in her head and felt it in her heart, and she ached at the realization that he didn't. Years of praying for Stephen hadn't opened the door, but Meghan wasn't giving up on him. God hadn't. *Please remind him to drive carefully. There have been enough tragedies on nights like this.*

Outdoor lights came on next door.

Jonathan Peters froze. Meghan was blind and couldn't see him, but if she had company coming over… He finished unlocking the side door of the dark house. He'd like to give Neil another stroke for not hiding the gems that needed to cool off in something straightforward like a box buried under the woodpile or beneath attic insulation. Neil's wife, now deep in the confusion of Alzheimer's, had sold her china doll collection to her sister without asking her husband—and with it a hidden ruby bracelet worth a small fortune.

In the interwoven friendships of Silverton there was a certain logic to Meghan's grandparents buying a vacation home next door to Neil's wife's sister. Jonathan eased open the door. Neil had given him a key. With the owners traveling, the house was empty tonight, and the storm was good cover.

Jonathan had no choice but to be the one who tried to recover the bracelet. He couldn't trust Craig now that it was clear his friend was frying his common sense on drugs, and Neil wouldn't be going more than a hundred feet from his sitting chair for the foreseeable future. The stroke had partially paralyzed Neil's left side and ended his craftsman ability and thus their profitable sideline career. Future income would have to come from selling pieces they had already taken. Because of that, it was important not to let the ruby bracelet be lost or to have the cops called in and asking questions.

How many pieces over the years had disappeared by accident as Neil's wife lost her sense of the present and gave away items?

Jonathan turned on his flashlight and looked around the living room, careful not to let the light pass across the windows. Shelves had been emptied and tables cleared of pictures and knickknacks. They were having the rooms redone— the project of a retired lady with too much time on her hands. Would the dolls be out or tucked in some boxes somewhere?

He would have to pressure Neil to tell him where the remaining pieces were hidden. He had no leverage with the man and didn't expect the pressure to yield much, but if he had to go to Silverton after Neil died and rip up his house and jewelry store—it would be a headache creating the block of free time in his schedule. His manager was already demanding to know what was so urgent that he had to fly back to the States for a long weekend and miss an opportunity to rehearse with the London symphony.

In a way he was glad of Neil's stroke. The stealing had run its course. Find the pieces, consider the income from their sale his nest egg, and wrap this up for good.

Neil was a tough old man. He'd probably live another ten years, but if he didn't? Jonathan wasn't looking to change things as much as create some insurance. Would Neil have kept so many pieces on his own property, among his own things? Or had he spread them out tucked in spots around town? Maybe at Meghan's—the fact she couldn't see would have made her home an ideal stash site.

The mere thought of being in a race with Craig to find the stones Neil had hidden wasn't something Jonathan wanted to contemplate. It was definitely time to start thinking about how to handle his friend before the occasion arose.

The china cabinet was empty. Couldn't she have waited another two or three days to begin redecorating? He sighed and started looking through the boxes that weren't taped closed.

Time crawled by as Meghan waited for Stephen to arrive. She paced back and forth in the living room. The power was out again. The radio in the bathroom might still have good batteries. She walked with her hand trailing along the wall into the hallway then to the stairway. Her dog bumped against her knee as she walked, pressing so close he interfered with her balance. She lowered her hand to stroke his head.

Meghan took the radio from the bathroom counter into the guest bedroom to try and find a location that got better reception. The local news crackled with static. A thunderbolt cracked overhead. Her dog yelped and she heard a door hit a wall.

"Blackie." He must have headed into his favorite hiding spot—the open walk-in closet. She tried to coax him out but he refused to come. She finally crawled in after him, shoving back the hanging coats to sit beside him. "I can't blame you, boy. It's loud enough to hurt your ears." She leaned her head against his warm coat.

Glass broke and Meghan flinched. Somewhere a tree limb had just pierced a window. She left Blackie to his temporary shelter, tossing a glove back at him to distract him. She followed the noise and realized it was the bathroom window. The rain was reaching her standing in the doorway, and she could tell from the wind it wasn't a little tap by a twig. Stepping on glass or cutting her hand was a bad idea. She gave up dealing with it herself and closed the bathroom door.

She thought there was plywood in the garage that could be used to patch the window for the night. Stephen was a good carpenter. Maybe it would help him out to have something to do tonight. She heard the potted fern in the bathroom shatter on the tiles. This was going to be a huge mess to clean up.

Jonathan found the china dolls wrapped in tissue paper in a box in the living room. He had unwrapped six before finding the one with painted black eyelashes, rosy cheeks, and a small red dimple on the right cheek. He opened up the base of the doll stand and the rubies tumbled out. The piece was gorgeous. He didn't remember who he had stolen it from. Had it really been that many years and that many pieces? He slipped the bracelet into his pocket. His percentage of the sale price would pay bills for a couple months.

Hearing a car slow, Jonathan clicked off his flashlight. Headlights crossed the windows. He walked over to the windows, staying back far enough from the curtains that his presence would remain unnoticed. The car pulled into Meghan's driveway. A man he didn't recognize with a baseball cap on his head dashed through the rain toward the house.

Jonathan wanted to check the other dolls and find out if Neil had tucked another piece in one of them and forgotten, but a guest noticing lights over here wasn't worth the risk. Tomorrow or the next day, he'd be back if necessary.

He walked through the room removing any signs of his presence. He slipped from the house. The entire subject of Neil and Craig needed to be thought through in detail.

Stephen wiped water off his face. He had gotten drenched from his run to the house. Meghan had left the door open as promised. He slipped off his wet jacket to hang on the coatrack, going off memory, for the kitchen was dark, the only illumination coming from lightning. "Meghan, where are you?"

"Up here. I left a flashlight on the stairs for you."

He hoped the power came on soon. He wasn't nearly as good at walking around in the dark as Meghan was. He found the flashlight and headed upstairs.

The first sight of her was one he would remember for quite a while. She was dragging a roll of heavy plastic from the spare bedroom. Her jeans were new and her sweatshirt was faded red. Her feet were bare, and her hair was blond. She'd been a brunette yesterday at Jennifer's visitation. She looked cute as a blonde.

"Watch the toolbox."

He spotted it in the hallway beside a piece of plywood and stopped on the top step to stay out of the way. "You're a trusting soul to leave the door unlocked."

"Who else is going to be out in this downpour? Your shoes are squishing."

"And my socks. It's a minor flood out there. Can I help?"

She settled the plastic against the wall. "The bathroom window got taken out by a tree limb. I'm going to let you do the hammering if you don't mind getting a little wetter."

"I doubt I'll notice more water. When did this happen?"

"Shortly after the power went out the second time." She took a step toward him and her hand found his chest. "I'm sorry about Jennifer."

He found it hard to look at eyes staring at his left shoulder. She couldn't see. It ripped his guts. He wanted—needed—to avoid the subject of Jennifer tonight. "Let's talk about it another day."

Her hand smoothed out the fabric of his shirt. "I'm really going to miss her too." She nodded down the hall. "The bathroom is the second door on your right."

He heard it now, the close sound of wind and rain. He covered her hand with his, squeezed it, and then stepped away. He walked down the hall and opened the door, using the flashlight to inspect the damage. "The branch took out the top pane of glass and cracked the other panel. And the shower curtain has seen better days; the wind has it wrapped around the towel rack." He stepped into the room, careful of the glass shards and the plant, to see how long the branch was and if he could tug it completely inside to remove it.

"Did it damage the walls?"

"No. And I don't see any chipped floor tiles, although it's hard to tell with the fern and dirt. Stand in the doorway, Meghan, and hold the light for me." He took her hand and placed the flashlight in her palm, showing her how he'd like it positioned. "Right there."

She leaned her shoulder against the doorpost and held the light steady. "I'm sorry to put you to work as soon as you walked in the door."

"Don't be. I'm thinking seriously about becoming a carpenter in my new career." He tugged the branch through the window, wishing he had brought gloves. He broke off smaller branches from the tree limb so he could set it sideways in the tub until he could carry it outside. Cleaning up the glass would be a challenge. He began taking down the ripped shower curtain. "Do you have a trash can or a box I can put these glass pieces in?"

"I've got a packing box that will work." Meghan held out the flashlight to him. "Be right back."

Her dog stayed in the doorway watching him rather than going with her. Stephen walked over to the doorway and without hurrying crouched down and held out his hand. The dog looked warily at him. "Blackie, how are you?"

Blackie wagged his tail and pushed against his hand.

Stephen warmed his hand in the canine's thick coat. "Taking good care of her, are you?" He pulled in the heavy plastic and began boarding up the window.

He stepped to the doorway when he heard Meghan coming back and turned the flashlight down the hallway to see if there was anything likely to trip her up. She ran her hand along the chair rail on the wall judging the distance. The box she carried was wide enough to take the larger glass pieces. "That should work, Meghan, thanks."

"I gather I should be glad I can't see that mess."

He looked back at the bathroom. "It's a mess all right. Give me twenty minutes. And maybe find something else to do so I can talk man-to-man with Blackie while I fight this."

She smiled at him as he'd hoped. "I'll find some dry towels to mop up the water."

"I appreciate it."

Stephen folded a towel for the side of the tub to give himself a place to sit. He picked up a piece of glass and dropped it in the box while Blackie lay in the doorway. Stephen angled his flashlight so it wouldn't shine in the animal's face. "I hear you don't like storms." Blackie wagged his tail. "Can't say I blame you. I'd rather see the storm blow over completely before we drive to Silverton."

Stephen picked up the destroyed fern and dumped it in the box. "Meghan's grandparents will need to buy another one, won't they, boy?" He was talking to a dog. *I miss you, Jennifer. You would have at least had something interesting to say about tonight.* He had to get a dog for his trip, or he'd be talking to *himself* before it was over.

When he was done with the repairs, Stephen carried the box of discarded pottery pieces and glass downstairs and out to the garage. He found Meghan in the kitchen wiping down the counter. "The patch should hold until the rain stops and someone can do something permanent. And the floor is once again safe for bare feet."

Her toes curled before she turned, drying her hands on the towel. "Thanks."

"You're very welcome." He leaned against the counter beside her.

"You smell like flowery soap. Sorry about that."

He lifted his hand and found she was right, then checked his shirtsleeve. "Better than smelling like sweat, smoke, or too much deodorant."

"Your shoes have finally stopped squeaking."

"But my socks are still wet." He reached up and brushed her hair behind her ear. She jolted at his touch.

"I like you as a blonde."

Her hand touched his. "I heard I was getting gray hair so it was time for some help."

"Not so I noticed. You look cute." She'd stopped wearing her sunglasses as a defensive shield at some point in the last year. Her eyes looked fine. He looked at them, haunted that there was no animation backing them. The police had never found the driver who ran her off the road. The injustice of it made him so angry.

"Have a seat, Stephen, and I'll get the tea."

He set his flashlight on the table and pulled out a chair. Meghan poured the tea. He made no attempt to take the cup from her hand but let her slide it on the table in front of him. She was fine getting around as long as no one tried to be helpful and interrupted her movements.

"The honey should already be out."

"It's here. Thanks."

She settled on the chair across from him and picked up her cup. She'd lost some weight in the last few years, gotten a little more assertive with her words and more deliberate in her movements. Just looking at her made him tired—he was having a hard time handling *this* moment in his life, while she dealt well with so much more.

"Do you have plans for your travels?" Meghan asked.

"See some of the countryside, do some fishing, maybe some hiking. If money gets low, I'll pick up some carpentry work. Maybe I'll make a few items for wedding gifts."

"Kate introduced me to Shari last night. She seems nice."

"Marcus found a wonderful lady," he agreed. "I figure they'll set a wedding date soon, as will Rachel and Cole, and Jack and Cassie. There's no more reason for them to delay. No one wanted to make plans while Jennifer was so sick."

"Give yourself time to accept the loss, Stephen. Jennifer's death is a huge hole in the fabric of your family."

"It feels like an abyss."

She nudged the honey toward him. "Have some more tea. The second cup you can fix yourself."

He rose. "Would you like more too?"

"Sure."

He handed her the refilled cup, careful to wait until she had it steady in her hands before releasing it. The appliances kicked on with a shudder and hum, and the weather channel was on TV. Stephen glanced around. "Finish your tea; I'll reset the blinking clocks and such."

She nodded.

He walked through the downstairs rooms. When he returned to the living room, Meghan was there resting against the doorjamb.

"Your suitcases are packed?" Stephen asked.

"They're in the bedroom. I'll show you." He walked beside her up the stairs. "I've just got one suitcase and a bag," Meghan said. "I'm glad you were here to deal with the window. The neighbor across the street was replacing one last month and cut himself rather badly. Blood was flowing and his wife was hysterical. I've never been so glad to hear the sound of ambulance sirens."

Stephen could feel his hands going cold as the memories returned—the drunk pinned in his car with his stomach opened up and his guts lying in his lap…the teenager shot for his new tennis shoes…the wife so battered her words slurred, who refused to admit her husband had beaten her up. He could see the blood. Smell it. "Change the subject, Meghan."

"Stephen?"

He'd left it too late. Her hand tightened on his arm as he wobbled, and he pushed her away to avoid taking her with him. The darkness deepened.

And then there was nothing.

SEVEN

He'd almost taken her down the stairs with him. The nausea that came with that fact overwhelmed him. "Are you okay?" Stephen whispered, struggling to focus.

"Lie still. I'm not the one who took the header down the stairs."

His head was in her lap and Blackie was resting his chin across Stephen's chest. He'd been here a while. He raised a shaky hand and rubbed his eyes. "How long was I out?"

"Two minutes, going on three." Her hand caught his and slid to his wrist to take his pulse. "Did you eat anything today?"

"Fed Ann's son Nathan M&M's, ate a few bites of dinner at Kate's. I bought a Polish sausage, but didn't get around to trying it."

"You passed out. Totally." She tightened her grip on his hand.

A nice headache was blooming and he didn't feel all that great, but it had nothing to do with the day. Meghan had been talking about her neighbor's accident, he saw it in his mind, and he felt himself mentally trying to step back from all the blood that was so near he could smell it. He'd fainted again—the second time in a week—at the description of blood. The realization made him cold.

Meghan rubbed his arm, chasing away the chill she felt. "Want to sit up?"

"Not particularly." It had been a long time since a woman held him in her arms and it was…nice.

She smiled down at him. "Since I can't see you, I want honest answers to the next questions. What hurts? And what happened?"

"I'm sorry I scared you."

"I admit that for a moment I forgot the storm."

He sighed. "I got light-headed and passed out. Hopefully I didn't do too much damage coming down the stairs." He slowly moved arms and legs, testing for broken bones.

"How many times have you passed out like that?"

He wanted to avoid the question. "A couple."

She checked for a fever. He thought about kissing her fingers as they passed by, anything to get that worry and fear off her face.

"You don't have a fever and your low pulse is improving." She lifted his head from her lap. "Up."

He reluctantly sat up and his head swam. This wasn't good.

She rubbed his neck. "Don't tense or you'll make it worse."

"I'm okay, Meghan."

She gave him a full minute sitting there. "Is it the memories? You asked me to change the subject."

He gave a rueful laugh. "I don't do blood very well anymore."

She rested her chin against his shoulder. "I'm sorry."

"So am I." He sighed. "It'll pass. I just need a vacation."

"You've needed a vacation for a long time." She got up behind him. "You want something to eat before we head out?"

"You're still okay riding with me?"

She smiled and offered a hand. "You'll do better behind the wheel than I will."

He stood, relieved to find the sense of weakness had passed. "Can you fix me a sandwich? Maybe food will help."

"Turkey and cheddar?"

"Please."

She oriented herself with a hand on the banister and turned toward the kitchen. "How about two aspirin for the headache as well?"

"Sounds good." He bent to stroke Blackie's head and then went to get Meghan's suitcases.

Fainting. It seemed a fitting end for a day he hoped simply to forget.

Stephen's car was comfortable, very warm, and smelled a bit like leather cleaner. It was reassuring in a way to find that he took care of his car like he did his ambulance. Some habits died hard. Meghan settled deeper in the seat, debating the odds she would soon be asleep. Blackie was already snoring, stretched out in the backseat. Stephen had turned on the radio for her. She tilted her head toward him. "I remember the time you ran away when you were fourteen."

"Meghan."

She smiled at his discomfort. "I wanted to go with you and you wouldn't let me."

"There wasn't much reason to run away if I was taking someone along."

"Why are you running away this time?"

"I thought the point of running away was not to have a reason."

"You're an O'Malley. You've probably got reasons stacked on top of each other."

"I'm looking for some space, some peace, and that needed vacation."

She listened to the rhythm of the wipers. She could push or not. *Jesus, which is best?* She reached over and either he found her hand or she got reasonably lucky reaching out. She squeezed his fingers. "I'd like postcards from the various stops you make. Mom can read them to me." He was feeling cornered by so many pressures.

"I can probably manage that."

"You know you're worrying your family."

"I know."

She sighed. "I'm not going to change your mind, am I?"

"Were you trying to?"

"Apparently not hard enough."

"I need this, Meg. A trip with no destination and no clock governing my time."

"I hope you find what you're looking for." She was afraid he wouldn't. The peace he sought could only be found in what he was avoiding: faith. Jesus. She tried last night at the visitation to mention heaven and what Jennifer believed but had gotten the politest of brush-offs. She knew a stubborn will when she met one. She had herself as a model. The O'Malleys were right. It was best to let him go. *Lord, this journey needs to end with his finding You. Please. He's hurting. Maybe he'll be ready to listen this time.* "Don't be gone too long, okay?"

He squeezed her hand. "Like I told Kate, I'll be back."

Meghan used the pillow she had brought along to cushion her head against the window. "Do you want help staying awake?"

"Go ahead and sleep while you can. I'm fine for now."

"I sleep more now that I'm blind. It's subtle but I've learned to love naps." She closed her eyes and let herself relax. Stephen was one of the few men she trusted to drive safely for the conditions.

She was going to help Stephen through the next few months, even if it meant postcards JoAnne helped her read and phone calls to keep him current on news at home. He wanted to leave, but what he really needed was to stay. He'd figure that out eventually.

Tiredness overwhelmed her and she didn't fight it. She slept.

"Meghan." Stephen rubbed her arm. "We're outside Silverton."

She awoke with a start, her dream filled with music. He'd changed the radio station she realized groggily. Whatever this station was, it was nice. "Do you need directions? Dad said he'd leave the porch light on."

"I remember it's two right turns then watch for a huge rock."

"The rock moved a bit when someone ran into it, but it's still a safe marker. Are you getting tired? Should I find you a hotel room? Silverton has its first really nice tourist hotel and restaurant now."

"I've gotten a second wind; I'll be okay through the dawn." She heard the blinkers come on. "The night has cleared, the sky is full of stars, and there's a full moon over the western sky."

"It sounds like a good night to drive."

The car slowed. "There's the rock." The pavement changed to gravel in the long driveway to her parents' house. Stephen parked. "I'll bring your bag."

Meghan gathered up her water bottle and pillow, opened her door, and let Blackie out of the car. The gravel driveway had a distinct edge and a moderate downward slope. It took her only a few steps to place her position and walk confidently up to the house. She stepped inside, reaching back to hold the door open for Stephen. "Just set the bag by the stairs. Are you sure you wouldn't like some coffee?"

"I'm fine, Meg. Is there anything else I can do for you before I go?"

He was ready to move on. She smiled at him, determined to make it easy for him. "I'm home; this is comfortable terrain. Thanks for the ride."

"You're welcome."

She put out a hand to find Stephen's chest, then stepped forward to hug him. "Promise me, no heights until you stop with the fainting."

He laughed and ran his hand across her hair, ruffling it in a gesture that was as affectionate as it was simple. "No heights. It was nice having company tonight."

"You're welcome." She wanted to make the hurt of this day go away but couldn't. She rested her head against his chest. "It's going to be okay," she whispered and felt the emotions shake him. He was close to losing it and he wouldn't want her to witness that. She squeezed him and then let him go. She didn't try to put words to her good-bye; Stephen absolutely hated good-byes.

He stepped outside and she stood in the doorway, waving when she heard him put the car into gear. "Come back soon, Stephen," she whispered, listening to the car pull out of the drive.

 EIGHT

Kate tugged open her desk drawer, looked with longing at the chocolate bar and regretfully pushed it aside, knowing her queasy stomach would never handle it. She reached for the bag of crackers that came with the soup she'd had at lunch. She wanted the man currently in jail for kidnapping to catch a bad bout of the stomach flu as payback. He'd held a busload of children hostage because he wanted to kill himself and do it with media attention. At least one of the kids had the stomach flu. By the time Kate talked him into releasing them, she'd caught the bug and hadn't been able to shake it off for the last week.

"Try this." Her FBI agent husband set a bottle of Diet 7 Up in front of her and then perched on the edge of her desk. He didn't bother to tell her to go home. They'd already battled that out this morning before she left. One weekend in bed sick had convinced her she'd rather be on her feet. When she could stay standing, that was. The light-headedness hit at the most unfortunate times.

Dave didn't have to tell her she wasn't worth much on the job today. She'd voluntarily put herself on desk duty for the day. They had a deal: She would work as a hostage negotiator until they had a family, and then she would have to suffer a pedestrian career in homicide, robbery, or fraud. A child deserved to have both parents come home from work. And a hostage negotiator role was a bit too much risk to accept—even for her. This day of paperwork was turning her mind into mush and reminding her why she so disliked those safer options.

She twisted off the top and took a long drink then leaned back in her chair to look at him. The man looked fine, but he was smothering her with all his care. "I thought you had a day in court."

"It got bumped to tomorrow; the lawyers are arguing motions. It's kind of hard for a mob boss to get away with murdering his wife when it's obvious from the evidence that he did it. But he can stall the trial a bit."

The crime was four years old, or was it five? She lost track of time. It was a case of Dave's from before she knew him. A mob boss killed his wife for having an affair—a pretty straightforward conviction assuming evidence didn't get tossed on a technicality. Dave and his team were too good at their jobs to have that happen. "What is this, his second or third trial?"

"He bribed a juror the first time. His lawyer died of a heart attack in the second one. He won't get so lucky a third time. What time did Marcus say he was coming into town?"

"I told him we'd pick him up at seven." Marcus was making a twenty-four-hour visit at her request so they could hash out plans—someone had to go after Stephen. It was one thing to be traveling to get some space, another to stay away over the Christmas holidays. She wanted him home.

"Would you like me to make myself scarce so you two can talk?"

"Stay around. I have a feeling I'm going to need the backup. Marcus has a different opinion than I do and it could be an interesting discussion."

"Stephen is okay." Dave nudged her hair back behind her ear and tipped up her chin. "He's an O'Malley. He may not often go this far afield, but it's not like he doesn't have your phone number."

Would Dave tag along if she decided to go knock on Stephen's motel room door? He probably would, just so he could sympathize with her brother. "Some space is one thing; hurting and hiding is another. It's time to give him a shove back to the land of the living."

"I'll fix barbeque ribs on the grill for dinner to soften Marcus up, and we'll see if you can keep down a salad. You won't succeed in changing Marcus's mind, but for what it's worth, I'm on your side."

"You just don't want to spend the next couple weeks listening to me worry about Stephen."

Dave smiled. "You worry very nicely. It's kind of cute." He picked up the last cracker. "Eat; you need to keep something down today."

"I want my coffee back, and my sugar."

His eyes narrowed. "Still that rocky?"

She drank more of the Diet 7 Up. "This stuff is one step away from being medicine. Find me some goldfish crackers, okay? Those little yellow things."

Dave laughed. "It will ruin your image."

"Probably. But no one will dare say anything to my face."

He glanced around the open office packed with desks and men. "Sure they will—" he looked back at her—"just not until you feel better."

Arizona

Stephen checked the straps tying down the cover on the fishing boat, confirming it was still tight and secured for the night. Arizona in December was an odd combination of cool weather, occasional rain, desert, and huge reservoirs that had some of the best fishing in the Southwest. He'd bought the boat and trailer last month from a couple at the nearby campground, and he planned to sell it next month when he was ready to move on. It was cheaper than renting a boat since he planned to use it each day.

He picked up the bucket of chicken from the front seat of his truck—a replacement for his car that had died in South Dakota. He lifted a hand to the motel owner, who was washing windows in the office, and walked down to room number eight. The motel wouldn't bankrupt him, so he'd put down semitemporary roots here.

The carpet was worn and the furniture old, but the linens were fresh, the bed neatly remade. The owner's wife had brought down his mail and set it on the round table along with a promised piece of her raspberry cobbler.

Stephen dropped his keys on the dresser and stepped out of his shoes, setting his dinner on the table, and out of habit turned on the TV. He didn't care much about local news, so he flipped to cable news to see what was going on in the world.

The national news wasn't interesting: a multicar pileup in Georgia, a line of ice and winter storms in Colorado, and a steady rain across Florida, causing some flooding. He clicked over to a rerun of *Quincy*.

Stephen fixed a plate for dinner. Chicken was a change from his own catch of fish, even if it was about the hundredth chicken meal he'd had since this trip began.

He still hadn't decided if he wanted to go back for the O'Malley Christmas gathering. The fact he was debating it when normally a family gathering was the highlight, told him the memories that had driven this journey were far from settled. He would be there for the weddings in June and July—Jack, Rachel, and Marcus in quick succession—then all of his family would be married except him.

It was time to make some decisions he'd been avoiding for months. He didn't want to go back to Chicago, back to being a paramedic. That life was distant now and he didn't miss it. But if not Chicago, then what? Keeping the O'Malleys out of trouble was a mission that had run its course.

He was getting tired of traveling. He'd visited national parks and Indian reservations, seen a lot of wildlife, walked through numerous art galleries, and studied beautiful homes. He'd met fishermen and hunters and retired couples and teens longing to head to the big city. He'd ridden horses, done some white-water rafting, tried his hand at skydiving, and got some practice at waterskiing. He had needed the downtime, but there had just been too much time to think during the long drives.

He could join a construction crew and earn some serious money for the summer, but what would he spend it on? He could buy a home in Chicago and fix it up to live in long term, but it would have him bouncing around a huge place alone. He could start a business of his own—carpentry, construction—but it just didn't spark any interest.

He was bored. And lonely.

No O'Malley handled bored very well. He set down his dinner plate and went to wax the truck.

He wished the loneliness had as easy a solution.

CHICAGO

Marcus O'Malley took his soda into the living room, impressed with the efforts Kate had gone to for this brief visit. She called; he came. He would have come anyway on Dave's word that Kate was still feeling pretty rocky after the bus hostage crisis. Children slid under her defenses like no other victims, and she bore the weight of those calls for months. And she had never been able to handle being sick.

He sat on the couch and looked across at Kate, curled up on one of the chairs. He'd been the guardian of the O'Malleys for over two decades. He'd walked through some very dark days with Kate and there was no one he trusted more. It had been hard since Jennifer died, for they both had been feeling their way through the weeks and months. "What's the family grapevine say?"

"That if Stephen isn't coming home, we skip Christmas as a family. No one wants to meet without him there."

He turned his glass in his hand, studying the ice. "Is that why you think we need to tug him back?" He looked up and caught an expression briefly crossing her face that he couldn't interpret. His eyes narrowed. Emotional control defined Kate and how she handled her life, her job, and that had been a very fascinating flash.

"It's time. His place is here, not miles away. Christmas will be miserable for him if he spends it alone."

"I know."

"I don't want that for him."

"He wants it for himself. He wants to feel again, Kate, and when he hits Christmas alone he's got an excuse to feel miserable. Tug him back here, and he'd just have to pretend he's okay."

"He doesn't need to rescue us from the hurt."

"Doesn't he?" Marcus set aside the glass. "He protects you and he always has. Protecting you from his grief—it matters to him."

He watched her rise. Kate had very few tells that gave away what she was thinking, but a break in eye contact, pacing—something more than a disrupted family gathering was behind her desire to have Stephen back in Chicago. "Something going on with Meghan?"

She glanced over, startled.

"She's the one other person he's been sending some letters to. I know the two of you have talked a few times. Did he say anything that has you concerned?"

"No."

"Then relax. Stephen was like this the year after his parents died, when he didn't want anyone close. Give him a year away. He'll be back for the weddings."

She leaned against the bookshelves, sipping a cup of tea Dave gave her, pensive in a way he didn't remember seeing in a long time. "Okay, Marcus. I won't chase him down."

"What else is going on?"

She looked over and shook her head. "Nothing."

"You sure?"

She came over to settle back in her seat. "Do you think he'll bring someone to Jack and Cassie's wedding?"

"Maybe Ann and the boys. It would be logical since she's already on the invitation list. Stephen will settle down when he's ready, when the desire for roots is larger than the fear of having them torn away by tragedy. Drink your tea," Marcus encouraged.

"Your flight is at ten tomorrow morning?"

"Yes."

"I'll drive you to the airport. Dave's got a court appearance."

"Let's talk more in the morning then. I'm ready for a few hours of sleep." He stood and picked up his glass, then paused by her chair to touch her shoulder. "I'm glad you called."

"So am I."

He'd figure out what was going on. He took his glass back to the kitchen and went to find Dave to start some quiet questioning.

NINE

Arizona didn't provide snow for Christmas. Stephen took a walk after breakfast on Christmas morning, and when he returned to the motel, he decided he would spend the day on the water fishing and reading a book from Lisa. It was a depressing day to spend alone, but he had chosen this over being with family. He had only himself to blame.

The phone rang as he unlocked his room. He reached it on the third ring. "Hello?"

"Stephen, Merry Christmas! I wasn't sure I'd catch you."

He rubbed his eyes. "Hey, lady." He didn't want to burst Meghan's happiness with his less-than-compelling company. "I'm just heading out, as a matter of fact."

"You sound down."

So much for keeping his voice steady. "I'm just tired." He pulled out a chair at the table.

"I won't keep you. I just wanted to thank you for the Christmas gift. The time you must have invested to carve an entire chess set—I'm honored. The queen feels like an elegant lady. And the knights, I can feel their armor."

He sank back in the chair; he hadn't been sure how she would take the gift. "Finding time to whittle is easy given how many hours I've spent watching a bobber and hoping for a fish to come by. I remember you said you loved to play."

"There's no need to downplay the effort. I love the gift. I'll practice with Dad, so when you return I'll be able to give you a decent game."

"I'll enjoy that, Meg."

"Is your Christmas Day going okay?"

He looked at the remaining unwrapped gifts from his family still on the table. He was trying to avoid the bittersweet joy that would come with opening them. They could wait until tonight when his sadness had worn off. At least he hoped it would. "I'm going fishing. It's a sunny day here and nice weather to be on the water," he said, trying to convince himself.

"Have you opened my gift yet?"

He moved around the packages on the table. The shoebox-size gift from her had a big red bow on it. "I'll open it tonight. I'm saving it for last."

"Oh, that's sweet. Call me later when you open it, okay? No matter what the time."

"It could be pretty late, Meg."

"That's okay. You'll understand later."

"All right. What are you doing with the rest of your day?"

"Thinking about furniture. I'm buying a house."

His hand stopped twisting the ribbon on her package. "When did this come about?"

Meghan laughed. "Suddenly. The current owners are moving to Nebraska for a job that starts January 1, and they have to sell quickly. We came to a fair price. It's the house I've dreamed about for years. It's in town, just off Main Street, so I can walk to work at the medical clinic. The house is small enough that I won't feel overwhelmed to maintain it, but the yard will be fine for Blackie. There's room for a craft area, an office, and a large bedroom suite. I'm not wild about the basement but I can use it for storage."

"I'm happy for you, Meg. Are your parents comfortable with the idea?"

"Not entirely, but it's time. You've got a standing invitation to see it when you come back to town."

"I'll take you up on that."

"Is there anything I can do to help make your day brighter?"

"You already have, Meghan. It was good to hear your voice. I'll call you later tonight."

"Then I'll let you go. Take care."

He hung up the phone, smiling, and picked up his keys. The day would pass peacefully if he didn't let himself think about what he'd lost. He had a conference call with his family arranged for this evening; he would look forward to that. *Jennifer, today I just miss your voice.*

Stephen opened the rest of the gifts from his family after dinner on Christmas Day, a cup of hot coffee on the table beside him, a piece of raspberry cobbler for dessert. It wasn't what they sent as much as the fact that they had plastered the wrapped gifts with stickers and all signed the funny Christmas card. He found his favorite salami, hot mustard, an assortment of cheeses, homemade cookies, new fishing lures, two new books, and a stack of prepaid phone cards. He smiled at the phone cards. He was missed. He was loved. And the gifts were comfort gifts.

Stephen picked up the large flat box from Jack. He tugged out a painting, and his laughter echoed around the room. Jack had sent him the fish painting. He should have predicted it; he'd given it to Jack five years ago. It had been passed around among the O'Malleys as the white elephant gift and had finally come full circle. Stephen took down a painting on the wall and hung the fish for its one day of the year on display.

He gathered up the wrapping paper and filled a garbage bag, then straightened the gifts on the table. Taking a couple homemade peanut butter cookies with him, he stretched out on the bed and picked up the phone. He dialed from memory. "Hello, Meghan. What am I interrupting?"

"I'm curled up in the chair between the fireplace and the Christmas tree, listening to the quiet house. I'll probably fall asleep here before I make it to bed."

He could see her there enjoying the fire. "A nice picture."

"Hmm, it is. Did your day turn out okay?"

"I had a good day fishing." He shifted to look at the shoebox beside him. "I opened your gift. I don't know what to say. I'm overwhelmed." The box was full of cassette tapes made by Meghan, recording her favorite songs and providing her own intros to the artists.

"I enjoyed being the deejay. I didn't want you falling asleep when you drove, so now you can have me for company."

"I wish I had been a better friend to you over the years."

"Would you stop? You're going to make me all teary tonight."

"The gift is great."

"You're very welcome." A comfortable silence stretched between them. "I wish I could take away the loneliness that comes with today, Stephen."

"Your voice helps."

"Has it helped, getting away for a while?"

He thought about the myriad ways he could answer that and couldn't put all the emotions into words. "Yes."

"Then I'm glad you went."

Life goes on. It was about the only thing he'd really learned, but it would do. "I think I might come home in the spring."

"Whenever you come I imagine you'll get quite an O'Malley welcome home party," Meghan finally replied.

She hadn't tried to lock him down on a return date. He relaxed. The idea had formed and been spoken in the same breath. "Will you come to the party?"

"Am I going to be jealous of a great tan, big fish tales, and generally wishing I could have seen all the sights you've seen?"

"Absolutely."

"Well in that case..."

It felt good to laugh with her. He thought of all the majestic sights he had seen and all the places he had visited. "Someday I'll take you to the Tetons. You'd love the way the wind blows through the canyons and words echo against the mountains. You need a vacation too." He'd probably have to haul her up the path when they got to the high altitudes, but she'd get a taste of a mountain so intense she'd almost be able to see it as she climbed those paths and encountered snow at the higher elevations.

"I'd like that."

"So would I." Silence stretched. "I should let you go. It's late there."

"If you can't sleep, try tape eight."

He leaned over the side of the bed and shifted cassettes. "I found it. Good night, beautiful."

"G'night."

She was the first to hang up. Stephen held the receiver, thinking a minute, smiling, then set it down. He'd been blessed in his friends.

He slipped the tape into the cassette player he carried with him when he went fishing and turned it on. "It was the night before Christmas and all through the house, not a single person was moving; except for a smart blind mouse." Stephen laughed and shut it off to listen to later. She was priceless. She'd known the silence of this place would get to him, and she solved it in a unique way.

There was one box yet to open. He glanced at it on the table occasionally as he prepared to turn in early. The box was square and heavy. It wasn't the desire to have one last package left that delayed him. The tag on the box said it was from Jennifer's husband Tom.

He finally sat at the table and picked up the accompanying envelope.

Stephen, Jennifer asked me to give you this after a year passed. After some thought, I decided you should have it for the holidays. — Tom

Stephen opened the envelope, his name written in Jennifer's familiar elegant script. The fragrance in the letter was faint but one he immediately associated with his sister. She loved lilacs.

Stephen, it's hard to write a note knowing it will be words from the grave. I love you. I know how hard this last year must have been for you. I'd like to help with a gentle nudge. You have so many facts about God, but you've never let yourself get to know Him. Please meet Him. Jesus is someone you can trust, and He's the only one who can help with the hurt you're feeling now. I miss you, my friend. With all my love, Jennifer.

The note was her voice.

His hand shook as he opened the box. After reading her words, he wasn't surprised at the contents. He picked up Jennifer's diary. It was dated in gold on the cover with last year's date. He remembered Tom had given her this new one at that last Christmas. Beneath the diary was her Bible. He carried the two items with him and stretched out on the bed. He couldn't open the diary, not yet. Whatever she had been feeling those last few weeks before she died would be so hard to read. He picked up the Bible instead. She'd left a bookmark in the fourth chapter of Luke.

Religion had always felt like false hope. He'd been disappointed too many times to want to put his faith in something tangible. But belief in God had become an important part of his siblings' lives. The topic would be there when he returned home whether he tried to run from it or not. He owed Jennifer. To ease the pain of how he'd disappointed her, he took her note to heart and accepted that he couldn't run anymore from the topic of God. He started reading at her bookmark.

TEN

CHICAGO

"This is the most depressing New Year's Eve party I've ever attended."

Kate glanced up from her Diet Coke, wondering if it was the crabmeat crackers or the lobster rolls that were making her queasy tonight. Great. She just got over the flu only to give herself food poisoning eating questionable hors d'oeuvres. She tugged out the chair beside her with her foot. "Sit, Jack. You're bored."

Her brother dropped into the chair, tugging at his tie. At the invitation of her captain, they were crashing a New Year's Eve party sponsored by the Police Retirement Association. She was on the job, but about the only crisis happening on New Year's Eve so far was an attempted shooting and barricade at a hotel down the block, which she'd settled in an hour. "Cassie will be here soon."

"I should have just gone to pick her up."

"Give her a chance to get beautiful. The night will be better when she arrives." Kate looked at her watch. Where was Dave? He got off at ten, and it was half an hour past when she thought he'd be here. She rubbed a headache growing worse with each hour. How much grief would Dave give her if she admitted red spots were dancing in the edge of her vision now? She was ready to go home.

"I heard Marcus is coming to town in a couple weeks. Maybe we can get a family basketball game in?"

How long had it been since they last gathered as a group to play some ball? The schedules for couples were never as easy to coordinate as the spur-of-the-moment games they used to have when everyone was single. They hadn't played in months. The night of Jennifer's funeral they had played a pick-up game, using it to wear off the stress of the day. But after Stephen left, it felt strange playing without him. Kate forced a smile, pretty sure she'd be flat on her face if she tried to run on a basketball court right now. "We'll do that."

She spotted Jack's fiancée walking across the hotel lobby. "There's Cassie."

He spun out of his chair before she finished the words.

Kate watched him reach Cassie and sweep her up in a greeting. It was good for the O'Malleys now to be couples. Jack and the others were happy; she was head over heels in love with her husband. But the price of their happiness was higher than she thought.

What was Stephen doing tonight? He was being left out as the family transformed itself. When he set out on his drive she should have gone with him, should have stopped him from leaving. She drank her Coke and brooded.

Kate shoved scrambled eggs onto two plates next to some toast. "Stephen spent New Year's Day helping a guy hang cabinets. We've got to get him, Marcus, and drag him back here. He isn't grieving; he's stuck in a hole and making a motel in Arizona his home. What does he think, that we don't want him here?" It was the middle of January, and she felt like she'd lost a brother as well as a sister. It had been wrong to let this go on so long.

Marcus took the plate she handed him and pulled out a chair across from hers. "It's more than grief over Jennifer and the memories from his past the funeral stirred. He absorbed the pressure of working in this town for years without a break. He needs some time to decide what he wants to do. That's not a crisis, Kate. It's just his way of figuring things out. You know he's a runner."

She scowled. "I remember." She had tried to tail him during one of his attempts to run away from Trevor House, and he intentionally lost her by doubling back through the school yard. Stephen had looked after her over the years; it was time she looked after him. "How much longer?"

"A few weeks."

She looked at Marcus and finally accepted it with a nod. She'd be one of those going after Stephen. She wanted so badly to get a hug from him and know they were okay. "Like some more coffee?"

"Sure."

Kate got up from the table and staggered.

Marcus shot out his hand to catch her arm. "Whoa, sit back down."

She sat and he pushed her head between her knees.

"Here." Marcus pressed her water glass into her hand.

She lifted clammy hands and gripped it hard.

"I saw what you didn't eat, so that's not what's causing this. Why didn't you let the doctor check you out last month when this started?"

She bobbled the glass and nearly spilled the water. "I don't want to hear I've got cancer like Jennifer."

His hand tightened on the back of her neck. "I wish you had said something to Dave." She looked up. Marcus looked like she'd punched him in the gut.

"Dave would have just taken me to see a doctor."

"What do you think I'm going to do?"

She lowered her head and tried to take deep breaths, knowing the day had just moved out of her control. She'd been trying so hard to keep Dave from seeing one of these spells. She should have known her luck would run out around Marcus.

"Seriously, can a doctor make you feel any worse?"

The light-headedness faded and she forced herself to sit up. "Call Meghan. Maybe she'll know the name of a good doctor who has a decent bedside manner." Between the headaches, the waves of light-headedness, and the recurring nausea, her symptoms were growing steadily worse. She couldn't avoid the reality any longer. She groaned and laid her head down on the table. "I feel awful."

"I'll be right back."

Meghan thanked JoAnne for the ride to Lake Forest, caught hold of Blackie's handle, and turned toward Dave and Kate's house. She was glad she'd already been in town when her mom passed along the call.

"Thanks for coming, Meghan."

"It's my pleasure." She walked toward Marcus's voice, grateful there was something she could do for the O'Malleys for a change. Blackie led her up two steps and into the house.

Marcus clasped her hand with his. "You look really good."

"Thank you. How's Kate doing?"

"I talked her into lying down upstairs."

"Take me to see her?"

"Sure. Can I get you a drink or something first?"

"I'm fine for now." She motioned Blackie to follow him and walked up the stairs, out of habit silently counting them. They reached the landing. "Let me see her alone."

Marcus hesitated. "Sure. Her room is the second door on your left."

Meghan squeezed his arm and walked down the hall, trailing a hand along the wall to the second doorway. She tapped on the door. "I hear you're feeling pretty awful."

"Like someone is trying to take out my guts from the inside out," Kate replied. "The bed is six feet straight ahead, then there's a chair on your left."

Meghan let Blackie escort her to the chair as she smiled at her friend. "That symptom sounds descriptive. What time's your appointment?"

"One o'clock. And you don't need to make sure I actually get there."

"JoAnne and I were in town shopping. I was ready for a break." Meghan reached for Kate's wrist, checked her pulse, and then rubbed her arm.

"Don't bother. I'm dying."

Meghan settled back in the chair but kept her hand on Kate's. "You're not dying. I've seen a lot of the flu this year that is laying out grown men. You could be slightly allergic to the type of cologne Dave uses for all we know, but we'll eliminate the obvious things first—stomach flu, a reaction to your birth control pills, the start of an ulcer. Do you really think you've got cancer like Jennifer?"

"It crossed my mind a few times," Kate muttered.

Meghan squeezed Kate's hand, understanding just how hard it was to push away irrational thoughts when it came down to scary *what ifs*. "We'll let Sandy sort it out. I promise you'll feel better tomorrow, if only because you won't need to worry about it anymore."

"I'm scared, Meg. And I am never scared."

Meg turned Kate's wedding ring. "You're not going to lose everything you love just because for the first time you have happiness with Dave, a job you enjoy, and peace with God. It's not about to get ripped away from you. I promise you that."

"Jennifer died. Stephen left. And the fear eats at me because I'm never sick and something is wrong."

"Jennifer's waiting for you in heaven, and Stephen will come back. Depend on God, and the fear will find its right size. He's bigger than whatever is wrong."

"Dave's going to meet us at the doctor's office. He'll have to break the speed limit to get back in time, but he's determined."

"He loves you."

"I know, Meghan. I'm depending on that." Kate sighed. "I'd better change and get ready to go." She eased to the edge of the bed. "You'll keep Marcus company in the waiting room?"

"I will," Meg said. "He's worried about you."

"Good. It serves him right for telling on me to Dave."

Meg laughed.

Meghan sat beside Marcus and listened to the sounds in the waiting room. She could hear pages quickly turning in a magazine—Marcus wasn't pausing to read anything. "Would you relax? Kate's going to be fine."

"She looked awful."

Meghan patted his arm.

She missed this, the pace and flow of patients. She faintly heard Kate's voice saying good-bye to the doctor. "Marcus, call Dave again and tell him not to bother to park but to come around front to the circle drive. Kate and I will meet you in the lobby."

She heard him set down the magazine. "You're right; she's coming and her color is better."

"I think she would prefer talking with Dave downstairs rather than here in a crowded waiting room."

"A good assumption, Meg. I'll go intercept him. Meet you by the entrance downstairs."

A few moments later Kate collapsed into the seat Marcus just vacated. Meghan turned toward her. "What's the verdict?"

Kate struggled to get the words out. "I'm pregnant."

Meghan reached over and gripped her friend's hand. She'd been hoping that was the case. Kate's hand turned in hers and about cut off the circulation.

Kate sighed and then laughed. "Dave is going to be thrilled. World class thrilled."

"How far along did she think you are?"

"Eight weeks? Ten? I didn't hear much of what she said after the word *pregnant.*" Kate leaned forward. "Am I going to be this sick the entire nine months?"

Meghan smiled as she rubbed Kate's back. "Cheer up. You've only got seven months to go."

Kate groaned.

"The first trimester is normally the worst of it. Are you happy about this?"

"Yeah. I think I'm going to start blubbering soon. What do I know about babies? I have no idea how to be a mom."

"You'll learn how just like everybody else. Marcus went to find Dave. He'll meet us at the entrance."

"He's going to pick me up, whirl me around, and I'm going to lose the crackers I had down the front of his shirt."

"Toast, hot tea, no caffeine. I'll take you through a whole list of things that will help." Meghan got to her feet and offered her hand. Kate took it. "You're going to make a great mom."

"At least my son or daughter will have two parents who never leave."

Meghan wrapped her arm around Kate's waist and hugged her, hearing the absolute promise. "And I'm going to throw you the biggest baby shower you've ever seen."

"Meg, don't you dare."

Meghan laughed. "I bet your fellow cops would come. What are friends for, if not to embarrass you?"

ARIZONA

Stephen drove back to the motel Friday night, one hand on the wheel, the other rubbing a blister forming on the side of his left thumb. Next time he volunteered to help install a garage door opener, he would make sure he had on better gloves. Homemade bread still warm from the oven rested in a sack beside him, filling the cab with a wonderful aroma. He'd miss this barter system after he moved on to a more formal job in Texas. He pulled into the motel parking lot and felt a jolt. Marcus was leaning against a BMW waiting for him. Stephen parked and shut off the truck. The solemn focus on his brother's face warned him.

"It's Kate," Stephen said, guessing what would send Marcus halfway across the country without a warning phone call.

Marcus just nodded.

Stephen picked up the sack and shut the door of the truck feeling like a very old man. He'd known a day like this would come when she walked into a crisis and got into serious trouble.

"She's pregnant, Stephen."

He stopped halfway across the parking lot at the quiet words. "Kate?"

An easy smile played at the corners of Marcus's mouth. "That was about her reaction too. Does this town have somewhere you can get a good meal?"

Stephen shifted the sack. "Grandy's down the road a bit."

"There's no close airport and I've been driving for hours. We need to talk."

Stephen drove him to Grandy's, taking along the homemade bread. They settled at the back table. "Is she doing okay?"

"She's sicker than I've ever seen a lady get and struggling to accept the change this will mean at work. She kept her promise to Dave—she's moving over to work robbery and fraud. Her days as a hostage negotiator are over. She's hoping an opening in homicide will become available."

"Kate is going to be a mom." Stephen tried to get his thoughts around that new reality and found it a stretch. "I didn't even know she wanted to start a family right away."

Marcus smiled. "She came out of the doctor's office in a bit of shock. She didn't even suspect it."

"Dave is okay with it?"

"Walking on air and so proud you'd figure the baby was already born."

Stephen could see that; Dave was head over heels in love with Kate and the type of guy to celebrate the fact that he'd soon be a father. Stephen thought about Kate being pregnant and the image caused his smile to grow. "When's she due?"

"The doctor gave her a date in mid-July."

"I appreciate your coming to tell me in person, but you could have called."

"And miss out on seeing your expression when you heard the news?" Marcus opened the ketchup for his French fries. "I also figured I could talk you into showing me a good fishing spot so I could get a day out on the water before I fly back. I've seen those recent pictures you sent Jack."

"I can provide a great couple hours of fishing," Stephen promised, pleased to hear Marcus would be able to stay.

Marcus's smile turned serious as he started his meal. "This is me asking, not Kate: Did you get through Christmas okay?"

Stephen thought about it and shrugged. "The day passed. It was sadder than the day Jennifer died and so incredibly long. Every time I thought about past Christmases, she was always center in the memories. You?"

"Shari and I spent it with her family in Virginia, and I tried not to slow down long enough to think."

Stephen hesitated, then said quietly, "I went to church the Sunday after Christmas and sang a few songs. It seemed the thing to do."

Marcus looked over at him for a long moment and then nodded. "Thanks, it means a lot. And Jennifer would have really appreciated it too." Marcus picked up his sandwich. "I saw Meghan the other day. She asked about you."

"Is she doing okay?"

"She seems to be. She mentioned that Ken was teaching her to ski."

Stephen tore off a chunk of bread. "That's a nice way to break her neck."

"I told her that. She laughed and said when she *could* see she inevitably closed her eyes, so it wasn't much different."

"She mentioned at Christmas that she was buying a house."

"She's moved in. Kate saw the house and said it's wonderful. It's been good for Kate to have Meghan back in her life."

"Meg's a good friend to have."

"I wish you had gotten serious about her years ago. I like her."

"A few months ago you were hoping Ann and her boys would be the right fit."

"Ann's a great lady and her boys are priceless, but you dated her and settling down didn't cross your mind, which rather disappointed me as well as Jennifer," Marcus remarked. "You were restless then and you're *still* restless."

"I don't know what I'm looking for, Marcus. If I knew, I would have already found it." Stephen picked up his glass. "Ann seems pretty content the last couple times we've talked. I heard Gage was over at her place for Christmas, helping her boys with their new bikes." As surprised as he was at Gage's involvement, he knew it was a good development. Gage had lost his wife and son in a fire. For him to have found peace enough to spend time with Ann and her boys—Stephen knew his sister Rachel would be relieved at that turn of events. And surprisingly he thought it would be a good fit for both Ann and Gage.

"True enough." Marcus twirled ice in his water glass. "I'd like you to come home."

"I'll be there if I'm needed, you know that."

"That's the other reason I'm here. You're needed. Kate is worried about you, and that I would like to end."

Stephen winced. "I don't know that I ever planned to be gone this long. I'm sorry if it caused you problems."

Marcus shrugged. "It gives me something to do."

"I'll head home after I finish up a roofing job here."

"Thanks, Stephen." Marcus took a drink of his soda.

"Think I'll get a homecoming party?"

Marcus laughed. "With Jack around? You'll be lucky not to get a parade."

"So maybe I shouldn't advertise my return date..."

"You can try, but you'll never surprise him." Marcus finished his meal and tugged out his wallet to leave the tip. "Come on; let's get me a place to crash and plan to meet for an early morning of fishing."

They returned to the motel. Stephen saw his brother settled in a room near his, then said good-night.

He tossed his keys on the table in his room and looked around. He dug out his suitcase from the bottom of the closet and began to pack. It would take a couple weeks to finish the roofing job and sell the boat, but it was time.

He was going to be an uncle. Stephen couldn't hold back a smile. That was enough of a mission for the near future. He would go back to Chicago, rejoin his family, and spend the next couple years spoiling the next generation of O'Malleys. It felt like the right decision. For all the things Chicago lacked—good or bad—it was the place he thought of as home. He would be an exceptionally good uncle.

ELEVEN

Stephen drove north into Illinois the morning of February 15, the sun bright in his eyes and his sunglasses a welcome shield. Snow remained on the roadsides and in patches beneath trees where the sun couldn't reach. Fields lay dormant for the winter, the ground covered with rows of short brown stalks from corn harvests the fall before. He had left the state in the heat of summer and was returning with the merest hint of pending spring.

He slipped in the fourth tape Meghan had made, enjoying the sound of her voice introducing the songs. Occasionally he heard JoAnne on the tapes, laughing with Meghan in the background as the two of them selected songs.

No one knew he was coming today. It was a good tactical decision. He would open up his apartment, unload his groceries, do some laundry, then go make peace with Kate. Of all of his family, Kate was the one who read him best, who knew how close he was to not coming back.

He glanced at the huge rabbit in the passenger seat kept upright by a seat belt. It would get a laugh. Kate would probably hug him then playfully hit him, but it would at least break the ice.

Lisa and her husband Quinn were in Montana; Marcus was in Washington; Rachel—he wasn't sure where she was. The last he heard she was traveling in Georgia for the Red Cross. That left Jack as the only other O'Malley in Chicago, and finding him would only require a stop at the fire station. The time would let Stephen ease back into the flow with family.

And after that?

Stephen chewed on a toothpick. Two of his remodeled homes were nearing their closing dates to the couples currently renting them. He'd have to make a decision about what property to roll the income into next. The realtor had three properties she thought he might like to look at. It would do for a short-term answer.

A semi loaded with new cars rolled past. Stephen picked up the map. He would be home today. But before he got there, he had one stop to make.

SILVERTON

Meghan scrubbed the skillet and the two pans she had used as she hummed along to the song on the radio. The kitchen was filled with the smell of baked lasagna and bubbling cheese. Dinner in exchange for Ken's help was a good deal. By nightfall her new home would be graced with a piano. Drying her hands, Meghan stopped to touch the timer and listen to the countdown. Five more minutes. She didn't want the lasagna to bake completely, so she could finish it when Ken and JoAnne arrived.

She ran a hand along the edge of the counter and walked from the kitchen into the living room. This was her home. After years of dreaming, it was now reality. Her things were on the counters, in the cupboards, placed so she would know exactly where they were. The darkness was replaced with a certain knowledge of the rooms and where she had left items.

The spot on the wall for the upright piano was cleared. She sized up the opening again and took a step back to mark how far out the bench would come. She would still have three steps before she touched the side of the couch. Yes, this would work.

Furniture was always a hard thing to figure out. A few inches one way or the other and she would find herself either brushing into things or losing her exact sense of position in the room. The more cues to give her perspective in a room the better.

She hated the reality of the darkness she now lived in and always walking forward on trust for what was ahead of her. No one who had a fear of falling could survive being blind. This home would be her sanctuary. She curled her bare toes into the warm carpet, able to tell the line in the room the sun had reached by the change in temperature. JoAnne said this room was white, bright, and lovely. Meghan loved that description.

Neil Coffer had blessed her by offering her the piano his wife had played for years. Live music would soon fill this house. Not very good music at first, but she made herself a long-term promise to learn to play.

Neil's wife had died this past September, succumbing to weakness in her lungs after a lingering case of pneumonia. Neil had been relieved his wife never reached the point that she needed to be placed in a nursing home. Her death was peaceful, and that was helping Neil cope with it more than anything else.

Over the past months Neil began slowly giving away things his wife valued. It mattered to him that her piano be used, and Meghan had heard relief in his voice when she accepted his offer. Music was one of the few things his wife held on to until her death, and the piano was special.

Meghan touched her watch and listened to the spoken time. There was time to stop by the bank before she went back to work. She was going to do a round of home follow-ups with Ashley this afternoon, then make a point of stopping by the jewelry store to see Neil.

She opened the front door. "Blackie, are you ready to go?" He wasn't at the front door waiting to come back in, which was a bit of a surprise as he had a habit of begging whenever she cooked.

"Hello, Meghan."

Her hand tightened on the doorknob. "Stephen!" She leaned against the doorjamb and just let the pleasure of his presence settle inside. He was back. She knew this day was coming, but now that it was here... She laughed. "Where *are* you?"

She heard the sound of a jacket as he twisted. "Seated on the bottom step of your porch saying hello to your dog."

She moved that direction, putting out her hand and getting the reassuring grip of his closing around hers. His hand was harder, stronger, and bigger than she remembered. Her memory had dulled with the passing of time. "Are you coming or going from Chicago?" she asked, wondering what else her memories had softened or forgotten about this man.

"I'm moseying that direction. I figured I would return via the same path I left."

He drew her down to sit on the step beside him. He had been only a voice at the end of a phone line for months, and now he was in the flesh and his presence had substance. She was aware of his broad shoulders as she shared the step.

Blackie pushed against her free hand, wiggling in between the two of them to share the joy. Stephen laughed. "You're speechless."

She smiled. "You didn't mention you were coming here."

"And miss this moment?" His shoulder leaned against hers. "It's great to see you, Meg."

She tried to remember what she was wearing, hoping she hadn't spilled lasagna fixings while making lunch, wishing like crazy that she'd at least had enough warning to brush her hair. "You'll have to take what you get then, because for the life of me, I don't know what I look like at the moment." He still held her hand. She suddenly realized she was sitting outside in February, and though there wasn't snow on the steps, it was still too close to winter. "And it's cold out here."

"You look as beautiful as ever, and the cold...I can help with that. I brought you something." He released her hand and turned away. "Here you go. I'll put it on your lap."

"You brought me a jacket?"

"Sheep's wool inside and a nice golden brown leather on the outside."

She stroked the coat, finding the pockets and then the collar. "It's so soft."

"I thought of you as soon as I saw it."

He took it and helped her put it on.

"Oh my." It was like slipping into a heated blanket.

Stephen turned up the collar. "It's a popular jacket in North Dakota for a reason. It gets really cold there."

"You shouldn't have."

"I know." She heard the smile in his voice. "I wanted to. There are matching gloves."

She slipped them on and they were a perfect fit. "Thank you, Stephen." She leaned over and hugged him hard, not only for the gift, but also for buying her mittens when he was fourteen. Hugging him hadn't been okay back then; she would have embarrassed him.

He rubbed her back. "You're very welcome. Ninety hours ago I was walking around in shirtsleeves in seventy-degree weather. I've been frozen since I crossed into the state. I'm remembering fast one of the reasons I left."

She laughed, hearing the old Stephen in his words and the tough edge of his humor. "Then why are we sitting out here?"

"The gift doesn't mean as much inside."

She felt the slight breeze and the cold on her face. "We might be able to find enough snow to have a really brief snowball fight if you like, just to give you a taste of the winter you missed."

"Me? Toss a snowball at a blind lady?"

She shoved him off the step.

"On second thought..." She heard him sit back up. "I missed you, Meg."

"Someone has been pampering you while you were gone."

"I gained a few pounds from the pies, cakes, and cookies offered. Speaking of which, something smells good."

"Dinner!" Meghan surged to her feet.

She yanked open the door and rushed through the house into the kitchen. She shut the oven off, then cracked the oven door to let the heat dissipate more quickly. Slipping off the jacket, she draped it over a chair, put the gloves on the table, and went to grab the hot pads.

"Everything okay?"

She set the hot dish down and closed the oven, aware her cheeks were flushed from the heat. "Ken and JoAnne are coming for dinner tonight. I thought I'd only partially bake it now, but it definitely smells done. Did the cheese overcook?"

"A nice golden brown on the edges. It will warm okay."

"Good. Thank you. You're welcome to stay for dinner if you like. As you can see, there's plenty." Blackie nudged her left knee, letting her know he had joined her. She held down her hand and stroked his fur. He offered more than just comfort, he was warm, furry, and affectionate.

"I'd enjoy dinner, Meg, but I'd best take a rain check. I need to be back in Chicago in time to see Kate tonight. I hear she turns in early these days."

Her smile softened. "I hear that too. Pregnancy was a huge change to her system the first few months, and she's had it pretty rough. It will be good for her to have you home."

"I'm looking forward to seeing her. I'm going to love being an uncle." She heard the floorboard creak as he moved away. "I like your new home."

She slipped her hands into her pockets, wishing she knew what he looked like after months away. Her memories were a mix of days of a teenage crush and from five years ago when he was a paramedic. His voice was different now…older maybe, though it was much more than that. "Speaking of which, how did you find my house?"

"I stopped by and saw your father at the clinic and he gave me directions. Would you give me a tour of your new house? Maybe take a walk and show me your town? I can linger a couple hours before I need to head to the city."

If he could give her a couple hours, she would take it. "Let me call the office and tell them I won't be in for a while."

"Already done. Ashley said she could handle the two urgent follow-up visits and move the others to tomorrow."

"Oh, okay," she said, surprised that he'd made the arrangements for her.

"You could also tell me to come back another day. We've been friends long enough I could probably take it."

She moved toward his voice, making a calculated guess where he was standing so she could invade his space but not run into him. She heard his half step back as she reached him, indicating she had guessed it right. She smiled privately as she lifted her hand to touch his jacket. Worn leather, aged, and comfortable to her touch. She had a feeling it was the same jacket she'd often tossed in the back of her car after he left it in the hospital employee lounge.

She wanted to grip it and hold on to that fleeting vivid flashback so she could see it. The memory shook her and her words didn't have the sassy fun tone she had planned but huskiness. "A brief tour of the house, and then we take a walk," she offered. "I've got one errand I need to do before I take the rest of the day off."

His hands settled on her shoulders. "Deal." He squeezed lightly then stepped back. She heard him pick up the jacket he had given her and the gloves. "You once called this your dream house. Why?"

She nodded toward the living room and he moved that direction. She followed him. "When I was in high school, I used to babysit for the people who lived here. I fell in love with the big bay windows and the sunlight in this room. They had a rocking chair…right here, and the sun during the summer months made it a cozy place to sit. When Jessie fussed I'd rock her in the chair and she'd always fall asleep. It was my chair, you know? My place. And I'd sit here rocking her, looking around the room, and think this place was so peaceful, the perfect home."

"Making it a dream."

She nodded. "I had it all planned when I was sixteen: married, kids, working for my dad, and living in this house." She thought of that dream, still wistful about how simple it was in those days, and turned to smile his direction. "I'll find the perfect rocking chair soon."

"What goes there on the east wall?"

Her joy fed her smile. "Ken is bringing my piano tonight."

"I didn't know you played."

"I'm taking piano lessons. Mrs. Teal sees me as a creative challenge. She's a great teacher. A few of her students have gone on to great things—Theresa is working in Hollywood composing original music for movies, and Jonathan is now in Europe playing with the London symphony and recording. I have a small goal, but the church needs a pianist next winter when the Carlsons go to Florida, and I want to know a few songs well enough to be able to play some Sundays."

"You will make a really good pianist; I already know it."

"I want to try. The music is mine, you know? That's the one thing that is the same before and after the blindness."

"I started to get that feeling as I listened to tape number six and realized you'd made it at about three in the morning. Those drumsticks you were tapping on the desk jarred the turntable, making the needle occasionally skip."

"JoAnne and I were crashed at her place going through a stack of old LPs she found. I liked making those tapes. That gift was something I didn't have to adapt because of my blindness."

"That's twice in the space of a few minutes you've drawn the line of before and after the accident. You're not compromising when you make life work, Meg."

"Sure I am."

"It's not 'good for someone who's blind'; it's just good."

She tilted her head, hearing under the quiet words a layer of steel. He'd taken her words personally and was offended at the idea on her behalf. "True. Maybe the compromises are more subtle. I don't try some things now that I once would have. The adjustments are too great."

"I hear you're learning to ski."

She laughed. "Two lessons and I about broke my leg." She smiled at him and tossed off the melancholy that came when she talked of unfulfilled dreams. "Come on, Stephen. Serious discussions can come later. Let's walk. I want to show you my town."

He helped her with the jacket. "Do you need to lock up the house?"

"Pull the door and it will lock. I've got keys in my pocket."

She snapped her fingers for Blackie. His harness was on a peg beside the door. He accepted it eagerly, his tail slapping against her jeans as she knelt beside him.

"He's been a good addition to your life."

"An excellent one. He's saved my life a few times when it comes to crazy drivers ignoring lights."

Stephen's hand touched her arm. "I hope he's not averse to working with a partner. There will be two of us watching for crazy drivers today."

She found the fact he was up front about it reassuring. "I think Blackie likes you. Just be careful not to confuse him and point left when I say right." He held the door and they stepped outside. She tightened her grip on the harness. "Let's walk toward Main Street; I need to stop by the bank."

"Sure."

The sidewalk wasn't wide enough to walk abreast without crowding Blackie. Stephen moved them to the street.

Meghan wasn't sure about it. "Walking on the street is dangerous."

"Silverton has how many cars total in the entire town?"

"Good point." She settled into a rhythm with Blackie, the dog's stride naturally fast. She liked heading somewhere with Blackie confidently leading the way. His assurance became hers, and she could move without worrying what was ahead of her.

"Tell me about your town."

She turned her head toward him and smiled. "I've decided there are three types of small towns: the sad ones that are dying because people are moving away; the confused ones formed by transplanted residents from big cities trying to learn to function in small communities; and the best kind, like Silverton."

She motioned to the houses on either side of the street. "Families have lived here for generations. The town is thriving but not trying to attract large numbers of new residents. The town has a heart to it in the library, post office, and restaurant. A center in its church. And functionality in its bank, general store, and pharmacy. The pace here is balanced between work and family."

"Silverton has always been part of your dream—a community that is part of your life."

"It's one of the reasons it was so hard to translate my dreams to a big city. I wanted this small-town background. And this place fits my nursing career so well. Working in the hospital was just about treating the sick or injured. Here I'm part of my patients' lives, and I know what's going on with their jobs and their families. I'm able to go with Ashley on her rounds and sit and talk with Dad's patients, have the follow-up conversations that can ferret out the small facts that can influence medication levels and recovery times."

"Ashley's been your father's head nurse for several years, right?"

"Forever it seems. She was the reason I wanted to be a nurse. I'd go hang out with Dad at the clinic, and Ashley would show me what she was doing and why. She's lived here for over twenty years; there are no secrets from her in this town. My blindness helps sometimes. Diabetes, age-related injuries, chronic pain—I understand the frustration of knowing what it's like to battle something day after day. People are more willing to listen to my suggestions because I've been there."

"You're happy back here, with your job, your house?"

"Yes. It's home, Stephen."

"I'm glad." He touched her arm. "The bank is just ahead."

"I'll be about ten minutes."

"No hurry. Why don't we meet at JoAnne's store?"

She nodded, wondering what her friend would think when Stephen walked in. At least JoAnne would be able to tell her what Stephen looked like after months away.

〜❈〜

Meghan walked toward JoAnne's store, glad Stephen had offered to stay a while. Spending the next hour with him would be the highlight of her week.

"I'm right here, Meghan."

She paused at the words.

"The bench by the restaurant. I got sidetracked."

She heard the smile in Stephen's voice. With a small signal she had Blackie take her to join him. She sat on the bench beside him.

"Your friend was giving away samples of her muffins. Slip off your glove."

She did so and he handed her a still-warm muffin. "Mmm...blueberry and wonderful."

She stretched out her legs, settled back, and grinned as she broke off a piece. "I stop and get one of these every morning on my way to work."

"If she makes pies like this too, I can see why you claim the restaurant makes the best pies in the state."

"Good enough I've learned to take a lot of walks. This is another reason Silverton is special. It's kind of hard to do this in Chicago."

"True. Any more errands you need to run?"

"That was the only one." The bench was freezing. She got up and stomped her feet to get some warmth back in them. "Let's head back to my place and walk fast so I can warm up."

He laughed and let her pull him to his feet. He didn't release her hand.

She was glad she knew the streets, for it was hard to concentrate with her hand in his. She had so many questions for him, but at the core there was only one. "Tell me about your travels, Stephen. Did you find what you were searching for?"

He didn't answer her for a long time. "No, I didn't. But the time away was the break I needed. For years life has been driven by my career, by close family ties. Both of those have changed now in permanent ways. I don't know yet what I want in their place."

"I'm an expert on building a new life. You start with the foundation, the things that matter the deepest in your heart. Everything else you fit in around them."

"A good perspective."

"Are you going to resume your paramedic job?"

"I don't think so, and that's a pretty hard pill to swallow. I don't want to walk away, and yet I don't want it back as it was."

"Give it time, Stephen. You'll make the right decision. I've known you for years and I haven't seen you make a strategic mistake yet."

"Oh, I think I've made a few."

He turned her direction—she heard in the change of his voice that he was looking at her. She squeezed his hand rather than say anything.

They were nearing her house. She took the lead, sitting on the top porch step to lean down and remove Blackie's harness. "I know you need to go soon if you're to get to Chicago to see Kate before it gets too late. I'm so glad you came."

He took a seat beside her. "I'm sorry I won't be here to help with your piano."

"Ken will bring at least a couple guys with him. Next time you're in town, you can hear it after it's tuned."

"I'll be back, Meghan. I've gotten pretty attached to the pace of small towns over the last few months."

"You'll find me at Dad's clinic, or here, and I would love to buy you a piece of that world famous pie." She folded Blackie's harness as he scampered away, free to roam the yard. "I have a favor to ask."

"Anything."

"Can I see what you've become while you were away?"

"What do you mean?"

"Let me see your face."

He stilled, which made her fear she'd asked that of him too soon. Then she heard his soft sigh and his hands clasped hers. He leaned over and lifted her hands to touch his face. "I'm older."

His smile wasn't perfect. It was a little bit higher on the right, but it leveled out as it grew to full breadth. She traced his mouth and that smile, ran her fingers across his cheekbones and around his eyes up to his forehead. "I like your face; it's solid with a little character added with your slightly crooked nose." She lifted her hands to trace the hairline around his face. "You haven't aged. My memory of what you look like is stuck in time from five years ago." She grinned as she lowered her hands. "I just thought you'd be flattered to know that."

"I'll take it. I've gone a bit gray, Meg, and the lines on my face are permanent now."

"Growing old isn't so bad." She liked the new image she had of him in her mind. "I'm more adventurous now that I can't see what my hair color looks like. I just go by the reactions I get from people to find out what works and what doesn't."

"Blond. I really like blond."

"It feels small to try to get your attention with my hair color."

"Nevertheless, a guy appreciates it." He took her hands and kissed her palms. "I have to leave." He stood.

Flustered by his actions, she tried to figure out where to set her hands without making it obvious she wanted to press them together to capture the kiss. "I know."

Blackie bounded up the stairs, pushed into her arms, and dropped a find in her lap. "Yuck." Stephen's kiss had just got slobbered. The baseball was nearly chewed up and it was cold all the way through. "I was really hoping you had lost this for good, Blackie."

He barked. She judged which direction her yard would be and tossed the ball. Blackie scrambled away. She wished she could see the chase she could hear.

"That dog loves you."

She smiled. Not only that, but he knew how to get her out of an awkward moment. "It's mutual. I hope you have a good welcome home. Call me tonight? Just to let me know you got there all right?"

"I will. Good-bye for now, Meg."

She listened to him leave, his footsteps growing fainter. She lifted her hand to wave as she heard his truck start, then got to her feet. *Jesus...thanks. I was worried about how he was doing.* Stephen would be back. Her life had just gotten a lot more interesting.

Blackie bounded up the stairs to join her. "Come on, friend. Company is coming for dinner."

TWELVE

"Welcome home!"

Stephen stopped, one hand on the light switch and the other holding his duffle bag. People were three deep in his home: the O'Malleys, guys from the fire department, former coworkers from emergency services. "Should I go away for a few more minutes so you can try to fit another person in here?"

Jack laughed and caught his arm to tug him inside. "The dynamic duo is back together, brother. Bring on the food!"

Laughter rippled around the room and the sea of people parted to let Stephen in his own home. His sister Rachel was in the center of things, directing food, drink, and people crowding the kitchen. She pushed through to meet him, and he hugged her tight. "How did you know when I was coming?"

"Meghan called and offered to hold you there a bit longer; she guessed your drive time back. This was the crew that was free on short notice. A bigger group will celebrate your arrival this weekend."

I should have just kept driving.

Rachel laughed at his expression. "You know how many people dream about just taking off and driving around the country for several months? Everyone wants to hear the details."

"I'm staggered."

Jack slapped him on the back. "You were gone for months and managed to come back with only one bag?"

Stephen dug out his keys. "You have got to see the new wheels. The truck is in the drive. You might want to bring up what's in the passenger seat for me." Kate was sure to be in this crowd somewhere, and he was going to need that gift.

"You got it."

Jack looked so smugly happy that Stephen wanted to drop a headlock on him and ask why, but he had a good idea of the cause. His brother had gotten himself engaged. "Where's Cassie?"

"That way." Jack nodded down the hall toward the rooms Stephen had turned into an office and workshop. "I made sure we had at least one quiet spot in this medley so she could keep her sanity and not damage her sensitive hearing. You weren't around to help me pick out the ring. Cassie calls it excessive."

Stephen laughed. "A good beginning, Jack. I'll find her."

He moved through the crowd, greeting friends, his hand getting mangled in handshakes and his shoulder thumped in welcome. He spotted Kate coming toward him and his smile became a touch uncertain as he assessed her first reaction. "Hi, Kate." She was beginning to show, just a little. He knew her well enough to see the subtle signs. Her face was beautiful. His smile broadened. He was so proud of her.

She laughed as she hugged him. "You were gone a long time."

"I brought a stack of photos from every town I passed through." Stephen looked around the crowded rooms, then reached down and picked up Kate. "Coming through," he warned people, walking down the hallway.

Her arms strangled him. "Stephen, put me down!"

"Quiet." He caught Dave's attention and saw his surprise, then got a laugh and a thumbs-up.

The noise dropped as he left the main gathering. He heard Cassie's laughter from somewhere ahead and elbowed open the guest-room door. He sat Kate on the bed and then spun a chair around so he could sit facing her. "I unerstand you have news. I want to hear it firsthand."

Her face softened. "I'm pregnant."

He brushed her hair back, studying the changes in her face. "How do you feel about that?"

Her smile about burst from her face. "Thrilled. Terrified. Dave is doing some major hand-holding. I'm sicker than a dog most of the day, but it's fine. I can do this. I'm going to be an awesome mom, Stephen."

"What's your due date?"

"July 10."

"You'll be early," he predicted. Her pregnancy was good news, but also news with so many implications. "I heard you made some major changes at work. I'm sorry it was such an abrupt transition."

"I'm now a detective in robbery, fraud, and white-collar crimes. The first rule of parenting is to watch out for your kids, and I guess it starts now with a safer job. You know how much is stolen every year in this city? There is more stolen jewelry and equipment floating around this city than you could pick up in a lifetime."

"And I bet you try to find it all. I heard you eventually want homicide."

"A dead body at least gives you a case with boundaries. Most robberies are nothing but paperwork, and the goods are easy to disperse."

"Homicide won't help the nausea any."

"A hurdle I'll cross when I get to it." She studied his face. "You look different, older. Was the trip okay?"

Stephen wasn't sure how to answer her. Every answer he gave to that question just suggested another. "Useful, but not everything I had hoped. Not having to wear a watch helped. The solitude made me realize how much I missed everyone." He smiled at her, not wanting to get into a deep discussion. "I came back as promised."

"Are you going to stay in Chicago now?"

He ran a knuckle along her chin. "A decision left for another day."

Jack tapped on the door. "If this family meeting is over, you might want to give her this thing."

"What in the world?" Kate said.

Stephen got up to take the huge rabbit. "I saw it and thought of you, Kate."

"You got that for *me?*"

Stephen laughed. "For my new niece or nephew. When are you going to know which it is, by the way?"

"I'm not telling. And I can't believe you bought that."

Stephen set it in her lap and it dwarfed his sister. "It's perfect."

"Come cut your cake, buddy," Jack said. "Oh, and priorities, man. We're playing basketball tonight. Anyone tell you that yet?"

Stephen looked around the rabbit to see Kate. "Are you providing the bleacher commentary?"

"Absolutely."

Stephen turned to Jack. "Can I plead out of practice now before the evidence becomes obvious?"

"As a homecoming gift I'll carry you this game," Jack offered. "Late night basketball will get you back in the swing of things fast."

The gym was hot and smelled of sweat and floor wax. Stephen couldn't get enough oxygen to his muscles to walk, let alone make a decent attempt at a jump shot. His legs, arms, and back muscles were quivering. It was a basketball game O'Malley style. The intensity over every point made it feel like a small war, nobly fought. The elbows and fouls were being tempered, but the pushing and shoving had an art to it.

He wasn't going to let Jack down. He wasn't going to... Stephen took the basketball in a snap throw and forced his feet to move again.

"You're a bit rusty," Marcus said, sweat dripping off his face as he checked Stephen's forward progress with an outstretched hand and backed toward the basket. Marcus had flown back just to say welcome home and to join the game. Only he would think that a good use of time and money.

It would take breath to be able to answer. Stephen replied by faking out Marcus and going around him. Dave blocked him and Stephen passed off to Jack, relieved to have the ball out of his hands. Jack slammed it down in a dunk.

"When did he learn to do that?" Stephen tried not to trip over his feet as he moved backward.

"He's been floating on air ever since he and Cassie got engaged."

"Good shot." Stephen slapped Jack on the back as he went past. They'd been the dynamic duo since their teens, one heading into a skirmish and the other backing him up. He had missed this.

Jack stole the ball and raced down the court. Stephen grabbed a breath and ran too. He was going to kill his brother for being gung ho at midnight.

"You're limping."

"Be quiet, Kate." Stephen crossed the spacious kitchen in her home and pulled an ice pack from the freezer. Dawn light was coming in the window; just looking in that direction gave him a headache. They'd landed at Dave and Kate's after the basketball game, and somehow the night had never ended.

She laughed, pushed him toward a chair, and brought him aspirin. She kissed his forehead. "I'm glad you're home."

"Did we have to make the welcome home celebration into a twelve-hour event?"

"You're the one who said yes when Jack mentioned there was an all-night one-hour photo place down the street from the gym."

"I didn't think he meant right then and that we'd develop *every picture* I had taken on the trip. It cost me a fortune. I noticed you bailed at 2 A.M."

"I gave up my overnight tendencies when I got out of hostage rescue."

He flicked water from his glass at her. "I was practically waving a white flag and you were ignoring the signals."

"You could have just told Jack you were going home."

"Not in this lifetime. He would have shown up at my place at six o'clock to wake me up." Stephen ran his hand through his hair then rested his chin on his palm. He laughed. "It was fun. He won't be able to play an all-nighter once he's married."

"Marriage does change things a bit. Speaking of which, where is my husband?"

"Crashed in the living room, I think. I stumbled over him somewhere. I vaguely remember him saying something about the sun coming up, then the next thing I knew some fat orange cat was landing on my belly and digging in claws. I can't believe you still have that beast."

"I normally don't let Marvel inside. Dave is the soft touch."

Stephen debated the merits of falling asleep at his sister's kitchen table. "Thanks for being kind about the welcome home."

"Dave said I moped without you around."

He grinned. "Did you?"

"You don't have to look so pleased at the idea."

Stephen laughed and twirled his glass. "I'll tell you a secret, K. I'm going to spoil my niece or nephew something crazy."

"Niece. I'm really hoping for a little girl."

He blinked moisture out of his eyes as he lifted his glass. "A little girl. It will be great." And he was going to be blubbering on her soon. "You'll find a good obstetrician and pediatrician?"

"Dave has already made sure of it."

"And follow their advice."

She kicked him under the table and he smiled back at her.

"Was your trip worth it, Stephen?"

His smile slowly faded. He was tired enough to be honest. "At least while I traveled I didn't have to face the sharpness of walking into places we had shared with Jennifer and dealing with the fact that she wasn't there anymore. Those first few weeks—my heart was bleeding. I'd sleep and see her face; I'd walk into a crowd of tourists and think I saw her. The ache of that doesn't go away, but at least it's not as sharp."

She rested her chin on her hand. "It was a double whammy for me. Jennifer was the one I'd call when I needed to know things were right with the world; she was always the optimist, while the rest of us are more realists. And then when you were gone too—I got used to your looking out for me and being there when I turned around. I missed you, Stephen. My days just weren't the same."

"I missed you too, more than I can put into words. It was part of my daily routine too, that ritual of listening to the scanner so I could find out if you had gotten yourself into a jam somewhere. Can I ask you something?"

"Sure."

"How much is it going to bother you and the rest of the family if I don't end up here in Chicago?"

"I don't know about the others, but if you decide to settle in Arizona, you'll have problems with me."

Stephen smiled. He flexed his sore wrist. "It'll probably be around here somewhere. I want to swing a hammer for a bit this summer, and I'd prefer doing it where there isn't a traffic jam outside my window at 2 A.M. I did find out during my travels that I like the slower pace of small-town living."

"You'll make a good carpenter." Kate got up, reached over, and caught his hand. "Come on. I want to show you what I'm thinking for the nursery."

"You've got months yet, and it's bad luck to start planning a nursery this early."

"I'm doing this my own way. Besides, you need time to make the furniture."

His eyes narrowed at her pleased expression. "Just how much furniture are we talking about?"

THIRTEEN

SILVERTON

JoAnne and Ken had a nice place outside of Silverton. Stephen slowed to look at an old windmill as he drove past. It had been restored and appeared to be in perfect condition—freshly painted and built ages before to feed power to the well below. Two birds were swooping between the turning blades. There must be an awesome view of land all the way to the Mississippi River from up there. In the two weeks since his last drive into town, a promise of spring had come to the landscape. This was pretty country. He reached for the car phone and called Dr. Delhart's office. "Meghan Delhart please."

His call was transferred.

"This is Meghan. May I help you?"

Her voice was so businesslike and crisp; he grinned and made the turn into town. "Hey, beautiful. Can I take you to lunch?"

"Stephen! Sure, where are you?"

"Cruising up Main Street on the way to your office."

She laughed. "Stop at the restaurant and get a table. I'll finish up what I'm doing and be right down."

"I'm celebrating, so bring your appetite."

"Oh, really?"

"I'll tell you all about it over lunch."

Stephen found a place by the bank to park his truck. He locked the doors.

Main Street could be walked in its entirety in two minutes. He didn't hurry as he walked. It was a beautiful town with a budget that allowed the curbs to be kept in good repair, the public buildings painted, and the streets swept of clutter. Benches were set out and trees planted along Main Street, and numerous neatly painted signs marked parking and tourist stops. No wonder Meghan thought of it as a town with a good heart.

Stephen opened the door to Coffer's jewelry store. He'd met the owner twice during his walks with Meghan. She considered Neil a friend. The man was cleaning a glass display case. "There's a piece in the window, a bracelet," Stephen commented.

"I know the piece." Taking his time, Neil moved toward the front window and retrieved the piece. He set the velvet and the piece on the glass countertop.

Stephen picked it up. "It's beautiful." Each link was engraved with either a vine or a rose with starbursts holding the links together.

"I made it for my wife, but she passed away before I could finish it."

"Can you bear to part with it?"

"It's in the window, isn't it?"

There was no price on it. Stephen set the piece down on the velvet and ran his finger along the gold links. To have finished it after she had passed away… He could just imagine the memories. It might be in the window, but he bet Neil wasn't ready to let it go yet. "Thank you for showing it to me."

The man studied him, gave a curt nod, then carried it back to the window.

Stephen looked over the display cases. Numerous packing boxes were stacked by the door leading into the back of the store. "Are you moving?" Stephen asked, making conversation, liking the man even though he suspected it would take years to get a smile from him. The stroke had left Neil's left side weak and his walk a bit unsteady, but the man's thoughts were still sharp.

"Keeping the house now that my wife is gone and that I'm limited in my movements isn't worth it. I figured I'd move permanently into the second-floor apartment here and sell the farm."

"Meghan mentioned your place during my last visit."

"It adjoins her parents' place. They're nice neighbors, the Delharts."

Stephen laid out the sketch of a bracelet he'd made on a napkin at dinner last night. "Could you make me something like this? Meghan's partial to silver."

Neil picked up the napkin. "It will take a few days. And I'm not so steady on the detail work any longer. I don't do much of this kind of work anymore."

"Your best effort. She'll love the fact that you made it." Stephen dug out a pen and jotted his cell phone number down. "I'll swing back to town when it's ready. And—" Stephen pointed to another bracelet in the case with a fine gold braided chain and a line of four linked hearts—"wrap that for me?"

Neil gave a rough bark of laughter. "You're either apologizing or courtin'."

"Celebrating." He pulled out his wallet.

"Same thing."

Neil wrapped the gift, added a bow to the box, and handed it over. "Come back anytime. I'll help you lighten more of that wallet."

Stephen laughed and nodded his thanks. He walked to the restaurant, the box in his hand, his finger curling the bow. Maybe it was a little much, but Meghan would like it and celebrations needed gifts.

Meghan was coming toward him, Blackie leading the way. Stephen slowed, enjoying the sight. She couldn't see, but she walked with a smile, head tilted up to enjoy the sun, her pace fast beside Blackie. He'd pretty much given up on lasting happiness—he'd seen too many people he loved get ripped away—but he wouldn't mind sharing Meghan's happiness on this day. She had a smile a man could get lost in. "I'm watching this really nice-looking lady out strolling without a jacket in February when it's only a few degrees above freezing out here."

She slowed as she heard his voice and then picked up her pace. She looked directly at him. It was a punch in the gut to have that gaze focused on him. For a moment it was as if she could see him. "I can feel spring in the air; whereas you've been traveling in all those warm places and forgotten this perfect moment that comes once a year."

"True. Hi there, Blackie."

"He loves the idea of spring too."

Stephen held the restaurant door for her. "Do you have a favorite table?"

"Third on the right." He settled her at the table and she double-checked that Blackie had his feet and tail tucked out of the way so he wouldn't get stepped on. "What are we celebrating?"

He pulled out a piece of paper from his pocket, looked at it, and then leaned over to hand her the check. "This. Across the top it says Stephen O'Malley. And on the next line is the sum of the proceeds of not only two home sales, but also a dining-room table I made. I should go away for a few months more often."

She traced her finger across the check and then offered it back to him. "That is so neat, Stephen. You deserve to have your carpentry skills recognized."

"Now comes the decision of what home to buy and fix up next. I want your opinion on some places."

He paused so they could order lunch. The waitress looked at the box with the bow he'd set on the table, then at Meghan, and then at him. The lady smiled and he smiled back. She didn't mention the box as she confirmed their order and went to get their drinks.

Stephen settled back in his chair, studying Meghan as her fingers skimmed the tabletop, placing items into her mental map. "The realtor has already found three properties for me to consider. Two of them are single family homes; the other is a duplex."

"All of them are in the city? All need a lot of work?"

"Yes and yes."

"They sound right up your alley."

"That's why I want your advice. Kate asked me to make the furniture for the baby's room."

"Oh, you should! What a wonderful idea."

"It would be time consuming, and I'd need a workshop with some space. I don't think any of these properties would give that kind of space."

"You know you want to make Kate's furniture."

He smiled at her assertion. "You're right; I do. I'll pass on these properties and keep looking." Their lunch arrived and he paused as the waitress positioned plates and Meghan got her bearings. "That's my last two weeks. What have you been up to?"

Her smile faded a bit. "Breaking in my piano and getting accustomed to being a home owner."

"Something wrong, Meghan?"

She quickly shook her head. "It's just strange, learning the sounds of a new house. It was windy last night." She gave a rueful laugh. "I spook at the smallest things, thinking someone is there. Blackie is sleeping peacefully and I'm jumping at every creak of a board."

"You do look a little tired."

"In a few months I'll know this house as well as my parents' place, and it won't be that big a deal anymore."

"Call me next time you're lying there listening to strange sounds. You can describe them to me and I can guess along with you. It would be nice to have the phone ring in the middle of the night again. I kind of miss the pager interruptions in my life."

She tilted her head as she considered the offer. "Okay."

"Take me up on it. Meg—" he smiled at her and gently ran a finger along her cheek—"I'm glad you were free."

She smiled tentatively back at him, then nodded to her pie. "Do you have time for a walk after lunch?"

"I'd enjoy it."

When their meal was completed, Stephen paid the bill and tucked the jewelry box in his pocket as she gathered up Blackie's harness. They wandered down Main Street together. He thought she might turn toward her place and show him her new piano, but instead she motioned Blackie to stay on Main Street.

"The church is up ahead," Stephen commented.

"Do you mind if we stop in?"

He did, but he agreed to anyway. "We can stop."

The church was open, but the sanctuary was empty. Meghan released Blackie's harness and let him go off duty. "I love this place."

It was obvious she knew the church well, for she walked the aisle without thinking about her steps. Stephen trailed her. "Why?"

"My earliest memories are of the organ music. I was baptized here, and JoAnne and I met in the youth group."

Stephen looked around the room and saw comfortable pews, the worn carpet in the front of the sanctuary, the stained glass by the baptistery. He had been in churches like this as a child. His parents had gone to church on Sunday mornings no matter what town they were in, even during vacations. It felt strange, and kind of sad to be back in a place so similar to what he remembered from his childhood and to find it made him uncomfortable just being there.

Meghan slid into the second row from the front. "I prayed for you while you were gone."

"What did you pray?"

She rested her chin on the back of a pew in front of her. "That you'd come back."

"Nothing else?"

"Running away doesn't solve the hurt."

"It didn't. It just reminded me of what loneliness feels like."

She turned her head toward him. "You need a friend, Stephen."

"I've got you."

"Yes, you do. But Jesus wants to be your friend too. I wish you'd let Him."

"The idea of a personal relationship with someone you can't even know is there for certain—" He didn't finish the thought. He had no desire to hurt her with his words. "Is this where you came, the first year after you went blind, to find the ability to smile again? You came back with an enviable sense of peace about you."

"Yes. I'm partial to sitting under the big willow tree out back and remembering the view."

He looked out the window. The view she remembered had changed to a parking lot addition and a storage building. "What did you think about while you were sitting out there?"

She slid from the pew, hitting her hip on the end post. She rubbed the sore area as she walked forward to the piano. She pulled out the bench and sat down, picking out a few notes. He recognized the simple melody of "Jesus Loves Me."

"Mom often says that life is what you make of it. It took about a year, but I decided I would survive being blind. It's not the worst thing that could happen."

Stephen leaned against the grand piano, watching her expression soften and her eyes close as she played. "You've been practicing."

"Every day."

He sat beside her on the bench and it wobbled under both their weights. "Remind me to tighten these bench legs for you."

"This song is called 'Blessings.'" She shifted into a new song he'd not heard before.

"And I'm honestly not ducking your conversation about God. I'm just saving us from a disagreement."

"You were never a coward, Stephen. Why are you about this subject?"

"I've already made my decision. I know what God expects of a man, and I'm not ready to meet my end of the deal."

"Well it's an honest answer at least. The basis of it is wrong, but it's honest. You can't earn your way to being okay with God—sin is too pervasive. And while God does expect a lot once you're a Christian, when you know Jesus the things you care about, the things you do, change. The changes God wants are a by-product of that friendship, not rules you have to meet in order to be accepted."

"Still, it's an agreement to follow and become like Him. That's a big promise."

"I know it's big. But it's worth it."

For her the agreement had been worth it, and over the last year the other O'Malleys had also decided it was a good deal. He just wasn't ready to take the same step. He put his hands on the keyboard and improvised notes over hers.

He risked asking a question he'd come back to Silverton to ask. "Are we ever going to be anything more than friends?"

Her fingers fumbled the song and then stilled on the piano keys. She tilted her head to look at him, and he knew her answer in the tension he saw before she spoke. "No."

She didn't even qualify it. That hurt, for he'd been letting himself hope that someday at least there was a possibility of more. She'd been the one he chose to stay in touch with, thought about the most, while he was away. She knew the most about his past outside of family, and there was comfort with Meghan he hadn't found elsewhere.

He'd hoped, maybe, that in coming home he could have a deeper relationship to help fill the void that was growing wider each day. He needed a place to belong. He'd decided that on the long drive back. "I'm sorry to hear that."

"I can't divide me, Stephen. God matters and we don't share that. It would rub a relationship raw over time. And my blindness is a pretty big hurdle too."

"Honest and direct, even if I don't like the answer." He'd been friends with her so long, and neither item was an insurmountable hurdle for him. But for Meghan, life didn't come with second chances very often. He rested his hands on the piano, considering her, and then set the wrapped box on the piano in front of her. "Don't take this the wrong way, but I got you something." He took her hand and lifted it to touch the box.

"Stephen..."

"No strings. I just wanted to share my day of celebration, okay?" He kept the words light and smiled. No matter how much he regretted her answer, he wasn't going to let this moment damage the friendship he valued. She was simply too important.

He was afraid she wouldn't even open it, but she tugged at the ribbon. She opened the box and lifted out the bracelet, running her fingers over the links. Her eyes blinked fast at sudden moisture. "This is beautiful."

"I thought you'd like it." He fastened it around her slender wrist. "It looks good."

She leaned against him. "You might not be speaking to my Best Friend, which is a shame, but you do make an awfully nice friend yourself. Thank you."

"You're welcome."

"And I'm not going to give up on you or stop talking about Jesus; it's not my nature."

He hugged her. "I know. It's why you're a good friend." He leaned over and picked up a songbook from the stack. "Jennifer made arrangements for Tom to send me her diary and Bible for Christmas."

"Really?"

"I've been reading the Bible." He set the songbook on the stand. "How's your memory?"

"Not bad."

He picked out the melody. "Pay attention. This lesson is going to cost you."

"How much?"

"It depends on how seriously you slaughter this tune."

She laughed. He patiently taught her the melody line of the song.

"What do you think about what you've read?"

"That I should read some more. It's something I'm doing for Jennifer—I owed her that—but I haven't found the courage to open the diary yet."

Her hand moved to cover his. "There's no hurry to open it."

"Listening to her words from her last days… I'm not ready." And he wasn't ready for this conversation either. He closed the songbook. "Come on; show me your willow tree, and then we'll walk back downtown. You're going to be late back to work if we don't head that direction."

"Will you surprise me for lunch and a walk again?"

He heard the uncertainty and tightened his hand on hers as he smiled. "You can count on it. If friends can't agree to disagree, what kind of friendship is that?" He tripped over Blackie and nearly took Meghan down with him. "Sorry about that."

"I need to put something on his collar to warn that Blackie is around. He's good at taking people by surprise." She clipped on Blackie's harness.

Stephen rubbed the dog's ears in apology. "More observant people would probably help too."

He walked with Meghan back to the clinic.

He would have stepped in to see her office, but the reception area was filling up with people. "There are patients waiting, and it looks like a full crowd."

"We're the place for everything from emergencies to earaches. It's too bad you aren't living here. We need a paramedic in this community."

He let the casual remark go by unanswered. "I'll call you, Meg. Thanks for today."

"I'm glad you came." She motioned her dog inside. He watched her enter the building, greet people, and then disappear from view. This day had not gone anything like he planned. He pushed his hands deep in his pockets as he walked back to his truck.

Disappointment didn't sit well with Stephen.

Half an hour later, he slowed his truck on the road that passed by Meghan's parents' home. The Delhart land, adjacent to Neil's, ran as far as he could see. He pulled to the side of the road and got out. Hands on his hips, he looked his fill of the open land. This was the place Meghan had spent the last several years, and he could feel the peacefulness of it in the pond and the path around it, the open fields.

Her last comment about being a paramedic had struck a nerve. He wasn't going back to that profession in the foreseeable future. He would enjoy being a carpenter for the summer, and it was more than a small decision. What he needed most now was a sense of permanence and a place to belong that was his.

He could head back to Chicago and return to see Meghan in a few days. Or maybe... He turned and walked back to the truck.

Stephen entered Neil's jewelry store. The store was empty and the sound of a radio came from a door in the back that was open a few inches. "Mr. Coffer?"

Neil came from the back work area. "Meghan didn't like the bracelet."

"Are you kidding? She loved it." Stephen knew of no way to lead into the conversation but simply to ask. "You mentioned you were considering selling your place next to the Delharts'."

Neil leaned against the counter, considering him. "I've been thinking on it."

"Would it be possible to see it? At your convenience?"

Neil crossed over to the window and turned the sign to say closed. "It's time for a break. Let's take a drive now."

Stephen knew enough about land to know that what he was seeing was roots, generations of roots in one place. "Are you sure you want to sell this place, Neil? There's history here."

They walked slowly along the rock driveway from the barn back toward the house. The place was so much more than Stephen had expected. He no longer wondered what he was doing but rather how he could possibly make this work. The barn would be a perfect workshop—there were outbuildings for supplies and equipment—and he'd have so much land to use for future projects. The potential here was overwhelming.

"My wife and I had good years here. I married her down there by the pond, and we had our twenty-fifth anniversary out at the barn with a good old-fashioned square dance. She started to lose her memory, but she never forgot the dance or the pond or how much she loved to pick blackberries from that patch down the way. For me…I'm not growing any younger, and since my stroke this place is more work than I can manage. It's not like I have family to inherit it.

"I'll spend my last years quite comfortable living above the store. I've already been staying there during the winter when the weather is bad. It's even got an elevator from when it was a bank. I'll be selling this place. The only real question is whether the house and land need to be divided in order to find buyers."

Stephen looked around the grounds. "What are your boundaries?"

"The pond is all on my property, Bill Delhart's place comes to that line of trees near the other bank, and the homestead plot goes south to the line of trees. I own the acres across the road down to the corn Nelson had planted. There's just over a hundred acres total. There are five buildings on the property between the house, barn, garage, and two storage buildings. It would probably be better to simply tear down the house and start over than try to rebuild it."

Stephen didn't know much about living in the country. He knew less about farming. But today neither mattered. "Neil, I'd like to buy your place."

"You feel like haggling the price over a cup of coffee?"

Stephen smiled. "It's been a long time since I haggled over anything more than fish bait, but I'll go a few rounds."

"Once you see inside the house, you'll change your mind about this place."

"The house is the one thing I'm capable of restoring. There's no sagging and settling with age; that says whoever built it did a good job."

"Come on; I'll show you. I've already taken the furniture that mattered to me out and the last of my personal bits and pieces. Everything that's left can either go with the property or be sold at auction. Some items in the house go back to my parents, and the farm equipment in the storage barns runs, but it's old enough I don't know who would be interested in buying it."

Stephen followed him up the porch and into the house. The heat was turned down and there was the feel of a place that had been unoccupied, despite rugs on the hardwood floors, aged curtains, and plants on the windowsill still soaking up the sun. It was a simple house, but the ceilings were tall, the doorways narrow, and the windows larger than he expected. Stephen saw past the first layers to the potential. "I just sold two remodeled homes in Chicago and I've got the proceeds to work with. The land will secure a loan for the rest."

"We'll haggle a price and handshake on a deal. Give me a lift back to the store, and then come back and walk the place. My wife would be pleased to know it was going to be a home again."

"This is a lot of place for just a handshake."

"I never did a deal with a man whose word I couldn't trust," Neil replied. "My banker and lawyer will make it work. I'm old enough I'd rather have a few years to enjoy the proceeds than make this a drawn-out sale."

Stephen looked around the house and smiled. "Let's go get that coffee."

Craig froze at the sound of people moving around inside the old house. The insulation in the attic was scratching his skin, and just the idea that he had to be still immediately started driving him crazy. He was hot, tired, and hadn't found anything, but Neil was not a man to make this easy.

Craig knew there were gems hidden somewhere on this property or at the store, and he had to start the hunt somewhere. How many pieces were still stashed to cool off was hard to figure out, but he thought it had to be at least forty.

He figured Neil wouldn't have been able to recover any pieces hidden in hard-to-reach places since his stroke. The attic had seemed logical, but so far Craig had come up dry. He moved farther back from the attic trapdoor that went down into the utility room. He'd have to wait them out.

Another few weeks to search this place and he'd have what was here. He couldn't believe Neil was moving so fast to sell the property.

Once voices faded and he heard the sound of a vehicle leaving, Craig lowered himself down through the trapdoor. He would come back when it was dark. There was no use being seen out here. He was too well known in town that if someone saw him, even briefly, they would recognize him. If Neil got wind that he was out here, he didn't want to predict what Neil would do. The man didn't like being double-crossed.

Knowing his luck, the pieces had probably been moved to the store and Craig would have to wait for the man's next stroke. He had to do something to get cash soon. Steal from the pharmacy, something. He was desperate for another fix, and he could only stretch out what he had for so long.

Stephen waited as Neil went into the back of his store and then came back with a ring of keys. "That barn will make you a good workshop. I had them run extra power circuits and breakers for the building."

The banker had been more than willing to accept the endorsed cashier's check, the lawyer a one-page agreement, and with a handshake Stephen found himself the owner of the homestead. A loan for the sale of the sixty acres of farmland would process at its own speed, but as of now he was the tenant on record. He had to admire the efficiency of men who already had their ducks in a row. All the banker and lawyer had been waiting on was a name and price to add to the paperwork.

Stephen accepted the keys from Neil and offered his hand. "Thank you."

"You wanted a challenge; now you have one."

Stephen walked the property. It was a huge place, and he would have to learn the art of caring for grounds that had everything from grapevines to blackberries and several dozen types of trees in the orchard. The yard would take a huge mower, and he'd have to sort out the condition of the equipment acquired from Neil. The man had taken good care of this place, but as his wife's health slipped and he'd had less time and energy to give it, the years of neglect showed as nature reclaimed its territory. Several seasons of work would be needed to prune and trim it back under control.

The gravel driveway extended from the main road to a detached garage behind and to the left of the house. A long walkway connected the garage to the house. To his left a fenced pasture hailed back to the days when livestock roamed the property. The huge barn was close to the house, and farther out were two storage buildings. He'd bought the property without an appraisal, bought the contents of the barn and storage buildings with merely a glance inside, and did the same with the house. He would have to go through each to see what he would keep and what he would sell. Stephen wasn't worried about the speed of his decision; he knew how to read a man, and the price arrived at had been fair to them both.

This was his new home.

He took a deep breath as the depth of that hit him and leaned back against the front bumper of his truck. Home. He had no thought of ever selling this land.

Mom, Dad, I wish you were here to see this.

At the thought he pulled out his phone to call the family he had. "Jack? What are you doing at the moment?"

"Debating the merits of which movie to see with Cassie."

"If you two have a couple days free in your work rotations, want to see my new place?"

"You picked one of the homes to fix up?"

Stephen grinned. "Nope—a house and a hundred acres of land. I'm looking at something I think is a sundial beside an ancient well, and I own them both."

"Where are you?"

"Silverton."

"You bought a farm? What do you know about farms?"

"That's what I said, then I shrugged and shook the man's hand. You want to come help me out here?"

"You'll have to give precise directions. I don't drive outside of concrete and pavement."

"Bring your phone along. I'll get you here."

"Do I need to pack a sleeping bag?"

Stephen laughed. "It's not *that* rural. The town has a nice hotel and also a bed-and-breakfast. See if Cassie wants to come and I'll get you both rooms. I need help moving furniture from the house out to the storage buildings. I'm going to gut the house back to its frame."

"Do you want me to bring your basic move-in gear, or are you coming back into town tonight?"

"I'd appreciate it if you could bring what you can."

Jack checked with Cassie. "We'll be there Friday afternoon. Have you told the others yet?"

"I'm making the calls now."

"I think this is great, Stephen."

He looked around his property as the sun was beginning to set. His new niece or nephew should have a chance to explore the country life, ride a horse, pet a chicken, and feed a cow. This was the perfect place. "So do I. Call when you get near town and I'll give you directions."

He understood why his siblings were all getting married, why they wanted to make relationships permanent. This was his own definition of permanence—a place that would show his sweat equity and maybe a future business, if he loved the carpentry work as much as he thought he would.

He considered calling Meghan but didn't. The speed of this decision, the unexpectedness of it, would make her cautious. His arrival into her community might feel like pressure, and he didn't want that. Their friendship would have to find new footing with the addition of the word *neighbor.*

He wanted the same peace she had in her life, and part of that had come from having a permanent home. He might have selected Silverton because she was here, but he'd made the decision on the land for reasons that had little to do with her.

He needed to make peace with life, and he would begin that process here. Stephen O'Malley, landowner. It was a good feeling.

Stephen elected to take a hotel room for the night rather than stay at the farmhouse, if only to allow himself a good night's sleep and a chance to think through a plan for the next days. He stretched out on the bed and listened to the evening news while he thought about sleeping. Would Meghan understand? He thought about calling her several times during the course of the evening but never reached for the phone. There was time to tell her he was now her neighbor, but he didn't know yet what the ramifications were for the two of them. In a small town they would be seeing each other often.

He rubbed his eyes and reached over to the nightstand. He'd brought Jennifer's diary with him. For the first time since Tom had sent it to him, Stephen opened the book. He had settled down to one place and given himself roots. Jennifer wasn't around to call and tell about his new home. Every milestone in his life for the last two decades had been marked by Jennifer's quiet words. He missed her tonight. He turned pages and randomly chose an entry.

Tom's up already; I can hear him in the hotel living room. I can't help but smile, listening to a man try to reason with a less-than-year-old puppy about the difference between shoes and toys. Tom's patience continues to be the most fascinating part of his character. I'm blessed. We're going to join Marcus and Shari for lunch if I have the energy, and I'm trying to be good and rest to conserve my energy. I'm oddly restless and wanting to get the day started, feeling each day now that time is getting short. May Tom's patience extend to a strong-willed wife. He loves me, and I fear I take unfair advantage of that some days.

I heard through the family grapevine that Stephen had a bad run last night. A two-year-old in a car seat didn't survive a car crash. It hurts to think about it. I'd have been bawling, doctor or not. I've cared for too many children. Knowing Stephen, he'd be the one comforting me.

Kate said he was at the gym shooting baskets late last night and not in the mood to talk about it. Oh, I wish I'd been there just to hug the big guy.

I know the feelings that resonate for him when a child dies, when he has to relive the stress of Peg dying and being unable to help his own sister. Losing a child brings back that pain. Maybe the fact he has seen so much is what keeps him sane and able to keep helping. I'm going to find him before this day is done. If he's not working a double shift, he'll be working on some house. I'd page him, but to see my number would just worry him needlessly. I wish I could send him a reason to smile today. I worry about him because he's kind enough to let me.

Tom just sent the puppy in to wake me up. My toes are kind of numb and the pain in my side is growing. He'll be forced to help me walk today. I get so tired of being ill. My mind still has me fit and mobile and reality is annoying. I need to send Stephen my puppy for a visit—Butterball is always good for a smile and a laugh.

Stephen paused after reading the two-page entry. The straightforwardness of the entry was a relief. Jennifer had never been one to focus inward, and the entry didn't trigger the emotional reaction he had feared. He remembered the child.

I got through the days because I had to. He wasn't sure what had triggered his breaking point, what had brought the fainting at the sight of blood to the forefront. All those emergency calls had built inside until he finally cracked.

He thought about turning the page but instead closed the diary. He had a strong suspicion that as Jennifer's days drew to the end, not all the entries would be so easy to read.

He was rebuilding his life. Reading Jennifer's diary would help him let go of the emotions. But it would best be done slowly. He put the book back on the bedside table and turned off the light.

FIFTEEN

Meghan set down a coffee cup next to her mom. She shifted fabric samples for her new drapes to one side so she could take a seat on the piano bench. After the finishing touches were done on the living room and bedroom, she planned to tackle remodeling the bathroom. The decisions were never ending, but it was one of the best things about having a place of her own. Everywhere would eventually be touched by her decisions.

"So what do you think?" Mom asked.

Meghan didn't have to ask about the subject. It was all she had heard about over the last four days as patients flowed through the office.

"I'm surprised," Meghan replied, trying not to let herself get sucked too far into the speculation going on. She wasn't sure what to think about Stephen becoming a permanent resident of Silverton. He had never settled down before. Why now? Why here? Stephen just liked to complicate her life.

"You can do better than that, Meghan."

"What am I supposed to say?"

"Take him a pie as a welcome gift."

"And walk my heart back into a mess?"

"Do the safe thing—accept that he's part of the community, welcome him, then establish the relationship on the terms you want."

"I've already told him we'll only be friends."

"You might have mentioned that to him, but it wouldn't hurt to remind yourself again." Her mom touched her hand. "Stephen's a nice guy, and I know this will be hard for you. You had a crush on him as a teenager for a reason."

"I wish he hadn't put that kind of cash down."

"I've known Stephen since he was twelve. The man didn't buy a place in Silverton just so he could stop by and say hi to you. That was just an extra bonus. Invite him to church and over for lunch with us on Sunday. Your dad wants to talk with him. Of anyone who could have moved in and become our new neighbor, I can't think of a more interesting person than Stephen."

"I'll ask him." Meghan thought it was likely he'd say yes. And if he came to her parents' place for lunch, her mom could ask Stephen some of the questions Meghan would love to have answered but wasn't sure she'd have the nerve to ask.

He hadn't even called her to mention that he was buying Neil's place. Was he that upset about the no she had given him? Or was he changing tactics? He was moving in next door to her parents, and it wasn't the kind of place to be bought and sold quickly. This was a long-term decision. He already had her off balance enough that she wasn't sure what to think. This was so confusing.

She set aside the fabric samples. She wasn't going to rush over to deliver that welcome gift. Let him wonder a bit how she was reacting to the news. Maybe in a few days she'd have figured out the answer.

"Coming over." Stephen tossed another bale of hay to Jack. It landed at the end of the flatbed trailer, tossing up a cloud of dust and hay bits. Jack got his hands around the baling wire and hoisted the bale onto the stack he was building. They'd figured out from trial and error that the tractor pulling the flatbed could handle the weight of about a hundred bales per load. Stephen lifted an arm and wiped sweat away from his eyes. Three hours of hauling hay, and he still couldn't see the floor and walls of the first storage building. His neighbor Nelson would buy all the hay they could haul and store it in his barn. It was a good offer; Stephen hoped they could get the job done today.

"This will help."

Stephen looked back over his shoulder. Cassie carried a huge pitcher of ice water. Walking beside her were Meghan and Blackie.

"Break time," Jack said, vaulting from the trailer bed to the ground and striding over to join his fiancée. "Hello, Meghan. You're looking good."

"Hi, Jack. I heard you answered the call to help Stephen out."

"It's the novelty factor. Although a few hours of pitching hay already seems like a lifetime, we're making good progress."

Stephen steadied himself on the stacked hay bales he stood on and carefully climbed down. He tugged off his work gloves, shoved them in his back pocket, and accepted a glass of water from Cassie. "Thanks. Welcome to my new place, Meg. You're out visiting your parents?"

"Yes."

He'd wondered when he would hear from her or see her. The news had passed around town the same evening he bought the place, and the visits of neighbors and town folks stopping by to welcome him and offer a hand had been steady. The fact that she'd waited until midweek to get in touch was interesting.

"We'll leave you two big guys to get back to work. We just wanted to bring down the pitcher and see how you were doing," Cassie said.

Stephen wasn't letting Meghan get away that quickly. "I'll walk back to the house with you. Jack can drive this load up to the road then we'll take it over to unload."

Jack nodded, and Stephen fell into step beside the ladies. "How's the kitchen coming, Cassie?"

"I'm starting on the dishes and pans. It's going fast since you said to just pack it."

"Once the remodeling is done, I'll figure out what I want back in the house. For now we'll box everything in the house and store it in the second storage building. I'm hoping Jack and I can take out the kitchen cabinets tomorrow morning."

"Speaking of packing, I'll need more tape soon," Cassie said.

Stephen dug keys to his truck out of his pocket. "Sorry, I forgot to carry in the supplies I picked up this morning. Check the passenger seat. There's tape there and in the bed of the truck are more boxes."

Cassie accepted the keys and headed toward the truck.

"I wasn't sure you were going to come by," Stephen said to Meghan.

"It wasn't that simple to arrange. And I was planning to bring you a pie as a welcome gift, but my two attempts flopped. I should have just picked one up at the diner. Why this place, Stephen? You could have knocked me over with a feather when I heard the news."

"I had the cash and Neil wanted to sell. The timing was right. I fell in love with the idea of having a big workshop, a place my niece or nephew can come spend summer vacations, and a home with no traffic outside the window."

"You move fast when you make a decision."

"Yes, I do."

Meghan laughed and Stephen let himself relax. She stopped walking to turn and listen to the sound of the tractor coming to life. "This will be a good place for you, big and spacious and full of projects that will never be done."

"It has potential. The barn is great. I want a huge workbench that I can walk around with all the tools out and easy to access, and cubbyholes for everything I need to store. The floor is in good shape and the lighting is good. I'm hoping in a month to have it set up."

"Can I come and watch some days when you're making Kate's furniture?"

"You're welcome anytime. I'll even put you to work helping me if you like."

"I'd enjoy that." She scuffed her shoe in the dirt, then looked toward him. "Mom would like you to come to lunch this Sunday, if you're available."

"Sure. I'd love to stop by."

"Say around quarter till noon for lunch? Unless you'd like to come to church with us. You can meet the rest of your neighbors."

"Another Sunday, Meghan. Let's start with lunch." The tractor came up to the road. "There's Jack; I need to go help him unload the hay at Nelson's."

"I'll stay and help Cassie a bit if you don't mind."

He touched her hand. "Stay and help as long as you like. I'm glad you came."

"So am I." Meghan motioned Blackie toward the house.

Stephen watched her walk away.

He went to join his brother. A hay bale had fallen off the stack and Jack sat on it, chewing on a piece of hay. "If I wasn't happily engaged..."

Stephen pushed him off the hay bale.

His brother laughed, picked himself up, dusted off his jeans, and pulled out his gloves. He tossed the bale back up with the others. "I'll drive the tractor; you can ride the stack."

Stephen climbed up to make sure everything stayed steady during the short drive. He'd bought the right place—close enough that family would be over often from Chicago, near enough that Meghan would once again be part of his world. Family, friends, a permanent place... He wouldn't be bored, and at least the loneliness was at bay.

Stephen grabbed a hay bale. "Jack! Watch where you're driving! I'd rather not end up in the ditch."

The sun shone through the big bay windows into the Delhart dining room, sending rainbows dancing on the table as the light passed through the crystal water glasses. Stephen turned his glass a fraction and directed one of the rainbows toward Meghan. Still dressed in her church finery, she looked gorgeous. His first formal meal in Silverton, and it was at the table of Meghan's parents. It didn't get better than this. "Thank you, Mrs. Delhart. It was a wonderful meal."

"You're welcome to join us any Sunday."

Meghan's mom began gathering the dessert plates. Meghan rose and helped her mom clear the table, her touch steady and smooth across the tabletop as she searched and found pieces to pick up. He would have offered a hand, but Dr. Delhart nodded toward his office and Stephen didn't feel he had much option but to accept the silent invitation. "It's good to have you here, Stephen."

"Thank you, sir."

Dr. Delhart moved around to have a seat at his desk. "Are you thinking about settling down here long term? Or are you just fixing up the place to sell later?"

Stephen took a seat across from him. He didn't mind the direct question. The subject had been raised during lunch but only briefly. Meghan's mom kept the conversation focused on his travels and the places he had seen. "I plan to stay, Dr. Delhart. I've got another generation of family to think about, and the land is a good investment."

"I'm not faulting your judgment. It's good land and you made a fair deal for it. And please, make it Bill. We've known each other a long time."

"It's a friendship I've appreciated." Stephen set down his glass and stood, feeling more at ease on his feet. He walked over to study the bookshelves. Dr. Delhart had a good medical library.

"We could use your skills, Stephen. EMS for this town is provided by the county, and right now the ambulance and crew comes from the next town over. With another paramedic in the mix, we could fix that and have an ambulance stationed here at the clinic, effectively cutting down response times by fifteen to twenty minutes."

Stephen hadn't seen that coming. He rubbed the back of his neck before turning to look at Meghan's father. "I'm going to be occupied with the house for the summer at least. And to be honest, I haven't thought about picking up that EMS jacket again."

"I know the profession nearly chewed you up and spit you out. I've watched you with some concern the last few years. But I know you pretty well, Stephen. You're going to miss it." Bill leaned back in his chair and held his gaze. "I won't pretend it's easier work out here. We may get fewer emergencies per day, but Silverton is a long way from any hospital. What happens if you put that EMS jacket back on and have a really nasty loss like five-year-old twins in a car accident, or a heart attack in the grocery store, and you can't keep them alive during the long drive to the hospital? Here, you're it. But you're a good paramedic, and someday you have to find peace with the profession you poured your heart and soul into for a decade. Being a paramedic is more than a job; it's part of who you are. Walking away may not be the right answer."

Stephen listened to the advice and nodded. Bill was offering him a way back to the work if he wanted it. "I'll think about it."

"If I get shorthanded in a crisis, will you help me out? Strictly volunteer; the pay is expenses. I'll get you a pager and put you on insurance coverage with the county so you don't need to worry about that. I'll only call if it's life and death."

Stephen smiled. "No pressure." The idea of someone dying because EMS support was too far away—he'd been in the profession too long not to feel the responsibility. And bottom line, in a situation like that it would be Meghan trying to help her father out if it wasn't him. "If you need me in a crisis, I'll be there."

Bill got to his feet and shook Stephen's hand to seal the deal, his grip firm. "Thank you." Bill smiled. "Now you've got an excuse to drop by and see Meghan at the clinic if you need one."

"I'm pretty good at creating reasons to stop by on my own."

"I hope you do."

They moved to rejoin the ladies.

They found Meghan and Elizabeth had moved into the living room. Meghan was sitting on the floor by the fireplace, sorting through a basket of supplies. She snapped her fingers for her dog to join her. "I've got the brush. Come on, Blackie." Stephen watched her dog move somewhat warily to her side. Meghan laughed and ruffled his ears. "You love having this done, you fraud." She started working out the tangles in his fur.

"I found the photo album I told you about," Elizabeth mentioned, reaching for it on the corner table. Stephen crossed over to the couch and took a seat beside her. "I knew I had a picture of you. Here it is." She turned the album toward him. "You must have been about thirteen."

He looked at the photo. "I was so skinny—I was a stick."

"You and Jack started hanging out together that year. I remember that's the bike the two of you shared."

"Meghan, there's one here with you in braids."

Her mouth twisted wryly. "Don't remind me."

She looked so incredibly young. He wanted to laugh at the era, but there were too many pictures of him in this album to risk it. He hadn't realized how much he and Jack hung out with Meghan in those days. She had certainly loved books. In many pictures there was one set down near her. He'd seen stacks of books on tape at her home—so the love was still there. If he could figure out how to make the offer without sounding stupid, he'd offer to read for her.

"I'm glad you kept these, Elizabeth."

"So am I."

Stephen turned pages. There were several photos of JoAnne and Meghan together through high school, most of them with Ken making up the threesome. He paused when he found a picture of Meghan in a rocking chair with a baby nestled on her shoulder. She looked about sixteen, and if he wasn't mistaken, the photo had been taken in the home she now owned. "May I borrow this?" Stephen asked her mom, turning the picture to show her.

"If you like."

He'd add a rocking chair for Meghan to the list of furniture he was making for Kate. He'd get the photo blown up and figure out what he could of the chair from the picture. It would make a perfect housewarming gift.

He eventually came to the end of the pages. "Thanks for digging this album out. It brings back memories. You were cute, Meghan."

"Please, don't remind me of the braces and bell-bottom jeans."

Stephen glanced at the clock. "Ken was going to bring over a load of lumber this afternoon. I need to be going in case he's early."

"I hope you'll consider joining us again," Elizabeth offered.

"I hope I can return the favor soon."

"Meghan, why don't you walk Stephen home," Elizabeth suggested.

Stephen looked over at Meghan to see that she'd stilled in her brushing of Blackie's coat. "If you have the time."

She glanced at her mom and then back toward him. "I've got the time."

He waited as she gathered her items together and held the door for her. The sun warmed his shirt as they walked along the path that ran between the two properties. "It's a blue sky today with a few white clouds. I like this arrival of spring."

Meghan leaned her head back as she walked, seeking the direction of the sun. "Beautiful. I love lazy days where you can curl up and enjoy the warmth of the sun and take a nap."

He reached to take her hand, felt her start, and smiled as he waited for her to get comfortable. "It was nice of your mom to invite me over. She's one incredible cook and a great hostess. You've got great parents."

"I think so." She shifted her hand on Blackie's harness. "What were you and Dad talking about for so long?"

"He wants me to take an EMS job with the county."

Her steps slowed. "I'm sorry he pushed, Stephen."

He stroked his thumb across the back of her hand. "Don't be. This town needs a paramedic on call who actually lives here rather than the next town over. He was right to ask. I said I'd think about it, and I agreed to be a backup in a crisis. I like the work, Meg. A lot of the problem in the past was the fact that the job consumed every hour of my life. There was never any margin."

"If you're sure. There have been a few close calls in the last year where it would have really helped to have you around."

"You'll add my phone number to your speed dial?"

She laughed. "Yes."

He led the way around the pond.

"Any buyer's remorse for having locked yourself in to this place?"

"None. In fact Kate is already wondering if she'll ever get me back to Chicago. I don't miss it at all." Stephen pulled out his keys. "Why don't you and I take a drive after I help Ken unload this lumber?"

"Can we make it another time? JoAnne and I are looking at options for my bathroom wallpaper this afternoon."

Schedule collisions… "I can see our respective fix-up projects are going to be a challenge to manage so they don't step on higher priorities."

"If you're going to live here for the next decade, I'm sure we'll eventually have time free at the same time." She turned to walk back along the path to her parents' home. "I'll see you later."

"Count on it," Stephen called after her. He might have to settle for a friendship, but he still wanted the groundwork laid for something more.

She waved back at him and kept going.

In the shadow of Ken's windmill, Stephen leaned down and retied his shoelaces before beginning his climb. Above him Ken was already at work. He had done Stephen a favor bringing the shipment of lumber over two weeks ago; now he was returning the favor. He climbed, careful to get a good grasp on the rungs. Stephen could make out the Mississippi River through the hazy humidity on the horizon. He clipped his safety line to the top crossbar and moved from the ladder to the narrow walkway. "Do you ever do things halfway, Ken?"

"Not if I can help it. When you grow up in a small town, sometimes you have to make your own excitement."

Stephen reached for the rope, which stretched down to the ground, and tied it to the crossbar. He'd secured the case at the other end before beginning his climb. He began hand over hand pulling the case and its well-cushioned microphone up to their perch. He held the equipment in place while Ken bolted it down.

"If I could talk JoAnne into moving to Oklahoma, I'd study the big storms and twisters. But since it's doubtful I'd ever get her to move from Silverton, I'll settle for figuring out how to predict where rain will fall." Ken ran a test strip on the humidity gauge. "Everyone should have a hobby that lasts a lifetime."

"Does Meghan still go out with you on storm chases?"

"We get out at least once a month. She can hear the hail long before I can. Come along on our next storm chase. You'd enjoy it."

"I'm game to try it once. Give me a call."

"You got it." Ken climbed up two more rungs on the ladder to check the rain gauges. "I hear you're stocking your pond next week."

"I'm thinking sunfish and some bass. Bill suggested I expand the pond into his land and the two of us would make it a real fishing attraction. Maybe co-op the costs for those who want to fish in it and have them pay based on how much they catch and take out so we can keep it restocked."

"I'll take a charter membership in that co-op," Ken offered. "When you fish, it's nice to actually catch something."

Stephen swung around to the other side of the equipment platform and started work on securing the wind gauges. "Any idea where I can find someone who has sheep?"

Ken leaned around to see him. "I thought you were planning for some cattle."

"Actually, I'm leaning toward a petting zoo. Meghan would enjoy it."

Ken laughed. "Nice idea. I'll ask around for you." He mounted the protective hood on the microphone. "I admit I'm a bit curious about the two of you. Back in the days when she first moved here, Meghan used to talk about you. It was Stephen this, Stephen that. Then one day she didn't mention you anymore."

Stephen was glad the safety harness had him securely held in place. He didn't need any surprises, like a former boyfriend. "When was that?"

"About the time you started going out with someone named Caitlyn? JoAnne fixed Meghan up with Jonathan that summer, and we were a foursome until he moved on to study his music with more prestigious musicians."

Stephen had heard the name before. "Jonathan's the piano player?"

"Concert pianist, if you please. I've heard him play. He's good, if a bit arrogant now that he's famous."

"What's his full name?"

"Jonathan Peters."

"You know, I think Meghan sent me some of his stuff on one of those tapes at Christmas. He is good. Isn't Meghan taking piano lessons from the person who taught him?"

"Mrs. Teal. You'll like her; she's basically the town grandmother."

Stephen finished his task and slipped his hammer back on his belt. "Was Meghan serious about Jonathan?"

"For a while. He was more serious about his music. I never did understand that priority, but you can't argue with his success. Mrs. Teal says he's playing in Chicago this summer. If JoAnne and I can get tickets, do you and Meghan want to come?"

Stephen liked the way that was phrased. "Sure."

Meghan had dated Jonathan Peters, yet she never mentioned the name to him. What else had been going on in her life that he didn't know about? As far as he knew he was the only guy interested in dating Meghan who happened to still be in Silverton. He needed to press that advantage before it was too late. He moved over to the ladder to descend to the ground. What would be his next best move?

SIXTEEN

Stephen picked up a piece of pine Ken had brought over. Maybe use it for a display case? He moved it to the stack of wood being set aside for furniture. A month of hard work had finally made it possible to turn his attention from clearing the outbuildings and gutting the house to getting his workshop put together. Stephen brushed away a bug. The barn doors were open and the mid-day sun made it comfortable working out there. The stacks of wood barely made a dent in the work space; this barn was huge.

Once the wood was sorted, he started to look at what he wanted to do for a workbench and shelving. Neil had built up one area of the barn under the loft with a wooden floor, workbench, and good electrical connections and lights. By raising the wooden floor from the concrete, Neil had taken the first steps to make this a year-round workroom.

Stephen tugged on the shelving to see how sturdy the joints were and could barely nudge it. This unit was not going to be taken apart. And it would be best used over by the door. He thought about the weight to move, accepted that it had to be done, and went to get the dolly. *Jack, where are you when I need a helping hand?* The shelves weighed enough, even with the straps and wheels providing leverage, that it still took everything he had to move it to the door.

The wall behind where the shelves had stood was coated with cobwebs and dust. Stephen batted them away with a paper towel as he struggled to catch his breath. He used a hammer to rip out the two nails exposed and bent to see what shape the electrical outlets were in.

He found a couple spots on the wooden floor that gave under his weight. The board looked solid enough until he stepped down and realized the joist beneath it must have worn away. Probably mice, termites, or both. He tapped with the hammer to see where flooring might have to be replaced. He pulled up the floorboard, expecting dirt, decayed wood, and sawdust. He found that—and more. Stephen tugged out a leather pouch nestled between floor joists.

The leather, dry and stiff with age, cracked at his touch. The brittle drawstring broke as he loosened it. It must have been down there over a decade. He tipped the pouch and out slid a ring. The gold band and the stones had dulled.

He carried it to the door to look at it in the afternoon light. It was a square-cut diamond of good size with two smaller diamonds and an emerald in a rather ornate setting. The band itself was etched. He lifted it to try to read what was engraved inside. The initials *T. R.*

Why had Neil hidden an expensive ring under the floor in his barn? Stephen polished it with the corner of his shirt. The stones looked real. Why hadn't it been in the safe at Neil's store? It would spend tonight in that bank vault, for Neil owned it. Stephen slipped the ring back into the leather pouch and zipped it inside his pocket.

His pager went off. Stephen unclipped it to read the number. Bill needed him. It had been silent for so long he'd begun to wonder if the pager worked.

He called the dispatcher as he dug out the keys to his truck. "I'm on my way." He had a possible heart attack at Neil's jewelry store.

Meghan picked up the clinic mail as she passed through the reception area. Blackie nearly tripped her as they wedged through the doorway into her back office. "Easy, boy."

She would have to get him in to see a vet. She was afraid his bruised back leg was still causing him problems. He'd stopped her from falling into a ditch Wednesday, and as a thank-you she managed to fall on him. Blackie curled up on his big pillow, and she knelt beside him to tug out several biscuits from the box in the cabinet. "How are you doing?" He licked her hand in answer. She laughed and gave him a back rub.

She squeezed between the corner of the desk and file cabinet to reach her chair. They would have to move the clinic to a larger facility soon. Meghan placed the first letter on the scanner and the software read the return address aloud. She filed it with bills to be paid that month. Dad was making rounds today, and it was her chance to get caught up on the office paperwork.

The door chimes rang.

"Meghan?" JoAnne sounded out of breath.

"In the office."

"Your dad needs you at Coffer's jewelry store. It looks as if Neil is having a heart attack. Bill said to make sure it's been called in and to bring the blue and red cases."

Meghan reached for the radio behind her and requested the county EMS to send the ambulance. "The cases are in the cabinet by the door in the reception-ist area." Meghan snapped her fingers for Blackie and swiftly slipped on his harness. She joined JoAnne and pulled on her jacket. "Who found him?"

"The FED-EX driver brought packages and saw Neil in the front of the shop on the floor."

That didn't help much to narrow down the time of onset. Neil would have had nitroglycerin tablets with him. If he'd been able to take them, maybe the attack had been arrested in time. "Was he conscious?"

"Yes."

Meghan took JoAnne's arm and they hurried down Main Street to the store. "Let us through," JoAnne urged. Meghan heard several voices she recognized among the gathering crowd.

"Thanks, Meg." Her dad opened the cases. She knelt at Neil's left side as her dad worked and listened as he attached the heart monitor and started an IV to give the first round of drugs. Neil's hand felt clammy, and the sound of his breathing told her he was in a lot of pain.

"Meg, come along..."

She rubbed the back of Neil's hand. "You know I will."

"The workbench..." He tried to say something but his voice tapered off.

"Save your breath, Neil," her dad cautioned. "You're going to come through this okay. Meghan, lift his head and let's slip on oxygen."

Meghan gently raised Neil's head. If he came through this, he'd probably need to be on oxygen full time. Just another tug-of-war she'd have with him when he started to feel better. She adjusted the mask for him. "JoAnne will make sure everything's locked up here, and the deputy will watch the place while you're gone. We'll make sure everything is as you left it."

His hand tightened on hers. She couldn't do much, but she could ensure he didn't have to worry about his business. She heard people near the doorway shuffle back.

"JoAnne, ask around. Let's get vehicles parked at the street moved so the ambulance crew has easier access." Meghan turned her head, hearing Stephen's voice, intensely relieved. Moments later a hand squeezed her shoulder. "How you doing here?"

"Glad you're around. I called dispatch, and the ambulance is on its way."

"Good. Bill, you ready for me to brace his knee?"

"Yes. He's got as much painkiller in him as he can handle."

"Meg, Neil twisted his left knee when he fell. It's swelling fast," Stephen said. "I need some scissors."

She reached for the blue case and found them by touch.

"Got it; thanks. Find me something we can use to immobilize the leg."

She heard fabric tear. "There are collapsible splints in the bottom of the red case."

"Neil, how bad is the burn in your knee?" Stephen asked.

"Bad," he gasped from under the oxygen mask.

"You may have dislocated part of your kneecap. Hold on; this will make it better. Meg, hold here." Her hands were pressed into position below the knee injury. She could feel the muscle and bone and the heat of the swelling above her hands.

"I'm going to splint above your hands."

She nodded and Stephen leaned past her to get supplies. She used her fingers to hold the edge of the brace as he put it in position. The heart monitor printer hummed as a strip of paper was pushed out. "What's it look like, Dad?"

"Decent. Neil, you're doing fine."

She turned her head. "EMS is here; I hear the sirens coming."

"About time. You were right, Bill," Stephen said. "Twenty minutes from the page."

"Let's get him ready to transport."

Meghan moved out of the way as two paramedics came in. She listened to Stephen working with them and her dad, fitting in as if he had been part of the team for years. Neil was moved to a stretcher.

"Would you ride along with him, Stephen? I'll follow in a car with Meghan."

"Sure."

"Neil, just relax and let the drugs work," her dad encouraged.

"Better already."

"I'll get you there comfortably," Stephen promised.

Meghan started as Stephen's hand squeezed her shoulder. "I'll see you there." She nodded, and he moved past her. Moments later she heard doors slam and the ambulance pull away.

Meghan helped her father repack the two cases. "What do you think, Dad?"

"His color is bad. He was down for at least half an hour before he got help. There's going to be some lasting heart damage from this one."

"Will he make it?"

"He's a tough man. He's got a good chance." Her dad dropped his arm around her shoulders. "There was nothing more you could have done to prevent this. Neil has to stop smoking if he wants to have a chance."

"Maybe this time he'll listen."

"I hope so. Come on; my car's at the clinic."

Meghan paced the hospital hallway, one finger running along the wall to keep her place. She hated that she wasn't able to bring Blackie to this floor. Neil had been at the hospital for over two hours now, and still there wasn't word from Stephen or her dad about Neil's prognosis. She reached the elevator and turned, then retraced her steps. The cane felt odd in her hand, but it was better than nothing.

"Meghan."

She turned at Stephen's voice and knew what he was going to say just by the tone of his voice. His hand settled on her shoulder and the warmth of it relaxed her muscles.

"I'm sorry. They were setting him up for an emergency angioplasty when he had another heart attack. It was massive."

"Oh no." Neil had been a friend despite the gruff personality that didn't let someone get close. And he'd liked her too; she knew it from the treats he always had for Blackie when she stopped by.

Elevator doors opened and the hall filled with the noise of other conversations, making her wish Blackie were with her now. The situation was disheartening. She wanted to lean against Stephen but used the wall instead. "He'd done so well surviving the challenge of losing his wife and his first heart attack."

"This was sudden. Maybe for him that was best. He wouldn't have enjoyed living with the restrictions that would have been inevitable."

"Did you see my father?"

"I'm right here, Meg." Her dad's voice came from her right. "Stephen is correct. Nothing else could have been done to pull him out of this one." His hand touched her arm. "There's nothing more we can do here. Let's go home. Stephen, can we give you a ride back to Silverton?"

"I'll help Joseph get the ambulance restocked and stay in town for the evening to see family. Jack will give me a lift out tomorrow with more stuff from my place here."

Meghan wished he would come with them, but she understood his desire to stay and see family while he was in town. If they were more than just friends, maybe he'd invite her to join him… She pushed aside the disquieting thought and forced herself to smile. "Thanks for what you did, Stephen. It helped having you there."

"Anytime. See you around, Meg."

Stephen asked around the police central building until someone could direct him to the robbery and fraud group. He finally located Kate's new office on the third floor down the hall from the water fountain.

Stephen paused at a door that had Kate's name stenciled on the glass and smiled. His sister had arrived. He knew she must already hate the bureaucracy of it. He tapped on the door and opened it. She looked up from some paperwork. Her concentration turned into an instant grin. "This is a surprise."

The speed at which she dropped the papers had him laughing. "A pleasant one I hope."

"Always."

"You look really good." He entered her office and did a 360-degree turn to study it. "I'm impressed. Four walls with actual artwork and not a lot of paper clutter. A calendar turned to the correct month. And if I'm not mistaken, that plant is not plastic. Are you sure you're not borrowing someone else's office?"

"Dave helped me decorate. I drew the line at accepting an autographed football from Dave's famous brother-in-law for the credenza. What brings you back to town? Not that I'm not thrilled, but I figured we would have to drag you back."

"Neil Coffer, the jeweler in Silverton, had a heart attack. He died a short while ago at the hospital."

"I'm sorry to hear that."

Stephen pushed his hands into his pockets, not sure what he thought about the loss other than disappointment that it happened. His first time back as a paramedic and his patient died after arriving at the hospital. At least the time away from his profession had given back a sense of perspective—he wasn't carrying the weight of this loss home with him. "He was a long-term smoker and had already had one heart attack last year. It wasn't likely that he'd die getting hit by a bus."

"Without meaning to downplay his death, will it complicate your life and the property sale?"

"It shouldn't. All the paperwork is signed and the land sale is contingent only on the final loan approval, and that's in process with the bank." Stephen finally stopped walking and took a seat in the chair across from her. "You're looking good, Kate."

"I'm feeling better." She swiveled her chair back and forth with her foot as she studied him. "You didn't go to the trouble to find my office because you were at loose ends for the afternoon."

"No." Stephen thought about what it would mean for the reputation of a man not able to defend himself if he answered Kate's question. He sighed and did what he had to. He unzipped his jacket pocket and pulled out the pouch. "I've got a mystery for you. I found this under a floorboard in the barn. Neil has owned that farm for over thirty years; he owns a jewelry store with a walk-in bank vault. Somehow I don't think this was in the barn by accident."

Kate took the pouch, opened it, and let the ring fall into her hand. She studied it and then looked back up at him. "Is it real?"

"You tell me. The man had a heart attack before I could even mention it to him."

"Did you find anything else?"

He started to say, "not so far" but stopped himself. "No. As an honest jeweler, realizing someone he knew sold him something stolen, he hid it and hoped to bury the incident rather than report it. The man just died, Kate. From everything I hear, he was a decent guy."

"Yet you didn't go to the local sheriff."

Stephen inclined his head, conceding. He wanted for now to keep this in the family. He had a suspicion he knew what would be found, and he didn't want the news spreading around Silverton until the implications were fully understood. "I don't know him. I know you."

"I'll look into it. Quietly," Kate promised.

"Thanks." He thought about staying to chat but his mission for the moment was over. Besides, Kate would start to look into that ring as soon as he left. He got to his feet.

"Are you in town for the evening?"

"I'm heading to the house to pack up another load. But I'll take an hour of your time tonight to look over some furniture sketches if you're free."

"I'm free. In this job the pager rarely goes off. Say about seven?"

"Perfect." He pulled out his keys.

"Stephen."

He stopped at the door to look back at her.

"Neil just died. If this isn't a one-time innocent thing, if there are more pieces, someone else may know that and try to find them. Watch yourself, okay?"

"I don't like the way you think."

"Sometimes I don't either."

He jiggled his keys and nodded. "I'll take care."

Craig searched carefully through the desk drawers in Meghan's home and found many receipts but not what he sought. She kept a neat house. Where were her credit cards, her checkbook? She hadn't had a purse with her when she left with her father for the hospital—he'd slipped quickly into her office at the clinic, and it hadn't been there. She might not carry a purse because she wanted her hands free for the dog harness, but she would still have the contents of a purse around.

He moved into the living room to check the path she would take when she came home, looking for the natural place she would set a bag. He found a large coin purse set beside the cookie jar on his second walk-through and unzipped it. Bingo. He sorted credit cards and chose the one with the longest expiration date. A stolen credit card would sell for some instant cash, and he needed fast cash.

He'd lifted forty dollars from the cash in the cigar box on her desk, and one of the two diamond earrings she left on the dresser. He had to be careful in his choices. He couldn't risk taking something so obvious she noticed the theft right away, and he had to make sure she had reasonable doubt that there really had been a theft. Having a blind lady move into town was a gift; he didn't want to spook her into installing an alarm. He planned to be back.

Craig needed to get into Neil's store, but a cop was watching the place for the night. And Craig had to have a fix to calm the jitters before he tried to rob the place. He didn't have long—a few days, a week—before Jonathan would hear that Neil was dead and came looking for jewels too. Craig would make sure he had them first.

Maybe during the funeral there would be a window of time to slip into the store. If the stones were in the vault, he was out of luck. But he suspected Neil had simply moved the hidden gems from his house to the second-floor apartment. The cop probably wouldn't think to check the apartment, so if Craig could get in, he'd find what he was after. With the number of gems stolen over the years, it would pile up into a fortune.

"Blackie, are you coming in?"

Craig froze. Meghan was home early. He looked toward the back door but couldn't get to it in time. He eased a step back toward the living room as the front door opened, reaching out for something to use as a weapon. His hand closed over a tall thin statue.

He hated dogs. He slid a hand across his mouth to quiet his breathing as she turned in the doorway less than twenty feet away and waved to someone at the street. She closed the door and moved into the room, humming softly. She paused at the closet to hang up her jacket and disappeared into the kitchen, sorting the mail she had carried in with her.

He took a breath. No dog—she'd left Blackie outside. He relaxed his grip on the statue and placed it silently back on the piano. He eased toward the back door at a snail's pace, wanting to run but not able to afford so much as a board creaking.

She turned on the faucet, and he turned the doorknob and eased open the back door. He slipped through and closed it slowly. That had been too close. He took two steps away from the house and let himself breathe again.

He'd have his fix tonight, he'd plan the robbery, and in a few days he would leave this town rich, and set for years to come.

The pesky dog growled at him as he walked around the side of the house. It began barking furiously and lunging at the fence. Craig walked away. Next time he'd bring something to handle the mutt.

Meghan opened her closet and sorted through her clothes to find the dress she would wear for Neil's funeral tomorrow at 10 A.M. She had a simple black dress that would be perfect with her pearls. She located the dress, relieved to find she had sent it to be dry cleaned before putting it away. She laid the dress out and looked for her shoes.

She picked up her pearls and felt around for her diamond earrings. She found one but as she kept searching she wasn't finding the second one. She knew she had put it here in the jewelry box. Meghan took the box over to the bed and carefully emptied it. She felt along the lining and every compartment. How did she lose just one earring?

She checked the other jewelry to see if it had become stuck in a brooch or tangled with a necklace but didn't find anything. If she'd snagged the back of the post on her clothing and lost the earring, she would have noticed when she removed them. She had put two earrings in the box but there was only one here.

Meghan went through the box again.

She was misplacing things; it had to be that simple. She lifted her head as Blackie rambled down the hall, trailing something of interest to him. The random noises in the house were suddenly not innocuous. She went to the dresser and opened the first drawer, systematically beginning a more thorough search.

SEVENTEEN

Stephen leaned against the door to the clinic office and watched Meghan work, her concentration on the document in front of her complete. She wore earphones, moving the cursor around on the screen and typing in spurts at a furious pace. She was so incredibly pretty… He wished life wasn't so complicated.

Taking her to dinner, inviting her to the next O'Malley basketball game—in the past he would have done so without a second thought. Now his actions would be clouded with how it would be interpreted. How did you just be friends when you wanted to be something so much more? The puzzle had no easy answer. She leaned over and replaced something on the scanner, then hit the button to activate the scan.

Stephen knelt and greeted her dog.

"Who's there?"

He looked up, startled to realize she'd slipped off the earphones and heard him. The anger and fear in her voice shook him. "I'm sorry, Meghan. You were working or I would have said something."

Her gaze dropped to focus toward him next to Blackie.

She was pale. He rose slowly. "Are you okay?"

She turned back to her work. "You just surprised me."

Meghan wasn't normally so spooked about being surprised by someone. And she had never been very good at lying. "I came to ask if I could take you to the funeral."

She took a deep breath and paused what she was doing, then glanced back at him. "Sure, just give me a moment and I'll be ready to go."

He leaned against the door again and waited as she shut down her equipment and reached for her bag. "Okay."

She was wearing the bracelet he had given her. With the elegant black dress and pearls, it looked good. He would have to buy her earrings to match. "You can leave Blackie off duty and walk with me to the church if you trust me for the details."

"I'd like that." She came around the desk.

He guided her hand to his arm and felt how cold her hand was. "Is there anything I can do to help you out today? Funerals aren't easy."

She glanced his way as they walked. "I was just about to ask you the same thing. This will resonate with Jennifer's funeral."

"And Peg's…and my parents'." Stephen set his hand above hers and squeezed it. "It's okay. I'm getting pretty good at knowing what funerals are like. I didn't know Neil more than casually. I'm sorry he didn't make it, but at least he had a full life before he died."

"I'm likely to need some Kleenex. I've known him all my life, and I'm going to miss his gruffness even if I didn't know him all that well."

Stephen patted her hand. "I came prepared."

Meghan moved around her mother's kitchen loading the dishwasher after dinner, thinking about the funeral. It had been so hard to listen to them lower Neil into the ground and wonder what else she could have done. Her hand touched something sharp and she jerked back. *Don't get distracted when handling knives.*

She finished loading the dishwasher and looked out where she knew the window was toward Stephen's property. What was he doing tonight? He'd been quiet after the funeral. The pastor had been talking about heaven and she picked up on Stephen's discomfort. He had walked her back to the office, then left to go back to work on his house. "What's the time, Mom?"

"Ten till seven."

Meghan dried her hands. She wanted to see the changes Stephen had made to the house. He invited her to stop by, but it looked like it would have to be a late visit. Neil's lawyer had asked to see both her and Dad tonight. There would inevitably be final items for the estate to settle up surrounding how he died. Meghan wished it could have been put off for another night.

"Walter's here, honey. Could you bring in the coffee?"

"I'll get it, Mom."

They settled in the living room, and Meghan listened politely to Walter as he talked over business items with her father. Meghan picked up the baby blanket squares her mom was putting together to make a quilt for Kate's baby shower. A teddy bear embroidered in each fourth square was within her skill level. The outline was already made and she simply needed to count stitches to fill the circles.

"Let me get to the reason I'm here," Walter said. "As you know, Neil had no surviving family members. I asked him what he would like to do with his estate, and he wanted the proceeds to go toward expanding the health care clinic of Silverton."

"That was generous of him," Dad remarked.

"He appreciated your help through the years, Bill. Since you already have the clinic structured as a nonprofit, it won't be that difficult to arrange in terms of complying with the trust bequest. After talking about a number of ways to make that wish happen, Neil went for simplicity. Meghan, Neil left you in charge of the jewelry store."

She stopped counting stitches. "He what?"

"The business and property are now in trust for the clinic, and they're yours to liquidate. The sale of the house and grounds to Stephen will go through, for the contracts are valid, but the proceeds will simply flow into the estate at settlement."

She couldn't get past the simple fact that he'd entrusted his jewelry business to a blind lady. "Why me?"

"Several reasons," she heard Walter smile as he explained. "He liked you, and he knew you'd care that it was done right and that you'd oversee the funds to get the best return possible. He also knew you would have the time this was going to take."

"But what do I know about jewelry?"

"Enough to ask good questions," Walter replied. "The problem won't be getting offers of help but in choosing the right people. Neil empowered his banker and me to help you with the details. He kept his own books, and from what I've seen they are meticulously maintained. You should have no problem following them. It is a very simple business at its heart.

"The trust provides for the immediate needs of the business, the chief one security. You may notice there have already been private security officers stationed at the store, taking over for the deputy who watched the store the first day. Neil had that already arranged and he hired a good firm. You'll have no worries there.

"The business will have to be closed and pieces that were on consignment for sale or for repair returned to their owners. That's the immediate concern. For the inventory owned outright by the business, you can either hold onto the pieces, reopen the store under your own name to facilitate their sale, or you may wish to sell the pieces to other dealers and accept the discount prices you'll get. Then you'll have to decide on the building and whether to sell the property or maintain it and rent it out."

"Did Neil use an accountant?" Meghan asked.

"A tax accountant. I have copies of the last several years of filings. I know this sounds overwhelming, Meghan, but it won't be. I have the keys at my office, and I can walk you through bank accounts and such. Come down when you feel ready. Feel free to bring along anyone you like to hear the details."

"When this estate is wrapped up, how much money are we talking about, Walter?" her father asked.

"I'm guessing a million, a million plus."

"Oh, my," her mother said into the silence.

Meghan felt shock to her toes at those kinds of numbers. And she was responsible for it?

"Neil had simple tastes, he reinvested in the stones he bought, and he did it for decades." Walter got to his feet. "I'll leave you to talk among yourselves. Meghan, call me when you're ready and I'll answer any questions you might have."

"What happens if I say no, if I don't want the responsibility?"

"He asked Stephen to do it."

She slowly nodded. Her third surprise of the night. "I'll call you."

Stephen left his workshop in the barn and strode back to the house, unable to focus on the task at hand. The funeral had been for someone he only casually knew, but it had been enough to make the memories return. Jennifer's funeral was too fresh in his mind. Stephen changed his shirt to one that didn't smell of varnish and set aside his work shirt to be laundered.

He sat on the bed and picked up the liniment he was using on a new blister. He applied it and a new Band-Aid. The funeral remarks had been close to a sermon on heaven. He sighed and picked up Jennifer's Bible from the bedside table. *Jenny, I wish you hadn't sent me this.* He had read the book of Luke from beginning to end, then had started the book of John. The more he read, the heavier his heart became.

He was willing to accept all of it, that God existed, that Jesus was His son and had risen from the dead, but it didn't change the problem he wrestled with the most—the life that came after the words "I'm a Christian." The idea of God having a personal relationship with people here on earth, for that relationship to continue for eternity simply didn't seem reasonable. God was well…God. A relationship of any real intimacy seemed far-fetched. And when it came right down to it, if he couldn't sort out what being a Christian meant after he said the words, it didn't make sense to take that step.

Meghan was one of those who came right out and called it a friendship.

It felt like a contradiction. Most Christians didn't live like they were best friends with God. Yet that relationship was described as the norm of what Christianity would be like. Maybe for a Moses who got the Ten Commandments or a King David who led Israel the word fit. But even if Stephen accepted it might be the norm for others, it didn't fit what he thought Christianity would be like for him. He was lousy at playing by team rules. And no matter how he cut it, Christianity came with a significant amount of expectations. Maybe it was cowardly to say he didn't want to try, but he didn't want to fail. And this looked like a failure waiting to happen.

He took the Bible with him out to the front porch and sat in the rocking chair, fulfilling his silent promise to Jennifer to keep reading until either his questions were addressed or he finished the book. He glanced at his watch. Meghan should be here within the hour. The meeting at her parents' had to be breaking up soon. He'd invited her to stop by, and he promised Bill he'd see her safely home. He hoped she could come.

Jenny, I'm not sure how I'm doing with Meghan. The last thing I want to do is ruin a good friendship; she's just so…I don't know…together with her life. I envy her the peace she's found. And you always liked her. I wish you were around to give me some personal advice.

He set his chair to rocking. He missed his sister. Maybe that was why Meghan had agreed to come by tonight. She had sensed how the funeral was lingering in his mind. She was able to read his mood better than he could read hers. *Why can't life be simple, Meg?*

"I'm sitting on the front porch, Meg." Stephen saw her coming around the path by the pond, walking at such a slow pace he knew she was lost in thought, depending on Blackie to take her safely where she was going.

She lifted her head and looked his direction. "Say where again?"

"Twenty some feet ahead and angle two to your left. Blackie is getting distracted by the flower garden I just planted."

Stephen lifted a hand to Bill, watching his daughter from the edge of his property. If Meghan knew silent angels often watched her, she never commented on it. She might live in a world of darkness where it was the same day or night, but for those who loved her, it helped to know she got safely from place to place. "There's a second chair on the porch free, we can go inside, or we can share the steps."

"Direct me to the chair. I'll let Blackie loose to get some exercise."

Stephen reached out a hand as she came up the stairs. "Here you go."

He waited until she was settled and comfortable. She rested her head against the back of the chair and sighed. He handed her a glass of iced tea. "Problems?"

"Neil left me in charge of the jewelry store, with the proceeds to be used to expand the clinic."

He stopped in the process of setting down the book in his lap. "That's a very generous bequest *and* a big job."

She smiled. "My first reaction was 'wow,' my second, 'what in the world am I going to do?'"

He picked up his glass. "You'll do fine."

"You better hope so, because if I say no, he left it to you to handle."

Stephen choked on his drink.

Meghan reached over and slapped him on the back.

Stephen alternated between coughing and laughing as he looked at her. "I am not letting you say no."

Meghan slid her hand down to his and squeezed his hand. "I may need some of your help."

"Whatever you need," Stephen said. "Just as long as you keep the project." There was nothing Meghan couldn't figure out given some time. He set his chair in motion, rocking as he watched Blackie roam around the yard.

"Is the sky clear?"

"Hmm. There's a big bright band of stars that mark the Milky Way, and the moon is very bright tonight."

"That fits with the image in my mind."

"I could never see stars like this in the city. I didn't know what I was missing."

She drank the iced tea and rocked her chair in rhythm with his. Stephen let the quiet between them linger, just enjoying her presence. "Blackie's wearing down, Meg. Come on inside and let me show you my home."

"I was here many times visiting Neil's wife."

He stood and smiled. "Somehow I don't think your memory of this place will be much help." He opened the door, offered his arm, and led her inside. "The four walls and the windows are the same, but that's about it. Jack and I removed the kitchen cabinets the first week. Since then we took down one interior wall between the kitchen and the living room. Until I figure out the layout I want, there is now one huge open room with a hallway going back to the bedrooms." He described his plans, somewhat nervous about what she might think.

She turned in a quarter circle as she tried to mentally visualize what he described. "No furniture?"

"Just whatever's in your imagination. Plus one sofa brought from my home, a stereo, and my ever-present lawn chairs for comfort. Jack still has my barrel tables for some shindig at the fire district."

"You can't be serious."

He smiled. "Absolutely. I can recommend the couch for sitting a spell. Other than that…well at least there isn't much you can trip over."

She stamped her foot on the wooden floor and listened to the echo. "I like it. Which direction to the couch?"

He took her shoulders and turned her a little more east. "Fifteen of your little paces, ten of my strides."

"Show off." She smiled and moved forward to sit down. "You've got big plans for this place."

"I do. I want my nephew or niece to spend a few weeks of his or her summers in the country. I've got it in mind to become one very doting uncle."

"You'll make a good one, Stephen."

"I plan to."

She laughed. "Nothing like a huge dose of self-confidence."

"You want some more of that iced tea? Your mom taught me how to make it with a jar in the sun and the whole bit."

"You're falling in love with my mom."

"I've had a crush on your mom since I was twelve. You're just now catching on?" He came back with a refill on the tea. ".I need a favor."

"What's that?"

"When you decide details for what to do with the jewelry store, can you keep me in mind for Neil's workbench? He built that one to last, and I'd hate to see it not find a good home."

"Sure."

He took a seat on the chair across from her, not wanting to push his luck with sharing the couch. "I'm glad you came."

She smiled back at him. "Me too."

He started his chair rocking again.

"Where do we start?" JoAnne asked.

Meghan set down the handheld tape player she'd used to record the conversation with Walter as he went over the business accounts. In the days since the funeral, she'd slowly been putting together a plan for where to begin. It was going to be a long Saturday.

"Let's locate the business records and paperwork first, inventory items second, appraise and evaluate third." With JoAnne's help, this job was doable. "We can tackle Neil's apartment and his personal effects later. Since we know he kept some fake pieces in his display cases and the real pieces in the vault, we'll need to have a gemologist make sure we don't misclassify a piece."

Meghan trailed her hand along the countertop, mentally putting a picture together of the store. "Let's find a place we can bring in a couple tables and set up a workstation and scanner and bring in a couple file cabinets to hold the records as we sort them out. I'd like you to photograph everything. We'll need a numbering system for the jewelry so they can be uniquely tagged."

"I've got an extra case of those clear plastic bags with closure tabs," JoAnne said. "We can use them and both slip tags around the pieces and number the bags as we take the pictures."

"Good. I have a feeling there will be several hundred pieces by the time we're done with this inventory. Are you ready for this?"

"I'm surrounded by jewelry. This is going to be fun."

Meghan laughed. "Let's see what you think in about six hours. Tell me about the layout in here."

Neil had placed an incredible trust in her, and she was determined to do her very best job. The time it would take to do the job right—maybe it was best.

Besides, if she was busy, she wouldn't be spending her evenings rocking on Stephen's porch and wondering where their relationship would go over the coming years. She'd enjoyed the evening almost too much for her peace of mind. *You're such a good guy, Stephen. Why did you have to land in my backyard? No one else compares anymore. And you're still out of reach.*

EIGHTEEN

A week after Neil's funeral, Jonathan Peters checked into the hotel on Broadway Street in Silverton making a point to chat with the front desk clerk. He remembered her from high school and even back then she had been a gossip. He wanted the news that he had arrived spread around town before he could finish unpacking. There was no hiding the fact a famous son had returned to town, and it would be worth using that to his advantage. Before long there would be a few people seeking autographs and asking about living in Europe, and the conversations would allow him to ask some questions in return and probe recent events in town.

He took the room key he was handed, nodded to the couple getting off the elevator, and carried his two bags up to the second floor. He would have normally let the hotel staff carry his bags, but there were some items he was carrying he would rather keep in his possession.

Neil had sold his farm. Jonathan hoped that was the last surprise of this trip. He had figured they would have to bury Neil there, that the man would never leave the land that had been in his family for decades. The stolen jewels must not be there anymore. That left the store or the strange places Neil had hidden gems in the past among his possessions. At least the heart attack would have given Neil no time to dispose of the jewels to buyers. They were still here somewhere.

Jonathan opened his bag and shook out his shirts and hung them up in the closet. The flight back from Europe had been a dash through airports on whatever seat he could get. He was going to kill Craig for not contacting him about Neil's death. The news had come from Mrs. Teal, calling to congratulate him for a splendid concert performance the week before in London. He sent her the recordings as a way to ensure he regularly heard news of what was happening in Silverton. She'd mentioned it in passing, a few days after Neil's funeral.

Mrs. Teal had been eager to pass on what she knew. Neil had left his estate for the new medical clinic, had put Meghan in charge of the liquidation. Jonathan was grateful to the man for that fact. It would be easy enough for him to stay in the loop, for Meghan was too open for her own good at times. If there had been anything out of the ordinary found in the estate thus far, it would have been on the town grapevine. It was what he wasn't hearing that was reassuring: No stolen pieces had been found and the sheriff wasn't investigating Neil for suspicious sales.

He had to find the recently stolen European pieces; the older pieces couldn't as easily be tied back to him. The diamond choker stolen in Germany led the list of gems to find. The replacement piece had been damaged less than forty-eight hours after the exchange had been made and the piece discovered to be a fake. A search for the stolen choker was underway in Europe. If that choker showed up here in his hometown, his name would be written all over the theft.

He wanted ten hours of sleep to fight the jet lag but couldn't afford the delay. He glanced at his watch. He bet he could find Meghan at the clinic or the store. He wanted to time his visit so he could invite her to dinner. She was his access to the hidden jewels; she just didn't know it.

He also had to find Craig. The man would be desperately searching for the stones. Craig acting rashly and getting caught was the real threat. If he thought it would help his own situation out, he'd talk about the years of stealing.

Jonathan had stolen the stones over the years. If they were going to fall to anyone now that Neil was dead, it would be to him. He had already been in contact with two buyers who had dealt with Neil in the past. They were interested in buying whatever he would care to pass on. He would take them up on it. Jonathan planned to return to Europe with a fortune tucked safely away. He slipped the key in his pocket and went to scope out the situation.

Craig could be handled. Jonathan had had a few months since his last trip to Silverton to figure out how. Craig *would* be handled.

CHICAGO

Kate picked up the ring Stephen had left with her: gold band, three diamonds and an emerald, the stones real. The initials T. R. inside. And the report had just come back verifying the piece as stolen.

Dave pushed a salad across the desk. "Eat, love."

"I'm not hungry," she replied, absently turning the ring. She pushed the open file toward her husband. "Five years ago a lady is having her ring cleaned before her thirty-fifth anniversary and learns it's actually an excellent fake. Last month the real ring is discovered hidden in Stephen's barn."

"And you said working robbery was boring." He stabbed an olive in his salad and used his other hand to flip open the file.

"The ring is worth a small fortune and Neil had it hidden in his barn. If he was the fence for the piece, surely he would have sold it by now. I don't want to wrongly accuse a dead man. He acquired the piece, realized it was stolen, and tried to make sure it disappeared for a lifetime. He wouldn't be the first honest shopkeeper to find out he had been sold stolen goods or end up in a quandary about what to do."

He turned pages in the file. "Maybe. But he didn't turn it in to the sheriff communicating his suspicions. Was that the only item recovered in a strange location?"

"So far." She compared the ring she held with the photo of the fake ring. They looked identical. "How many thieves go to the trouble of replacing a ring with a high-quality fake?"

"A thief who steals a lot and is covering his tracks. You don't go to all that trouble and cost if you intend to snatch only one or two pieces. How many good-quality fakes have shown up over the last few years?"

Kate flipped open her notepad. "I went back ten years and found two other local cases; those original pieces have never turned up. I'm still trying to get any national information."

"Stay with the case you have—that diamond ring. If the others are connected, they'll fall into place."

"Who made the fake? How did he know how to design the piece? Who pulled off the swap? When? And where?"

Dave smiled at her. "I'd say you've got an interesting case."

"One that may quickly become a quagmire. It's old, and from the filed report, the owner won't be much help identifying where and when it was swapped."

"Stay with where it was found; that's the opening."

"If he's deeply involved in this, Neil might have been the one making the fake pieces."

"A good possibility. There's only one way to find out, and it's not sitting here in an office. Let's go check out that bed-and-breakfast in Silverton. You can nose around this case for Stephen quietly as promised."

"As long as you're coming along off duty. No offense, but I'd rather do this investigation without FBI help."

Dave slid the file back across her desk. "You'd rather, but you won't because I have one similar national case for you. My mob boss case where he murdered his wife Marie? Her emerald earrings, a square-cut diamond ring, and a diamond and emerald bracelet and necklace were all discovered to be excellent fakes. Only her brooch was real. Her husband thought she had been having an affair and was selling the jewelry he bought her to make a nest egg for herself before she bolted."

Kate stared at her husband. "Let's try to keep the mob out of this one, okay?"

He smiled. "It could be a coincidence."

"Right." The ring in her hand felt warm now. "I may have a lead on a thief who stole from a mob boss's wife."

"One step at a time, Kate. We need to know if there's more than just that one ring among Neil's things before we speculate on how far this might go."

She handed him the phone. "Make us reservations in Silverton. The last thing I need is for Stephen to be in the dark on this. If there are more pieces, he may be the first to stumble on them. And if not Stephen, then Meghan. Neil put her in charge of wrapping up the jewelry store."

SILVERTON

Meghan stretched her hands high over her head, flexing her stiff back. "JoAnne, you about ready to go?" They'd been working on cataloging the gems for a week, and it felt like they had barely made a dent in the project. She couldn't concentrate any longer tonight.

"Just about."

Meghan shut down the computer and scanner and pushed her chair back under the table.

"Anything you need me to store in the vault?"

"No. Go ahead and lock it up." Meghan knelt and slipped on Blackie's harness.

She followed JoAnne through the showroom to the front door. "Good night, Lou."

"Miss Delhart. Have a good evening. I'll get the door."

"Thanks." It helped, knowing there was a security guard present around the clock. She didn't have to worry about getting accustomed to the sounds in the building. Security made sure the store and valuable contents stayed safe.

"Neil bought a lot of jewelry."

"Little by little, we'll get it done," JoAnne reassured. "I'm going to stop by and order that pizza. Do you want to come with me or should I pick you up in about forty minutes?"

Ken was tracking an incoming storm, and a night sharing a meal and debating weather data with her friends beat returning home alone to listen to the storm come in. "Blackie needs to stretch his legs, and I could use a good walk. Why don't you pick me up at the church after you pick up the pizza?"

"Sure. Pepperoni and mushrooms okay with you?"

"Excellent." Meghan turned to walk Main Street and let Blackie set the pace. The heat of the store and her slight headache faded as the fresh air revived her.

The church doors were open as Meghan expected. She entered the sanctuary and walked toward the front. Someday she'd play the piano for Sunday services. The dream felt so far off. She pulled out the bench and sat, picking her way through two songs she had memorized. She turned her attention to playing scales. It felt clumsy. She frowned in concentration and slowly the B-flat scale smoothed out.

"You're improving, Meg."

She tilted her head, vaguely recognizing the voice.

"It's Jonathan. I was wondering if I might find you here."

She smiled and finished the scale. "I have a piano at home to practice on now, but I love hearing the sound of the baby grand. I heard you were back in town, Jon." It had been a long time since she had been sixteen and going out with him, but the comfort level was still there. She'd come to really appreciate music since she had gone blind, and he'd been one of the few friends who hadn't let the change in her eyesight change how he acted around her. "I didn't think you'd be back until after the London recording sessions were finished."

"Mrs. Teal's birthday is this weekend. There are some things a man should honor in his life, and the teacher who opened doors to the world is one of them."

She finished the scale and dropped her hands to her lap as she heard Jonathan move up the aisle.

"Please, don't stop playing on my account."

"I'm finished. Have you come down to the church to practice?"

"I try to get in my four hours a day even when I'm traveling," he replied, and she heard him lean against the piano. "We can play duets if you like."

"Why don't you start your practice time, and I'll just sit in a pew and listen."

"I'd love an audience. So what have you been doing with your life since I last saw you? Getting more beautiful, I see. I like you as a blonde."

"So does Stephen."

"The guy who bought Neil's place the month before he died?"

She laughed. "The grapevine is working fine I see."

She moved to the second pew and rested her hands on the back of the first pew, listening as the music began. "You make that sound so easy."

"It is." He added a flourish to a melody. "Mrs. Teal mentioned Neil had passed away. I was sorry to hear that. He was a fixture in town even when I lived here. I understand you are working on settling some of his estate?"

"The jewelry store. He left his estate to the medical clinic so it could be expanded."

"That must be a challenge."

"JoAnne's helping me. We've been working on it about a week, and we're making slow but steady progress. Will you be in town for long?"

"Four or five days. Since I was making a trip back, I said yes to a concert in Chicago and then I have a music clinic to teach. I'll be back in June to do a series of performances in Chicago."

"I know Mrs. Teal will be thrilled to have you back for a visit."

He switched to playing scales. "I'm trying to keep it a surprise for tomorrow morning, but the odds of that happening are slim. Would you be interested in joining me for dinner tonight, Meghan?"

"I'm afraid I have plans. A storm is coming through tonight and I'm helping Ken with his research."

Jonathan laughed. "Ken always was thrilled by a good storm. Another day for dinner perhaps?"

"I would like that."

He shifted to a sonata.

"You did well with your gift. You turned it into everything it could be."

"Thanks, Meg. I've tried."

She stayed and listened to him practice until JoAnne arrived, then gathered up Blackie's harness. "It was good to see you, Jon."

"For me as well. I'll look forward to that dinner."

"So will I."

He began playing a jazz piece as she left.

Stephen rubbed an aching shoulder as he walked through his rather sparsely furnished house listening to Meghan's phone keep ringing. Her machine finally answered. So much for suggesting he would see her today. He left a second message and hung up. It was getting depressing how hard it was to coordinate schedules. She spent her days at the jewelry store; he spent his tied up with deliveries for the remodeling work. Shingles had arrived today. He'd call her parents to see if she was there, but he figured she would have called to say hi if she was so close by.

She'd be at church in the morning. He sat on the couch, willing to consider going to church if only to have a chance to see Meghan and maybe get invited to lunch afterward. What a lousy reason to go. He was faintly ashamed for being so crass about it but he was getting squeezed. Kate and Dave were coming tomorrow afternoon, which meant he had to scratch the idea of seeing Meghan then. Kate must finally have some news about the ring, or else Dave was trying to get her away for the weekend. At six months pregnant, Kate needed to start taking more weekends off.

His new guest butted his ankles. Stephen looked down. "Would you relax and think about getting some sleep?"

The baby goat chewed at his bootlaces. Stephen had the fenced-in area finished and the covered pens done, but the kid would be the only living thing out there tonight. Stephen listened to the wind whip outside and wondered what Ken's equipment was registering. The storm was blowing in fast. Surely Meghan wouldn't sit at home alone tonight listening to this storm come in.

"I wish you were a baby lamb or at least something soft. You're all knobby knees and shedding hair." He scratched the animal's back anyway. The utility room would work for the night. There wasn't anything the goat could butt in there that wasn't already slated to come out during the remodeling.

His phone rang and he leaned over for it.

"Is there hail by you?"

"Meghan?"

"Yes, sorry. Is there hail by you? Or rain?"

He was thinking about romance and she was thinking about the weather. He couldn't catch a break tonight. But he had to smile at the contrast—at least she would never be predictable. "Where are you?"

"With Ken tracking this storm data. The rain is coming. He thinks it will hit your place in four minutes."

Stephen carried the phone with him to the door off the kitchen and stepped outside under the overhang. "There's wind, a lot of wind, but no rain."

"Wait for it."

"You sound like you're having fun."

"I am. You should be here. JoAnne and I brought a pizza back for dinner and started helping Ken plot his numbers. The new equipment is working out great. You should see the data streaming in from the windmill."

He wished he was with her. He heard something in the trees growing louder as it approached. "Here comes the hail." It started slapping the ground, small white chunks bouncing on the grass showing in the lights from the house.

"Ken called that within five minutes. Not too bad. We need another data station on the west side of town. The small set of equipment he has at his parents' isn't as good as what he has on the windmill. I've got to go. I need to call Mrs. Teal and see if the rain has reached her place yet. Thanks for the news."

"No problem. Talk to you later, Meg." He set down the phone and thumped his hand against the wall before walking into the kitchen. She was blissfully unaware of any romantic undercurrents as she called and started talking about storm data. It was time to get with reality. From the casualness in her voice, she wasn't even thinking of something more than friendship. And if he was smart, he'd let it remain that way.

Out the window a light flickered in the distance. He stopped and watched.

Someone was in the barn.

Stephen hunched his shoulders, his jacket lifted high to protect his head from the pounding hail and rain. Mud clung to his boots. A small river now ran across the yard, covering the walkway. Wind buffeted his back. The light, if that was what he had seen, was gone. He walked down to the barn, convinced he had probably seen headlights from the road.

He reached the barn as the first lightning flashed and thunder rolled instantaneously overhead. He pulled the door open. A man slammed into him. They tumbled back, hitting the ground with a splash. Stephen grabbed at coarse fabric of the coat smashed into his face and tried to shove the intruder off him. The smell of sweat and desperation clung to the man, and a weight pressed against Stephen's chest trying to keep him down on the ground.

Coming from the barn…the thought that it must be a vagrant flashed by as Stephen grabbed an arm and twisted it away. He had to put this man down, or one of them was going to really get hurt. It had been too long since he was in a knock-down-drag-out fight. Stephen threw the man off him like a stubborn bale of hay and got leverage to rise to his knees. He blocked the coming blow and charged from his kneeling position, knocking the guy back through the doors and into the barn. It was like slamming into a steer, the impact numbing his arm.

He ducked a fist thrown at his face and threw a punch back, sending the guy into the shelves he had moved beside the door. There was barely time to get his hands up before the handle of the rake connected, catching him across the face. Stephen rolled with the force of it and scrambled back up. The barn door swung wildly in the wind.

The man was gone.

Stephen staggered to the door and caught it, wrestling to hold it. The thick tree branches whipped back and forth in the wind, darker moving shadows in a dark night. He couldn't see anyone out there. Stephen wiped his bleeding nose; leaned over, his hands resting against his knees; and sucked in air. Fading adrenaline left white spots in front of his eyes. He heard a car start somewhere far down the road. The idea to give chase lasted only as long as it took for the thought to form. Stephen instead reentered the barn and turned on the lights.

Holes had been punched into the walls and a few places in the floor. Stephen kicked wood out of his way. Had a sledgehammer been swung with great delight at the walls? What had the guy been doing? The floorboard where the pouch had been found now rested upright in the empty crevice. Stephen saw an empty bottle of whisky on the floor and several tossed beer cans. That hadn't been a kid, and it hadn't been an old vagrant. It had been a man with at least a bit of muscle on him.

The ring.

If he'd been searching for it, there was some comfort in knowing it wasn't there to be found. But had something else been here? Stephen had searched this portion of the barn with care, but he hadn't ripped into the walls.

He went to check his workbench and equipment. At least it appeared to have been left undamaged. The far end of the barn he'd yet to clear of equipment didn't look disturbed.

Stephen sat on the pile of lumber and looked around. What else had Neil hidden? And who was looking for it?

Puzzles. The others in his family loved them; he hated them. He touched his sore face. Puzzles left people getting hurt.

Meghan. If tonight was related to the jewelry, that meant the store was also a prime target. She was with JoAnne and Ken for the evening, would be at church with her family in the morning, and Kate and Dave would be here by the afternoon. They'd help him figure out what to do.

Stephen wearily pushed himself to his feet. What a way to end a miserable day. He dug out a padlock for the barn doors. He would call the sheriff, but with this weather the man probably had his hands full with accidents. Stephen expected his own pager to sound before long. The morning would be early enough to investigate this.

He needed an ice pack.

NINETEEN

Stephen worked his way across the barn roof carrying another bundle of shingles, taking care to find good footing. The breeze still carried a fine drizzle in it. The bundle of shingles weighed eighty pounds, and they were as likely to send him crashing through a soft spot in the roof as tumbling off of it. It would be another month before he wanted to risk replacing the roof. His repairs would hold that long, assuming they didn't get another burst of sixty-mile-per-hour winds coming through. A vandal damaged the inside of the barn; the storm damaged the outside. His first look in daylight hadn't been promising.

There had to be an easier definition of home ownership. He wiped sweat and water off his face with the back of his hand and then pulled on his gloves. He ripped open the package of shingles. The staple gun was battery powered, and years of practice meant it took less time to line up and place three rows of shingles than it took to haul them up to the roof.

A blue Lexus came down the road and slowed. Stephen paused to watch as the car pulled into his drive. He picked up his tools. The ladder sank deeper into the ground as he descended. "Welcome to my place," he called, watching Kate get out of the car. She moved slowly, the six months of pregnancy no longer something that could be hidden.

"Hi, Dave."

Kate's husband nodded toward the barn. "How much damage did you get last night?"

"Wind, a little hail, enough to leave its mark."

Kate walked over to join him and her smile disappeared as she neared him. "Who'd you get into a fight with?" she asked softly; a dangerous softness that hardened her eyes.

He touched his face. Between his left eye and his jaw his face was simply sore. "It looks as black as that?"

"Be glad Meghan can't see."

"I had some unwelcome company last night." He pulled the tarp over the supplies so the packaging wouldn't turn into a wet lump of paper mess. "You've had a long drive. Before you hit me with the questions, why don't I get you two something to drink while you stretch your legs and look around? It's not like the details will change."

Kate looked over at Dave then back at him. "Give me the CliffsNotes first then."

Stephen touched her determined chin, smiled, and pointed to the barn. "Come on in; I'll show you. I didn't fix anything inside yet, figuring you'd want to see it for yourself. My guest was looking for something."

He reached around her and turned on lights as she entered the barn.

"What a mess," Dave said.

"I'll say." Stephen walked over to look at one of the deepest strikes against the wall. "He punched holes but didn't come back around to try and pry off the drywall. I'm guessing he was pretty drunk or high, maybe both, and I interrupted him."

"Any idea who it was?"

Stephen shrugged. "Male, medium height, medium build. He hadn't had a bath recently. I never got a good look at him. There were beer cans and a whisky bottle left tossed about so there may be prints." Stephen pointed to the box he'd put them into.

"I'll have the lab take a look. Does it seem like he found anything?" Kate asked.

Stephen looked around at the dozen or so holes. "Not that I can tell."

"I'm glad he wasn't swinging that sledgehammer at *you.*"

"The rake handle was enough. He ran, and I heard a car start shortly thereafter down by the east pasture, but in the rain I never got a look at the make or model."

"I'll go check the area," Dave suggested. "If he was drinking here, he may have been also drinking and pitching beer bottles while he waited for it to get late enough to start snooping. Maybe he left more trash behind that will help us identify him."

"Good idea."

Dave left the barn.

Kate settled on the stool by Stephen's workbench. "Where did you find the pouch with the ring?"

Stephen pointed. "That floorboard was pried up. He either knew about that spot or saw where I'd recently pulled it up."

"The ring was stolen."

"As I nursed my aching jaw last night, I figured that was probably the case," Stephen agreed. "Who was it stolen from? And when?"

"Five years ago a lady was having her ring cleaned before her thirty-fifth anniversary. She found out then that it was a fake. A really good counterfeit of the piece you handed me. When and where the swap had been made?" Kate shook her head. "It could have been years before. We've got no good way to tell."

"Was it a ring she wore often?"

"Yes. What are you thinking?"

"So the fake was durable." Stephen rested a boot against the stacked lumber. "I've heard about the fake pieces Neil displayed in the front of his store while he kept the real pieces in the safe. They're so good that Meghan had to bring in two appraisers to help with the store inventory to figure out what is real and what's a brilliant copy."

"I pulled Neil's records and he's clean," Kate said. "Nothing shows up for receiving or dealing stolen property. There were no financial or tax problems, no suggestions of anything criminal."

"He wouldn't get to be an old thief by making mistakes."

"Have you found any more pieces?" Kate asked.

"No."

"Any indication more pieces were hidden here that Neil removed before he sold this place? Maybe he simply forgot the piece you found in the barn?"

Stephen started to shake his head then stopped.

"What?"

"Before I started ripping into the house and barn, I did a pretty thorough assessment of what needed to be repaired or replaced. The attic insulation in the house was disturbed. I remember wondering if a squirrel had gotten trapped up there and panicked before finding a way out."

"Could something still be hidden up there that you didn't find?"

"Most of the insulation came up when I looked at the wiring. I would have found something."

"Show me," Kate said.

"The trapdoor to the attic is in the utility room. You don't need to be crawling around up there pregnant. I'll show Dave and he can check it out."

"That's fine with me. Let's walk up to the house now. I could use a drink and a chance to stretch my legs."

He closed up the barn and slipped on the padlock. They walked to the house.

"You need security out here," Kate said. "Word gets out that there is a treasure hunt underway and you'll have more than just one unwanted guest."

"That's one of the reasons I didn't call the sheriff—nothing in this town stays quiet. Word may already be out for all I know. The guy was drunk enough he probably talked about it before he came out here. At least it shouldn't be that hard to find who around town has an eye to match mine. What we need to do is talk with Meghan. If Neil has more pieces hidden, the probable place he put them isn't here but at the store or the apartment over it. She's the one most likely to find something."

"I agree it's better we keep this quiet. I'm afraid you may be sitting on a cache site, Stephen, and that more pieces are here even more valuable than that ring. I don't want to add more worry, but you need to know this could get complex fast. Dave had a case that could factor in: A mob boss killed his wife when he found out she was having an affair. Since he went at her in the master bedroom and bashed in her head, it was open and shut. But one of the things that turned up was that some of her rather priceless jewelry were elegant fakes. If one of those stolen pieces shows up here…"

"A thief that messed with a mob boss? Now living in Silverton?" Stephen shook his head. "I thought I left behind big city crime when I got out of Chicago. You just described it being in my backyard."

"We need to figure out what's going on here. If there are more pieces found, if word leaks back to the jail system… In that scenario, we don't catch a thief; we end up finding a body."

"Miss Delhart, there's a Stephen O'Malley to see you," the security guard said. Meghan leaned back from her intense focus tracing numbers through the inventory books. She was not in any shape for company, but it wasn't polite to say no. "Please send him back."

She heard footsteps coming and keyed the software to record her place on the page, then turned on her stool. "Hi, Stephen."

"I brought along a surprise guest."

"Hi, Meg."

"Kate!" Meghan spun her stool the rest of the way around. "Stephen, find her a chair somewhere."

Kate laughed and Meghan heard rollers on a chair move. "I brought Dave along too."

"Hey, Meghan."

"Oh, it's great to see you both." She struggled to sort out sounds as the three of them came into the room. "How are you feeling Kate? You're at…six months?"

"I'm doing lovely. I'm still sick every morning, tired in the afternoon, and walking on swollen ankles—"

"Fussing at being pampered, craving pickles and black walnut ice cream, already rearranging the house to start nesting—" Dave added.

Meghan laughed. She loved it. "Oh, I'm so glad you came for a visit."

"I heard about your project," Kate said. "It looks like you are making good progress."

Meghan gestured to her worktable. "JoAnne and I have cataloged every piece of jewelry in the store and had them appraised. Now it's a matter of tracking down every piece here through Neil's paperwork so I know what he owns and what was on consignment. So far his paperwork is holding up."

"No surprises?"

"Only one. Would you like to see what a million dollars in jewelry looks like?" She stood and crossed over to the walk-in vault. She had changed the combination so it stopped on only major digits, and on the old huge dial it was easy to check by touch. She centered the last number and pulled open the large door.

The jewelry pieces, numbered and sealed in plastic bags, rested on platters lined in velvet. She counted down to the fourth tray and pulled it out. "These are a few of the expensive pieces he had collected."

"Wow," Stephen breathed to her left. His reaction made her smile. She couldn't see the pieces, but she'd noted JoAnne's reaction, the appraisers', and her touch told her a lot.

"May I?" Dave asked.

She stepped back to let him access the pieces.

Kate beside her hadn't said anything. "What do you think, Dave?"

"The pieces he bought—he was a collector. That explains a lot."

"What do you mean?"

"They're all chokers or necklaces, all emeralds, rubies, or diamonds. He liked a particular look. I wish you could see them, Meg. They are quite spectacular."

"I've got a good imagination."

"How much progress have you made identifying these pieces?" Kate asked.

"The bags that have red tags on them have been located in the paperwork. Neil kept a registry. When he bought a piece he wrote down a line in the book. When he sold a piece he wrote it in the book and made a notation back on the purchase line to show that the piece had passed out of his inventory. It's pretty basic, but it matches up—one line in, one line out throughout the book."

"Is the registry complete?"

Meghan shook her head. "I'm not sure yet, Dave. I know Neil handled a few pieces for which I haven't been able to find a record: JoAnne's brooch for example. Neil bought a piece from JoAnne a few years back; it's what let them be able to afford a vacation cruise. Ken and JoAnne had found a brooch and a locket in an old music box stored in their attic. They kept the locket and sold Neil the brooch. We didn't find the brooch in his inventory, and I can't find lines in the registry recording its purchase or sale. It's possible he handled a few pieces like those as favors and was buying them out of his own pocket."

"I hate to ask this question so bluntly, but I'll explain in a moment. Was Neil honest?" Kate asked.

Meghan frowned. She had been Kate's friend for a very long time. It sounded like the cop in Kate asking the question. She was looking for something. "I've found no indication he cheated in his cash flow or on his taxes. Nor are there more pieces here than he has records for. The value he placed on pieces is in line with what the other appraisers judged them to be. The repair shop records are more nebulous, for he often bought gold and silver, even loose stones, to repair another piece. There are some records where a piece was taken apart and its diamonds reused. What's going on, Kate?"

"Stephen found a ring hidden under the floor of Neil's barn. It's a diamond ring, and we've confirmed it was stolen."

Stolen. Meghan leaned against the wall, absorbing that hurt. The suggestion that Neil had handled stolen gems didn't fit what she knew about him. "There's no indication within the store that any stolen goods flowed through here, either in the inventory or the records."

"Was the business in the black? Was it generating good cash flow?"

"It was generating more cash than he could spend. The checking account and savings accounts for the business are very healthy."

"How well have you searched this store to locate any pieces that might be here?" Stephen asked.

She looked his direction. "We weren't trying to find something hidden, but we've been through every display case, drawer, box, and file cabinet while doing the inventory. JoAnne put white dots on the furniture as we went through them."

"Has security been here every day since Neil's death?" Kate asked.

"Around the clock. It was part of the arrangements Neil had made in his will and with his attorney. It's a good security firm." Meghan hated where this was leading. "What do you want to do, Kate?"

"Find out if that ring recovered in the barn was a one-of-a-kind incident or the first of several stolen items. We need to do another search of Neil's possessions with an eye toward finding something concealed. Have you started working through his personal belongings upstairs?"

"Just the basics of disposing of perishables, finding paperwork to close out bills, and the like." Meghan rubbed her forehead. "I don't believe he could have been involved in something like you're suggesting, Kate. So let's prove it one way or the other. I'm responsible for everything in this building, and Stephen owns Neil's former land. You've got full access. How do you want to start the search?"

"I'm not interested in trashing Neil's reputation. We can do the search ourselves, and there's no time like the present to get started," Kate suggested.

"You don't want to bring in the sheriff?"

"Not yet, Meghan. We're worried that this might be bigger than just Neil. Someone tried to search Stephen's barn last night and took a sledgehammer to the walls and floors. Someone local is involved in this, and we'd rather not tip him off until we know who that is."

Meghan spun toward Stephen.

"I had a bit of a tussle and acquired a black eye that I'm very glad you are not able to see," Stephen said, answering her unspoken question.

"You should tell the sheriff."

"No. It's important that word not get out and trigger the start of a treasure hunt," Stephen replied. "We know there's one person out there to worry about—the guy who searched the barn. I'd rather not add a layer of idiots trying to find jewelry we only suspect might be out there."

"What about your place, Stephen? Who's watching it while you're in town?"

"Marcus is coming to help out," Kate replied for him.

"He's what?" Stephen protested.

"Marcus and Shari will be here Monday. Shari's going to assist with your new kitchen while Marcus helps us conduct a complete search."

"When was *this* decided?"

"A 2 A.M. phone call," Kate said.

Before Stephen could protest the fact his family was stepping in, Meghan settled her hand on his arm. "Kate, I suggest we divide and conquer. Why don't you and I work down here, and Dave and Stephen can take the upstairs."

Jonathan tugged out another of Craig's dresser drawers and rifled through it. This place was a dump. Craig hadn't been seen this weekend, and Jonathan had run out of patience tracking him down. The man was likely bingeing somewhere on drugs, booze, or both, assuming he had scrounged up enough cash or stolen anything of value. The barkeeper told him Craig had been rambling on about cobwebs, bugs, and barns. There was enough truth in that drunken babbling to suggest Craig had been exploring for the jewelry on his own since Neil's death.

Jonathan stepped over piles of trash to shove open the closet door. The odds Craig had actually destroyed all the pictures of the jewelry taken over the years as he was ordered were nil. The man took his money and got high. It was a wonder he hadn't had a head-on car wreck, leaving real jewels and evidence of a robbery lying around to be picked up. It was the price of small-town crime that he ended up with an excellent partner in Neil and a nearly incompetent partner in his friend Craig.

Jonathan heard the sound of a car that badly needed a tune-up approaching. He left the bedroom and strode through the rooms. He shoved open the front door and walked outside as the car went off the driveway and came to a stop half over a bush.

Craig got out of the car while Jonathan waited. He caught hold of the man's shirt, spun him around, and slammed him against the car. "What have you been doing, Craig? Acting on your own?" His friend's bruised face and knuckles told their own story. "You've been out to the farm searching? Getting yourself spotted?"

"The pieces are out there," Craig said, his mouth swollen and his words nearly impossible to make out. His eyes were still wild with whatever drug he was on.

"And if we're going to retrieve them, it's necessary that the authorities not know we're looking for them! You think Stephen won't react to you prowling around his land? There will probably be dogs and every kind of hassle to get past now."

"You can't stop me. I earned the right to those jewels just as much as you."

"Well you're not looking for them anymore. You are going back to Chicago or wherever you crawled home from and cool your heels. If you so much as think about looking for the gems again, you'll be sporting more than bruises."

Craig tried to wrestle away from Jonathan's grasp.

He pressed against Craig's chest so he couldn't draw a breath. "You listen to me, punk. We don't want a *single* piece found; we want *them all.* I'll get them my own way. You push me on this and you will regret it."

He waited until Craig stuttered an agreement.

Jonathan shoved an envelope into Craig's shirt pocket. "Go get high somewhere. Just stay out of my way."

TWENTY

Stephen lowered his frame into one of the lawn chairs that along with the couch comprised the extent of his living room furniture. A long frustrating day of searching had led to nothing of substance. "It's good that we didn't find anything."

Kate swung her feet up onto the couch and reached to rub her ankle. "Maybe. Neil either had no other pieces to hide or he had a very cautious plan for hiding them. Meghan and I didn't get very far in our search. If we go two more days without finding anything else, then I'll start to relax." She moved around the pillows. "I'm impressed with your home. This is going to be a great place."

Stephen set down his iced tea. "Where the walls will go is marked on the floor in chalk, and the furniture locations are marked out in squares on the carpet. You have to use a lot of imagination."

"The plan is there." Kate settled back on the couch. "And Dave really likes that baby goat you bought. He was calling his office to check in, but he was walking toward the barn as he dialed. I bet he's gotten lost playing with the goat again."

"That animal does kind of grow on you. The kid will have company soon; I've got feelers out for some lambs."

"You couldn't just buy a dog?"

Stephen laughed. "It's called freedom to do stuff I couldn't contemplate in the city. I'm thinking a llama might be a nice addition at some point."

"Stick to raising fish in your pond."

"Meghan will enjoy the petting zoo more."

Kate studied him. "Any movement on that front?"

"We're both so busy it's hard to get time together." He couldn't hold back a sigh. "We're friends. She's made it pretty clear that's all it will be until I'm a Christian."

"Good. She's not offering you false hope that she's going to change her mind."

"Thanks a lot, sis."

"She's right. A compromise wouldn't last. You might respect what she believes and the importance of church in her life, but inevitably you'd feel left out. She can't love Jesus and you too without eventually being forced to choose between you. She won't walk into that quicksand."

He didn't want to have this conversation, but maybe it would be better to simply get it over with. He'd been reading Jennifer's Bible, and his questions were still much the same. "Why does it feel like God has conditions on loving me?"

"He doesn't. You're projecting your own list of what you think He should expect. It gets pretty intense when you realize He accepts you despite the fact you're a mess at the moment."

He scowled at her. "I appreciate the endorsement."

"Face it, Stephen, you are. You took off after Jennifer died and left in chaos. You came back and you're still in chaos. Jesus is the kind who moves in, says I love you anyway, and then starts helping repair the mess. He means it when He says He loves you as you are, not based on what you've done. But He loves you too much to leave you in that chaos once you know Him."

"Just like that."

"Pretty much. Stephen, there are not many times in life when we get a chance to hear 'I love you and it has nothing to do with what you can do for me.' Don't let wrong assumptions cause you to mishandle the most important decision of your life."

"All the O'Malleys believe but me; therefore, I'm missing something."

"We just went first and figured out the ground on this side of believing is safe."

"Is it really?"

"Yes, it is. Jesus is a good friend. I don't regret for a moment the decision I made to believe." Kate reached for her iced tea. "You and I have been friends for ages. If I tell you I'm going to do something, you don't waste a lot of time wondering if I'm going to keep my word. Because we're friends, you trust my word to be good. And when I suggest to Marcus that he come and help out, when I push you to talk about a bad day at work, you take it in the spirit it's intended. I do it because I care an enormous amount about how you're doing and I want to help."

Kate relaxed her head back against the pillows. "That's the kind of friendship I have with Jesus. He keeps His word, and He cares about my welfare. You're so tense around the subject of religion and God that you can't envision what a friendship with Him is like. You're waiting to be let down, don't you see? You can't have both. You either trust His word and the fact that He cares about you or you don't. Until you approach Jesus with the intention of finding a trustworthy friend waiting to respond, you'll never be able to connect and get to know Him."

Stephen turned his empty glass in his hand and sighed, then set it on the floor. "I appreciate how real this is for you. I really do. It just doesn't ring true for me."

Kate tried hard to hide her disappointment. He was grateful for that as she smiled at him. "Well when it finally does ring true, will you at least promise me you'll act on it? It's tough watching you stuck there with all your questions and no answer resonating." She tugged one of the pillows out from behind her. "I know it's not an easy step, Stephen, to believe. It took Dave months to help me figure out answers to my questions. Please, keep searching for the answers instead of pushing aside the questions. When family keeps coming back to this subject, please understand—it's not because we think less of you. It's because we're convinced life is better this way. We want you to have that peace and assurance too."

"I promise I'm still listening."

"Good enough." Kate smiled. "What are the odds I might be able to talk you into finding me some ice cream?"

"Decent, assuming I can move to get out of this chair."

"You really look like someone bopped you one."

"It's been too long since I was in a street fight." Stephen pushed himself to his feet. "I'll get you some ice cream and myself an ice pack. I'm glad you came, Kate."

"So am I."

Stephen followed Kate and Dave to the bed-and-breakfast where they were staying, lifted a hand in farewell, and drove to the pharmacy. He didn't immediately need the bottle of aspirin and new ice packs he bought, but it gave him an excuse to come into town.

He drove by the jewelry store to check that all was quiet, and then he went around an extra block to check on Meghan's place. He was surprised to see her lights still on and Blackie sitting on the front porch. Stephen pulled over to the curb and stopped.

He walked up the sidewalk. Stephen held out his hand to Blackie, rubbed the dog's head, and leaned past him to knock on the door. "Meghan, it's Stephen," he called, wanting to avoid her worrying about who was knocking on her door at this time of night.

"Stephen?" He heard movement inside, then the door opened. "Is something wrong?"

"Everything's fine. I happened to be in town and saw your lights were still on."

"I was just listening to a book on tape. Would you like to come in?"

He wanted her advice on what he was thinking about Kate's comments. He knew Meghan would listen and not take offense if he asked some tough questions. He shifted his hands in his pockets. "It's a pretty night. Why don't you get a jacket and sit out on the porch with me."

She hesitated and then nodded. "Give me a minute."

Stephen settled on the top step of the porch. Blackie moved over to join him.

Meghan sat beside him a few minutes later, offering a cup of coffee. "I don't want you getting chilled sitting out here this time of night."

"Thanks. The moon is about half full right now, very white, and hanging low in the eastern sky."

She closed her eyes and smiled. "I can see it." She took a sip of tea. "Did you have a good evening with Dave and Kate?"

"I always have a good time with them," Stephen said, switching the mug to warm both hands. "Kate's happy. When they got married I wondered how smoothly she could make the adjustment to being half of a couple. Dave's good with her—he's figured out the right mix of giving her space and taking care of her without being smothering."

"She's trying hard to put on a good front, but she's nervous about the idea of being a mom."

"Kate gets very quiet when she's trying to figure out an unknown. She never had a mom around as a role model. I figure her confidence will go through the roof and she'll get a bit smug after she's figured out what she's doing. Kate feeling smug—it just begs for me to tease her a bit."

Meghan laughed. "Still glad you're going to be an uncle?"

"The idea of a child trailing me around expecting me to know answers to life's questions—like why caterpillars crawl, the sunset turns color, and raindrops don't collide with each other—I'm going to enjoy it." Just thinking about it caused him to relax. "There's going to be a second generation of O'Malleys. That's a good feeling." He set down his coffee mug. "The conversation tonight turned serious with Kate. She pretty much gave me both barrels about why I push away God."

Meghan rested her chin on her up-drawn knees. "Sorry about that."

"It's okay. We dance around the subject of religion every few months. I should have predicted the conversation." He sighed and nudged back Blackie so he could rest his hands behind him on the porch to take his weight. "I don't know if I'll ever believe, Meg. I wish I could say it would be different, but I may never make that step my family has." The reality of that decision was hurting him and his family. It was why they were after him, why Jennifer had left the gift she had. He didn't know what to do.

"I know Jennifer's primary goal near the end of her life was to help each of you come to believe. I hope her death hasn't been a stumbling block."

"I miss her, and it is part of this. Jennifer's Bible is marked up with underlines and dates and scribbled-in notes."

"Mine is too; those underlined verses and notes are memories of conversations."

"What do you mean?"

"The Bible is a living book, and her notes are records of an ongoing dialogue between her and the Lord. She'd start reading having a question or with something going on in her life that concerned her, then as she read, verses would stand out that brought answers, comfort, or insight. It's a friendship. God provides His side of the conversation through His written words. I know God enjoys my company and I enjoy His. That's what Jennifer found too."

"You talk as if it's a day-to-day friendship. I don't understand how you get to that point. I've read parts of the Bible, and it's like reading history and a kind of daily journal of Jesus as He traveled through towns around Jerusalem."

Her expression softened. "You keep reading. You listen. You hold onto what you do understand and continue to pursue what's still confusing. God then steps in and makes that dialogue alive. There's no secret; it's not intended to be hard. The Bible reassures us on that point—those who seek God will find Him." She reached over and touched his knee. "Why don't you want Jesus as a friend?"

She was breaking his heart pushing against that question. "He's not always there, Meg. Not when you really need Him."

"Yes, He is," she whispered. "He was there when Jennifer died, when Peg died, when they came to tell you your parents had been killed. Jesus was there." He looked over and caught a glimpse of deep emotion before her expression became calm. "Just like He was there the night I went blind. I know He's good and that He loves me. He didn't give me back my sight, but He gave me something more precious—a full and joyous life in the midst of this. I would have chosen my sight, but that decision was His to make. I trust Him, even in this."

"I wish I had that peace in spite of circumstances."

"You can't find the happiness you want and the peace you seek by borrowing from mine. It doesn't work that way. As much as you know about Jesus, you've never let yourself accept Him. Please, stop hiding behind the fear that you might be let down. You won't be."

She pushed her hands into her pockets. "I'll always be your friend, Stephen. Whether you believe or not, that isn't going to change. But if you don't believe, you limit our relationship to friends only. And I'll be forced to spend eternity without you. That grieves me."

"I know it does. I often wonder what I'm holding out for, but I'm not sure."

"When you can answer that, you'll have this resolved." She smiled at him. "Let it go for tonight."

Stephen smiled back. "For a day or two." He nudged Blackie away from his coffee cup. "Would you like to come out to the farm this week? Maybe Wednesday, after we do another round of searching the jewelry store? I have something to show you."

"I'd enjoy that."

"I think I'll invite JoAnne and Ken, whichever O'Malley's can make it, your parents and have my first open house."

"Oh, this sounds like fun. Let me know if I can help with food or such."

"You got it."

Neil had turned the second bedroom in the apartment into a storage room. Stephen steadied a stack of boxes and lifted off the top three. He carried the boxes into the living room where Dave had set up a worktable. Neil could have hidden jewelry in practically anything from the flour canister to a box buried behind dozens of other boxes. The only way to make sure they didn't miss something was to look through everything.

"If Neil was deeply involved in these thefts, he'd have pictures of the pieces he was duplicating, someplace to store the stolen jewels until they cooled off, and a buyer. Can we also work this problem by figuring out if he traveled? Who his regular customers were?"

"When did he have his first stroke?" Dave asked.

"A little over a year ago. I know the paralysis he was suffering on his left side made it difficult for him to do the jewelry repair work any longer."

"So that first stroke would have basically ended the creation of fakes. If Neil was dealing with stolen gems, he had a year to plan how he would close it down."

"We still don't know if Neil ever took more than the one piece I found in the barn, Dave."

"We know that diamond ring was stolen and replaced with a high-quality fake. And we know the guy who blackened your eye had an idea something was there to find. That's enough to suggest we're on the right track."

Stephen looked around the room. "He's had a stroke, he has decided he's going to move, and he knows he basically wants to shut down whatever he'd been involved with. He could either sell the stolen pieces at a big discount and move them all on to buyers or wrap them up and put them away somewhere he would consider safe."

"He didn't need money," Dave said. "What if he decided to keep the last pieces rather than sell them? His wife is dead, his health is fading, and he's got one interest left in his life: the jewelry. If he decided to keep them just because they were beautiful pieces, he's going to keep them somewhere he can see them occasionally."

"If he went to the trouble of making a final place to hide them, he'd design it to be exactly what he needed."

Dave stopped his search. "If he's got several pieces, he'd have them stored together."

"It's what I would do."

Dave sighed. "I agree with you. I'm just not sure what we do next. Searching in boxes, cupboards, behind furniture, and in walls is doable. Getting inside Neil's head is not."

Stephen circled the room. "How many pieces of jewelry would you suspect might be stashed?"

"Rings, bracelets, a couple necklaces, maybe a few really expensive pieces like he had in the vault."

"So they could fit in something about the size of a shoebox? Maybe flatter and longer?"

"That sounds about right."

"Maybe inside a piece of furniture then." Stephen picked up cushions from the couch. He tipped up the couch to check the framing to see if it looked like anything had been modified. Stephen turned over the chair by the window. The fabric had been taped to the frame in a couple places. He pulled aside the tape and used his small pocketknife to pry up a couple staples holding the fabric. "It's got to be inside something."

"Try this one," Dave tossed over his pocketknife.

"What is this, the Boy Scout special deluxe model?"

"You never know with Kate what you're going to need."

Stephen thought about that a moment and laughed. "You're right." He used the pinchers to tug up the edge of the cushion. "This works." He didn't find the box he sought, but he picked up a penny. "Nineteen forty-two. It's still got a shine. Meghan loves old coins."

"Does she?"

"Something about the idea of holding something really old." Stephen tucked the penny in his pocket. "I'm having a gathering out at the farm Wednesday afternoon, a kind of house warming party. Could you and Kate stay over another night and come?"

"We'll be there. I'm worried her blood pressure is a little high, and that job of hers isn't helping. She could use another day or two here."

"What's going on? I thought it was a pretty low-key job."

"She's not in control anymore. She hears her friends on the SWAT team and the emergency response group are out on a tough call and she's listening to hear if they're okay. I think it would be easier on her to be at the scene in the communication van making suggestions than being so far out of the loop."

"They're comrades on the front line and it feels like she's abandoned them."

"Something like that. She doesn't want an emergency response job and those risks now that we're having a family, but I don't think either one of us thought through the ramifications of it."

"She's trying for homicide."

"I know." Dave sighed. "I'm praying she doesn't get it, Stephen, and you may not tell her that. She was a great hostage negotiator because she walked right up to the line between life and death and put herself between death and the innocents caught up in events. She survived her job because she won and people walked out alive. For Kate to be working homicides—I'd give her about six months before she brought the job home with her, unable to shut it off."

Dave shook his head. "I don't know what might be best right now. Robbery is burying her in bureaucracy and cases so old and numerous that she can't solve enough of them to feel like she is successful and contributing something worthwhile."

Stephen tipped over another chair. "She isn't supervisor material."

"What she is, is one of the best hostage negotiators I've ever seen. I think she would make a brilliant teacher. I want her working at FBI and teaching at Quantico."

Stephen burst out laughing. "Kate, a Fed?"

"I haven't figured out how to approach her with the idea."

"My suggestion: stand far across the room when you do."

"She's not going to like the idea of working for a federal bureaucracy?" Dave teased.

"It will never happen. She's not good at working according to anyone else's script."

"Well Kate and I have got to figure out a solution."

Stephen moved from inspecting the furniture to checking the walls for any signs of construction in the last few years. He lifted down the wall clock. "We need to find at least one more hidden gem; then you'll have part of your solution. Kate can stay here a few more days to give you more time to think."

"How about four square diamonds and three emeralds set in a silver and gold starburst brooch?"

Stephen turned.

Dave had a piece of jewelry about the size of a small sand dollar resting in the palm of his hand.

"He had it wrapped in velvet and slid into a closed case along with his wife's diary. This one was sentimental."

TWENTY-ONE

Stephen watched from his hammock as Meghan walked the path from her parents' home toward the pond and the path that led to his house. He reached down and lazily moved a piece on the chessboard resting on an overturned shipping case. "Check."

Jack scowled.

"It's the bishops. You keep forgetting I like to go deep," Stephen remarked. "We're over this direction, Meg."

She paused Blackie.

"I hung a hammock under the oak trees beside the pond."

Blackie led her toward them.

"Do you have a fishing line in the water?" she asked, drawing closer.

He glanced over at the pond. "The bobber is getting poked a few times as baby fish check out my worm. I can cast while lying in my hammock. It doesn't get better than this." He nudged his fishing pole a little more upright in the holder driven into the ground to tighten the slack in the line created by the light breeze.

"This is going to be his hiding place, or so he says," Jack added, moving his rook.

Stephen looked at the board. "Do you really want to do that?"

"Just move."

Stephen moved his pawn. "Checkmate."

Jack sat back and studied the board. "I'm not playing you again until we figure out an adequate handicap."

"Hey, I gave you a queen."

"And decimated me before I could ever use mine," Jack replied.

Blackie stopped to check out the board. "Am I early? Or are the party plans already done?" Meghan asked.

Stephen smiled. "I've got the grill ready, the chicken marinating, the salad, rolls, and pies from the restaurant now in the refrigerator. I know how to arrange a party in an hour."

"I'm impressed."

"There are two chairs about three feet straight ahead, and a blanket spread out on the bank of the pond. Take your pick."

"I smell freshly cut grass." She took a seat on the blanket and unclipped Blackie's harness to let him go off duty.

"Jack helped me get the big mower going. We only managed to knock over a couple posts and about five feet of fencing while we figured out how to execute turns." Stephen touched her shoulder and offered her a soda from the cooler. "We're relaxing after hard labor."

"Sweaty hard labor," Jack added, greeting Blackie.

"I'm glad you came over, Jack."

"Cassie and I had a rare scheduling agreement to have the same day off. And I'm for starting up that grill. I'm getting hungry."

Stephen checked his watch. "Yes, it would be good to at least head that direction." He reeled in his fishing line.

"I'll take the chairs back to the house."

"Thanks, Jack."

Meghan folded up the blanket. "We're going to have to break in that chess set you made for me. I've been practicing with Dad."

"I'd like that. If you want to take my arm, Blackie can keep wandering." She complied and he led her to the house.

"Do you know if Kate heard anything yet about the brooch Dave found?" Meghan asked.

"She hasn't mentioned anything."

"I hope it's not stolen."

"It could have been a gift Neil made for his wife, Meg. Don't borrow trouble until we know something for sure."

"I'm trying not to. It's just unsettling to realize I didn't know Neil like I thought I did. And as executor it gets strange, knowing some of the jewels he has might be stolen."

"The sheriff was out to the house this morning, and he's agreed it's best to keep news about these pieces quiet. There is no benefit to having it discussed at the diner. Kate will stay a few more days and help us with the search. Once there are more facts to work with, they'll decide the next course of action."

"Good. I'd really like to keep this quiet."

"Meg, remember that I'm listed in Neil's trust document. If this becomes public knowledge and you need me to finish wrapping up the work at the store, I'd be glad to step in and help you out."

"Would you?"

"You bet."

She relaxed. "I've known Neil all my life, been in his home, helped care for his wife. I don't want to learn he was a felon through all those years."

"Then you have my promise. If you need to step back, just ask."

"I will."

Stephen opened the gate for them.

"Have Marcus and Shari arrived yet?"

"They'll be here anytime. They flew into Chicago this morning and are driving out." He paused her before she could turn toward the house. "Leave the blanket here on the gate. What I want to show you is down by the barn."

She left the folded blanket over the top railing.

"This way." He led with her hand tucked in his arm.

"Do you have your carpentry shop up and running?"

"Yes. I'm starting my first piece for Kate, a cubbyhole storage unit she wants for beside the crib. You're welcome to come over and keep me company as I work anytime."

"I'll do that."

Stephen stopped by the fenced-in area he had repaired and completed. "Why don't you wait here? I'll be right back." The sounds would give him away soon and he would prefer to have this be a surprise. He walked over to the enclosed pen and brought back his surprise.

"Hold out your arms, about a foot apart."

She did so and he smiled. She was a trusting lady.

He handed her the surprise. "Stephen?" Her whispered delight was worth every bit of the effort to make the moment happen. She sat on the ground where she had stood, cradling the animal. "You got a lamb."

"Three, and their mothers."

Her hands gently ran across the animal. "Keep Blackie away so he won't scare this baby."

"Blackie is over by the pen getting acquainted with the others. It looks like a calm greeting session all around."

"You bought lambs—I'm delighted, but why?"

He laughed at the stunned way she repeated it. "I also bought a baby goat. I'm creating a petting zoo."

She leaned her head back to look at him. "You aren't."

He crouched beside her. "Yep, I am. And the answer to your question is easy: Why not?"

She laughed. "Good point. Fish…animals. You're making good use of this place."

"It's fun, Meg. I don't think I've done enough fun things in my life."

"Well this is a good start."

"The goat is a rambunctious little guy. I'll take you to meet him next."

She buried her face in the soft coat of the lamb. "I'm glad you came to Silverton."

"So am I." He reached over and brushed back her hair, slipping her sunglasses up on top of her head. "So am I," he whispered. "It's a good place to find some peace in life, not that you're helping that much." He let his thumb trace her smile. "I'd love to kiss you right now."

She blinked at him.

"Stephen, where's the charcoal for the grill?" Dave called.

Meghan averted her face. He was going to murder his brother-in-law. Stephen let his hand drop. "I'd better go help him. You want me to take you down to the enclosure to meet the other animals?"

She looked up at him, a smile playing around her mouth again. "Yes, please. And there's no need to spill blood over Dave's timing."

"The moment he interrupted is indelibly printed in my memory as another of my life's unfortunate *if onlys...*" Blackie about tripped him as he darted back to Meghan's side. Stephen caught himself before he stumbled into Meghan. "I'm going to get the party started now before something else untimely happens."

She patted his chest. "Go."

Like her mom, Meghan made a wonderful hostess. Stephen watched her mingle with his family and stop to talk with Shari. The group had moved inside as darkness fell. Marcus rested his arm around Shari's shoulders, and something he said had Meghan tipping her head back as she laughed. She had relaxed after a comprehensive walk-through of the large room and how he had set up chairs for the party. She paused to touch the corner of the couch, orient herself, and then walked toward where he had put the table with drinks. He'd have to remember to provide more location cues for her next time he had a gathering.

Meghan's parents joined him. "It's been a great evening, Stephen."

"Thank you, Bill."

"We're going to head on home. Would you stop by the office tomorrow? The new extraction gear arrived. We're going to load it so it will be available on the ambulance. I'd like your opinion."

"I'll be there about nine," Stephen said, pleased Bill made the request. When the nights were quiet and long, he was beginning to miss the paramedic work. Maybe part-time wouldn't be such a bad idea, just to keep his skills up-to-date. He walked Elizabeth and Bill to their car and thought about sounding Bill out tomorrow about the idea.

The night was gorgeous. As soon as he could reasonably slip away from his own party, he would have to talk Meghan into walking with him. Going back to work as a paramedic even part time had some risks with it. Was he ready to be responsible for someone's life or death? Before he pursued the idea, he wanted to know Meghan's reaction. If she had reservations, she'd be a good enough friend to be honest about it.

Stephen looked around the party. Kate and Dave were down by the fire ring where a few logs had been tossed together so marshmallows could be toasted. Stephen picked up two glasses left on the picnic table and walked their direction.

Dave leaned over and kissed Kate. Stephen stopped, quietly turned, and went back toward the house.

He found the group inside had moved to the living room where Jack was telling some story and gesturing to a chorus of laughter. Smiling, Stephen turned into the kitchen area to return the glasses. Meghan was ahead of him, walking over to the cooler filled with ice and pop cans.

The barrier he had put around the cutout flooring where the sink and dishwasher used to be had slipped forward and her hand held palm out would pass over it.

"Stop, Meg!" He could see her catching her foot on that opening and pitching into the cut-off pipes sticking up into the air, impaling herself. He caught her around the waist and swung her away from the danger. For a moment, all he could hear was the sound of his own heartbeat. "Sorry. The barrier had moved. There was a hole."

She rested her head against his chest and his heart came out of his throat. The image of blood flowing made him cold.

Her hands came up to settle around his. "I knew the pipes were there, Stephen. I'm okay. You can let me go now." Her words finally registered. He eased his grip and she stepped back.

The glass had spilled, staining her top. Her hand touched the wet fabric. "Thanks for stopping me."

She hadn't needed his help. He'd overreacted. And he'd been the one to embarrass her. "I'm sorry, Meg."

She looked up and gave him a rueful smile. "It's fine. It will dry."

"I'll get you a towel."

"That would be good." She put out her hand and felt for the wall, reorienting herself.

She accepted the hand towel he brought her. Her hand reached out and touched his chest. "Go get me a Diet Pepsi please, and I was getting Kate a 7 Up."

"Sure."

She walked back into the living room, only a slight hesitation to her first steps until she reached the change in flooring marking where the wall used to be. She moved to the couch and took a seat beside Shari, who leaned over to ask Meghan something and got a small shake of the head in reply.

Stephen sighed. It wasn't the first time he'd embarrassed her; it wouldn't be the last. It just wasn't a great lead-in for asking her to go for a moonlit walk.

He got her soda and Kate's then went to join them.

The party broke up shortly after ten. In the sorting out of people heading to both the bed-and-breakfast and the hotel, Meghan accepted an offer from Marcus and Shari to drop her off at home. Stephen ended up saying good-night to her in a snatched moment between the three of them stepping outside and the ringing phone pulling him back inside.

It wasn't how he wanted the evening to end.

Later Stephen walked the property one last time, checking his animals, confirming the barn was padlocked, and the alarm system installed with Jack's help was turned on. He wanted the pager he wore to go off so he would have an excuse to drive into town. After the emergency was done, he'd drive by to see if Meghan was still up and ask her what she'd think of his being a paramedic again part-time. He wanted a full life back—with the job he had run from and with something that was more than just a friendship with Meghan.

It was a night for wishful thinking. The clock didn't turn back easily. And just the thought of seeing Meghan bleeding had been enough to make him cold. The sight of anyone bleeding like that… He wasn't sure he'd be able to handle it. She'd come so close to stumbling into an accident.

He kicked at a fence post. He knew why he overreacted. Would his past never leave him alone?

He could have at least apologized better for the spilled drink. Stephen pushed his hand through his hair. He could walk around deciding on what he should have said and done, or he could see if she was still up and tell her. He wouldn't get much sleep tonight while he pondered the issues of his future.

Stephen walked back to the house, picked up his keys, and took the truck into town. He drove down her street, expecting her to have already turned in but hoping luck was with him.

Meghan was sitting on her front steps, Blackie beside her.

He parked the truck and stepped out, closing the door and pocketing the keys. "Meghan? Is something wrong?"

"No, I was just hoping you might stop by." She was still nursing the soda she had taken with her an hour before. "This is one of the few times I really hate the fact I can no longer drive. I really miss it."

His steps slowed as he reached her. He'd known her for a long time. His eyes narrowed as he studied her. "You were praying for me to show up."

She gave him a small smile. "It worked didn't it? If I need something, I find it makes life easier to pray and give God a chance to intervene if He'd like to. I bet you started thinking about me? I love how that just happens."

"In this case I don't think it takes God to make me think of you. Maybe to make me not think about you…"

She laughed at that gentle rejoinder and patted the step beside her. "I need to talk to you and was hoping to do it face-to-face. Another half hour and I would have just called you."

He sat down beside her. "Okay. I'm here. What's going on?"

"I'm sorry I embarrassed you."

He about slid off the step turning toward her. "You didn't—"

Her hand on his arm stopped him. "It was nice that you acted like you did. You don't know how many people hesitate when they should say something, and I end up walking around with two different-colored socks or with a twisted ankle or a jammed finger. I'm glad you acted, even if it was unnecessary."

"And I was coming over to apologize for how many things I didn't think through before tonight—the room cues, the moved furniture, the path down to the barn. You had to do several saves just to be able to enjoy the party."

Her hand on his arm tightened. "Let's call it even."

Her smile settled deep inside his heart where it made him feel like a knight in shining armor, saving her with his fumbled attempt to help her. He laughed softly as he relaxed. "You've got a deal, Meg."

He stretched out his legs and settled back leaning against his elbows. Should he tell her why he had acted as he did, or simply close the subject? Honesty on a night like this mattered. And the one thing he'd rarely let himself talk about with Meghan was the past.

"I'll apologize in advance for the next time I embarrass you because I overreact, Meg. It's instinct to watch out for you. It's got nothing to do with whether or not you can take care of yourself. I spent years watching out for Kate too, and it's got nothing to do with her skills as a cop. If you get in trouble, I just need to be near enough so I can help."

"I truly appreciate the sentiment, but why?"

He should have said something years ago. "Peg."

"Tell me about what happened. You've never talked much about that day."

"I was nine, my sister was just six. I was watching her that day for an hour while Mom went grocery shopping and Dad worked in the garage." The sounds of that afternoon still echoed in his mind like yesterday. Why, oh why, did he have to remember so well? "She was playing with her dolls in the living room, the dolls lined up in front of the couch, using the one I gave her for Christmas to direct her choir while Peg sang some made-up song. The phone rang. I remember the phone rang and I yelled at Peg to quiet down so I could hear."

Meghan's grip began to hurt and he rubbed the back of her hand with his. He was okay...he had to be. He couldn't change the memory. "Mom called checking on something I wanted her to get at the grocery store for a sleepover I was having with friends from school. Peg slipped outside while I was on the phone."

He sighed and the overwhelming emotions quieted. The rest just was. He didn't let himself feel it. "She was always fascinated with our neighbor's swimming pool. She could swim like a fish. But on that day, something went wrong. When I found her Peg was facedown in the water. I didn't know CPR."

He smiled at the pain that her grip caused, for it kept him in the present. "Ease up a bit, honey."

Meg opened her hand so fast he was pretty sure she hadn't even been aware she'd tightened her grip again. Her silence helped. Meg cared more about listening than trying to soothe with premature words.

"The paramedics that came worked on Peg forever and never gave up, even as they took her to the ambulance. They were still working on her when they reached the hospital. I never forgot that. They got her breathing again, but it wasn't enough to save her life. She died three days later."

Meg leaned her head against his shoulder. "You were nine. And you know CPR now."

"No one ever blamed me—Mom reassured me and hugged me so much it was embarrassing. She tried so hard to convince me it wasn't my fault, that Peg had had an accident. Of course it was my fault. We all knew it. An accident, but my negligence."

"I'm not six years old. I can holler with the best of them, and I've got Blackie who can bark up a storm and get help."

"I know that, Meg. It's not that. You were up on the ladder helping Kate get boxes down at the store the other day. I watched you and I was nine again inside. It's not that I think you might fall; it's more subtle than that. But if you fall, what will I do and where will I be. The more someone matters, the more intense the emotion that I have to be there. To back off, I have to care less, and that's a vicious line to try to walk."

She smiled. "That's so romantic."

"Quit changing the subject."

She laughed and leaned against him. "Thank you. The close attention and your choice to eventually be a paramedic are starting to make sense. You can't not hover over Kate unless you love her less. And you're starting to hover over me because I'm slipping into your heart too."

It was more like a full invasion, but he would let her think it was something softer. Neither of them knew what to do with this emotion pushing them beyond just being friends. She didn't want it, and he didn't know what to do with the feelings that kept getting stronger. "I just wanted to make sure you knew that your being blind has nothing to do with it. I don't think in any way that you can't handle yourself. I didn't hover in the first years after you went blind."

"You didn't care what happened to me?" she teased.

"Not so much my heart was in my throat at the thought of not being there. And I see that smile you're trying to hide."

"So what are we going to do about this new development?"

"You'll be kind enough to pat my arm, smile, and let me hover. And I'll see what I can do about shoving my heart out of my throat when you get yourself close to trouble."

"Why don't you just trust Jesus to take care of me?"

"I don't think He cares as much about you as I do."

"He loves me more actually."

"Then maybe it's the fact that it just doesn't feel like He does. We've already established the feeling in my gut is driving this."

"Would you just relax your grip and let God be God? Jesus is the one person you'll never have to rescue. If He wants the weather still, He makes it still. He wants the dead to come to life, He raises them. He wants to feed a multitude, He does it. That nine-year-old's sense of panic in your gut will never ease unless you accept there is someone bigger and more comforting in control. Jesus can watch out for me just fine."

Her eloquence had never been the problem; his doubts were, and he had no answer left to give her. He wanted to lean over and kiss her just to change the subject, then was ashamed of that thought. His struggle over religion wasn't going to be answered with logic. His parents had believed, all the O'Malleys believed, Meghan did— Logic said he should listen and come to the same conclusion they did, for his respect ran deep for each one of them. But the resistance ran deeper into his emotions and memories, and he did not want to go back into those memories again tonight. He leaned his head against hers. Her hand crept around his waist and she leaned back. And for once Blackie didn't interrupt.

He let himself kiss her, felt the jolt of her surprise, and deepened the kiss, drawing her closer. Years of history with Meghan and he'd never imagined something this sweet.

Meghan broke off their kiss and pressed her hand against his chest. "You're going to break my heart," she whispered. "Don't do this. I already made my choice. If I had to make it again, I'm sorry but you'd lose."

"I know." He eased back. "And I'm not going to put you in that position. I'll give us both some space." He watched her touch her lips, and the softness in her smile was enough to become a priceless memory of this night. "Could I ask a favor?"

"Sure."

He asked it fast, while he thought she might say yes. "I'd like you to remove yourself from the jewelry search. I don't want to worry about your getting into trouble with the same idiot who broke into my barn. My heart can't take it, Meg."

She stilled.

"Please. I know it's a big favor, but do it for me. Put your focus back on the nursing work at the clinic and let Kate and Dave deal with the search."

She rubbed his arm. "I can't. Someone was in my house last week."

TWENTY-TWO

Stephen studied all the doors from the kitchen to the garage, looking for any signs of tampering. He tightened the doorknob screws until the Phillips head screwdriver began to strip the metal, his anger simmering just below the surface. "Why didn't you say something earlier?"

Meghan circled her finger around the coaster on the kitchen table, not looking over at him. "I thought it was my just misplacing things."

Someone in her place… He had felt guilty about keeping a secret from her about what had happened when he was nine years old and she'd been hiding *this*. "What else besides the earring is missing?"

"A bag of chips I bought. I checked: It was on my grocery receipt, I know I put the bag away in the cupboard, and it's gone." She shifted in her chair and leaned down to rub Blackie's back. "And I think some cash is missing, but it's hard to tell how much. It's probably a kid. I could have lost the earring, but why take only one earring and not two?"

Stephen didn't want to scare her to death, but what if she really had someone watching her, someone feeling comfortable coming and going from her house, taking items to keep as mementos and putting her off balance…? Stephen looked at the dog. Blackie would take a man down if he thought Meghan was threatened. That was the one point of comfort in this.

Maybe it was a kid; the chips would suggest that. Maybe she had simply lost one of the earrings. Maybe she had miscounted the cash. There were a lot of maybes… "Has Blackie ever acted unusual when you got home?"

"No. And you know he would if anyone was here. He's very territorial. When we get home I let him run around the yard or he prowls through the house. At a minimum he's going to bark like mad when he senses something is wrong, get his back up, and stand between potential danger and me. He's trained for it, and it's also his nature."

Stephen walked past Meghan into the living room. He checked the front door. There was no sign of tampering. If someone was stealing from her, how were they getting in? He checked the windows. The alarm system was good—it would catch a door or window opening. "What's down in the basement?"

"Darkness." She smiled. "It's a place I rarely go because the stairs are narrow and steep. It's also concrete with a lot of odd things to touch such as the furnace and the hot-water heater. The door is by the utility room."

"Any windows down there?"

"Just two small eight-inch half windows at ground level."

Stephen opened the door to the basement, turned on the light switch, and found the bulb had good wattage. "I'll take a look."

"I'm staying right here."

He found the basement sparse; the water heater, furnace, and sump pump were in the east corner. The windows had a reassuring layer of cobwebs and accumulated dirt on the panes. The lighting was good, and he inspected the stairs while he was there, looking for any signs they were weakening or that the banister had loosened in case Meghan ever needed to come down here. He walked back upstairs, shut off the light, and closed the door. "The basement looks fine. How do you get into the attic?"

"Stephen, that's not necessary."

"Then it will just take a couple minutes to confirm it."

She led the way down the hall and stopped by the linen closet, then pointed up. "The ladder tugs down."

He opened the access panel and went up to check the attic. There wasn't much clearance and one glance told him based on the layer of dust that nothing around the access door had been disturbed in months if not years.

"Everything okay?"

"It's okay." He closed the access door. Meghan stood in the hallway, arms crossed, leaning against the wall, a combination of weariness and uncertainty in her expression. "I'm adding my phone number to that list of automatic dials the alarm system makes."

She nodded.

"I want your word you'll let Blackie go into the house ahead of you, and if there's anything at all you question that is missing, moved, or just doesn't feel right, you'll call me."

"You've got my word."

He reached out and ran his hand down her arm. "Then I'll let this rest."

"The alarm system is good, and I've got Blackie. There's Mace in the bedside table, a phone in the bathroom, and good locks on that door if I decide I have to bolt somewhere. I'm not letting a possibility drive me out of my own home."

"I'll worry about you anyway."

She half smiled. "At least I didn't acquire a black eye."

He leaned over and planted a quick kiss on her lips, unable to resist that smile. "I'm going home."

Stephen walked his land, not bothering to try to sleep for the remaining hours of the night. *The precious idiot.* She didn't think it was worth mentioning that something felt wrong at her home. She was blind, but she had moved so far beyond it in how she structured her life that it took nights like tonight to remind him just how vulnerable she was to trouble. At least with Blackie and that alarm system this was contained. She really was invading his heart. What was he going to do now?

I'm in over my head.

It wasn't his job this time; it was his personal life, or lack thereof. And what he had to do now was intensely more complex. He wanted what was best for Meghan. Her faith had allowed her to survive being blind and was the foundation of the peace in her life. She felt incredibly loved by her God, but he wasn't on speaking terms with her best friend.

The bind he put Meghan in because of that was huge. He wanted to deny it was that big of a deal. God was spirit, and it shouldn't be that big a deal if he knew Him or not, but Stephen was kidding himself. She'd made the right choice by saying it was an insurmountable problem. She wouldn't be able to talk freely about God and share that bond with him. If he fell in love with a lady who wasn't on speaking terms with one of the O'Malleys, it would have ripped him apart trying to choose between them.

He was already feeling the stress of being the only holdout in a family of Christians. There was a growing sense of a distance because he just didn't get it. He hated that void. They were working so hard not to let the relationship change, and yet it was happening. He wanted to belong. He'd been searching for that his whole life—in his profession, his family—and all he knew for certain was that he hadn't found the perfect answer yet. Maybe it was God who filled that void. The other O'Malleys thought so.

He looked at the land he called home and the stars displayed overhead.

"I don't know what to say to You."

He stopped walking. He'd just acknowledged that there was someone there to listen to his words, whom he expected to respond. He'd spoken without thinking, and now it was out there lingering as if there was someone listening. Maybe a relationship with God might be personal, even for him.

He couldn't think of anything to say.

He started walking again.

Meghan and his family all had personal relationships with God that were enviable for their closeness. He had friends whom he knew in a distant kind of way, enough to call them friends even if he didn't hang out with them twenty-four/seven. And he had friends like the O'Malleys whom he could count on with absolute confidence they would always be there if he needed anything.

"Which kind of friendship is this going to be, God? I can't make the choice on Your side. Distant or close? For years I've avoided knowing You for the simple reason that I don't want a distant relationship, struggling to meet Your expectations and never quite feeling accepted. My family expects a lot of me, but they give me plenty in return. You are a high expectations God. I've read the verses:

'Be holy, for I am holy,' and 'Love your enemies.'"

Stephen hesitated. Was it okay to be bluntly honest with God? Or were you supposed to be polite for a while and diplomatic? This was not as straightforward as Meghan claimed. All he really knew how to be was himself, and that meant blunt honesty. "I'm afraid to take the step to be a Christian. I know what is expected of me, but I don't know if I can meet it. So what do we do now?"

It felt odd to talk aloud, alone, as he walked the property, but he remembered his mom praying aloud at dinner, and he'd feel even sillier stopping and closing his eyes. "Kate says she figured out the ground on the other side of believing is safe, that it's the relationship that makes believing work. I'll admit I'd like to understand what she means."

He stopped at the fenced-in area where his sheep were lying down for the night and leaned against the railing, finding peace just looking at the animals. He had come to love them. The baby goat was a splotch of gray with a white streak curled up, sleeping and dreaming if that was what baby goats did at night.

Either he found peace with the God Meghan called her best friend or…what? To stay and let the emotions grow between them when they were at an impasse would just hurt them both. And he couldn't handle being the one to hurt Meghan. He was falling in love with her.

There were no good options.

He walked back to the house, not sure what he should do next. The house was quiet, and he went through the rooms turning off lights and checking locks, then headed back to his bedroom.

He pushed off his boots and stretched out atop the bedspread and out of habit reached for Jennifer's Bible. He turned pages in it absently, having already read through Luke. He felt as though he were eavesdropping at times as he read Jennifer's notes and what she had underlined. Meghan was right. They were echoes of a conversation Jennifer had been having with God.

He turned to where he had left the bookmark in the book of John. He'd spoken his piece tonight, and Meghan said God did His talking primarily through His Word. He didn't understand what she meant when she said the Bible was a living book, that the words "came alive." What he'd read so far was interesting, but it was ancient history. Since the New Testament was Jesus' biography, he started reading in John.

As the father has loved me, so have I loved you; abide in my love. If you keep my commandments, you will abide in my love, just as I have kept my Father's commandments and abide in his love. These things I have spoken to you, that my joy may be in you, and that your joy may be full. This is my commandment, that you love one another as I have loved you. Greater love has no man than this, that a man lay down his life for his friends. You are my friends if you do what I command you. No longer do I call you servants, for the servant does not know what his master is doing; but I have called you friends, for all that I have heard from my Father I have made known to you.

Stephen turned the Bible to read Jennifer's note written in the margin in her flowing handwriting. *The great love relationship for eternity; mine; so much joy!*

She'd lived her last year with a joy that he'd had a hard time understanding given the cancer she fought. Her note was dated a month before she died. Jennifer's joy had come from within.

He read again the verse she'd underlined. *Greater love has no man than this, that a man lay down his life for his friends.* He knew what that verse meant, and more than just theoretically. Of all the emergency calls he had answered as a paramedic, the most heartbreaking were those where someone had died trying to rescue a friend. It spoke of a love so deep that person's own safety no longer mattered, of a will to help so strong that no obstacle would stop them even if it meant rushing into a burning building or a collapsing structure. It was an absolute love that had no limits. Did Jesus offer to be a friend like that?

Hope stirred.

He rolled onto his back and looked toward the ceiling, imagining the stars above the house and the vastness of that vista he'd been walking under a few minutes ago. "Jesus, I didn't understand why You would come to the earth, die on a cross, and then walk out of a tomb. But maybe now I'm beginning to. The laying down Your life for another—I understand that. I know in my gut what it takes to put it all on the line to rescue someone else.

"I know for a fact I'm a sinner: I live with me; I know how many times I blow it every day. Was dying for me the only way You could save me? Did You make that ultimate sacrifice on just the hope that we would one day be friends?

"It speaks volumes about Your character if You did, and it blows me away with its generosity. If You're willing to die for me, I should be able to trust You." He flexed his fingers and watched the veins move on the back of his hand. "You know trust is not something I easily give, but this feels real.

"My family and Meghan have been trying so hard to get me to see the truth. And I think I just saw a bit of it. But what now, Jesus? I don't have much to offer You in return." He thought about the last decades of his life. "Not much at all. I'm a burned-out paramedic who's a decent carpenter." He picked up the Bible and tried to read through the rest of the page where the bookmark rested but couldn't concentrate on the words. He closed the Bible.

He didn't have much to offer at all. And the baggage of his past was still there. A tear built in the corner of his eye. So much baggage. "Is Peg happy in heaven?"

TWENTY-THREE

Meghan shifted pharmacy sacks in her satchel Friday afternoon. The number of holes in the attached punch card was her system for identifying them. She made rounds with Ashley delivering medicines and doing follow-up care visits, but errands like this to drop off supplies like gauze strips or diabetic blood sugar test strips was something Meghan could do on her own.

Craig Fulton was a borderline diabetic. Add to that the fact he had a drug addiction he didn't want to beat, and his health was fading fast. He'd missed his last two appointments with her dad, and the supplies were an excuse to stop by, check on him, and encourage him to make a third appointment. If she let him give up, there would never be a recovery.

She walked up his porch steps and opened the screen door. She knocked on the main door, startled when it moved under her hand. "Craig? It's Meghan. I brought you more supplies."

Blackie lunged forward in his harness, whining. She held him back and raised her voice. "Craig, are you home?"

Blackie came close to pulling her off balance. "Okay, boy, okay. Take me to a person," she urged, opening the door wider. He tugged her inside.

The smell of oil, burnt toast, and rotting garbage came from all directions. Blackie pulled her forward to her right. Under her feet she could feel places where the carpet was worn and frayed. Blackie sat and whined.

"Craig?"

Her searching hands found no furniture turned over. Blackie pushed at her knee nearly buckling her. Her foot touched something hard that gave. She reached down and her hand hit flannel and warmth and...deadweight. She jerked back and her elbow collided with the side of Blackie's head. The dog yelped. Her hands searched in front of her and encountered rough denim, and she struggled to figure out how Craig had fallen. "Craig!" His body began to shake—he must be having a seizure.

She grabbed for her phone and scrambled to push the right buttons.

Stephen pushed through the narrow doorway into Craig's apartment, carrying the gray medical supply case. The weight of the case rubbed against jeans still muddy from work rebuilding the water piping from the old well on his farm.

He'd managed an eight-minute response to get here, and from the look on Meghan's face it hadn't been fast enough. "I've got the backup kit, Bill."

"Bring it over."

Stephen shoved a card table out of his way and stepped over Blackie to squeeze in beside Meghan's father. Stephen looked at their patient, then turned startled eyes toward Bill, who shook his head. It was hopeless. Craig's eyes were still open, but life was gone. Bill was doing CPR, but it wasn't for the patient he was attempting to treat.

No...not this. Stephen closed his eyes, took a deep breath, and steadied himself. He reached over to rub Meghan's shoulder. "You need a hand?" She was rhythmically squeezing the air bag.

"I've got it. I found him on the floor where he had fallen. His pulse was racing; he was still breathing. Seizures, three of them, hard."

"Okay. Slow down, honey. We're here now."

He tugged on latex gloves and studied Craig. There were signs of seizure-induced bleeding: muscles locked and blood vessels ruptured behind his eyes. Stephen scanned the room. The drugs on the dresser and the trace on the floorboards marked the cause. He didn't need a chemical test to tell him the powder was cocaine and overly pure. He'd seen this death before—the overdose had exploded his heart. Craig was a dead man the moment he inhaled the drug, taking it straight through the back of the nasal cavity and rapidly into the brain. Even a doctor with the full suite of drugs available couldn't have stopped it.

A terrible death. And Meghan had been here when those death rattles came.

Stephen pushed aside the footstool and stepped around to get closer to Meghan. He nodded to her father.

"Craig overdosed, honey," Bill said softly. "We can stop now." He discontinued his compressions and reached over to still her hands on the air bag. "There's no way to bring him back."

"No. Do something! He was alive when I got here, when Blackie found him."

Stephen moved her back and nearly got his chin clipped with the top of her head when she tried to ward him off. He turned her head into his shoulder. Meghan was shaking. "He overdosed, Meg. There was nothing you could have done," he murmured, trying to comfort her.

She'd seen death before as an ER nurse. But this time—unable to see what was happening and why, with no medical equipment available, and Craig dying—those minutes alone must have felt like an eternity.

He stood, lifting her with him.

The sheriff came in with the county paramedic. Stephen looked over at her father. "We'll be outside."

Bill looked at his daughter, then back at him, and nodded. "I'll need to be here a while. Why don't you take her home?"

"If I've got any questions, I'll come by later," the sheriff said.

"Thanks, guys. Come on, Meg."

She didn't want to go, but he insisted and led her out of the room. Blackie pushed against her leg and she reached a hand down, seeking his reassurance. Stephen opened the door and her dog led the way outside.

Meghan pulled away from him and sat on the top step. She wrapped her arms around Blackie and buried her face in his fur. Stephen hoped she would cry, but she just clenched her hands in that warm fur. Slowly the shakes stilled. Blackie whined and pushed at her. "What did he take?"

"It looks like cocaine."

Stephen tugged over the small medical kit the paramedic had left on the porch and found wet wipes. He ripped three open and cleaned the blood from her hands. "You came to see Craig?"

"To drop off supplies," she said tiredly. "And Jonathan left Craig tickets for the benefit. Not that it was likely he would have come to the symphony but maybe to the gathering afterward. The two were friends since high school… You hope for the best of a friend. Jonathan thought he might come. I offered to drop the tickets off."

"Was he in seizures when you arrived?"

"Yes."

"He probably ingested the drugs in the hour before. Seizures like you described mark the final moments." He wrapped his arm around her and hugged her. "At least he didn't die alone. You were there with him."

Her tears finally came. He wiped them away as they ran down her cheeks.

"I wish I'd been able to help him more than that."

"If he'd wanted help with his drug problem, he would have let you help months ago." Stephen got to his feet. "Come on. I'm taking you home."

"I'd rather not go home," she whispered. "I don't want to take this with me."

"My place then. You can walk for a while."

Stephen stirred the chili and put it back in the microwave, then got out dishes from the cabinet. Meghan might not feel like eating but it would distract her. He saw the sheriff's car turn into the drive. Meghan didn't need more hard information hitting her tonight, or questions. Stephen set down the dishes, stopped the microwave, and went outside to meet the man.

The sheriff leaned against the side of the squad car and waited for him. "Whoever sold him that packet might as well have shot him. It was 90 percent pure, not cut down much at all. I sure hope it was only a small batch and the dealer figures it out soon, or we're going to learn the hard way just how many in this community he's selling to."

"I was afraid of that."

"I wish I had more to tell you, Stephen. We're inventorying Craig's things, looking for whatever leads that indicate where he's been and who he's been dealing with. Craig's been acquiring cash to feed his habit from somewhere, and if he's turned to dealing, I figure we'll find a trail. I would have never placed him as a dealer, but then I also didn't see him as stupid enough to die from it."

"He's been getting cash from somewhere, Sheriff. Do you think he's connected to the stolen jewelry we found?"

"Maybe. The one thing Craig did a lot of was spend his weekends away from here, often driving to Chicago and Davenport. He could have been couriering pieces and getting cash that way." The sheriff pointed to Stephen's barn. "Now that damage fits what I would expect of Craig."

"He fits the general size and build of the guy who gave me the shiner."

"And if you look below the overdose, it's pretty obvious he's been in a fight recently."

"I saw the bruises." Stephen pushed his hands into his pockets. "Does it end here if Craig was the one searching my barn and the courier for stolen pieces Neil was fencing? Both of them are now dead and we're finding the remaining jewels."

The sheriff pushed back his hat. "I'd be relieved if it was just the two of them. The barn suggests Craig knew about the jewelry, and Neil had to be the one creating those excellent replicas. Maybe it does end here. We'll see what the investigation turns up to further connect them."

"You'll let me know what you find?"

"Sure thing. How is Meghan?"

Stephen glanced back to the house. "She doesn't like people dying."

"I've got no questions that can't wait for another day." He opened the squad car door.

Stephen saw the sheriff off, then turned and went back to the house. He could also see Craig going through Meghan's house while she was away, lifting things he could use to pay for his habit. As tragic as this day had been, it may have just removed a few serious worries.

Stephen let the door close softly behind him and walked through the house. Meghan had shifted on the sofa and her eyes were closed, her hand resting down to curl in Blackie's coat. The dog was watching her, a vigil that hadn't changed since they arrived. He stood watching the two of them for a moment, then grinned.

He was jealous of a dog.

He tugged her sock to wake her. "How you doing?"

She moved her feet to let him have a seat on the couch. "Do I need to go home?"

"What?"

"I lost track of time. Do I need to go home?"

"It's only about eight."

She sighed. "Okay."

She slid the pillow up over her face. Dwelling on the memories was the last thing she needed, and sleep wouldn't come without images to disturb it. He wouldn't be shaking Meghan out of this silent depression easily.

"Still chilly?"

"A little."

He added the blanket the baby goat had been playing with on top of the throw she was already using. The dust might make Meghan sneeze, but it was better than letting her end up with a chill.

"This is what you dealt with for years in Chicago—overdoses, guys splattered in car wrecks, and images like it," she observed, her voice heavy.

"Yes."

"No wonder your system said enough and forced you to take that vacation. I thought I understood what it was like to deal with trauma from working in the ER. I didn't even have a taste of it. Not the frontline weight of being first on the scene."

"You'll notice I'm now raising fish and pretending to be a farmer." Stephen reached over and clicked on the music, put the CDs on random play, then turned the volume down. "When I walked away from days like this as a paramedic, I'd go play basketball to wear away the memories. What would you like to do?"

She shrugged.

Letting her rest here wasn't going to help her get over it. "Come on down to my shop. I'm working on a chest of drawers for Kate."

"Can I do something to help?"

"Want to help make the knobs for me? It's a little work with a whittling knife and a lot of work with sandpaper."

She opened her eyes and moved her head, making the effort to look toward him. "Do you have something warm I could borrow to wear?"

"I've still got my North Dakota jacket around here somewhere. It's bigger than yours, but it'll keep you snuggly warm. I'll get it for you."

She offered her hand. "Put me to work."

Stephen tightened a piece of wood in the vice and then reached for his measuring tape and a pencil. "I like having you down here keeping me company, but if you fall asleep at that workbench, you'll fall off the stool and give us both a scare. What do you say I take you home now?"

Meghan ran her hand across the round drawer knobs she had sorted, sanded, measured, and confirmed were identical. "I like being here. How come you're not getting tired?"

"Because I like working on a piece until late into the night. It's therapy; gives me time to think. You on the other hand stop moving and the thinking stops; then you start nodding off to sleep."

She smiled at him. He was falling in love with that smile, and it had taken its time to finally reappear tonight. He didn't really want to take her home, but it was getting late.

"Did you know Jesus was a carpenter?"

Stephen opened the vice and nudged the piece of wood farther down. "Jennifer mentioned it." The sadness that came just with saying her name didn't hit with its normal intensity. It was progress. "I bet He was a good one."

"I wish you were comfortable with the fact Jesus loves you."

"I'm working on it. I'm comfortable that Jesus loves *you.*" He knew she'd be overjoyed to learn he had crossed the line to believe in Jesus, but that conversation would inevitably lead to his mentioning his revelation about Peg and the tears that had ended his night. He wasn't ready for that yet, and Meghan had already absorbed too much emotion today. A peaceful conversation tomorrow would do just fine.

Stephen walked over and got out the cushion foams from his cabinet of supplies. "Why don't you toss your towel over this cushion, and you'll have yourself a pillow so you can close your eyes and rest them a moment."

"Thanks."

"Hold still a minute." He knelt and used his tape to measure the distance from her shoe soles to the back of her knee.

She reached down and touched his hand. "What are you doing?"

"You're about Kate's height. It helps if custom chairs are at least within the ballpark of the right height for comfort."

He walked back over to his workbench and jotted down the figures. "I was thinking I might pick you up next Sunday and go to services with you."

He glanced over, hoping it might catch her speechless, but that small smile appeared and she just rested her chin on her hand as she looked at him. "I'm thinking I would like it if you did."

She'd been praying for him again; he was starting to recognize that small smile. Stephen softly whistled as he measured a piece of wood to Meghan's height. Yes, he could certainly get used to more nights like this one. "Would you like to come to Chicago with me next month for two weddings? Cole and Rachel are having a quiet ceremony on Friday afternoon, the twenty-eighth, and Jack and Cassie are getting married the next day. I'd enjoy your company for the weekend."

"Can I think about the invitation for a few days?"

"Sure. As long as you say yes."

"I like the changes you're making out here," Bill commented, walking along the new fence Stephen built.

"Thanks."

Stephen followed Meghan's father, watching the man as he reached out to touch a post, shake a board, confirming just how solid the work had been done then nod with approval.

Stephen pulled his hand from his pocket and pointed ahead to where the walk to the pond joined their two properties. "I'm thinking about making the path to the pond into something more defined, with woodchips and edging and the occasional post with a different pattern to each top knob, so Meghan doesn't have to wonder about her location on the path. If I do, would you like me to extend it over to your orchard fence?"

"Please. Come over anytime and I'll help you mark it out." Bill paused to watch the sheep. "I appreciate what you did yesterday. I knew it was hopeless as soon as I saw Craig, but I saw how invested she was in saving him—" Bill shook his head.

"You did the right thing. When an infant died of SIDS, we'd often do the same attempts to resuscitate even though it was useless effort just to give the parents a little more time to accept what was happening. You treat the living, and the shock they are experiencing. Meghan did what she could, but nothing could have saved Craig's life. Accepting that doesn't come easy, not when she's blind and having to take our word for it."

"I shared coffee with her this morning. She's dealing with it."

Stephen leaned against the fence, watching the baby goat race through the grazing sheep, running off energy. "I've been thinking about picking up that paramedic's jacket, returning to the job part-time. It wouldn't solve all the response-time problems given just the sheer distances out here, but it would help."

"It would let us get one of the county ambulances stationed at the clinic in Silverton, if not as its permanent hub then as a rotating one. Are you sure you're ready, Stephen? The job chewed you up the last time."

"I don't know if I'll ever be really ready. But the last two pages—they've felt right. I'm a good paramedic and I'm comfortable with the pressure of being the one who's responsible. It's not my job to determine the outcome; it's God's. I can live with that."

Bill looked over at him thoughtfully and nodded. "I'm glad you found that perspective. You sound at peace with it."

"I am."

Bill held out his hand. "I'd be honored to have you on the team. We can do the paperwork with the county EMS this afternoon and make it official."

Stephen appreciated the confidence offered, but he wasn't sure he had earned it yet. "I won't let you down."

"I don't expect you will."

As momentous as the change, it was finalized in merely a minute. Stephen kicked at a fence post and figured he'd better get himself a phone to carry with him, maybe get that jacket of his repaired so the emblem didn't pull away. "I haven't told Meghan yet; I'd appreciate if you let me break the news."

"Sure. She'll be glad to have you coming in and out of the office occasionally."

"Will she?"

Bill smiled and patted him on the back. "You're going to settle your questions about God, find the peace you're after, and start making my life havoc by asking Meghan out. I'm an old man, but I still notice the obvious. Ever since you bought this place, you've begun setting down roots."

"I'm well on my way to being there. I'll make her happy, Bill."

"I know you will. Would you like to come over for lunch Sunday?"

"I'm planning to give Meg a lift to church; I'll be glad to join you for lunch afterward. Your wife makes a great pie."

"That she does. How's the remodeling coming along?"

"Good. Come on up to the house and I'll show you around. I could use your opinion on my future office. I want to build shelves like those you have."

TWENTY-FOUR

Meghan agreed to a picnic lunch on Saturday, and Stephen chose a place over by the river, hoping even the few miles of distance would help her shake the sadness of the last few days.

The quilt covered the grass and the ground wasn't that uncomfortable for an hour. At least the ants had yet to appear. Stephen finished his second croissant sandwich and speared one of the olives in the relish tray.

Meghan nibbled her way around the last of a pear. "You make a nice lunch."

"Thanks." He leaned over and nudged Blackie, offering him the last piece of cheese. The dog was doing his best not to beg but this had to be tough—the food was spread out to one side of the blanket in front of him. The pepper cheese disappeared in one bite.

"He's a mooch, and you're just going to make him sick."

Stephen rubbed Blackie's ears. "Hard work deserves a reward occasionally."

He packed away the remains of their lunch and placed them in the picnic basket. "I told your father I'd start working more formally as one of the county paramedics. It won't prevent days like yesterday, but maybe in the next crisis I'll be able to help you more."

"You're comfortable doing that?"

"It's time, Meg. And I'm not as queasy at the sight of blood anymore."

"I'm glad. You'll do a wonderful job, and the town residents will welcome you to the job with open arms."

"Think you can handle me wandering in and out of the clinic when I'm in town?"

"Are you going to make a point of letting me know you're around?"

"Hmm."

She smiled. "I was afraid of that."

He rolled onto his back. He was in the mood to close his eyes and catch a nap.

"Something is different today, Stephen. I can hear it in your voice. You sound…I don't know the right word. Calm."

"I'm falling asleep," he clarified. "It's good to have the decision made. And I made another big one just before it." He turned his head to look at her, interested in watching her face. "The Bible is starting to make sense, Meg. I understand now how you know Jesus as a friend."

The pear juice got ahead of her and had to be rubbed off her chin. He watched the emotions on her face—joy, curiosity, hesitancy to make too much of his words. "You believe."

He smiled at her caution. "Yes, what I understand so far. I was reading through John and it started to come alive as you described, and the pieces began to make sense. Your description of it as a conversation—it fit. The fact Jesus would come and die on a cross for me, when it began to click that He could love me that much— There's something powerful in that, Meg, that overrides so many of the questions that still linger."

"He loves completely, and every time I think I've figured that out, I find I've barely scratched the surface. On the questions, a suggestion? Take your time and keep searching for answers. He's not bothered by honest conversation when we hurt."

"It was the first time I thought about Peg being in heaven where I would get to see her again. It got pretty emotional."

"Peg's there and it will be a good reunion. She's going to be everything you remember, and more. Only her body died. And Jesus promised a new one for heaven and eternity."

"You'll see again in heaven."

"Heaven is described as being so beautiful. A few years without sight here on earth will make the joy of seeing heaven so incredible." She lifted a sleeve to wipe at her eyes. "Oh, I'm going to cry, and that's not fair."

He rolled toward her. "Here, I've got more napkins. And your happy tears aren't so bad."

She took a handful of the napkins. "I've been praying for you so long." She scrubbed at her face and then just buried her head in her hands. "Oh, look somewhere else will you? My nose is going red; I can tell."

He laughed. "It's kind of endearing, but it's not like all that many people are out here to notice." He waited until she pushed her hair back and looked up. "I'm glad you kept praying."

"I figured the O'Malleys were trying to do enough of the explaining." She mopped her eyes and gave him a smile. "Did you bring dessert? I could use a distraction."

"First-class dessert: cheesecake." He pulled over the picnic basket. "How about we rent a movie tonight? Something you remember well and hopefully not too mushy. We can see if Ken and JoAnne are free. I need his help with the new kitchen cabinets."

He watched her relax.

"Could I feed your sheep?"

"Sure. You'll have to watch out for the baby goat; he loves shoelaces." Stephen touched her hand and offered a plate. "Dessert is served."

❧❦❧

Jonathan sat in the diner at a corner table near the front window, watching people coming and going along Main Street. Craig was no longer a threat. Jonathan had to swallow hard to eat without choking. He'd done what he had to do. It cost him seven thousand to buy that envelope and its contents. He'd given Craig a chance; he hadn't forced his friend to open the envelope and use what it contained…but Jonathan had known he would do it. Craig had betrayed him and tried to take the jewelry for himself. There had been no other choice.

He'd never killed before.

He wasn't sure he liked how it felt.

He pushed the emotions aside, for it was over and done. He had a decision to make, and it was his own life on the line this time. The stolen gems were still out there somewhere.

If the jewels were not going to be found, then the correct tactical decision was to walk away and leave them behind—unsold, unfound, and the knowledge of them buried with Neil and Craig. But if Meghan or the cops had a chance of finding the gems, then recovering them had to be his top priority and would be worth any risk short of being discovered.

Neil, where did you put them?

The owner of some of those pieces might— He should have never let Neil talk him into stealing them from the wife of a mob boss. Rumor had it the man liked his victims to bleed to death. Slowly.

The jewelry could never be found. He would have to ensure that. So far they had been hidden well enough, even though in the last few days several people were looking for them. The authorities didn't have tangible proof yet that more pieces existed, so eventually they'd give up and figure they had already found everything. If he tried to search and revealed that someone else was involved beyond Neil and Craig, it would create trouble and keep the search going.

Maybe Neil had done one thing right and hidden them well enough they would never be found. Maybe it was better to do nothing. Jonathan pushed his coffee cup aside. He was taking a nasty risk no matter which he chose. Was this over?

He left the restaurant and walked back to the hotel, then stopped at the desk to ask for messages and that his bill be prepared.

If he did come back to Silverton, it would be because trouble had arrived and the jewels had been found. He'd be forced again to act to protect himself.

They said the second murder was easier than the first. He didn't want to have to find out…

TWENTY-FIVE

SILVERTON
Monday, June 10

Meghan curled her bare feet into the living-room carpet, enjoying the warmth of the sun. In the last few weeks as summer arrived, this room had become her favorite place to spend her afternoons. She walked over and nudged out her piano bench with her foot, reached forward to search the piano top to find her coaster, and carefully set down her glass of ice water. She turned on the cassette player and listened to Mrs. Teal's last lesson in order to hear the song played correctly. Mrs. Teal made this sound so easy.

Meghan found the opening chords and began her hour of practice. Someday she'd be able to play the song without jarring mistakes. She loved "Amazing Grace." And the fact Stephen had mentioned it had been a favorite of his mom's, she so wanted to be able to play it smoothly.

He likes me…he likes me a lot…he loves me… She paused to run a scale. Jesus, where's this heading? Stephen has got me so off balance. She loved her job, her home, and the hope for a husband and family was a lifelong dream. Maybe it was finally drawing near…she sure hoped so.

Blackie barked. Meghan pushed back the bench and shut off the cassette player. JoAnne was coming over this morning to help her hang pictures. She knocked over the water glass. Meghan instinctively shoved her arm across the top of the piano to push the water off the piano top before it flowed down and into the keyboard. She knocked the metronome, the empty cassette box, her little bear, and the photo she kept there of Jonathan and Mrs. Teal from a high school concert to the floor.

She hurried into the kitchen and grabbed the roll of paper towels. She tore off squares to dry the spill. Accidents happened, even to people who could see. It just *had* to be the piano, the one thing she treasured most in her house.

As she came back into the living room she missed her location cues and struck her knee hard on the piano bench, then yelped as it tumbled over and struck her foot. She pulled back and stepped on something.

Meghan froze. Wanting to kick something in frustration, she forced herself to stand still and absorb the wave of emotion that came at such blindness-caused clumsiness. She eased back from the disaster, knelt to see what she had just destroyed, hoping it wasn't the picture frame, and reached out toward broken glass fragments.

She had broken the metronome. The wood had cracked at the base. She tried to sort out how badly the wood had separated and if the metronome would still keep time. The bar that swung back and forth wouldn't move. She pushed at it and felt the device come apart in her hands. Something that landed in her palm felt wrong. *What in the world?*

Velvet. She closed her hand around the unexpected item and set the rest of the broken device on the floor. The velvet was taped and when she opened it, she found herself holding a ring. It felt like a woman's ring—slender, a big stone, and what felt like a modern setting. A ring, in her metronome. Neil's piano...Neil's metronome.

She was holding a stolen ring.

Neil, no. Why did you have to be a thief?

She had thought it was over, the searches having turned up only the ring in the barn and the brooch in Neil's apartment. Dave and Kate had gone back to Chicago weeks ago, comfortable they had found everything.

Should she call Stephen? The sheriff?

She tucked the ring in her pocket, carefully stood, and walked into the kitchen. She dialed from memory. Dave would be back in town this weekend to do her a favor regarding the jewelry store as she prepared to complete her work with the estate. "Kate, I've got a ring in my hand that is likely another of Neil's stashed pieces. Could you come with Dave this weekend and take a look?"

Joseph looked over the edge of the ravine and shook his head as he stepped back.

"The boy just had to break his leg when he was all the way down there, instead of tripping at the top of the trail."

Stephen hoisted the ropes to his shoulder and smiled at his new partner. "Want me to lead the way to break your fall, or shall I hold the safety rope so you don't crash to the bottom like he did?"

"The kid is my nephew, so I guess I should do the honors. I'll take the lead. You would figure he'd have listened when I warned him. This loose shale will do it to you every time."

"What's down there that's so fascinating?"

"An old coal mine. It's kind of like Silverton's equivalent to a haunted house. A couple miners died down there in the 1930s, and their ghosts are the legend behind all kinds of stories the kids tell to spook each other."

Stephen accepted the water bottle from Joseph.

"I've got the splints and litter. Let's go get him." Joseph moved over to the start of the steep trail and began his descent. Stephen watched his footing and followed. A cop and two other teens were already down there with the boy. It was good to be back working as a paramedic. And his partner had been doing the job for decades. Stephen liked being the junior man on the team for a change.

Splint the boy's leg, carry him out, transport him to the hospital to get his leg x-rayed and set— They'd be done with this run by two. That left plenty of time to stop by and see Meghan and tease a smile out of her when he turned in paperwork.

He started whistling as he slid down a particularly steep six feet of the path. Meg liked to hear about the job runs and he enjoyed talking to her about his day. He slapped at a mosquito and scowled at the swarm of them ahead of him. He'd forgotten the bug spray again.

Kate pushed open the door to the jewelry store Saturday morning, smiling as she caught Meghan and Stephen standing a step closer than just friends, Stephen's hand idly rubbing Meghan's shoulder as they talked. Her brother looked...content. Kate hadn't seen that relaxed expression and stance since before Jennifer died. She nearly stepped back outside rather than interrupt them.

Stephen half turned. "Hi, Kate." He reached for a spot below his shoulder. "Right about there." Meghan scratched his back. "Oh...perfect, now down a bit to the left." He sighed. "I walked through a swarm of mosquitoes this week and the bites are driving me crazy."

"He forgot to use repellant and now he's paying for it. But I think he just wants to be pampered a bit," Meghan added, leaning against Stephen's back to rest her chin on his shoulder. "You made good time, Kate. Was the drive okay?"

Kate looked from Meg to Stephen and walked over to the table and set down her coffee. "Dave and I left early so we could stop often. Are we the first ones here, or has Jack arrived?"

"He's measuring the truck now to figure out how to load the workbench. I'd better go help him out." Stephen reached back and held Meg's hand. "You've got everything you need?"

"Yes. Don't drop that thing on someone's foot when you haul it out."

"We won't."

Stephen shook his finger in silent caution as he went by and Kate smiled back, planning to ignore the warning. Something had definitely changed here in the last few weeks, and Stephen wasn't talking.

Meghan touched the counter and oriented herself. "Kate, I've got the ring back in the vault. Would you like to see it now or does Dave need me to do paperwork?"

"He's still making a couple calls squaring away details, so we've got time. How does Stephen like being a paramedic again?"

Meg laughed. "He loves it, even though he takes every opportunity to make a big deal about the calls." She led the way through the jewelry store to the back repair room. The shelves were about empty and the worktables cleared.

Meghan opened the vault door and retrieved the box from the second shelf. "Here's the ring I found."

Kate turned on the powerful lighted magnifying glass and Meghan brought her the ring. Kate turned it slowly, studying every detail. "It's gold with the inscription: *I have, I hold.* The words don't strike me as a particularly romantic phrase. The diamond is nice size though."

"It didn't show up anywhere in Neil's registry. Do you think it was stolen?"

"It's a more modern setting than the last stone, and the inscription should be easy enough to track down if a report was filed. I'll take it with me, if that's okay."

"Of course. Given this is the third piece found, I have to figure there will be more pieces turning up in random places. We never stopped to think about the number of items Neil gave away over the years."

"It's hard to know when these discoveries will end. Thanks for calling me." Kate carefully put the ring away.

Jack strode into the workroom, followed by Stephen. Jack leaned over the massive workbench in the center of the room to see how the brace was secured. "Do you really have to have this workbench?" He shoved it and barely moved the bench a few inches.

"It will be perfect at the barn," Stephen said.

"And I need the floor space," Meghan added. "I can't sell this building with that thing still here."

"Well if we do get it to the barn, it's going to stay there," Jack declared. "This is a monster. How do we do this?"

"Tip it on its side and shove it through the door?"

"Getting it on the truck will be the tricky part." Jack put his entire weight against one end of the bench to get it to tip. "Meg, you might want to keep Blackie back. I'd hate to step on a foot or a tail."

She snapped her fingers and the dog moved to her side.

Stephen shoved and the bench began to move. They walked it toward the doorway.

"Watch the door frame," Jack cautioned.

"I'm watching it. There's no clearance for fingers." Stephen heaved to get it over the rise.

Kate leaned back against the wall. "Guys look good flexing muscles and sweating," she commented for Meghan's benefit. "I've got good-looking brothers."

"Thanks for the visual."

Kate laughed.

"Hold it, Jack. This isn't going to work. We can't clear the display case."

"Let me see." He shoved the workbench back. "We can fix this. Meg, where's the power screwdriver?" Jack called. "I need to take out a glass door and two handles."

"The toolbox is behind the counter."

"Thanks."

The security guard squeezed around the guys. "Miss Delhart, the armored truck is here."

"Thanks, Lou. Kate, JoAnne left the tally sheets in the top drawer of the file cabinet."

Kate pushed away from the wall to stand straight. She would be so glad when she delivered this child. She couldn't see her feet and her balance was off. She felt great for the first time in months; she just couldn't walk without thinking about her balance. She found the documents and flipped to the final page. "Wow. You weren't kidding about the appraisals."

"Neil had some good pieces."

Kate looked up as her husband came in. "It's a good thing they sent two security guards."

Dave accepted the list. "Are you sure you're ready to do this, Meghan?"

"I'll be incredibly relieved to have it over. You'll need to check each piece against the list, make sure we didn't miss anything." Meghan opened the vault door and picked up two black hard-sided cases stored inside. "Thank you for this."

"I'm riding back to Chicago with my wife and following an armored truck with a million dollars in jewels. I can think of harder ways to spend an afternoon. We'll sign them over to the wholesale buyer and call you when the delivery is complete."

"It's a huge load off my shoulders to have this done."

"Have you decided on the next step here?" Dave asked.

"Dad has decided to use some of the estate gift to expand the clinic. We'll start looking for a doctor to join the practice."

"That sounds like a good plan. Kate, hold on to the list and I'll take these cases outside."

Meghan used a brick to brace open the vault door so it would air out. "Would you check to make sure I haven't missed anything?"

"Sure." Kate found a flashlight and checked the back corners of the drawers and edges of the shelves. "I think you were smart to work with one dealer to take all the pieces."

"It ends it at least. It's awful to say after all Neil's years of effort that I'll be relieved to have his business liquidated, but I will. The realtor already has a possible buyer for the property."

Kate looked around to make sure Stephen was still outside. "Have you decided if you'll come with Stephen to Jack's wedding?"

"I'm still thinking about it."

"Come, please. We'd love for you to be there."

"It's a big deal, Kate."

"I know. I need you to come, Meg. Stephen will be the last O'Malley not married, and I don't want him to be there alone. I don't know how he'll be feeling at the end of the weekend when he leaves to drive back here. I'd rather he had someone with him."

"When you put it that way—yes, I'll talk to Stephen and come."

Meghan pushed a broom across the now open floor area, finishing the cleanup. She was amazed that Jack and Stephen had been able to move the workbench in one piece. She was sure they'd have to take it apart to have any chance of getting it out of the room.

The problem with going to the O'Malley weddings was the drive to town and back with Stephen, being the focus of his attention for the weekend. That amount of time would either move them a huge step closer together or something would happen that brought out just how hard it really was to have a relationship with a blind lady. She bit her bottom lip and shoved at the broom.

It was one thing to dream, another to realize a dream might be coming true. What had been easy to dismiss earlier now had to be dealt with. She'd be on unfamiliar territory and would have to depend on Stephen for so many details just to get around.

Her broom caught on an uneven point in the floor. Meghan stepped forward to see if a nail had worked upwards or if it was a loose board. The board moved on her.

She leaned down and found a board was more than loose; it sat slightly below the floor level. She tried to remove it only to find it was actually pivoting. She felt under the board, expecting cobwebs, sawdust, and concrete but touched a hard-sided book.

She lifted it out, realizing as she rubbed off the dust that the dimensions and the heavy weight of the paper were similar to a book she'd been handling every day for the last few weeks. She laughed. Neil had kept a second registry. He has kept meticulous records for the store; it made sense that he'd do the same for the pieces he was forging.

She carried it over to the table with the computer and scanner she had used as she went through his first registry. She turned on the equipment. As she waited impatiently for it to warm up, she found her phone and dialed.

"Stephen! You have to come back to the store. I found it. Neil's registry of stolen goods, at least that's what I think it is. It was under a floorboard where the workbench used to be and it feels like a similar ledger. I haven't scanned it yet, but I can tell it's been well-used over the years."

"I'll be there just as soon as Jack and I get this workbench off the back of the truck."

"Thanks."

She opened the registry, laid it on the glass, and scanned the first page.

Neil must have printed in a tight hand because the software had a hard time deciphering every letter, but it could read enough of each line to let her fill in the blanks. She listened as the software read dates, descriptions of pieces, and dollar amounts. Occasionally there was a second line with an annotated reference about the piece.

Neil had been stealing and forging pieces for years. She started jumping forward to pages at random, looking for the year Neil would have bought the brooch from JoAnne. Had it been a stolen piece that her friend had found in that music box years ago?

Stephen parked the truck in front of the jewelry store and grabbed his keys. The front door was locked. "Meghan?" He knocked, surprised the security guard was no longer on duty.

Blackie began to bark inside.

"I'm coming!"

He opened the door and his greeting died. Tears traced down Meghan's cheeks. "What's wrong?"

She shook her head and trailed a hand along the display cases that headed to the back room. "Come back and see the registry."

Stephen locked the front door behind him and followed her. "Where's the security guard?"

"There's nothing else here of value now that the vault is empty. Today was his last day."

Those didn't look like her happy tears. "Meghan, why are you crying?"

"Tell me about the ledger first." The floorboard piece she'd found was propped open. She was right. The bench would have concealed it, and it was heavy enough that no one would have looked underneath it. Meghan lifted the lid on the scanner and picked up the registry and offered it to him.

He tugged a Kleenex from his pocket and pressed it into her hand, then looked at what she'd found. "The ledger is black leather binding, legal-size pages with the light green guide lines. There are about sixty pages, the first ten pages or so with entries." She wiped at her eyes. "What's wrong, Meghan? Is it this book?"

"Read the line for Friday, August 16, 1996."

He ran his hand down the page to find the entry.

August 16, Wilshire Hotel, Chicago, midnight. Three pieces switched: emerald earrings, a square-cut diamond ring, a bracelet and necklace with diamonds and emeralds in twenty-four carat gold. Fakes. 18 hours labor.

Two columns labeled simply E and T respectively showed the words advance 10,000. The next line in the ledger was a note.

Advance Craig additional 2,000—clipped bridge railing, bumper damage on father's car.

Neil had known a great deal about the robbery—he listed when and where the stones were taken, the specifics of the pieces taken, the time it took him to create the replicas. Did *T* stand for *transport?* Maybe *E* for who had made the exchange? "The ledger proves Craig had been the courier Neil used for the robberies." He looked over lines in the registry. No other names were mentioned on the page. He didn't understand.

Stephen rubbed Meghan's back, for she was still wiping away tears. "You're breaking my heart, honey. What is it?"

"Friday, August 16, 1996, is the night I went blind."

TWENTY-SIX

Stephen felt as though he'd taken another punch as her words registered.

"Craig had to be at the Wilshire Hotel in Chicago at midnight," Meghan said. "He would have been coming from Silverton. Sometime during that trip he damaged his dad's car on a bridge railing. You want to figure the odds of two people traveling to and from Silverton on a Friday night six years ago, who both have accidents on a bridge, and have it be two different bridges?"

She wrapped her arms tight across her waist. "The other car accelerated at me. Craig was probably high; even back then he was a heavy user. He ran me off the bridge and left me blind."

Stephen set down the ledger, his gaze never leaving her. "What do you want to do? Throw something? I'll get out of the way. Scream? I'll hold my ears. Just please do something with that anger but stand there rocking on your feet. You're going to have a coronary on me here." Stephen reached out to grip her arm. She'd begun to tremble.

Her hand clung to his and cut into the circulation. And rather than speak she just moved into his arms. Stephen winced at the sobs that shook her. "It's okay. Shh." There was nothing that made this better. She'd gone blind because of a robbery. "Don't, Meg."

He closed his eyes against his own tears and rocked with her where they stood. *Jesus, how do You heal this pain she's in? Couldn't You have sent Craig into that ditch instead of Meghan?* There were some events that simply didn't square up and make sense. *You could have but You didn't. And Meg lives blind. That's hard to accept.* "You're worrying Blackie, honey, crying this hard. Let's go sit down." He led her toward a chair and wished he knew what to do that would help.

A storm wasn't much of a distraction, but it was all Stephen could come up with to get Meghan away from Silverton and the topic of the stolen jewelry. He was relieved Ken was going storm chasing today. Kate could sort out the ledger for them. He had a more pressing problem helping Meghan shake the depression.

He tended to run when life overwhelmed him; she just got quiet, and it wasn't easy to shift her out of that sad place. He couldn't remember the last time he ate lunch literally at the side of the road, sitting on lawn chairs and eating sandwiches. The wind blowing toward them was brisk. He watched her and was glad they came.

"The sound in the trees is changing," Meghan commented.

Ken lowered his camera. "The front is coming against blue sky and it's vast, with thunderheads blowing upward for tens of thousands of feet."

"Are we going to get hail?"

Ken studied the laptop screen beside him. "Probably. There's a big humidity and temperature change as the front crosses the Mississippi River. It looks as if the front is already beginning to generate its own wind. By the time it reaches Silverton we're going to have a serious storm on our hands."

Stephen tossed a tennis ball into the field for Blackie to chase. "I can see why you like to spend Saturdays out doing this, Ken. What got you started?"

"Where else can you watch something this magnificent, enjoy it for several hours, and it's free? It was great in college when I wanted JoAnne's time for several hours but didn't have more than a couple bucks in my pocket."

The wind began to pick up pieces of roadside gravel. Stephen shielded his eyes.

"Are the clouds beginning to roll at the leading edge of the storm?" Meghan asked, holding down the papers on the makeshift table.

Ken snapped more pictures. "Oh yeah. The front edge is beginning to lead the main storm like a pressure wave."

"Let's head for the Lookout," JoAnne suggested.

"Good idea. Pile back in the van; let's move before we get wet."

Ken and Stephen quickly collapsed lawn chairs. JoAnne laughed and chased the cooler as the wind blew it toward the field.

Meghan slid into the backseat and Blackie scrambled in with her. "Don't you love this?"

Stephen slid in beside her. "It's memorable, I'll give you."

Ken turned the van around and they drove away from the storm front. He pulled into the Lookout Restaurant west of Davenport. Stephen understood the name when he saw the layout of the restaurant. Windows stretched along the west wall and gave a panoramic view of the incoming storm. Their presence doubled the number of patrons in the restaurant.

"Is our table free?" Meghan asked.

"Yes," JoAnne confirmed.

Meghan and Blackie set off across the restaurant for the center booth by the windows.

"I gather you come here often?" Stephen asked Ken.

"It's the halfway point for most storm chasing trips," Ken explained. "That's one of my photographs, taken from this parking lot in '98."

Stephen walked over to see. The sky was a roiling gray and green with a clear funnel cloud beginning to drop at the south end of the photo.

"It came in fast and furious and about took the roof of the restaurant off when it dropped to the ground. You can still see some of its path where it decimated trees across the interstate. It ripped up and tossed eighty-year-old oaks around like they were twigs."

Stephen glanced back outside. "Any chance this storm front will be that violent?"

"It's generating its own wind; the cumulus clouds are rising into the low edges of the jet stream. All it needs now is energy to feed on, and the humid air held in place by the high pressure over Ohio fits the bill. They might get some twister action a state or two over tonight."

"You sound regretful."

"It's hard to chase storms after sunset and get decent photos; otherwise I'd be planning to go after it. Once you've been close to a twister, you'll understand the pull." He and Ken ordered for the group then carried trays over to the booth.

Stephen slid in beside Meghan and shared a milkshake with her as they watched the storm come in. In half an hour, rain began to thump against the roof. "I vote we get back to Silverton so you can babysit your windmill, Ken."

"Agreed. This is going to be a good test."

Jonathan drove toward Silverton, rain and wind buffeting his van. He'd gambled and lost. They had found a ring. Mrs. Teal had only known the most cursory of details and about the inscription on the ring, but it was enough to know he was in serious trouble.

That ring was his death warrant.

He wiped sweaty hands and turned the windshield wipers up on high to push away the rain faster.

The mob boss would murder him for having an affair with Marie and would make it painfully slow for also having robbed from him. Somehow Jonathan had to get the ring back and locate the other items from that robbery—earrings, a bracelet, and a necklace.

Why did it have to be Meghan who found it, someone he knew and liked? The idea of hurting her... He had to get that ring back, and somehow he doubted she would give it to him and not tell anyone he had it. She was blind; there had to be a way to use that to his advantage. She probably had it stored in the bank vault. If he could get Meghan to open the vault for some reason, maybe he could slide the ring into his pocket and she'd never be the wiser.

And if the ring had already been turned over to the cops? He'd have to somehow force them to return it without revealing his identity. He couldn't send someone else to get the ring, and there was no one else alive who knew the truth. The cops would have to bring the ring to him...and he had no idea how to make that happen.

It would be better all around if Meghan still had the ring.

If it had been in the metronome, there was a good chance the other pieces would be nearby. Maybe somewhere in Neil's piano. He'd start there. He didn't have much time to get this done.

Kate shifted in the front car seat, trying to find a comfortable position.

"Are you sure you don't want me to stop and let you have a chance to walk around for a few minutes?" Dave asked.

Her back ached, her feet were swollen, she was eight months and four days pregnant, and she was ready to have this over. She hadn't been comfortable in weeks. "I'm okay. I'd rather get to Silverton before this storm does." She made a notation on the enlarged copies of the registry pages she had been working on since Meg found the book.

"What are you planning to tell Meghan?"

"Something other than the fact the ring was stolen from a mob boss. But we have to find the other stones, even if we have to break up every piece of furniture Neil ever owned."

"Agreed."

Stephen turned up the radio to try to drown out the noise outside as the rain reached the barn. Meghan, smoothing the edges of the baby cradle he had made for Kate, set aside the sandpaper and looked up at the roof. "It sounds nasty out there."

"We can go up to the house if you like. If we go now we can probably make it before the heaviest rain arrives."

"I'm okay out here. As long as the barn roof stays on."

"It will. Your dog is not very happy right now though; he just disappeared underneath the table."

"Blackie hates thunder, and I can't blame him."

Stephen rubbed a soft cloth over the piece of furniture on the workbench, checking that the glue had dried, then set it on the ground. "Come over here a minute. I'd like you to try something."

Meghan got up, her hand trailing along the worktable. "What do you have?"

Stephen took her hand and set it on the back of the chair. She rubbed her hand along the edges trying to figure out what it was. She smiled. "You made Kate a rocking chair."

He guided her into the chair. "Actually...I made *you* a rocking chair."

She stopped rocking. "Me?"

"Your mom gave me a photo of the rocking chair you used when you were a teen and babysat in the house you now own."

Meghan ran her hands along the armrests and the spokes, then she laughed. "It's an incredible rocking chair."

"The wood is unpainted right now, a light oak. I can either varnish it or paint it for you."

"Maybe a light varnish. Why did you decide to make this?"

He rested his hands on the arms of the rocking chair. "Your smile." Stephen leaned down and kissed her, enjoying the blush. "There are times I like the fact you're blind," he whispered.

Her hand curled in his shirt as her smile grew. "There are times I like being surprised."

He eased back. "You're dangerous."

"Hmm." She released his shirt and smoothed the wrinkles out. "What else do we have to work on tonight? I'm about done with the cradle."

His thoughts were too muddled with ideas of kissing her again to think about work, and at his long pause she laughed. "Focus, Stephen."

"I'm trying, but you're intoxicating." He took a deep breath and took a full step back. "I need the slats sanded for the display case, and I've got a couple repair projects to work on."

"Let me work on the slats."

"Sure." He looked away to get his thoughts back to the work at hand. "Sanding. You'll need more sandpaper."

"I love it when you're flustered."

He glanced over at her. "It's nice to have your smile back."

"It's hard to stay sad around you. Thanks, Stephen. Today meant a lot."

"You're very welcome."

He set her up at the workbench and then moved to pick up the first repair project. He'd brought her damaged piano bench back with him to the workshop to tighten the legs and remove the wobble. He turned it upside down on the work-table and got out the wood glue, working with small shims to tighten the joints. The fabric was worn through around the staples and had begun to tear. He studied the fabric and realized the original staples had been inserted over a double fold of material. He could move the staples and give the bench another few years of life.

He found a pair of needle-nose pliers and tugged up the staples.

The wood underneath the staples shifted. He stopped. If he removed these staples the bench was so old it might come apart. Better to fix it than have it give way on Meghan someday. He pulled up the staples and rather than a solid piece of wood supporting the seat cushion found a flat piece of wood covering a hollow space.

Intrigued, he pulled the wood back. "Meghan, set down what you're doing and come over here. I just found something."

He tugged out a backgammon-sized case secured inside the bench.

Meghan joined him.

"Inside the piano bench there was a slim compartment and a case." He used a knife to force the clasp open. "Oh, my."

"What is it?"

He reached inside the box. "It's not everything we've been searching for, but it's quite a sight. Three pieces—emerald earrings and a diamond-and-emerald bracelet and necklace. Assuming these are real, compared to the pieces you had appraised, these would be in the exceptional category."

"I doubt Neil would hide fakes." Meghan reached out and Stephen took her hand, showed her the pieces. "Is it too late to call Kate?"

"For this she'll appreciate a call. I'll get my phone."

The pager he wore went off.

"There's been an accident caused by the storm," Meghan predicted. He squeezed her hand as he dialed the dispatch center instead of his sister. It was a car wreck on the highway, police were responding, but he was the only one available for EMS. He confirmed he was on his way and closed the phone. "The jewels have been here for a long time; they can wait a little longer. Come with me. I can drop you at the clinic." He didn't want to leave her here alone.

"Why don't I take the case and you can drop me at the store on the way to the clinic to get the ambulance. This barn doesn't have a good track record for storing valuables and the wind here is scary."

The store was brick and originally built to be a bank. It was a better place on a stormy night than this barn. "Agreed." He closed the box clasp. "I'm afraid you're about to get somewhat wet."

She snapped her fingers for Blackie. "I won't melt, and I can run. Let's go."

Stephen stepped on the truck brakes as his headlights picked out a huge limb of a fallen tree. It stretched across the road. Meghan tightened her arms draped around her dog sitting on the seat between them, and Stephen reached over to steady him too.

"What is it?"

"The road's blocked." There was not enough clearance around either end to drive around the fallen tree. "This is going to be a longer trip than I planned." He backed up and found a place he could turn the truck around. "I'll have to get to the accident scene the long way around. I'm sorry, Meghan. You'll have to come with me."

"Do it. Blackie and I will survive."

Stephen called the dispatcher to find out if Joseph could get through to Silverton to bring the ambulance and to ask if there was any chance of fire and rescue being available. He didn't want to think about having to transport victims in the back of a police car. Wind pummeled the truck. Lightning snapped overhead and the thunder sounded like it was right over them. Meghan flinched. "The worst has to pass over us soon," Stephen reassured. If not for the jewels in the case at her feet, he would have left her at his house.

"I'd say there is a bit of hail in that rain."

"I think you could be right."

Stephen finally saw the flashing lights ahead in the rain. "At least one cop car has made it here. Stay in the truck, Meg. If I can use your help, I'll send someone to get you." He parked off the side of the road as far as he could get and wished there were at least a few drivers out tonight who might stop and render assistance. He wanted Meghan to stay with someone rather than sit here on her own.

"I'll be fine. Go do your job."

Stephen squeezed her hand, grabbed his powerful torchlight, his EMS jacket, and slipped out of the truck.

The rain beat at him, the wind tried to blow him over, and Meghan had been right about the hail. He was getting a few strikes harder than just rain.

Two cars had clipped each other in an off-center head-on collision. "Over here!" The cop shouted from the car off the west side of the road.

The officer came around the back of the car to meet him. "This driver is trapped with a broken left leg; the driver of the other car looks more like straight shock and a broken wrist when the air bag went off. I moved him over here to keep him dry and watch him since I couldn't be two places at the same time."

"Good thinking. Trees are down; the ambulance may not be able to get here, and fire and rescue is currently committed to other accidents. For now it's just us. Let's get this driver freed, then we can transport one in my truck and one in your car. My date has some medical training, so she can ride with you."

"Fine. Anything is better than drowning out here."

Stephen circled the wreck. With a broken leg, they needed options that didn't involve twisting the driver around. "While I check their conditions, head back to your squad car and get on the radio. See if you can raise another driver, a semi truck, anybody out on the roads to give us a hand. Once we get the injured moved, we need to push these cars off the highway. And I need a tire iron, a jack, and whatever you might have in your squad car that won't bend when we use it as a wedge to force that metal."

"I'll get on it."

Stephen opened the driver-side door and slid in to check the conditions of one of the two drivers. Both drivers were now his responsibility.

Meghan hunched in the front seat of the truck, using the length of the seat to stretch out her legs and give Blackie room to lie down. He still whined when thunder rumbled and about exhausted himself shaking.

God, I know You made the lightning, thunder, rain, and hail, but this is awful. Please tone it down.

Stephen had been gone half an hour—in this weather it seemed like an eternity. The wreck and the injuries must be bad or he would have been back by now. She wished she could go offer to help without being in his way.

She jerked as a brisk rap on the window behind her seized her breathing and scared a decade off her life.

"Meghan! I'm parked nearby and the ambulance is arriving behind me. Let's get you out of here!"

Relieved to hear a familiar voice, she turned and opened the door.

Stephen headed back down the road to get Meghan, fighting the wind and rubbing a bruised wrist, relieved to have Joseph here with the ambulance. His two patients were loaded and ready to head to the hospital. She could ride in the passenger seat of the ambulance with Blackie while he rode in back.

The truck passenger door was open, the overhead light on, and the dashboard chime was dinging a warning for an open door with the truck running.

The vehicle was empty. "Meghan!" He turned in a full circle, only to see nothing but night. "Meghan!" The wind blew his shout back to him. Where had she gone? Why? How long had she been gone? He leaned into the door of the truck and found the seat wet but that told him little. Blackie was gone and she'd taken the jewelry case with her.

He looked around for any other cars that had stopped, anyone else she might have gone to help. The wreck had blocked both lanes of traffic. A car was completing a three-point turn on the road in order to turn around and go back the way they had come; another car pulled to the side, the driver waiting his turn to make the same maneuver. Stephen hurried toward it.

The girl on the passenger side lowered the window. "Is the wreck bad?"

"The ambulance crew has it covered. Have you seen a lady walking this direction with a collie?"

"We haven't seen anything but the cop lights ahead and the cars turning around. The ambulance came around us, but everyone else has been turning around."

"Did you see anyone get out of a car, walk around, go to see the wreck?"

She shook her head. "Sorry. Nothing."

Stephen stepped back from the car and went to ask the next driver. He couldn't believe Meghan would leave the scene to go back to town with another driver without coming to let him know.

No one had seen Meghan or Blackie. Stephen walked back toward his truck and the accident scene, his torch sweeping both sides of the road. She'd left the door open. Had Blackie darted out ahead of her when she intended to slip on his harness? "Meghan!" The dog was having a rough time in the storm, maybe that was it.

Maybe she'd heard something? Thought someone else needed help?

He reached his truck and searched it again, looking to see what was missing—her jacket, and a cursory look under the seats and in the glove box didn't turn up the jewelry case. He headed toward the accident scene. She got worried and must have left the truck to come and help him. He shone his light back and forth to both sides of the road searching as he headed toward the wreck. The noise would have been enough to help her go the right direction. "Meghan!"

She couldn't have just disappeared.

Blackie appeared through the rain running toward him, barking ferociously.

"What's going on?"

"An accident of some sort." Dave slowed the car. Traffic wasn't getting past. "That looks like a county cop car and ambulance lights." He pulled to the shoulder and activated the hazard lights. "I'll go see if they need help."

"I'd help but..."

Dave squeezed her hand. "Eight-month pregnant ladies can leave helping at accidents to their husbands. I love you. Stay put."

"Go."

Dave grabbed his jacket and climbed out into the wind and rain.

TWENTY-SEVEN

"What do you mean Meghan's missing?" Kate demanded as Dave leaned in the passenger window of their car.

"Exactly that. She was in Stephen's truck; now she's missing. Blackie bolted, she went after the dog and got lost off the side of the road or in the field. Something." Dave reached in past her and opened the glove box and pulled out the extra package of batteries and the flashlight inside.

Kate reached around to the backseat for her jacket. The ambulance doing a point-by-point turn shone lights into her eyes. "Help me out of the car."

"Just a minute," Dave said. "As soon as the ambulance clears I'll drive us up next to Stephen's truck. The cop is going to drive the ambulance while Joseph rides in back with the two patients, so Stephen and I can set up a search to find Meghan."

"We need more help."

"It's coming, but we're in the middle of nowhere and trees are down. Getting here isn't easy. Sit tight, Kate. I'll be right back."

Dave disappeared back into the rain.

Meghan was missing. Kate fought the nausea that now came in overwhelming speed when she was under stress. *Jesus, I don't know what's going on, but Meghan… Please help us find her quickly.*

The radio broke in with another weather alert: a severe storm warning with heavy rain, hail, and tornado watch continuing until 11 P.M.

We need lightning, Lord, as much of it as You can send. We need to be able to see.

The driver's door pulled open and Dave slid into the seat. He drove the car forward to beside Stephen's truck.

The rear driver's side door opened and Stephen tossed a blanket on the seat and lifted in Meghan's wet and shivering dog. Kate leaned over to help hold Blackie.

"Stephen, get in too, please." Kate caught his wet sleeve and tugged him in. "You're as wet as Blackie is." She spent her life negotiating her way through emotionally charged situations, and one glance told her Stephen needed her skills. "So many people are coming there will be an army here soon to help," she promised, knowing Dave would call in favors to make it happen. If he didn't calm down soon, he wouldn't be thinking clearly and might leave out details that would make the difference between their finding Meghan or not.

"She's been gone at least an hour now."

"Tell me what happened."

"I left her in the truck with Blackie and went to help the cop at the wreck. I told her I would send someone back if I needed her. The ambulance arrived about a half hour later. I went back to get Meghan." Stephen took a deep breath. "The passenger side door was open, the truck was still running, the seat was wet. Meghan and Blackie were gone. Blackie came running from the direction of the wreck, barking furiously. There's no sign of Meghan, Kate."

"The likely reality is she opened the truck door, Blackie bolted, she went after him and got farther than she realized, and is sitting waiting for someone to find her. She may have even sent Blackie back to get us. She'll be okay, Stephen." Kate held his gaze until she saw him accept that and relax just a bit. "We'll start a systematic search outward from your truck as soon as enough help arrives."

They needed ideas for how to direct the search. "Or a second possibility: She went with someone back to town and she left a note for you. Someone else coming onto the scene found the truck abandoned, opened the door, and the note was blown away by the wind. For that matter, maybe they decided to steal the truck and got interrupted."

"Meghan wouldn't leave here without Blackie. Even if he bolted in the thunder, she would not leave without him."

"Okay. Third option: If she did go with someone else and it wasn't voluntary, why?"

"The jewels." Stephen leaned his head down against the front seat. "We found a case hidden in the lining of the piano bench Neil gave her. It's the reason Meghan was traveling with me to begin with. The page came in and she didn't want to stay out at my place with them. I was going to drop her off at the jewelry store on the way to the clinic to get the ambulance so she could put them in the vault. That case is not in the truck."

"Who knew she had them?" Dave asked.

"No one. We found them literally minutes before the page for the wreck came in."

"What were the stones?"

"Emerald earrings, a diamond-and-emerald bracelet and necklace."

Kate looked over at Dave, her own alarm hard to check. Those pieces went with the ring Meghan had given her to check out. They'd been stolen from the wife of a mob boss. Had he heard about the ring being discovered? That inscription *I have, I hold*—he would have known immediately it was the real piece. Kate could just hear the simple direct order: *Find that blind lady and get my ring.* And as they had discovered tonight, the only road into Silverton was this one.

Headlights shone across them as several cars arrived. "Let's get this search underway." She didn't want to explain the implications of option number three to Stephen.

Jonathan parked the car in the alley behind the jewelry store, waiting until lightning showed they were alone before shutting off the car. "Come on."

Meghan didn't move.

He circled the car, opened the door, and pulled her out. "The passive aggression isn't going to help so I suggest you start cooperating. Give me your keys."

He tugged around her jacket to get to the pocket and she pulled out her hand to give them to him. "Why are you doing this?"

He ignored the question. He opened the door to the store and pushed her inside. He shook rain off his jacket.

Without the dog, controlling her was simple. She couldn't see him, so she couldn't fight him, and she couldn't run. And so far they had been on territory she didn't know. This store she knew and he saw the change as she reached out one hand behind her to touch the wall, feel the door frame, and get her bearings.

"The faster I get what I want, the faster this is over." He caught her elbow and led her into the back room. "Since the security guard is gone and you have pretty much cleared this room of furniture, I gather the vault is also empty?"

"It's empty."

"Then you won't mind showing me. Open it."

She tugged against his hand.

"Don't push me, Meghan. You don't know what's going on here tonight. If the vault is empty, just show me. It makes no sense to resist on principle when there is nothing to protect."

She moved to the vault and began turning the tumblers.

He set the case she had with her in the truck on the worktable next to a computer she must have brought in, for Neil had never owned one. He opened the clasp on the case.

The luck of the evening was with him—he had three of the four pieces. Marie's earrings, necklace, and bracelet. Five years had dulled his memory of their beauty. He picked up the necklace. Now that he had the pieces, what was he going to do with them? Dump them in the river, bury them, somehow make them disappear.

He needed the ring.

He sat down and turned on her computer. While it booted, he looked through the papers on the table. Anything incriminating he was going to burn. And given the rain, he couldn't just torch the store and be confident that everything would burn before the rain extinguished the fire. The computer came on and he set it to not just delete files but also to wipe the data.

He pulled over the two registries Neil kept. He was startled to see in one the stolen pieces over the years. He scanned for his name and didn't see it, but someone matching his itinerary to this list would see too many similarities for comfort. Burn it.

Meghan opened the vault door.

Jonathan joined her. "Ladies first." He didn't want her closing him inside the vault; she'd do it if given a chance. He kept a hand on her arm as he pulled trays out and confirmed they were empty.

"Not even a loose clasp left in here…you did a thorough job." He steered her out of the vault and walked her over to a chair. "Who has the ring you found? You know the one; the inscription says: *I Have, I Hold.*"

She set her jaw and didn't answer.

He left her sitting in the chair. The electrical box in the corner of the room gave him water and fire alarm circuits. He cut both. He tugged the metal garbage can into the center of the room. Jonathan tossed a match onto the pages in the trash can, and while it burned, he ripped pages from the ledger and tossed them into the flames.

She shoved the chair back as she smelled smoke.

"Where's the ring, Meghan? Or should I just leave you in this building?"

"I don't have the ring. Stephen's sister Kate has it."

"But you can get it." He picked up the phone, walked over, and handed it to her. "Call Kate and tell her to bring the ring."

"What?"

"It's a simple deal; the ring for your location."

"You wouldn't—"

"I'm dead if that ring is left out there. Get me the ring, Meghan. Or you're not going to see tomorrow."

Kate shoved maps to the side and arched her back as best she could in the car seat to ease the ache that had become nearly a cramp. The problem with being this pregnant was everything in her body protested being in the same position for more than ten minutes at a time.

The radio crackled as another searcher called back his grid number. She marked off another square on her hand-drawn map of the road, the wreck, and the area they needed to search. Dave and Stephen were out with Blackie, and nine others had now arrived to help with the search. They would find Meghan. They wouldn't stop looking until they did, but it was taking longer than expected. She wished the sheriff would call and say Meghan was in Silverton and this was a mix up.

Radio tones sounded and the updated weather warnings were read. Kate grabbed the knob and turned up the volume as the town list was read again. She found the map and struggled to read the fine print of town names. She closed her eyes and wanted to swear, but instead put her hand on the car horn and gave a fifteen-second-long blast, paused for five seconds, and gave another long blast.

She forced her arms into her coat and wrestled open the door. The wind slammed the door back at her. The nearest officer coming her way had a radio. "There's hail coming, quarter of an inch. Get everyone back in!"

Blackie pawed at the car door. Stephen wrapped his arms around the wet animal and pulled him back. "I know you want to go out there and find her, but you can't go, boy."

The dog shook water off his coat and rested his head on Stephen's arm. "I know." Stephen shared the dog's depression. The hail on the roof was deafening. "If she's out in this—" Stephen couldn't finish that thought.

"We pray." Kate said from the front seat. "We pray, we hope, and when it eases up, I'm joining the search too."

Stephen buried his head in the dog's fur. *Jesus, Meghan loves You, and I love her. I failed to keep her safe. Please, help me rescue her. Wherever she is, help me find her.*

Car lights swept across the rear window. Stephen looked back to see if it was more help arriving, but the car drove past.

"We've got another theory beyond she got lost and is out there somewhere in this," Kate offered.

He turned toward his sister. Anything was better than the image of Meghan out there getting pounded by this hail. "I'm listening."

"The ring Meghan found, the pieces you found in the piano bench—they're from the same robbery. If the original owner heard about the ring, he may have sent someone to retrieve his property. He'll be after the four pieces, and Meghan has three of them with her. She knows I've got the fourth."

Dave nodded. "Or another possibility: The ledger had a column of payments to someone who made the exchange. The person who originally swapped the pieces could have heard the jewelry had been found and is trying to get hold of them."

Kate looked at her husband. "Good point."

"I know you're making up these hypothetical scenarios to help me out," Stephen said, "but why would the ring be so important to justify snatching Meghan?"

"Steal something from a mob boss, you kind of hope it never reappears in your lifetime. The guy who made the exchange needs the pieces back no matter what the cost. Jail is an easier alternative than death. And if the mob boss wants them back, I don't think he's going to wait for the cops to return them."

"I don't care who or why, we just have to get Meghan back safe."

The car phone rang and they all froze. It had been a hypothetical idea to keep his mind off the fact Meghan was out getting bloodied by this hail, but suddenly he wasn't sure, and neither were they.

Dave looked at Kate. "You're the negotiator."

Surprise crossed her face as Dave offered her the lead in this, and then her expression smoothed out and became impassive as Kate mentally shifted to work mode. No matter what happened, she'd try to calmly shape events. She picked up the phone and answered in a smooth and cheerful voice, "This is Kate."

"Let's go, Meghan. We've got an exchange to make." Jonathan pulled her to her feet. The smoke was choking them now as it settled in the room. The pieces he had taken recently in Europe were marked on that ledger page as sold. A surprise, but Neil apparently had been moving pieces taken on other continents as soon as they came in. It was his second lucky break of the night. That left the ring and its chilling inscription as the final piece to find before he could safely disappear.

He opened the driver's door and pushed Meghan's head down to put her into the car. "Slide over." He wouldn't put it past her to try to bolt on him into the darkness.

"No matter where you run, they'll find you."

"You're the only one who knows my identity, and you won't be talking."

"I won't cover for you."

He started the car. "Stephen will be dead if you don't. These stones were stolen from a man who would think nothing of murdering to get them back. You try to suggest I'm involved, and I'll make sure one of those pieces in that case is delivered to the owner by courier, and I'll point at Stephen as the thief. He'll kill Stephen slowly and ask questions later. Do you understand me?"

"I hear you."

He drove north. There was one good thing about having known Craig. If this town had a shadier side and hiding places, Craig had known them. Jonathan knew where they could wait without risk of being found.

The sheriff's office was crowded. Kate rested her hip against the desk and sipped at the 7 Up Dave had gotten her for the nausea. "He knows this town. Look at directions to the drop-off point: *'Leave the ring east end of the bridge, in a briefcase on the concrete bench honoring the flood victims of 1913.'* This has got to be the guy who worked with Craig and Neil. Meghan didn't give any indication she knew the person who took her, but I bet she's got an idea. With this weather, we can't track him from the air, and on country roads we'll have a very hard time staying with his car without revealing our presence. You can't be stealthy in a downpour."

"Meghan's location and safety is the only thing that matters," Stephen insisted. Kate reached over and squeezed his arm. "It's the first thing that matters. He's got every incentive to make this trade and make it fast. He'll want to get away under cover of the storm. I doubt Meghan will be close to the exchange site. He'll want to use the fact we have to go get her as a way to buy himself more time to get away. Lying to us and taking her with him—it would only add to the intensity of the manhunt. It's in his best interests to tell us where she is. Stephen, do you want to stay here, and we call the location in so you can go with the cops to get her, or do you want to go out to the drop site?"

"I'm going with you," Stephen said. "Where are Meg's parents?"

"On their way back from Chicago. Bill was at the hospital with a patient when we got word to him. Elizabeth had gone along to help the patient's wife. I sent an officer to drive them back," the sheriff replied.

"Can you divert them to their home? After this is over Meghan will need a safe place to decompress, and I'd rather take her to her parents' home than back here for the debriefing. Anything short of serious medical needs, her father can best handle."

"Done."

"Who do you suggest should leave the briefcase with the ring at the bench?" Kate asked.

The Sheriff nodded to his deputy. "Tom. He knows that area well. He can leave the briefcase, drive away, and find the nearest secluded spot to stop and observe. My guess is the guy will try to cross the Mississippi and head into Iowa. This weather is going to cut off a lot of his options. We've got power lines down and numerous trees. We can get resources on the most likely crossing points."

"What if this guy goes to ground somewhere around here after he picks up the ring? Just sits and waits for the search to cool off?" Stephen asked.

"He'd be risking Meghan being able to tell us who he is."

The front door of the sheriff's office slammed open. "The jewelry store is on fire!"

Stephen surged outside with the officers. The store…the vault. If the guy had locked Meghan in the vault and tossed a match on some gasoline… Meghan's dog bolted away from him and into the night, heading in the direction of Meghan's house.

"Blackie!"

He couldn't go after the animal but couldn't lose him either. Meghan would need Blackie when they found her.

The wind whipped around and smoke blanketed the street. He choked and raised his arm to breathe through his sleeve. The inferno inside the jewelry store flashed over, and windows in the upper apartment exploded. An interior wall collapsed. Stephen tried to get near the building but was forced back by officers. The volunteer firemen began to arrive.

Anyone inside that building was dead.

Kate wrapped her arm around him. "She's not in there."

"You don't know that."

"We have to believe it." She tugged at his arm. "Come on; let's go. We'll leave the ring at the bench and wait for the call."

TWENTY-EIGHT

"Don't leave me here," Meghan pleaded against being abandoned. As much as she wanted to be away from Jonathan, she didn't want it happening like this. The cues from the trip, how long the car ride was, the road surfaces, nothing gave her a clue for where she was. She couldn't hear traffic or the sounds of town life. Just the whistle of the wind and the intense crack of thunder.

"Sit down."

Her hand felt a quilt and the edge of a bed; she touched an old iron headboard.

"The place just smells musty from lack of use. It's dry and there are no bugs or mice. The refrigerator is still running; you can hear its hum. There are plenty of sodas still in it, and there are peanut butter and tubes of crackers on the top shelf of the refrigerator. Craig used this place all the time."

"Where are we? Please, I need to know."

"You are safer if you don't know, if you simply stay here. Don't try to get yourself home, Meghan. On a night like this you'll break your neck in those woods. When I have the ring and am away from here, I'll let them know where you are." He walked away. The fury of the storm whipped inside when he opened the door. "I'm sorry about this."

"If you were sorry about it, you wouldn't be doing this."

The door closed. Meghan sat frozen, listening to the unknown stillness around her. She drew her feet up on the bed and wrapped her arms around her knees. The shaking started and then the tears. *Oh, Lord, what am I going to do?*

She tasted blood as she bit her lower lip. Gulping air, she forced herself to calm down. *Jesus...* She rubbed her arms to try and stop the shaking. Jonathan was gone. She was alone, but she was okay.

Kate was somewhere in Silverton. Stephen must have called his family for help as soon as he realized she wasn't in the truck. They'd find her. Stephen wouldn't stop searching until he found her.

She had to get up and explore this place. If there was power for a refrigerator then someone was paying utility bills. There might be a phone. Stephen and her parents had to be nearly frantic by now. She cautiously moved a foot down to the floor. A wind gust rattled a plane of glass so hard it sounded as if it cracked.

⤜⤛⤚⤙

"Did he take the ring or not?" Stephen demanded, feeling every minute past midnight tick by as an eternity. "The briefcase and ring were left as ordered. Why hasn't he taken it and called?"

Dave focused his binoculars out the open driver's side window. "I can't tell if the case is still there or not. The rain is too heavy to see with night vision goggles any better than straight binoculars. Kate?"

"Nothing."

Dave picked up the radio. "Tom, do you see anything?"

"Negative."

Stephen leaned across from the backseat, peering into the rain. "One of us needs to go down there to see if he already took the case and left us sitting here without a lead on Meghan."

Kate squeezed his hand. "We wait."

Stephen leaned his head down against the front seat. Five hours. Meghan had been missing close to five hours. *Jesus, I can't stand this wait. Where is she?* He was trying hard to trust God to be a faithful friend and help him. It wasn't easy.

The phone rang and Kate grabbed it. "Yes, this is Kate."

She dropped the phone and grabbed the radio. "Tom, she's at the old mill house! Where is that?"

"The northeast side of town, near the old water tower."

"We'll go. You've got this scene. Don't move in to check that bench until we know for sure we have Meghan."

"Roger."

Dave put the car in reverse, leaving the headlights off until he had slowly moved away from their lookout spot. Then he turned around, switched on the headlights, and put his foot down on the gas. Kate scrambled to search the map.

"Okay. Go east at this next interchange," Kate pointed out.

"What exactly did he say?" Stephen asked.

"Just the location and he hung up. There wasn't enough for me to be able to recognize the voice."

The car hit a pothole and Kate shifted uncomfortably. Stephen put his hand down on her shoulder, silently sympathizing with the discomfort she was in.

"When we get there, you and Dave go on ahead and rescue her. Just don't rush forward until you have a feel for what the situation is."

"We'll be careful," Stephen promised. *Meghan, we're coming. Just hold on.*

The radio broke in for a weather update. A tornado watch and flash flood warning were added to the severe storm warning. Meghan hated storms. And without Blackie available to help her... They had to find her soon.

⤜⤛

"There it is!" Stephen spotted the old water tower first. "The gravel road has to be just ahead."

Dave slowed the car. The car rocked in the powerful wind gusts. Stephen strained to look through the darkness and rain. There were few visual clues to mark the area—no homes, few side roads. The sheriff described the old mill house as a one-room hunting lodge rarely used by its owners.

Kate pointed. "On your left. There's the private drive."

It was narrow gravel and disappeared into the trees. Dave turned down the road. "How far back in these woods do you guess it is?"

"A hunting lodge could be a mile back," Stephen guessed. The road began to head up a steep incline.

"This is far enough, Dave," Kate warned. "Look at the phone poles. Power and phone lines just joined together. It's probably not that far ahead."

"Agreed. From here we walk." Dave pulled to the side and stopped the car. He turned off the headlights. The howling wind immediately dominated every sound. Dave tried his phone. "I've still got a signal. I'll call you, Kate, and you can drive up once we know what we're dealing with."

Stephen picked up the extra torchlight and the medical kit backpack. He pushed open the door and the wind about ripped the door off its hinges. To the left of the road was an open field and the tall grass was whipping first east and then flattening to the west. Gravel was beginning to stir on the road.

A tree crashed nearby in an explosion of wood. Stephen had been out in a lot of bad weather but this was scary. "Kate, we need to park the car elsewhere." A tree would land on her if they left it here.

Kate opened her door. "Take me with you. When we find Meghan, we'd best be prepared to hunker down and stay put until this blows over."

Dave looked around and nodded. "I don't like it but yes, come with us. If we drive up to the house, we risk getting shot at. If I leave you here, it may be very hard to get back to you later. I don't want you sitting in a car for the rest of the night. Just stay back when the fun starts."

They set off along the road, Kate walking between them. If the mill house was set back in those trees there were no lights on. The only sign something was there was the road and the power lines. Meghan alone, in a place she didn't know… "I can't believe he just left her out here."

"We'll find her, Stephen," Kate promised.

"I hope she didn't try to get to help on her own."

"She's a wise lady, even when scared to death. She will sit and wait for us."

Stephen wasn't so sure. If Meghan thought the man might come back, she'd get away while she could.

Stephen felt a sudden updraft. Seconds passed and it did not dissipate. He looked up at the sky hearing a faint rumble of distant thunder and something else. The updraft intensified.

Kate stopped. "What is *that?*"

Dave shoved his wife toward the open field as a tree ahead of them snapped. "We are not moving to the country!"

Stephen heard it then, the sound of a freight train coming. He grabbed Kate and swung her over the roadside ditch as Dave jumped it. Dave picked Kate up and ran. Stephen spotted the culvert and pushed Dave toward it. They hit the ground as the wind started lifting anything it could. Stephen pushed Kate's head down and prayed the depression was deep enough. He grabbed his phone from his pocket and felt like swearing when he couldn't get a signal. Then he reached across and grabbed Dave's and had better luck getting through to the sheriff's office. "There's a tornado on the ground north of water tower! Sound the sirens, warn people!"

The noise turned deafening. Trees lifted from the ground. Dave sheltered Kate's body as debris began to rain down. The tornado tore through ahead of them, cutting apart the land. Stephen put his face into the wet earth.

Meghan. Oh, God, please, keep her safe.

Meghan hit a table hard, bruising her thigh. She pushed the table aside, grabbed the chair and shoved it ahead of her, using it to clear her way. She knew that frightening sound.

The roof groaned above her. It would be ripped away any moment. Under the bed was no protection. Outside would be worse as trees came down.

Lord, what do I do?

She was a sitting duck.

Her hand touched brick.

A fireplace. She searched frantically to find out if there was a built-in wood box or something strong and sturdy near this wall of bricks.

The roof peeled up and began breaking apart. Meghan covered her head with one arm as she tried to protect herself. Water cascaded inside. She whimpered and struggled with the only thing she could find. She tipped the heavy couch over and shoved it near the brick wall. She crawled beneath it for shelter, hoping it was heavy enough it would be buried in the rubble and not lifted away in the wind. Glass exploded.

"Meghan! Where are you?!" Stephen's torchlight lit up a broken bedroom door leaning drunkenly against an oak tree. Curtains wrapped around a fallen tree branch fluttered. The kitchen table was twenty yards ahead sitting among the grass as if set up there in a normal place for a meal. Stephen helped Kate over a tree trunk.

Kate's torchlight illuminated a shattered lamp resting ten feet up in a tree. The old mill house was now pieces of wood and brick and furniture strewn on the ground through the trees.

"There!" Dave focused his light ahead of them. The skeleton of the house was still there—two outside walls were still standing and part of the roof tipped in on its side. Stephen released Kate's arm, looked to make sure she was steady, and then surged ahead of her to join Dave.

He picked his way around the foundation of the house. "Meghan!"

"Is there a basement or a shelter somewhere she would have dove for cover?" Dave asked, his light running across the building remains.

Stephen wedged his light in a crevice. "Dig!" He started tossing drywall and broken furniture away. Tears tracked down his face. *She was in this!* A nail on a board pierced his glove and drew blood. He tossed the board away. He climbed over the remains of the refrigerator and with Dave's help shoved it off the debris pile. They needed more help, light, time. Minutes counted when someone was hurt. Dawn was still hours away, and he was afraid there would be no extra hands to help them. Destruction marked the path of the tornado as it cut toward town.

Meghan pushed her hand against the fabric of the couch, her head aching, nearly deaf from the noise. "Here." Someone was out there. She tried to call and could barely whisper. She tried to get a deeper breath but it made her dizzy. Something was covering the opening she had used when she slipped under the sofa. Bricks. Those were bricks. The fireplace had come down over the couch.

She was getting hot. She lifted her head a few inches from the floor and realized her mouth was bleeding again. "Over here." Her hand felt the cool metal of the fire poker near the couch arm. She couldn't lift it, but she could wiggle it. She moved it as much as she could, trying to dislodge what it had struck. She heard something fall.

"Meghan!"

The voices were getting louder. She pushed the poker again and realized she could move the bricks. She rested her head back down on the floor and put her energy into moving out bricks.

"She's under here!"

Stephen. She let her head rest back against the floorboard. He'd come. She gulped air around the tears of relief, then she reached a hand toward where she could hear them digging. She waited for her rescuer to reach her.

Stephen tugged his sweater over Meghan's head, turning her into a mummy of wool. "Better?" He wiped at the remaining traces of tears.

"Much." She wrapped her arms around the warmth. They sat in the shelter of the remaining wall, out of the wind and the tapering-off rain. Stephen checked her pulse again and this time she didn't try to push his hand away. She had a cut on her lip, a few bruises, and he was still worried about her hearing, but she'd come through this night in better shape than he could have hoped.

He dug through his pockets looking for anything else that might help, or at least bring comfort. He found a piece of gum, not sure how old it was. It wouldn't do her sore jaw any good. He set it aside.

She laughed weakly. "I wish I'd been able to see the tornado. Ken has been trying to get near one for years and I ended up under one."

"A little too close for my comfort." He ran his finger along her hairline, pushing back her dripping bangs and wishing he had a hat to offer her. "That couch is about the only piece of furniture still actually left in the house. We passed the mattress stuck up in a tree and the bed frame wrapped around a snapped telephone pole."

"I prayed for an angel to sit on it for me to keep it from moving."

Stephen leaned down and kissed her forehead. "I'll take it, however it happened. I did a lot of praying too."

She smiled toward him, and then her expression turned distant. "Did they catch him?"

Stephen didn't let himself dwell on what he would like to do to the man who had kidnapped her. "I don't know. I was coming to rescue you."

"I appreciate your priorities." She leaned against his chest and wrapped her arms around him. "I knew you would come."

He rubbed his hand across her back. "You wanna talk about it?"

She instantly shook her head.

He leaned down to see her face. The separation from Blackie, the storm, being snatched, going through it blind—they had to talk about it sometime soon, or the memories would just mess with her head. Now wasn't the right time to push. "Maybe later," he offered and she didn't reject the idea.

"Where's Blackie?"

"I had him with me at the sheriff's office when word came in the jewelry store was on fire. He bolted on me, heading toward your house. He's been frantically looking for you."

"He'll crawl under the porch—he's got a blanket pulled under there—or if he can get into the house and head under my bed, he'll be there."

"I'll find him as soon as we get to town," he promised. The weight of the day was catching up with him. He hugged her and sighed. "Let's not do this again, okay?"

"I'm exhausted enough to fall asleep right here. I don't think I'll worry about hearing just a little wind and thunder anymore."

"I agree with that."

Dave's torchlight appeared as he helped Kate over the uneven ground.

"Kate is pretty wiped out too. She's coming over with Dave now."

"You let her out in this?"

"Saying no wasn't an option."

Meghan struggled to sit up. "The couch was upside down; it will still be pretty dry. Dig it out and give us somewhere more comfortable to sit than the ground."

It was a good idea. Stephen squeezed Meghan's hand and stood. He tugged the couch out of the remaining rubble of the fireplace. Kate joined Meghan and Dave came over to help him.

"What are the odds we'll find the car still drivable?" Stephen asked Dave as he flipped over the couch cushions to find the driest side.

"I'll hike back to the road and find out," Dave said. "I'll drive in as close as I can. I'd rather not spend the rest of the night out here."

"Take the extra batteries for the flashlight."

"Will do." Dave stopped and hugged Kate, then headed for the road.

"Meghan, let's move you to the couch." Stephen helped her up. She held onto his hand and Kate's arm and picked her way through the debris. She gripped the arm of the couch and moved to sit down. "Okay, this is good."

Meghan tugged Kate down to sit beside her. "Swing your feet up on the couch and breathe deeply. Stephen, can you find the throw pillows? They were near the couch earlier. And we need a blanket."

"What's wrong?"

Kate groaned and started to pant.

Meghan laughed. "She's in labor."

TWENTY-NINE

Dave pushed the car keys into his pocket and walked through the trees back to the destroyed hunting lodge. They had transportation out of here. Meghan needed to get back on familiar turf, and he had to get Kate somewhere she could get some rest. Ahead of him Meghan and Stephen both hovered over Kate. He broke into a jog over the rough ground.

"What's wrong?" He looked from Stephen to Meghan and then at his wife, and he forgot everything else going on around him. Her face was bunched in a tight grimace, her eyes closed, the strain showing in her body. "She's in labor!"

"Yes."

The contraction shook his wife. "Kate—" Dave knelt beside the couch, his hand gripping hers tight. He was going to be a dad too early, and far from the hospital where he had her preregistered. "Breathe, love, like they showed you."

The contraction eased off and her eyes opened as she sucked in a deep breath. "I'm having this baby. Now!"

His hand shook as he pushed back her hair. "And you're going to be fine; I'm right here, just like I promised. Why didn't you say something earlier?"

"I didn't know. My back ached, but then the contractions just started."

"The car survived; we've got transportation to get us back to Silverton."

"That would be good," she whispered, breathing out. "Assuming Stephen doesn't want to deliver his niece or nephew right here."

Stephen paled. "Dave, give me the keys to the car. I'll check how much gas we've got left and see if phones still work, find out which roads are passable. We either try for Silverton, or we head the extra miles to Ridgefield. Don't move her until I get back and can help."

Dave dug out his keys and handed them to Stephen. "Just getting back to the highway is going to be the biggest challenge."

"I'm willing to shove aside a downed tree if you are. Meghan, come with me. Let's see what we can do about getting the backseat cleared for Kate to recline."

"Guys, relax. She's got plenty of time." Meghan hugged Kate. "I'll be back." She reached for Stephen's hand. "Let's go."

Dave watched Stephen and Meghan walk toward the car. "They make a nice couple."

"It's about time he settled down."

Dave turned back to his wife, leaned forward and kissed her. "No chance this is a false alarm and the little one is just making sure we're paying attention?"

"None."

"I was afraid of that." He leaned his head forward against hers. His wife handled a kidnapping first and pushed aside the fact she was in labor until after the job was done. "Good job, Kate." He laughed. "Just think of the story we'll have to tell at birthdays."

"I want a little girl."

"As long as she is just like you, that would be okay with me."

She looked around. "I really do not want to have this baby here."

"I'll carry you back to town if I have to. Lie back and relax while you can. The car ride will be tough."

The tornado had hit the town. Stephen drove slowly through the debris-filled main street, easing the car over bricks and boards and stripped tree limbs. The smoke rising from the jewelry store added to the sense of its being a war zone. Two bulldozers were literally pushing debris out of the roadway. "It's bad, Meghan." There wasn't panic among those directing the cleanup. Men would be digging by hand through that rubble if someone was thought buried under there. The tornado sirens must have given the residents just enough warning to get to cover.

"Get us as close to the side door of the clinic as you can," Meghan urged.

"I'll try. The road is crowded with cars, and deputies are bringing what looks like the walking injured into the clinic," Stephen said. "The building is in good shape, just a couple toppled trees. Ahh, here we go. Joseph has triage set up in the parking lot. He can help us get Kate inside."

Kate arched her back to ease a contraction. "It's good timing. We don't have much time!"

"Dave, support her back. Breathe, Kate. Pant. Stay ahead of it," Meghan said.

"I'm trying."

Stephen didn't dare look back. He concentrated on getting through the vehicles.

"That's good. Keep with it. It's going to ease off," Meghan encouraged.

Kate groaned. "It is not. And I want to push."

"Not yet!" Dave ordered. "Just squeeze my hand and don't push."

"Kate, it's early yet. The sensation is just the baby moving. You've still got several hours of labor ahead of you, I'm afraid."

"Oh, don't say that, Meg. I won't survive it."

Stephen threw the car in park and rushed around to open the back door. "Okay, sis, we're here." She was panting as the contraction faded away.

"We've got a couple minutes before the next one hits. Let's get you comfortable inside, love," Dave encouraged. Stephen helped Dave ease her out of the car. Dave swept her up into his arms.

Stephen rushed ahead of him to open the door.

"This way." Meghan directed them through the back hall of the clinic. "I'll get Dad. He's wonderful at delivering babies."

Stephen caught her hand to pause her at the doorway. "I'm needed out there with Joseph. I hate to leave you here, but..." His lips brushed against hers. "Remember I love you."

Her hands framed his face and she kissed him back. "I love you too. Now go to work."

Stephen struggled to get around the downed trees and power lines to reach Meghan's street. She desperately needed Blackie with her.

Her house was gone. He stood and stared at the destruction, feeling sick. All that remained was the fireplace, an interior wall, and part of the roof bracing. There were no discernable rooms, no sign of her piano. The flooring had gone into the basement area. The next house on the street was merely a smooth foundation. She'd loved this house and all the dreams it represented.

"Blackie!" Meghan had suggested under the porch or under her bed. Stephen didn't have much hope for either.

The answering bark was faint but joyous. And it was somewhere from the far left side of this mess. "Blackie, where are you?"

Stephen climbed over the debris and got down on his belly as he realized the sound was coming from below him in what had once been the basement. He shoved aside loose boards. The dog was down there in two feet of water. Blackie desperately tried to jump and get a foothold on the debris only to slide back into the water with a splash.

"Easy, boy. Let me come to you." A beam had protected the dog from being buried in the debris. He was behind what looked like the hot-water heater, the white metal giving the animal no traction. Plaster pieces floated in the water around him.

Stephen locked his feet around a beam and wiggled another six inches over the edge. He got a hand around the dog's front leg and another in the fur behind his neck and he did the only thing he could—hauling the animal out even as he yelped. "Sorry, boy, sorry."

He got a drenching as the wet animal slammed against him and then a hot bath as the dog licked every inch of his face he could reach. Stephen held the dog off his chest and heaved a deep breath as he laughed. "I'm glad you're alive too. And there's someone who is going to be very happy to see you."

The sun rose into a pink dawn. Stephen held a towel against a lady's badly gashed arm as he walked with her into the clinic, grateful the sight of blood was no longer causing him problems. A nurse met them before they had even crossed the waiting room. Doctors and nurses from surrounding towns poured into Silverton to help, and for the first time since this had begun, Stephen felt as though they were getting ahead of the rescue efforts.

"Thank you, Stephen."

"My pleasure, Mrs. Heath. They'll have you fixed up in no time." He handed his patient off.

He saw Meghan step out of an exam room at the end of the hall and he whistled as he headed her direction. Her head came up and she swiveled her head to locate the direction of the sound, and then a private smile appeared just for him.

"Hey there, beautiful." Blackie was pressed so tight against her left knee she had to take cautious steps.

She pushed back her hair with both hands. "Hardly beautiful after this night, but I'll take the kind words."

"How's Kate doing?"

Her face lit up with her smile. "Good. Ashley is coaching her, and she's the expert. Maybe in the next half hour. If the ambulances weren't so urgently needed for the injured, Dad would have transferred Kate to the hospital, but I think the plan now is to let her deliver here. Two obstetricians are among the medical teams helping out, so she'll be in good hands when the time comes. Dave's with her. Would you like to see them?"

"In a bit. Can you take a couple minutes and share the back steps and a cup of coffee?"

"I would love to."

Volunteers had set up coffee, tea, toast, and donuts on the table in the receptionist area. Stephen got them coffee and walked Meghan out through the back of the clinic. "I'm glad you can't see this damage. The town took a direct hit."

She pushed off her tennis shoes and worked a rock out. "There were no casualties, so it could have been much worse. Dad said their place and yours are pretty much untouched."

Stephen rested a hand against her face to turn her toward him. "I'm sorry about your house."

"So am I. Everything I dreamed about from the curtains over the kitchen sink to the wind chimes by the front door. It was a house kept alive in my memories all these years. I can't believe it's just gone."

"I'll rebuild it for you. Every detail."

Her eyes filled with tears. "You would do that for me?"

"You bet." He would love to have her one day sharing his farm, but he wasn't going to use this timing to even suggest she think that direction.

Her smile appeared. "I'll think about it some. Maybe the next house shouldn't have a basement. Or that step into the garage I kept missing."

He wiped away her tears. "We'll make it right, okay? Of everything you have to be sad about right now, the loss of the house is one thing we can fix." Stephen picked up her hand and looked at how the scrapes were healing. She'd been wearing latex gloves and the powder had irritated the scrapes. He soothed his thumb across them and made a note to get some lotion. "How else are you doing?"

"I'm okay, just very tired."

An understatement if he'd ever heard one. She looked exhausted.

A car door in the parking lot slammed and her coffee sloshed. She was still very nervous under that fatigue. "Would you tell me about what happened?"

"I'd rather not."

He let her drink her coffee. "Why?"

"I was so scared…" she whispered.

"Then share it, let me at least soften the memories."

"I hate being blind. There was no reference point for where I was, what the surroundings were like. Without Blackie—I was petrified to move. And when I heard that sound of the wind… I just want to forget."

He rubbed her arm. "Did you know your abductor?"

She didn't answer him.

Stephen turned her face toward him and brushed his hand along her cheek. "You can trust me with whatever that answer is."

"I trust you. I just don't want to talk about it."

Someone she knew. It must be someone she knew. And if he pushed, he'd be adding to the pressure she felt. "We'll talk later, then. I may be gone a good part of this morning. I'll be going up soon with the police helicopter to comb the area for others who need help. Jack is part of that area search team and he needs another paramedic out there. If you get done here, would you head out to your parents and I'll meet you there later?"

"Yes. I'll stop by with Mom and take care of your animals if you like."

"I'd appreciate that. Maybe I'll just say a brief hi to Kate from the doorway. Labor is hard to watch."

Meghan laughed and got to her feet. "It's hard to endure too. Come on; I'll hold your hand."

Because her smile had returned, Stephen took her up on the offer. They went back into the clinic and walked through to a comfortable room at the back.

Dave was sitting by Kate's side, feeding her ice chips. Both looked like they had been through a battle. Uncertain about this, wishing he hadn't asked, Stephen walked over to Kate. He gently touched her sweaty hand. "Hi."

She opened her eyes enough to smile at him. "I'm having a baby, not dying. This is just tiring work."

Dave fed her more ice. "We have a baby who has decided to take her time in coming."

Kate groaned as another contraction hit.

Meghan slipped her hand in his and Stephen squeezed it, appreciating the comfort.

Ashley timed the latest contraction. "Why don't you go find your dad, Meg? I think this little one is finally ready to make an appearance."

"About time," Kate panted.

Dave wiped her forehead. "Tomorrow you'll be saying it wasn't so bad."

"Then I'd be lying."

Dave laughed and kissed her forehead.

THIRTY

The police helicopter landed east of the bank and Stephen hurried toward it. Jack shoved open the door for him. "We've got to rush it—they've only got fuel for another forty minutes before they have to divert to the airport, and there's a lot of territory to cover."

Stephen clipped on the seat restraints. "I'm good."

The pilot lifted off.

Jack handed over a map. "We've been searching the tornado path west along the highway and it's a wide swath. They think a couple secondary twisters in the storm front added to the damage. Teams of searchers are fanning out along the roads to check damaged structures, but some of the remote homes can only be reached by air."

"How many injuries so far?"

"Twelve, nothing serious. We're transporting to the nearest ground team if it's not life threatening."

Stephen found a place to store the extra gloves he'd brought. "Where's Tom working?"

"South of here, at a collapsed silo. Two teams are trying to reach a trapped man."

"Did Tom have anything to pass on regarding last night?"

"Tom spotted a car leaving the area where the ring was left, but he lost it right about here in this cloverleaf of roads. I'm betting the guy headed toward the river. But that road, at that time of night—he was driving across the path of the twister. He would have been hit with the brunt of this storm front."

"Do we know anything about the make and model of the car?"

"Tom saw enough to place it as a late model tan Toyota."

"Keep your eyes peeled for it just in case we get lucky and the guy had a flat tire or drove himself into a ditch." The odds they would find the car eight hours later were slim, but Stephen couldn't stand the idea of Meghan's abductor getting away.

"Will do." Jack dug out a second pair of binoculars and handed them over.

The helicopter passed over the path of the tornado. The ground had been stripped down to the dirt, and a long trail of debris adorned the path. Stephen started searching the area for signs of anyone needing help.

"Jack, down there!" Stephen slapped his brother's shoulder and pointed to the country road to their east. From the air the vehicle was a shiny reflection in the sun against the water. It rested upside down on the banks of an overflowing stream, shoved there during the night by a powerful flow of water. "It's not tagged."

Searchers had been leaving bright fluorescent stickers on structures and vehicles they checked to mark them as cleared. Stephen was pretty sure even at these angles that the vehicle had tan paint.

"Let's check it out."

The helicopter pilot nodded and banked them toward the stream. Stephen reached for a couple fluorescent tags. As soon as the helicopter touched ground, Jack shoved open the door. Stephen unclipped his restraints and followed his brother. They jogged toward the crash.

"The car isn't stable," Jack warned, seeing the water rock it.

"Help me down over there. I can get near enough to check if it's empty." Stephen pulled on his gloves. It was a tan Toyota. He wanted to check this vehicle for more reasons than just an injured driver. Jack tested how secure the tree was at the top of the incline and nodded, then got a good hold and offered Stephen a hand to help ease his way down.

Stephen scrambled not to topple into the water as his feet hit the stream bank. "This water is freezing." He picked his way downstream to reach the car and knelt to peer through the broken-out side window. "It's empty!"

"He probably abandoned the vehicle before the worst of the storm came through."

"Maybe. The river water did a number on the inside—there's nothing in the car not fastened down." He tried to reach in and open the glove box but it was jammed. Stephen pushed himself away from the car, disappointed. If this was the car Meghan had been in, there was nothing here to help him. He slapped the fluorescent tags on so they could be seen from the air.

Stephen elected to pass the car and go up the bank farther downstream. He saw the case as he reached for a low-lying tree limb. Open, wedged against the tree roots, the velvet was destroyed by the water. It was the case he'd held last night, found in the piano bench. He reached for it.

The hinge had broken and the top of the case had cracked. Beyond water and mud it was empty. He searched the stream bank and nothing caught his attention. If the jewelry was anywhere here to be found, it would take a miracle to find it.

"This is the car." Stephen held up the box. "This is the jewelry box."

"There isn't going to be much forensic evidence worth finding. The river ran through the car for the night." Jack leaned down to help him out of the ravine. "Stay and search?" Jack asked. "The guy may be around here."

"If a driver's injured out here, we'll have better luck spotting him from the air," Stephen said. "Call Tom so he can mark the car and have it hauled in for evidence. Maybe they can trace the license plate. I bet the guy had another vehicle waiting and this car was abandoned here. There'd be no need to take an empty box along when he could stuff the jewels in his pocket."

"At least it's a solid lead."

Stephen had the feeling that it was the last clue they would get. The guy was gone.

THIRTY-ONE

Stephen cradled his two-and-a-half-week-old niece against his chest and walked around the hotel banquet room, lulling Holly back to sleep. Jennifer had asked that he be happy, settled, and at peace with life. He couldn't get more content than this. Holly was perfection. Dark hair like Kate's, perfect eyelashes, cute fingers. Her skin was so incredibly soft.

He was an uncle.

Cole and Rachel's wedding this afternoon had been perfect in its simplicity and Jack and Cassie's tomorrow would be a day-long party. Tonight Kate, Dave, and their new daughter were stealing the show.

"Stephen, come over here."

He turned. Kate patted the open spot on the couch beside her. "I think Holly already has you wrapped around her little finger. I've never seen you so relaxed."

"Your daughter might have something to do with it." He smiled at Meghan seated beside Kate. She had a lot more to do with it. "Want to hold Holly, Meg?"

"Please."

He carefully transferred the sleeping infant and then sat on the couch beside Meghan. He stretched out his arm and rested it along the back of the couch and around her shoulders. He idly twirled a lock of Meghan's hair around his finger. "Jack wants to go shoot a few baskets tonight to run off some nerves. Do you think you'll be okay here with Blackie for an hour? I'd better go along to keep him out of trouble." The dog lifted his head at the sound of his name, and Stephen reached down to rub his ears. Blackie was still showing the aftereffects of having lost Meghan. He did not let her leave a room without going after her.

"I'll be fine here; you don't have to hurry back."

He smiled at her. "You just want to tug more stories out of Kate." Stephen leaned over and kissed her. "I'll be back in an hour."

Stephen slapped the basketball away from Jack, took off for the basket, and made a layup. "That's sixteen."

Jack chased down the ball. "Lucky grab." Jack tossed him the ball and Stephen tossed it back, putting it in play. This was the way they had formed their friendship decades ago, doing friendly battle over a basketball court.

"So are you ready to get married tomorrow?"

"Past ready." Jack cut around him and tried to dunk the ball. "I was pleased to see Meghan came with you."

"You'll forgive me if my attention as best man tomorrow is not entirely on my duties."

The gym door opened. Marcus walked in but not dressed to play ball; he was still in a suit from the party. "Hey, guys. Stephen, I need you a minute."

Stephen offered his hand to Jack. "Call it a draw?"

"Deal." Jack headed over to the bench where Cassie sat watching the game.

Stephen jogged over to Marcus. "What's happening?"

"Maybe a few answers." Marcus offered a file he held. "Kate wants to know if you happen to recognize these. They were couriered over tonight."

Stephen took the file. He was looking at a photo of the jewelry that had nearly cost him Meghan's life. The emerald earrings in particular were brilliant. His gaze shot up to hold Marcus's.

"You recognize them?"

Stephen closed the file and handed it to Marcus. "Those are the pieces we found in the piano bench, that Meghan was carrying the night she was snatched."

"Someone tried to resell them in St. Louis."

"Who was it?"

"The recovered car was rented to Jonathan Peters, and the description of the guy in St. Louis fits him."

"The pianist?" Stephen said.

"Yes. He's using his credit cards, but we haven't been able to put our hands on him yet."

"Meghan is going to be horrified."

Marcus gave a small smile. "Nice standing up for your lady. You know she already knows it was him."

"She'll never testify against him."

"That's pretty obvious." Marcus tucked the file under his arm.

Meghan was trying so hard to keep it quiet rather than say it had been a friend. "Does she have to know the stones were recovered?"

"For now the photos become part of the file. If we catch Jonathan, then we'll see what kind of case can be made."

Stephen relaxed. "Thanks."

"Don't mention it." Marcus nodded to Jack. "Letting him win as a wedding present?"

Stephen looked over at his brother. "Now would I do that?"

Marcus laughed and strolled toward Cassie. "I think I'll stick around and watch the end of this game."

≫≈≪

Stephen stopped by his hotel room to clean up and retrieve a package from his suitcase before returning to the gathering. Kate looked to be asleep. Stephen paused by the couch to look down at her and then over at Dave sitting in the chair just watching his wife sleep. He shared a smile with him. Stephen looked around for Holly. Meghan had her, strolling back and forth in front of the windows as she rocked the infant. Stephen moved to join them, whistling softly.

Her head came up and she gave a half turn toward him.

"You look very comfortable."

She smiled as she rested her head against Holly. "I am. How was the game?"

"I let Jack win, but don't tell him that." He hesitated, but knew it was only a matter of time before the police apprehended Jonathan. "They found the jewelry, Meg. They know it was Jonathan."

Her sudden tension woke Holly and Stephen rested a hand on Meghan's shoulder to ease the reaction.

"They picked him up?"

"Not yet, but they likely will soon."

Meghan sighed and rocked Holly to calm the infant. "He threatened to use the jewels he did have to point the mob boss toward you as the thief. I've known Jonathan a long time. He was desperate, and I couldn't figure what he might do. And I didn't want to be the one to turn him in for kidnapping. He was a friend, even if he'd forgotten that fact. I wish I had been able to talk him into giving himself up."

"Don't, honey. You can't protect him from the results of his own choices."

"Will I have to testify against him?"

He stroked her shoulder with his thumb. "If you do, I'll be there with you. At least this ends it. The theft ring was Neil and Craig and Jonathan. It's finally over."

"Yes." Meghan smiled slightly. "I'm glad. I want my peaceful life back."

"So do I, as long as I get to be part of your peaceful future." He touched his niece's little hand. "I have something for you, but you'll have to trade me Holly."

"That's going to have to be something pretty special."

"Hmm, it is."

She carefully handed him the infant and Stephen settled his niece against his chest. "I'm in love with this little lady." He tucked the blanket snugly around the child. "Months ago, I had Neil make me something."

"I remember the receipt in the register. He just noted it was a customized piece."

"Don't look so flustered; I sketched it in the first days I came back. I just wanted it for a night we had something to celebrate. I wish Neil had done more of this kind of creating pieces than getting involved in what he did. He had a lot of talent." He half turned. "Slip your hand into my left jacket pocket."

She retrieved the tissue-paper-wrapped gift.

"I asked Neil to do it in silver."

"Oh, Stephen." The heart pendant was swirled in silver, with a script *M* inside.

He leaned over and kissed her forehead. "I would have added an *S* if it wouldn't have seemed too forward at the time." Stephen nudged her arm. "Hey, I've got my hands full. You can't cry on me."

She blinked back the tears even as she laughed. "I'm thinking I'll add it as a superman *S*, right behind my heart."

"Really?"

She slid her hand around his arm. "Did I just fluster you?"

"A bit." It was hard to think coherently when she was invading his space. "You rescued me, Meg, by leading me to the ultimate Rescuer. I thought we'd celebrate that tonight. I wish I'd figured out you were what I was searching for years ago." He bent to tenderly kiss her. "I wasted so much time."

"I love you, Stephen."

He smiled and wiped one of her tears, then shifted Holly so he could hug Meghan. He was tired of waiting when he finally found what he wanted. "When we get home, what do you say you come walk through the farmhouse and decide on a place for a new piano? What would you say about marrying me someday, Meghan?"

She about hugged the breath out of him. "I'd say yes."

He laughed and caught her close. The night was complete, and nearly perfect. "I wish Jennifer were here so I could tell her first."

"She knows," Meghan whispered against his shirt, then leaned back. "What do you say we wake up Kate to tell her next? Then call my parents."

Stephen looked over at his sister and smiled. "Yes, let's do that. This should be an O'Malley family celebration."

Dear Reader,

Thank you for reading this story. Stephen opened the O'Malley series with Kate in *The Negotiator*, and now in *The Rescuer* brings this set of books to a close. He's the last O'Malley to settle down, and his loneliness after the death of Jennifer is intense. His friendship with Meghan was the thing he turned to, and as I got to know Meghan, I understood why Stephen chose her. She's been through hard times and found the peace he seeks.

Stephen is the last O'Malley to believe. He knows who God is, knows what religion asks of a man, and his struggle is a matter of will. What Stephen needs most to hear is that Jesus wants to be his friend. He has to see the truth become personal: That Jesus wants to rescue him because God wants more than a servant; He wants a friendship. Is God trustworthy to be our deepest, closest Friend? Exploring that question with Stephen made this one of the richest O'Malley books to write.

Thank you for reading the O'Malley series and getting to know this special family.

As always, I love to hear from my readers. Feel free to write me at:

Dee Henderson
c/o Multnomah Fiction
P.O. Box 1720
Sisters, Oregon 97759
E-mail: dee@deehenderson.com
or on-line: http://www.deehenderson.com

God bless,

Dee Henderson

The publisher would love to hear your
comments about this book. *Please contact us at:*
www.deefiction.com

DISCUSSION QUESTIONS

1. When Meghan went blind, she struggled but still had a peace that people noticed and admired. What gave her that peace? When tragedy has struck in your life, what helped you overcome your adversity, gave you peace?

2. Why was Stephen running away? Are there any issues in your life that you are ignoring or avoiding? If so, how are you going to face them?

3. What aspects of Meghan's personality make her so likable? What's likable about Stephen? What qualities do you appreciate and admire in your mate?

4. What factors contributed to Stephen's resistance to church and God? The Bible tells us that those who seek God will find Him (Jeremiah 29:13). Do you tend to resist God or do you seek Him? Why?

5. How did Stephen's childhood affect his life choices? Work choices? The kind of girl to whom he was attracted? What kind of influence does your childhood have on the choices you've made as an adult?

6. How do you think Meghan felt when people she considered to be trustworthy friends (Neil and Jonathan) turned out to be criminals? Has anyone you've known ever betrayed your trust? How did that make you feel?

7. How did reading Jennifer's diary help Stephen deal with his struggles? How was Jennifer's battle with cancer similar to Stephen's search for contentment? How was it different? Do you have friends or family members who've dealt with a serious illness? If so, how did his or her struggle impact your life?

8. Even though Stephen was antisocial for quite a while, his family, especially Kate, fought to keep him from isolating himself too much. In what ways has your family ever had to keep you "in line"? How did that make you feel? How did that affect your relationships?

9. Why does Stephen have such a hard time trusting others? Do you tend to be more or less trusting? Why? How does that affect your relationships with others?

10. Why didn't Meghan want to talk about the storm and her abduction? Why is it hard to talk about painful experiences?

11. What do you think Stephen and Meghan's future will be like after they get married? What kinds of adjustments do they need to make individually? Together? In your relationship with your spouse or significant other, what kinds of changes have you made since being together? How can you improve and strengthen your relationship even more?

THE O'MALLEY SERIES

The Negotiator—**Book One:** FBI agent Dave Richman from *Danger in the Shadows* is back. He's about to meet Kate O'Malley, and his life will never be the same. She's a hostage negotiator. He protects people. Dave's about to find out that falling in love with a hostage negotiator is one thing, but keeping her safe is another!
ISBN 1-57673-819-1
Audio book also available
CD: 1-59052-101-3/Cassette: 1-59052-100-5

The Guardian—**Book Two:** A federal judge has been murdered. There is only one witness. And an assassin wants her dead. U.S. Marshal Marcus O'Malley thought he knew the risks of the assignment... He was wrong.
ISBN 1-57673-642-3
Audio book also available
CD: 1-59052-105-6/Cassette: 1-59052-104-8

The Truth Seeker—**Book Three:** Women are turning up dead. Lisa O'Malley is a forensic pathologist and mysteries are her domain. When she's investigating a crime, it means trouble is soon to follow. U.S. Marshal Quinn Diamond has found that loving her is easier than keeping her out of danger. Lisa's found the killer, and now she's missing too...
ISBN 1-57673-753-5
Audio book also available
CD: 1-59052-107-2/Cassette: 1-59052-106-4

THE O'MALLEY SERIES

The Protector—**Book Four:** Jack O'Malley is a fireman. He's fearless when it comes to facing an inferno. But when an arsonist begins targeting his district, his shift, his friends, Jack faces the ultimate challenge: protecting the lady who saw the arsonist before she pays an even higher price...
ISBN 1-57673-846-9
Audio book also available
CD: 1-59052-116-1/Cassette: 1-59052-115-3

The Healer—**Book Five:** Rachel O'Malley makes her living as a trauma psychologist, working disaster relief for the Red Cross. Her specialty is helping children. When a school shooting rips through her community, she finds herself dealing with more than just grief among the children she's trying to help. There's a secret. One of them witnessed the shooting. And the murder weapon is still missing...
ISBN 1-57673-925-2
Audio book also available
CD: 1-59052-103-X/Cassette: 1-59052-102-1

The Rescuer—**Book Six:** Stephen O'Malley is a paramedic who has been rescuing people all his life. But now he's running—from job burnout, from the grief of losing his sister, and from a God he doesn't want to trust. He's run into a mystery. Stolen jewels are turning up in unexpected places, and Meghan is caught in the middle of the trouble. Can Stephen rescue the woman he loves before catastrophe strikes?
ISBN 1-59052-073-4
Audio book also available
CD: 1-59052-114-5/Cassette: 1-59052-113-7

"I highly recommend this book to anyone who likes suspense."

—Terri Blackstock, bestselling author of *Trial by Fire*

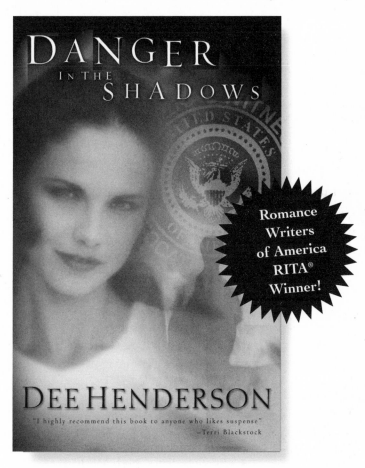

Don't miss the prequel to the O'Malley series!

Sara's terrified. She's doing the one thing she cannot afford to do: fall in love with former pro football player Adam Black, a man everyone knows. Sara's been hidden away in the witness protection program, her safety dependent on being invisible—and loving Adam could get her killed.

ISBN 1-57673-927-9

JOIN US IN AN ALL NEW DEE HENDERSON WEBSITE AT www.deefiction.com

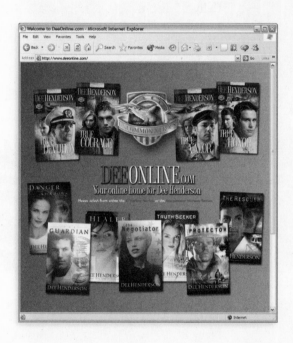

This site is packed with information, sample chapters,
and consumer activities on the
O'Malley and Uncommon Heroes series
by Dee Henderson.

THE UNCOMMON HEROES SERIES
by Dee Henderson

TRUE DEVOTION
Uncommon Heroes series, book one
While Navy SEAL Joe Baker struggles with asking Kelly to risk loving a soldier again, Kelly's in danger from her husband's killer, and Joe may not be able to save her...
1-57673-886-8
Audio book also available
CD: 1-59052-123-4/Cassette: 1-59052-1226

TRUE VALOR
Uncommon Heroes series, book two
Gracie is a Navy pilot; Bruce works Air Force pararescue. When she is shot down behind enemy lines, Bruce has got one mission: get Gracie out alive...
1-57673-887-6
Audio book also available
CD: 1-59052-178-1/Cassette: 1-59052-177-3

TRUE HONOR
Uncommon Heroes series, book three
Navy SEAL Sam "Cougar" Houston is in love with a CIA agent. But it may be a short relationship, for terrorists have chosen their next targets, and Darcy's name is high on the list...
1-59052-043-2
Audio book also available
CD: 1-59052-118-8/Cassette: 1-59052-117-X

TRUE COURAGE
Uncommon Heroes series, book four
FBI agent Luke Falcon is hunting his extended family's kidnappers. He fears that if his family never returns, his own chance at love may vanish as well.
1-59052-082-3
Audio book also available
CD: 1-59052-121-8